THE IDIOT

D1716943

Fyodor Dostoevsky

CONTENTS

THE IDIOT

PART I

CHAPTER I. 1

CHAPTER II. 7

CHAPTER III. 13

CHAPTER IV. 20

CHAPTER V. 27

CHAPTER VI. 36

CHAPTER VII. 41

CHAPTER VIII. 49

CHAPTER IX. 57

CHAPTER X. 62

CHAPTER XI. 66

CHAPTER XII. 70

CHAPTER XIII. 76

CHAPTER XIV. 81

CHAPTER XV. 86

CHAPTER XVI. 91

PART II

CHAPTER I. 99

CHAPTER II. 104

CHAPTER III. 112

CHAPTER IV. 120

CHAPTER V. 123

CHAPTER VI. 129

CHAPTER VII. 137

CHAPTER VIII. 142

CHAPTER IX. 151

CHAPTER X. 158

CHAPTER XI. 166

CHAPTER XII. 173

PART III

CHAPTER I. 179

CHAPTER II. 187

CHAPTER III. 195

CHAPTER IV. 204

CHAPTER V. 212

CHAPTER VI. 220

CHAPTER VII. 229

CHAPTER VIII. 237

CHAPTER IX. 245

CHAPTER X. 253

PART IV

Chapter I. 258
Chapter II. 265
Chapter III. 270
Chapter IV. 276
Chapter V. 283
Chapter VI. 294
Chapter VII. 303
Chapter VIII. 313
Chapter IX. 323
Chapter X. 330
Chapter XI. 337
Chapter XII. 345

PART I

CHAPTER I.

Towards the end of November, during a thaw, at nine o'clock one morning, a train on the Warsaw and Petersburg railway was approaching the latter city at full speed. The morning was so damp and misty that it was only with great difficulty that the day succeeded in breaking; and it was impossible to distinguish anything more than a few yards away from the carriage windows.

Some of the passengers by this particular train were returning from abroad; but the third-class carriages were the best filled, chiefly with insignificant persons of various occupations and degrees, picked up at the different stations nearer town. All of them seemed weary, and most of them had sleepy eyes and a shivering expression, while their complexions generally appeared to have taken on the colour of the fog outside.

When day dawned, two passengers in one of the third-class carriages found themselves opposite each other. Both were young fellows, both were rather poorly dressed, both had remarkable faces, and both were evidently anxious to start a conversation. If they had but known why, at this particular moment, they were both remarkable persons, they would undoubtedly have wondered at the strange chance which had set them down opposite to one another in a third-class carriage of the Warsaw Railway Company.

One of them was a young fellow of about twenty-seven, not tall, with black curling hair, and small, grey, fiery eyes. His nose was broad and flat, and he had high cheek bones; his thin lips were constantly compressed into an impudent, ironical—it might almost be called a malicious—smile; but his forehead was high and well formed, and atoned for a good deal of the ugliness of the lower part of his face. A special feature of this physiognomy was its death-like pallor, which gave to the whole man an indescribably emaciated appearance in spite of his hard look, and at the same time a sort of passionate and suffering expression which did not harmonize with his impudent, sarcastic smile and keen, self-satisfied bearing. He wore a large fur—or rather astrachan—overcoat, which had kept him warm all night, while his neighbour had been obliged to bear the full severity of a Russian November night entirely unprepared. His wide sleeveless mantle with a large cape to it—the sort of cloak one sees upon travellers during the winter months in Switzerland or North Italy—was by no means adapted to the long cold journey through Russia, from Eydkuhnen to St. Petersburg.

The wearer of this cloak was a young fellow, also of about twenty-six or twenty-seven years of age, slightly above the middle height, very fair, with a thin, pointed and very light coloured beard; his eyes were large and blue, and had an intent look about them, yet that heavy expression which some people affirm to be a peculiarity as well as evidence, of an epileptic subject. His face was decidedly a pleasant one for all that; refined, but quite colourless, except for the circumstance that at this moment it was blue with cold. He held a bundle made up of an old faded silk handkerchief that apparently contained all his travelling wardrobe, and wore thick shoes and gaiters, his whole appearance being very un-Russian.

His black-haired neighbour inspected these peculiarities, having nothing better to do, and at length remarked, with that rude enjoyment of the discomforts of others which the common classes so often show:

"Cold?"

"Very," said his neighbour, readily, "and this is a thaw, too. Fancy if it had been a hard frost! I never thought it would be so cold in the old country. I've grown quite out of the way of it."

"What, been abroad, I suppose?"

"Yes, straight from Switzerland."

"Wheugh! my goodness!" The black-haired young fellow whistled, and then laughed.

The conversation proceeded. The readiness of the fair-haired young man in the cloak to answer all his opposite neighbour's questions was surprising. He seemed to have no suspicion of any impertinence or inappropriateness in the fact of such questions being put to him. Replying to them, he made known to the inquirer that he certainly had been long absent from Russia, more than four years; that he had been sent abroad for his health; that he had suffered from some strange nervous malady—a kind of epilepsy, with convulsive spasms. His interlocutor burst out laughing several times at his answers; and more than ever, when to the question, "whether he had been cured?" the patient replied:

"No, they did not cure me."

"Hey! that's it! You stumped up your money for nothing, and we believe in those fellows, here!" remarked the black-haired individual, sarcastically.

"Gospel truth, sir, Gospel truth!" exclaimed another passenger, a shabbily dressed man of about forty, who looked like a clerk, and possessed a red nose and a very blotchy face. "Gospel truth! All they do is to get hold of our good Russian money free, gratis, and for nothing."

"Oh, but you're quite wrong in my particular instance," said the Swiss patient, quietly. "Of course I can't argue the matter, because I know only my own case; but my doctor gave me money—and he had very little—to pay my journey back, besides having kept me at his own expense, while there, for nearly two years."

"Why? Was there no one else to pay for you?" asked the black-haired one.

"No—Mr. Pavlicheff, who had been supporting me there, died a couple of years ago. I wrote to Mrs. General Epanchin at the time (she is a distant relative of mine), but she did not answer my letter. And so eventually I came back."

"And where have you come to?"

"That is—where am I going to stay? I—I really don't quite know yet, I—"

Both the listeners laughed again.

"I suppose your whole set-up is in that bundle, then?" asked the first.

"I bet anything it is!" exclaimed the red-nosed passenger, with extreme satisfaction, "and that he has precious little in the luggage van!—though of course poverty is no crime—we must remember that!"

It appeared that it was indeed as they had surmised. The young fellow hastened to admit the fact with wonderful readiness.

"Your bundle has some importance, however," continued the clerk, when they had laughed their fill (it was observable that the subject of their mirth joined in the laughter when he saw them laughing); "for though I dare say it is not stuffed full of friedrichs d'or and louis d'or—judge from your costume and gaiters—still—if you can add to your possessions such a valuable property as a relation like Mrs. General Epanchin, then your bundle becomes a significant object at once. That is, of course, if you really are a relative of Mrs. Epanchin's, and have not made a little error through—well, absence of mind, which is very common to human beings; or, say—through a too luxuriant fancy?"

"Oh, you are right again," said the fair-haired traveller, "for I really am *almost* wrong when I say she and I are related. She is hardly a relation at all; so little, in fact, that I was not in the least surprised to have no answer to my letter. I expected as much."

"H'm! you spent your postage for nothing, then. H'm! you are candid, however—and that is commendable. H'm! Mrs. Epanchin—oh yes! a most eminent person. I know her. As for Mr. Pavlicheff, who supported you in Switzerland, I know him too—at least, if it was Nicolai Andreevitch of that name? A fine fellow he was—and had a property of four thousand souls in his day."

"Yes, Nicolai Andreevitch—that was his name," and the young fellow looked earnestly and with curiosity at the all-knowing gentleman with the red nose.

This sort of character is met with pretty frequently in a certain class. They are people who know everyone—that is, they know where a man is employed, what his salary is, whom he knows, whom he married, what money his wife had, who are his cousins, and second cousins, etc., etc. These men generally have about a hundred pounds a year to live on, and they spend their whole time and talents in the amassing of this style of knowledge, which they reduce—or raise—to the standard of a science.

During the latter part of the conversation the black-haired young man had become very impatient. He stared out of the window, and fidgeted, and evidently longed for the end of the journey. He was very absent; he would appear to listen—and heard nothing; and he would laugh of a sudden, evidently with no idea of what he was laughing about.

"Excuse me," said the red-nosed man to the young fellow with the bundle, rather suddenly; "whom have I the honour to be talking to?"

"Prince Lef Nicolaievitch Muishkin," replied the latter, with perfect readiness.

"Prince Muishkin? Lef Nicolaievitch? H'm! I don't know, I'm sure! I may say I have never heard of such a person," said the clerk, thoughtfully. "At least, the name, I admit, is historical. Karamsin must mention the family name, of course, in his history—but as an individual—one never hears of any Prince Muishkin nowadays."

"Of course not," replied the prince; "there are none, except myself. I believe I am the last and only one. As to my forefathers, they have always been a poor lot; my own father was a sublieutenant in the army. I don't know how Mrs. Epanchin comes into the Muishkin family, but she is descended from the Princess Muishkin, and she, too, is the last of her line."

"And did you learn science and all that, with your professor over there?" asked the black-haired passenger.

"Oh yes—I did learn a little, but—"

"I've never learned anything whatever," said the other.

"Oh, but I learned very little, you know!" added the prince, as though excusing himself. "They could not teach me very much on account of my illness."

"Do you know the Rogojins?" asked his questioner, abruptly.

"No, I don't—not at all! I hardly know anyone in Russia. Why, is that your name?"

"Yes, I am Rogojin, Parfen Rogojin."

"Parfen Rogojin? dear me—then don't you belong to those very Rogojins, perhaps—" began the clerk, with a very perceptible increase of civility in his tone.

"Yes—those very ones," interrupted Rogojin, impatiently, and with scant courtesy. I may remark that he had not once taken any notice of the blotchy-faced passenger, and had hitherto addressed all his remarks direct to the prince.

"Dear me—is it possible?" observed the clerk, while his face assumed an expression of great deference and servility—if not of absolute alarm: "what, a son of that very Semen Rogojin—hereditary honourable citizen—who died a month or so ago and left two million and a half of roubles?"

"And how do *you* know that he left two million and a half of roubles?" asked Rogojin, disdainfully, and not deigning so much as to look at the other. "However, it's true enough that my father died a month ago, and that here am I returning from Pskoff, a month after, with hardly a boot to my foot. They've treated me like a dog! I've been ill of fever at Pskoff the whole time, and not a line, nor farthing of money, have I received from my mother or my confounded brother!"

"And now you'll have a million roubles, at least—goodness gracious me!" exclaimed the clerk, rubbing his hands.

"Five weeks since, I was just like yourself," continued Rogojin, addressing the prince, "with nothing but a bundle and the clothes I wore. I ran away from my father and came to Pskoff to my aunt's house, where I caved in at once with fever, and he went and died while I was away. All honour to my respected father's memory—but he uncommonly nearly killed me, all the same. Give you my word, prince, if I hadn't cut and run then, when I did, he'd have murdered me like a dog."

"I suppose you angered him somehow?" asked the prince, looking at the millionaire with considerable curiosity. But though there may have been something remarkable in the fact that this man was heir to millions of roubles there was something about him which surprised and interested the prince more than that. Rogojin, too, seemed to have taken up the conversation with unusual alacrity it appeared that he was still in a considerable state of excitement, if not absolutely feverish, and was in real need of someone to talk to for the mere sake of talking, as safety-valve to his agitation.

As for his red-nosed neighbour, the latter—since the information as to the identity of Rogojin—hung over him, seemed to be living on the honey of his words and in the breath of his nostrils, catching at every syllable as though it were a pearl of great price.

"Oh, yes; I angered him—I certainly did anger him," replied Rogojin. "But what puts me out so is my brother. Of course my mother couldn't do anything—she's too old—and whatever brother Senka says is law for her! But why couldn't he let me know? He sent a telegram, they say. What's the good of a telegram? It frightened my aunt so that she sent it back to the office unopened, and there it's been ever since! It's only thanks to Konief that I heard at all; he wrote me all about it. He says my brother cut off the gold tassels from my father's coffin, at night 'because they're worth a lot of money!' says he. Why, I can get him sent off to Siberia for that alone, if I like; it's sacrilege. Here, you—scarecrow!" he added, addressing the clerk at his side, "is it sacrilege or not, by law?"

"Sacrilege, certainly—certainly sacrilege," said the latter.

"And it's Siberia for sacrilege, isn't it?"

"Undoubtedly so; Siberia, of course!"

"They will think that I'm still ill," continued Rogojin to the prince, "but I sloped off quietly, seedy as I was, took the train and came away. Aha, brother Senka, you'll have to open your gates and let me in, my boy! I know he told tales about me to my father—I know that well enough but I certainly did rile my father about Nastasia Philipovna that's very sure, and that was my own doing."

"Nastasia Philipovna?" said the clerk, as though trying to think out something.

"Come, you know nothing about _her_," said Rogojin, impatiently.

"And supposing I do know something?" observed the other, triumphantly.

"Bosh! there are plenty of Nastasia Philipovnas. And what an impertinent beast you are!" he added angrily. "I thought some creature like you would hang on to me as soon as I got hold of my money."

"Oh, but I do know, as it happens," said the clerk in an aggravating manner. "Lebedeff knows all about her. You are pleased to reproach me, your excellency, but what if I prove that I am right after all? Nastasia Phillpovna's family name is Barashkoff—I know, you see—and she is a very well known lady, indeed, and comes of a good family, too. She is connected with one Totski, Afanasy Ivanovitch, a man of considerable property, a director of companies, and so on, and a great friend of General Epanchin, who is interested in the same matters as he is."

"My eyes!" said Rogojin, really surprised at last. "The devil take the fellow, how does he know that?"

"Why, he knows everything—Lebedeff knows everything! I was a month or two with Lihachof after his father died, your excellency, and while he was knocking about—he's in the debtor's prison now—I was with him, and he couldn't do a thing without Lebedeff; and I got to know Nastasia Philipovna and several people at that time."

"Nastasia Philipovna? Why, you don't mean to say that she and Lihachof—" cried Rogojin, turning quite pale.

"No, no, no, no, no! Nothing of the sort, I assure you!" said Lebedeff, hastily. "Oh dear no, not for the world! Totski's the only man with any chance there. Oh, no! He takes her to his box at the opera at the French theatre of an evening, and the officers and people all look at her and say, 'By Jove, there's the famous Nastasia Philipovna!' but no one ever gets any further than that, for there is nothing more to say."

"Yes, it's quite true," said Rogojin, frowning gloomily; "so Zaleshoff told me. I was walking about the Nefsky one fine day, prince, in my father's old coat, when she suddenly came out of a shop and stepped into her carriage. I swear I was all of a blaze at once. Then I met Zaleshoff—looking like a hair-dresser's assistant, got up as fine as I don't know who, while I looked like a tinker. 'Don't flatter yourself, my boy,' said he; 'she's not for such as you; she's a princess, she is, and her name is Nastasia Philipovna Barashkoff, and she lives with Totski, who wishes to get rid of her because he's growing rather old—fifty-five or so—and wants to marry a certain beauty, the loveliest woman in all Petersburg.' And then he told me that I could see Nastasia Philipovna at the opera-house that evening, if I liked, and described which was her box. Well, I'd like to see my father allowing any of us to go to the theatre; he'd sooner have killed us, any day. However, I went for an hour or so and saw Nastasia Philipovna, and I never slept a wink all night after. Next morning my father happened to give me two government loan bonds to sell, worth nearly five thousand roubles each. 'Sell them,' said he, 'and then take seven thousand five hundred roubles to the office, give them to the cashier, and bring me back the rest of the ten thousand, without looking in anywhere on the way; look sharp, I shall be waiting for you.' Well, I sold the bonds, but I didn't take the seven thousand roubles to the office; I went straight to the English shop and chose a pair of earrings, with a diamond the size of a nut in each. They cost four hundred roubles more than I had, so I gave my name, and they trusted me. With the earrings I went at once to Zaleshoff's. 'Come on!' I said, 'come on to Nastasia Philipovna's,' and off we went without more ado. I tell you I hadn't a notion of what was about me or before me or below my feet all the way; I saw nothing whatever. We went straight into her drawing-room, and then she came out to us.

"I didn't say right out who I was, but Zaleshoff said: 'From Parfen Rogojin, in memory of his first meeting with you yesterday; be so kind as to accept these!'

"She opened the parcel, looked at the earrings, and laughed.

"'Thank your friend Mr. Rogojin for his kind attention,' says she, and bowed and went off. Why didn't I die there on the spot? The worst of it all was, though, that the beast Zaleshoff got all the credit of it! I was short and abominably dressed, and stood and stared in her face and never said a word, because I was shy, like an ass! And there was he all in the fashion, pomaded and dressed out, with a smart tie on, bowing and scraping; and I bet anything she took him for me all the while!

"'Look here now,' I said, when we came out, 'none of your interference here after this—do you understand?' He laughed: 'And how are you going to settle up with your father?' says he. I thought I might as well jump into the Neva at once without going home first; but it struck me that I wouldn't, after all, and I went home feeling like one of the damned."

"My goodness!" shivered the clerk. "And his father," he added, for the prince's instruction, "and his father would have given a man a ticket to the other world for ten roubles any day—not to speak of ten thousand!"

The prince observed Rogojin with great curiosity; he seemed paler than ever at this moment.

"What do you know about it?" cried the latter. "Well, my father learned the whole story at once, and Zaleshoff blabbed it all over the town besides. So he took me upstairs and locked me up, and swore at me for an hour. 'This is only a foretaste,' says he; 'wait a bit till night comes, and I'll come back and talk to you again.'

"Well, what do you think? The old fellow went straight off to Nastasia Philipovna, touched the floor with his forehead, and began blubbering and beseeching her on his knees to give him back the diamonds. So after awhile she brought the box and flew out at him. 'There,' she says, 'take your earrings, you wretched old miser; although they are ten times dearer than their value to me now that I know what it must have cost Parfen to get them! Give Parfen my compliments,' she says, 'and thank him very much!' Well, I meanwhile had borrowed twenty-five roubles from a friend, and off I went to Pskoff to my aunt's. The old woman there lectured me so that I left the house and went on a drinking tour round the public-houses of the place. I was in a high fever when I got to Pskoff, and by nightfall I was lying delirious in the streets somewhere or other!"

"Oho! we'll make Nastasia Philipovna sing another song now!" giggled Lebedeff, rubbing his hands with glee. "Hey, my boy, we'll get her some proper earrings now! We'll get her such earrings that—"

"Look here," cried Rogojin, seizing him fiercely by the arm, "look here, if you so much as name Nastasia Philipovna again, I'll tan your hide as sure as you sit there!"

"Aha! do—by all means! if you tan my hide you won't turn me away from your society. You'll bind me to you, with your lash, for ever. Ha, ha! here we are at the station, though."

Sure enough, the train was just steaming in as he spoke.

Though Rogojin had declared that he left Pskoff secretly, a large collection of friends had assembled to greet him, and did so with profuse waving of hats and shouting.

"Why, there's Zaleshoff here, too!" he muttered, gazing at the scene with a sort of triumphant but unpleasant smile. Then he suddenly turned to the prince: "Prince, I don't know why I have taken a fancy to you; perhaps because I met you just when I did. But no, it can't be that, for I met this fellow" (nodding at Lebedeff) "too, and I have not taken a fancy to him by any means. Come to see me, prince; we'll take off those gaiters of yours and dress you up in a smart fur coat, the best we can buy. You shall have a dress coat, best quality, white waistcoat, anything you like, and your pocket shall be full of money. Come, and you shall go with me to Nastasia Philipovna's. Now then will you come or no?"

"Accept, accept, Prince Lef Nicolaievitch" said Lebedef solemnly; "don't let it slip! Accept, quick!"

Prince Muishkin rose and stretched out his hand courteously, while he replied with some cordiality:

"I will come with the greatest pleasure, and thank you very much for taking a fancy to me. I dare say I may even come today if I have time, for I tell you frankly that I like you very much too. I liked you especially when you told us about the diamond earrings; but I liked you before that as well, though you have such a dark-clouded sort of face. Thanks very much for the offer of clothes and a fur coat; I certainly shall require both clothes and coat very soon. As for money, I have hardly a copeck about me at this moment."

"You shall have lots of money; by the evening I shall have plenty; so come along!"

"That's true enough, he'll have lots before evening!" put in Lebedeff.

"But, look here, are you a great hand with the ladies? Let's know that first?" asked Rogojin.

"Oh no, oh no!" said the prince; "I couldn't, you know—my illness—I hardly ever saw a soul."

"H'm! well—here, you fellow—you can come along with me now if you like!" cried Rogojin to Lebedeff, and so they all left the carriage.

Lebedeff had his desire. He went off with the noisy group of Rogojin's friends towards the Voznesensky, while the prince's route lay towards the Litaynaya. It was damp and wet. The prince asked his way of passers-by, and finding that he was a couple of miles or so from his destination, he determined to take a droshky.

CHAPTER II.

General Epanchin lived in his own house near the Litaynaya. Besides this large residence—five-sixths of which was let in flats and lodgings—the general was owner of another enormous house in the Sadovaya bringing in even more rent than the first. Besides these houses he had a delightful little estate just out of town, and some sort of factory in another part of the city. General Epanchin, as everyone knew, had a good deal to do with certain government monopolies; he was also a voice, and an important one, in many rich public companies of various descriptions; in fact, he enjoyed the reputation of being a well-to-do man of busy habits, many ties, and affluent means. He had made himself indispensable in several quarters, amongst others in his department of the government; and yet it was a known fact that Fedor Ivanovitch Epanchin was a man of no education whatever, and had absolutely risen from the ranks.

This last fact could, of course, reflect nothing but credit upon the general; and yet, though unquestionably a sagacious man, he had his own little weaknesses—very excusable ones,—one of which was a dislike to any allusion to the above circumstance. He was undoubtedly clever. For instance, he made a point of never asserting himself when he would gain more by keeping in the background; and in consequence many exalted personages valued him principally for his humility and simplicity, and because "he knew his place." And yet if these good people could only have had a peep into the mind of this excellent fellow who "knew his place" so well! The fact is that, in spite of his knowledge of the world and his really remarkable abilities, he always liked to appear to be carrying out other people's ideas rather than his own. And also, his luck seldom failed him, even at cards, for which he had a passion that he did not attempt to conceal. He played for high stakes, and moved, altogether, in very varied society.

As to age, General Epanchin was in the very prime of life; that is, about fifty-five years of age,—the flowering time of existence, when real enjoyment of life begins. His healthy appearance, good colour, sound, though discoloured teeth, sturdy figure, preoccupied air during business hours, and jolly good humour during his game at cards in the evening, all bore witness to his success in life, and combined to make existence a bed of roses to his excellency. The general was lord of a flourishing family, consisting of his wife and three grown-up daughters. He had married young, while still a lieutenant, his wife being a girl of about his own age, who possessed neither beauty nor education, and who brought him no more than fifty souls of landed property, which little estate served, however, as a nest-egg for far more important accumulations. The general never regretted his early marriage, or regarded it as a foolish youthful escapade; and he so respected and feared his wife that he was very near loving her. Mrs. Epanchin came of the princely stock of Muishkin, which if not a brilliant, was, at all events, a decidedly ancient family; and she was extremely proud of her descent.

With a few exceptions, the worthy couple had lived through their long union very happily. While still young the wife had been able to make important friends among the aristocracy, partly by virtue of her family descent, and partly by her own exertions; while, in after life, thanks to their wealth and to the position of her husband in the service, she took her place among the higher circles as by right.

During these last few years all three of the general's daughters—Alexandra, Adelaida, and Aglaya—had grown up and matured. Of course they were only Epanchins, but their mother's family was noble; they might expect considerable fortunes; their father had hopes of attaining to very high rank indeed in his country's service—all of which was satisfactory. All three of the girls were decidedly pretty, even the eldest, Alexandra, who was just twenty-five years old. The middle daughter was now twenty-three, while the youngest, Aglaya, was twenty. This youngest girl was absolutely a beauty, and had begun of late to attract considerable attention in society. But this was not all, for every one of the three was clever, well educated, and accomplished.

It was a matter of general knowledge that the three girls were very fond of one another, and supported each other in every way; it was even said that the two elder ones had made certain sacrifices for the sake of the idol of the household, Aglaya. In society they not only disliked asserting themselves, but were actually retiring. Certainly no one could blame them for being too arrogant or haughty, and yet everybody was well aware that they were proud and quite understood their own value. The eldest was musical, while the second was a clever artist, which fact she had concealed until lately. In a word, the world spoke well of the girls; but they were not without their enemies, and occasionally people talked with horror of the number of books they had read.

They were in no hurry to marry. They liked good society, but were not too keen about it. All this was the more remarkable, because everyone was well aware of the hopes and aims of their parents.

It was about eleven o'clock in the forenoon when the prince rang the bell at General Epanchin's door. The general lived on the first floor or flat of the house, as modest a lodging as his position permitted. A liveried servant opened the door, and the prince was obliged to enter into long explanations with this gentleman, who, from the first glance, looked at him and his bundle with grave suspicion. At last, however, on the repeated positive assurance that he really was Prince Muishkin, and must absolutely see the general on business, the bewildered domestic showed him into a little ante-chamber leading to a waiting-room that adjoined the general's study, there handing him over to another servant, whose duty it was to be in this ante-chamber all the morning, and announce visitors to the general. This second individual wore a dress coat, and was some forty years of age; he was the general's special study servant, and well aware of his own importance.

"Wait in the next room, please; and leave your bundle here," said the door-keeper, as he sat down comfortably in his own easy-chair in the ante-chamber. He looked at the prince in severe surprise as the latter settled himself in another chair alongside, with his bundle on his knees.

"If you don't mind, I would rather sit here with you," said the prince; "I should prefer it to sitting in there."

"Oh, but you can't stay here. You are a visitor—a guest, so to speak. Is it the general himself you wish to see?"

The man evidently could not take in the idea of such a shabby-looking visitor, and had decided to ask once more.

"Yes—I have business—" began the prince.

"I do not ask you what your business may be, all I have to do is to announce you; and unless the secretary comes in here I cannot do that."

The man's suspicions seemed to increase more and more. The prince was too unlike the usual run of daily visitors; and although the general certainly did receive, on business, all sorts and conditions of men, yet in spite of this fact the servant felt great doubts on the subject of this particular visitor. The presence of the secretary as an intermediary was, he judged, essential in this case.

"Surely you—are from abroad?" he inquired at last, in a confused sort of way. He had begun his sentence intending to say, "Surely you are not Prince Muishkin, are you?"

"Yes, straight from the train! Did not you intend to say, 'Surely you are not Prince Muishkin?' just now, but refrained out of politeness?"

"H'm!" grunted the astonished servant.

"I assure you I am not deceiving you; you shall not have to answer for me. As to my being dressed like this, and carrying a bundle, there's nothing surprising in that—the fact is, my circumstances are not particularly rosy at this moment."

"H'm!—no, I'm not afraid of that, you see; I have to announce you, that's all. The secretary will be out directly—that is, unless you—yes, that's the rub—unless you—come, you must allow me to ask you—you've not come to beg, have you?"

"Oh dear no, you can be perfectly easy on that score. I have quite another matter on hand."

"You must excuse my asking, you know. Your appearance led me to think—but just wait for the secretary; the general is busy now, but the secretary is sure to come out."

"Oh—well, look here, if I have some time to wait, would you mind telling me, is there any place about where I could have a smoke? I have my pipe and tobacco with me."

"*Smoke?*" said the man, in shocked but disdainful surprise, blinking his eyes at the prince as though he could not believe his senses. "No, sir, you cannot smoke here, and I wonder you are not ashamed of the very suggestion. Ha, ha! a cool idea that, I declare!"

"Oh, I didn't mean in this room! I know I can't smoke here, of course. I'd adjourn to some other room, wherever you like to show me to. You see, I'm used to smoking a good deal, and now I haven't had a puff for three hours; however, just as you like."

"Now how on earth am I to announce a man like that?" muttered the servant. "In the first place, you've no right in here at all; you ought to be in the waiting-room, because you're a sort of visitor— a guest, in fact—and I shall catch it for this. Look here, do you intend to take up you abode with us?" he added, glancing once more at the prince's bundle, which evidently gave him no peace.

"No, I don't think so. I don't think I should stay even if they were to invite me. I've simply come to make their acquaintance, and nothing more."

"Make their acquaintance?" asked the man, in amazement, and with redoubled suspicion. "Then why did you say you had business with the general?"

"Oh well, very little business. There is one little matter—some advice I am going to ask him for; but my principal object is simply to introduce myself, because I am Prince Muishkin, and Madame Epanchin is the last of her branch of the house, and besides herself and me there are no other Muishkins left."

"What—you're a relation then, are you?" asked the servant, so bewildered that he began to feel quite alarmed.

"Well, hardly so. If you stretch a point, we are relations, of course, but so distant that one cannot really take cognizance of it. I once wrote to your mistress from abroad, but she did not reply. However, I have thought it right to make acquaintance with her on my arrival. I am telling you all this in order to ease your mind, for I see you are still far from comfortable on my account. All you have to do is to announce me as Prince Muishkin, and the object of my visit will be plain enough. If I am received—very good; if not, well, very good again. But they are sure to receive me, I should think; Madame Epanchin will naturally be curious to see the only remaining representative of her family. She values her Muishkin descent very highly, if I am rightly informed."

The prince's conversation was artless and confiding to a degree, and the servant could not help feeling that as from visitor to common serving-man this state of things was highly improper. His conclusion was that one of two things must be the explanation—either that this was a begging impostor, or that the prince, if prince he were, was simply a fool, without the slightest ambition; for a sensible prince with any ambition would certainly not wait about in ante-rooms with servants, and talk of his own private affairs like this. In either case, how was he to announce this singular visitor?

"I really think I must request you to step into the next room!" he said, with all the insistence he could muster.

"Why? If I had been sitting there now, I should not have had the opportunity of making these personal explanations. I see you are still uneasy about me and keep eyeing my cloak and bundle. Don't you think you might go in yourself now, without waiting for the secretary to come out?"

"No, no! I can't announce a visitor like yourself without the secretary. Besides the general said he was not to be disturbed—he is with the Colonel C—. Gavrila Ardalionovitch goes in without announcing."

"Who may that be? a clerk?"

"What? Gavrila Ardalionovitch? Oh no; he belongs to one of the companies. Look here, at all events put your bundle down, here."

"Yes, I will if I may; and—can I take off my cloak"

"Of course; you can't go in *there* with it on, anyhow."

The prince rose and took off his mantle, revealing a neat enough morning costume—a little worn, but well made. He wore a steel watch chain and from this chain there hung a silver Geneva watch. Fool the prince might be, still, the general's servant felt that it was not correct for him to continue to converse thus with a visitor, in spite of the fact that the prince pleased him somehow.

"And what time of day does the lady receive?" the latter asked, reseating himself in his old place.

"Oh, that's not in *my* province! I believe she receives at any time; it depends upon the visitors. The dressmaker goes in at eleven. Gavrila Ardalionovitch is allowed much earlier than other people, too; he is even admitted to early lunch now and then."

"It is much warmer in the rooms here than it is abroad at this season," observed the prince; "but it is much warmer there out of doors. As for the houses—a Russian can't live in them in the winter until he gets accustomed to them."

"Don't they heat them at all?"

"Well, they do heat them a little; but the houses and stoves are so different to ours."

"H'm! were you long away?"

"Four years! and I was in the same place nearly all the time,—in one village."

"You must have forgotten Russia, hadn't you?"

"Yes, indeed I had—a good deal; and, would you believe it, I often wonder at myself for not having forgotten how to speak Russian? Even now, as I talk to you, I keep saying to myself 'how well I am speaking it.' Perhaps that is partly why I am so talkative this morning. I assure you, ever since yesterday evening I have had the strongest desire to go on and on talking Russian."

"H'm! yes; did you live in Petersburg in former years?"

This good flunkey, in spite of his conscientious scruples, really could not resist continuing such a very genteel and agreeable conversation.

"In Petersburg? Oh no! hardly at all, and now they say so much is changed in the place that even those who did know it well are obliged to relearn what they knew. They talk a good deal about the new law courts, and changes there, don't they?"

"H'm! yes, that's true enough. Well now, how is the law over there, do they administer it more justly than here?"

"Oh, I don't know about that! I've heard much that is good about our legal administration, too. There is no capital punishment here for one thing."

"Is there over there?"

"Yes—I saw an execution in France—at Lyons. Schneider took me over with him to see it."

"What, did they hang the fellow?"

"No, they cut off people's heads in France."

"What did the fellow do?—yell?"

"Oh no—it's the work of an instant. They put a man inside a frame and a sort of broad knife falls by machinery—they call the thing a guillotine—it falls with fearful force and weight—the head springs off so quickly that you can't wink your eye in between. But all the preparations are so dreadful. When they announce the sentence, you know, and prepare the criminal and tie his hands, and cart him off to the scaffold—that's the fearful part of the business. The people all crowd round—even women—though they don't at all approve of women looking on."

"No, it's not a thing for women."

"Of course not—of course not!—bah! The criminal was a fine intelligent fearless man; Le Gros was his name; and I may tell you—believe it or not, as you like—that when that man stepped upon the scaffold he *cried*, he did indeed,—he was as white as a bit of paper. Isn't it a dreadful idea that he should have cried—cried! Whoever heard of a grown man crying from fear—not a child, but a man who never had cried before—a grown man of forty-five years. Imagine what must have been going on in that man's mind at such a moment; what dreadful convulsions his whole spirit must have endured; it is an outrage on the soul that's what it is. Because it is said 'thou shalt not kill,' is he to be killed because he murdered some one else? No, it is not right, it's an impossible theory. I assure you, I saw the sight a month ago and it's dancing before my eyes to this moment. I dream of it, often."

The prince had grown animated as he spoke, and a tinge of colour suffused his pale face, though his way of talking was as quiet as ever. The servant followed his words with sympathetic interest.

Clearly he was not at all anxious to bring the conversation to an end. Who knows? Perhaps he too was a man of imagination and with some capacity for thought.

"Well, at all events it is a good thing that there's no pain when the poor fellow's head flies off," he remarked.

"Do you know, though," cried the prince warmly, "you made that remark now, and everyone says the same thing, and the machine is designed with the purpose of avoiding pain, this guillotine I mean; but a thought came into my head then: what if it be a bad plan after all? You may laugh at my idea, perhaps—but I could not help its occurring to me all the same. Now with the rack and tortures and so on—you suffer terrible pain of course; but then your torture is bodily pain only (although no doubt you have plenty of that) until you die. But *here* I should imagine the most terrible part of the whole punishment is, not the bodily pain at all—but the certain knowledge that in an hour,—then in ten minutes, then in half a minute, then now—this very *instant*—your soul must quit your body and that you will no longer be a man—and that this is certain, *certain!* That's the point— the certainty of it. Just that instant when you place your head on the block and hear the iron grate over your head—then—that quarter of a second is the most awful of all.

"This is not my own fantastical opinion—many people have thought the same; but I feel it so deeply that I'll tell you what I think. I believe that to execute a man for murder is to punish him immeasurably more dreadfully than is equivalent to his crime. A murder by sentence is far more dreadful than a murder committed by a criminal. The man who is attacked by robbers at night, in a dark wood, or anywhere, undoubtedly hopes and hopes that he may yet escape until the very moment of his death. There are plenty of instances of a man running away, or imploring for mercy— at all events hoping on in some degree—even after his throat was cut. But in the case of an execution, that last hope—having which it is so immeasurably less dreadful to die,—is taken away from the wretch and *certainty* substituted in its place! There is his sentence, and with it that terrible certainty that he cannot possibly escape death—which, I consider, must be the most dreadful anguish in the world. You may place a soldier before a cannon's mouth in battle, and fire upon him—and he will still hope. But read to that same soldier his death-sentence, and he will either go mad or burst into tears. Who dares to say that any man can suffer this without going mad? No, no! it is an abuse, a shame, it is unnecessary—why should such a thing exist? Doubtless there may be men who have been sentenced, who have suffered this mental anguish for a while and then have been reprieved; perhaps such men may have been able to relate their feelings afterwards. Our Lord Christ spoke of this anguish and dread. No! no! no! No man should be treated so, no man, no man!"

The servant, though of course he could not have expressed all this as the prince did, still clearly entered into it and was greatly conciliated, as was evident from the increased amiability of his expression. "If you are really very anxious for a smoke," he remarked, "I think it might possibly be managed, if you are very quick about it. You see they might come out and inquire for you, and you wouldn't be on the spot. You see that door there? Go in there and you'll find a little room on the right; you can smoke there, only open the window, because I ought not to allow it really, and—." But there was no time, after all.

A young fellow entered the ante-room at this moment, with a bundle of papers in his hand. The footman hastened to help him take off his overcoat. The new arrival glanced at the prince out of the corners of his eyes.

"This gentleman declares, Gavrila Ardalionovitch," began the man, confidentially and almost familiarly, "that he is Prince Muishkin and a relative of Madame Epanchin's. He has just arrived from abroad, with nothing but a bundle by way of luggage—."

The prince did not hear the rest, because at this point the servant continued his communication in a whisper.

Gavrila Ardalionovitch listened attentively, and gazed at the prince with great curiosity. At last he motioned the man aside and stepped hurriedly towards the prince.

"Are you Prince Muishkin?" he asked, with the greatest courtesy and amiability.

He was a remarkably handsome young fellow of some twenty-eight summers, fair and of middle height; he wore a small beard, and his face was most intelligent. Yet his smile, in spite of its sweetness, was a little thin, if I may so call it, and showed his teeth too evenly; his gaze though decidedly good-humoured and ingenuous, was a trifle too inquisitive and intent to be altogether agreeable.

"Probably when he is alone he looks quite different, and hardly smiles at all!" thought the prince.

He explained about himself in a few words, very much the same as he had told the footman and Rogojin beforehand.

Gavrila Ardalionovitch meanwhile seemed to be trying to recall something.

"Was it not you, then, who sent a letter a year or less ago—from Switzerland, I think it was—to Elizabetha Prokofievna (Mrs. Epanchin)?"

"It was."

"Oh, then, of course they will remember who you are. You wish to see the general? I'll tell him at once—he will be free in a minute; but you—you had better wait in the ante-chamber,—hadn't you? Why is he here?" he added, severely, to the man.

"I tell you, sir, he wished it himself!"

At this moment the study door opened, and a military man, with a portfolio under his arm, came out talking loudly, and after bidding good-bye to someone inside, took his departure.

"You there, Gania?" cried a voice from the study, "come in here, will you?"

Gavrila Ardalionovitch nodded to the prince and entered the room hastily.

A couple of minutes later the door opened again and the affable voice of Gania cried:

"Come in please, prince!"

Chapter III.

General Ivan Fedorovitch Epanchin was standing in the middle of the room, and gazed with great curiosity at the prince as he entered. He even advanced a couple of steps to meet him.

The prince came forward and introduced himself.

"Quite so," replied the general, "and what can I do for you?"

"Oh, I have no special business; my principal object was to make your acquaintance. I should not like to disturb you. I do not know your times and arrangements here, you see, but I have only just arrived. I came straight from the station. I am come direct from Switzerland."

The general very nearly smiled, but thought better of it and kept his smile back. Then he reflected, blinked his eyes, stared at his guest once more from head to foot; then abruptly motioned him to a chair, sat down himself, and waited with some impatience for the prince to speak.

Gania stood at his table in the far corner of the room, turning over papers.

"I have not much time for making acquaintances, as a rule," said the general, "but as, of course, you have your object in coming, I—"

"I felt sure you would think I had some object in view when I resolved to pay you this visit," the prince interrupted; "but I give you my word, beyond the pleasure of making your acquaintance I had no personal object whatever."

"The pleasure is, of course, mutual; but life is not all pleasure, as you are aware. There is such a thing as business, and I really do not see what possible reason there can be, or what we have in common to—"

"Oh, there is no reason, of course, and I suppose there is nothing in common between us, or very little; for if I am Prince Muishkin, and your wife happens to be a member of my house, that can hardly be called a 'reason.' I quite understand that. And yet that was my whole motive for coming. You see I have not been in Russia for four years, and knew very little about anything when I left. I had been very ill for a long time, and I feel now the need of a few good friends. In fact, I have a certain question upon which I much need advice, and do not know whom to go to for it. I thought of your family when I was passing through Berlin. 'They are almost relations,' I said to myself, 'so I'll begin with them; perhaps we may get on with each other, I with them and they with me, if they are kind people;' and I have heard that you are very kind people!"

"Oh, thank you, thank you, I'm sure," replied the general, considerably taken aback. "May I ask where you have taken up your quarters?"

"Nowhere, as yet."

"What, straight from the station to my house? And how about your luggage?"

"I only had a small bundle, containing linen, with me, nothing more. I can carry it in my hand, easily. There will be plenty of time to take a room in some hotel by the evening."

"Oh, then you *do* intend to take a room?"

"Of course."

"To judge from your words, you came straight to my house with the intention of staying there."

"That could only have been on your invitation. I confess, however, that I should not have stayed here even if you had invited me, not for any particular reason, but because it is—well, contrary to my practice and nature, somehow."

"Oh, indeed! Then it is perhaps as well that I neither *did* invite you, nor *do* invite you now. Excuse me, prince, but we had better make this matter clear, once for all. We have just agreed that with regard to our relationship there is not much to be said, though, of course, it would have been very delightful to us to feel that such relationship did actually exist; therefore, perhaps—"

"Therefore, perhaps I had better get up and go away?" said the prince, laughing merrily as he rose from his place; just as merrily as though the circumstances were by no means strained or difficult.

"And I give you my word, general, that though I know nothing whatever of manners and customs of society, and how people live and all that, yet I felt quite sure that this visit of mine would end exactly as it has ended now. Oh, well, I suppose it's all right; especially as my letter was not answered. Well, good-bye, and forgive me for having disturbed you!"

The prince's expression was so good-natured at this moment, and so entirely free from even a suspicion of unpleasant feeling was the smile with which he looked at the general as he spoke, that the latter suddenly paused, and appeared to gaze at his guest from quite a new point of view, all in an instant.

"Do you know, prince," he said, in quite a different tone, "I do not know you at all, yet, and after all, Elizabetha Prokofievna would very likely be pleased to have a peep at a man of her own name. Wait a little, if you don't mind, and if you have time to spare?"

"Oh, I assure you I've lots of time, my time is entirely my own!" And the prince immediately replaced his soft, round hat on the table. "I confess, I thought Elizabetha Prokofievna would very likely remember that I had written her a letter. Just now your servant—outside there—was dreadfully suspicious that I had come to beg of you. I noticed that! Probably he has very strict instructions on that score; but I assure you I did not come to beg. I came to make some friends. But I am rather bothered at having disturbed you; that's all I care about.—"

"Look here, prince," said the general, with a cordial smile, "if you really are the sort of man you appear to be, it may be a source of great pleasure to us to make your better acquaintance; but, you see, I am a very busy man, and have to be perpetually sitting here and signing papers, or off to see his excellency, or to my department, or somewhere; so that though I should be glad to see more of people, nice people—you see, I—however, I am sure you are so well brought up that you will see at once, and—but how old are you, prince?"

"Twenty-six."

"No? I thought you very much younger."

"Yes, they say I have a 'young' face. As to disturbing you I shall soon learn to avoid doing that, for I hate disturbing people. Besides, you and I are so differently constituted, I should think, that there must be very little in common between us. Not that I will ever believe there is *nothing* in common between any two people, as some declare is the case. I am sure people make a great mistake in sorting each other into groups, by appearances; but I am boring you, I see, you—"

"Just two words: have you any means at all? Or perhaps you may be intending to undertake some sort of employment? Excuse my questioning you, but—"

"Oh, my dear sir, I esteem and understand your kindness in putting the question. No; at present I have no means whatever, and no employment either, but I hope to find some. I was living on other people abroad. Schneider, the professor who treated me and taught me, too, in Switzerland, gave me just enough money for my journey, so that now I have but a few copecks left. There certainly is one question upon which I am anxious to have advice, but—"

"Tell me, how do you intend to live now, and what are your plans?" interrupted the general.

"I wish to work, somehow or other."

"Oh yes, but then, you see, you are a philosopher. Have you any talents, or ability in any direction—that is, any that would bring in money and bread? Excuse me again—"

"Oh, don't apologize. No, I don't think I have either talents or special abilities of any kind; on the contrary. I have always been an invalid and unable to learn much. As for bread, I should think—"

The general interrupted once more with questions; while the prince again replied with the narrative we have heard before. It appeared that the general had known Pavlicheff; but why the latter had taken an interest in the prince, that young gentleman could not explain; probably by virtue of the old friendship with his father, he thought.

The prince had been left an orphan when quite a little child, and Pavlicheff had entrusted him to an old lady, a relative of his own, living in the country, the child needing the fresh air and exercise of country life. He was educated, first by a governess, and afterwards by a tutor, but could not remember much about this time of his life. His fits were so frequent then, that they made almost an idiot of him (the prince used the expression "idiot" himself). Pavlicheff had met Professor Schneider in Berlin, and the latter had persuaded him to send the boy to Switzerland, to Schneider's establishment there, for the cure of his epilepsy, and, five years before this time, the prince was sent off. But Pavlicheff had died two or three years since, and Schneider had himself supported the young fellow, from that day to this, at his own expense. Although he had not quite cured him, he had greatly improved his condition; and now, at last, at the prince's own desire, and because of a certain matter which came to the ears of the latter, Schneider had despatched the young man to Russia.

The general was much astonished.

"Then you have no one, absolutely *no* one in Russia?" he asked.

"No one, at present; but I hope to make friends; and then I have a letter from—"

"At all events," put in the general, not listening to the news about the letter, "at all events, you must have learned *something*, and your malady would not prevent your undertaking some easy work, in one of the departments, for instance?"

"Oh dear no, oh no! As for a situation, I should much like to find one for I am anxious to discover what I really am fit for. I have learned a good deal in the last four years, and, besides, I read a great many Russian books."

"Russian books, indeed? Then, of course, you can read and write quite correctly?"

"Oh dear, yes!"

"Capital! And your handwriting?"

"Ah, there I am *really* talented! I may say I am a real caligraphist. Let me write you something, just to show you," said the prince, with some excitement.

"With pleasure! In fact, it is very necessary. I like your readiness, prince; in fact, I must say—I—I—like you very well, altogether," said the general.

"What delightful writing materials you have here, such a lot of pencils and things, and what beautiful paper! It's a charming room altogether. I know that picture, it's a Swiss view. I'm sure the artist painted it from nature, and that I have seen the very place—"

"Quite likely, though I bought it here. Gania, give the prince some paper. Here are pens and paper; now then, take this table. What's this?" the general continued to Gania, who had that moment taken a large photograph out of his portfolio, and shown it to his senior. "Halloa! Nastasia Philipovna! Did she send it you herself? Herself?" he inquired, with much curiosity and great animation.

"She gave it me just now, when I called in to congratulate her. I asked her for it long ago. I don't know whether she meant it for a hint that I had come empty-handed, without a present for her birthday, or what," added Gania, with an unpleasant smile.

"Oh, nonsense, nonsense," said the general, with decision. "What extraordinary ideas you have, Gania! As if she would hint; that's not her way at all. Besides, what could *you* give her, without having thousands at your disposal? You might have given her your portrait, however. Has she ever asked you for it?"

"No, not yet. Very likely she never will. I suppose you haven't forgotten about tonight, have you, Ivan Fedorovitch? You were one of those specially invited, you know."

"Oh no, I remember all right, and I shall go, of course. I should think so! She's twenty-five years old today! And, you know, Gania, you must be ready for great things; she has promised both myself and Afanasy Ivanovitch that she will give a decided answer tonight, yes or no. So be prepared!"

Gania suddenly became so ill at ease that his face grew paler than ever.

"Are you sure she said that?" he asked, and his voice seemed to quiver as he spoke.

"Yes, she promised. We both worried her so that she gave in; but she wished us to tell you nothing about it until the day."

The general watched Gania's confusion intently, and clearly did not like it.

"Remember, Ivan Fedorovitch," said Gania, in great agitation, "that I was to be free too, until her decision; and that even then I was to have my 'yes or no' free."

"Why, don't you, aren't you—" began the general, in alarm.

"Oh, don't misunderstand—"

"But, my dear fellow, what are you doing, what do you mean?"

"Oh, I'm not rejecting her. I may have expressed myself badly, but I didn't mean that."

"Reject her! I should think not!" said the general with annoyance, and apparently not in the least anxious to conceal it. "Why, my dear fellow, it's not a question of your rejecting her, it is whether you are prepared to receive her consent joyfully, and with proper satisfaction. How are things going on at home?"

"At home? Oh, I can do as I like there, of course; only my father will make a fool of himself, as usual. He is rapidly becoming a general nuisance. I don't ever talk to him now, but I hold him in check, safe enough. I swear if it had not been for my mother, I should have shown him the way out, long ago. My mother is always crying, of course, and my sister sulks. I had to tell them at last that I intended to be master of my own destiny, and that I expect to be obeyed at home. At least, I gave my sister to understand as much, and my mother was present."

"Well, I must say, I cannot understand it!" said the general, shrugging his shoulders and dropping his hands. "You remember your mother, Nina Alexandrovna, that day she came and sat here and groaned—and when I asked her what was the matter, she says, 'Oh, it's such a *dishonour* to us!' dishonour! Stuff and nonsense! I should like to know who can reproach Nastasia Philipovna, or who can say a word of any kind against her. Did she mean because Nastasia had been living with Totski? What nonsense it is! You would not let her come near your daughters, says Nina Alexandrovna. What next, I wonder? I don't see how she can fail to—to understand—"

"Her own position?" prompted Gania. "She does understand. Don't be annoyed with her. I have warned her not to meddle in other people's affairs. However, although there's comparative peace at home at present, the storm will break if anything is finally settled tonight."

The prince heard the whole of the foregoing conversation, as he sat at the table, writing. He finished at last, and brought the result of his labour to the general's desk.

"So this is Nastasia Philipovna," he said, looking attentively and curiously at the portrait. "How wonderfully beautiful!" he immediately added, with warmth. The picture was certainly that of an unusually lovely woman. She was photographed in a black silk dress of simple design, her hair was evidently dark and plainly arranged, her eyes were deep and thoughtful, the expression of her face passionate, but proud. She was rather thin, perhaps, and a little pale. Both Gania and the general gazed at the prince in amazement.

"How do you know it's Nastasia Philipovna?" asked the general; "you surely don't know her already, do you?"

"Yes, I do! I have only been one day in Russia, but I have heard of the great beauty!" And the prince proceeded to narrate his meeting with Rogojin in the train and the whole of the latter's story.

"There's news!" said the general in some excitement, after listening to the story with engrossed attention.

"Oh, of course it's nothing but humbug!" cried Gania, a little disturbed, however. "It's all humbug; the young merchant was pleased to indulge in a little innocent recreation! I have heard something of Rogojin!"

"Yes, so have I!" replied the general. "Nastasia Philipovna told us all about the earrings that very day. But now it is quite a different matter. You see the fellow really has a million of roubles, and he is passionately in love. The whole story smells of passion, and we all know what this class of gentry is capable of when infatuated. I am much afraid of some disagreeable scandal, I am indeed!"

"You are afraid of the million, I suppose," said Gania, grinning and showing his teeth.

"And you are *not*, I presume, eh?"

"How did he strike you, prince?" asked Gania, suddenly. "Did he seem to be a serious sort of a man, or just a common rowdy fellow? What was your own opinion about the matter?"

While Gania put this question, a new idea suddenly flashed into his brain, and blazed out, impatiently, in his eyes. The general, who was really agitated and disturbed, looked at the prince too, but did not seem to expect much from his reply.

"I really don't quite know how to tell you," replied the prince, "but it certainly did seem to me that the man was full of passion, and not, perhaps, quite healthy passion. He seemed to be still far from well. Very likely he will be in bed again in a day or two, especially if he lives fast."

"No! do you think so?" said the general, catching at the idea.

"Yes, I do think so!"

"Yes, but the sort of scandal I referred to may happen at any moment. It may be this very evening," remarked Gania to the general, with a smile.

"Of course; quite so. In that case it all depends upon what is going on in her brain at this moment."

"You know the kind of person she is at times."

"How? What kind of person is she?" cried the general, arrived at the limits of his patience. "Look here, Gania, don't you go annoying her tonight. What you are to do is to be as agreeable towards her as ever you can. Well, what are you smiling at? You must understand, Gania, that I have no interest whatever in speaking like this. Whichever way the question is settled, it will be to my advantage. Nothing will move Totski from his resolution, so I run no risk. If there is anything I desire, you must know that it is your benefit only. Can't you trust me? You are a sensible fellow, and I have been counting on you; for, in this matter, that, that—"

"Yes, that's the chief thing," said Gania, helping the general out of his difficulties again, and curling his lips in an envenomed smile, which he did not attempt to conceal. He gazed with his fevered eyes straight into those of the general, as though he were anxious that the latter might read his thoughts.

The general grew purple with anger.

"Yes, of course it is the chief thing!" he cried, looking sharply at Gania. "What a very curious man you are, Gania! You actually seem to be *glad* to hear of this millionaire fellow's arrival—just as though you wished for an excuse to get out of the whole thing. This is an affair in which you ought to act honestly with both sides, and give due warning, to avoid compromising others. But, even now, there is still time. Do you understand me? I wish to know whether you desire this arrangement or whether you do not? If not, say so,—and—and welcome! No one is trying to force you into the snare, Gavrila Ardalionovitch, if you see a snare in the matter, at least."

"I do desire it," murmured Gania, softly but firmly, lowering his eyes; and he relapsed into gloomy silence.

The general was satisfied. He had excited himself, and was evidently now regretting that he had gone so far. He turned to the prince, and suddenly the disagreeable thought of the latter's presence struck him, and the certainty that he must have heard every word of the conversation. But he felt at ease in another moment; it only needed one glance at the prince to see that in that quarter there was nothing to fear.

"Oh!" cried the general, catching sight of the prince's specimen of caligraphy, which the latter had now handed him for inspection. "Why, this is simply beautiful; look at that, Gania, there's real talent there!"

On a sheet of thick writing-paper the prince had written in medieval characters the legend:

"The gentle Abbot Pafnute signed this."

"There," explained the prince, with great delight and animation, "there, that's the abbot's real signature—from a manuscript of the fourteenth century. All these old abbots and bishops used to write most beautifully, with such taste and so much care and diligence. Have you no copy of Pogodin, general? If you had one I could show you another type. Stop a bit—here you have the large round writing common in France during the eighteenth century. Some of the letters are shaped quite differently from those now in use. It was the writing current then, and employed by public writers generally. I copied this from one of them, and you can see how good it is. Look at the well-rounded a and d. I have tried to translate the French character into the Russian letters—a difficult thing to do, but I think I have succeeded fairly. Here is a fine sentence, written in a good, original hand— 'Zeal triumphs over all.' That is the script of the Russian War Office. That is how official documents addressed to important personages should be written. The letters are round, the type black, and the style somewhat remarkable. A stylist would not allow these ornaments, or attempts at flourishes— just look at these unfinished tails!—but it has distinction and really depicts the soul of the writer. He would like to give play to his imagination, and follow the inspiration of his genius, but a soldier is only at ease in the guard-room, and the pen stops half-way, a slave to discipline. How delightful! The first time I met an example of this handwriting, I was positively astonished, and where do you think I chanced to find it? In Switzerland, of all places! Now that is an ordinary English hand. It can hardly be improved, it is so refined and exquisite—almost perfection. This is an example of another kind, a mixture of styles. The copy was given me by a French commercial traveller. It is founded on the English, but the downstrokes are a little blacker, and more marked. Notice that the oval has some slight modification—it is more rounded. This writing allows for flourishes; now a flourish is a dangerous thing! Its use requires such taste, but, if successful, what a distinction it gives to the whole! It results in an incomparable type—one to fall in love with!"

"Dear me! How you have gone into all the refinements and details of the question! Why, my dear fellow, you are not a caligraphist, you are an artist! Eh, Gania?"

"Wonderful!" said Gania. "And he knows it too," he added, with a sarcastic smile.

"You may smile,—but there's a career in this," said the general. "You don't know what a great personage I shall show this to, prince. Why, you can command a situation at thirty-five roubles per month to start with. However, it's half-past twelve," he concluded, looking at his watch; "so to business, prince, for I must be setting to work and shall not see you again today. Sit down a minute. I have told you that I cannot receive you myself very often, but I should like to be of some assistance to you, some small assistance, of a kind that would give you satisfaction. I shall find you a place in one of the State departments, an easy place—but you will require to be accurate. Now, as to your plans—in the house, or rather in the family of Gania here—my young friend, whom I hope you will know better—his mother and sister have prepared two or three rooms for lodgers, and let them to highly recommended young fellows, with board and attendance. I am sure Nina Alexandrovna will take you in on my recommendation. There you will be comfortable and well taken care of; for I do not think, prince, that you are the sort of man to be left to the mercy of Fate in a town like Petersburg. Nina Alexandrovna, Gania's mother, and Varvara Alexandrovna, are ladies for whom I have the highest possible esteem and respect. Nina Alexandrovna is the wife of General Ardalion Alexandrovitch, my old brother in arms, with whom, I regret to say, on account of certain circumstances, I am no longer acquainted. I give you all this information, prince, in order to make it clear to you that I am personally recommending you to this family, and that in so doing, I am more or less taking upon myself to answer for you. The terms are most reasonable, and I trust that your salary will very shortly prove amply sufficient for your expenditure. Of course pocket-money is a necessity, if only a little; do not be angry, prince, if I strongly recommend you to avoid carrying money in your pocket. But as your purse is quite empty at the present moment, you must allow me to press these twenty-five roubles upon your acceptance, as something to begin with. Of course we will settle this little matter another time, and if you are the upright, honest man you look, I anticipate very little trouble between us on that score. Taking so much interest in you as you may perceive I do, I am not without my object, and you shall know it in good time. You see, I am perfectly candid with you. I hope, Gania, you have nothing to say against the prince's taking up his abode in your house?"

"Oh, on the contrary! my mother will be very glad," said Gania, courteously and kindly.

"I think only one of your rooms is engaged as yet, is it not? That fellow Ferd-Ferd—"

"Ferdishenko."

"Yes—I don't like that Ferdishenko. I can't understand why Nastasia Philipovna encourages him so. Is he really her cousin, as he says?"

"Oh dear no, it's all a joke. No more cousin than I am."

"Well, what do you think of the arrangement, prince?"

"Thank you, general; you have behaved very kindly to me; all the more so since I did not ask you to help me. I don't say that out of pride. I certainly did not know where to lay my head tonight. Rogojin asked me to come to his house, of course, but—"

"Rogojin? No, no, my good fellow. I should strongly recommend you, paternally,—or, if you prefer it, as a friend,—to forget all about Rogojin, and, in fact, to stick to the family into which you are about to enter."

"Thank you," began the prince; "and since you are so very kind there is just one matter which I—"

"You must really excuse me," interrupted the general, "but I positively haven't another moment now. I shall just tell Elizabetha Prokofievna about you, and if she wishes to receive you at once—as I shall advise her—I strongly recommend you to ingratiate yourself with her at the first opportunity, for my wife may be of the greatest service to you in many ways. If she cannot receive you now, you must be content to wait till another time. Meanwhile you, Gania, just look over these accounts, will you? We mustn't forget to finish off that matter—"

The general left the room, and the prince never succeeded in broaching the business which he had on hand, though he had endeavoured to do so four times.

Gania lit a cigarette and offered one to the prince. The latter accepted the offer, but did not talk, being unwilling to disturb Gania's work. He commenced to examine the study and its contents. But Gania hardly so much as glanced at the papers lying before him; he was absent and thoughtful, and his smile and general appearance struck the prince still more disagreeably now that the two were left alone together.

Suddenly Gania approached our hero who was at the moment standing over Nastasia Philipovna's portrait, gazing at it.

"Do you admire that sort of woman, prince?" he asked, looking intently at him. He seemed to have some special object in the question.

"It's a wonderful face," said the prince, "and I feel sure that her destiny is not by any means an ordinary, uneventful one. Her face is smiling enough, but she must have suffered terribly—hasn't she? Her eyes show it—those two bones there, the little points under her eyes, just where the cheek begins. It's a proud face too, terribly proud! And I—I can't say whether she is good and kind, or not. Oh, if she be but good! That would make all well!"

"And would you marry a woman like that, now?" continued Gania, never taking his excited eyes off the prince's face.

"I cannot marry at all," said the latter. "I am an invalid."

"Would Rogojin marry her, do you think?"

"Why not? Certainly he would, I should think. He would marry her tomorrow!—marry her tomorrow and murder her in a week!"

Hardly had the prince uttered the last word when Gania gave such a fearful shudder that the prince almost cried out.

"What's the matter?" said he, seizing Gania's hand.

"Your highness! His excellency begs your presence in her excellency's apartments!" announced the footman, appearing at the door.

The prince immediately followed the man out of the room.

Chapter IV.

All three of the Miss Epanchins were fine, healthy girls, well-grown, with good shoulders and busts, and strong—almost masculine—hands; and, of course, with all the above attributes, they enjoyed capital appetites, of which they were not in the least ashamed.

Elizabetha Prokofievna sometimes informed the girls that they were a little too candid in this matter, but in spite of their outward deference to their mother these three young women, in solemn conclave, had long agreed to modify the unquestioning obedience which they had been in the habit of according to her; and Mrs. General Epanchin had judged it better to say nothing about it, though, of course, she was well aware of the fact.

It is true that her nature sometimes rebelled against these dictates of reason, and that she grew yearly more capricious and impatient; but having a respectful and well-disciplined husband under her thumb at all times, she found it possible, as a rule, to empty any little accumulations of spleen upon his head, and therefore the harmony of the family was kept duly balanced, and things went as smoothly as family matters can.

Mrs. Epanchin had a fair appetite herself, and generally took her share of the capital mid-day lunch which was always served for the girls, and which was nearly as good as a dinner. The young ladies used to have a cup of coffee each before this meal, at ten o'clock, while still in bed. This was a favourite and unalterable arrangement with them. At half-past twelve, the table was laid in the small dining-room, and occasionally the general himself appeared at the family gathering, if he had time.

Besides tea and coffee, cheese, honey, butter, pan-cakes of various kinds (the lady of the house loved these best), cutlets, and so on, there was generally strong beef soup, and other substantial delicacies.

On the particular morning on which our story has opened, the family had assembled in the dining-room, and were waiting the general's appearance, the latter having promised to come this day. If he had been one moment late, he would have been sent for at once; but he turned up punctually.

As he came forward to wish his wife good-morning and kiss her hands, as his custom was, he observed something in her look which boded ill. He thought he knew the reason, and had expected it, but still, he was not altogether comfortable. His daughters advanced to kiss him, too, and though they did not look exactly angry, there was something strange in their expression as well.

The general was, owing to certain circumstances, a little inclined to be too suspicious at home, and needlessly nervous; but, as an experienced father and husband, he judged it better to take measures at once to protect himself from any dangers there might be in the air.

However, I hope I shall not interfere with the proper sequence of my narrative too much, if I diverge for a moment at this point, in order to explain the mutual relations between General Epanchin's family and others acting a part in this history, at the time when we take up the thread of their destiny. I have already stated that the general, though he was a man of lowly origin, and of poor education, was, for all that, an experienced and talented husband and father. Among other things, he considered it undesirable to hurry his daughters to the matrimonial altar and to worry them too much with assurances of his paternal wishes for their happiness, as is the custom among parents of many grown-up daughters. He even succeeded in ranging his wife on his side on this question, though he found the feat very difficult to accomplish, because unnatural; but the general's arguments were conclusive, and founded upon obvious facts. The general considered that the girls' taste and good sense should be allowed to develop and mature deliberately, and that the parents' duty should merely be to keep watch, in order that no strange or undesirable choice be made; but that the selection once effected, both father and mother were bound from that moment to enter heart and soul into the cause, and to see that the matter progressed without hindrance until the altar should be happily reached.

Besides this, it was clear that the Epanchins' position gained each year, with geometrical accuracy, both as to financial solidity and social weight; and, therefore, the longer the girls waited, the better was their chance of making a brilliant match.

But again, amidst the incontrovertible facts just recorded, one more, equally significant, rose up to confront the family; and this was, that the eldest daughter, Alexandra, had imperceptibly arrived at her twenty-fifth birthday. Almost at the same moment, Afanasy Ivanovitch Totski, a man of immense wealth, high connections, and good standing, announced his intention of marrying. Afanasy Ivanovitch was a gentleman of fifty-five years of age, artistically gifted, and of most refined tastes. He wished to marry well, and, moreover, he was a keen admirer and judge of beauty.

Now, since Totski had, of late, been upon terms of great cordiality with Epanchin, which excellent relations were intensified by the fact that they were, so to speak, partners in several financial enterprises, it so happened that the former now put in a friendly request to the general for counsel with regard to the important step he meditated. Might he suggest, for instance, such a thing as a marriage between himself and one of the general's daughters?

Evidently the quiet, pleasant current of the family life of the Epanchins was about to undergo a change.

The undoubted beauty of the family, *par excellence*, was the youngest, Aglaya, as aforesaid. But Totski himself, though an egotist of the extremest type, realized that he had no chance there; Aglaya was clearly not for such as he.

Perhaps the sisterly love and friendship of the three girls had more or less exaggerated Aglaya's chances of happiness. In their opinion, the latter's destiny was not merely to be very happy; she was to live in a heaven on earth. Aglaya's husband was to be a compendium of all the virtues, and of all success, not to speak of fabulous wealth. The two elder sisters had agreed that all was to be sacrificed by them, if need be, for Aglaya's sake; her dowry was to be colossal and unprecedented.

The general and his wife were aware of this agreement, and, therefore, when Totski suggested himself for one of the sisters, the parents made no doubt that one of the two elder girls would probably accept the offer, since Totski would certainly make no difficulty as to dowry. The general valued the proposal very highly. He knew life, and realized what such an offer was worth.

The answer of the sisters to the communication was, if not conclusive, at least consoling and hopeful. It made known that the eldest, Alexandra, would very likely be disposed to listen to a proposal.

Alexandra was a good-natured girl, though she had a will of her own. She was intelligent and kind-hearted, and, if she were to marry Totski, she would make him a good wife. She did not care for a brilliant marriage; she was eminently a woman calculated to soothe and sweeten the life of any man; decidedly pretty, if not absolutely handsome. What better could Totski wish?

So the matter crept slowly forward. The general and Totski had agreed to avoid any hasty and irrevocable step. Alexandra's parents had not even begun to talk to their daughters freely upon the subject, when suddenly, as it were, a dissonant chord was struck amid the harmony of the proceedings. Mrs. Epanchin began to show signs of discontent, and that was a serious matter. A certain circumstance had crept in, a disagreeable and troublesome factor, which threatened to overturn the whole business.

This circumstance had come into existence eighteen years before. Close to an estate of Totski's, in one of the central provinces of Russia, there lived, at that time, a poor gentleman whose estate was of the wretchedest description. This gentleman was noted in the district for his persistent ill-fortune; his name was Barashkoff, and, as regards family and descent, he was vastly superior to Totski, but his estate was mortgaged to the last acre. One day, when he had ridden over to the town to see a creditor, the chief peasant of his village followed him shortly after, with the news that his house had been burnt down, and that his wife had perished with it, but his children were safe.

Even Barashkoff, inured to the storms of evil fortune as he was, could not stand this last stroke. He went mad and died shortly after in the town hospital. His estate was sold for the creditors; and the little girls—two of them, of seven and eight years of age respectively,—were adopted by Totski, who undertook their maintenance and education in the kindness of his heart. They were brought up together with the children of his German bailiff. Very soon, however, there was only one of them left—Nastasia Philipovna—for the other little one died of whooping-cough. Totski, who was living abroad at this time, very soon forgot all about the child; but five years after, returning to Russia, it struck him that he would like to look over his estate and see how matters were going there, and, arrived at his bailiff's house, he was not long in discovering that among the children of the latter there now dwelt a most lovely little girl of twelve, sweet and intelligent, and bright, and promising to develop beauty of most unusual quality—as to which last Totski was an undoubted authority.

He only stayed at his country seat a few days on this occasion, but he had time to make his arrangements. Great changes took place in the child's education; a good governess was engaged, a Swiss lady of experience and culture. For four years this lady resided in the house with little Nastia, and then the education was considered complete. The governess took her departure, and another lady came down to fetch Nastia, by Totski's instructions. The child was now transported to another of Totski's estates in a distant part of the country. Here she found a delightful little house, just built, and prepared for her reception with great care and taste; and here she took up her abode together with the lady who had accompanied her from her old home. In the house there were two experienced maids, musical instruments of all sorts, a charming "young lady's library," pictures, paint-boxes, a lap-dog, and everything to make life agreeable. Within a fortnight Totski himself arrived, and from that time he appeared to have taken a great fancy to this part of the world and came down each summer, staying two and three months at a time. So passed four years peacefully and happily, in charming surroundings.

At the end of that time, and about four months after Totski's last visit (he had stayed but a fortnight on this occasion), a report reached Nastasia Philipovna that he was about to be married in St. Petersburg, to a rich, eminent, and lovely woman. The report was only partially true, the marriage project being only in an embryo condition; but a great change now came over Nastasia Philipovna. She suddenly displayed unusual decision of character; and without wasting time in thought, she left her country home and came up to St. Petersburg, straight to Totski's house, all alone.

The latter, amazed at her conduct, began to express his displeasure; but he very soon became aware that he must change his voice, style, and everything else, with this young lady; the good old times were gone. An entirely new and different woman sat before him, between whom and the girl he had left in the country last July there seemed nothing in common.

In the first place, this new woman understood a good deal more than was usual for young people of her age; so much indeed, that Totski could not help wondering where she had picked up her knowledge. Surely not from her "young lady's library"? It even embraced legal matters, and the "world" in general, to a considerable extent.

Her character was absolutely changed. No more of the girlish alternations of timidity and petulance, the adorable naivete, the reveries, the tears, the playfulness... It was an entirely new and hitherto unknown being who now sat and laughed at him, and informed him to his face that she had never had the faintest feeling for him of any kind, except loathing and contempt—contempt which had followed closely upon her sensations of surprise and bewilderment after her first acquaintance with him.

This new woman gave him further to understand that though it was absolutely the same to her whom he married, yet she had decided to prevent this marriage—for no particular reason, but that she *chose* to do so, and because she wished to amuse herself at his expense for that it was "quite her turn to laugh a little now!"

Such were her words—very likely she did not give her real reason for this eccentric conduct; but, at all events, that was all the explanation she deigned to offer.

Meanwhile, Totski thought the matter over as well as his scattered ideas would permit. His meditations lasted a fortnight, however, and at the end of that time his resolution was taken. The fact was, Totski was at that time a man of fifty years of age; his position was solid and respectable; his place in society had long been firmly fixed upon safe foundations; he loved himself, his personal comforts, and his position better than all the world, as every respectable gentleman should!

At the same time his grasp of things in general soon showed Totski that he now had to deal with a being who was outside the pale of the ordinary rules of traditional behaviour, and who would not only threaten mischief but would undoubtedly carry it out, and stop for no one.

There was evidently, he concluded, something at work here; some storm of the mind, some paroxysm of romantic anger, goodness knows against whom or what, some insatiable contempt—in a word, something altogether absurd and impossible, but at the same time most dangerous to be met with by any respectable person with a position in society to keep up.

For a man of Totski's wealth and standing, it would, of course, have been the simplest possible matter to take steps which would rid him at once from all annoyance; while it was obviously impossible for Nastasia Philipovna to harm him in any way, either legally or by stirring up a scandal, for, in case of the latter danger, he could so easily remove her to a sphere of safety. However, these arguments would only hold good in case of Nastasia acting as others might in such an emergency. She was much more likely to overstep the bounds of reasonable conduct by some extraordinary eccentricity.

Here the sound judgment of Totski stood him in good stead. He realized that Nastasia Philipovna must be well aware that she could do nothing by legal means to injure him, and that her flashing eyes betrayed some entirely different intention.

Nastasia Philipovna was quite capable of ruining herself, and even of perpetrating something which would send her to Siberia, for the mere pleasure of injuring a man for whom she had developed so inhuman a sense of loathing and contempt. He had sufficient insight to understand that she valued nothing in the world—herself least of all—and he made no attempt to conceal the fact that he was a coward in some respects. For instance, if he had been told that he would be stabbed at the altar, or publicly insulted, he would undoubtedly have been frightened; but not so much at the idea of being murdered, or wounded, or insulted, as at the thought that if such things were to happen he would be made to look ridiculous in the eyes of society.

He knew well that Nastasia thoroughly understood him and where to wound him and how, and therefore, as the marriage was still only in embryo, Totski decided to conciliate her by giving it up. His decision was strengthened by the fact that Nastasia Philipovna had curiously altered of late. It would be difficult to conceive how different she was physically, at the present time, to the girl of a few years ago. She was pretty then... but now!... Totski laughed angrily when he thought how short-sighted he had been. In days gone by he remembered how he had looked at her beautiful eyes, how even then he had marvelled at their dark mysterious depths, and at their wondering gaze which seemed to seek an answer to some unknown riddle. Her complexion also had altered. She was now exceedingly pale, but, curiously, this change only made her more beautiful. Like most men of the world, Totski had rather despised such a cheaply-bought conquest, but of late years he had begun to think differently about it. It had struck him as long ago as last spring that he ought to be finding a good match for Nastasia; for instance, some respectable and reasonable young fellow serving in a government office in another part of the country. How maliciously Nastasia laughed at the idea of such a thing, now!

However, it appeared to Totski that he might make use of her in another way; and he determined to establish her in St. Petersburg, surrounding her with all the comforts and luxuries that his wealth could command. In this way he might gain glory in certain circles.

Five years of this Petersburg life went by, and, of course, during that time a great deal happened. Totski's position was very uncomfortable; having "funked" once, he could not totally regain his ease. He was afraid, he did not know why, but he was simply *afraid* of Nastasia Philipovna. For the first two years or so he had suspected that she wished to marry him herself, and that only her vanity prevented her telling him so. He thought that she wanted him to approach her with a humble proposal from his own side. But to his great, and not entirely pleasurable amazement, he discovered that this was by no means the case, and that were he to offer himself he would be refused. He could not understand such a state of things, and was obliged to conclude that it was pride, the pride of an injured and imaginative woman, which had gone to such lengths that it preferred to sit and nurse its contempt and hatred in solitude rather than mount to heights of hitherto unattainable splendour. To make matters worse, she was quite impervious to mercenary considerations, and could not be bribed in any way.

Finally, Totski took cunning means to try to break his chains and be free. He tried to tempt her in various ways to lose her heart; he invited princes, hussars, secretaries of embassies, poets, novelists, even Socialists, to see her; but not one of them all made the faintest impression upon Nastasia. It was as though she had a pebble in place of a heart, as though her feelings and affections were dried up and withered for ever.

She lived almost entirely alone; she read, she studied, she loved music. Her principal acquaintances were poor women of various grades, a couple of actresses, and the family of a poor schoolteacher. Among these people she was much beloved.

She received four or five friends sometimes, of an evening. Totski often came. Lately, too, General Epanchin had been enabled with great difficulty to introduce himself into her circle. Gania made her acquaintance also, and others were Ferdishenko, an ill-bred, and would-be witty, young clerk, and Ptitsin, a money-lender of modest and polished manners, who had risen from poverty. In fact, Nastasia Philipovna's beauty became a thing known to all the town; but not a single man could boast of anything more than his own admiration for her; and this reputation of hers, and her wit and culture and grace, all confirmed Totski in the plan he had now prepared.

And it was at this moment that General Epanchin began to play so large and important a part in the story.

When Totski had approached the general with his request for friendly counsel as to a marriage with one of his daughters, he had made a full and candid confession. He had said that he intended to stop at no means to obtain his freedom; even if Nastasia were to promise to leave him entirely alone in future, he would not (he said) believe and trust her; words were not enough for him; he must have solid guarantees of some sort. So he and the general determined to try what an attempt to appeal to her heart would effect. Having arrived at Nastasia's house one day, with Epanchin, Totski immediately began to speak of the intolerable torment of his position. He admitted that he was to blame for all, but candidly confessed that he could not bring himself to feel any remorse for his original guilt towards herself, because he was a man of sensual passions which were inborn and ineradicable, and that he had no power over himself in this respect; but that he wished, seriously, to marry at last, and that the whole fate of the most desirable social union which he contemplated, was in her hands; in a word, he confided his all to her generosity of heart.

General Epanchin took up his part and spoke in the character of father of a family; he spoke sensibly, and without wasting words over any attempt at sentimentality, he merely recorded his full admission of her right to be the arbiter of Totski's destiny at this moment. He then pointed out that the fate of his daughter, and very likely of both his other daughters, now hung upon her reply.

To Nastasia's question as to what they wished her to do, Totski confessed that he had been so frightened by her, five years ago, that he could never now be entirely comfortable until she herself married. He immediately added that such a suggestion from him would, of course, be absurd, unless accompanied by remarks of a more pointed nature. He very well knew, he said, that a certain young gentleman of good family, namely, Gavrila Ardalionovitch Ivolgin, with whom she was acquainted, and whom she received at her house, had long loved her passionately, and would give his life for some response from her. The young fellow had confessed this love of his to him (Totski) and had also admitted it in the hearing of his benefactor, General Epanchin. Lastly, he could not help being of opinion that Nastasia must be aware of Gania's love for her, and if he (Totski) mistook not, she had looked with some favour upon it, being often lonely, and rather tired of her present life. Having remarked how difficult it was for him, of all people, to speak to her of these matters, Totski concluded by saying that he trusted Nastasia Philipovna would not look with contempt upon him if he now expressed his sincere desire to guarantee her future by a gift of seventy-five thousand roubles. He added that the sum would have been left her all the same in his will, and that therefore she must not consider the gift as in any way an indemnification to her for anything, but that there was no reason, after all, why a man should not be allowed to entertain a natural desire to lighten his conscience, etc., etc.; in fact, all that would naturally be said under the circumstances. Totski was very eloquent all through, and, in conclusion, just touched on the fact that not a soul in the world, not even General Epanchin, had ever heard a word about the above seventy-five thousand roubles, and that this was the first time he had ever given expression to his intentions in respect to them.

Nastasia Philipovna's reply to this long rigmarole astonished both the friends considerably.

Not only was there no trace of her former irony, of her old hatred and enmity, and of that dreadful laughter, the very recollection of which sent a cold chill down Totski's back to this very day; but she seemed charmed and really glad to have the opportunity of talking seriously with him for once in a way. She confessed that she had long wished to have a frank and free conversation and to ask for friendly advice, but that pride had hitherto prevented her; now, however, that the ice was broken, nothing could be more welcome to her than this opportunity.

First, with a sad smile, and then with a twinkle of merriment in her eyes, she admitted that such a storm as that of five years ago was now quite out of the question. She said that she had long since changed her views of things, and recognized that facts must be taken into consideration in spite of the feelings of the heart. What was done was done and ended, and she could not understand why Totski should still feel alarmed.

She next turned to General Epanchin and observed, most courteously, that she had long since known of his daughters, and that she had heard none but good report; that she had learned to think of them with deep and sincere respect. The idea alone that she could in any way serve them, would be to her both a pride and a source of real happiness.

It was true that she was lonely in her present life; Totski had judged her thoughts aright. She longed to rise, if not to love, at least to family life and new hopes and objects, but as to Gavrila Ardalionovitch, she could not as yet say much. She thought it must be the case that he loved her; she felt that she too might learn to love him, if she could be sure of the firmness of his attachment to herself; but he was very young, and it was a difficult question to decide. What she specially liked about him was that he worked, and supported his family by his toil.

She had heard that he was proud and ambitious; she had heard much that was interesting of his mother and sister, she had heard of them from Mr. Ptitsin, and would much like to make their acquaintance, but—another question!—would they like to receive her into their house? At all events, though she did not reject the idea of this marriage, she desired not to be hurried. As for the seventy-five thousand roubles, Mr. Totski need not have found any difficulty or awkwardness about the matter; she quite understood the value of money, and would, of course, accept the gift. She thanked him for his delicacy, however, but saw no reason why Gavrila Ardalionovitch should not know about it.

She would not marry the latter, she said, until she felt persuaded that neither on his part nor on the part of his family did there exist any sort of concealed suspicions as to herself. She did not intend to ask forgiveness for anything in the past, which fact she desired to be known. She did not consider herself to blame for anything that had happened in former years, and she thought that Gavrila Ardalionovitch should be informed as to the relations which had existed between herself and Totski during the last five years. If she accepted this money it was not to be considered as indemnification for her misfortune as a young girl, which had not been in any degree her own fault, but merely as compensation for her ruined life.

She became so excited and agitated during all these explanations and confessions that General Epanchin was highly gratified, and considered the matter satisfactorily arranged once for all. But the once bitten Totski was twice shy, and looked for hidden snakes among the flowers. However, the special point to which the two friends particularly trusted to bring about their object (namely, Gania's attractiveness for Nastasia Philipovna), stood out more and more prominently; the pourparlers had commenced, and gradually even Totski began to believe in the possibility of success.

Before long Nastasia and Gania had talked the matter over. Very little was said—her modesty seemed to suffer under the infliction of discussing such a question. But she recognized his love, on the understanding that she bound herself to nothing whatever, and that she reserved the right to say "no" up to the very hour of the marriage ceremony. Gania was to have the same right of refusal at the last moment.

It soon became clear to Gania, after scenes of wrath and quarrellings at the domestic hearth, that his family were seriously opposed to the match, and that Nastasia was aware of this fact was equally evident. She said nothing about it, though he daily expected her to do so.

There were several rumours afloat, before long, which upset Totski's equanimity a good deal, but we will not now stop to describe them; merely mentioning an instance or two. One was that Nastasia had entered into close and secret relations with the Epanchin girls—a most unlikely rumour; another was that Nastasia had long satisfied herself of the fact that Gania was merely marrying her for money, and that his nature was gloomy and greedy, impatient and selfish, to an extraordinary degree; and that although he had been keen enough in his desire to achieve a conquest before, yet since the two friends had agreed to exploit his passion for their own purposes, it was clear enough that he had begun to consider the whole thing a nuisance and a nightmare.

In his heart passion and hate seemed to hold divided sway, and although he had at last given his consent to marry the woman (as he said), under the stress of circumstances, yet he promised himself that he would "take it out of her," after marriage.

Nastasia seemed to Totski to have divined all this, and to be preparing something on her own account, which frightened him to such an extent that he did not dare communicate his views even to the general. But at times he would pluck up his courage and be full of hope and good spirits again, acting, in fact, as weak men do act in such circumstances.

However, both the friends felt that the thing looked rosy indeed when one day Nastasia informed them that she would give her final answer on the evening of her birthday, which anniversary was due in a very short time.

A strange rumour began to circulate, meanwhile; no less than that the respectable and highly respected General Epanchin was himself so fascinated by Nastasia Philipovna that his feeling for her amounted almost to passion. What he thought to gain by Gania's marriage to the girl it was difficult to imagine. Possibly he counted on Gania's complaisance; for Totski had long suspected that there existed some secret understanding between the general and his secretary. At all events the fact was known that he had prepared a magnificent present of pearls for Nastasia's birthday, and that he was looking forward to the occasion when he should present his gift with the greatest excitement and impatience. The day before her birthday he was in a fever of agitation.

Mrs. Epanchin, long accustomed to her husband's infidelities, had heard of the pearls, and the rumour excited her liveliest curiosity and interest. The general remarked her suspicions, and felt that a grand explanation must shortly take place—which fact alarmed him much.

This is the reason why he was so unwilling to take lunch (on the morning upon which we took up this narrative) with the rest of his family. Before the prince's arrival he had made up his mind to plead business, and "cut" the meal; which simply meant running away.

He was particularly anxious that this one day should be passed—especially the evening—without unpleasantness between himself and his family; and just at the right moment the prince turned up— "as though Heaven had sent him on purpose," said the general to himself, as he left the study to seek out the wife of his bosom.

CHAPTER V.

Mrs. General Epanchin was a proud woman by nature. What must her feelings have been when she heard that Prince Muishkin, the last of his and her line, had arrived in beggar's guise, a wretched idiot, a recipient of charity—all of which details the general gave out for greater effect! He was anxious to steal her interest at the first swoop, so as to distract her thoughts from other matters nearer home.

Mrs. Epanchin was in the habit of holding herself very straight, and staring before her, without speaking, in moments of excitement.

She was a fine woman of the same age as her husband, with a slightly hooked nose, a high, narrow forehead, thick hair turning a little grey, and a sallow complexion. Her eyes were grey and wore a very curious expression at times. She believed them to be most effective—a belief that nothing could alter.

"What, receive him! Now, at once?" asked Mrs. Epanchin, gazing vaguely at her husband as he stood fidgeting before her.

"Oh, dear me, I assure you there is no need to stand on ceremony with him," the general explained hastily. "He is quite a child, not to say a pathetic-looking creature. He has fits of some sort, and has just arrived from Switzerland, straight from the station, dressed like a German and without a farthing in his pocket. I gave him twenty-five roubles to go on with, and am going to find him some easy place in one of the government offices. I should like you to ply him well with the victuals, my dears, for I should think he must be very hungry."

"You astonish me," said the lady, gazing as before. "Fits, and hungry too! What sort of fits?"

"Oh, they don't come on frequently, besides, he's a regular child, though he seems to be fairly educated. I should like you, if possible, my dears," the general added, making slowly for the door, "to put him through his paces a bit, and see what he is good for. I think you should be kind to him; it is a good deed, you know—however, just as you like, of course—but he is a sort of relation, remember, and I thought it might interest you to see the young fellow, seeing that this is so."

"Oh, of course, mamma, if we needn't stand on ceremony with him, we must give the poor fellow something to eat after his journey; especially as he has not the least idea where to go to," said Alexandra, the eldest of the girls.

"Besides, he's quite a child; we can entertain him with a little hide-and-seek, in case of need," said Adelaida.

"Hide-and-seek? What do you mean?" inquired Mrs. Epanchin.

"Oh, do stop pretending, mamma," cried Aglaya, in vexation. "Send him up, father; mother allows."

The general rang the bell and gave orders that the prince should be shown in.

"Only on condition that he has a napkin under his chin at lunch, then," said Mrs. Epanchin, "and let Fedor, or Mavra, stand behind him while he eats. Is he quiet when he has these fits? He doesn't show violence, does he?"

"On the contrary, he seems to be very well brought up. His manners are excellent—but here he is himself. Here you are, prince—let me introduce you, the last of the Muishkins, a relative of your own, my dear, or at least of the same name. Receive him kindly, please. They'll bring in lunch directly, prince; you must stop and have some, but you must excuse me. I'm in a hurry, I must be off—"

"We all know where *you* must be off to!" said Mrs. Epanchin, in a meaning voice.

"Yes, yes—I must hurry away, I'm late! Look here, dears, let him write you something in your albums; you've no idea what a wonderful caligraphist he is, wonderful talent! He has just written out 'Abbot Pafnute signed this' for me. Well, *au revoir!*"

"Stop a minute; where are you off to? Who is this abbot?" cried Mrs. Epanchin to her retreating husband in a tone of excited annoyance.

"Yes, my dear, it was an old abbot of that name—I must be off to see the count, he's waiting for me, I'm late—Good-bye! *Au revoir*, prince!"—and the general bolted at full speed.

"Oh, yes—I know what count you're going to see!" remarked his wife in a cutting manner, as she turned her angry eyes on the prince. "Now then, what's all this about?—What abbot—Who's Pafnute?" she added, brusquely.

"Mamma!" said Alexandra, shocked at her rudeness.

Aglaya stamped her foot.

"Nonsense! Let me alone!" said the angry mother. "Now then, prince, sit down here, no, nearer, come nearer the light! I want to have a good look at you. So, now then, who is this abbot?"

"Abbot Pafnute," said our friend, seriously and with deference.

"Pafnute, yes. And who was he?"

Mrs. Epanchin put these questions hastily and brusquely, and when the prince answered she nodded her head sagely at each word he said.

"The Abbot Pafnute lived in the fourteenth century," began the prince; "he was in charge of one of the monasteries on the Volga, about where our present Kostroma government lies. He went to Oreol and helped in the great matters then going on in the religious world; he signed an edict there, and I have seen a print of his signature; it struck me, so I copied it. When the general asked me, in his study, to write something for him, to show my handwriting, I wrote 'The Abbot Pafnute signed this,' in the exact handwriting of the abbot. The general liked it very much, and that's why he recalled it just now."

"Aglaya, make a note of 'Pafnute,' or we shall forget him. H'm! and where is this signature?"

"I think it was left on the general's table."

"Let it be sent for at once!"

"Oh, I'll write you a new one in half a minute," said the prince, "if you like!"

"Of course, mamma!" said Alexandra. "But let's have lunch now, we are all hungry!"

"Yes; come along, prince," said the mother, "are you very hungry?"

"Yes; I must say that I am pretty hungry, thanks very much."

"H'm! I like to see that you know your manners; and you are by no means such a person as the general thought fit to describe you. Come along; you sit here, opposite to me," she continued, "I wish to be able to see your face. Alexandra, Adelaida, look after the prince! He doesn't seem so very ill, does he? I don't think he requires a napkin under his chin, after all; are you accustomed to having one on, prince?"

"Formerly, when I was seven years old or so. I believe I wore one; but now I usually hold my napkin on my knee when I eat."

"Of course, of course! And about your fits?"

"Fits?" asked the prince, slightly surprised. "I very seldom have fits nowadays. I don't know how it may be here, though; they say the climate may be bad for me."

"He talks very well, you know!" said Mrs. Epanchin, who still continued to nod at each word the prince spoke. "I really did not expect it at all; in fact, I suppose it was all stuff and nonsense on the general's part, as usual. Eat away, prince, and tell me where you were born, and where you were brought up. I wish to know all about you, you interest me very much!"

The prince expressed his thanks once more, and eating heartily the while, recommended the narrative of his life in Switzerland, all of which we have heard before. Mrs. Epanchin became more and more pleased with her guest; the girls, too, listened with considerable attention. In talking over the question of relationship it turned out that the prince was very well up in the matter and knew his pedigree off by heart. It was found that scarcely any connection existed between himself and Mrs. Epanchin, but the talk, and the opportunity of conversing about her family tree, gratified the latter exceedingly, and she rose from the table in great good humour.

"Let's all go to my boudoir," she said, "and they shall bring some coffee in there. That's the room where we all assemble and busy ourselves as we like best," she explained. "Alexandra, my eldest, here, plays the piano, or reads or sews; Adelaida paints landscapes and portraits (but never finishes any); and Aglaya sits and does nothing. I don't work too much, either. Here we are, now; sit down, prince, near the fire and talk to us. I want to hear you relate something. I wish to make sure of you first and then tell my old friend, Princess Bielokonski, about you. I wish you to know all the good people and to interest them. Now then, begin!"

"Mamma, it's rather a strange order, that!" said Adelaida, who was fussing among her paints and paint-brushes at the easel. Aglaya and Alexandra had settled themselves with folded hands on a sofa, evidently meaning to be listeners. The prince felt that the general attention was concentrated upon himself.

"I should refuse to say a word if *I* were ordered to tell a story like that!" observed Aglaya.

"Why? what's there strange about it? He has a tongue. Why shouldn't he tell us something? I want to judge whether he is a good story-teller; anything you like, prince—how you liked Switzerland, what was your first impression, anything. You'll see, he'll begin directly and tell us all about it beautifully."

"The impression was forcible—" the prince began.

"There, you see, girls," said the impatient lady, "he *has* begun, you see."

"Well, then, *let* him talk, mamma," said Alexandra. "This prince is a great humbug and by no means an idiot," she whispered to Aglaya.

"Oh, I saw that at once," replied the latter. "I don't think it at all nice of him to play a part. What does he wish to gain by it, I wonder?"

"My first impression was a very strong one," repeated the prince. "When they took me away from Russia, I remember I passed through many German towns and looked out of the windows, but did not trouble so much as to ask questions about them. This was after a long series of fits. I always used to fall into a sort of torpid condition after such a series, and lost my memory almost entirely; and though I was not altogether without reason at such times, yet I had no logical power of thought. This would continue for three or four days, and then I would recover myself again. I remember my melancholy was intolerable; I felt inclined to cry; I sat and wondered and wondered uncomfortably; the consciousness that everything was strange weighed terribly upon me; I could understand that it was all foreign and strange. I recollect I awoke from this state for the first time at Basle, one evening; the bray of a donkey aroused me, a donkey in the town market. I saw the donkey and was extremely pleased with it, and from that moment my head seemed to clear."

"A donkey? How strange! Yet it is not strange. Anyone of us might fall in love with a donkey! It happened in mythological times," said Madame Epanchin, looking wrathfully at her daughters, who had begun to laugh. "Go on, prince."

"Since that evening I have been specially fond of donkeys. I began to ask questions about them, for I had never seen one before; and I at once came to the conclusion that this must be one of the most useful of animals—strong, willing, patient, cheap; and, thanks to this donkey, I began to like the whole country I was travelling through; and my melancholy passed away."

"All this is very strange and interesting," said Mrs. Epanchin. "Now let's leave the donkey and go on to other matters. What are you laughing at, Aglaya? and you too, Adelaida? The prince told us his experiences very cleverly; he saw the donkey himself, and what have you ever seen? *You* have never been abroad."

"I have seen a donkey though, mamma!" said Aglaya.

"And I've heard one!" said Adelaida. All three of the girls laughed out loud, and the prince laughed with them.

"Well, it's too bad of you," said mamma. "You must forgive them, prince; they are good girls. I am very fond of them, though I often have to be scolding them; they are all as silly and mad as march hares."

"Oh, why shouldn't they laugh?" said the prince. "I shouldn't have let the chance go by in their place, I know. But I stick up for the donkey, all the same; he's a patient, good-natured fellow."

"Are you a patient man, prince? I ask out of curiosity," said Mrs. Epanchin.

All laughed again.

"Oh, that wretched donkey again, I see!" cried the lady. "I assure you, prince, I was not guilty of the least—"

"Insinuation? Oh! I assure you, I take your word for it." And the prince continued laughing merrily.

"I must say it's very nice of you to laugh. I see you really are a kind-hearted fellow," said Mrs. Epanchin.

"I'm not always kind, though."

"I am kind myself, and *always* kind too, if you please!" she retorted, unexpectedly; "and that is my chief fault, for one ought not to be always kind. I am often angry with these girls and their father; but the worst of it is, I am always kindest when I am cross. I was very angry just before you came, and Aglaya there read me a lesson—thanks, Aglaya, dear—come and kiss me—there—that's enough" she added, as Aglaya came forward and kissed her lips and then her hand. "Now then, go on, prince. Perhaps you can think of something more exciting than about the donkey, eh?"

"I must say, again, *I* can't understand how you can expect anyone to tell you stories straight away, so," said Adelaida. "I know I never could!"

"Yes, but the prince can, because he is clever—cleverer than you are by ten or twenty times, if you like. There, that's so, prince; and seriously, let's drop the donkey now—what else did you see abroad, besides the donkey?"

"Yes, but the prince told us about the donkey very cleverly, all the same," said Alexandra. "I have always been most interested to hear how people go mad and get well again, and that sort of thing. Especially when it happens suddenly."

"Quite so, quite so!" cried Mrs. Epanchin, delighted. "I see you *can* be sensible now and then, Alexandra. You were speaking of Switzerland, prince?"

"Yes. We came to Lucerne, and I was taken out in a boat. I felt how lovely it was, but the loveliness weighed upon me somehow or other, and made me feel melancholy."

"Why?" asked Alexandra.

"I don't know; I always feel like that when I look at the beauties of nature for the first time; but then, I was ill at that time, of course!"

"Oh, but I should like to see it!" said Adelaida; "and I don't know *when* we shall ever go abroad. I've been two years looking out for a good subject for a picture. I've done all I know. 'The North and South I know by heart,' as our poet observes. Do help me to a subject, prince."

"Oh, but I know nothing about painting. It seems to me one only has to look, and paint what one sees."

"But I don't know *how* to see!"

"Nonsense, what rubbish you talk!" the mother struck in. "Not know how to see! Open your eyes and look! If you can't see here, you won't see abroad either. Tell us what you saw yourself, prince!"

"Yes, that's better," said Adelaida; "the prince *learned to see* abroad."

"Oh, I hardly know! You see, I only went to restore my health. I don't know whether I learned to see, exactly. I was very happy, however, nearly all the time."

"Happy! you can be happy?" cried Aglaya. "Then how can you say you did not learn to see? I should think you could teach *us* to see!"

"Oh! *do* teach us," laughed Adelaida.

"Oh! I can't do that," said the prince, laughing too. "I lived almost all the while in one little Swiss village; what can I teach you? At first I was only just not absolutely dull; then my health began to improve—then every day became dearer and more precious to me, and the longer I stayed, the dearer became the time to me; so much so that I could not help observing it; but why this was so, it would be difficult to say."

"So that you didn't care to go away anywhere else?"

"Well, at first I did; I was restless; I didn't know however I should manage to support life—you know there are such moments, especially in solitude. There was a waterfall near us, such a lovely thin streak of water, like a thread but white and moving. It fell from a great height, but it looked quite low, and it was half a mile away, though it did not seem fifty paces. I loved to listen to it at night, but it was then that I became so restless. Sometimes I went and climbed the mountain and stood there in the midst of the tall pines, all alone in the terrible silence, with our little village in the distance, and the sky so blue, and the sun so bright, and an old ruined castle on the mountain-side, far away. I used to watch the line where earth and sky met, and longed to go and seek there the key of all mysteries, thinking that I might find there a new life, perhaps some great city where life should be grander and richer—and then it struck me that life may be grand enough even in a prison."

"I read that last most praiseworthy thought in my manual, when I was twelve years old," said Aglaya.

"All this is pure philosophy," said Adelaida. "You are a philosopher, prince, and have come here to instruct us in your views."

"Perhaps you are right," said the prince, smiling. "I think I am a philosopher, perhaps, and who knows, perhaps I do wish to teach my views of things to those I meet with?"

"Your philosophy is rather like that of an old woman we know, who is rich and yet does nothing but try how little she can spend. She talks of nothing but money all day. Your great philosophical idea of a grand life in a prison and your four happy years in that Swiss village are like this, rather," said Aglaya.

"As to life in a prison, of course there may be two opinions," said the prince. "I once heard the story of a man who lived twelve years in a prison—I heard it from the man himself. He was one of the persons under treatment with my professor; he had fits, and attacks of melancholy, then he would weep, and once he tried to commit suicide. *His* life in prison was sad enough; his only acquaintances were spiders and a tree that grew outside his grating—but I think I had better tell you of another man I met last year. There was a very strange feature in this case, strange because of its extremely rare occurrence. This man had once been brought to the scaffold in company with several others, and had had the sentence of death by shooting passed upon him for some political crime. Twenty minutes later he had been reprieved and some other punishment substituted; but the interval between the two sentences, twenty minutes, or at least a quarter of an hour, had been passed in the certainty that within a few minutes he must die. I was very anxious to hear him speak of his impressions during that dreadful time, and I several times inquired of him as to what he thought and felt. He remembered everything with the most accurate and extraordinary distinctness, and declared that he would never forget a single iota of the experience.

"About twenty paces from the scaffold, where he had stood to hear the sentence, were three posts, fixed in the ground, to which to fasten the criminals (of whom there were several). The first three criminals were taken to the posts, dressed in long white tunics, with white caps drawn over their faces, so that they could not see the rifles pointed at them. Then a group of soldiers took their stand opposite to each post. My friend was the eighth on the list, and therefore he would have been among the third lot to go up. A priest went about among them with a cross: and there was about five minutes of time left for him to live.

"He said that those five minutes seemed to him to be a most interminable period, an enormous wealth of time; he seemed to be living, in these minutes, so many lives that there was no need as yet to think of that last moment, so that he made several arrangements, dividing up the time into portions—one for saying farewell to his companions, two minutes for that; then a couple more for thinking over his own life and career and all about himself; and another minute for a last look around. He remembered having divided his time like this quite well. While saying good-bye to his friends he recollected asking one of them some very usual everyday question, and being much interested in the answer. Then having bade farewell, he embarked upon those two minutes which he had allotted to looking into himself; he knew beforehand what he was going to think about. He wished to put it to himself as quickly and clearly as possible, that here was he, a living, thinking man, and that in three minutes he would be nobody; or if somebody or something, then what and where? He thought he would decide this question once for all in these last three minutes. A little way off there stood a church, and its gilded spire glittered in the sun. He remembered staring stubbornly at this spire, and at the rays of light sparkling from it. He could not tear his eyes from these rays of light; he got the idea that these rays were his new nature, and that in three minutes he would become one of them, amalgamated somehow with them.

"The repugnance to what must ensue almost immediately, and the uncertainty, were dreadful, he said; but worst of all was the idea, 'What should I do if I were not to die now? What if I were to return to life again? What an eternity of days, and all mine! How I should grudge and count up every minute of it, so as to waste not a single instant!' He said that this thought weighed so upon him and became such a terrible burden upon his brain that he could not bear it, and wished they would shoot him quickly and have done with it."

The prince paused and all waited, expecting him to go on again and finish the story.

"Is that all?" asked Aglaya.

"All? Yes," said the prince, emerging from a momentary reverie.

"And why did you tell us this?"

"Oh, I happened to recall it, that's all! It fitted into the conversation—"

"You probably wish to deduce, prince," said Alexandra, "that moments of time cannot be reckoned by money value, and that sometimes five minutes are worth priceless treasures. All this is very praiseworthy; but may I ask about this friend of yours, who told you the terrible experience of his life? He was reprieved, you say; in other words, they did restore to him that 'eternity of days.' What did he do with these riches of time? Did he keep careful account of his minutes?"

"Oh no, he didn't! I asked him myself. He said that he had not lived a bit as he had intended, and had wasted many, and many a minute."

"Very well, then there's an experiment, and the thing is proved; one cannot live and count each moment; say what you like, but one *cannot.*"

"That is true," said the prince, "I have thought so myself. And yet, why shouldn't one do it?"

"You think, then, that you could live more wisely than other people?" said Aglaya.

"I have had that idea."

"And you have it still?"

"Yes—I have it still," the prince replied.

He had contemplated Aglaya until now, with a pleasant though rather timid smile, but as the last words fell from his lips he began to laugh, and looked at her merrily.

"You are not very modest!" said she.

"But how brave you are!" said he. "You are laughing, and I—that man's tale impressed me so much, that I dreamt of it afterwards; yes, I dreamt of those five minutes..."

He looked at his listeners again with that same serious, searching expression.

"You are not angry with me?" he asked suddenly, and with a kind of nervous hurry, although he looked them straight in the face.

"Why should we be angry?" they cried.

"Only because I seem to be giving you a lecture, all the time!"

At this they laughed heartily.

"Please don't be angry with me," continued the prince. "I know very well that I have seen less of life than other people, and have less knowledge of it. I must appear to speak strangely sometimes..."

He said the last words nervously.

"You say you have been happy, and that proves you have lived, not less, but more than other people. Why make all these excuses?" interrupted Aglaya in a mocking tone of voice. "Besides, you need not mind about lecturing us; you have nothing to boast of. With your quietism, one could live happily for a hundred years at least. One might show you the execution of a felon, or show you one's little finger. You could draw a moral from either, and be quite satisfied. That sort of existence is easy enough."

"I can't understand why you always fly into a temper," said Mrs. Epanchin, who had been listening to the conversation and examining the faces of the speakers in turn. "I do not understand what you mean. What has your little finger to do with it? The prince talks well, though he is not amusing. He began all right, but now he seems sad."

"Never mind, mamma! Prince, I wish you had seen an execution," said Aglaya. "I should like to ask you a question about that, if you had."

"I have seen an execution," said the prince.

"You have!" cried Aglaya. "I might have guessed it. That's a fitting crown to the rest of the story. If you have seen an execution, how can you say you lived happily all the while?"

"But is there capital punishment where you were?" asked Adelaida.

"I saw it at Lyons. Schneider took us there, and as soon as we arrived we came in for that."

"Well, and did you like it very much? Was it very edifying and instructive?" asked Aglaya.

"No, I didn't like it at all, and was ill after seeing it; but I confess I stared as though my eyes were fixed to the sight. I could not tear them away."

"I, too, should have been unable to tear my eyes away," said Aglaya.

"They do not at all approve of women going to see an execution there. The women who do go are condemned for it afterwards in the newspapers."

"That is, by contending that it is not a sight for women they admit that it is a sight for men. I congratulate them on the deduction. I suppose you quite agree with them, prince?"

"Tell us about the execution," put in Adelaida.

"I would much rather not, just now," said the prince, a little disturbed and frowning slightly.

"You don't seem to want to tell us," said Aglaya, with a mocking air.

"No,—the thing is, I was telling all about the execution a little while ago, and—"

"Whom did you tell about it?"

"The man-servant, while I was waiting to see the general."

"Our man-servant?" exclaimed several voices at once.

"Yes, the one who waits in the entrance hall, a greyish, red-faced man—"

"The prince is clearly a democrat," remarked Aglaya.

"Well, if you could tell Aleksey about it, surely you can tell us too."

"I do so want to hear about it," repeated Adelaida.

"Just now, I confess," began the prince, with more animation, "when you asked me for a subject for a picture, I confess I had serious thoughts of giving you one. I thought of asking you to draw the face of a criminal, one minute before the fall of the guillotine, while the wretched man is still standing on the scaffold, preparatory to placing his neck on the block."

"What, his face? only his face?" asked Adelaida. "That would be a strange subject indeed. And what sort of a picture would that make?"

"Oh, why not?" the prince insisted, with some warmth. "When I was in Basle I saw a picture very much in that style—I should like to tell you about it; I will some time or other; it struck me very forcibly."

"Oh, you shall tell us about the Basle picture another time; now we must have all about the execution," said Adelaida. "Tell us about that face as it appeared to your imagination—how should it be drawn?—just the face alone, do you mean?"

"It was just a minute before the execution," began the prince, readily, carried away by the recollection and evidently forgetting everything else in a moment; "just at the instant when he stepped off the ladder on to the scaffold. He happened to look in my direction: I saw his eyes and understood all, at once—but how am I to describe it? I do so wish you or somebody else could draw it, you, if possible. I thought at the time what a picture it would make. You must imagine all that went before, of course, all—all. He had lived in the prison for some time and had not expected that the execution would take place for at least a week yet—he had counted on all the formalities and so on taking time; but it so happened that his papers had been got ready quickly. At five o'clock in the morning he was asleep—it was October, and at five in the morning it was cold and dark. The governor of the prison comes in on tip-toe and touches the sleeping man's shoulder gently. He starts up. 'What is it?' he says. 'The execution is fixed for ten o'clock.' He was only just awake, and would not believe at first, but began to argue that his papers would not be out for a week, and so on. When he was wide awake and realized the truth, he became very silent and argued no more—so they say; but after a bit he said: 'It comes very hard on one so suddenly' and then he was silent again and said nothing.

"The three or four hours went by, of course, in necessary preparations—the priest, breakfast, (coffee, meat, and some wine they gave him; doesn't it seem ridiculous?) And yet I believe these people give them a good breakfast out of pure kindness of heart, and believe that they are doing a good action. Then he is dressed, and then begins the procession through the town to the scaffold. I think he, too, must feel that he has an age to live still while they cart him along. Probably he thought, on the way, 'Oh, I have a long, long time yet. Three streets of life yet! When we've passed this street there'll be that other one; and then that one where the baker's shop is on the right; and when shall we get there? It's ages, ages!' Around him are crowds shouting, yelling—ten thousand faces, twenty thousand eyes. All this has to be endured, and especially the thought: 'Here are ten thousand men, and not one of them is going to be executed, and yet I am to die.' Well, all that is preparatory.

"At the scaffold there is a ladder, and just there he burst into tears—and this was a strong man, and a terribly wicked one, they say! There was a priest with him the whole time, talking; even in the cart as they drove along, he talked and talked. Probably the other heard nothing; he would begin to listen now and then, and at the third word or so he had forgotten all about it.

"At last he began to mount the steps; his legs were tied, so that he had to take very small steps. The priest, who seemed to be a wise man, had stopped talking now, and only held the cross for the wretched fellow to kiss. At the foot of the ladder he had been pale enough; but when he set foot on the scaffold at the top, his face suddenly became the colour of paper, positively like white notepaper. His legs must have become suddenly feeble and helpless, and he felt a choking in his throat—you know the sudden feeling one has in moments of terrible fear, when one does not lose one's wits, but is absolutely powerless to move? If some dreadful thing were suddenly to happen; if a house were just about to fall on one;—don't you know how one would long to sit down and shut one's eyes and wait, and wait? Well, when this terrible feeling came over him, the priest quickly pressed the cross to his lips, without a word—a little silver cross it was—and he kept on pressing it to the man's lips every second. And whenever the cross touched his lips, the eyes would open for a moment, and the legs moved once, and he kissed the cross greedily, hurriedly—just as though he were anxious to catch hold of something in case of its being useful to him afterwards, though he could hardly have had any connected religious thoughts at the time. And so up to the very block.

"How strange that criminals seldom swoon at such a moment! On the contrary, the brain is especially active, and works incessantly—probably hard, hard, hard—like an engine at full pressure. I imagine that various thoughts must beat loud and fast through his head—all unfinished ones, and strange, funny thoughts, very likely!—like this, for instance: 'That man is looking at me, and he has a wart on his forehead! and the executioner has burst one of his buttons, and the lowest one is all rusty!' And meanwhile he notices and remembers everything. There is one point that cannot be forgotten, round which everything else dances and turns about; and because of this point he cannot faint, and this lasts until the very final quarter of a second, when the wretched neck is on the block and the victim listens and waits and *knows*—that's the point, he *knows* that he is just *now* about to die, and listens for the rasp of the iron over his head. If I lay there, I should certainly listen for that grating sound, and hear it, too! There would probably be but the tenth part of an instant left to hear it in, but one would certainly hear it. And imagine, some people declare that when the head flies off it is *conscious* of having flown off! Just imagine what a thing to realize! Fancy if consciousness were to last for even five seconds!

"Draw the scaffold so that only the top step of the ladder comes in clearly. The criminal must be just stepping on to it, his face as white as note-paper. The priest is holding the cross to his blue lips, and the criminal kisses it, and knows and sees and understands everything. The cross and the head—there's your picture; the priest and the executioner, with his two assistants, and a few heads and eyes below. Those might come in as subordinate accessories—a sort of mist. There's a picture for you." The prince paused, and looked around.

"Certainly that isn't much like quietism," murmured Alexandra, half to herself.

"Now tell us about your love affairs," said Adelaida, after a moment's pause.

The prince gazed at her in amazement.

"You know," Adelaida continued, "you owe us a description of the Basle picture; but first I wish to hear how you fell in love. Don't deny the fact, for you did, of course. Besides, you stop philosophizing when you are telling about anything."

"Why are you ashamed of your stories the moment after you have told them?" asked Aglaya, suddenly.

"How silly you are!" said Mrs. Epanchin, looking indignantly towards the last speaker.

"Yes, that wasn't a clever remark," said Alexandra.

"Don't listen to her, prince," said Mrs. Epanchin; "she says that sort of thing out of mischief. Don't think anything of their nonsense, it means nothing. They love to chaff, but they like you. I can see it in their faces—I know their faces."

"I know their faces, too," said the prince, with a peculiar stress on the words.

"How so?" asked Adelaida, with curiosity.

"What do *you* know about our faces?" exclaimed the other two, in chorus.

But the prince was silent and serious. All awaited his reply.

"I'll tell you afterwards," he said quietly.

"Ah, you want to arouse our curiosity!" said Aglaya. "And how terribly solemn you are about it!"

"Very well," interrupted Adelaida, "then if you can read faces so well, you *must* have been in love. Come now; I've guessed—let's have the secret!"

"I have not been in love," said the prince, as quietly and seriously as before. "I have been happy in another way."

"How, how?"

"Well, I'll tell you," said the prince, apparently in a deep reverie.

CHAPTER VI.

"Here you all are," began the prince, "settling yourselves down to listen to me with so much curiosity, that if I do not satisfy you you will probably be angry with me. No, no! I'm only joking!" he added, hastily, with a smile.

"Well, then—they were all children there, and I was always among children and only with children. They were the children of the village in which I lived, and they went to the school there—all of them. I did not teach them, oh no; there was a master for that, one Jules Thibaut. I may have taught them some things, but I was among them just as an outsider, and I passed all four years of my life there among them. I wished for nothing better; I used to tell them everything and hid nothing from them. Their fathers and relations were very angry with me, because the children could do nothing without me at last, and used to throng after me at all times. The schoolmaster was my greatest enemy in the end! I had many enemies, and all because of the children. Even Schneider reproached me. What were they afraid of? One can tell a child everything, anything. I have often been struck by the fact that parents know their children so little. They should not conceal so much from them. How well even little children understand that their parents conceal things from them, because they consider them too young to understand! Children are capable of giving advice in the most important matters. How can one deceive these dear little birds, when they look at one so sweetly and confidingly? I call them birds because there is nothing in the world better than birds!

"However, most of the people were angry with me about one and the same thing; but Thibaut simply was jealous of me. At first he had wagged his head and wondered how it was that the children understood what I told them so well, and could not learn from him; and he laughed like anything when I replied that neither he nor I could teach them very much, but that *they* might teach us a good deal.

"How he could hate me and tell scandalous stories about me, living among children as he did, is what I cannot understand. Children soothe and heal the wounded heart. I remember there was one poor fellow at our professor's who was being treated for madness, and you have no idea what those children did for him, eventually. I don't think he was mad, but only terribly unhappy. But I'll tell you all about him another day. Now I must get on with this story.

"The children did not love me at first; I was such a sickly, awkward kind of a fellow then—and I know I am ugly. Besides, I was a foreigner. The children used to laugh at me, at first; and they even went so far as to throw stones at me, when they saw me kiss Marie. I only kissed her once in my life—no, no, don't laugh!" The prince hastened to suppress the smiles of his audience at this point. "It was not a matter of *love* at all! If only you knew what a miserable creature she was, you would have pitied her, just as I did. She belonged to our village. Her mother was an old, old woman, and they used to sell string and thread, and soap and tobacco, out of the window of their little house, and lived on the pittance they gained by this trade. The old woman was ill and very old, and could hardly move. Marie was her daughter, a girl of twenty, weak and thin and consumptive; but still she did heavy work at the houses around, day by day. Well, one fine day a commercial traveller betrayed her and carried her off; and a week later he deserted her. She came home dirty, draggled, and shoeless; she had walked for a whole week without shoes; she had slept in the fields, and caught a terrible cold; her feet were swollen and sore, and her hands torn and scratched all over. She never had been pretty even before; but her eyes were quiet, innocent, kind eyes.

"She was very quiet always—and I remember once, when she had suddenly begun singing at her work, everyone said, 'Marie tried to sing today!' and she got so chaffed that she was silent for ever after. She had been treated kindly in the place before; but when she came back now—ill and shunned and miserable—not one of them all had the slightest sympathy for her. Cruel people! Oh, what hazy understandings they have on such matters! Her mother was the first to show the way. She received her wrathfully, unkindly, and with contempt. 'You have disgraced me,' she said. She was the first to cast her into ignominy; but when they all heard that Marie had returned to the village, they ran out to see her and crowded into the little cottage—old men, children, women, girls—such a hurrying, stamping, greedy crowd. Marie was lying on the floor at the old woman's feet, hungry, torn, draggled, crying, miserable.

"When everyone crowded into the room she hid her face in her dishevelled hair and lay cowering on the floor. Everyone looked at her as though she were a piece of dirt off the road. The old men scolded and condemned, and the young ones laughed at her. The women condemned her too, and looked at her contemptuously, just as though she were some loathsome insect.

"Her mother allowed all this to go on, and nodded her head and encouraged them. The old woman was very ill at that time, and knew she was dying (she really did die a couple of months later), and though she felt the end approaching she never thought of forgiving her daughter, to the very day of her death. She would not even speak to her. She made her sleep on straw in a shed, and hardly gave her food enough to support life.

"Marie was very gentle to her mother, and nursed her, and did everything for her; but the old woman accepted all her services without a word and never showed her the slightest kindness. Marie bore all this; and I could see when I got to know her that she thought it quite right and fitting, considering herself the lowest and meanest of creatures.

"When the old woman took to her bed finally, the other old women in the village sat with her by turns, as the custom is there; and then Marie was quite driven out of the house. They gave her no food at all, and she could not get any work in the village; none would employ her. The men seemed to consider her no longer a woman, they said such dreadful things to her. Sometimes on Sundays, if they were drunk enough, they used to throw her a penny or two, into the mud, and Marie would silently pick up the money. She had began to spit blood at that time.

"At last her rags became so tattered and torn that she was ashamed of appearing in the village any longer. The children used to pelt her with mud; so she begged to be taken on as assistant cowherd, but the cowherd would not have her. Then she took to helping him without leave; and he saw how valuable her assistance was to him, and did not drive her away again; on the contrary, he occasionally gave her the remnants of his dinner, bread and cheese. He considered that he was being very kind. When the mother died, the village parson was not ashamed to hold Marie up to public derision and shame. Marie was standing at the coffin's head, in all her rags, crying.

"A crowd of people had collected to see how she would cry. The parson, a young fellow ambitious of becoming a great preacher, began his sermon and pointed to Marie. 'There,' he said, 'there is the cause of the death of this venerable woman'—(which was a lie, because she had been ill for at least two years)—'there she stands before you, and dares not lift her eyes from the ground, because she knows that the finger of God is upon her. Look at her tatters and rags—the badge of those who lose their virtue. Who is she? her daughter!' and so on to the end.

"And just fancy, this infamy pleased them, all of them, nearly. Only the children had altered—for then they were all on my side and had learned to love Marie.

"This is how it was: I had wished to do something for Marie; I longed to give her some money, but I never had a farthing while I was there. But I had a little diamond pin, and this I sold to a travelling pedlar; he gave me eight francs for it—it was worth at least forty.

"I long sought to meet Marie alone; and at last I did meet her, on the hillside beyond the village. I gave her the eight francs and asked her to take care of the money because I could get no more; and then I kissed her and said that she was not to suppose I kissed her with any evil motives or because I was in love with her, for that I did so solely out of pity for her, and because from the first I had not accounted her as guilty so much as unfortunate. I longed to console and encourage her somehow, and to assure her that she was not the low, base thing which she and others strove to make out; but I don't think she understood me. She stood before me, dreadfully ashamed of herself, and with downcast eyes; and when I had finished she kissed my hand. I would have kissed hers, but she drew it away. Just at this moment the whole troop of children saw us. (I found out afterwards that they had long kept a watch upon me.) They all began whistling and clapping their hands, and laughing at us. Marie ran away at once; and when I tried to talk to them, they threw stones at me. All the village heard of it the same day, and Marie's position became worse than ever. The children would not let her pass now in the streets, but annoyed her and threw dirt at her more than before. They used to run after her—she racing away with her poor feeble lungs panting and gasping, and they pelting her and shouting abuse at her.

"Once I had to interfere by force; and after that I took to speaking to them every day and whenever I could. Occasionally they stopped and listened; but they teased Marie all the same.

"I told them how unhappy Marie was, and after a while they stopped their abuse of her, and let her go by silently. Little by little we got into the way of conversing together, the children and I. I concealed nothing from them, I told them all. They listened very attentively and soon began to be sorry for Marie. At last some of them took to saying 'Good-morning' to her, kindly, when they met her. It is the custom there to salute anyone you meet with 'Good-morning' whether acquainted or not. I can imagine how astonished Marie was at these first greetings from the children.

"Once two little girls got hold of some food and took it to her, and came back and told me. They said she had burst into tears, and that they loved her very much now. Very soon after that they all became fond of Marie, and at the same time they began to develop the greatest affection for myself. They often came to me and begged me to tell them stories. I think I must have told stories well, for they did so love to hear them. At last I took to reading up interesting things on purpose to pass them on to the little ones, and this went on for all the rest of my time there, three years. Later, when everyone—even Schneider—was angry with me for hiding nothing from the children, I pointed out how foolish it was, for they always knew things, only they learnt them in a way that soiled their minds but not so from me. One has only to remember one's own childhood to admit the truth of this. But nobody was convinced... It was two weeks before her mother died that I had kissed Marie; and when the clergyman preached that sermon the children were all on my side.

"When I told them what a shame it was of the parson to talk as he had done, and explained my reason, they were so angry that some of them went and broke his windows with stones. Of course I stopped them, for that was not right, but all the village heard of it, and how I caught it for spoiling the children! Everyone discovered now that the little ones had taken to being fond of Marie, and their parents were terribly alarmed; but Marie was so happy. The children were forbidden to meet her; but they used to run out of the village to the herd and take her food and things; and sometimes just ran off there and kissed her, and said, '*Je vous aime, Marie!*' and then trotted back again. They imagined that I was in love with Marie, and this was the only point on which I did not undeceive them, for they got such enjoyment out of it. And what delicacy and tenderness they showed!

"In the evening I used to walk to the waterfall. There was a spot there which was quite closed in and hidden from view by large trees; and to this spot the children used to come to me. They could not bear that their dear Leon should love a poor girl without shoes to her feet and dressed all in rags and tatters. So, would you believe it, they actually clubbed together, somehow, and bought her shoes and stockings, and some linen, and even a dress! I can't understand how they managed it, but they did it, all together. When I asked them about it they only laughed and shouted, and the little girls clapped their hands and kissed me. I sometimes went to see Marie secretly, too. She had become very ill, and could hardly walk. She still went with the herd, but could not help the herdsman any longer. She used to sit on a stone near, and wait there almost motionless all day, till the herd went home. Her consumption was so advanced, and she was so weak, that she used to sit with closed eyes, breathing heavily. Her face was as thin as a skeleton's, and sweat used to stand on her white brow in large drops. I always found her sitting just like that. I used to come up quietly to look at her; but Marie would hear me, open her eyes, and tremble violently as she kissed my hands. I did not take my hand away because it made her happy to have it, and so she would sit and cry quietly. Sometimes she tried to speak; but it was very difficult to understand her. She was almost like a madwoman, with excitement and ecstasy, whenever I came. Occasionally the children came with me; when they did so, they would stand some way off and keep guard over us, so as to tell me if anybody came near. This was a great pleasure to them.

"When we left her, Marie used to relapse at once into her old condition, and sit with closed eyes and motionless limbs. One day she could not go out at all, and remained at home all alone in the empty hut; but the children very soon became aware of the fact, and nearly all of them visited her that day as she lay alone and helpless in her miserable bed.

"For two days the children looked after her, and then, when the village people got to know that Marie was really dying, some of the old women came and took it in turns to sit by her and look after her a bit. I think they began to be a little sorry for her in the village at last; at all events they did not interfere with the children any more, on her account.

"Marie lay in a state of uncomfortable delirium the whole while; she coughed dreadfully. The old women would not let the children stay in the room; but they all collected outside the window each morning, if only for a moment, and shouted '*Bon jour, notre bonne Marie!*' and Marie no sooner caught sight of, or heard them, and she became quite animated at once, and, in spite of the old women, would try to sit up and nod her head and smile at them, and thank them. The little ones used to bring her nice things and sweets to eat, but she could hardly touch anything. Thanks to them, I assure you, the girl died almost perfectly happy. She almost forgot her misery, and seemed to accept their love as a sort of symbol of pardon for her offence, though she never ceased to consider herself a dreadful sinner. They used to flutter at her window just like little birds, calling out: '*Nous t'aimons, Marie!*'

"She died very soon; I had thought she would live much longer. The day before her death I went to see her for the last time, just before sunset. I think she recognized me, for she pressed my hand.

"Next morning they came and told me that Marie was dead. The children could not be restrained now; they went and covered her coffin with flowers, and put a wreath of lovely blossoms on her head. The pastor did not throw any more shameful words at the poor dead woman; but there were very few people at the funeral. However, when it came to carrying the coffin, all the children rushed up, to carry it themselves. Of course they could not do it alone, but they insisted on helping, and walked alongside and behind, crying.

"They have planted roses all round her grave, and every year they look after the flowers and make Marie's resting-place as beautiful as they can. I was in ill odour after all this with the parents of the children, and especially with the parson and schoolmaster. Schneider was obliged to promise that I should not meet them and talk to them; but we conversed from a distance by signs, and they used to write me sweet little notes. Afterwards I came closer than ever to those little souls, but even then it was very dear to me, to have them so fond of me.

"Schneider said that I did the children great harm by my pernicious 'system'; what nonsense that was! And what did he mean by my system? He said afterwards that he believed I was a child myself—just before I came away. 'You have the form and face of an adult' he said, 'but as regards soul, and character, and perhaps even intelligence, you are a child in the completest sense of the word, and always will be, if you live to be sixty.' I laughed very much, for of course that is nonsense. But it is a fact that I do not care to be among grown-up people and much prefer the society of children. However kind people may be to me, I never feel quite at home with them, and am always glad to get back to my little companions. Now my companions have always been children, not because I was a child myself once, but because young things attract me. On one of the first days of my stay in Switzerland, I was strolling about alone and miserable, when I came upon the children rushing noisily out of school, with their slates and bags, and books, their games, their laughter and shouts—and my soul went out to them. I stopped and laughed happily as I watched their little feet moving so quickly. Girls and boys, laughing and crying; for as they went home many of them found time to fight and make peace, to weep and play. I forgot my troubles in looking at them. And then, all those three years, I tried to understand why men should be for ever tormenting themselves. I lived the life of a child there, and thought I should never leave the little village; indeed, I was far from thinking that I should ever return to Russia. But at last I recognized the fact that Schneider could not keep me any longer. And then something so important happened, that Schneider himself urged me to depart. I am going to see now if can get good advice about it. Perhaps my lot in life will be changed; but that is not the principal thing. The principal thing is the entire change that has already come over me. I left many things behind me—too many. They have gone. On the journey I said to myself, 'I am going into the world of men. I don't know much, perhaps, but a new life has begun for me.' I made up my mind to be honest, and steadfast in accomplishing my task. Perhaps I shall meet with troubles and many disappointments, but I have made up my mind to be polite and sincere to everyone; more cannot be asked of me. People may consider me a child if they like. I am often called an idiot, and at one time I certainly was so ill that I was nearly as bad as an idiot; but I am not an idiot now. How can I possibly be so when I know myself that I am considered one?

"When I received a letter from those dear little souls, while passing through Berlin, I only then realized how much I loved them. It was very, very painful, getting that first little letter. How melancholy they had been when they saw me off! For a month before, they had been talking of my departure and sorrowing over it; and at the waterfall, of an evening, when we parted for the night, they would hug me so tight and kiss me so warmly, far more so than before. And every now and then they would turn up one by one when I was alone, just to give me a kiss and a hug, to show their love for me. The whole flock went with me to the station, which was about a mile from the village, and every now and then one of them would stop to throw his arms round me, and all the little girls had tears in their voices, though they tried hard not to cry. As the train steamed out of the station, I saw them all standing on the platform waving to me and crying 'Hurrah!' till they were lost in the distance.

"I assure you, when I came in here just now and saw your kind faces (I can read faces well) my heart felt light for the first time since that moment of parting. I think I must be one of those who are born to be in luck, for one does not often meet with people whom one feels he can love from the first sight of their faces; and yet, no sooner do I step out of the railway carriage than I happen upon you!

"I know it is more or less a shamefaced thing to speak of one's feelings before others; and yet here am I talking like this to you, and am not a bit ashamed or shy. I am an unsociable sort of fellow and shall very likely not come to see you again for some time; but don't think the worse of me for that. It is not that I do not value your society; and you must never suppose that I have taken offence at anything.

"You asked me about your faces, and what I could read in them; I will tell you with the greatest pleasure. You, Adelaida Ivanovna, have a very happy face; it is the most sympathetic of the three. Not to speak of your natural beauty, one can look at your face and say to one's self, 'She has the face of a kind sister.' You are simple and merry, but you can see into another's heart very quickly. That's what I read in your face.

"You too, Alexandra Ivanovna, have a very lovely face; but I think you may have some secret sorrow. Your heart is undoubtedly a kind, good one, but you are not merry. There is a certain suspicion of 'shadow' in your face, like in that of Holbein's Madonna in Dresden. So much for your face. Have I guessed right?

"As for your face, Lizabetha Prokofievna, I not only think, but am perfectly *sure*, that you are an absolute child—in all, in all, mind, both good and bad—and in spite of your years. Don't be angry with me for saying so; you know what my feelings for children are. And do not suppose that I am so candid out of pure simplicity of soul. Oh dear no, it is by no means the case! Perhaps I have my own very profound object in view."

CHAPTER VII.

When the prince ceased speaking all were gazing merrily at him—even Aglaya; but Lizabetha Prokofievna looked the jolliest of all.

"Well!" she cried, "we *have* 'put him through his paces,' with a vengeance! My dears, you imagined, I believe, that you were about to patronize this young gentleman, like some poor *protégé* picked up somewhere, and taken under your magnificent protection. What fools we were, and what a specially big fool is your father! Well done, prince! I assure you the general actually asked me to put you through your paces, and examine you. As to what you said about my face, you are absolutely correct in your judgment. I am a child, and know it. I knew it long before you said so; you have expressed my own thoughts. I think your nature and mine must be extremely alike, and I am very glad of it. We are like two drops of water, only you are a man and I a woman, and I've not been to Switzerland, and that is all the difference between us."

"Don't be in a hurry, mother; the prince says that he has some motive behind his simplicity," cried Aglaya.

"Yes, yes, so he does," laughed the others.

"Oh, don't you begin bantering him," said mamma. "He is probably a good deal cleverer than all three of you girls put together. We shall see. Only you haven't told us anything about Aglaya yet, prince; and Aglaya and I are both waiting to hear."

"I cannot say anything at present. I'll tell you afterwards."

"Why? Her face is clear enough, isn't it?"

"Oh yes, of course. You are very beautiful, Aglaya Ivanovna, so beautiful that one is afraid to look at you."

"Is that all? What about her character?" persisted Mrs. Epanchin.

"It is difficult to judge when such beauty is concerned. I have not prepared my judgment. Beauty is a riddle."

"That means that you have set Aglaya a riddle!" said Adelaida. "Guess it, Aglaya! But she's pretty, prince, isn't she?"

"Most wonderfully so," said the latter, warmly, gazing at Aglaya with admiration. "Almost as lovely as Nastasia Philipovna, but quite a different type."

All present exchanged looks of surprise.

"As lovely as *who?*" said Mrs. Epanchin. "As *Nastasia Philipovna?* Where have you seen Nastasia Philipovna? What Nastasia Philipovna?"

"Gavrila Ardalionovitch showed the general her portrait just now."

"How so? Did he bring the portrait for my husband?"

"Only to show it. Nastasia Philipovna gave it to Gavrila Ardalionovitch today, and the latter brought it here to show to the general."

"I must see it!" cried Mrs. Epanchin. "Where is the portrait? If she gave it to him, he must have it; and he is still in the study. He never leaves before four o'clock on Wednesdays. Send for Gavrila Ardalionovitch at once. No, I don't long to see *him* so much. Look here, dear prince, *be* so kind, will you? Just step to the study and fetch this portrait! Say we want to look at it. Please do this for me, will you?"

"He is a nice fellow, but a little too simple," said Adelaida, as the prince left the room.

"He is, indeed," said Alexandra; "almost laughably so at times."

Neither one nor the other seemed to give expression to her full thoughts.

"He got out of it very neatly about our faces, though," said Aglaya. "He flattered us all round, even mamma."

"Nonsense!" cried the latter. "He did not flatter me. It was I who found his appreciation flattering. I think you are a great deal more foolish than he is. He is simple, of course, but also very knowing. Just like myself."

"How stupid of me to speak of the portrait," thought the prince as he entered the study, with a feeling of guilt at his heart, "and yet, perhaps I was right after all." He had an idea, unformed as yet, but a strange idea.

Gavrila Ardalionovitch was still sitting in the study, buried in a mass of papers. He looked as though he did not take his salary from the public company, whose servant he was, for a sinecure.

He grew very wroth and confused when the prince asked for the portrait, and explained how it came about that he had spoken of it.

"Oh, curse it all," he said; "what on earth must you go blabbing for? You know nothing about the thing, and yet—idiot!" he added, muttering the last word to himself in irrepressible rage.

"I am very sorry; I was not thinking at the time. I merely said that Aglaya was almost as beautiful as Nastasia Philipovna."

Gania asked for further details; and the prince once more repeated the conversation. Gania looked at him with ironical contempt the while.

"Nastasia Philipovna," he began, and there paused; he was clearly much agitated and annoyed. The prince reminded him of the portrait.

"Listen, prince," said Gania, as though an idea had just struck him, "I wish to ask you a great favour, and yet I really don't know—"

He paused again, he was trying to make up his mind to something, and was turning the matter over. The prince waited quietly. Once more Gania fixed him with intent and questioning eyes.

"Prince," he began again, "they are rather angry with me, in there, owing to a circumstance which I need not explain, so that I do not care to go in at present without an invitation. I particularly wish to speak to Aglaya, but I have written a few words in case I shall not have the chance of seeing her" (here the prince observed a small note in his hand), "and I do not know how to get my communication to her. Don't you think you could undertake to give it to her at once, but only to her, mind, and so that no one else should see you give it? It isn't much of a secret, but still—Well, will you do it?"

"I don't quite like it," replied the prince.

"Oh, but it is absolutely necessary for me," Gania entreated. "Believe me, if it were not so, I would not ask you; how else am I to get it to her? It is most important, dreadfully important!"

Gania was evidently much alarmed at the idea that the prince would not consent to take his note, and he looked at him now with an expression of absolute entreaty.

"Well, I will take it then."

"But mind, nobody is to see!" cried the delighted Gania "And of course I may rely on your word of honour, eh?"

"I won't show it to anyone," said the prince.

"The letter is not sealed—" continued Gania, and paused in confusion.

"Oh, I won't read it," said the prince, quite simply.

He took up the portrait, and went out of the room.

Gania, left alone, clutched his head with his hands.

"One word from her," he said, "one word from her, and I may yet be free."

He could not settle himself to his papers again, for agitation and excitement, but began walking up and down the room from corner to corner.

The prince walked along, musing. He did not like his commission, and disliked the idea of Gania sending a note to Aglaya at all; but when he was two rooms distant from the drawing-room, where they all were, he stopped as though recalling something; went to the window, nearer the light, and began to examine the portrait in his hand.

He longed to solve the mystery of something in the face of Nastasia Philipovna, something which had struck him as he looked at the portrait for the first time; the impression had not left him. It was partly the fact of her marvellous beauty that struck him, and partly something else. There was a suggestion of immense pride and disdain in the face almost of hatred, and at the same time something confiding and very full of simplicity. The contrast aroused a deep sympathy in his heart as he looked at the lovely face. The blinding loveliness of it was almost intolerable, this pale thin face with its flaming eyes; it was a strange beauty.

The prince gazed at it for a minute or two, then glanced around him, and hurriedly raised the portrait to his lips. When, a minute after, he reached the drawing-room door, his face was quite composed. But just as he reached the door he met Aglaya coming out alone.

"Gavrila Ardalionovitch begged me to give you this," he said, handing her the note.

Aglaya stopped, took the letter, and gazed strangely into the prince's eyes. There was no confusion in her face; a little surprise, perhaps, but that was all. By her look she seemed merely to challenge the prince to an explanation as to how he and Gania happened to be connected in this matter. But her expression was perfectly cool and quiet, and even condescending.

So they stood for a moment or two, confronting one another. At length a faint smile passed over her face, and she passed by him without a word.

Mrs. Epanchin examined the portrait of Nastasia Philipovna for some little while, holding it critically at arm's length.

"Yes, she is pretty," she said at last, "even very pretty. I have seen her twice, but only at a distance. So you admire this kind of beauty, do you?" she asked the prince, suddenly.

"Yes, I do—this kind."

"Do you mean especially this kind?"

"Yes, especially this kind."

"Why?"

"There is much suffering in this face," murmured the prince, more as though talking to himself than answering the question.

"I think you are wandering a little, prince," Mrs. Epanchin decided, after a lengthened survey of his face; and she tossed the portrait on to the table, haughtily.

Alexandra took it, and Adelaida came up, and both the girls examined the photograph. Just then Aglaya entered the room.

"What a power!" cried Adelaida suddenly, as she earnestly examined the portrait over her sister's shoulder.

"Whom? What power?" asked her mother, crossly.

"Such beauty is real power," said Adelaida. "With such beauty as that one might overthrow the world." She returned to her easel thoughtfully.

Aglaya merely glanced at the portrait—frowned, and put out her underlip; then went and sat down on the sofa with folded hands. Mrs. Epanchin rang the bell.

"Ask Gavrila Ardalionovitch to step this way," said she to the man who answered.

"Mamma!" cried Alexandra, significantly.

"I shall just say two words to him, that's all," said her mother, silencing all objection by her manner; she was evidently seriously put out. "You see, prince, it is all secrets with us, just now—all secrets. It seems to be the etiquette of the house, for some reason or other. Stupid nonsense, and in a matter which ought to be approached with all candour and open-heartedness. There is a marriage being talked of, and I don't like this marriage—"

"Mamma, what are you saying?" said Alexandra again, hurriedly.

"Well, what, my dear girl? As if you can possibly like it yourself? The heart is the great thing, and the rest is all rubbish—though one must have sense as well. Perhaps sense is really the great thing. Don't smile like that, Aglaya. I don't contradict myself. A fool with a heart and no brains is just as unhappy as a fool with brains and no heart. I am one and you are the other, and therefore both of us suffer, both of us are unhappy."

"Why are you so unhappy, mother?" asked Adelaida, who alone of all the company seemed to have preserved her good temper and spirits up to now.

"In the first place, because of my carefully brought-up daughters," said Mrs. Epanchin, cuttingly; "and as that is the best reason I can give you we need not bother about any other at present. Enough of words, now! We shall see how both of you (I don't count Aglaya) will manage your business, and whether you, most revered Alexandra Ivanovna, will be happy with your fine mate."

"Ah!" she added, as Gania suddenly entered the room, "here's another marrying subject. How do you do?" she continued, in response to Gania's bow; but she did not invite him to sit down. "You are going to be married?"

"Married? how—what marriage?" murmured Gania, overwhelmed with confusion.

"Are you about to take a wife? I ask,—if you prefer that expression."

"No, no I—I—no!" said Gania, bringing out his lie with a tell-tale blush of shame. He glanced keenly at Aglaya, who was sitting some way off, and dropped his eyes immediately.

Aglaya gazed coldly, intently, and composedly at him, without taking her eyes off his face, and watched his confusion.

"No? You say no, do you?" continued the pitiless Mrs. General. "Very well, I shall remember that you told me this Wednesday morning, in answer to my question, that you are not going to be married. What day is it, Wednesday, isn't it?"

"Yes, I think so!" said Adelaida.

"You never know the day of the week; what's the day of the month?"

"Twenty-seventh!" said Gania.

"Twenty-seventh; very well. Good-bye now; you have a good deal to do, I'm sure, and I must dress and go out. Take your portrait. Give my respects to your unfortunate mother, Nina Alexandrovna. *Au revoir*, dear prince, come in and see us often, do; and I shall tell old Princess Bielokonski about you. I shall go and see her on purpose. And listen, my dear boy, I feel sure that God has sent you to Petersburg from Switzerland on purpose for me. Maybe you will have other things to do, besides, but you are sent chiefly for my sake, I feel sure of it. God sent you to me! *Au revoir!* Alexandra, come with me, my dear."

Mrs. Epanchin left the room.

Gania—confused, annoyed, furious—took up his portrait, and turned to the prince with a nasty smile on his face.

"Prince," he said, "I am just going home. If you have not changed your mind as to living with us, perhaps you would like to come with me. You don't know the address, I believe?"

"Wait a minute, prince," said Aglaya, suddenly rising from her seat, "do write something in my album first, will you? Father says you are a most talented caligraphist; I'll bring you my book in a minute." She left the room.

"Well, *au revoir*, prince," said Adelaida, "I must be going too." She pressed the prince's hand warmly, and gave him a friendly smile as she left the room. She did not so much as look at Gania.

"This is your doing, prince," said Gania, turning on the latter so soon as the others were all out of the room. "This is your doing, sir! *You* have been telling them that I am going to be married!" He said this in a hurried whisper, his eyes flashing with rage and his face ablaze. "You shameless tattler!"

"I assure you, you are under a delusion," said the prince, calmly and politely. "I did not even know that you were to be married."

"You heard me talking about it, the general and me. You heard me say that everything was to be settled today at Nastasia Philipovna's, and you went and blurted it out here. You lie if you deny it. Who else could have told them? Devil take it, sir, who could have told them except yourself? Didn't the old woman as good as hint as much to me?"

"If she hinted to you who told her you must know best, of course; but I never said a word about it."

"Did you give my note? Is there an answer?" interrupted Gania, impatiently.

But at this moment Aglaya came back, and the prince had no time to reply.

"There, prince," said she, "there's my album. Now choose a page and write me something, will you? There's a pen, a new one; do you mind a steel one? I have heard that you caligraphists don't like steel pens."

Conversing with the prince, Aglaya did not even seem to notice that Gania was in the room. But while the prince was getting his pen ready, finding a page, and making his preparations to write, Gania came up to the fireplace where Aglaya was standing, to the right of the prince, and in trembling, broken accents said, almost in her ear:

"One word, just one word from you, and I'm saved."

The prince turned sharply round and looked at both of them. Gania's face was full of real despair; he seemed to have said the words almost unconsciously and on the impulse of the moment.

Aglaya gazed at him for some seconds with precisely the same composure and calm astonishment as she had shown a little while before, when the prince handed her the note, and it appeared that this calm surprise and seemingly absolute incomprehension of what was said to her, were more terribly overwhelming to Gania than even the most plainly expressed disdain would have been.

"What shall I write?" asked the prince.

"I'll dictate to you," said Aglaya, coming up to the table. "Now then, are you ready? Write, 'I never condescend to bargain!' Now put your name and the date. Let me see it."

The prince handed her the album.

"Capital! How beautifully you have written it! Thanks so much. *Au revoir*, prince. Wait a minute," she added, "I want to give you something for a keepsake. Come with me this way, will you?"

The prince followed her. Arrived at the dining-room, she stopped.

"Read this," she said, handing him Gania's note.

The prince took it from her hand, but gazed at her in bewilderment.

"Oh! I *know* you haven't read it, and that you could never be that man's accomplice. Read it, I wish you to read it."

The letter had evidently been written in a hurry:

"My fate is to be decided today" (it ran), "you know how. This day I must give my word irrevocably. I have no right to ask your help, and I dare not allow myself to indulge in any hopes; but once you said just one word, and that word lighted up the night of my life, and became the beacon of my days. Say one more such word, and save me from utter ruin. Only tell me, 'break off the whole thing!' and I will do so this very day. Oh! what can it cost you to say just this one word? In doing so you will but be giving me a sign of your sympathy for me, and of your pity; only this, only this; nothing more, nothing. I dare not indulge in any hope, because I am unworthy of it. But if you say but this word, I will take up my cross again with joy, and return once more to my battle with poverty. I shall meet the storm and be glad of it; I shall rise up with renewed strength.

"Send me back then this one word of sympathy, only sympathy, I swear to you; and oh! do not be angry with the audacity of despair, with the drowning man who has dared to make this last effort to save himself from perishing beneath the waters.

"*G.L.*"

"This man assures me," said Aglaya, scornfully, when the prince had finished reading the letter, "that the words 'break off everything' do not commit me to anything whatever; and himself gives me a written guarantee to that effect, in this letter. Observe how ingenuously he underlines certain words, and how crudely he glosses over his hidden thoughts. He must know that if he 'broke off everything,' *first*, by himself, and without telling me a word about it or having the slightest hope on my account, that in that case I should perhaps be able to change my opinion of him, and even accept his—friendship. He must know that, but his soul is such a wretched thing. He knows it and cannot make up his mind; he knows it and yet asks for guarantees. He cannot bring himself to *trust*, he wants me to give him hopes of myself before he lets go of his hundred thousand roubles. As to the 'former word' which he declares 'lighted up the night of his life,' he is simply an impudent liar; I merely pitied him once. But he is audacious and shameless. He immediately began to hope, at that very moment. I saw it. He has tried to catch me ever since; he is still fishing for me. Well, enough of this. Take the letter and give it back to him, as soon as you have left our house; not before, of course."

"And what shall I tell him by way of answer?"

"Nothing—of course! That's the best answer. Is it the case that you are going to live in his house?"

"Yes, your father kindly recommended me to him."

"Then look out for him, I warn you! He won't forgive you easily, for taking back the letter."

Aglaya pressed the prince's hand and left the room. Her face was serious and frowning; she did not even smile as she nodded good-bye to him at the door.

"I'll just get my parcel and we'll go," said the prince to Gania, as he re-entered the drawing-room. Gania stamped his foot with impatience. His face looked dark and gloomy with rage.

At last they left the house behind them, the prince carrying his bundle.

"The answer—quick—the answer!" said Gania, the instant they were outside. "What did she say? Did you give the letter?" The prince silently held out the note. Gania was struck motionless with amazement.

"How, what? my letter?" he cried. "He never delivered it! I might have guessed it, oh! curse him! Of course she did not understand what I meant, naturally! Why—why—*why* didn't you give her the note, you—"

"Excuse me; I was able to deliver it almost immediately after receiving your commission, and I gave it, too, just as you asked me to. It has come into my hands now because Aglaya Ivanovna has just returned it to me."

"How? When?"

"As soon as I finished writing in her album for her, and when she asked me to come out of the room with her (you heard?), we went into the dining-room, and she gave me your letter to read, and then told me to return it."

"To *read*?" cried Gania, almost at the top of his voice; "to *read*, and you read it?"

And again he stood like a log in the middle of the pavement; so amazed that his mouth remained open after the last word had left it.

"Yes, I have just read it."

"And she gave it you to read herself—*herself*?"

"Yes, herself; and you may believe me when I tell you that I would not have read it for anything without her permission."

Gania was silent for a minute or two, as though thinking out some problem. Suddenly he cried:

"It's impossible, she cannot have given it to you to read! You are lying. You read it yourself!"

"I am telling you the truth," said the prince in his former composed tone of voice; "and believe me, I am extremely sorry that the circumstance should have made such an unpleasant impression upon you!"

"But, you wretched man, at least she must have said something? There must be *some* answer from her!"

"Yes, of course, she did say something!"

"Out with it then, damn it! Out with it at once!" and Gania stamped his foot twice on the pavement.

"As soon as I had finished reading it, she told me that you were fishing for her; that you wished to compromise her so far as to receive some hopes from her, trusting to which hopes you might break with the prospect of receiving a hundred thousand roubles. She said that if you had done this without bargaining with her, if you had broken with the money prospects without trying to force a guarantee out of her first, she might have been your friend. That's all, I think. Oh no, when I asked her what I was to say, as I took the letter, she replied that 'no answer is the best answer.' I think that was it. Forgive me if I do not use her exact expressions. I tell you the sense as I understood it myself."

Ungovernable rage and madness took entire possession of Gania, and his fury burst out without the least attempt at restraint.

"Oh! that's it, is it!" he yelled. "She throws my letters out of the window, does she! Oh! and she does not condescend to bargain, while I *do*, eh? We shall see, we shall see! I shall pay her out for this."

He twisted himself about with rage, and grew paler and paler; he shook his fist. So the pair walked along a few steps. Gania did not stand on ceremony with the prince; he behaved just as though he were alone in his room. He clearly counted the latter as a nonentity. But suddenly he seemed to have an idea, and recollected himself.

"But how was it?" he asked, "how was it that you (idiot that you are)," he added to himself, "were so very confidential a couple of hours after your first meeting with these people? How was that, eh?"

Up to this moment jealousy had not been one of his torments; now it suddenly gnawed at his heart.

"That is a thing I cannot undertake to explain," replied the prince. Gania looked at him with angry contempt.

"Oh! I suppose the present she wished to make to you, when she took you into the dining-room, was her confidence, eh?"

"I suppose that was it; I cannot explain it otherwise."

"But why, *why*? Devil take it, what did you do in there? Why did they fancy you? Look here, can't you remember exactly what you said to them, from the very beginning? Can't you remember?"

"Oh, we talked of a great many things. When first I went in we began to speak of Switzerland."

"Oh, the devil take Switzerland!"

"Then about executions."

"Executions?"

"Yes—at least about one. Then I told the whole three years' story of my life, and the history of a poor peasant girl—"

"Oh, damn the peasant girl! go on, go on!" said Gania, impatiently.

"Then how Schneider told me about my childish nature, and—"

"Oh, *curse* Schneider and his dirty opinions! Go on."

"Then I began to talk about faces, at least about the *expressions* of faces, and said that Aglaya Ivanovna was nearly as lovely as Nastasia Philipovna. It was then I blurted out about the portrait—"

"But you didn't repeat what you heard in the study? You didn't repeat that—eh?"

"No, I tell you I did *not*."

"Then how did they—look here! Did Aglaya show my letter to the old lady?"

"Oh, there I can give you my fullest assurance that she did *not*. I was there all the while—she had no time to do it!"

"But perhaps you may not have observed it, oh, you damned idiot, you!" he shouted, quite beside himself with fury. "You can't even describe what went on."

Gania having once descended to abuse, and receiving no check, very soon knew no bounds or limit to his licence, as is often the way in such cases. His rage so blinded him that he had not even been able to detect that this "idiot," whom he was abusing to such an extent, was very far from being slow of comprehension, and had a way of taking in an impression, and afterwards giving it out again, which was very un-idiotic indeed. But something a little unforeseen now occurred.

"I think I ought to tell you, Gavrila Ardalionovitch," said the prince, suddenly, "that though I once was so ill that I really was little better than an idiot, yet now I am almost recovered, and that, therefore, it is not altogether pleasant to be called an idiot to my face. Of course your anger is excusable, considering the treatment you have just experienced; but I must remind you that you have twice abused me rather rudely. I do not like this sort of thing, and especially so at the first time of meeting a man, and, therefore, as we happen to be at this moment standing at a crossroad, don't you think we had better part, you to the left, homewards, and I to the right, here? I have twenty-five roubles, and I shall easily find a lodging."

Gania was much confused, and blushed for shame "Do forgive me, prince!" he cried, suddenly changing his abusive tone for one of great courtesy. "For Heaven's sake, forgive me! You see what a miserable plight I am in, but you hardly know anything of the facts of the case as yet. If you did, I am sure you would forgive me, at least partially. Of course it was inexcusable of me, I know, but—"

"Oh, dear me, I really do not require such profuse apologies," replied the prince, hastily. "I quite understand how unpleasant your position is, and that is what made you abuse me. So come along to your house, after all. I shall be delighted—"

"I am not going to let him go like this," thought Gania, glancing angrily at the prince as they walked along. "The fellow has sucked everything out of me, and now he takes off his mask—there's something more than appears, here we shall see. It shall all be as clear as water by tonight, everything!"

But by this time they had reached Gania's house.

Chapter VIII.

The flat occupied by Gania and his family was on the third floor of the house. It was reached by a clean light staircase, and consisted of seven rooms, a nice enough lodging, and one would have thought a little too good for a clerk on two thousand roubles a year. But it was designed to accommodate a few lodgers on board terms, and had been taken a few months since, much to the disgust of Gania, at the urgent request of his mother and his sister, Varvara Ardalionovna, who longed to do something to increase the family income a little, and fixed their hopes upon letting lodgings. Gania frowned upon the idea. He thought it *infra dig*, and did not quite like appearing in society afterwards—that society in which he had been accustomed to pose up to now as a young man of rather brilliant prospects. All these concessions and rebuffs of fortune, of late, had wounded his spirit severely, and his temper had become extremely irritable, his wrath being generally quite out of proportion to the cause. But if he had made up his mind to put up with this sort of life for a while, it was only on the plain understanding with his inner self that he would very soon change it all, and have things as he chose again. Yet the very means by which he hoped to make this change threatened to involve him in even greater difficulties than he had had before.

The flat was divided by a passage which led straight out of the entrance-hall. Along one side of this corridor lay the three rooms which were designed for the accommodation of the "highly recommended" lodgers. Besides these three rooms there was another small one at the end of the passage, close to the kitchen, which was allotted to General Ivolgin, the nominal master of the house, who slept on a wide sofa, and was obliged to pass into and out of his room through the kitchen, and up or down the back stairs. Colia, Gania's young brother, a school-boy of thirteen, shared this room with his father. He, too, had to sleep on an old sofa, a narrow, uncomfortable thing with a torn rug over it; his chief duty being to look after his father, who needed to be watched more and more every day.

The prince was given the middle room of the three, the first being occupied by one Ferdishenko, while the third was empty.

But Gania first conducted the prince to the family apartments. These consisted of a "salon," which became the dining-room when required; a drawing-room, which was only a drawing-room in the morning, and became Gania's study in the evening, and his bedroom at night; and lastly Nina Alexandrovna's and Varvara's bedroom, a small, close chamber which they shared together.

In a word, the whole place was confined, and a "tight fit" for the party. Gania used to grind his teeth with rage over the state of affairs; though he was anxious to be dutiful and polite to his mother. However, it was very soon apparent to anyone coming into the house, that Gania was the tyrant of the family.

Nina Alexandrovna and her daughter were both seated in the drawing-room, engaged in knitting, and talking to a visitor, Ivan Petrovitch Ptitsin.

The lady of the house appeared to be a woman of about fifty years of age, thin-faced, and with black lines under the eyes. She looked ill and rather sad; but her face was a pleasant one for all that; and from the first word that fell from her lips, any stranger would at once conclude that she was of a serious and particularly sincere nature. In spite of her sorrowful expression, she gave the idea of possessing considerable firmness and decision.

Her dress was modest and simple to a degree, dark and elderly in style; but both her face and appearance gave evidence that she had seen better days.

Varvara was a girl of some twenty-three summers, of middle height, thin, but possessing a face which, without being actually beautiful, had the rare quality of charm, and might fascinate even to the extent of passionate regard.

She was very like her mother: she even dressed like her, which proved that she had no taste for smart clothes. The expression of her grey eyes was merry and gentle, when it was not, as lately, too full of thought and anxiety. The same decision and firmness was to be observed in her face as in her mother's, but her strength seemed to be more vigorous than that of Nina Alexandrovna. She was subject to outbursts of temper, of which even her brother was a little afraid.

The present visitor, Ptitsin, was also afraid of her. This was a young fellow of something under thirty, dressed plainly, but neatly. His manners were good, but rather ponderously so. His dark beard bore evidence to the fact that he was not in any government employ. He could speak well, but preferred silence. On the whole he made a decidedly agreeable impression. He was clearly attracted by Varvara, and made no secret of his feelings. She trusted him in a friendly way, but had not shown him any decided encouragement as yet, which fact did not quell his ardour in the least.

Nina Alexandrovna was very fond of him, and had grown quite confidential with him of late. Ptitsin, as was well known, was engaged in the business of lending out money on good security, and at a good rate of interest. He was a great friend of Gania's.

After a formal introduction by Gania (who greeted his mother very shortly, took no notice of his sister, and immediately marched Ptitsin out of the room), Nina Alexandrovna addressed a few kind words to the prince and forthwith requested Colia, who had just appeared at the door, to show him to the "middle room."

Colia was a nice-looking boy. His expression was simple and confiding, and his manners were very polite and engaging.

"Where's your luggage?" he asked, as he led the prince away to his room.

"I had a bundle; it's in the entrance hall."

"I'll bring it you directly. We only have a cook and one maid, so I have to help as much as I can. Varia looks after things, generally, and loses her temper over it. Gania says you have only just arrived from Switzerland?"

"Yes."

"Is it jolly there?"

"Very."

"Mountains?"

"Yes."

"I'll go and get your bundle."

Here Varvara joined them.

"The maid shall bring your bed-linen directly. Have you a portmanteau?"

"No; a bundle—your brother has just gone to the hall for it."

"There's nothing there except this," said Colia, returning at this moment. "Where did you put it?"

"Oh! but that's all I have," said the prince, taking it.

"Ah! I thought perhaps Ferdishenko had taken it."

"Don't talk nonsense," said Varia, severely. She seemed put out, and was only just polite with the prince.

"Oho!" laughed the boy, "you can be nicer than that to *me*, you know—I'm not Ptitsin!"

"You ought to be whipped, Colia, you silly boy. If you want anything" (to the prince) "please apply to the servant. We dine at half-past four. You can take your dinner with us, or have it in your room, just as you please. Come along, Colia, don't disturb the prince."

At the door they met Gania coming in.

"Is father in?" he asked. Colia whispered something in his ear and went out.

"Just a couple of words, prince, if you'll excuse me. Don't blab over *there* about what you may see here, or in this house as to all that about Aglaya and me, you know. Things are not altogether pleasant in this establishment—devil take it all! You'll see. At all events keep your tongue to yourself for *today*."

"I assure you I 'blabbed' a great deal less than you seem to suppose," said the prince, with some annoyance. Clearly the relations between Gania and himself were by no means improving.

"Oh well; I caught it quite hot enough today, thanks to you. However, I forgive you."

"I think you might fairly remember that I was not in any way bound, I had no reason to be silent about that portrait. You never asked me not to mention it."

"Pfu! what a wretched room this is—dark, and the window looking into the yard. Your coming to our house is, in no respect, opportune. However, it's not *my* affair. I don't keep the lodgings."

Ptitsin here looked in and beckoned to Gania, who hastily left the room, in spite of the fact that he had evidently wished to say something more and had only made the remark about the room to gain time. The prince had hardly had time to wash and tidy himself a little when the door opened once more, and another figure appeared.

This was a gentleman of about thirty, tall, broad-shouldered, and red-haired; his face was red, too, and he possessed a pair of thick lips, a wide nose, small eyes, rather bloodshot, and with an ironical expression in them; as though he were perpetually winking at someone. His whole appearance gave one the idea of impudence; his dress was shabby.

He opened the door just enough to let his head in. His head remained so placed for a few seconds while he quietly scrutinized the room; the door then opened enough to admit his body; but still he did not enter. He stood on the threshold and examined the prince carefully. At last he gave the door a final shove, entered, approached the prince, took his hand and seated himself and the owner of the room on two chairs side by side.

"Ferdishenko," he said, gazing intently and inquiringly into the prince's eyes.

"Very well, what next?" said the latter, almost laughing in his face.

"A lodger here," continued the other, staring as before.

"Do you wish to make acquaintance?" asked the prince.

"Ah!" said the visitor, passing his fingers through his hair and sighing. He then looked over to the other side of the room and around it. "Got any money?" he asked, suddenly.

"Not much."

"How much?"

"Twenty-five roubles."

"Let's see it."

The prince took his banknote out and showed it to Ferdishenko. The latter unfolded it and looked at it; then he turned it round and examined the other side; then he held it up to the light.

"How strange that it should have browned so," he said, reflectively. "These twenty-five rouble notes brown in a most extraordinary way, while other notes often grow paler. Take it."

The prince took his note. Ferdishenko rose.

"I came here to warn you," he said. "In the first place, don't lend me any money, for I shall certainly ask you to."

"Very well."

"Shall you pay here?"

"Yes, I intend to."

"Oh! I *don't* intend to. Thanks. I live here, next door to you; you noticed a room, did you? Don't come to me very often; I shall see you here quite often enough. Have you seen the general?"

"No."

"Nor heard him?"

"No; of course not."

"Well, you'll both hear and see him soon; he even tries to borrow money from me. *Avis au lecteur.* Good-bye; do you think a man can possibly live with a name like Ferdishenko?"

"Why not?"

"Good-bye."

And so he departed. The prince found out afterwards that this gentleman made it his business to amaze people with his originality and wit, but that it did not as a rule "come off." He even produced a bad impression on some people, which grieved him sorely; but he did not change his ways for all that.

As he went out of the prince's room, he collided with yet another visitor coming in. Ferdishenko took the opportunity of making several warning gestures to the prince from behind the new arrival's back, and left the room in conscious pride.

This next arrival was a tall red-faced man of about fifty-five, with greyish hair and whiskers, and large eyes which stood out of their sockets. His appearance would have been distinguished had it not been that he gave the idea of being rather dirty. He was dressed in an old coat, and he smelled of vodka when he came near. His walk was effective, and he clearly did his best to appear dignified, and to impress people by his manner.

This gentleman now approached the prince slowly, and with a most courteous smile; silently took his hand and held it in his own, as he examined the prince's features as though searching for familiar traits therein.

"'Tis he, 'tis he!" he said at last, quietly, but with much solemnity. "As though he were alive once more. I heard the familiar name—the dear familiar name—and, oh! how it reminded me of the irrevocable past—Prince Muishkin, I believe?"

"Exactly so."

"General Ivolgin—retired and unfortunate. May I ask your Christian and generic names?"

"Lef Nicolaievitch."

"So, so—the son of my old, I may say my childhood's friend, Nicolai Petrovitch."

"My father's name was Nicolai Lvovitch."

"Lvovitch," repeated the general without the slightest haste, and with perfect confidence, just as though he had not committed himself the least in the world, but merely made a little slip of the tongue. He sat down, and taking the prince's hand, drew him to a seat next to himself.

"I carried you in my arms as a baby," he observed.

"Really?" asked the prince. "Why, it's twenty years since my father died."

"Yes, yes—twenty years and three months. We were educated together; I went straight into the army, and he—"

"My father went into the army, too. He was a sub-lieutenant in the Vasiliefsky regiment."

"No, sir—in the Bielomirsky; he changed into the latter shortly before his death. I was at his bedside when he died, and gave him my blessing for eternity. Your mother—" The general paused, as though overcome with emotion.

"She died a few months later, from a cold," said the prince.

"Oh, not cold—believe an old man—not from a cold, but from grief for her prince. Oh—your mother, your mother! heigh-ho! Youth—youth! Your father and I—old friends as we were—nearly murdered each other for her sake."

The prince began to be a little incredulous.

"I was passionately in love with her when she was engaged—engaged to my friend. The prince noticed the fact and was furious. He came and woke me at seven o'clock one morning. I rise and dress in amazement; silence on both sides. I understand it all. He takes a couple of pistols out of his pocket—across a handkerchief—without witnesses. Why invite witnesses when both of us would be walking in eternity in a couple of minutes? The pistols are loaded; we stretch the handkerchief and stand opposite one another. We aim the pistols at each other's hearts. Suddenly tears start to our eyes, our hands shake; we weep, we embrace—the battle is one of self-sacrifice now! The prince shouts, 'She is yours;' I cry, 'She is yours—' in a word, in a word—You've come to live with us, hey?"

"Yes—yes—for a while, I think," stammered the prince.

"Prince, mother begs you to come to her," said Colia, appearing at the door.

The prince rose to go, but the general once more laid his hand in a friendly manner on his shoulder, and dragged him down on to the sofa.

"As the true friend of your father, I wish to say a few words to you," he began. "I have suffered—there was a catastrophe. I suffered without a trial; I had no trial. Nina Alexandrovna my wife, is an excellent woman, so is my daughter Varvara. We have to let lodgings because we are poor—a dreadful, unheard-of come-down for us—for me, who should have been a governor-general; but we are very glad to have *you*, at all events. Meanwhile there is a tragedy in the house."

The prince looked inquiringly at the other.

"Yes, a marriage is being arranged—a marriage between a questionable woman and a young fellow who might be a flunkey. They wish to bring this woman into the house where my wife and daughter reside, but while I live and breathe she shall never enter my doors. I shall lie at the threshold, and she shall trample me underfoot if she does. I hardly talk to Gania now, and avoid him as much as I can. I warn you of this beforehand, but you cannot fail to observe it. But you are the son of my old friend, and I hope—"

"Prince, be so kind as to come to me for a moment in the drawing-room," said Nina Alexandrovna herself, appearing at the door.

"Imagine, my dear," cried the general, "it turns out that I have nursed the prince on my knee in the old days." His wife looked searchingly at him, and glanced at the prince, but said nothing. The prince rose and followed her; but hardly had they reached the drawing-room, and Nina Alexandrovna had begun to talk hurriedly, when in came the general. She immediately relapsed into silence. The master of the house may have observed this, but at all events he did not take any notice of it; he was in high good humour.

"A son of my old friend, dear," he cried; "surely you must remember Prince Nicolai Lvovitch? You saw him at—at Tver."

"I don't remember any Nicolai Lvovitch. Was that your father?" she inquired of the prince.

"Yes, but he died at Elizabethgrad, not at Tver," said the prince, rather timidly. "So Pavlicheff told me."

"No, Tver," insisted the general; "he removed just before his death. You were very small and cannot remember; and Pavlicheff, though an excellent fellow, may have made a mistake."

"You knew Pavlicheff then?"

"Oh, yes—a wonderful fellow; but I was present myself. I gave him my blessing."

"My father was just about to be tried when he died," said the prince, "although I never knew of what he was accused. He died in hospital."

"Oh! it was the Kolpakoff business, and of course he would have been acquitted."

"Yes? Do you know that for a fact?" asked the prince, whose curiosity was aroused by the general's words.

"I should think so indeed!" cried the latter. "The court-martial came to no decision. It was a mysterious, an impossible business, one might say! Captain Larionoff, commander of the company, had died; his command was handed over to the prince for the moment. Very well. This soldier, Kolpakoff, stole some leather from one of his comrades, intending to sell it, and spent the money on drink. Well! The prince—you understand that what follows took place in the presence of the sergeant-major, and a corporal—the prince rated Kolpakoff soundly, and threatened to have him flogged. Well, Kolpakoff went back to the barracks, lay down on a camp bedstead, and in a quarter of an hour was dead: you quite understand? It was, as I said, a strange, almost impossible, affair. In due course Kolpakoff was buried; the prince wrote his report, the deceased's name was removed from the roll. All as it should be, is it not? But exactly three months later at the inspection of the brigade, the man Kolpakoff was found in the third company of the second battalion of infantry, Novozemlianski division, just as if nothing had happened!"

"What?" said the prince, much astonished.

"It did not occur—it's a mistake!" said Nina Alexandrovna quickly, looking, at the prince rather anxiously. "*Mon mari se trompe,*" she added, speaking in French.

"My dear, '*se trompe*' is easily said. Do you remember any case at all like it? Everybody was at their wits' end. I should be the first to say '*qu'on se trompe*,' but unfortunately I was an eye-witness, and was also on the commission of inquiry. Everything proved that it was really he, the very same soldier Kolpakoff who had been given the usual military funeral to the sound of the drum. It is of course a most curious case—nearly an impossible one. I recognize that... but—"

"Father, your dinner is ready," said Varvara at this point, putting her head in at the door.

"Very glad, I'm particularly hungry. Yes, yes, a strange coincidence—almost a psychological—"

"Your soup'll be cold; do come."

"Coming, coming," said the general. "Son of my old friend—" he was heard muttering as he went down the passage.

"You will have to excuse very much in my husband, if you stay with us," said Nina Alexandrovna; "but he will not disturb you often. He dines alone. Everyone has his little peculiarities, you know, and some people perhaps have more than those who are most pointed at and laughed at. One thing I must beg of you—if my husband applies to you for payment for board and lodging, tell him that you have already paid me. Of course anything paid by you to the general would be as fully settled as if paid to me, so far as you are concerned; but I wish it to be so, if you please, for convenience' sake. What is it, Varia?"

Varia had quietly entered the room, and was holding out the portrait of Nastasia Philipovna to her mother.

Nina Alexandrovna started, and examined the photograph intently, gazing at it long and sadly. At last she looked up inquiringly at Varia.

"It's a present from herself to him," said Varia; "the question is to be finally decided this evening."

"This evening!" repeated her mother in a tone of despair, but softly, as though to herself. "Then it's all settled, of course, and there's no hope left to us. She has anticipated her answer by the present of her portrait. Did he show it you himself?" she added, in some surprise.

"You know we have hardly spoken to each other for a whole month. Ptitsin told me all about it; and the photo was lying under the table, and I picked it up."

"Prince," asked Nina Alexandrovna, "I wanted to inquire whether you have known my son long? I think he said that you had only arrived today from somewhere."

The prince gave a short narrative of what we have heard before, leaving out the greater part. The two ladies listened intently.

"I did not ask about Gania out of curiosity," said the elder, at last. "I wish to know how much you know about him, because he said just now that we need not stand on ceremony with you. What, exactly, does that mean?"

At this moment Gania and Ptitsin entered the room together, and Nina Alexandrovna immediately became silent again. The prince remained seated next to her, but Varia moved to the other end of the room; the portrait of Nastasia Philipovna remained lying as before on the work-table. Gania observed it there, and with a frown of annoyance snatched it up and threw it across to his writing-table, which stood at the other end of the room.

"Is it today, Gania?" asked Nina Alexandrovna, at last.

"Is what today?" cried the former. Then suddenly recollecting himself, he turned sharply on the prince. "Oh," he growled, "I see, you are here, that explains it! Is it a disease, or what, that you can't hold your tongue? Look here, understand once for all, prince—"

"I am to blame in this, Gania—no one else," said Ptitsin.

Gania glanced inquiringly at the speaker.

"It's better so, you know, Gania—especially as, from one point of view, the matter may be considered as settled," said Ptitsin; and sitting down a little way from the table he began to study a paper covered with pencil writing.

Gania stood and frowned, he expected a family scene. He never thought of apologizing to the prince, however.

"If it's all settled, Gania, then of course Mr. Ptitsin is right," said Nina Alexandrovna. "Don't frown. You need not worry yourself, Gania; I shall ask you no questions. You need not tell me anything you don't like. I assure you I have quite submitted to your will." She said all this, knitting away the while as though perfectly calm and composed.

Gania was surprised, but cautiously kept silence and looked at his mother, hoping that she would express herself more clearly. Nina Alexandrovna observed his cautiousness and added, with a bitter smile:

"You are still suspicious, I see, and do not believe me; but you may be quite at your ease. There shall be no more tears, nor questions—not from my side, at all events. All I wish is that you may be happy, you know that. I have submitted to my fate; but my heart will always be with you, whether we remain united, or whether we part. Of course I only answer for myself—you can hardly expect your sister—"

"My sister again," cried Gania, looking at her with contempt and almost hate. "Look here, mother, I have already given you my word that I shall always respect you fully and absolutely, and so shall everyone else in this house, be it who it may, who shall cross this threshold."

Gania was so much relieved that he gazed at his mother almost affectionately.

"I was not at all afraid for myself, Gania, as you know well. It was not for my own sake that I have been so anxious and worried all this time! They say it is all to be settled to-day. What is to be settled?"

"She has promised to tell me tonight at her own house whether she consents or not," replied Gania.

"We have been silent on this subject for three weeks," said his mother, "and it was better so; and now I will only ask you one question. How can she give her consent and make you a present of her portrait when you do not love her? How can such a—such a—"

"Practised hand—eh?"

"I was not going to express myself so. But how could you so blind her?"

Nina Alexandrovna's question betrayed intense annoyance. Gania waited a moment and then said, without taking the trouble to conceal the irony of his tone:

"There you are, mother, you are always like that. You begin by promising that there are to be no reproaches or insinuations or questions, and here you are beginning them at once. We had better drop the subject—we had, really. I shall never leave you, mother; any other man would cut and run from such a sister as this. See how she is looking at me at this moment! Besides, how do you know that I am blinding Nastasia Philipovna? As for Varia, I don't care—she can do just as she pleases. There, that's quite enough!"

Gania's irritation increased with every word he uttered, as he walked up and down the room. These conversations always touched the family sores before long.

"I have said already that the moment she comes in I go out, and I shall keep my word," remarked Varia.

"Out of obstinacy" shouted Gania. "You haven't married, either, thanks to your obstinacy. Oh, you needn't frown at me, Varvara! You can go at once for all I care; I am sick enough of your company. What, you are going to leave us are you, too?" he cried, turning to the prince, who was rising from his chair.

Gania's voice was full of the most uncontrolled and uncontrollable irritation.

The prince turned at the door to say something, but perceiving in Gania's expression that there was but that one drop wanting to make the cup overflow, he changed his mind and left the room without a word. A few minutes later he was aware from the noisy voices in the drawing room, that the conversation had become more quarrelsome than ever after his departure.

He crossed the salon and the entrance-hall, so as to pass down the corridor into his own room. As he came near the front door he heard someone outside vainly endeavouring to ring the bell, which was evidently broken, and only shook a little, without emitting any sound.

The prince took down the chain and opened the door. He started back in amazement—for there stood Nastasia Philipovna. He knew her at once from her photograph. Her eyes blazed with anger as she looked at him. She quickly pushed by him into the hall, shouldering him out of her way, and said, furiously, as she threw off her fur cloak:

"If you are too lazy to mend your bell, you should at least wait in the hall to let people in when they rattle the bell handle. There, now, you've dropped my fur cloak—dummy!"

Sure enough the cloak was lying on the ground. Nastasia had thrown it off her towards the prince, expecting him to catch it, but the prince had missed it.

"Now then—announce me, quick!"

The prince wanted to say something, but was so confused and astonished that he could not. However, he moved off towards the drawing-room with the cloak over his arm.

"Now then, where are you taking my cloak to? Ha, ha, ha! Are you mad?"

The prince turned and came back, more confused than ever. When she burst out laughing, he smiled, but his tongue could not form a word as yet. At first, when he had opened the door and saw her standing before him, he had become as pale as death; but now the red blood had rushed back to his cheeks in a torrent.

"Why, what an idiot it is!" cried Nastasia, stamping her foot with irritation. "Go on, do! Whom are you going to announce?"

"Nastasia Philipovna," murmured the prince.

"And how do you know that?" she asked him, sharply.

"I have never seen you before!"

"Go on, announce me—what's that noise?"

"They are quarrelling," said the prince, and entered the drawing-room, just as matters in there had almost reached a crisis. Nina Alexandrovna had forgotten that she had "submitted to everything!" She was defending Varia. Ptitsin was taking her part, too. Not that Varia was afraid of standing up for herself. She was by no means that sort of a girl; but her brother was becoming ruder and more intolerable every moment. Her usual practice in such cases as the present was to say nothing, but stare at him, without taking her eyes off his face for an instant. This manoeuvre, as she well knew, could drive Gania distracted.

Just at this moment the door opened and the prince entered, announcing:

"Nastasia Philipovna!"

CHAPTER IX.

Silence immediately fell on the room; all looked at the prince as though they neither understood, nor hoped to understand. Gania was motionless with horror.

Nastasia's arrival was a most unexpected and overwhelming event to all parties. In the first place, she had never been before. Up to now she had been so haughty that she had never even asked Gania to introduce her to his parents. Of late she had not so much as mentioned them. Gania was partly glad of this; but still he had put it to her debit in the account to be settled after marriage.

He would have borne anything from her rather than this visit. But one thing seemed to him quite clear—her visit now, and the present of her portrait on this particular day, pointed out plainly enough which way she intended to make her decision!

The incredulous amazement with which all regarded the prince did not last long, for Nastasia herself appeared at the door and passed in, pushing by the prince again.

"At last I've stormed the citadel! Why do you tie up your bell?" she said, merrily, as she pressed Gania's hand, the latter having rushed up to her as soon as she made her appearance. "What are you looking so upset about? Introduce me, please!"

The bewildered Gania introduced her first to Varia, and both women, before shaking hands, exchanged looks of strange import. Nastasia, however, smiled amiably; but Varia did not try to look amiable, and kept her gloomy expression. She did not even vouchsafe the usual courteous smile of etiquette. Gania darted a terrible glance of wrath at her for this, but Nina Alexandrovna mended matters a little when Gania introduced her at last. Hardly, however, had the old lady begun about her "highly gratified feelings," and so on, when Nastasia left her, and flounced into a chair by Gania's side in the corner by the window, and cried: "Where's your study? and where are the—the lodgers? You do take in lodgers, don't you?"

Gania looked dreadfully put out, and tried to say something in reply, but Nastasia interrupted him:

"Why, where are you going to squeeze lodgers in here? Don't you use a study? Does this sort of thing pay?" she added, turning to Nina Alexandrovna.

"Well, it is troublesome, rather," said the latter; "but I suppose it will 'pay' pretty well. We have only just begun, however—"

Again Nastasia Philipovna did not hear the sentence out. She glanced at Gania, and cried, laughing, "What a face! My goodness, what a face you have on at this moment!"

Indeed, Gania did not look in the least like himself. His bewilderment and his alarmed perplexity passed off, however, and his lips now twitched with rage as he continued to stare evilly at his laughing guest, while his countenance became absolutely livid.

There was another witness, who, though standing at the door motionless and bewildered himself, still managed to remark Gania's death-like pallor, and the dreadful change that had come over his face. This witness was the prince, who now advanced in alarm and muttered to Gania:

"Drink some water, and don't look like that!"

It was clear that he came out with these words quite spontaneously, on the spur of the moment. But his speech was productive of much—for it appeared that all Gania's rage now overflowed upon the prince. He seized him by the shoulder and gazed with an intensity of loathing and revenge at him, but said nothing—as though his feelings were too strong to permit of words.

General agitation prevailed. Nina Alexandrovna gave a little cry of anxiety; Ptitsin took a step forward in alarm; Colia and Ferdishenko stood stock still at the door in amazement;—only Varia remained coolly watching the scene from under her eyelashes. She did not sit down, but stood by her mother with folded hands. However, Gania recollected himself almost immediately. He let go of the prince and burst out laughing.

"Why, are you a doctor, prince, or what?" he asked, as naturally as possible. "I declare you quite frightened me! Nastasia Philipovna, let me introduce this interesting character to you—though I have only known him myself since the morning."

Nastasia gazed at the prince in bewilderment. "Prince? He a Prince? Why, I took him for the footman, just now, and sent him in to announce me! Ha, ha, ha, isn't that good!"

"Not bad that, not bad at all!" put in Ferdishenko, "*se non è vero—*"

"I rather think I pitched into you, too, didn't I? Forgive me—do! Who is he, did you say? What prince? Muishkin?" she added, addressing Gania.

"He is a lodger of ours," explained the latter.

"An idiot!"—the prince distinctly heard the word half whispered from behind him. This was Ferdishenko's voluntary information for Nastasia's benefit.

"Tell me, why didn't you put me right when I made such a dreadful mistake just now?" continued the latter, examining the prince from head to foot without the slightest ceremony. She awaited the answer as though convinced that it would be so foolish that she must inevitably fail to restrain her laughter over it.

"I was astonished, seeing you so suddenly—" murmured the prince.

"How did you know who I was? Where had you seen me before? And why were you so struck dumb at the sight of me? What was there so overwhelming about me?"

"Oho! ho, ho, ho!" cried Ferdishenko. "*Now* then, prince! My word, what things I would say if I had such a chance as that! My goodness, prince—go on!"

"So should I, in your place, I've no doubt!" laughed the prince to Ferdishenko; then continued, addressing Nastasia: "Your portrait struck me very forcibly this morning; then I was talking about you to the Epanchins; and then, in the train, before I reached Petersburg, Parfen Rogojin told me a good deal about you; and at the very moment that I opened the door to you I happened to be thinking of you, when—there you stood before me!"

"And how did you recognize me?"

"From the portrait!"

"What else?"

"I seemed to imagine you exactly as you are—I seemed to have seen you somewhere."

"Where—where?"

"I seem to have seen your eyes somewhere; but it cannot be! I have not seen you—I never was here before. I may have dreamed of you, I don't know."

The prince said all this with manifest effort—in broken sentences, and with many drawings of breath. He was evidently much agitated. Nastasia Philipovna looked at him inquisitively, but did not laugh.

"Bravo, prince!" cried Ferdishenko, delighted.

At this moment a loud voice from behind the group which hedged in the prince and Nastasia Philipovna, divided the crowd, as it were, and before them stood the head of the family, General Ivolgin. He was dressed in evening clothes; his moustache was dyed.

This apparition was too much for Gania. Vain and ambitious almost to morbidness, he had had much to put up with in the last two months, and was seeking feverishly for some means of enabling himself to lead a more presentable kind of existence. At home, he now adopted an attitude of absolute cynicism, but he could not keep this up before Nastasia Philipovna, although he had sworn to make her pay after marriage for all he suffered now. He was experiencing a last humiliation, the bitterest of all, at this moment—the humiliation of blushing for his own kindred in his own house. A question flashed through his mind as to whether the game was really worth the candle.

For that had happened at this moment, which for two months had been his nightmare; which had filled his soul with dread and shame—the meeting between his father and Nastasia Philipovna. He had often tried to imagine such an event, but had found the picture too mortifying and exasperating, and had quietly dropped it. Very likely he anticipated far worse things than was at all necessary; it is often so with vain persons. He had long since determined, therefore, to get his father out of the way, anywhere, before his marriage, in order to avoid such a meeting; but when Nastasia entered the room just now, he had been so overwhelmed with astonishment, that he had not thought of his father, and had made no arrangements to keep him out of the way. And now it was too late—there he was, and got up, too, in a dress coat and white tie, and Nastasia in the very humour to heap ridicule on him and his family circle; of this last fact, he felt quite persuaded. What else had she come for? There were his mother and his sister sitting before her, and she seemed to have forgotten their very existence already; and if she behaved like that, he thought, she must have some object in view.

Ferdishenko led the general up to Nastasia Philipovna.

"Ardalion Alexandrovitch Ivolgin," said the smiling general, with a low bow of great dignity, "an old soldier, unfortunate, and the father of this family; but happy in the hope of including in that family so exquisite—"

He did not finish his sentence, for at this moment Ferdishenko pushed a chair up from behind, and the general, not very firm on his legs, at this post-prandial hour, flopped into it backwards. It was always a difficult thing to put this warrior to confusion, and his sudden descent left him as composed as before. He had sat down just opposite to Nastasia, whose fingers he now took, and raised to his lips with great elegance, and much courtesy. The general had once belonged to a very select circle of society, but he had been turned out of it two or three years since on account of certain weaknesses, in which he now indulged with all the less restraint; but his good manners remained with him to this day, in spite of all.

Nastasia Philipovna seemed delighted at the appearance of this latest arrival, of whom she had of course heard a good deal by report.

"I have heard that my son—" began Ardalion Alexandrovitch.

"Your son, indeed! A nice papa you are! *You* might have come to see me anyhow, without compromising anyone. Do you hide yourself, or does your son hide you?"

"The children of the nineteenth century, and their parents—" began the general, again.

"Nastasia Philipovna, will you excuse the general for a moment? Someone is inquiring for him," said Nina Alexandrovna in a loud voice, interrupting the conversation.

"Excuse him? Oh no, I have wished to see him too long for that. Why, what business can he have? He has retired, hasn't he? You won't leave me, general, will you?"

"I give you my word that he shall come and see you—but he—he needs rest just now."

"General, they say you require rest," said Nastasia Philipovna, with the melancholy face of a child whose toy is taken away.

Ardalion Alexandrovitch immediately did his best to make his foolish position a great deal worse.

"My dear, my dear!" he said, solemnly and reproachfully, looking at his wife, with one hand on his heart.

"Won't you leave the room, mamma?" asked Varia, aloud.

"No, Varia, I shall sit it out to the end."

Nastasia must have overheard both question and reply, but her vivacity was not in the least damped. On the contrary, it seemed to increase. She immediately overwhelmed the general once more with questions, and within five minutes that gentleman was as happy as a king, and holding forth at the top of his voice, amid the laughter of almost all who heard him.

Colia jogged the prince's arm.

"Can't *you* get him out of the room, somehow? *Do*, please," and tears of annoyance stood in the boy's eyes. "Curse that Gania!" he muttered, between his teeth.

"Oh yes, I knew General Epanchin well," General Ivolgin was saying at this moment; "he and Prince Nicolai Ivanovitch Muishkin—whose son I have this day embraced after an absence of twenty years—and I, were three inseparables. Alas one is in the grave, torn to pieces by calumnies and bullets; another is now before you, still battling with calumnies and bullets—"

"Bullets?" cried Nastasia.

"Yes, here in my chest. I received them at the siege of Kars, and I feel them in bad weather now. And as to the third of our trio, Epanchin, of course after that little affair with the poodle in the railway carriage, it was all *up* between us."

"Poodle? What was that? And in a railway carriage? Dear me," said Nastasia, thoughtfully, as though trying to recall something to mind.

"Oh, just a silly, little occurrence, really not worth telling, about Princess Bielokonski's governess, Miss Smith, and—oh, it is really not worth telling!"

"No, no, we must have it!" cried Nastasia merrily.

"Yes, of course," said Ferdishenko. "C'est du nouveau."

"Ardalion," said Nina Alexandrovitch, entreatingly.

"Papa, you are wanted!" cried Colia.

"Well, it is a silly little story, in a few words," began the delighted general. "A couple of years ago, soon after the new railway was opened, I had to go somewhere or other on business. Well, I took a first-class ticket, sat down, and began to smoke, or rather *continued* to smoke, for I had lighted up before. I was alone in the carriage. Smoking is not allowed, but is not prohibited either; it is half allowed—so to speak, winked at. I had the window open."

"Suddenly, just before the whistle, in came two ladies with a little poodle, and sat down opposite to me; not bad-looking women; one was in light blue, the other in black silk. The poodle, a beauty with a silver collar, lay on light blue's knee. They looked haughtily about, and talked English together. I took no notice, just went on smoking. I observed that the ladies were getting angry—over my cigar, doubtless. One looked at me through her tortoise-shell eyeglass.

"I took no notice, because they never said a word. If they didn't like the cigar, why couldn't they say so? Not a word, not a hint! Suddenly, and without the very slightest suspicion of warning, 'light blue' seizes my cigar from between my fingers, and, wheugh! out of the window with it! Well, on flew the train, and I sat bewildered, and the young woman, tall and fair, and rather red in the face, too red, glared at me with flashing eyes.

"I didn't say a word, but with extreme courtesy, I may say with most refined courtesy, I reached my finger and thumb over towards the poodle, took it up delicately by the nape of the neck, and chucked it out of the window, after the cigar. The train went flying on, and the poodle's yells were lost in the distance."

"Oh, you naughty man!" cried Nastasia, laughing and clapping her hands like a child.

"Bravo!" said Ferdishenko. Ptitsin laughed too, though he had been very sorry to see the general appear. Even Colia laughed and said, "Bravo!"

"And I was right, truly right," cried the general, with warmth and solemnity, "for if cigars are forbidden in railway carriages, poodles are much more so."

"Well, and what did the lady do?" asked Nastasia, impatiently.

"She—ah, that's where all the mischief of it lies!" replied Ivolgin, frowning. "Without a word, as it were, of warning, she slapped me on the cheek! An extraordinary woman!"

"And you?"

The general dropped his eyes, and elevated his brows; shrugged his shoulders, tightened his lips, spread his hands, and remained silent. At last he blurted out:

"I lost my head!"

"Did you hit her?"

"No, oh no!—there was a great flare-up, but I didn't hit her! I had to struggle a little, purely to defend myself; but the very devil was in the business. It turned out that 'light blue' was an Englishwoman, governess or something, at Princess Bielokonski's, and the other woman was one of the old-maid princesses Bielokonski. Well, everybody knows what great friends the princess and Mrs. Epanchin are, so there was a pretty kettle of fish. All the Bielokonskis went into mourning for the poodle. Six princesses in tears, and the Englishwoman shrieking!

"Of course I wrote an apology, and called, but they would not receive either me or my apology, and the Epanchins cut me, too!"

"But wait," said Nastasia. "How is it that, five or six days since, I read exactly the same story in the paper, as happening between a Frenchman and an English girl? The cigar was snatched away exactly as you describe, and the poodle was chucked out of the window after it. The slapping came off, too, as in your case; and the girl's dress was light blue!"

The general blushed dreadfully; Colia blushed too; and Ptitsin turned hastily away. Ferdishenko was the only one who laughed as gaily as before. As to Gania, I need not say that he was miserable; he stood dumb and wretched and took no notice of anybody.

"I assure you," said the general, "that exactly the same thing happened to myself!"

"I remembered there was some quarrel between father and Miss Smith, the Bielokonski's governess," said Colia.

"How very curious, point for point the same anecdote, and happening at different ends of Europe! Even the light blue dress the same," continued the pitiless Nastasia. "I must really send you the paper."

"You must observe," insisted the general, "that my experience was two years earlier."

"Ah! that's it, no doubt!"

Nastasia Philipovna laughed hysterically.

"Father, will you hear a word from me outside!" said Gania, his voice shaking with agitation, as he seized his father by the shoulder. His eyes shone with a blaze of hatred.

At this moment there was a terrific bang at the front door, almost enough to break it down. Some most unusual visitor must have arrived. Colia ran to open.

CHAPTER X.

The entrance-hall suddenly became full of noise and people. To judge from the sounds which penetrated to the drawing-room, a number of people had already come in, and the stampede continued. Several voices were talking and shouting at once; others were talking and shouting on the stairs outside; it was evidently a most extraordinary visit that was about to take place.

Everyone exchanged startled glances. Gania rushed out towards the dining-room, but a number of men had already made their way in, and met him.

"Ah! here he is, the Judas!" cried a voice which the prince recognized at once. "How d'ye do, Gania, you old blackguard?"

"Yes, that's the man!" said another voice.

There was no room for doubt in the prince's mind: one of the voices was Rogojin's, and the other Lebedeff's.

Gania stood at the door like a block and looked on in silence, putting no obstacle in the way of their entrance, and ten or a dozen men marched in behind Parfen Rogojin. They were a decidedly mixed-looking collection, and some of them came in in their furs and caps. None of them were quite drunk, but all appeared to be considerably excited.

They seemed to need each other's support, morally, before they dared come in; not one of them would have entered alone but with the rest each one was brave enough. Even Rogojin entered rather cautiously at the head of his troop; but he was evidently preoccupied. He appeared to be gloomy and morose, and had clearly come with some end in view. All the rest were merely chorus, brought in to support the chief character. Besides Lebedeff there was the dandy Zalesheff, who came in without his coat and hat, two or three others followed his example; the rest were more uncouth. They included a couple of young merchants, a man in a great-coat, a medical student, a little Pole, a small fat man who laughed continuously, and an enormously tall stout one who apparently put great faith in the strength of his fists. A couple of "ladies" of some sort put their heads in at the front door, but did not dare come any farther. Colia promptly banged the door in their faces and locked it.

"Hallo, Gania, you blackguard! You didn't expect Rogojin, eh?" said the latter, entering the drawing-room, and stopping before Gania.

But at this moment he saw, seated before him, Nastasia Philipovna. He had not dreamed of meeting her here, evidently, for her appearance produced a marvellous effect upon him. He grew pale, and his lips became actually blue.

"I suppose it is true, then!" he muttered to himself, and his face took on an expression of despair. "So that's the end of it! Now you, sir, will you answer me or not?" he went on suddenly, gazing at Gania with ineffable malice. "Now then, you—"

He panted, and could hardly speak for agitation. He advanced into the room mechanically; but perceiving Nina Alexandrovna and Varia he became more or less embarrassed, in spite of his excitement. His followers entered after him, and all paused a moment at sight of the ladies. Of course their modesty was not fated to be long-lived, but for a moment they were abashed. Once let them begin to shout, however, and nothing on earth should disconcert them.

"What, you here too, prince?" said Rogojin, absently, but a little surprised all the same "Still in your gaiters, eh?" He sighed, and forgot the prince next moment, and his wild eyes wandered over to Nastasia again, as though attracted in that direction by some magnetic force.

Nastasia looked at the new arrivals with great curiosity. Gania recollected himself at last.

"Excuse me, sirs," he said, loudly, "but what does all this mean?" He glared at the advancing crowd generally, but addressed his remarks especially to their captain, Rogojin. "You are not in a stable, gentlemen, though you may think it—my mother and sister are present."

"Yes, I see your mother and sister," muttered Rogojin, through his teeth; and Lebedeff seemed to feel himself called upon to second the statement.

"At all events, I must request you to step into the salon," said Gania, his rage rising quite out of proportion to his words, "and then I shall inquire—"

"What, he doesn't know me!" said Rogojin, showing his teeth disagreeably. "He doesn't recognize Rogojin!" He did not move an inch, however.

"I have met you somewhere, I believe, but—"

"Met me somewhere, pfu! Why, it's only three months since I lost two hundred roubles of my father's money to you, at cards. The old fellow died before he found out. Ptitsin knows all about it. Why, I've only to pull out a three-rouble note and show it to you, and you'd crawl on your hands and knees to the other end of the town for it; that's the sort of man you are. Why, I've come now, at this moment, to buy you up! Oh, you needn't think that because I wear these boots I have no money. I have lots of money, my beauty,—enough to buy up you and all yours together. So I shall, if I like to! I'll buy you up! I will!" he yelled, apparently growing more and more intoxicated and excited. "Oh, Nastasia Philipovna! don't turn me out! Say one word, do! Are you going to marry this man, or not?"

Rogojin asked his question like a lost soul appealing to some divinity, with the reckless daring of one appointed to die, who has nothing to lose.

He awaited the reply in deadly anxiety.

Nastasia Philipovna gazed at him with a haughty, ironical expression of face; but when she glanced at Nina Alexandrovna and Varia, and from them to Gania, she changed her tone, all of a sudden.

"Certainly not; what are you thinking of? What could have induced you to ask such a question?" she replied, quietly and seriously, and even, apparently, with some astonishment.

"No? No?" shouted Rogojin, almost out of his mind with joy. "You are not going to, after all? And they told me—oh, Nastasia Philipovna—they said you had promised to marry him, *him!* As if you *could* do it!—him—pooh! I don't mind saying it to everyone—I'd buy him off for a hundred roubles, any day pfu! Give him a thousand, or three if he likes, poor devil, and he'd cut and run the day before his wedding, and leave his bride to me! Wouldn't you, Gania, you blackguard? You'd take three thousand, wouldn't you? Here's the money! Look, I've come on purpose to pay you off and get your receipt, formally. I said I'd buy you up, and so I will."

"Get out of this, you drunken beast!" cried Gania, who was red and white by turns.

Rogojin's troop, who were only waiting for an excuse, set up a howl at this. Lebedeff stepped forward and whispered something in Parfen's ear.

"You're right, clerk," said the latter, "you're right, tipsy spirit—you're right!—Nastasia Philipovna," he added, looking at her like some lunatic, harmless generally, but suddenly wound up to a pitch of audacity, "here are eighteen thousand roubles, and—and you shall have more—." Here he threw a packet of bank-notes tied up in white paper, on the table before her, not daring to say all he wished to say.

"No—no—no!" muttered Lebedeff, clutching at his arm. He was clearly aghast at the largeness of the sum, and thought a far smaller amount should have been tried first.

"No, you fool—you don't know whom you are dealing with—and it appears I am a fool, too!" said Parfen, trembling beneath the flashing glance of Nastasia. "Oh, curse it all! What a fool I was to listen to you!" he added, with profound melancholy.

Nastasia Philipovna, observing his woe-begone expression, suddenly burst out laughing.

"Eighteen thousand roubles, for me? Why, you declare yourself a fool at once," she said, with impudent familiarity, as she rose from the sofa and prepared to go. Gania watched the whole scene with a sinking of the heart.

"Forty thousand, then—forty thousand roubles instead of eighteen! Ptitsin and another have promised to find me forty thousand roubles by seven o'clock tonight. Forty thousand roubles—paid down on the nail!"

The scene was growing more and more disgraceful; but Nastasia Philipovna continued to laugh and did not go away. Nina Alexandrovna and Varia had both risen from their places and were waiting, in silent horror, to see what would happen. Varia's eyes were all ablaze with anger; but the scene had a different effect on Nina Alexandrovna. She paled and trembled, and looked more and more like fainting every moment.

"Very well then, a *hundred* thousand! a hundred thousand! paid this very day. Ptitsin! find it for me. A good share shall stick to your fingers—come!"

"You are mad!" said Ptitsin, coming up quickly and seizing him by the hand. "You're drunk—the police will be sent for if you don't look out. Think where you are."

"Yes, he's boasting like a drunkard," added Nastasia, as though with the sole intention of goading him.

"I do *not* boast! You shall have a hundred thousand, this very day. Ptitsin, get the money, you gay usurer! Take what you like for it, but get it by the evening! I'll show that I'm in earnest!" cried Rogojin, working himself up into a frenzy of excitement.

"Come, come; what's all this?" cried General Ivolgin, suddenly and angrily, coming close up to Rogojin. The unexpectedness of this sally on the part of the hitherto silent old man caused some laughter among the intruders.

"Halloa! what's this now?" laughed Rogojin. "You come along with me, old fellow! You shall have as much to drink as you like."

"Oh, it's too horrible!" cried poor Colia, sobbing with shame and annoyance.

"Surely there must be someone among all of you here who will turn this shameless creature out of the room?" cried Varia, suddenly. She was shaking and trembling with rage.

"That's me, I suppose. I'm the shameless creature!" cried Nastasia Philipovna, with amused indifference. "Dear me, and I came—like a fool, as I am—to invite them over to my house for the evening! Look how your sister treats me, Gavrila Ardalionovitch."

For some moments Gania stood as if stunned or struck by lightning, after his sister's speech. But seeing that Nastasia Philipovna was really about to leave the room this time, he sprang at Varia and seized her by the arm like a madman.

"What have you done?" he hissed, glaring at her as though he would like to annihilate her on the spot. He was quite beside himself, and could hardly articulate his words for rage.

"What have I done? Where are you dragging me to?"

"Do you wish me to beg pardon of this creature because she has come here to insult our mother and disgrace the whole household, you low, base wretch?" cried Varia, looking back at her brother with proud defiance.

A few moments passed as they stood there face to face, Gania still holding her wrist tightly. Varia struggled once—twice—to get free; then could restrain herself no longer, and spat in his face.

"There's a girl for you!" cried Nastasia Philipovna. "Mr. Ptitsin, I congratulate you on your choice."

Gania lost his head. Forgetful of everything he aimed a blow at Varia, which would inevitably have laid her low, but suddenly another hand caught his. Between him and Varia stood the prince.

"Enough—enough!" said the latter, with insistence, but all of a tremble with excitement.

"Are you going to cross my path for ever, damn you!" cried Gania; and, loosening his hold on Varia, he slapped the prince's face with all his force.

Exclamations of horror arose on all sides. The prince grew pale as death; he gazed into Gania's eyes with a strange, wild, reproachful look; his lips trembled and vainly endeavoured to form some words; then his mouth twisted into an incongruous smile.

"Very well—never mind about me; but I shall not allow you to strike her!" he said, at last, quietly. Then, suddenly, he could bear it no longer, and covering his face with his hands, turned to the wall, and murmured in broken accents:

"Oh! how ashamed you will be of this afterwards!"

Gania certainly did look dreadfully abashed. Colia rushed up to comfort the prince, and after him crowded Varia, Rogojin and all, even the general.

"It's nothing, it's nothing!" said the prince, and again he wore the smile which was so inconsistent with the circumstances.

"Yes, he will be ashamed!" cried Rogojin. "You will be properly ashamed of yourself for having injured such a—such a sheep" (he could not find a better word). "Prince, my dear fellow, leave this and come away with me. I'll show you how Rogojin shows his affection for his friends."

Nastasia Philipovna was also much impressed, both with Gania's action and with the prince's reply.

Her usually thoughtful, pale face, which all this while had been so little in harmony with the jests and laughter which she had seemed to put on for the occasion, was now evidently agitated by new feelings, though she tried to conceal the fact and to look as though she were as ready as ever for jesting and irony.

"I really think I must have seen him somewhere!" she murmured seriously enough.

"Oh, aren't you ashamed of yourself—aren't you ashamed? Are you really the sort of woman you are trying to represent yourself to be? Is it possible?" The prince was now addressing Nastasia, in a tone of reproach, which evidently came from his very heart.

Nastasia Philipovna looked surprised, and smiled, but evidently concealed something beneath her smile and with some confusion and a glance at Gania she left the room.

However, she had not reached the outer hall when she turned round, walked quickly up to Nina Alexandrovna, seized her hand and lifted it to her lips.

"He guessed quite right. I am not that sort of woman," she whispered hurriedly, flushing red all over. Then she turned again and left the room so quickly that no one could imagine what she had come back for. All they saw was that she said something to Nina Alexandrovna in a hurried whisper, and seemed to kiss her hand. Varia, however, both saw and heard all, and watched Nastasia out of the room with an expression of wonder.

Gania recollected himself in time to rush after her in order to show her out, but she had gone. He followed her to the stairs.

"Don't come with me," she cried, "*Au revoir*, till the evening—do you hear? *Au revoir!*"

He returned thoughtful and confused; the riddle lay heavier than ever on his soul. He was troubled about the prince, too, and so bewildered that he did not even observe Rogojin's rowdy band crowd past him and step on his toes, at the door as they went out. They were all talking at once. Rogojin went ahead of the others, talking to Ptitsin, and apparently insisting vehemently upon something very important.

"You've lost the game, Gania" he cried, as he passed the latter.

Gania gazed after him uneasily, but said nothing.

CHAPTER XI.

The prince now left the room and shut himself up in his own chamber. Colia followed him almost at once, anxious to do what he could to console him. The poor boy seemed to be already so attached to him that he could hardly leave him.

"You were quite right to go away!" he said. "The row will rage there worse than ever now; and it's like this every day with us—and all through that Nastasia Philipovna."

"You have so many sources of trouble here, Colia," said the prince.

"Yes, indeed, and it is all our own fault. But I have a great friend who is much worse off even than we are. Would you like to know him?"

"Yes, very much. Is he one of your school-fellows?"

"Well, not exactly. I will tell you all about him some day.... What do you think of Nastasia Philipovna? She is beautiful, isn't she? I had never seen her before, though I had a great wish to do so. She fascinated me. I could forgive Gania if he were to marry her for love, but for money! Oh dear! that is horrible!"

"Yes, your brother does not attract me much."

"I am not surprised at that. After what you... But I do hate that way of looking at things! Because some fool, or a rogue pretending to be a fool, strikes a man, that man is to be dishonoured for his whole life, unless he wipes out the disgrace with blood, or makes his assailant beg forgiveness on his knees! I think that so very absurd and tyrannical. Lermontoff's Bal Masque is based on that idea—a stupid and unnatural one, in my opinion; but he was hardly more than a child when he wrote it."

"I like your sister very much."

"Did you see how she spat in Gania's face! Varia is afraid of no one. But you did not follow her example, and yet I am sure it was not through cowardice. Here she comes! Speak of a wolf and you see his tail! I felt sure that she would come. She is very generous, though of course she has her faults."

Varia pounced upon her brother.

"This is not the place for you," said she. "Go to father. Is he plaguing you, prince?"

"Not in the least; on the contrary, he interests me."

"Scolding as usual, Varia! It is the worst thing about her. After all, I believe father may have started off with Rogojin. No doubt he is sorry now. Perhaps I had better go and see what he is doing," added Colia, running off.

"Thank God, I have got mother away, and put her to bed without another scene! Gania is worried—and ashamed—not without reason! What a spectacle! I have come to thank you once more, prince, and to ask you if you knew Nastasia Philipovna before?"

"No, I have never known her."

"Then what did you mean, when you said straight out to her that she was not really 'like that'? You guessed right, I fancy. It is quite possible she was not herself at the moment, though I cannot fathom her meaning. Evidently she meant to hurt and insult us. I have heard curious tales about her before now, but if she came to invite us to her house, why did she behave so to my mother? Ptitsin knows her very well; he says he could not understand her today. With Rogojin, too! No one with a spark of self-respect could have talked like that in the house of her... Mother is extremely vexed on your account, too...

"That is nothing!" said the prince, waving his hand.

"But how meek she was when you spoke to her!"

"Meek! What do you mean?"

"You told her it was a shame for her to behave so, and her manner changed at once; she was like another person. You have some influence over her, prince," added Varia, smiling a little.

The door opened at this point, and in came Gania most unexpectedly.

He was not in the least disconcerted to see Varia there, but he stood a moment at the door, and then approached the prince quietly.

"Prince," he said, with feeling, "I was a blackguard. Forgive me!" His face gave evidence of suffering. The prince was considerably amazed, and did not reply at once. "Oh, come, forgive me, forgive me!" Gania insisted, rather impatiently. "If you like, I'll kiss your hand. There!"

The prince was touched; he took Gania's hands, and embraced him heartily, while each kissed the other.

"I never, never thought you were like that," said Muishkin, drawing a deep breath. "I thought you—you weren't capable of—"

"Of what? Apologizing, eh? And where on earth did I get the idea that you were an idiot? You always observe what other people pass by unnoticed; one could talk sense to you, but—"

"Here is another to whom you should apologize," said the prince, pointing to Varia.

"No, no! they are all enemies! I've tried them often enough, believe me," and Gania turned his back on Varia with these words.

"But if I beg you to make it up?" said Varia.

"And you'll go to Nastasia Philipovna's this evening—"

"If you insist: but, judge for yourself, can I go, ought I to go?"

"But she is not that sort of woman, I tell you!" said Gania, angrily. "She was only acting."

"I know that—I know that; but what a part to play! And think what she must take *you* for, Gania! I know she kissed mother's hand, and all that, but she laughed at you, all the same. All this is not good enough for seventy-five thousand roubles, my dear boy. You are capable of honourable feelings still, and that's why I am talking to you so. Oh! *do* take care what you are doing! Don't you know yourself that it will end badly, Gania?"

So saying, and in a state of violent agitation, Varia left the room.

"There, they are all like that," said Gania, laughing, "just as if I do not know all about it much better than they do."

He sat down with these words, evidently intending to prolong his visit.

"If you know it so well," said the prince a little timidly, "why do you choose all this worry for the sake of the seventy-five thousand, which, you confess, does not cover it?"

"I didn't mean that," said Gania; "but while we are upon the subject, let me hear your opinion. Is all this worry worth seventy-five thousand or not?"

"Certainly not."

"Of course! And it would be a disgrace to marry so, eh?"

"A great disgrace."

"Oh, well, then you may know that I shall certainly do it, now. I shall certainly marry her. I was not quite sure of myself before, but now I am. Don't say a word: I know what you want to tell me—"

"No. I was only going to say that what surprises me most of all is your extraordinary confidence."

"How so? What in?"

"That Nastasia Philipovna will accept you, and that the question is as good as settled; and secondly, that even if she did, you would be able to pocket the money. Of course, I know very little about it, but that's my view. When a man marries for money it often happens that the wife keeps the money in her own hands."

"Of course, you don't know all; but, I assure you, you needn't be afraid, it won't be like that in our case. There are circumstances," said Gania, rather excitedly. "And as to her answer to me, there's no doubt about that. Why should you suppose she will refuse me?"

"Oh, I only judge by what I see. Varvara Ardalionovna said just now—"

"Oh she—they don't know anything about it! Nastasia was only chaffing Rogojin. I was alarmed at first, but I have thought better of it now; she was simply laughing at him. She looks on me as a fool because I show that I meant her money, and doesn't realize that there are other men who would deceive her in far worse fashion. I'm not going to pretend anything, and you'll see she'll marry me, all right. If she likes to live quietly, so she shall; but if she gives me any of her nonsense, I shall leave her at once, but I shall keep the money. I'm not going to look a fool; that's the first thing, not to look a fool."

"But Nastasia Philipovna seems to me to be such a *sensible* woman, and, as such, why should she run blindly into this business? That's what puzzles me so," said the prince.

"You don't know all, you see; I tell you there are things—and besides, I'm sure that she is persuaded that I love her to distraction, and I give you my word I have a strong suspicion that she loves me, too—in her own way, of course. She thinks she will be able to make a sort of slave of me all my life; but I shall prepare a little surprise for her. I don't know whether I ought to be confidential with you, prince; but, I assure you, you are the only decent fellow I have come across. I have not spoken so sincerely as I am doing at this moment for years. There are uncommonly few honest people about, prince; there isn't one honester than Ptitsin, he's the best of the lot. Are you laughing? You don't know, perhaps, that blackguards like honest people, and being one myself I like you. *Why* am I a blackguard? Tell me honestly, now. They all call me a blackguard because of her, and I have got into the way of thinking myself one. That's what is so bad about the business."

"*I* for one shall never think you a blackguard again," said the prince. "I confess I had a poor opinion of you at first, but I have been so joyfully surprised about you just now; it's a good lesson for me. I shall never judge again without a thorough trial. I see now that you are not only not a blackguard, but are not even quite spoiled. I see that you are quite an ordinary man, not original in the least degree, but rather weak."

Gania laughed sarcastically, but said nothing. The prince, seeing that he did not quite like the last remark, blushed, and was silent too.

"Has my father asked you for money?" asked Gania, suddenly.

"No."

"Don't give it to him if he does. Fancy, he was a decent, respectable man once! He was received in the best society; he was not always the liar he is now. Of course, wine is at the bottom of it all; but he is a good deal worse than an innocent liar now. Do you know that he keeps a mistress? I can't understand how mother is so long-suffering. Did he tell you the story of the siege of Kars? Or perhaps the one about his grey horse that talked? He loves to enlarge on these absurd histories." And Gania burst into a fit of laughter. Suddenly he turned to the prince and asked: "Why are you looking at me like that?"

"I am surprised to see you laugh in that way, like a child. You came to make friends with me again just now, and you said, 'I will kiss your hand, if you like,' just as a child would have said it. And then, all at once you are talking of this mad project—of these seventy-five thousand roubles! It all seems so absurd and impossible."

"Well, what conclusion have you reached?"

"That you are rushing madly into the undertaking, and that you would do well to think it over again. It is more than possible that Varvara Ardalionovna is right."

"Ah! now you begin to moralize! I know that I am only a child, very well," replied Gania impatiently. "That is proved by my having this conversation with you. It is not for money only, prince, that I am rushing into this affair," he continued, hardly master of his words, so closely had his vanity been touched. "If I reckoned on that I should certainly be deceived, for I am still too weak in mind and character. I am obeying a passion, an impulse perhaps, because I have but one aim, one that overmasters all else. You imagine that once I am in possession of these seventy-five thousand roubles, I shall rush to buy a carriage... No, I shall go on wearing the old overcoat I have worn for three years, and I shall give up my club. I shall follow the example of men who have made their fortunes. When Ptitsin was seventeen he slept in the street, he sold pen-knives, and began with a copeck; now he has sixty thousand roubles, but to get them, what has he not done? Well, I shall be spared such a hard beginning, and shall start with a little capital. In fifteen years people will say, 'Look,

68

that's Ivolgin, the king of the Jews!' You say that I have no originality. Now mark this, prince—there is nothing so offensive to a man of our time and race than to be told that he is wanting in originality, that he is weak in character, has no particular talent, and is, in short, an ordinary person. You have not even done me the honour of looking upon me as a rogue. Do you know, I could have knocked you down for that just now! You wounded me more cruelly than Epanchin, who thinks me capable of selling him my wife! Observe, it was a perfectly gratuitous idea on his part, seeing there has never been any discussion of it between us! This has exasperated me, and I am determined to make a fortune! I will do it! Once I am rich, I shall be a genius, an extremely original man. One of the vilest and most hateful things connected with money is that it can buy even talent; and will do so as long as the world lasts. You will say that this is childish—or romantic. Well, that will be all the better for me, but the thing shall be done. I will carry it through. He laughs most, who laughs last. Why does Epanchin insult me? Simply because, socially, I am a nobody. However, enough for the present. Colia has put his nose in to tell us dinner is ready, twice. I'm dining out. I shall come and talk to you now and then; you shall be comfortable enough with us. They are sure to make you one of the family. I think you and I will either be great friends or enemies. Look here now, supposing I had kissed your hand just now, as I offered to do in all sincerity, should I have hated you for it afterwards?"

"Certainly, but not always. You would not have been able to keep it up, and would have ended by forgiving me," said the prince, after a pause for reflection, and with a pleasant smile.

"Oho, how careful one has to be with you, prince! Haven't you put a drop of poison in that remark now, eh? By the way—ha, ha, ha!—I forgot to ask, was I right in believing that you were a good deal struck yourself with Nastasia Philipovna."

"Ye-yes."

"Are you in love with her?"

"N-no."

"And yet you flush up as red as a rosebud! Come—it's all right. I'm not going to laugh at you. Do you know she is a very virtuous woman? Believe it or not, as you like. You think she and Totski—not a bit of it, not a bit of it! Not for ever so long! *Au revoir!*"

Gania left the room in great good humour. The prince stayed behind, and meditated alone for a few minutes. At length, Colia popped his head in once more.

"I don't want any dinner, thanks, Colia. I had too good a lunch at General Epanchin's."

Colia came into the room and gave the prince a note; it was from the general and was carefully sealed up. It was clear from Colia's face how painful it was to him to deliver the missive. The prince read it, rose, and took his hat.

"It's only a couple of yards," said Colia, blushing.

"He's sitting there over his bottle—and how they can give him credit, I cannot understand. Don't tell mother I brought you the note, prince; I have sworn not to do it a thousand times, but I'm always so sorry for him. Don't stand on ceremony, give him some trifle, and let that end it."

"Come along, Colia, I want to see your father. I have an idea," said the prince.

CHAPTER XII.

Colia took the prince to a public-house in the Litaynaya, not far off. In one of the side rooms there sat at a table—looking like one of the regular guests of the establishment—Ardalion Alexandrovitch, with a bottle before him, and a newspaper on his knee. He was waiting for the prince, and no sooner did the latter appear than he began a long harangue about something or other; but so far gone was he that the prince could hardly understand a word.

"I have not got a ten-rouble note," said the prince; "but here is a twenty-five. Change it and give me back the fifteen, or I shall be left without a farthing myself."

"Oh, of course, of course; and you quite understand that I—"

"Yes; and I have another request to make, general. Have you ever been at Nastasia Philipovna's?"

"I? I? Do you mean me? Often, my friend, often! I only pretended I had not in order to avoid a painful subject. You saw today, you were a witness, that I did all that a kind, an indulgent father could do. Now a father of altogether another type shall step into the scene. You shall see; the old soldier shall lay bare this intrigue, or a shameless woman will force her way into a respectable and noble family."

"Yes, quite so. I wished to ask you whether you could show me the way to Nastasia Philipovna's tonight. I must go; I have business with her; I was not invited but I was introduced. Anyhow I am ready to trespass the laws of propriety if only I can get in somehow or other."

"My dear young friend, you have hit on my very idea. It was not for this rubbish I asked you to come over here" (he pocketed the money, however, at this point), "it was to invite your alliance in the campaign against Nastasia Philipovna tonight. How well it sounds, 'General Ivolgin and Prince Muishkin.' That'll fetch her, I think, eh? Capital! We'll go at nine; there's time yet."

"Where does she live?"

"Oh, a long way off, near the Great Theatre, just in the square there—It won't be a large party."

The general sat on and on. He had ordered a fresh bottle when the prince arrived; this took him an hour to drink, and then he had another, and another, during the consumption of which he told pretty nearly the whole story of his life. The prince was in despair. He felt that though he had but applied to this miserable old drunkard because he saw no other way of getting to Nastasia Philipovna's, yet he had been very wrong to put the slightest confidence in such a man.

At last he rose and declared that he would wait no longer. The general rose too, drank the last drops that he could squeeze out of the bottle, and staggered into the street.

Muishkin began to despair. He could not imagine how he had been so foolish as to trust this man. He only wanted one thing, and that was to get to Nastasia Philipovna's, even at the cost of a certain amount of impropriety. But now the scandal threatened to be more than he had bargained for. By this time Ardalion Alexandrovitch was quite intoxicated, and he kept his companion listening while he discoursed eloquently and pathetically on subjects of all kinds, interspersed with torrents of recrimination against the members of his family. He insisted that all his troubles were caused by their bad conduct, and time alone would put an end to them.

At last they reached the Litaynaya. The thaw increased steadily, a warm, unhealthy wind blew through the streets, vehicles splashed through the mud, and the iron shoes of horses and mules rang on the paving stones. Crowds of melancholy people plodded wearily along the footpaths, with here and there a drunken man among them.

"Do you see those brightly-lighted windows?" said the general. "Many of my old comrades-in-arms live about here, and I, who served longer, and suffered more than any of them, am walking on foot to the house of a woman of rather questionable reputation! A man, look you, who has thirteen bullets on his breast!... You don't believe it? Well, I can assure you it was entirely on my account that Pirogoff telegraphed to Paris, and left Sebastopol at the greatest risk during the siege. Nelaton, the Tuileries surgeon, demanded a safe conduct, in the name of science, into the besieged city in order to attend my wounds. The government knows all about it. 'That's the Ivolgin with thirteen bullets in him!' That's how they speak of me.... Do you see that house, prince? One of my old friends lives on the first floor, with his large family. In this and five other houses, three overlooking Nevsky, two in the Morskaya, are all that remain of my personal friends. Nina Alexandrovna gave them up long ago, but I keep in touch with them still... I may say I find refreshment in this little coterie, in thus meeting my old acquaintances and subordinates, who worship me still, in spite of all. General Sokolovitch (by the way, I have not called on him lately, or seen Anna Fedorovna)... You know, my dear prince, when a person does not receive company himself, he gives up going to other people's houses involuntarily. And yet... well... you look as if you didn't believe me.... Well now, why should I not present the son of my old friend and companion to this delightful family—General Ivolgin and Prince Muishkin? You will see a lovely girl—what am I saying—a lovely girl? No, indeed, two, three! Ornaments of this city and of society: beauty, education, culture—the woman question—poetry—everything! Added to which is the fact that each one will have a dot of at least eighty thousand roubles. No bad thing, eh?... In a word I absolutely must introduce you to them: it is a duty, an obligation. General Ivolgin and Prince Muishkin. Tableau!"

"At once? Now? You must have forgotten..." began the prince.

"No, I have forgotten nothing. Come! This is the house—up this magnificent staircase. I am surprised not to see the porter, but .... it is a holiday... and the man has gone off... Drunken fool! Why have they not got rid of him? Sokolovitch owes all the happiness he has had in the service and in his private life to me, and me alone, but... here we are."

The prince followed quietly, making no further objection for fear of irritating the old man. At the same time he fervently hoped that General Sokolovitch and his family would fade away like a mirage in the desert, so that the visitors could escape, by merely returning downstairs. But to his horror he saw that General Ivolgin was quite familiar with the house, and really seemed to have friends there. At every step he named some topographical or biographical detail that left nothing to be desired on the score of accuracy. When they arrived at last, on the first floor, and the general turned to ring the bell to the right, the prince decided to run away, but a curious incident stopped him momentarily.

"You have made a mistake, general," said he. "The name on the door is Koulakoff, and you were going to see General Sokolovitch."

"Koulakoff... Koulakoff means nothing. This is Sokolovitch's flat, and I am ringing at his door.... What do I care for Koulakoff?... Here comes someone to open."

In fact, the door opened directly, and the footman informed the visitors that the family were all away.

"What a pity! What a pity! It's just my luck!" repeated Ardalion Alexandrovitch over and over again, in regretful tones. "When your master and mistress return, my man, tell them that General Ivolgin and Prince Muishkin desired to present themselves, and that they were extremely sorry, excessively grieved..."

Just then another person belonging to the household was seen at the back of the hall. It was a woman of some forty years, dressed in sombre colours, probably a housekeeper or a governess. Hearing the names she came forward with a look of suspicion on her face.

"Marie Alexandrovna is not at home," said she, staring hard at the general. "She has gone to her mother's, with Alexandra Michailovna."

"Alexandra Michailovna out, too! How disappointing! Would you believe it, I am always so unfortunate! May I most respectfully ask you to present my compliments to Alexandra Michailovna, and remind her... tell her, that with my whole heart I wish for her what she wished for herself on Thursday evening, while she was listening to Chopin's Ballade. She will remember. I wish it with all sincerity. General Ivolgin and Prince Muishkin!"

The woman's face changed; she lost her suspicious expression.

"I will not fail to deliver your message," she replied, and bowed them out.

As they went downstairs the general regretted repeatedly that he had failed to introduce the prince to his friends.

"You know I am a bit of a poet," said he. "Have you noticed it? The poetic soul, you know." Then he added suddenly—"But after all... after all I believe we made a mistake this time! I remember that the Sokolovitch's live in another house, and what is more, they are just now in Moscow. Yes, I certainly was at fault. However, it is of no consequence."

"Just tell me," said the prince in reply, "may I count still on your assistance? Or shall I go on alone to see Nastasia Philipovna?"

"Count on my assistance? Go alone? How can you ask me that question, when it is a matter on which the fate of my family so largely depends? You don't know Ivolgin, my friend. To trust Ivolgin is to trust a rock; that's how the first squadron I commanded spoke of me. 'Depend upon Ivolgin,' said they all, 'he is as steady as a rock.' But, excuse me, I must just call at a house on our way, a house where I have found consolation and help in all my trials for years."

"You are going home?"

"No... I wish... to visit Madame Terentieff, the widow of Captain Terentieff, my old subordinate and friend. She helps me to keep up my courage, and to bear the trials of my domestic life, and as I have an extra burden on my mind today..."

"It seems to me," interrupted the prince, "that I was foolish to trouble you just now. However, at present you... Good-bye!"

"Indeed, you must not go away like that, young man, you must not!" cried the general. "My friend here is a widow, the mother of a family; her words come straight from her heart, and find an echo in mine. A visit to her is merely an affair of a few minutes; I am quite at home in her house. I will have a wash, and dress, and then we can drive to the Grand Theatre. Make up your mind to spend the evening with me.... We are just there—that's the house... Why, Colia! you here! Well, is Marfa Borisovna at home or have you only just come?"

"Oh no! I have been here a long while," replied Colia, who was at the front door when the general met him. "I am keeping Hippolyte company. He is worse, and has been in bed all day. I came down to buy some cards. Marfa Borisovna expects you. But what a state you are in, father!" added the boy, noticing his father's unsteady gait. "Well, let us go in."

On meeting Colia the prince determined to accompany the general, though he made up his mind to stay as short a time as possible. He wanted Colia, but firmly resolved to leave the general behind. He could not forgive himself for being so simple as to imagine that Ivolgin would be of any use. The three climbed up the long staircase until they reached the fourth floor where Madame Terentieff lived.

"You intend to introduce the prince?" asked Colia, as they went up.

"Yes, my boy. I wish to present him: General Ivolgin and Prince Muishkin! But what's the matter?... what?... How is Marfa Borisovna?"

"You know, father, you would have done much better not to come at all! She is ready to eat you up! You have not shown yourself since the day before yesterday and she is expecting the money. Why did you promise her any? You are always the same! Well, now you will have to get out of it as best you can."

They stopped before a somewhat low doorway on the fourth floor. Ardalion Alexandrovitch, evidently much out of countenance, pushed Muishkin in front.

"I will wait here," he stammered. "I should like to surprise her. ...."

Colia entered first, and as the door stood open, the mistress of the house peeped out. The surprise of the general's imagination fell very flat, for she at once began to address him in terms of reproach.

Marfa Borisovna was about forty years of age. She wore a dressing-jacket, her feet were in slippers, her face painted, and her hair was in dozens of small plaits. No sooner did she catch sight of Ardalion Alexandrovitch than she screamed:

"There he is, that wicked, mean wretch! I knew it was he! My heart misgave me!"

The old man tried to put a good face on the affair.

"Come, let us go in—it's all right," he whispered in the prince's ear.

But it was more serious than he wished to think. As soon as the visitors had crossed the low dark hall, and entered the narrow reception-room, furnished with half a dozen cane chairs, and two small card-tables, Madame Terentieff, in the shrill tones habitual to her, continued her stream of invectives.

"Are you not ashamed? Are you not ashamed? You barbarian! You tyrant! You have robbed me of all I possessed—you have sucked my bones to the marrow. How long shall I be your victim? Shameless, dishonourable man!"

"Marfa Borisovna! Marfa Borisovna! Here is... the Prince Muishkin! General Ivolgin and Prince Muishkin," stammered the disconcerted old man.

"Would you believe," said the mistress of the house, suddenly addressing the prince, "would you believe that that man has not even spared my orphan children? He has stolen everything I possessed, sold everything, pawned everything; he has left me nothing—nothing! What am I to do with your IOU's, you cunning, unscrupulous rogue? Answer, devourer! answer, heart of stone! How shall I feed my orphans? with what shall I nourish them? And now he has come, he is drunk! He can scarcely stand. How, oh how, have I offended the Almighty, that He should bring this curse upon me! Answer, you worthless villain, answer!"

But this was too much for the general.

"Here are twenty-five roubles, Marfa Borisovna... it is all that I can give... and I owe even these to the prince's generosity—my noble friend. I have been cruelly deceived. Such is... life... Now... Excuse me, I am very weak," he continued, standing in the centre of the room, and bowing to all sides. "I am faint; excuse me! Lenotchka... a cushion... my dear!"

Lenotchka, a little girl of eight, ran to fetch the cushion at once, and placed it on the rickety old sofa. The general meant to have said much more, but as soon as he had stretched himself out, he turned his face to the wall, and slept the sleep of the just.

With a grave and ceremonious air, Marfa Borisovna motioned the prince to a chair at one of the card-tables. She seated herself opposite, leaned her right cheek on her hand, and sat in silence, her eyes fixed on Muishkin, now and again sighing deeply. The three children, two little girls and a boy, Lenotchka being the eldest, came and leant on the table and also stared steadily at him. Presently Colia appeared from the adjoining room.

"I am very glad indeed to have met you here, Colia," said the prince. "Can you do something for me? I must see Nastasia Philipovna, and I asked Ardalion Alexandrovitch just now to take me to her house, but he has gone to sleep, as you see. Will you show me the way, for I do not know the street? I have the address, though; it is close to the Grand Theatre."

"Nastasia Philipovna? She does not live there, and to tell you the truth my father has never been to her house! It is strange that you should have depended on him! She lives near Wladimir Street, at the Five Corners, and it is quite close by. Will you go directly? It is just half-past nine. I will show you the way with pleasure."

Colia and the prince went off together. Alas! the latter had no money to pay for a cab, so they were obliged to walk.

"I should have liked to have taken you to see Hippolyte," said Colia. "He is the eldest son of the lady you met just now, and was in the next room. He is ill, and has been in bed all day. But he is rather strange, and extremely sensitive, and I thought he might be upset considering the circumstances in which you came... Somehow it touches me less, as it concerns my father, while it is *his* mother. That, of course, makes a great difference. What is a terrible disgrace to a woman, does not disgrace a man, at least not in the same way. Perhaps public opinion is wrong in condemning one sex, and excusing the other. Hippolyte is an extremely clever boy, but so prejudiced. He is really a slave to his opinions."

"Do you say he is consumptive?"

"Yes. It really would be happier for him to die young. If I were in his place I should certainly long for death. He is unhappy about his brother and sisters, the children you saw. If it were possible, if we only had a little money, we should leave our respective families, and live together in a little apartment of our own. It is our dream. But, do you know, when I was talking over your affair with him, he was angry, and said that anyone who did not call out a man who had given him a blow was a coward. He is very irritable to-day, and I left off arguing the matter with him. So Nastasia Philipovna has invited you to go and see her?"

"To tell the truth, she has not."

"Then how do you come to be going there?" cried Colia, so much astonished that he stopped short in the middle of the pavement. "And... and are you going to her 'At Home' in that costume?"

"I don't know, really, whether I shall be allowed in at all. If she will receive me, so much the better. If not, the matter is ended. As to my clothes—what can I do?"

"Are you going there for some particular reason, or only as a way of getting into her society, and that of her friends?"

"No, I have really an object in going... That is, I am going on business it is difficult to explain, but..."

"Well, whether you go on business or not is your affair, I do not want to know. The only important thing, in my eyes, is that you should not be going there simply for the pleasure of spending your evening in such company—cocottes, generals, usurers! If that were the case I should despise and laugh at you. There are terribly few honest people here, and hardly any whom one can respect, although people put on airs—Varia especially! Have you noticed, prince, how many adventurers there are nowadays? Especially here, in our dear Russia. How it has happened I never can understand. There used to be a certain amount of solidity in all things, but now what happens? Everything is exposed to the public gaze, veils are thrown back, every wound is probed by careless fingers. We are for ever present at an orgy of scandalous revelations. Parents blush when they remember their old-fashioned morality. At Moscow lately a father was heard urging his son to stop at nothing—at nothing, mind you!—to get money! The press seized upon the story, of course, and now it is public property. Look at my father, the general! See what he is, and yet, I assure you, he is an honest man! Only... he drinks too much, and his morals are not all we could desire. Yes, that's true! I pity him, to tell the truth, but I dare not say so, because everybody would laugh at me—but I do pity him! And who are the really clever men, after all? Money-grubbers, every one of them, from the first to the last. Hippolyte finds excuses for money-lending, and says it is a necessity. He talks about the economic movement, and the ebb and flow of capital; the devil knows what he means. It makes me angry to hear him talk so, but he is soured by his troubles. Just imagine—the general keeps his mother—but she lends him money! She lends it for a week or ten days at very high interest! Isn't it disgusting? And then, you would hardly believe it, but my mother—Nina Alexandrovna—helps Hippolyte in all sorts of ways, sends him money and clothes. She even goes as far as helping the children, through Hippolyte, because their mother cares nothing about them, and Varia does the same."

"Well, just now you said there were no honest nor good people about, that there were only money-grubbers—and here they are quite close at hand, these honest and good people, your mother and Varia! I think there is a good deal of moral strength in helping people in such circumstances."

"Varia does it from pride, and likes showing off, and giving herself airs. As to my mother, I really do admire her—yes, and honour her. Hippolyte, hardened as he is, feels it. He laughed at first, and thought it vulgar of her—but now, he is sometimes quite touched and overcome by her kindness. H'm! You call that being strong and good? I will remember that! Gania knows nothing about it. He would say that it was encouraging vice."

"Ah, Gania knows nothing about it? It seems there are many things that Gania does not know," exclaimed the prince, as he considered Colia's last words.

"Do you know, I like you very much indeed, prince? I shall never forget about this afternoon."

"I like you too, Colia."

"Listen to me! You are going to live here, are you not?" said Colia. "I mean to get something to do directly, and earn money. Then shall we three live together? You, and I, and Hippolyte? We will hire a flat, and let the general come and visit us. What do you say?"

"It would be very pleasant," returned the prince. "But we must see. I am really rather worried just now. What! are we there already? Is that the house? What a long flight of steps! And there's a porter! Well, Colia I don't know what will come of it all."

The prince seemed quite distracted for the moment.

"You must tell me all about it tomorrow! Don't be afraid. I wish you success; we agree so entirely that I can do so, although I do not understand why you are here. Good-bye!" cried Colia excitedly. "Now I will rush back and tell Hippolyte all about our plans and proposals! But as to your getting in—don't be in the least afraid. You will see her. She is so original about everything. It's the first floor. The porter will show you."

CHAPTER XIII.

The prince was very nervous as he reached the outer door; but he did his best to encourage himself with the reflection that the worst thing that could happen to him would be that he would not be received, or, perhaps, received, then laughed at for coming.

But there was another question, which terrified him considerably, and that was: what was he going to do when he *did* get in? And to this question he could fashion no satisfactory reply.

If only he could find an opportunity of coming close up to Nastasia Philipovna and saying to her: "Don't ruin yourself by marrying this man. He does not love you, he only loves your money. He told me so himself, and so did Aglaya Ivanovna, and I have come on purpose to warn you"— but even that did not seem quite a legitimate or practicable thing to do. Then, again, there was another delicate question, to which he could not find an answer; dared not, in fact, think of it; but at the very idea of which he trembled and blushed. However, in spite of all his fears and heart-quakings he went in, and asked for Nastasia Philipovna.

Nastasia occupied a medium-sized, but distinctly tasteful, flat, beautifully furnished and arranged. At one period of these five years of Petersburg life, Totski had certainly not spared his expenditure upon her. He had calculated upon her eventual love, and tried to tempt her with a lavish outlay upon comforts and luxuries, knowing too well how easily the heart accustoms itself to comforts, and how difficult it is to tear one's self away from luxuries which have become habitual and, little by little, indispensable.

Nastasia did not reject all this, she even loved her comforts and luxuries, but, strangely enough, never became, in the least degree, dependent upon them, and always gave the impression that she could do just as well without them. In fact, she went so far as to inform Totski on several occasions that such was the case, which the latter gentleman considered a very unpleasant communication indeed.

But, of late, Totski had observed many strange and original features and characteristics in Nastasia, which he had neither known nor reckoned upon in former times, and some of these fascinated him, even now, in spite of the fact that all his old calculations with regard to her were long ago cast to the winds.

A maid opened the door for the prince (Nastasia's servants were all females) and, to his surprise, received his request to announce him to her mistress without any astonishment. Neither his dirty boots, nor his wide-brimmed hat, nor his sleeveless cloak, nor his evident confusion of manner, produced the least impression upon her. She helped him off with his cloak, and begged him to wait a moment in the ante-room while she announced him.

The company assembled at Nastasia Philipovna's consisted of none but her most intimate friends, and formed a very small party in comparison with her usual gatherings on this anniversary.

In the first place there were present Totski, and General Epanchin. They were both highly amiable, but both appeared to be labouring under a half-hidden feeling of anxiety as to the result of Nastasia's deliberations with regard to Gania, which result was to be made public this evening.

Then, of course, there was Gania who was by no means so amiable as his elders, but stood apart, gloomy, and miserable, and silent. He had determined not to bring Varia with him; but Nastasia had not even asked after her, though no sooner had he arrived than she had reminded him of the episode between himself and the prince. The general, who had heard nothing of it before, began to listen with some interest, while Gania, drily, but with perfect candour, went through the whole history, including the fact of his apology to the prince. He finished by declaring that the prince was a most extraordinary man, and goodness knows why he had been considered an idiot hitherto, for he was very far from being one.

Nastasia listened to all this with great interest; but the conversation soon turned to Rogojin and his visit, and this theme proved of the greatest attraction to both Totski and the general.

Ptitsin was able to afford some particulars as to Rogojin's conduct since the afternoon. He declared that he had been busy finding money for the latter ever since, and up to nine o'clock, Rogojin having declared that he must absolutely have a hundred thousand roubles by the evening. He added that Rogojin was drunk, of course; but that he thought the money would be forthcoming, for the excited and intoxicated rapture of the fellow impelled him to give any interest or premium that was asked of him, and there were several others engaged in beating up the money, also.

All this news was received by the company with somewhat gloomy interest. Nastasia was silent, and would not say what she thought about it. Gania was equally uncommunicative. The general seemed the most anxious of all, and decidedly uneasy. The present of pearls which he had prepared with so much joy in the morning had been accepted but coldly, and Nastasia had smiled rather disagreeably as she took it from him. Ferdishenko was the only person present in good spirits.

Totski himself, who had the reputation of being a capital talker, and was usually the life and soul of these entertainments, was as silent as any on this occasion, and sat in a state of, for him, most uncommon perturbation.

The rest of the guests (an old tutor or schoolmaster, goodness knows why invited; a young man, very timid, and shy and silent; a rather loud woman of about forty, apparently an actress; and a very pretty, well-dressed German lady who hardly said a word all the evening) not only had no gift for enlivening the proceedings, but hardly knew what to say for themselves when addressed. Under these circumstances the arrival of the prince came almost as a godsend.

The announcement of his name gave rise to some surprise and to some smiles, especially when it became evident, from Nastasia's astonished look, that she had not thought of inviting him. But her astonishment once over, Nastasia showed such satisfaction that all prepared to greet the prince with cordial smiles of welcome.

"Of course," remarked General Epanchin, "he does this out of pure innocence. It's a little dangerous, perhaps, to encourage this sort of freedom; but it is rather a good thing that he has arrived just at this moment. He may enliven us a little with his originalities."

"Especially as he asked himself," said Ferdishenko.

"What's that got to do with it?" asked the general, who loathed Ferdishenko.

"Why, he must pay toll for his entrance," explained the latter.

"H'm! Prince Muishkin is not Ferdishenko," said the general, impatiently. This worthy gentleman could never quite reconcile himself to the idea of meeting Ferdishenko in society, and on an equal footing.

"Oh general, spare Ferdishenko!" replied the other, smiling. "I have special privileges."

"What do you mean by special privileges?"

"Once before I had the honour of stating them to the company. I will repeat the explanation to-day for your excellency's benefit. You see, excellency, all the world is witty and clever except myself. I am neither. As a kind of compensation I am allowed to tell the truth, for it is a well-known fact that only stupid people tell 'the truth.' Added to this, I am a spiteful man, just because I am not clever. If I am offended or injured I bear it quite patiently until the man injuring me meets with some misfortune. Then I remember, and take my revenge. I return the injury sevenfold, as Ivan Petrovitch Ptitsin says. (Of course he never does so himself.) Excellency, no doubt you recollect Kryloff's fable, 'The Lion and the Ass'? Well now, that's you and I. That fable was written precisely for us."

"You seem to be talking nonsense again, Ferdishenko," growled the general.

"What is the matter, excellency? I know how to keep my place. When I said just now that we, you and I, were the lion and the ass of Kryloff's fable, of course it is understood that I take the role of the ass. Your excellency is the lion of which the fable remarks:

'A mighty lion, terror of the woods,
Was shorn of his great prowess by old age.'

And I, your excellency, am the ass."

"I am of your opinion on that last point," said Ivan Fedorovitch, with ill-concealed irritation.

All this was no doubt extremely coarse, and moreover it was premeditated, but after all Ferdishenko had persuaded everyone to accept him as a buffoon.

"If I am admitted and tolerated here," he had said one day, "it is simply because I talk in this way. How can anyone possibly receive such a man as I am? I quite understand. Now, could I, a Ferdishenko, be allowed to sit shoulder to shoulder with a clever man like Afanasy Ivanovitch? There is one explanation, only one. I am given the position because it is so entirely inconceivable!"

But these vulgarities seemed to please Nastasia Philipovna, although too often they were both rude and offensive. Those who wished to go to her house were forced to put up with Ferdishenko. Possibly the latter was not mistaken in imagining that he was received simply in order to annoy Totski, who disliked him extremely. Gania also was often made the butt of the jester's sarcasms, who used this method of keeping in Nastasia Philipovna's good graces.

"The prince will begin by singing us a fashionable ditty," remarked Ferdishenko, and looked at the mistress of the house, to see what she would say.

"I don't think so, Ferdishenko; please be quiet," answered Nastasia Philipovna dryly.

"A-ah! if he is to be under special patronage, I withdraw my claws."

But Nastasia Philipovna had now risen and advanced to meet the prince.

"I was so sorry to have forgotten to ask you to come, when I saw you," she said, "and I am delighted to be able to thank you personally now, and to express my pleasure at your resolution."

So saying she gazed into his eyes, longing to see whether she could make any guess as to the explanation of his motive in coming to her house. The prince would very likely have made some reply to her kind words, but he was so dazzled by her appearance that he could not speak.

Nastasia noticed this with satisfaction. She was in full dress this evening; and her appearance was certainly calculated to impress all beholders. She took his hand and led him towards her other guests. But just before they reached the drawing-room door, the prince stopped her, and hurriedly and in great agitation whispered to her:

"You are altogether perfection; even your pallor and thinness are perfect; one could not wish you otherwise. I did so wish to come and see you. I—forgive me, please—"

"Don't apologize," said Nastasia, laughing; "you spoil the whole originality of the thing. I think what they say about you must be true, that you are so original.—So you think me perfection, do you?"

"Yes."

"H'm! Well, you may be a good reader of riddles but you are wrong *there*, at all events. I'll remind you of this, tonight."

Nastasia introduced the prince to her guests, to most of whom he was already known.

Totski immediately made some amiable remark. All seemed to brighten up at once, and the conversation became general. Nastasia made the prince sit down next to herself.

"Dear me, there's nothing so very curious about the prince dropping in, after all," remarked Ferdishenko.

"It's quite a clear case," said the hitherto silent Gania. "I have watched the prince almost all day, ever since the moment when he first saw Nastasia Philipovna's portrait, at General Epanchin's. I remember thinking at the time what I am now pretty sure of; and what, I may say in passing, the prince confessed to myself."

Gania said all this perfectly seriously, and without the slightest appearance of joking; indeed, he seemed strangely gloomy.

"I did not confess anything to you," said the prince, blushing. "I only answered your question."

"Bravo! That's frank, at any rate!" shouted Ferdishenko, and there was general laughter.

"Oh prince, prince! I never should have thought it of you;" said General Epanchin. "And I imagined you a philosopher! Oh, you silent fellows!"

"Judging from the fact that the prince blushed at this innocent joke, like a young girl, I should think that he must, as an honourable man, harbour the noblest intentions," said the old toothless schoolmaster, most unexpectedly; he had not so much as opened his mouth before. This remark provoked general mirth, and the old fellow himself laughed loudest of the lot, but ended with a stupendous fit of coughing.

Nastasia Philipovna, who loved originality and drollery of all kinds, was apparently very fond of this old man, and rang the bell for more tea to stop his coughing. It was now half-past ten o'clock.

"Gentlemen, wouldn't you like a little champagne now?" she asked. "I have it all ready; it will cheer us up—do now—no ceremony!"

This invitation to drink, couched, as it was, in such informal terms, came very strangely from Nastasia Philipovna. Her usual entertainments were not quite like this; there was more style about them. However, the wine was not refused; each guest took a glass excepting Gania, who drank nothing.

It was extremely difficult to account for Nastasia's strange condition of mind, which became more evident each moment, and which none could avoid noticing.

She took her glass, and vowed she would empty it three times that evening. She was hysterical, and laughed aloud every other minute with no apparent reason—the next moment relapsing into gloom and thoughtfulness.

Some of her guests suspected that she must be ill; but concluded at last that she was expecting something, for she continued to look at her watch impatiently and unceasingly; she was most absent and strange.

"You seem to be a little feverish tonight," said the actress.

"Yes; I feel quite ill. I have been obliged to put on this shawl—I feel so cold," replied Nastasia. She certainly had grown very pale, and every now and then she tried to suppress a trembling in her limbs.

"Had we not better allow our hostess to retire?" asked Totski of the general.

"Not at all, gentlemen, not at all! Your presence is absolutely necessary to me tonight," said Nastasia, significantly.

As most of those present were aware that this evening a certain very important decision was to be taken, these words of Nastasia Philipovna's appeared to be fraught with much hidden interest. The general and Totski exchanged looks; Gania fidgeted convulsively in his chair.

"Let's play at some game!" suggested the actress.

"I know a new and most delightful game, added Ferdishenko.

"What is it?" asked the actress.

"Well, when we tried it we were a party of people, like this, for instance; and somebody proposed that each of us, without leaving his place at the table, should relate something about himself. It had to be something that he really and honestly considered the very worst action he had ever committed in his life. But he was to be honest—that was the chief point! He wasn't to be allowed to lie."

"What an extraordinary idea!" said the general.

"That's the beauty of it, general!"

"It's a funny notion," said Totski, "and yet quite natural—it's only a new way of boasting."

"Perhaps that is just what was so fascinating about it."

"Why, it would be a game to cry over—not to laugh at!" said the actress.

"Did it succeed?" asked Nastasia Philipovna. "Come, let's try it, let's try it; we really are not quite so jolly as we might be—let's try it! We may like it; it's original, at all events!"

"Yes," said Ferdishenko; "it's a good idea—come along—the men begin. Of course no one need tell a story if he prefers to be disobliging. We must draw lots! Throw your slips of paper, gentlemen, into this hat, and the prince shall draw for turns. It's a very simple game; all you have to do is to tell the story of the worst action of your life. It's as simple as anything. I'll prompt anyone who forgets the rules!"

No one liked the idea much. Some smiled, some frowned; some objected, but faintly, not wishing to oppose Nastasia's wishes; for this new idea seemed to be rather well received by her. She was still in an excited, hysterical state, laughing convulsively at nothing and everything. Her eyes were blazing, and her cheeks showed two bright red spots against the white. The melancholy appearance of some of her guests seemed to add to her sarcastic humour, and perhaps the very cynicism and cruelty of the game proposed by Ferdishenko pleased her. At all events she was attracted by the idea, and gradually her guests came round to her side; the thing was original, at least, and might turn out to be amusing. "And supposing it's something that one—one can't speak about before ladies?" asked the timid and silent young man.

"Why, then of course, you won't say anything about it. As if there are not plenty of sins to your score without the need of those!" said Ferdishenko.

"But I really don't know which of my actions is the worst," said the lively actress.

"Ladies are exempted if they like."

"And how are you to know that one isn't lying? And if one lies the whole point of the game is lost," said Gania.

"Oh, but think how delightful to hear how one's friends lie! Besides you needn't be afraid, Gania; everybody knows what your worst action is without the need of any lying on your part. Only think, gentlemen,"—and Ferdishenko here grew quite enthusiastic, "only think with what eyes we shall observe one another tomorrow, after our tales have been told!"

"But surely this is a joke, Nastasia Philipovna?" asked Totski. "You don't really mean us to play this game."

"Whoever is afraid of wolves had better not go into the wood," said Nastasia, smiling.

"But, pardon me, Mr. Ferdishenko, is it possible to make a game out of this kind of thing?" persisted Totski, growing more and more uneasy. "I assure you it can't be a success."

"And why not? Why, the last time I simply told straight off about how I stole three roubles."

"Perhaps so; but it is hardly possible that you told it so that it seemed like truth, or so that you were believed. And, as Gavrila Ardalionovitch has said, the least suggestion of a falsehood takes all point out of the game. It seems to me that sincerity, on the other hand, is only possible if combined with a kind of bad taste that would be utterly out of place here."

"How subtle you are, Afanasy Ivanovitch! You astonish me," cried Ferdishenko. "You will remark, gentlemen, that in saying that I could not recount the story of my theft so as to be believed, Afanasy Ivanovitch has very ingeniously implied that I am not capable of thieving—(it would have been bad taste to say so openly); and all the time he is probably firmly convinced, in his own mind, that I am very well capable of it! But now, gentlemen, to business! Put in your slips, ladies and gentlemen—is yours in, Mr. Totski? So—then we are all ready; now prince, draw, please." The prince silently put his hand into the hat, and drew the names. Ferdishenko was first, then Ptitsin, then the general, Totski next, his own fifth, then Gania, and so on; the ladies did not draw.

"Oh, dear! oh, dear!" cried Ferdishenko. "I did so hope the prince would come out first, and then the general. Well, gentlemen, I suppose I must set a good example! What vexes me much is that I am such an insignificant creature that it matters nothing to anybody whether I have done bad actions or not! Besides, which am I to choose? It's an *embarras de richesse*. Shall I tell how I became a thief on one occasion only, to convince Afanasy Ivanovitch that it is possible to steal without being a thief?"

"Do go on, Ferdishenko, and don't make unnecessary preface, or you'll never finish," said Nastasia Philipovna. All observed how irritable and cross she had become since her last burst of laughter; but none the less obstinately did she stick to her absurd whim about this new game. Totski sat looking miserable enough. The general lingered over his champagne, and seemed to be thinking of some story for the time when his turn should come.

CHAPTER XIV.

"I have no wit, Nastasia Philipovna," began Ferdishenko, "and therefore I talk too much, perhaps. Were I as witty, now, as Mr. Totski or the general, I should probably have sat silent all the evening, as they have. Now, prince, what do you think?—are there not far more thieves than honest men in this world? Don't you think we may say there does not exist a single person so honest that he has never stolen anything whatever in his life?"

"What a silly idea," said the actress. "Of course it is not the case. I have never stolen anything, for one."

"H'm! very well, Daria Alexeyevna; you have not stolen anything—agreed. But how about the prince, now—look how he is blushing!"

"I think you are partially right, but you exaggerate," said the prince, who had certainly blushed up, of a sudden, for some reason or other.

"Ferdishenko—either tell us your story, or be quiet, and mind your own business. You exhaust all patience," cuttingly and irritably remarked Nastasia Philipovna.

"Immediately, immediately! As for my story, gentlemen, it is too stupid and absurd to tell you.

"I assure you I am not a thief, and yet I have stolen; I cannot explain why. It was at Semeon Ivanovitch Ishenka's country house, one Sunday. He had a dinner party. After dinner the men stayed at the table over their wine. It struck me to ask the daughter of the house to play something on the piano; so I passed through the corner room to join the ladies. In that room, on Maria Ivanovna's writing-table, I observed a three-rouble note. She must have taken it out for some purpose, and left it lying there. There was no one about. I took up the note and put it in my pocket; why, I can't say. I don't know what possessed me to do it, but it was done, and I went quickly back to the dining-room and reseated myself at the dinner-table. I sat and waited there in a great state of excitement. I talked hard, and told lots of stories, and laughed like mad; then I joined the ladies.

"In half an hour or so the loss was discovered, and the servants were being put under examination. Daria, the housemaid was suspected. I exhibited the greatest interest and sympathy, and I remember that poor Daria quite lost her head, and that I began assuring her, before everyone, that I would guarantee her forgiveness on the part of her mistress, if she would confess her guilt. They all stared at the girl, and I remember a wonderful attraction in the reflection that here was I sermonizing away, with the money in my own pocket all the while. I went and spent the three roubles that very evening at a restaurant. I went in and asked for a bottle of Lafite, and drank it up; I wanted to be rid of the money.

"I did not feel much remorse either then or afterwards; but I would not repeat the performance—believe it or not as you please. There—that's all."

"Only, of course that's not nearly your worst action," said the actress, with evident dislike in her face.

"That was a psychological phenomenon, not an action," remarked Totski.

"And what about the maid?" asked Nastasia Philipovna, with undisguised contempt.

"Oh, she was turned out next day, of course. It's a very strict household, there!"

"And you allowed it?"

"I should think so, rather! I was not going to return and confess next day," laughed Ferdishenko, who seemed a little surprised at the disagreeable impression which his story had made on all parties.

"How mean you were!" said Nastasia.

"Bah! you wish to hear a man tell of his worst actions, and you expect the story to come out goody-goody! One's worst actions always are mean. We shall see what the general has to say for himself now. All is not gold that glitters, you know; and because a man keeps his carriage he need not be specially virtuous, I assure you, all sorts of people keep carriages. And by what means?"

In a word, Ferdishenko was very angry and rapidly forgetting himself; his whole face was drawn with passion. Strange as it may appear, he had expected much better success for his story. These little errors of taste on Ferdishenko's part occurred very frequently. Nastasia trembled with rage, and looked fixedly at him, whereupon he relapsed into alarmed silence. He realized that he had gone a little too far.

"Had we not better end this game?" asked Totski.

"It's my turn, but I plead exemption," said Ptitsin.

"You don't care to oblige us?" asked Nastasia.

"I cannot, I assure you. I confess I do not understand how anyone can play this game."

"Then, general, it's your turn," continued Nastasia Philipovna, "and if you refuse, the whole game will fall through, which will disappoint me very much, for I was looking forward to relating a certain 'page of my own life.' I am only waiting for you and Afanasy Ivanovitch to have your turns, for I require the support of your example," she added, smiling.

"Oh, if you put it in that way," cried the general, excitedly, "I'm ready to tell the whole story of my life, but I must confess that I prepared a little story in anticipation of my turn."

Nastasia smiled amiably at him; but evidently her depression and irritability were increasing with every moment. Totski was dreadfully alarmed to hear her promise a revelation out of her own life.

"I, like everyone else," began the general, "have committed certain not altogether graceful actions, so to speak, during the course of my life. But the strangest thing of all in my case is, that I should consider the little anecdote which I am now about to give you as a confession of the worst of my 'bad actions.' It is thirty-five years since it all happened, and yet I cannot to this very day recall the circumstances without, as it were, a sudden pang at the heart.

"It was a silly affair—I was an ensign at the time. You know ensigns—their blood is boiling water, their circumstances generally penurious. Well, I had a servant Nikifor who used to do everything for me in my quarters, economized and managed for me, and even laid hands on anything he could find (belonging to other people), in order to augment our household goods; but a faithful, honest fellow all the same.

"I was strict, but just by nature. At that time we were stationed in a small town. I was quartered at an old widow's house, a lieutenant's widow of eighty years of age. She lived in a wretched little wooden house, and had not even a servant, so poor was she.

"Her relations had all died off—her husband was dead and buried forty years since; and a niece, who had lived with her and bullied her up to three years ago, was dead too; so that she was quite alone.

"Well, I was precious dull with her, especially as she was so childish that there was nothing to be got out of her. Eventually, she stole a fowl of mine; the business is a mystery to this day; but it could have been no one but herself. I requested to be quartered somewhere else, and was shifted to the other end of the town, to the house of a merchant with a large family, and a long beard, as I remember him. Nikifor and I were delighted to go; but the old lady was not pleased at our departure.

"Well, a day or two afterwards, when I returned from drill, Nikifor says to me: 'We oughtn't to have left our tureen with the old lady, I've nothing to serve the soup in.'

"I asked how it came about that the tureen had been left. Nikifor explained that the old lady refused to give it up, because, she said, we had broken her bowl, and she must have our tureen in place of it; she had declared that I had so arranged the matter with herself.

"This baseness on her part of course aroused my young blood to fever heat; I jumped up, and away I flew.

"I arrived at the old woman's house beside myself. She was sitting in a corner all alone, leaning her face on her hand. I fell on her like a clap of thunder. 'You old wretch!' I yelled and all that sort of thing, in real Russian style. Well, when I began cursing at her, a strange thing happened. I looked at her, and she stared back with her eyes starting out of her head, but she did not say a word. She seemed to sway about as she sat, and looked and looked at me in the strangest way. Well, I soon stopped swearing and looked closer at her, asked her questions, but not a word could I get out of her. The flies were buzzing about the room and only this sound broke the silence; the sun was setting outside; I didn't know what to make of it, so I went away.

"Before I reached home I was met and summoned to the major's, so that it was some while before I actually got there. When I came in, Nikifor met me. 'Have you heard, sir, that our old lady is dead?' '*dead*, when?' 'Oh, an hour and a half ago.' That meant nothing more nor less than that she was dying at the moment when I pounced on her and began abusing her.

"This produced a great effect upon me. I used to dream of the poor old woman at nights. I really am not superstitious, but two days after, I went to her funeral, and as time went on I thought more and more about her. I said to myself, 'This woman, this human being, lived to a great age. She had children, a husband and family, friends and relations; her household was busy and cheerful; she was surrounded by smiling faces; and then suddenly they are gone, and she is left alone like a solitary fly... like a fly, cursed with the burden of her age. At last, God calls her to Himself. At sunset, on a lovely summer's evening, my little old woman passes away—a thought, you will notice, which offers much food for reflection—and behold! instead of tears and prayers to start her on her last journey, she has insults and jeers from a young ensign, who stands before her with his hands in his pockets, making a terrible row about a soup tureen!' Of course I was to blame, and even now that I have time to look back at it calmly, I pity the poor old thing no less. I repeat that I wonder at myself, for after all I was not really responsible. Why did she take it into her head to die at that moment? But the more I thought of it, the more I felt the weight of it upon my mind; and I never got quite rid of the impression until I put a couple of old women into an almshouse and kept them there at my own expense. There, that's all. I repeat I dare say I have committed many a grievous sin in my day; but I cannot help always looking back upon this as the worst action I have ever perpetrated."

"H'm! and instead of a bad action, your excellency has detailed one of your noblest deeds," said Ferdishenko. "Ferdishenko is 'done.'"

"Dear me, general," said Nastasia Philipovna, absently, "I really never imagined you had such a good heart."

The general laughed with great satisfaction, and applied himself once more to the champagne.

It was now Totski's turn, and his story was awaited with great curiosity—while all eyes turned on Nastasia Philipovna, as though anticipating that his revelation must be connected somehow with her. Nastasia, during the whole of his story, pulled at the lace trimming of her sleeve, and never once glanced at the speaker. Totski was a handsome man, rather stout, with a very polite and dignified manner. He was always well dressed, and his linen was exquisite. He had plump white hands, and wore a magnificent diamond ring on one finger.

"What simplifies the duty before me considerably, in my opinion," he began, "is that I am bound to recall and relate the very worst action of my life. In such circumstances there can, of course, be no doubt. One's conscience very soon informs one what is the proper narrative to tell. I admit, that among the many silly and thoughtless actions of my life, the memory of one comes prominently forward and reminds me that it lay long like a stone on my heart. Some twenty years since, I paid a visit to Platon Ordintzeff at his country-house. He had just been elected marshal of the nobility, and had come there with his young wife for the winter holidays. Anfisa Alexeyevna's birthday came off just then, too, and there were two balls arranged. At that time Dumas-fils' beautiful work, *La Dame aux Camélias*—a novel which I consider imperishable—had just come into fashion. In the provinces all the ladies were in raptures over it, those who had read it, at least. Camellias were all the fashion. Everyone inquired for them, everybody wanted them; and a grand lot of camellias are to be got in a country town—as you all know—and two balls to provide for!

"Poor Peter Volhofskoi was desperately in love with Anfisa Alexeyevna. I don't know whether there was anything—I mean I don't know whether he could possibly have indulged in any hope. The poor fellow was beside himself to get her a bouquet of camellias. Countess Sotski and Sophia Bespalova, as everyone knew, were coming with white camellia bouquets. Anfisa wished for red ones, for effect. Well, her husband Platon was driven desperate to find some. And the day before the ball, Anfisa's rival snapped up the only red camellias to be had in the place, from under Platon's nose, and Platon—wretched man—was done for. Now if Peter had only been able to step in at this moment with a red bouquet, his little hopes might have made gigantic strides. A woman's gratitude under such circumstances would have been boundless—but it was practically an impossibility.

"The night before the ball I met Peter, looking radiant. 'What is it?' I ask. 'I've found them, Eureka!' 'No! where, where?' 'At Ekshaisk (a little town fifteen miles off) there's a rich old merchant, who keeps a lot of canaries, has no children, and he and his wife are devoted to flowers. He's got some camellias.' 'And what if he won't let you have them?' 'I'll go on my knees and implore till I get them. I won't go away.' 'When shall you start?' 'Tomorrow morning at five o'clock.' 'Go on,' I said, 'and good luck to you.'

"I was glad for the poor fellow, and went home. But an idea got hold of me somehow. I don't know how. It was nearly two in the morning. I rang the bell and ordered the coachman to be waked up and sent to me. He came. I gave him a tip of fifteen roubles, and told him to get the carriage ready at once. In half an hour it was at the door. I got in and off we went.

"By five I drew up at the Ekshaisky inn. I waited there till dawn, and soon after six I was off, and at the old merchant Trepalaf's.

"'Camellias!' I said, 'father, save me, save me, let me have some camellias!' He was a tall, grey old man—a terrible-looking old gentleman. 'Not a bit of it,' he says. 'I won't.' Down I went on my knees. 'Don't say so, don't—think what you're doing!' I cried; 'it's a matter of life and death!' 'If that's the case, take them,' says he. So up I get, and cut such a bouquet of red camellias! He had a whole greenhouse full of them—lovely ones. The old fellow sighs. I pull out a hundred roubles. 'No, no!' says he, 'don't insult me that way.' 'Oh, if that's the case, give it to the village hospital,' I say. 'Ah,' he says, 'that's quite a different matter; that's good of you and generous. I'll pay it in there for you with pleasure.' I liked that old fellow, Russian to the core, *de la vraie souche*. I went home in raptures, but took another road in order to avoid Peter. Immediately on arriving I sent up the bouquet for Anfisa to see when she awoke.

"You may imagine her ecstasy, her gratitude. The wretched Platon, who had almost died since yesterday of the reproaches showered upon him, wept on my shoulder. Of course poor Peter had no chance after this.

"I thought he would cut my throat at first, and went about armed ready to meet him. But he took it differently; he fainted, and had brain fever and convulsions. A month after, when he had hardly recovered, he went off to the Crimea, and there he was shot.

"I assure you this business left me no peace for many a long year. Why did I do it? I was not in love with her myself; I'm afraid it was simply mischief—pure 'cussedness' on my part.

"If I hadn't seized that bouquet from under his nose he might have been alive now, and a happy man. He might have been successful in life, and never have gone to fight the Turks."

Totski ended his tale with the same dignity that had characterized its commencement.

Nastasia Philipovna's eyes were flashing in a most unmistakable way, now; and her lips were all a-quiver by the time Totski finished his story.

All present watched both of them with curiosity.

"You were right, Totski," said Nastasia, "it is a dull game and a stupid one. I'll just tell my story, as I promised, and then we'll play cards."

"Yes, but let's have the story first!" cried the general.

"Prince," said Nastasia Philipovna, unexpectedly turning to Muishkin, "here are my old friends, Totski and General Epanchin, who wish to marry me off. Tell me what you think. Shall I marry or not? As you decide, so shall it be."

Totski grew white as a sheet. The general was struck dumb. All present started and listened intently. Gania sat rooted to his chair.

"Marry whom?" asked the prince, faintly.

"Gavrila Ardalionovitch Ivolgin," said Nastasia, firmly and evenly.

There were a few seconds of dead silence.

The prince tried to speak, but could not form his words; a great weight seemed to lie upon his breast and suffocate him.

"N-no! don't marry him!" he whispered at last, drawing his breath with an effort.

"So be it, then. Gavrila Ardalionovitch," she spoke solemnly and forcibly, "you hear the prince's decision? Take it as my decision; and let that be the end of the matter for good and all."

"Nastasia Philipovna!" cried Totski, in a quaking voice.

"Nastasia Philipovna!" said the general, in persuasive but agitated tones.

Everyone in the room fidgeted in their places, and waited to see what was coming next.

"Well, gentlemen!" she continued, gazing around in apparent astonishment; "what do you all look so alarmed about? Why are you so upset?"

"But—recollect, Nastasia Philipovna," stammered Totski, "you gave a promise, quite a free one, and—and you might have spared us this. I am confused and bewildered, I know; but, in a word, at such a moment, and before company, and all so-so-irregular, finishing off a game with a serious matter like this, a matter of honour, and of heart, and—"

"I don't follow you, Afanasy Ivanovitch; you are losing your head. In the first place, what do you mean by 'before company'? Isn't the company good enough for you? And what's all that about 'a game'? I wished to tell my little story, and I told it! Don't you like it? You heard what I said to the prince? 'As you decide, so it shall be!' If he had said 'yes,' I should have given my consent! But he said 'no,' so I refused. Here was my whole life hanging on his one word! Surely I was serious enough?"

"The prince! What on earth has the prince got to do with it? Who the deuce is the prince?" cried the general, who could conceal his wrath no longer.

"The prince has this to do with it—that I see in him for the first time in all my life, a man endowed with real truthfulness of spirit, and I trust him. He trusted me at first sight, and I trust him!"

"It only remains for me, then, to thank Nastasia Philipovna for the great delicacy with which she has treated me," said Gania, as pale as death, and with quivering lips. "That is my plain duty, of course; but the prince—what has he to do in the matter?"

"I see what you are driving at," said Nastasia Philipovna. "You imply that the prince is after the seventy-five thousand roubles—I quite understand you. Mr. Totski, I forgot to say, 'Take your seventy-five thousand roubles'—I don't want them. I let you go free for nothing—take your freedom! You must need it. Nine years and three months' captivity is enough for anybody. Tomorrow I shall start afresh—today I am a free agent for the first time in my life.

"General, you must take your pearls back, too—give them to your wife—here they are! Tomorrow I shall leave this flat altogether, and then there'll be no more of these pleasant little social gatherings, ladies and gentlemen."

So saying, she scornfully rose from her seat as though to depart.

"Nastasia Philipovna! Nastasia Philipovna!"

The words burst involuntarily from every mouth. All present started up in bewildered excitement; all surrounded her; all had listened uneasily to her wild, disconnected sentences. All felt that something had happened, something had gone very far wrong indeed, but no one could make head or tail of the matter.

At this moment there was a furious ring at the bell, and a great knock at the door—exactly similar to the one which had startled the company at Gania's house in the afternoon.

"Ah, ah! here's the climax at last, at half-past twelve!" cried Nastasia Philipovna. "Sit down, gentlemen, I beg you. Something is about to happen."

So saying, she reseated herself; a strange smile played on her lips. She sat quite still, but watched the door in a fever of impatience.

"Rogojin and his hundred thousand roubles, no doubt of it," muttered Ptitsin to himself.

CHAPTER XV.

Katia, the maid-servant, made her appearance, terribly frightened.

"Goodness knows what it means, ma'am," she said. "There is a whole collection of men come—all tipsy—and want to see you. They say that 'it's Rogojin, and she knows all about it.'"

"It's all right, Katia, let them all in at once."

"Surely not *all*, ma'am? They seem so disorderly—it's dreadful to see them."

"Yes *all*, Katia, all—every one of them. Let them in, or they'll come in whether you like or no. Listen! what a noise they are making! Perhaps you are offended, gentlemen, that I should receive such guests in your presence? I am very sorry, and ask your forgiveness, but it cannot be helped—and I should be very grateful if you could all stay and witness this climax. However, just as you please, of course."

The guests exchanged glances; they were annoyed and bewildered by the episode; but it was clear enough that all this had been pre-arranged and expected by Nastasia Philipovna, and that there was no use in trying to stop her now—for she was little short of insane.

Besides, they were naturally inquisitive to see what was to happen. There was nobody who would be likely to feel much alarm. There were but two ladies present; one of whom was the lively actress, who was not easily frightened, and the other the silent German beauty who, it turned out, did not understand a word of Russian, and seemed to be as stupid as she was lovely.

Her acquaintances invited her to their "At Homes" because she was so decorative. She was exhibited to their guests like a valuable picture, or vase, or statue, or firescreen. As for the men, Ptitsin was one of Rogojin's friends; Ferdishenko was as much at home as a fish in the sea, Gania, not yet recovered from his amazement, appeared to be chained to a pillory. The old professor did not in the least understand what was happening; but when he noticed how extremely agitated the mistress of the house, and her friends, seemed, he nearly wept, and trembled with fright: but he would rather have died than leave Nastasia Philipovna at such a crisis, for he loved her as if she were his own granddaughter. Afanasy Ivanovitch greatly disliked having anything to do with the affair, but he was too much interested to leave, in spite of the mad turn things had taken; and a few words that had dropped from the lips of Nastasia puzzled him so much, that he felt he could not go without an explanation. He resolved therefore, to see it out, and to adopt the attitude of silent spectator, as most suited to his dignity. General Epanchin alone determined to depart. He was annoyed at the manner in which his gift had been returned, as though he had condescended, under the influence of passion, to place himself on a level with Ptitsin and Ferdishenko, his self-respect and sense of duty now returned together with a consciousness of what was due to his social rank and official importance. In short, he plainly showed his conviction that a man in his position could have nothing to do with Rogojin and his companions. But Nastasia interrupted him at his first words.

"Ah, general!" she cried, "I was forgetting! If I had only foreseen this unpleasantness! I won't insist on keeping you against your will, although I should have liked you to be beside me now. In any case, I am most grateful to you for your visit, and flattering attention... but if you are afraid..."

"Excuse me, Nastasia Philipovna," interrupted the general, with chivalric generosity. "To whom are you speaking? I have remained until now simply because of my devotion to you, and as for danger, I am only afraid that the carpets may be ruined, and the furniture smashed!... You should shut the door on the lot, in my opinion. But I confess that I am extremely curious to see how it ends."

"Rogojin!" announced Ferdishenko.

"What do you think about it?" said the general in a low voice to Totski. "Is she mad? I mean mad in the medical sense of the word .... eh?"

"I've always said she was predisposed to it," whispered Afanasy Ivanovitch slyly. "Perhaps it is a fever!"

Since their visit to Gania's home, Rogojin's followers had been increased by two new recruits—a dissolute old man, the hero of some ancient scandal, and a retired sub-lieutenant. A laughable story was told of the former. He possessed, it was said, a set of false teeth, and one day when he wanted money for a drinking orgy, he pawned them, and was never able to reclaim them! The officer appeared to be a rival of the gentleman who was so proud of his fists. He was known to none of Rogojin's followers, but as they passed by the Nevsky, where he stood begging, he had joined their ranks. His claim for the charity he desired seemed based on the fact that in the days of his prosperity he had given away as much as fifteen roubles at a time. The rivals seemed more than a little jealous of one another. The athlete appeared injured at the admission of the "beggar" into the company. By nature taciturn, he now merely growled occasionally like a bear, and glared contemptuously upon the "beggar," who, being somewhat of a man of the world, and a diplomatist, tried to insinuate himself into the bear's good graces. He was a much smaller man than the athlete, and doubtless was conscious that he must tread warily. Gently and without argument he alluded to the advantages of the English style in boxing, and showed himself a firm believer in Western institutions. The athlete's lips curled disdainfully, and without honouring his adversary with a formal denial, he exhibited, as if by accident, that peculiarly Russian object—an enormous fist, clenched, muscular, and covered with red hairs! The sight of this pre-eminently national attribute was enough to convince anybody, without words, that it was a serious matter for those who should happen to come into contact with it.

None of the band were very drunk, for the leader had kept his intended visit to Nastasia in view all day, and had done his best to prevent his followers from drinking too much. He was sober himself, but the excitement of this chaotic day—the strangest day of his life—had affected him so that he was in a dazed, wild condition, which almost resembled drunkenness.

He had kept but one idea before him all day, and for that he had worked in an agony of anxiety and a fever of suspense. His lieutenants had worked so hard from five o'clock until eleven, that they actually had collected a hundred thousand roubles for him, but at such terrific expense, that the rate of interest was only mentioned among them in whispers and with bated breath.

As before, Rogojin walked in advance of his troop, who followed him with mingled self-assertion and timidity. They were specially frightened of Nastasia Philipovna herself, for some reason.

Many of them expected to be thrown downstairs at once, without further ceremony, the elegant and irresistible Zaleshoff among them. But the party led by the athlete, without openly showing their hostile intentions, silently nursed contempt and even hatred for Nastasia Philipovna, and marched into her house as they would have marched into an enemy's fortress. Arrived there, the luxury of the rooms seemed to inspire them with a kind of respect, not unmixed with alarm. So many things were entirely new to their experience—the choice furniture, the pictures, the great statue of Venus. They followed their chief into the salon, however, with a kind of impudent curiosity. There, the sight of General Epanchin among the guests, caused many of them to beat a hasty retreat into the adjoining room, the "boxer" and "beggar" being among the first to go. A few only, of whom Lebedeff made one, stood their ground; he had contrived to walk side by side with Rogojin, for he quite understood the importance of a man who had a fortune of a million odd roubles, and who at this moment carried a hundred thousand in his hand. It may be added that the whole company, not excepting Lebedeff, had the vaguest idea of the extent of their powers, and of how far they could safely go. At some moments Lebedeff was sure that right was on their side; at others he tried uneasily to remember various cheering and reassuring articles of the Civil Code.

Rogojin, when he stepped into the room, and his eyes fell upon Nastasia, stopped short, grew white as a sheet, and stood staring; it was clear that his heart was beating painfully. So he stood, gazing intently, but timidly, for a few seconds. Suddenly, as though bereft of his senses, he moved forward, staggering helplessly, towards the table. On his way he collided against Ptitsin's chair, and put his dirty foot on the lace skirt of the silent lady's dress; but he neither apologized for this, nor even noticed it.

On reaching the table, he placed upon it a strange-looking object, which he had carried with him into the drawing-room. This was a paper packet, some six or seven inches thick, and eight or nine in length, wrapped in an old newspaper, and tied round three or four times with string.

Having placed this before her, he stood with drooped arms and head, as though awaiting his sentence.

His costume was the same as it had been in the morning, except for a new silk handkerchief round his neck, bright green and red, fastened with a huge diamond pin, and an enormous diamond ring on his dirty forefinger.

Lebedeff stood two or three paces behind his chief; and the rest of the band waited about near the door.

The two maid-servants were both peeping in, frightened and amazed at this unusual and disorderly scene.

"What is that?" asked Nastasia Philipovna, gazing intently at Rogojin, and indicating the paper packet.

"A hundred thousand," replied the latter, almost in a whisper.

"Oh! so he kept his word—there's a man for you! Well, sit down, please—take that chair. I shall have something to say to you presently. Who are all these with you? The same party? Let them come in and sit down. There's room on that sofa, there are some chairs and there's another sofa! Well, why don't they sit down?"

Sure enough, some of the brave fellows entirely lost their heads at this point, and retreated into the next room. Others, however, took the hint and sat down, as far as they could from the table, however; feeling braver in proportion to their distance from Nastasia.

Rogojin took the chair offered him, but he did not sit long; he soon stood up again, and did not reseat himself. Little by little he began to look around him and discern the other guests. Seeing Gania, he smiled venomously and muttered to himself, "Look at that!"

He gazed at Totski and the general with no apparent confusion, and with very little curiosity. But when he observed that the prince was seated beside Nastasia Philipovna, he could not take his eyes off him for a long while, and was clearly amazed. He could not account for the prince's presence there. It was not in the least surprising that Rogojin should be, at this time, in a more or less delirious condition; for not to speak of the excitements of the day, he had spent the night before in the train, and had not slept more than a wink for forty-eight hours.

"This, gentlemen, is a hundred thousand roubles," said Nastasia Philipovna, addressing the company in general, "here, in this dirty parcel. This afternoon Rogojin yelled, like a madman, that he would bring me a hundred thousand in the evening, and I have been waiting for him all the while. He was bargaining for me, you know; first he offered me eighteen thousand; then he rose to forty, and then to a hundred thousand. And he has kept his word, see! My goodness, how white he is! All this happened this afternoon, at Gania's. I had gone to pay his mother a visit—my future family, you know! And his sister said to my very face, surely somebody will turn this shameless creature out. After which she spat in her brother Gania's face—a girl of character, that!"

"Nastasia Philipovna!" began the general, reproachfully. He was beginning to put his own interpretation on the affair.

"Well, what, general? Not quite good form, eh? Oh, nonsense! Here have I been sitting in my box at the French theatre for the last five years like a statue of inaccessible virtue, and kept out of the way of all admirers, like a silly little idiot! Now, there's this man, who comes and pays down his hundred thousand on the table, before you all, in spite of my five years of innocence and proud virtue, and I dare be sworn he has his sledge outside waiting to carry me off. He values me at a hundred thousand! I see you are still angry with me, Gania! Why, surely you never really wished to take *me* into your family? *me*, Rogojin's mistress! What did the prince say just now?"

"I never said you were Rogojin's mistress—you are *not!*" said the prince, in trembling accents.

"Nastasia Philipovna, dear soul!" cried the actress, impatiently, "do be calm, dear! If it annoys you so—all this—do go away and rest! Of course you would never go with this wretched fellow, in spite of his hundred thousand roubles! Take his money and kick him out of the house; that's the way to treat him and the likes of him! Upon my word, if it were my business, I'd soon clear them all out!"

The actress was a kind-hearted woman, and highly impressionable. She was very angry now.

"Don't be cross, Daria Alexeyevna!" laughed Nastasia. "I was not angry when I spoke; I wasn't reproaching Gania. I don't know how it was that I ever could have indulged the whim of entering an honest family like his. I saw his mother—and kissed her hand, too. I came and stirred up all that fuss, Gania, this afternoon, on purpose to see how much you could swallow—you surprised me, my friend—you did, indeed. Surely you could not marry a woman who accepts pearls like those you knew the general was going to give me, on the very eve of her marriage? And Rogojin! Why, in your own house and before your own brother and sister, he bargained with me! Yet you could come here and expect to be betrothed to me before you left the house! You almost brought your sister, too. Surely what Rogojin said about you is not really true: that you would crawl all the way to the other end of the town, on hands and knees, for three roubles?"

"Yes, he would!" said Rogojin, quietly, but with an air of absolute conviction.

"H'm! and he receives a good salary, I'm told. Well, what should you get but disgrace and misery if you took a wife you hated into your family (for I know very well that you do hate me)? No, no! I believe now that a man like you would murder anyone for money—sharpen a razor and come up behind his best friend and cut his throat like a sheep—I've read of such people. Everyone seems money-mad nowadays. No, no! I may be shameless, but you are far worse. I don't say a word about that other—"

"Nastasia Philipovna, is this really you? You, once so refined and delicate of speech. Oh, what a tongue! What dreadful things you are saying," cried the general, wringing his hands in real grief.

"I am intoxicated, general. I am having a day out, you know—it's my birthday! I have long looked forward to this happy occasion. Daria Alexeyevna, you see that nosegay-man, that Monsieur aux Camelias, sitting there laughing at us?"

"I am not laughing, Nastasia Philipovna; I am only listening with all my attention," said Totski, with dignity.

"Well, why have I worried him, for five years, and never let him go free? Is he worth it? He is only just what he ought to be—nothing particular. He thinks I am to blame, too. He gave me my education, kept me like a countess. Money—my word! What a lot of money he spent over me! And he tried to find me an honest husband first, and then this Gania, here. And what do you think? All these five years I did not live with him, and yet I took his money, and considered I was quite justified.

"You say, take the hundred thousand and kick that man out. It is true, it is an abominable business, as you say. I might have married long ago, not Gania—Oh, no!—but that would have been abominable too.

"Would you believe it, I had some thoughts of marrying Totski, four years ago! I meant mischief, I confess—but I could have had him, I give you my word; he asked me himself. But I thought, no! it's not worthwhile to take such advantage of him. No! I had better go on to the streets, or accept Rogojin, or become a washerwoman or something—for I have nothing of my own, you know. I shall go away and leave everything behind, to the last rag—he shall have it all back. And who would take me without anything? Ask Gania, there, whether he would. Why, even Ferdishenko wouldn't have me!"

"No, Ferdishenko would not; he is a candid fellow, Nastasia Philipovna," said that worthy. "But the prince would. You sit here making complaints, but just look at the prince. I've been observing him for a long while."

Nastasia Philipovna looked keenly round at the prince.

"Is that true?" she asked.

"Quite true," whispered the prince.

"You'll take me as I am, with nothing?"

"I will, Nastasia Philipovna."

"Here's a pretty business!" cried the general. "However, it might have been expected of him."

The prince continued to regard Nastasia with a sorrowful, but intent and piercing, gaze.

"Here's another alternative for me," said Nastasia, turning once more to the actress; "and he does it out of pure kindness of heart. I know him. I've found a benefactor. Perhaps, though, what they say about him may be true—that he's an—we know what. And what shall you live on, if you are really so madly in love with Rogojin's mistress, that you are ready to marry her—eh?"

"I take you as a good, honest woman, Nastasia Philipovna—not as Rogojin's mistress."

"Who? I?—good and honest?"

"Yes, you."

"Oh, you get those ideas out of novels, you know. Times are changed now, dear prince; the world sees things as they really are. That's all nonsense. Besides, how can you marry? You need a nurse, not a wife."

The prince rose and began to speak in a trembling, timid tone, but with the air of a man absolutely sure of the truth of his words.

"I know nothing, Nastasia Philipovna. I have seen nothing. You are right so far; but I consider that you would be honouring me, and not I you. I am a nobody. You have suffered, you have passed through hell and emerged pure, and that is very much. Why do you shame yourself by desiring to go with Rogojin? You are delirious. You have returned to Mr. Totski his seventy-five thousand roubles, and declared that you will leave this house and all that is in it, which is a line of conduct that not one person here would imitate. Nastasia Philipovna, I love you! I would die for you. I shall never let any man say one word against you, Nastasia Philipovna! and if we are poor, I can work for both."

As the prince spoke these last words a titter was heard from Ferdishenko; Lebedeff laughed too. The general grunted with irritation; Ptitsin and Totski barely restrained their smiles. The rest all sat listening, open-mouthed with wonder.

"But perhaps we shall not be poor; we may be very rich, Nastasia Philipovna," continued the prince, in the same timid, quivering tones. "I don't know for certain, and I'm sorry to say I haven't had an opportunity of finding out all day; but I received a letter from Moscow, while I was in Switzerland, from a Mr. Salaskin, and he acquaints me with the fact that I am entitled to a very large inheritance. This letter—"

The prince pulled a letter out of his pocket.

"Is he raving?" said the general. "Are we really in a mad-house?"

There was silence for a moment. Then Ptitsin spoke.

"I think you said, prince, that your letter was from Salaskin? Salaskin is a very eminent man, indeed, in his own world; he is a wonderfully clever solicitor, and if he really tells you this, I think you may be pretty sure that he is right. It so happens, luckily, that I know his handwriting, for I have lately had business with him. If you would allow me to see it, I should perhaps be able to tell you."

The prince held out the letter silently, but with a shaking hand.

"What, what?" said the general, much agitated.

"What's all this? Is he really heir to anything?"

All present concentrated their attention upon Ptitsin, reading the prince's letter. The general curiosity had received a new fillip. Ferdishenko could not sit still. Rogojin fixed his eyes first on the prince, and then on Ptitsin, and then back again; he was extremely agitated. Lebedeff could not stand it. He crept up and read over Ptitsin's shoulder, with the air of a naughty boy who expects a box on the ear every moment for his indiscretion.

CHAPTER XVI.

"It's good business," said Ptitsin, at last, folding the letter and handing it back to the prince. "You will receive, without the slightest trouble, by the last will and testament of your aunt, a very large sum of money indeed."

"Impossible!" cried the general, starting up as if he had been shot.

Ptitsin explained, for the benefit of the company, that the prince's aunt had died five months since. He had never known her, but she was his mother's own sister, the daughter of a Moscow merchant, one Paparchin, who had died a bankrupt. But the elder brother of this same Paparchin, had been an eminent and very rich merchant. A year since it had so happened that his only two sons had both died within the same month. This sad event had so affected the old man that he, too, had died very shortly after. He was a widower, and had no relations left, excepting the prince's aunt, a poor woman living on charity, who was herself at the point of death from dropsy; but who had time, before she died, to set Salaskin to work to find her nephew, and to make her will bequeathing her newly-acquired fortune to him.

It appeared that neither the prince, nor the doctor with whom he lived in Switzerland, had thought of waiting for further communications; but the prince had started straight away with Salaskin's letter in his pocket.

"One thing I may tell you, for certain," concluded Ptitsin, addressing the prince, "that there is no question about the authenticity of this matter. Anything that Salaskin writes you as regards your unquestionable right to this inheritance, you may look upon as so much money in your pocket. I congratulate you, prince; you may receive a million and a half of roubles, perhaps more; I don't know. All I *do* know is that Paparchin was a very rich merchant indeed."

"Hurrah!" cried Lebedeff, in a drunken voice. "Hurrah for the last of the Muishkins!"

"My goodness me! and I gave him twenty-five roubles this morning as though he were a beggar," blurted out the general, half senseless with amazement. "Well, I congratulate you, I congratulate you!" And the general rose from his seat and solemnly embraced the prince. All came forward with congratulations; even those of Rogojin's party who had retreated into the next room, now crept softly back to look on. For the moment even Nastasia Philipovna was forgotten.

But gradually the consciousness crept back into the minds of each one present that the prince had just made her an offer of marriage. The situation had, therefore, become three times as fantastic as before.

Totski sat and shrugged his shoulders, bewildered. He was the only guest left sitting at this time; the others had thronged round the table in disorder, and were all talking at once.

It was generally agreed, afterwards, in recalling that evening, that from this moment Nastasia Philipovna seemed entirely to lose her senses. She continued to sit still in her place, looking around at her guests with a strange, bewildered expression, as though she were trying to collect her thoughts, and could not. Then she suddenly turned to the prince, and glared at him with frowning brows; but this only lasted one moment. Perhaps it suddenly struck her that all this was a jest, but his face seemed to reassure her. She reflected, and smiled again, vaguely.

"So I am really a princess," she whispered to herself, ironically, and glancing accidentally at Daria Alexeyevna's face, she burst out laughing.

"Ha, ha, ha!" she cried, "this is an unexpected climax, after all. I didn't expect this. What are you all standing up for, gentlemen? Sit down; congratulate me and the prince! Ferdishenko, just step out and order some more champagne, will you? Katia, Pasha," she added suddenly, seeing the servants at the door, "come here! I'm going to be married, did you hear? To the prince. He has a million and a half of roubles; he is Prince Muishkin, and has asked me to marry him. Here, prince, come and sit by me; and here comes the wine. Now then, ladies and gentlemen, where are your congratulations?"

"Hurrah!" cried a number of voices. A rush was made for the wine by Rogojin's followers, though, even among them, there seemed some sort of realization that the situation had changed. Rogojin stood and looked on, with an incredulous smile, screwing up one side of his mouth.

"Prince, my dear fellow, do remember what you are about," said the general, approaching Muishkin, and pulling him by the coat sleeve.

Nastasia Philipovna overheard the remark, and burst out laughing.

"No, no, general!" she cried. "You had better look out! I am the princess now, you know. The prince won't let you insult me. Afanasy Ivanovitch, why don't you congratulate me? I shall be able to sit at table with your new wife, now. Aha! you see what I gain by marrying a prince! A million and a half, and a prince, and an idiot into the bargain, they say. What better could I wish for? Life is only just about to commence for me in earnest. Rogojin, you are a little too late. Away with your paper parcel! I'm going to marry the prince; I'm richer than you are now."

But Rogojin understood how things were tending, at last. An inexpressibly painful expression came over his face. He wrung his hands; a groan made its way up from the depths of his soul.

"Surrender her, for God's sake!" he said to the prince.

All around burst out laughing.

"What? Surrender her to *you?*" cried Daria Alexeyevna. "To a fellow who comes and bargains for a wife like a moujik! The prince wishes to marry her, and you—"

"So do I, so do I! This moment, if I could! I'd give every farthing I have to do it."

"You drunken moujik," said Daria Alexeyevna, once more. "You ought to be kicked out of the place."

The laughter became louder than ever.

"Do you hear, prince?" said Nastasia Philipovna. "Do you hear how this moujik of a fellow goes on bargaining for your bride?"

"He is drunk," said the prince, quietly, "and he loves you very much."

"Won't you be ashamed, afterwards, to reflect that your wife very nearly ran away with Rogojin?"

"Oh, you were raving, you were in a fever; you are still half delirious."

"And won't you be ashamed when they tell you, afterwards, that your wife lived at Totski's expense so many years?"

"No; I shall not be ashamed of that. You did not so live by your own will."

"And you'll never reproach me with it?"

"Never."

"Take care, don't commit yourself for a whole lifetime."

"Nastasia Philipovna." said the prince, quietly, and with deep emotion, "I said before that I shall esteem your consent to be my wife as a great honour to myself, and shall consider that it is you who will honour me, not I you, by our marriage. You laughed at these words, and others around us laughed as well; I heard them. Very likely I expressed myself funnily, and I may have looked funny, but, for all that, I believe I understand where honour lies, and what I said was but the literal truth. You were about to ruin yourself just now, irrevocably; you would never have forgiven yourself for so doing afterwards; and yet, you are absolutely blameless. It is impossible that your life should be altogether ruined at your age. What matter that Rogojin came bargaining here, and that Gavrila Ardalionovitch would have deceived you if he could? Why do you continually remind us of these facts? I assure you once more that very few could find it in them to act as you have acted this day. As for your wish to go with Rogojin, that was simply the idea of a delirious and suffering brain. You are still quite feverish; you ought to be in bed, not here. You know quite well that if you had gone with Rogojin, you would have become a washer-woman next day, rather than stay with him. You are proud, Nastasia Philipovna, and perhaps you have really suffered so much that you imagine yourself to be a desperately guilty woman. You require a great deal of petting and looking after, Nastasia Philipovna, and I will do this. I saw your portrait this morning, and it seemed quite a familiar face to me; it seemed to me that the portrait-face was calling to me for help. I—I shall respect you all my life, Nastasia Philipovna," concluded the prince, as though suddenly recollecting himself, and blushing to think of the sort of company before whom he had said all this.

Ptitsin bowed his head and looked at the ground, overcome by a mixture of feelings. Totski muttered to himself: "He may be an idiot, but he knows that flattery is the best road to success here."

The prince observed Gania's eyes flashing at him, as though they would gladly annihilate him then and there.

"That's a kind-hearted man, if you like," said Daria Alexeyevna, whose wrath was quickly evaporating.

"A refined man, but—lost," murmured the general.

Totski took his hat and rose to go. He and the general exchanged glances, making a private arrangement, thereby, to leave the house together.

"Thank you, prince; no one has ever spoken to me like that before," began Nastasia Philipovna. "Men have always bargained for me, before this; and not a single respectable man has ever proposed to marry me. Do you hear, Afanasy Ivanovitch? What do *you* think of what the prince has just been saying? It was almost immodest, wasn't it? You, Rogojin, wait a moment, don't go yet! I see you don't intend to move however. Perhaps I may go with you yet. Where did you mean to take me to?"

"To Ekaterinhof," replied Lebedeff. Rogojin simply stood staring, with trembling lips, not daring to believe his ears. He was stunned, as though from a blow on the head.

"What are you thinking of, my dear Nastasia?" said Daria Alexeyevna in alarm. "What are you saying?" "You are not going mad, are you?"

Nastasia Philipovna burst out laughing and jumped up from the sofa.

"You thought I should accept this good child's invitation to ruin him, did you?" she cried. "That's Totski's way, not mine. He's fond of children. Come along, Rogojin, get your money ready! We won't talk about marrying just at this moment, but let's see the money at all events. Come! I may not marry you, either. I don't know. I suppose you thought you'd keep the money, if I did! Ha, ha, ha! nonsense! I have no sense of shame left. I tell you I have been Totski's concubine. Prince, you must marry Aglaya Ivanovna, not Nastasia Philipovna, or this fellow Ferdishenko will always be pointing the finger of scorn at you. You aren't afraid, I know; but I should always be afraid that I had ruined you, and that you would reproach me for it. As for what you say about my doing you honour by marrying you—well, Totski can tell you all about that. You had your eye on Aglaya, Gania, you know you had; and you might have married her if you had not come bargaining. You are all like this. You should choose, once for all, between disreputable women, and respectable ones, or you are sure to get mixed. Look at the general, how he's staring at me!"

"This is too horrible," said the general, starting to his feet. All were standing up now. Nastasia was absolutely beside herself.

"I am very proud, in spite of what I am," she continued. "You called me 'perfection' just now, prince. A nice sort of perfection to throw up a prince and a million and a half of roubles in order to be able to boast of the fact afterwards! What sort of a wife should I make for you, after all I have said? Afanasy Ivanovitch, do you observe I have really and truly thrown away a million of roubles? And you thought that I should consider your wretched seventy-five thousand, with Gania thrown in for a husband, a paradise of bliss! Take your seventy-five thousand back, sir; you did not reach the hundred thousand. Rogojin cut a better dash than you did. I'll console Gania myself; I have an idea about that. But now I must be off! I've been in prison for ten years. I'm free at last! Well, Rogojin, what are you waiting for? Let's get ready and go."

"Come along!" shouted Rogojin, beside himself with joy. "Hey! all of you fellows! Wine! Round with it! Fill the glasses!"

"Get away!" he shouted frantically, observing that Daria Alexeyevna was approaching to protest against Nastasia's conduct. "Get away, she's mine, everything's mine! She's a queen, get away!"

He was panting with ecstasy. He walked round and round Nastasia Philipovna and told everybody to "keep their distance."

All the Rogojin company were now collected in the drawing-room; some were drinking, some laughed and talked: all were in the highest and wildest spirits. Ferdishenko was doing his best to unite himself to them; the general and Totski again made an attempt to go. Gania, too stood hat in hand ready to go; but seemed to be unable to tear his eyes away from the scene before him.

"Get out, keep your distance!" shouted Rogojin.

"What are you shouting about there!" cried Nastasia "I'm not yours yet. I may kick you out for all you know I haven't taken your money yet; there it all is on the table. Here, give me over that packet! Is there a hundred thousand roubles in that one packet? Pfu! what abominable stuff it looks! Oh! nonsense, Daria Alexeyevna; you surely did not expect me to ruin *him?*" (indicating the prince). "Fancy him nursing me! Why, he needs a nurse himself! The general, there, will be his nurse now, you'll see. Here, prince, look here! Your bride is accepting money. What a disreputable woman she must be! And you wished to marry her! What are you crying about? Is it a bitter dose? Never mind, you shall laugh yet. Trust to time." (In spite of these words there were two large tears rolling down Nastasia's own cheeks.) "It's far better to think twice of it now than afterwards. Oh! you mustn't cry like that! There's Katia crying, too. What is it, Katia, dear? I shall leave you and Pasha a lot of things, I've laid them out for you already; but good-bye, now. I made an honest girl like you serve a low woman like myself. It's better so, prince, it is indeed. You'd begin to despise me afterwards—we should never be happy. Oh! you needn't swear, prince, I shan't believe you, you know. How foolish it would be, too! No, no; we'd better say good-bye and part friends. I am a bit of a dreamer myself, and I used to dream of you once. Very often during those five years down at his estate I used to dream and think, and I always imagined just such a good, honest, foolish fellow as you, one who should come and say to me: 'You are an innocent woman, Nastasia Philipovna, and I adore you.' I dreamt of you often. I used to think so much down there that I nearly went mad; and then this fellow here would come down. He would stay a couple of months out of the twelve, and disgrace and insult and deprave me, and then go; so that I longed to drown myself in the pond a thousand times over; but I did not dare do it. I hadn't the heart, and now—well, are you ready, Rogojin?"

"Ready—keep your distance, all of you!"

"We're all ready," said several of his friends. "The troikas [Sledges drawn by three horses abreast.] are at the door, bells and all."

Nastasia Philipovna seized the packet of bank-notes.

"Gania, I have an idea. I wish to recompense you—why should you lose all? Rogojin, would he crawl for three roubles as far as the Vassiliostrof?"

"Oh, wouldn't he just!"

"Well, look here, Gania. I wish to look into your heart once more, for the last time. You've worried me for the last three months—now it's my turn. Do you see this packet? It contains a hundred thousand roubles. Now, I'm going to throw it into the fire, here—before all these witnesses. As soon as the fire catches hold of it, you put your hands into the fire and pick it out—without gloves, you know. You must have bare hands, and you must turn your sleeves up. Pull it out, I say, and it's all yours. You may burn your fingers a little, of course; but then it's a hundred thousand roubles, remember—it won't take you long to lay hold of it and snatch it out. I shall so much admire you if you put your hands into the fire for my money. All here present may be witnesses that the whole packet of money is yours if you get it out. If you don't get it out, it shall burn. I will let no one else come; away—get away, all of you—it's my money! Rogojin has bought me with it. Is it my money, Rogojin?"

"Yes, my queen; it's your own money, my joy."

"Get away then, all of you. I shall do as I like with my own—don't meddle! Ferdishenko, make up the fire, quick!"

"Nastasia Philipovna, I can't; my hands won't obey me," said Ferdishenko, astounded and helpless with bewilderment.

"Nonsense," cried Nastasia Philipovna, seizing the poker and raking a couple of logs together. No sooner did a tongue of flame burst out than she threw the packet of notes upon it.

Everyone gasped; some even crossed themselves.

"She's mad—she's mad!" was the cry.

"Oughtn't-oughtn't we to secure her?" asked the general of Ptitsin, in a whisper; "or shall we send for the authorities? Why, she's mad, isn't she—isn't she, eh?"

"N-no, I hardly think she is actually mad," whispered Ptitsin, who was as white as his handkerchief, and trembling like a leaf. He could not take his eyes off the smouldering packet.

"She's mad surely, isn't she?" the general appealed to Totski.

"I told you she wasn't an ordinary woman," replied the latter, who was as pale as anyone.

"Oh, but, positively, you know—a hundred thousand roubles!"

"Goodness gracious! good heavens!" came from all quarters of the room.

All now crowded round the fire and thronged to see what was going on; everyone lamented and gave vent to exclamations of horror and woe. Some jumped up on chairs in order to get a better view. Daria Alexeyevna ran into the next room and whispered excitedly to Katia and Pasha. The beautiful German disappeared altogether.

"My lady! my sovereign!" lamented Lebedeff, falling on his knees before Nastasia Philipovna, and stretching out his hands towards the fire; "it's a hundred thousand roubles, it is indeed, I packed it up myself, I saw the money! My queen, let me get into the fire after it—say the word—I'll put my whole grey head into the fire for it! I have a poor lame wife and thirteen children. My father died of starvation last week. Nastasia Philipovna, Nastasia Philipovna!" The wretched little man wept, and groaned, and crawled towards the fire.

"Away, out of the way!" cried Nastasia. "Make room, all of you! Gania, what are you standing there for? Don't stand on ceremony. Put in your hand! There's your whole happiness smouldering away, look! Quick!"

But Gania had borne too much that day, and especially this evening, and he was not prepared for this last, quite unexpected trial.

The crowd parted on each side of him and he was left face to face with Nastasia Philipovna, three paces from her. She stood by the fire and waited, with her intent gaze fixed upon him.

Gania stood before her, in his evening clothes, holding his white gloves and hat in his hand, speechless and motionless, with arms folded and eyes fixed on the fire.

A silly, meaningless smile played on his white, death-like lips. He could not take his eyes off the smouldering packet; but it appeared that something new had come to birth in his soul—as though he were vowing to himself that he would bear this trial. He did not move from his place. In a few seconds it became evident to all that he did not intend to rescue the money.

"Hey! look at it, it'll burn in another minute or two!" cried Nastasia Philipovna. "You'll hang yourself afterwards, you know, if it does! I'm not joking."

The fire, choked between a couple of smouldering pieces of wood, had died down for the first few moments after the packet was thrown upon it. But a little tongue of fire now began to lick the paper from below, and soon, gathering courage, mounted the sides of the parcel, and crept around it. In another moment, the whole of it burst into flames, and the exclamations of woe and horror were redoubled.

"Nastasia Philipovna!" lamented Lebedeff again, straining towards the fireplace; but Rogojin dragged him away, and pushed him to the rear once more.

The whole of Rogojin's being was concentrated in one rapturous gaze of ecstasy. He could not take his eyes off Nastasia. He stood drinking her in, as it were. He was in the seventh heaven of delight.

"Oh, what a queen she is!" he ejaculated, every other minute, throwing out the remark for anyone who liked to catch it. "That's the sort of woman for me! Which of you would think of doing a thing like that, you blackguards, eh?" he yelled. He was hopelessly and wildly beside himself with ecstasy.

The prince watched the whole scene, silent and dejected.

"I'll pull it out with my teeth for one thousand," said Ferdishenko.

"So would I," said another, from behind, "with pleasure. Devil take the thing!" he added, in a tempest of despair, "it will all be burnt up in a minute—It's burning, it's burning!"

"It's burning, it's burning!" cried all, thronging nearer and nearer to the fire in their excitement.

"Gania, don't be a fool! I tell you for the last time."

"Get on, quick!" shrieked Ferdishenko, rushing wildly up to Gania, and trying to drag him to the fire by the sleeve of his coat. "Get it, you dummy, it's burning away fast! Oh—*damn* the thing!"

Gania hurled Ferdishenko from him; then he turned sharp round and made for the door. But he had not gone a couple of steps when he tottered and fell to the ground.

"He's fainted!" the cry went round.

"And the money's burning still," Lebedeff lamented.

"Burning for nothing," shouted others.

"Katia-Pasha! Bring him some water!" cried Nastasia Philipovna. Then she took the tongs and fished out the packet.

Nearly the whole of the outer covering was burned away, but it was soon evident that the contents were hardly touched. The packet had been wrapped in a threefold covering of newspaper, and the notes were safe. All breathed more freely.

"Some dirty little thousand or so may be touched," said Lebedeff, immensely relieved, "but there's very little harm done, after all."

"It's all his—the whole packet is for him, do you hear—all of you?" cried Nastasia Philipovna, placing the packet by the side of Gania. "He restrained himself, and didn't go after it; so his self-respect is greater than his thirst for money. All right—he'll come to directly—he must have the packet or he'll cut his throat afterwards. There! He's coming to himself. General, Totski, all of you, did you hear me? The money is all Gania's. I give it to him, fully conscious of my action, as recompense for—well, for anything he thinks best. Tell him so. Let it lie here beside him. Off we go, Rogojin! Goodbye, prince. I have seen a man for the first time in my life. Goodbye, Afanasy Ivanovitch—and thanks!"

The Rogojin gang followed their leader and Nastasia Philipovna to the entrance-hall, laughing and shouting and whistling.

In the hall the servants were waiting, and handed her her fur cloak. Martha, the cook, ran in from the kitchen. Nastasia kissed them all round.

"Are you really throwing us all over, little mother? Where, where are you going to? And on your birthday, too!" cried the four girls, crying over her and kissing her hands.

"I am going out into the world, Katia; perhaps I shall be a laundress. I don't know. No more of Afanasy Ivanovitch, anyhow. Give him my respects. Don't think badly of me, girls."

The prince hurried down to the front gate where the party were settling into the troikas, all the bells tinkling a merry accompaniment the while. The general caught him up on the stairs:

"Prince, prince!" he cried, seizing hold of his arm, "recollect yourself! Drop her, prince! You see what sort of a woman she is. I am speaking to you like a father."

The prince glanced at him, but said nothing. He shook himself free, and rushed on downstairs.

The general was just in time to see the prince take the first sledge he could get, and, giving the order to Ekaterinhof, start off in pursuit of the troikas. Then the general's fine grey horse dragged that worthy home, with some new thoughts, and some new hopes and calculations developing in his brain, and with the pearls in his pocket, for he had not forgotten to bring them along with him, being a man of business. Amid his new thoughts and ideas there came, once or twice, the image of Nastasia Philipovna. The general sighed.

"I'm sorry, really sorry," he muttered. "She's a ruined woman. Mad! mad! However, the prince is not for Nastasia Philipovna now,—perhaps it's as well."

Two more of Nastasia's guests, who walked a short distance together, indulged in high moral sentiments of a similar nature.

"Do you know, Totski, this is all very like what they say goes on among the Japanese?" said Ptitsin. "The offended party there, they say, marches off to his insulter and says to him, 'You insulted me, so I have come to rip myself open before your eyes;' and with these words he does actually rip his stomach open before his enemy, and considers, doubtless, that he is having all possible and necessary satisfaction and revenge. There are strange characters in the world, sir!"

"H'm! and you think there was something of this sort here, do you? Dear me—a very remarkable comparison, you know! But you must have observed, my dear Ptitsin, that I did all I possibly could. I could do no more than I did. And you must admit that there are some rare qualities in this woman. I felt I could not speak in that Bedlam, or I should have been tempted to cry out, when she reproached me, that she herself was my best justification. Such a woman could make anyone forget all reason—everything! Even that moujik, Rogojin, you saw, brought her a hundred thousand roubles! Of course, all that happened tonight was ephemeral, fantastic, unseemly—yet it lacked neither colour nor originality. My God! What might not have been made of such a character combined with such beauty! Yet in spite of all efforts—in spite of all education, even—all those gifts are wasted! She is an uncut diamond.... I have often said so."

And Afanasy Ivanovitch heaved a deep sigh.

PART II

CHAPTER I.

Two days after the strange conclusion to Nastasia Philipovna's birthday party, with the record of which we concluded the first part of this story, Prince Muishkin hurriedly left St. Petersburg for Moscow, in order to see after some business connected with the receipt of his unexpected fortune.

It was said that there were other reasons for his hurried departure; but as to this, and as to his movements in Moscow, and as to his prolonged absence from St. Petersburg, we are able to give very little information.

The prince was away for six months, and even those who were most interested in his destiny were able to pick up very little news about him all that while. True, certain rumours did reach his friends, but these were both strange and rare, and each one contradicted the last.

Of course the Epanchin family was much interested in his movements, though he had not had time to bid them farewell before his departure. The general, however, had had an opportunity of seeing him once or twice since the eventful evening, and had spoken very seriously with him; but though he had seen the prince, as I say, he told his family nothing about the circumstance. In fact, for a month or so after his departure it was considered not the thing to mention the prince's name in the Epanchin household. Only Mrs. Epanchin, at the commencement of this period, had announced that she had been "cruelly mistaken in the prince!" and a day or two after, she had added, evidently alluding to him, but not mentioning his name, that it was an unalterable characteristic of hers to be mistaken in people. Then once more, ten days later, after some passage of arms with one of her daughters, she had remarked sententiously. "We have had enough of mistakes. I shall be more careful in future!" However, it was impossible to avoid remarking that there was some sense of oppression in the household—something unspoken, but felt; something strained. All the members of the family wore frowning looks. The general was unusually busy; his family hardly ever saw him.

As to the girls, nothing was said openly, at all events; and probably very little in private. They were proud damsels, and were not always perfectly confidential even among themselves. But they understood each other thoroughly at the first word on all occasions; very often at the first glance, so that there was no need of much talking as a rule.

One fact, at least, would have been perfectly plain to an outsider, had any such person been on the spot; and that was, that the prince had made a very considerable impression upon the family, in spite of the fact that he had but once been inside the house, and then only for a short time. Of course, if analyzed, this impression might have proved to be nothing more than a feeling of curiosity; but be it what it might, there it undoubtedly was.

Little by little, the rumours spread about town became lost in a maze of uncertainty. It was said that some foolish young prince, name unknown, had suddenly come into possession of a gigantic fortune, and had married a French ballet dancer. This was contradicted, and the rumour circulated that it was a young merchant who had come into the enormous fortune and married the great ballet dancer, and that at the wedding the drunken young fool had burned seventy thousand roubles at a candle out of pure bravado.

However, all these rumours soon died down, to which circumstance certain facts largely contributed. For instance, the whole of the Rogojin troop had departed, with him at their head, for Moscow. This was exactly a week after a dreadful orgy at the Ekaterinhof gardens, where Nastasia Philipovna had been present. It became known that after this orgy Nastasia Philipovna had entirely disappeared, and that she had since been traced to Moscow; so that the exodus of the Rogojin band was found consistent with this report.

There were rumours current as to Gania, too; but circumstances soon contradicted these. He had fallen seriously ill, and his illness precluded his appearance in society, and even at business, for over a month. As soon as he had recovered, however, he threw up his situation in the public company under General Epanchin's direction, for some unknown reason, and the post was given to another. He never went near the Epanchins' house at all, and was exceedingly irritable and depressed.

Varvara Ardalionovna married Ptitsin this winter, and it was said that the fact of Gania's retirement from business was the ultimate cause of the marriage, since Gania was now not only unable to support his family, but even required help himself.

We may mention that Gania was no longer mentioned in the Epanchin household any more than the prince was; but that a certain circumstance in connection with the fatal evening at Nastasia's house became known to the general, and, in fact, to all the family the very next day. This fact was that Gania had come home that night, but had refused to go to bed. He had awaited the prince's return from Ekaterinhof with feverish impatience.

On the latter's arrival, at six in the morning, Gania had gone to him in his room, bringing with him the singed packet of money, which he had insisted that the prince should return to Nastasia Philipovna without delay. It was said that when Gania entered the prince's room, he came with anything but friendly feelings, and in a condition of despair and misery; but that after a short conversation, he had stayed on for a couple of hours with him, sobbing continuously and bitterly the whole time. They had parted upon terms of cordial friendship.

The Epanchins heard about this, as well as about the episode at Nastasia Philipovna's. It was strange, perhaps, that the facts should become so quickly, and fairly accurately, known. As far as Gania was concerned, it might have been supposed that the news had come through Varvara Ardalionovna, who had suddenly become a frequent visitor of the Epanchin girls, greatly to their mother's surprise. But though Varvara had seen fit, for some reason, to make friends with them, it was not likely that she would have talked to them about her brother. She had plenty of pride, in spite of the fact that in thus acting she was seeking intimacy with people who had practically shown her brother the door. She and the Epanchin girls had been acquainted in childhood, although of late they had met but rarely. Even now Varvara hardly ever appeared in the drawing-room, but would slip in by a back way. Lizabetha Prokofievna, who disliked Varvara, although she had a great respect for her mother, was much annoyed by this sudden intimacy, and put it down to the general "contrariness" of her daughters, who were "always on the lookout for some new way of opposing her." Nevertheless, Varvara continued her visits.

A month after Muishkin's departure, Mrs. Epanchin received a letter from her old friend Princess Bielokonski (who had lately left for Moscow), which letter put her into the greatest good humour. She did not divulge its contents either to her daughters or the general, but her conduct towards the former became affectionate in the extreme. She even made some sort of confession to them, but they were unable to understand what it was about. She actually relaxed towards the general a little— he had been long disgraced—and though she managed to quarrel with them all the next day, yet she soon came round, and from her general behaviour it was to be concluded that she had had good news of some sort, which she would like, but could not make up her mind, to disclose.

However, a week later she received another letter from the same source, and at last resolved to speak.

She solemnly announced that she had heard from old Princess Bielokonski, who had given her most comforting news about "that queer young prince." Her friend had hunted him up, and found that all was going well with him. He had since called in person upon her, making an extremely favourable impression, for the princess had received him each day since, and had introduced him into several good houses.

The girls could see that their mother concealed a great deal from them, and left out large pieces of the letter in reading it to them.

However, the ice was broken, and it suddenly became possible to mention the prince's name again. And again it became evident how very strong was the impression the young man had made in the household by his one visit there. Mrs. Epanchin was surprised at the effect which the news from Moscow had upon the girls, and they were no less surprised that after solemnly remarking that her most striking characteristic was "being mistaken in people" she should have troubled to obtain for the prince the favour and protection of so powerful an old lady as the Princess Bielokonski. As soon as the ice was thus broken, the general lost no time in showing that he, too, took the greatest interest in the subject. He admitted that he was interested, but said that it was merely in the business side of the question. It appeared that, in the interests of the prince, he had made arrangements in Moscow for a careful watch to be kept upon the prince's business affairs, and especially upon Salaskin.

All that had been said as to the prince being an undoubted heir to a fortune turned out to be perfectly true; but the fortune proved to be much smaller than was at first reported. The estate was considerably encumbered with debts; creditors turned up on all sides, and the prince, in spite of all advice and entreaty, insisted upon managing all matters of claim himself—which, of course, meant satisfying everybody all round, although half the claims were absolutely fraudulent.

Mrs. Epanchin confirmed all this. She said the princess had written to much the same effect, and added that there was no curing a fool. But it was plain, from her expression of face, how strongly she approved of this particular young fool's doings. In conclusion, the general observed that his wife took as great an interest in the prince as though he were her own son; and that she had commenced to be especially affectionate towards Aglaya was a self-evident fact.

All this caused the general to look grave and important. But, alas! this agreeable state of affairs very soon changed once more.

A couple of weeks went by, and suddenly the general and his wife were once more gloomy and silent, and the ice was as firm as ever. The fact was, the general, who had heard first, how Nastasia Philipovna had fled to Moscow and had been discovered there by Rogojin; that she had then disappeared once more, and been found again by Rogojin, and how after that she had almost promised to marry him, now received news that she had once more disappeared, almost on the very day fixed for her wedding, flying somewhere into the interior of Russia this time, and that Prince Muishkin had left all his affairs in the hands of Salaskin and disappeared also—but whether he was with Nastasia, or had only set off in search of her, was unknown.

Lizabetha Prokofievna received confirmatory news from the princess—and alas, two months after the prince's first departure from St. Petersburg, darkness and mystery once more enveloped his whereabouts and actions, and in the Epanchin family the ice of silence once more formed over the subject. Varia, however, informed the girls of what had happened, she having received the news from Ptitsin, who generally knew more than most people.

To make an end, we may say that there were many changes in the Epanchin household in the spring, so that it was not difficult to forget the prince, who sent no news of himself.

The Epanchin family had at last made up their minds to spend the summer abroad, all except the general, who could not waste time in "travelling for enjoyment," of course. This arrangement was brought about by the persistence of the girls, who insisted that they were never allowed to go abroad because their parents were too anxious to marry them off. Perhaps their parents had at last come to the conclusion that husbands might be found abroad, and that a summer's travel might bear fruit. The marriage between Alexandra and Totski had been broken off. Since the prince's departure from St. Petersburg no more had been said about it; the subject had been dropped without ceremony, much to the joy of Mrs. General, who, announced that she was "ready to cross herself with both hands" in gratitude for the escape. The general, however, regretted Totski for a long while. "Such a fortune!" he sighed, "and such a good, easy-going fellow!"

After a time it became known that Totski had married a French marquise, and was to be carried off by her to Paris, and then to Brittany.

"Oh, well," thought the general, "he's lost to us for good, now."

So the Epanchins prepared to depart for the summer.

But now another circumstance occurred, which changed all the plans once more, and again the intended journey was put off, much to the delight of the general and his spouse.

A certain Prince S—— arrived in St. Petersburg from Moscow, an eminent and honourable young man. He was one of those active persons who always find some good work with which to employ themselves. Without forcing himself upon the public notice, modest and unobtrusive, this young prince was concerned with much that happened in the world in general.

He had served, at first, in one of the civil departments, had then attended to matters connected with the local government of provincial towns, and had of late been a corresponding member of several important scientific societies. He was a man of excellent family and solid means, about thirty-five years of age.

Prince S—— made the acquaintance of the general's family, and Adelaida, the second girl, made a great impression upon him. Towards the spring he proposed to her, and she accepted him. The general and his wife were delighted. The journey abroad was put off, and the wedding was fixed for a day not very distant.

The trip abroad might have been enjoyed later on by Mrs. Epanchin and her two remaining daughters, but for another circumstance.

It so happened that Prince S—— introduced a distant relation of his own into the Epanchin family—one Evgenie Pavlovitch, a young officer of about twenty-eight years of age, whose conquests among the ladies in Moscow had been proverbial. This young gentleman no sooner set eyes on Aglaya than he became a frequent visitor at the house. He was witty, well-educated, and extremely wealthy, as the general very soon discovered. His past reputation was the only thing against him.

Nothing was said; there were not even any hints dropped; but still, it seemed better to the parents to say nothing more about going abroad this season, at all events. Aglaya herself perhaps was of a different opinion.

All this happened just before the second appearance of our hero upon the scene.

By this time, to judge from appearances, poor Prince Muishkin had been quite forgotten in St. Petersburg. If he had appeared suddenly among his acquaintances, he would have been received as one from the skies; but we must just glance at one more fact before we conclude this preface.

Colia Ivolgin, for some time after the prince's departure, continued his old life. That is, he went to school, looked after his father, helped Varia in the house, and ran her errands, and went frequently to see his friend, Hippolyte.

The lodgers had disappeared very quickly—Ferdishenko soon after the events at Nastasia Philipovna's, while the prince went to Moscow, as we know. Gania and his mother went to live with Varia and Ptitsin immediately after the latter's wedding, while the general was housed in a debtor's prison by reason of certain IOU's given to the captain's widow under the impression that they would never be formally used against him. This unkind action much surprised poor Ardalion Alexandrovitch, the victim, as he called himself, of an "unbounded trust in the nobility of the human heart."

When he signed those notes of hand he never dreamt that they would be a source of future trouble. The event showed that he was mistaken. "Trust in anyone after this! Have the least confidence in man or woman!" he cried in bitter tones, as he sat with his new friends in prison, and recounted to them his favourite stories of the siege of Kars, and the resuscitated soldier. On the whole, he accommodated himself very well to his new position. Ptitsin and Varia declared that he was in the right place, and Gania was of the same opinion. The only person who deplored his fate was poor Nina Alexandrovna, who wept bitter tears over him, to the great surprise of her household, and, though always in feeble health, made a point of going to see him as often as possible.

Since the general's "mishap," as Colia called it, and the marriage of his sister, the boy had quietly possessed himself of far more freedom. His relations saw little of him, for he rarely slept at home. He made many new friends; and was moreover, a frequent visitor at the debtor's prison, to which he invariably accompanied his mother. Varia, who used to be always correcting him, never spoke to him now on the subject of his frequent absences, and the whole household was surprised to see Gania, in spite of his depression, on quite friendly terms with his brother. This was something new, for Gania had been wont to look upon Colia as a kind of errand-boy, treating him with contempt, threatening to "pull his ears," and in general driving him almost wild with irritation. It seemed now that Gania really needed his brother, and the latter, for his part, felt as if he could forgive Gania much since he had returned the hundred thousand roubles offered to him by Nastasia Philipovna. Three months after the departure of the prince, the Ivolgin family discovered that Colia had made acquaintance with the Epanchins, and was on very friendly terms with the daughters. Varia heard of it first, though Colia had not asked her to introduce him. Little by little the family grew quite fond of him. Madame Epanchin at first looked on him with disdain, and received him coldly, but in a short time he grew to please her, because, as she said, he "was candid and no flatterer"—a very true description. From the first he put himself on an equality with his new friends, and though he sometimes read newspapers and books to the mistress of the house, it was simply because he liked to be useful.

One day, however, he and Lizabetha Prokofievna quarrelled seriously about the "woman question," in the course of a lively discussion on that burning subject. He told her that she was a tyrant, and that he would never set foot in her house again. It may seem incredible, but a day or two after, Madame Epanchin sent a servant with a note begging him to return, and Colia, without standing on his dignity, did so at once.

Aglaya was the only one of the family whose good graces he could not gain, and who always spoke to him haughtily, but it so happened that the boy one day succeeded in giving the proud maiden a surprise.

It was about Easter, when, taking advantage of a momentary tête-à-tête Colia handed Aglaya a letter, remarking that he "had orders to deliver it to her privately." She stared at him in amazement, but he did not wait to hear what she had to say, and went out. Aglaya broke the seal, and read as follows:

"Once you did me the honour of giving me your confidence. Perhaps you have quite forgotten me now! How is it that I am writing to you? I do not know; but I am conscious of an irresistible desire to remind you of my existence, especially you. How many times I have needed all three of you; but only you have dwelt always in my mind's eye. I need you—I need you very much. I will not write about myself. I have nothing to tell you. But I long for you to be happy. Are you happy? That is all I wished to say to you—Your brother,

"Pr. L. Muishkin."

On reading this short and disconnected note, Aglaya suddenly blushed all over, and became very thoughtful.

It would be difficult to describe her thoughts at that moment. One of them was, "Shall I show it to anyone?" But she was ashamed to show it. So she ended by hiding it in her table drawer, with a very strange, ironical smile upon her lips.

Next day, she took it out, and put it into a large book, as she usually did with papers which she wanted to be able to find easily. She laughed when, about a week later, she happened to notice the name of the book, and saw that it was Don Quixote, but it would be difficult to say exactly why.

I cannot say, either, whether she showed the letter to her sisters.

But when she had read it herself once more, it suddenly struck her that surely that conceited boy, Colia, had not been the one chosen correspondent of the prince all this while. She determined to ask him, and did so with an exaggerated show of carelessness. He informed her haughtily that though he had given the prince his permanent address when the latter left town, and had offered his services, the prince had never before given him any commission to perform, nor had he written until the following lines arrived, with Aglaya's letter. Aglaya took the note, and read it.

"*Dear Colia*,—Please be so kind as to give the enclosed sealed letter to Aglaya Ivanovna. Keep well—Ever your loving,

"Pr. L. Muishkin."

"It seems absurd to trust a little pepper-box like you," said Aglaya, as she returned the note, and walked past the "pepper-box" with an expression of great contempt.

This was more than Colia could bear. He had actually borrowed Gania's new green tie for the occasion, without saying why he wanted it, in order to impress her. He was very deeply mortified.

CHAPTER II.

It was the beginning of June, and for a whole week the weather in St. Petersburg had been magnificent. The Epanchins had a luxurious country-house at Pavlofsk, [One of the fashionable summer resorts near St. Petersburg.] and to this spot Mrs. Epanchin determined to proceed without further delay. In a couple of days all was ready, and the family had left town. A day or two after this removal to Pavlofsk, Prince Muishkin arrived in St. Petersburg by the morning train from Moscow. No one met him; but, as he stepped out of the carriage, he suddenly became aware of two strangely glowing eyes fixed upon him from among the crowd that met the train. On endeavouring to re-discover the eyes, and see to whom they belonged, he could find nothing to guide him. It must have been a hallucination. But the disagreeable impression remained, and without this, the prince was sad and thoughtful already, and seemed to be much preoccupied.

His cab took him to a small and bad hotel near the Litaynaya. Here he engaged a couple of rooms, dark and badly furnished. He washed and changed, and hurriedly left the hotel again, as though anxious to waste no time. Anyone who now saw him for the first time since he left Petersburg would judge that he had improved vastly so far as his exterior was concerned. His clothes certainly were very different; they were more fashionable, perhaps even too much so, and anyone inclined to mockery might have found something to smile at in his appearance. But what is there that people will not smile at?

The prince took a cab and drove to a street near the Nativity, where he soon discovered the house he was seeking. It was a small wooden villa, and he was struck by its attractive and clean appearance; it stood in a pleasant little garden, full of flowers. The windows looking on the street were open, and the sound of a voice, reading aloud or making a speech, came through them. It rose at times to a shout, and was interrupted occasionally by bursts of laughter.

Prince Muishkin entered the court-yard, and ascended the steps. A cook with her sleeves turned up to the elbows opened the door. The visitor asked if Mr. Lebedeff were at home.

"He is in there," said she, pointing to the salon.

The room had a blue wall-paper, and was well, almost pretentiously, furnished, with its round table, its divan, and its bronze clock under a glass shade. There was a narrow pier-glass against the wall, and a chandelier adorned with lustres hung by a bronze chain from the ceiling.

When the prince entered, Lebedeff was standing in the middle of the room, his back to the door. He was in his shirt-sleeves, on account of the extreme heat, and he seemed to have just reached the peroration of his speech, and was impressively beating his breast.

His audience consisted of a youth of about fifteen years of age with a clever face, who had a book in his hand, though he was not reading; a young lady of twenty, in deep mourning, stood near him with an infant in her arms; another girl of thirteen, also in black, was laughing loudly, her mouth wide open; and on the sofa lay a handsome young man, with black hair and eyes, and a suspicion of beard and whiskers. He frequently interrupted the speaker and argued with him, to the great delight of the others.

"Lukian Timofeyovitch! Lukian Timofeyovitch! Here's someone to see you! Look here!... a gentleman to speak to you!... Well, it's not my fault!" and the cook turned and went away red with anger.

Lebedeff started, and at sight of the prince stood like a statue for a moment. Then he moved up to him with an ingratiating smile, but stopped short again.

"Prince! ex-ex-excellency!" he stammered. Then suddenly he ran towards the girl with the infant, a movement so unexpected by her that she staggered and fell back, but next moment he was threatening the other child, who was standing, still laughing, in the doorway. She screamed, and ran towards the kitchen. Lebedeff stamped his foot angrily; then, seeing the prince regarding him with amazement, he murmured apologetically—"Pardon to show respect!... he-he!"

"You are quite wrong..." began the prince.

"At once... at once... in one moment!"

He rushed like a whirlwind from the room, and Muishkin looked inquiringly at the others.

They were all laughing, and the guest joined in the chorus.

"He has gone to get his coat," said the boy.

"How annoying!" exclaimed the prince. "I thought... Tell me, is he..."

"You think he is drunk?" cried the young man on the sofa. "Not in the least. He's only had three or four small glasses, perhaps five; but what is that? The usual thing!"

As the prince opened his mouth to answer, he was interrupted by the girl, whose sweet face wore an expression of absolute frankness.

"He never drinks much in the morning; if you have come to talk business with him, do it now. It is the best time. He sometimes comes back drunk in the evening; but just now he passes the greater part of the evening in tears, and reads passages of Holy Scripture aloud, because our mother died five weeks ago."

"No doubt he ran off because he did not know what to say to you," said the youth on the divan. "I bet he is trying to cheat you, and is thinking how best to do it."

Just then Lebedeff returned, having put on his coat.

"Five weeks!" said he, wiping his eyes. "Only five weeks! Poor orphans!"

"But why wear a coat in holes," asked the girl, "when your new one is hanging behind the door? Did you not see it?"

"Hold your tongue, dragon-fly!" he scolded. "What a plague you are!" He stamped his foot irritably, but she only laughed, and answered:

"Are you trying to frighten me? I am not Tania, you know, and I don't intend to run away. Look, you are waking Lubotchka, and she will have convulsions again. Why do you shout like that?"

"Well, well! I won't again," said the master of the house, his anxiety getting the better of his temper. He went up to his daughter, and looked at the child in her arms, anxiously making the sign of the cross over her three times. "God bless her! God bless her!" he cried with emotion. "This little creature is my daughter Luboff," addressing the prince. "My wife, Helena, died—at her birth; and this is my big daughter Vera, in mourning, as you see; and this, this, oh, this," pointing to the young man on the divan...

"Well, go on! never mind me!" mocked the other. "Don't be afraid!"

"Excellency! Have you read that account of the murder of the Zemarin family, in the newspaper?" cried Lebedeff, all of a sudden.

"Yes," said Muishkin, with some surprise.

"Well, that is the murderer! It is he—in fact—"

"What do you mean?" asked the visitor.

"I am speaking allegorically, of course; but he will be the murderer of a Zemarin family in the future. He is getting ready. ..."

They all laughed, and the thought crossed the prince's mind that perhaps Lebedeff was really trifling in this way because he foresaw inconvenient questions, and wanted to gain time.

"He is a traitor! a conspirator!" shouted Lebedeff, who seemed to have lost all control over himself. "A monster! a slanderer! Ought I to treat him as a nephew, the son of my sister Anisia?"

"Oh! do be quiet! You must be drunk! He has taken it into his head to play the lawyer, prince, and he practices speechifying, and is always repeating his eloquent pleadings to his children. And who do you think was his last client? An old woman who had been robbed of five hundred roubles, her all, by some rogue of a usurer, besought him to take up her case, instead of which he defended the usurer himself, a Jew named Zeidler, because this Jew promised to give him fifty roubles...."

"It was to be fifty if I won the case, only five if I lost," interrupted Lebedeff, speaking in a low tone, a great contrast to his earlier manner.

"Well! naturally he came to grief: the law is not administered as it used to be, and he only got laughed at for his pains. But he was much pleased with himself in spite of that. 'Most learned judge!' said he, 'picture this unhappy man, crippled by age and infirmities, who gains his living by honourable toil—picture him, I repeat, robbed of his all, of his last mouthful; remember, I entreat you, the words of that learned legislator, "Let mercy and justice alike rule the courts of law."' Now, would you believe it, excellency, every morning he recites this speech to us from beginning to end, exactly as he spoke it before the magistrate. To-day we have heard it for the fifth time. He was just starting again when you arrived, so much does he admire it. He is now preparing to undertake another case. I think, by the way, that you are Prince Muishkin? Colia tells me you are the cleverest man he has ever known...."

"The cleverest in the world," interrupted his uncle hastily.

"I do not pay much attention to that opinion," continued the young man calmly. "Colia is very fond of you, but he," pointing to Lebedeff, "is flattering you. I can assure you I have no intention of flattering you, or anyone else, but at least you have some common-sense. Well, will you judge between us? Shall we ask the prince to act as arbitrator?" he went on, addressing his uncle.

"I am so glad you chanced to come here, prince."

"I agree," said Lebedeff, firmly, looking round involuntarily at his daughter, who had come nearer, and was listening attentively to the conversation.

"What is it all about?" asked the prince, frowning. His head ached, and he felt sure that Lebedeff was trying to cheat him in some way, and only talking to put off the explanation that he had come for.

"I will tell you all the story. I am his nephew; he did speak the truth there, although he is generally telling lies. I am at the University, and have not yet finished my course. I mean to do so, and I shall, for I have a determined character. I must, however, find something to do for the present, and therefore I have got employment on the railway at twenty-four roubles a month. I admit that my uncle has helped me once or twice before. Well, I had twenty roubles in my pocket, and I gambled them away. Can you believe that I should be so low, so base, as to lose money in that way?"

"And the man who won it is a rogue, a rogue whom you ought not to have paid!" cried Lebedeff.

"Yes, he is a rogue, but I was obliged to pay him," said the young man. "As to his being a rogue, he is assuredly that, and I am not saying it because he beat you. He is an ex-lieutenant, prince, dismissed from the service, a teacher of boxing, and one of Rogojin's followers. They are all lounging about the pavements now that Rogojin has turned them off. Of course, the worst of it is that, knowing he was a rascal, and a card-sharper, I none the less played palki with him, and risked my last rouble. To tell the truth, I thought to myself, 'If I lose, I will go to my uncle, and I am sure he will not refuse to help me.' Now that was base—cowardly and base!"

"That is so," observed Lebedeff quietly; "cowardly and base."

"Well, wait a bit, before you begin to triumph," said the nephew viciously; for the words seemed to irritate him. "He is delighted! I came to him here and told him everything: I acted honourably, for I did not excuse myself. I spoke most severely of my conduct, as everyone here can witness. But I must smarten myself up before I take up my new post, for I am really like a tramp. Just look at my boots! I cannot possibly appear like this, and if I am not at the bureau at the time appointed, the job will be given to someone else; and I shall have to try for another. Now I only beg for fifteen roubles, and I give my word that I will never ask him for anything again. I am also ready to promise to repay my debt in three months' time, and I will keep my word, even if I have to live on bread and water. My salary will amount to seventy-five roubles in three months. The sum I now ask, added to what I have borrowed already, will make a total of about thirty-five roubles, so you see I shall have enough to pay him and confound him! if he wants interest, he shall have that, too! Haven't I always paid back the money he lent me before? Why should he be so mean now? He grudges my having paid that lieutenant; there can be no other reason! That's the kind he is—a dog in the manger!"

"And he won't go away!" cried Lebedeff. "He has installed himself here, and here he remains!"

"I have told you already, that I will not go away until I have got what I ask. Why are you smiling, prince? You look as if you disapproved of me."

"I am not smiling, but I really think you are in the wrong, somewhat," replied Muishkin, reluctantly.

"Don't shuffle! Say plainly that you think that I am quite wrong, without any 'somewhat'! Why 'somewhat'?"

"I will say you are quite wrong, if you wish."

"If I wish! That's good, I must say! Do you think I am deceived as to the flagrant impropriety of my conduct? I am quite aware that his money is his own, and that my action—is much like an attempt at extortion. But you–you don't know what life is! If people don't learn by experience, they never understand. They must be taught. My intentions are perfectly honest; on my conscience he will lose nothing, and I will pay back the money with interest. Added to which he has had the moral satisfaction of seeing me disgraced. What does he want more? and what is he good for if he never helps anyone? Look what he does himself! just ask him about his dealings with others, how he deceives people! How did he manage to buy this house? You may cut off my head if he has not let you in for something—and if he is not trying to cheat you again. You are smiling. You don't believe me?"

"It seems to me that all this has nothing to do with your affairs," remarked the prince.

"I have lain here now for three days," cried the young man without noticing, "and I have seen a lot! Fancy! he suspects his daughter, that angel, that orphan, my cousin—he suspects her, and every evening he searches her room, to see if she has a lover hidden in it! He comes here too on tiptoe, creeping softly—oh, so softly—and looks under the sofa—my bed, you know. He is mad with suspicion, and sees a thief in every corner. He runs about all night long; he was up at least seven times last night, to satisfy himself that the windows and doors were barred, and to peep into the oven. That man who appears in court for scoundrels, rushes in here in the night and prays, lying prostrate, banging his head on the ground by the half-hour—and for whom do you think he prays? Who are the sinners figuring in his drunken petitions? I have heard him with my own ears praying for the repose of the soul of the Countess du Barry! Colia heard it too. He is as mad as a March hare!"

"You hear how he slanders me, prince," said Lebedeff, almost beside himself with rage. "I may be a drunkard, an evil-doer, a thief, but at least I can say one thing for myself. He does not know—how should he, mocker that he is?—that when he came into the world it was I who washed him, and dressed him in his swathing-bands, for my sister Anisia had lost her husband, and was in great poverty. I was very little better off than she, but I sat up night after night with her, and nursed both mother and child; I used to go downstairs and steal wood for them from the house-porter. How often did I sing him to sleep when I was half dead with hunger! In short, I was more than a father to him, and now—now he jeers at me! Even if I did cross myself, and pray for the repose of the soul of the Comtesse du Barry, what does it matter? Three days ago, for the first time in my life, I read her biography in an historical dictionary. Do you know who she was? You there!" addressing his nephew. "Speak! do you know?"

"Of course no one knows anything about her but you," muttered the young man in a would-be jeering tone.

"She was a Countess who rose from shame to reign like a Queen. An Empress wrote to her, with her own hand, as 'Ma chère cousine.' At a lever-du-roi one morning (do you know what a lever-du-roi was?)—a Cardinal, a Papal legate, offered to put on her stockings; a high and holy person like that looked on it as an honour! Did you know this? I see by your expression that you did not! Well, how did she die? Answer!"

"Oh! do stop—you are too absurd!"

"This is how she died. After all this honour and glory, after having been almost a Queen, she was guillotined by that butcher, Samson. She was quite innocent, but it had to be done, for the satisfaction of the fishwives of Paris. She was so terrified, that she did not understand what was happening. But when Samson seized her head, and pushed her under the knife with his foot, she cried out: 'Wait a moment! wait a moment, monsieur!' Well, because of that moment of bitter suffering, perhaps the Saviour will pardon her other faults, for one cannot imagine a greater agony. As I read the story my heart bled for her. And what does it matter to you, little worm, if I implored the Divine mercy for her, great sinner as she was, as I said my evening prayer? I might have done it because I doubted if anyone had ever crossed himself for her sake before. It may be that in the other world she will rejoice to think that a sinner like herself has cried to heaven for the salvation of her soul. Why are you laughing? You believe nothing, atheist! And your story was not even correct! If you had listened to what I was saying, you would have heard that I did not only pray for the Comtesse du Barry. I said, 'Oh Lord! give rest to the soul of that great sinner, the Comtesse du Barry, and to all unhappy ones like her.' You see that is quite a different thing, for how many sinners there are, how many women, who have passed through the trials of this life, are now suffering and groaning in purgatory! I prayed for you, too, in spite of your insolence and impudence, also for your fellows, as it seems that you claim to know how I pray..."

"Oh! that's enough in all conscience! Pray for whom you choose, and the devil take them and you! We have a scholar here; you did not know that, prince?" he continued, with a sneer. "He reads all sorts of books and memoirs now."

"At any rate, your uncle has a kind heart," remarked the prince, who really had to force himself to speak to the nephew, so much did he dislike him.

"Oh, now you are going to praise him! He will be set up! He puts his hand on his heart, and he is delighted! I never said he was a man without heart, but he is a rascal—that's the pity of it. And then, he is addicted to drink, and his mind is unhinged, like that of most people who have taken more than is good for them for years. He loves his children—oh, I know that well enough! He respected my aunt, his late wife... and he even has a sort of affection for me. He has remembered me in his will."

"I shall leave you nothing!" exclaimed his uncle angrily.

"Listen to me, Lebedeff," said the prince in a decided voice, turning his back on the young man. "I know by experience that when you choose, you can be business-like... I have very little time to spare, and if you... By the way—excuse me—what is your Christian name? I have forgotten it."

"Ti-Ti-Timofey."

"And?"

"Lukianovitch."

Everyone in the room began to laugh.

"He is telling lies!" cried the nephew. "Even now he cannot speak the truth. He is not called Timofey Lukianovitch, prince, but Lukian Timofeyovitch. Now do tell us why you must needs lie about it? Lukian or Timofey, it is all the same to you, and what difference can it make to the prince? He tells lies without the least necessity, simply by force of habit, I assure you."

"Is that true?" said the prince impatiently.

"My name really is Lukian Timofeyovitch," acknowledged Lebedeff, lowering his eyes, and putting his hand on his heart.

"Well, for God's sake, what made you say the other?"

"To humble myself," murmured Lebedeff.

"What on earth do you mean? Oh I if only I knew where Colia was at this moment!" cried the prince, standing up, as if to go.

"I can tell you all about Colia," said the young man

"Oh! no, no!" said Lebedeff, hurriedly.

"Colia spent the night here, and this morning went after his father, whom you let out of prison by paying his debts—Heaven only knows why! Yesterday the general promised to come and lodge here, but he did not appear. Most probably he slept at the hotel close by. No doubt Colia is there, unless he has gone to Pavlofsk to see the Epanchins. He had a little money, and was intending to go there yesterday. He must be either at the hotel or at Pavlofsk."

"At Pavlofsk! He is at Pavlofsk, undoubtedly!" interrupted Lebedeff.... "But come—let us go into the garden—we will have coffee there...." And Lebedeff seized the prince's arm, and led him from the room. They went across the yard, and found themselves in a delightful little garden with the trees already in their summer dress of green, thanks to the unusually fine weather. Lebedeff invited his guest to sit down on a green seat before a table of the same colour fixed in the earth, and took a seat facing him. In a few minutes the coffee appeared, and the prince did not refuse it. The host kept his eyes fixed on Muishkin, with an expression of passionate servility.

"I knew nothing about your home before," said the prince absently, as if he were thinking of something else.

"Poor orphans," began Lebedeff, his face assuming a mournful air, but he stopped short, for the other looked at him inattentively, as if he had already forgotten his own remark. They waited a few minutes in silence, while Lebedeff sat with his eyes fixed mournfully on the young man's face.

"Well!" said the latter, at last rousing himself. "Ah! yes! You know why I came, Lebedeff. Your letter brought me. Speak! Tell me all about it."

The clerk, rather confused, tried to say something, hesitated, began to speak, and again stopped. The prince looked at him gravely.

"I think I understand, Lukian Timofeyovitch: you were not sure that I should come. You did not think I should start at the first word from you, and you merely wrote to relieve your conscience. However, you see now that I have come, and I have had enough of trickery. Give up serving, or trying to serve, two masters. Rogojin has been here these three weeks. Have you managed to sell her to him as you did before? Tell me the truth."

"He discovered everything, the monster... himself......"

"Don't abuse him; though I dare say you have something to complain of...."

"He beat me, he thrashed me unmercifully!" replied Lebedeff vehemently. "He set a dog on me in Moscow, a bloodhound, a terrible beast that chased me all down the street."

"You seem to take me for a child, Lebedeff. Tell me, is it a fact that she left him while they were in Moscow?"

"Yes, it is a fact, and this time, let me tell you, on the very eve of their marriage! It was a question of minutes when she slipped off to Petersburg. She came to me directly she arrived—'Save me, Lukian! find me some refuge, and say nothing to the prince!' She is afraid of you, even more than she is of him, and in that she shows her wisdom!" And Lebedeff slily put his finger to his brow as he said the last words.

"And now it is you who have brought them together again?"

"Excellency, how could I, how could I prevent it?"

"That will do. I can find out for myself. Only tell me, where is she now? At his house? With him?"

"Oh no! Certainly not! 'I am free,' she says; you know how she insists on that point. 'I am entirely free.' She repeats it over and over again. She is living in Petersburgskaia, with my sister-in-law, as I told you in my letter."

"She is there at this moment?"

"Yes, unless she has gone to Pavlofsk: the fine weather may have tempted her, perhaps, into the country, with Daria Alexeyevna. 'I am quite free,' she says. Only yesterday she boasted of her freedom to Nicolai Ardalionovitch—a bad sign," added Lebedeff, smiling.

"Colia goes to see her often, does he not?"

"He is a strange boy, thoughtless, and inclined to be indiscreet."

"Is it long since you saw her?"

"I go to see her every day, every day."

"Then you were there yesterday?"

"N–no: I have not been these three last days."

"It is a pity you have taken too much wine, Lebedeff I want to ask you something... but..."

"All right! all right! I am not drunk," replied the clerk, preparing to listen.

"Tell me, how was she when you left her?"

"She is a woman who is seeking..."

"Seeking?"

"She seems always to be searching about, as if she had lost something. The mere idea of her coming marriage disgusts her; she looks on it as an insult. She cares as much for *him* as for a piece of orange-peel—not more. Yet I am much mistaken if she does not look on him with fear and trembling. She forbids his name to be mentioned before her, and they only meet when unavoidable. He understands, well enough! But it must be gone through. She is restless, mocking, deceitful, violent...."

"Deceitful and violent?"

"Yes, violent. I can give you a proof of it. A few days ago she tried to pull my hair because I said something that annoyed her. I tried to soothe her by reading the Apocalypse aloud."

"What?" exclaimed the prince, thinking he had not heard aright.

"By reading the Apocalypse. The lady has a restless imagination, he-he! She has a liking for conversation on serious subjects, of any kind; in fact they please her so much, that it flatters her to discuss them. Now for fifteen years at least I have studied the Apocalypse, and she agrees with me in thinking that the present is the epoch represented by the third horse, the black one whose rider holds a measure in his hand. It seems to me that everything is ruled by measure in our century; all men are clamouring for their rights; 'a measure of wheat for a penny, and three measures of barley for a penny.' But, added to this, men desire freedom of mind and body, a pure heart, a healthy life, and all God's good gifts. Now by pleading their rights alone, they will never attain all this, so the white horse, with his rider Death, comes next, and is followed by Hell. We talked about this matter when we met, and it impressed her very much."

"Do you believe all this?" asked Muishkin, looking curiously at his companion.

"I both believe it and explain it. I am but a poor creature, a beggar, an atom in the scale of humanity. Who has the least respect for Lebedeff? He is a target for all the world, the butt of any fool who chooses to kick him. But in interpreting revelation I am the equal of anyone, great as he may be! Such is the power of the mind and the spirit. I have made a lordly personage tremble, as he sat in his armchair... only by talking to him of things concerning the spirit. Two years ago, on Easter Eve, His Excellency Nil Alexeyovitch, whose subordinate I was then, wished to hear what I had to say, and sent a message by Peter Zakkaritch to ask me to go to his private room. 'They tell me you expound the prophecies relating to Antichrist,' said he, when we were alone. 'Is that so?' 'Yes,' I answered unhesitatingly, and I began to give some comments on the Apostle's allegorical vision. At first he smiled, but when we reached the numerical computations and correspondences, he trembled, and turned pale. Then he begged me to close the book, and sent me away, promising to put my name on the reward list. That took place as I said on the eve of Easter, and eight days later his soul returned to God."

"What?"

"It is the truth. One evening after dinner he stumbled as he stepped out of his carriage. He fell, and struck his head on the curb, and died immediately. He was seventy-three years of age, and had a red face, and white hair; he deluged himself with scent, and was always smiling like a child. Peter Zakkaritch recalled my interview with him, and said, '*you foretold his death.*'"

The prince rose from his seat, and Lebedeff, surprised to see his guest preparing to go so soon, remarked: "You are not interested?" in a respectful tone.

"I am not very well, and my head aches. Doubtless the effect of the journey," replied the prince, frowning.

"You should go into the country," said Lebedeff timidly.

The prince seemed to be considering the suggestion.

"You see, I am going into the country myself in three days, with my children and belongings. The little one is delicate; she needs change of air; and during our absence this house will be done up. I am going to Pavlofsk."

"You are going to Pavlofsk too?" asked the prince sharply. "Everybody seems to be going there. Have you a house in that neighbourhood?"

"I don't know of many people going to Pavlofsk, and as for the house, Ivan Ptitsin has let me one of his villas rather cheaply. It is a pleasant place, lying on a hill surrounded by trees, and one can live there for a mere song. There is good music to be heard, so no wonder it is popular. I shall stay in the lodge. As to the villa itself..."

"Have you let it?"

"N-no—not exactly."

"Let it to me," said the prince.

Now this was precisely what Lebedeff had made up his mind to do in the last three minutes. Not that he had any difficulty in finding a tenant; in fact the house was occupied at present by a chance visitor, who had told Lebedeff that he would perhaps take it for the summer months. The clerk knew very well that this "*perhaps*" meant "*certainly*," but as he thought he could make more out of a tenant like the prince, he felt justified in speaking vaguely about the present inhabitant's intentions. "This is quite a coincidence," thought he, and when the subject of price was mentioned, he made a gesture with his hand, as if to waive away a question of so little importance.

"Oh well, as you like!" said Muishkin. "I will think it over. You shall lose nothing!"

They were walking slowly across the garden.

"But if you... I could..." stammered Lebedeff, "if... if you please, prince, tell you something on the subject which would interest you, I am sure." He spoke in wheedling tones, and wriggled as he walked along.

Muishkin stopped short.

"Daria Alexeyevna also has a villa at Pavlofsk."

"Well?"

"A certain person is very friendly with her, and intends to visit her pretty often."

"Well?"

"Aglaya Ivanovna..."

"Oh stop, Lebedeff!" interposed Muishkin, feeling as if he had been touched on an open wound. "That... that has nothing to do with me. I should like to know when you are going to start. The sooner the better as far as I am concerned, for I am at an hotel."

They had left the garden now, and were crossing the yard on their way to the gate.

"Well, leave your hotel at once and come here; then we can all go together to Pavlofsk the day after tomorrow."

"I will think about it," said the prince dreamily, and went off.

The clerk stood looking after his guest, struck by his sudden absent-mindedness. He had not even remembered to say goodbye, and Lebedeff was the more surprised at the omission, as he knew by experience how courteous the prince usually was.

CHAPTER III.

It was now close on twelve o'clock.

The prince knew that if he called at the Epanchins' now he would only find the general, and that the latter might probably carry him straight off to Pavlofsk with him; whereas there was one visit he was most anxious to make without delay.

So at the risk of missing General Epanchin altogether, and thus postponing his visit to Pavlofsk for a day, at least, the prince decided to go and look for the house he desired to find.

The visit he was about to pay was, in some respects, a risky one. He was in two minds about it, but knowing that the house was in the Gorohovaya, not far from the Sadovaya, he determined to go in that direction, and to try to make up his mind on the way.

Arrived at the point where the Gorohovaya crosses the Sadovaya, he was surprised to find how excessively agitated he was. He had no idea that his heart could beat so painfully.

One house in the Gorohovaya began to attract his attention long before he reached it, and the prince remembered afterwards that he had said to himself: "That is the house, I'm sure of it." He came up to it quite curious to discover whether he had guessed right, and felt that he would be disagreeably impressed to find that he had actually done so. The house was a large gloomy-looking structure, without the slightest claim to architectural beauty, in colour a dirty green. There are a few of these old houses, built towards the end of the last century, still standing in that part of St. Petersburg, and showing little change from their original form and colour. They are solidly built, and are remarkable for the thickness of their walls, and for the fewness of their windows, many of which are covered by gratings. On the ground-floor there is usually a money-changer's shop, and the owner lives over it. Without as well as within, the houses seem inhospitable and mysterious—an impression which is difficult to explain, unless it has something to do with the actual architectural style. These houses are almost exclusively inhabited by the merchant class.

Arrived at the gate, the prince looked up at the legend over it, which ran:

"House of Rogojin, hereditary and honourable citizen."

He hesitated no longer; but opened the glazed door at the bottom of the outer stairs and made his way up to the second storey. The place was dark and gloomy-looking; the walls of the stone staircase were painted a dull red. Rogojin and his mother and brother occupied the whole of the second floor. The servant who opened the door to Muishkin led him, without taking his name, through several rooms and up and down many steps until they arrived at a door, where he knocked.

Parfen Rogojin opened the door himself.

On seeing the prince he became deadly white, and apparently fixed to the ground, so that he was more like a marble statue than a human being. The prince had expected some surprise, but Rogojin evidently considered his visit an impossible and miraculous event. He stared with an expression almost of terror, and his lips twisted into a bewildered smile.

"Parfen! perhaps my visit is ill-timed. I—I can go away again if you like," said Muishkin at last, rather embarrassed.

"No, no; it's all right, come in," said Parfen, recollecting himself.

They were evidently on quite familiar terms. In Moscow they had had many occasions of meeting; indeed, some few of those meetings were but too vividly impressed upon their memories. They had not met now, however, for three months.

The deathlike pallor, and a sort of slight convulsion about the lips, had not left Rogojin's face. Though he welcomed his guest, he was still obviously much disturbed. As he invited the prince to sit down near the table, the latter happened to turn towards him, and was startled by the strange expression on his face. A painful recollection flashed into his mind. He stood for a time, looking straight at Rogojin, whose eyes seemed to blaze like fire. At last Rogojin smiled, though he still looked agitated and shaken.

"What are you staring at me like that for?" he muttered. "Sit down."

The prince took a chair.

"Parfen," he said, "tell me honestly, did you know that I was coming to Petersburg or no?"

"Oh, I supposed you were coming," the other replied, smiling sarcastically, "and I was right in my supposition, you see; but how was I to know that you would come *today?*"

A certain strangeness and impatience in his manner impressed the prince very forcibly.

"And if you had known that I was coming today, why be so irritated about it?" he asked, in quiet surprise.

"Why did you ask me?"

"Because when I jumped out of the train this morning, two eyes glared at me just as yours did a moment since."

"Ha! and whose eyes may they have been?" said Rogojin, suspiciously. It seemed to the prince that he was trembling.

"I don't know; I thought it was a hallucination. I often have hallucinations nowadays. I feel just as I did five years ago when my fits were about to come on."

"Well, perhaps it was a hallucination, I don't know," said Parfen.

He tried to give the prince an affectionate smile, and it seemed to the latter as though in this smile of his something had broken, and that he could not mend it, try as he would.

"Shall you go abroad again then?" he asked, and suddenly added, "Do you remember how we came up in the train from Pskoff together? You and your cloak and leggings, eh?"

And Rogojin burst out laughing, this time with unconcealed malice, as though he were glad that he had been able to find an opportunity for giving vent to it.

"Have you quite taken up your quarters here?" asked the prince

"Yes, I'm at home. Where else should I go to?"

"We haven't met for some time. Meanwhile I have heard things about you which I should not have believed to be possible."

"What of that? People will say anything," said Rogojin drily.

"At all events, you've disbanded your troop—and you are living in your own house instead of being fast and loose about the place; that's all very good. Is this house all yours, or joint property?"

"It is my mother's. You get to her apartments by that passage."

"Where's your brother?"

"In the other wing."

"Is he married?"

"Widower. Why do you want to know all this?"

The prince looked at him, but said nothing. He had suddenly relapsed into musing, and had probably not heard the question at all. Rogojin did not insist upon an answer, and there was silence for a few moments.

"I guessed which was your house from a hundred yards off," said the prince at last.

"Why so?"

"I don't quite know. Your house has the aspect of yourself and all your family; it bears the stamp of the Rogojin life; but ask me why I think so, and I can tell you nothing. It is nonsense, of course. I am nervous about this kind of thing troubling me so much. I had never before imagined what sort of a house you would live in, and yet no sooner did I set eyes on this one than I said to myself that it must be yours."

"Really!" said Rogojin vaguely, not taking in what the prince meant by his rather obscure remarks.

The room they were now sitting in was a large one, lofty but dark, well furnished, principally with writing-tables and desks covered with papers and books. A wide sofa covered with red morocco evidently served Rogojin for a bed. On the table beside which the prince had been invited to seat himself lay some books; one containing a marker where the reader had left off, was a volume of Solovieff's History. Some oil-paintings in worn gilded frames hung on the walls, but it was impossible to make out what subjects they represented, so blackened were they by smoke and age. One, a life-sized portrait, attracted the prince's attention. It showed a man of about fifty, wearing a long riding-coat of German cut. He had two medals on his breast; his beard was white, short and thin; his face yellow and wrinkled, with a sly, suspicious expression in the eyes.

"That is your father, is it not?" asked the prince.

"Yes, it is," replied Rogojin with an unpleasant smile, as if he had expected his guest to ask the question, and then to make some disagreeable remark.

"Was he one of the Old Believers?"

"No, he went to church, but to tell the truth he really preferred the old religion. This was his study and is now mine. Why did you ask if he were an Old Believer?"

"Are you going to be married here?"

"Ye-yes!" replied Rogojin, starting at the unexpected question.

"Soon?"

"You know yourself it does not depend on me."

"Parfen, I am not your enemy, and I do not intend to oppose your intentions in any way. I repeat this to you now just as I said it to you once before on a very similar occasion. When you were arranging for your projected marriage in Moscow, I did not interfere with you—you know I did not. That first time she fled to me from you, from the very altar almost, and begged me to 'save her from you.' Afterwards she ran away from me again, and you found her and arranged your marriage with her once more; and now, I hear, she has run away from you and come to Petersburg. Is it true? Lebedeff wrote me to this effect, and that's why I came here. That you had once more arranged matters with Nastasia Philipovna I only learned last night in the train from a friend of yours, Zaleshoff—if you wish to know.

"I confess I came here with an object. I wished to persuade Nastasia to go abroad for her health; she requires it. Both mind and body need a change badly. I did not intend to take her abroad myself. I was going to arrange for her to go without me. Now I tell you honestly, Parfen, if it is true that all is made up between you, I will not so much as set eyes upon her, and I will never even come to see you again.

"You know quite well that I am telling the truth, because I have always been frank with you. I have never concealed my own opinion from you. I have always told you that I consider a marriage between you and her would be ruin to her. You would also be ruined, and perhaps even more hopelessly. If this marriage were to be broken off again, I admit I should be greatly pleased; but at the same time I have not the slightest intention of trying to part you. You may be quite easy in your mind, and you need not suspect me. You know yourself whether I was ever really your rival or not, even when she ran away and came to me.

"There, you are laughing at me—I know why you laugh. It is perfectly true that we lived apart from one another all the time, in different towns. I told you before that I did not love her with love, but with pity! You said then that you understood me; did you really understand me or not? What hatred there is in your eyes at this moment! I came to relieve your mind, because you are dear to me also. I love you very much, Parfen; and now I shall go away and never come back again. Goodbye."

The prince rose.

"Stay a little," said Parfen, not leaving his chair and resting his head on his right hand. "I haven't seen you for a long time."

The prince sat down again. Both were silent for a few moments.

"When you are not with me I hate you, Lef Nicolaievitch. I have loathed you every day of these three months since I last saw you. By heaven I have!" said Rogojin. "I could have poisoned you at any minute. Now, you have been with me but a quarter of an hour, and all my malice seems to have melted away, and you are as dear to me as ever. Stay here a little longer."

"When I am with you you trust me; but as soon as my back is turned you suspect me," said the prince, smiling, and trying to hide his emotion.

"I trust your voice, when I hear you speak. I quite understand that you and I cannot be put on a level, of course."

"Why did you add that?—There! Now you are cross again," said the prince, wondering.

"We were not asked, you see. We were made different, with different tastes and feelings, without being consulted. You say you love her with pity. I have no pity for her. She hates me—that's the plain truth of the matter. I dream of her every night, and always that she is laughing at me with another man. And so she does laugh at me. She thinks no more of marrying me than if she were changing her shoe. Would you believe it, I haven't seen her for five days, and I daren't go near her. She asks me what I come for, as if she were not content with having disgraced me—"

"Disgraced you! How?"

"Just as though you didn't know! Why, she ran away from me, and went to you. You admitted it yourself, just now."

"But surely you do not believe that she..."

"That she did not disgrace me at Moscow with that officer, Zemtuznikoff? I know for certain she did, after having fixed our marriage-day herself!"

"Impossible!" cried the prince.

"I know it for a fact," replied Rogojin, with conviction.

"It is not like her, you say? My friend, that's absurd. Perhaps such an act would horrify her, if she were with you, but it is quite different where I am concerned. She looks on me as vermin. Her affair with Keller was simply to make a laughing-stock of me. You don't know what a fool she made of me in Moscow; and the money I spent over her! The money! the money!"

"And you can marry her now, Parfen! What will come of it all?" said the prince, with dread in his voice.

Rogojin gazed back gloomily, and with a terrible expression in his eyes, but said nothing.

"I haven't been to see her for five days," he repeated, after a slight pause. "I'm afraid of being turned out. She says she's still her own mistress, and may turn me off altogether, and go abroad. She told me this herself," he said, with a peculiar glance at Muishkin. "I think she often does it merely to frighten me. She is always laughing at me, for some reason or other; but at other times she's angry, and won't say a word, and that's what I'm afraid of. I took her a shawl one day, the like of which she might never have seen, although she did live in luxury and she gave it away to her maid, Katia. Sometimes when I can keep away no longer, I steal past the house on the sly, and once I watched at the gate till dawn—I thought something was going on—and she saw me from the window. She asked me what I should do if I found she had deceived me. I said, 'You know well enough.'"

"What did she know?" cried the prince.

"How was I to tell?" replied Rogojin, with an angry laugh. "I did my best to catch her tripping in Moscow, but did not succeed. However, I caught hold of her one day, and said: 'You are engaged to be married into a respectable family, and do you know what sort of a woman you are? *That's* the sort of woman you are,' I said."

"You told her that?"

"Yes."

"Well, go on."

"She said, 'I wouldn't even have you for a footman now, much less for a husband.' 'I shan't leave the house,' I said, 'so it doesn't matter.' 'Then I shall call somebody and have you kicked out,' she cried. So then I rushed at her, and beat her till she was bruised all over."

"Impossible!" cried the prince, aghast.

"I tell you it's true," said Rogojin quietly, but with eyes ablaze with passion.

"Then for a day and a half I neither slept, nor ate, nor drank, and would not leave her. I knelt at her feet: 'I shall die here,' I said, 'if you don't forgive me; and if you have me turned out, I shall drown myself; because, what should I be without you now?' She was like a madwoman all that day; now she would cry; now she would threaten me with a knife; now she would abuse me. She called in Zaleshoff and Keller, and showed me to them, shamed me in their presence. 'Let's all go to the theatre,' she says, 'and leave him here if he won't go—it's not my business. They'll give you some tea, Parfen Semeonovitch, while I am away, for you must be hungry.' She came back from the theatre alone. 'Those cowards wouldn't come,' she said. 'They are afraid of you, and tried to frighten me, too. "He won't go away as he came," they said, "he'll cut your throat—see if he doesn't." Now, I shall go to my bedroom, and I shall not even lock my door, just to show you how much I am afraid of you. You must be shown that once for all. Did you have tea?' 'No,' I said, 'and I don't intend to.' 'Ha, ha! you are playing off your pride against your stomach! That sort of heroism doesn't sit well on you,' she said.

"With that she did as she had said she would; she went to bed, and did not lock her door. In the morning she came out. 'Are you quite mad?' she said, sharply. 'Why, you'll die of hunger like this.' 'Forgive me,' I said. 'No, I won't, and I won't marry you. I've said it. Surely you haven't sat in this chair all night without sleeping?' 'I didn't sleep,' I said. 'H'm! how sensible of you. And are you going to have no breakfast or dinner today?' 'I told you I wouldn't. Forgive me!' 'You've no idea how unbecoming this sort of thing is to you,' she said, 'it's like putting a saddle on a cow's back. Do you think you are frightening me? My word, what a dreadful thing that you should sit here and eat no food! How terribly frightened I am!' She wasn't angry long, and didn't seem to remember my offence at all. I was surprised, for she is a vindictive, resentful woman—but then I thought that perhaps she despised me too much to feel any resentment against me. And that's the truth.

"She came up to me and said, 'Do you know who the Pope of Rome is?' 'I've heard of him,' I said. 'I suppose you've read the Universal History, Parfen Semeonovitch, haven't you?' she asked. 'I've learned nothing at all,' I said. 'Then I'll lend it to you to read. You must know there was a Roman Pope once, and he was very angry with a certain Emperor; so the Emperor came and neither ate nor drank, but knelt before the Pope's palace till he should be forgiven. And what sort of vows do you think that Emperor was making during all those days on his knees? Stop, I'll read it to you!' Then she read me a lot of verses, where it said that the Emperor spent all the time vowing vengeance against the Pope. 'You don't mean to say you don't approve of the poem, Parfen Semeonovitch,' she says. 'All you have read out is perfectly true,' say I. 'Aha!' says she, 'you admit it's true, do you? And you are making vows to yourself that if I marry you, you will remind me of all this, and take it out of me.' 'I don't know,' I say, 'perhaps I was thinking like that, and perhaps I was not. I'm not thinking of anything just now.' 'What are your thoughts, then?' 'I'm thinking that when you rise from your chair and go past me, I watch you, and follow you with my eyes; if your dress does but rustle, my heart sinks; if you leave the room, I remember every little word and action, and what your voice sounded like, and what you said. I thought of nothing all last night, but sat here listening to your sleeping breath, and heard you move a little, twice.' 'And as for your attack upon me,' she says, 'I suppose you never once thought of *that?*' 'Perhaps I did think of it, and perhaps not,' I say. 'And what if I don't either forgive you or marry you?' 'I tell you I shall go and drown myself.' 'H'm!' she said, and then relapsed into silence. Then she got angry, and went out. 'I suppose you'd murder me before you drowned yourself, though!' she cried as she left the room.

"An hour later, she came to me again, looking melancholy. 'I will marry you, Parfen Semeonovitch,' she says, not because I'm frightened of you, but because it's all the same to me how I ruin myself. And how can I do it better? Sit down; they'll bring you some dinner directly. And if I do marry you, I'll be a faithful wife to you—you need not doubt that.' Then she thought a bit, and said, 'At all events, you are not a flunkey; at first, I thought you were no better than a flunkey.' And she arranged the wedding and fixed the day straight away on the spot.

"Then, in another week, she had run away again, and came here to Lebedeff's; and when I found her here, she said to me, 'I'm not going to renounce you altogether, but I wish to put off the wedding a bit longer yet—just as long as I like—for I am still my own mistress; so you may wait, if you like.' That's how the matter stands between us now. What do you think of all this, Lef Nicolaievitch?"

"'What do you think of it yourself?" replied the prince, looking sadly at Rogojin.

"As if I can think anything about it! I—" He was about to say more, but stopped in despair.

The prince rose again, as if he would leave.

"At all events, I shall not interfere with you!" he murmured, as though making answer to some secret thought of his own.

"I'll tell you what!" cried Rogojin, and his eyes flashed fire. "I can't understand your yielding her to me like this; I don't understand it. Have you given up loving her altogether? At first you suffered badly—I know it—I saw it. Besides, why did you come post-haste after us? Out of pity, eh? He, he, he!" His mouth curved in a mocking smile.

"Do you think I am deceiving you?" asked the prince.

"No! I trust you—but I can't understand. It seems to me that your pity is greater than my love." A hungry longing to speak his mind out seemed to flash in the man's eyes, combined with an intense anger.

"Your love is mingled with hatred, and therefore, when your love passes, there will be the greater misery," said the prince. "I tell you this, Parfen—"

"What! that I'll cut her throat, you mean?"

The prince shuddered.

"You'll hate her afterwards for all your present love, and for all the torment you are suffering on her account now. What seems to me the most extraordinary thing is, that she can again consent to marry you, after all that has passed between you. When I heard the news yesterday, I could hardly bring myself to believe it. Why, she has run twice from you, from the very altar rails, as it were. She must have some presentiment of evil. What can she want with you now? Your money? Nonsense! Besides, I should think you must have made a fairly large hole in your fortune already. Surely it is not because she is so very anxious to find a husband? She could find many a one besides yourself. Anyone would be better than you, because you will murder her, and I feel sure she must know that but too well by now. Is it because you love her so passionately? Indeed, that may be it. I have heard that there are women who want just that kind of love... but still..." The prince paused, reflectively.

"What are you grinning at my father's portrait again for?" asked Rogojin, suddenly. He was carefully observing every change in the expression of the prince's face.

"I smiled because the idea came into my head that if it were not for this unhappy passion of yours you might have, and would have, become just such a man as your father, and that very quickly, too. You'd have settled down in this house of yours with some silent and obedient wife. You would have spoken rarely, trusted no one, heeded no one, and thought of nothing but making money."

"Laugh away! She said exactly the same, almost word for word, when she saw my father's portrait. It's remarkable how entirely you and she are at one now-a-days."

"What, has she been here?" asked the prince with curiosity.

"Yes! She looked long at the portrait and asked all about my father. 'You'd be just such another,' she said at last, and laughed. 'You have such strong passions, Parfen,' she said, 'that they'd have taken you to Siberia in no time if you had not, luckily, intelligence as well. For you have a good deal of intelligence.' (She said this—believe it or not. The first time I ever heard anything of that sort from her.) 'You'd soon have thrown up all this rowdyism that you indulge in now, and you'd have settled down to quiet, steady money-making, because you have little education; and here you'd have stayed just like your father before you. And you'd have loved your money so that you'd amass not two million, like him, but ten million; and you'd have died of hunger on your money bags to finish up with, for you carry everything to extremes.' There, that's exactly word for word as she said it to me. She never talked to me like that before. She always talks nonsense and laughs when she's with me. We went all over this old house together. 'I shall change all this,' I said, 'or else I'll buy a new house for the wedding.' 'No, no!' she said, 'don't touch anything; leave it all as it is; I shall live with your mother when I marry you.'

"I took her to see my mother, and she was as respectful and kind as though she were her own daughter. Mother has been almost demented ever since father died—she's an old woman. She sits and bows from her chair to everyone she sees. If you left her alone and didn't feed her for three days, I don't believe she would notice it. Well, I took her hand, and I said, 'Give your blessing to this lady, mother, she's going to be my wife.' So Nastasia kissed mother's hand with great feeling. 'She must have suffered terribly, hasn't she?' she said. She saw this book here lying before me. 'What! have you begun to read Russian history?' she asked. She told me once in Moscow, you know, that I had better get Solovieff's Russian History and read it, because I knew nothing. 'That's good,' she said, 'you go on like that, reading books. I'll make you a list myself of the books you ought to read first—shall I?' She had never once spoken to me like this before; it was the first time I felt I could breathe before her like a living creature."

"I'm very, very glad to hear of this, Parfen," said the prince, with real feeling. "Who knows? Maybe God will yet bring you near to one another."

"Never, never!" cried Rogojin, excitedly.

"Look here, Parfen; if you love her so much, surely you must be anxious to earn her respect? And if you do so wish, surely you may hope to? I said just now that I considered it extraordinary that she could still be ready to marry you. Well, though I cannot yet understand it, I feel sure she must have some good reason, or she wouldn't do it. She is sure of your love; but besides that, she must attribute *something* else to you—some good qualities, otherwise the thing would not be. What you have just said confirms my words. You say yourself that she found it possible to speak to you quite differently from her usual manner. You are suspicious, you know, and jealous, therefore when anything annoying happens to you, you exaggerate its significance. Of course, of course, she does not think so ill of you as you say. Why, if she did, she would simply be walking to death by drowning or by the knife, with her eyes wide open, when she married you. It is impossible! As if anybody would go to their death deliberately!"

Rogojin listened to the prince's excited words with a bitter smile. His conviction was, apparently, unalterable.

"How dreadfully you look at me, Parfen!" said the prince, with a feeling of dread.

"Water or the knife?" said the latter, at last. "Ha, ha—that's exactly why she is going to marry me, because she knows for certain that the knife awaits her. Prince, can it be that you don't even yet see what's at the root of it all?"

"I don't understand you."

"Perhaps he really doesn't understand me! They do say that you are a—you know what! She loves another—there, you can understand that much! Just as I love her, exactly so she loves another man. And that other man is—do you know who? It's you. There—you didn't know that, eh?"

"I?"

"You, you! She has loved you ever since that day, her birthday! Only she thinks she cannot marry you, because it would be the ruin of you. 'Everybody knows what sort of a woman I am,' she says. She told me all this herself, to my very face! She's afraid of disgracing and ruining you, she says, but it doesn't matter about me. She can marry me all right! Notice how much consideration she shows for me!"

"But why did she run away to me, and then again from me to—"

"From you to me? Ha, ha! that's nothing! Why, she always acts as though she were in a delirium now-a-days! Either she says, 'Come on, I'll marry you! Let's have the wedding quickly!' and fixes the day, and seems in a hurry for it, and when it begins to come near she feels frightened; or else some other idea gets into her head—goodness knows! you've seen her—you know how she goes on—laughing and crying and raving! There's nothing extraordinary about her having run away from you! She ran away because she found out how dearly she loved you. She could not bear to be near you. You said just now that I had found her at Moscow, when she ran away from you. I didn't do anything of the sort; she came to me herself, straight from you. 'Name the day—I'm ready!' she said. 'Let's have some champagne, and go and hear the gipsies sing!' I tell you she'd have thrown herself into the water long ago if it were not for me! She doesn't do it because I am, perhaps, even more dreadful to her than the water! She's marrying me out of spite; if she marries me, I tell you, it will be for spite!"

"But how do you, how can you—" began the prince, gazing with dread and horror at Rogojin.

"Why don't you finish your sentence? Shall I tell you what you were thinking to yourself just then? You were thinking, 'How can she marry him after this? How can it possibly be permitted?' Oh, I know what you were thinking about!"

"I didn't come here for that purpose, Parfen. That was not in my mind—"

"That may be! Perhaps you didn't *come* with the idea, but the idea is certainly there *now!* Ha, ha! well, that's enough! What are you upset about? Didn't you really know it all before? You astonish me!"

"All this is mere jealousy—it is some malady of yours, Parfen! You exaggerate everything," said the prince, excessively agitated. "What are you doing?"

"Let go of it!" said Parfen, seizing from the prince's hand a knife which the latter had at that moment taken up from the table, where it lay beside the history. Parfen replaced it where it had been.

"I seemed to know it—I felt it, when I was coming back to Petersburg," continued the prince, "I did not want to come, I wished to forget all this, to uproot it from my memory altogether! Well, good-bye—what is the matter?"

He had absently taken up the knife a second time, and again Rogojin snatched it from his hand, and threw it down on the table. It was a plain looking knife, with a bone handle, a blade about eight inches long, and broad in proportion, it did not clasp.

Seeing that the prince was considerably struck by the fact that he had twice seized this knife out of his hand, Rogojin caught it up with some irritation, put it inside the book, and threw the latter across to another table.

"Do you cut your pages with it, or what?" asked Muishkin, still rather absently, as though unable to throw off a deep preoccupation into which the conversation had thrown him.

"Yes."

"It's a garden knife, isn't it?"

"Yes. Can't one cut pages with a garden knife?"

"It's quite new."

"Well, what of that? Can't I buy a new knife if I like?" shouted Rogojin furiously, his irritation growing with every word.

The prince shuddered, and gazed fixedly at Parfen. Suddenly he burst out laughing.

"Why, what an idea!" he said. "I didn't mean to ask you any of these questions; I was thinking of something quite different! But my head is heavy, and I seem so absent-minded nowadays! Well, good-bye—I can't remember what I wanted to say—good-bye!"

"Not that way," said Rogojin.

"There, I've forgotten that too!"

"This way—come along—I'll show you."

CHAPTER IV.

They passed through the same rooms which the prince had traversed on his arrival. In the largest there were pictures on the walls, portraits and landscapes of little interest. Over the door, however, there was one of strange and rather striking shape; it was six or seven feet in length, and not more than a foot in height. It represented the Saviour just taken from the cross.

The prince glanced at it, but took no further notice. He moved on hastily, as though anxious to get out of the house. But Rogojin suddenly stopped underneath the picture.

"My father picked up all these pictures very cheap at auctions, and so on," he said; "they are all rubbish, except the one over the door, and that is valuable. A man offered five hundred roubles for it last week."

"Yes—that's a copy of a Holbein," said the prince, looking at it again, "and a good copy, too, so far as I am able to judge. I saw the picture abroad, and could not forget it—what's the matter?"

Rogojin had dropped the subject of the picture and walked on. Of course his strange frame of mind was sufficient to account for his conduct; but, still, it seemed queer to the prince that he should so abruptly drop a conversation commenced by himself. Rogojin did not take any notice of his question.

"Lef Nicolaievitch," said Rogojin, after a pause, during which the two walked along a little further, "I have long wished to ask you, do you believe in God?"

"How strangely you speak, and how odd you look!" said the other, involuntarily.

"I like looking at that picture," muttered Rogojin, not noticing, apparently, that the prince had not answered his question.

"That picture! That picture!" cried Muishkin, struck by a sudden idea. "Why, a man's faith might be ruined by looking at that picture!"

"So it is!" said Rogojin, unexpectedly. They had now reached the front door.

The prince stopped.

"How?" he said. "What do you mean? I was half joking, and you took me up quite seriously! Why do you ask me whether I believe in God?"

"Oh, no particular reason. I meant to ask you before—many people are unbelievers nowadays, especially Russians, I have been told. You ought to know—you've lived abroad."

Rogojin laughed bitterly as he said these words, and opening the door, held it for the prince to pass out. Muishkin looked surprised, but went out. The other followed him as far as the landing of the outer stairs, and shut the door behind him. They both now stood facing one another, as though oblivious of where they were, or what they had to do next.

"Well, good-bye!" said the prince, holding out his hand.

"Good-bye," said Rogojin, pressing it hard, but quite mechanically.

The prince made one step forward, and then turned round.

"As to faith," he said, smiling, and evidently unwilling to leave Rogojin in this state—"as to faith, I had four curious conversations in two days, a week or so ago. One morning I met a man in the train, and made acquaintance with him at once. I had often heard of him as a very learned man, but an atheist; and I was very glad of the opportunity of conversing with so eminent and clever a person. He doesn't believe in God, and he talked a good deal about it, but all the while it appeared to me that he was speaking *outside the subject*. And it has always struck me, both in speaking to such men and in reading their books, that they do not seem really to be touching on that at all, though on the surface they may appear to do so. I told him this, but I dare say I did not clearly express what I meant, for he could not understand me.

"That same evening I stopped at a small provincial hotel, and it so happened that a dreadful murder had been committed there the night before, and everybody was talking about it. Two peasants—elderly men and old friends—had had tea together there the night before, and were to occupy the same bedroom. They were not drunk but one of them had noticed for the first time that his friend possessed a silver watch which he was wearing on a chain. He was by no means a thief, and was, as peasants go, a rich man; but this watch so fascinated him that he could not restrain himself. He took a knife, and when his friend turned his back, he came up softly behind, raised his eyes to heaven, crossed himself, and saying earnestly—'God forgive me, for Christ's sake!' he cut his friend's throat like a sheep, and took the watch."

Rogojin roared with laughter. He laughed as though he were in a sort of fit. It was strange to see him laughing so after the sombre mood he had been in just before.

"Oh, I like that! That beats anything!" he cried convulsively, panting for breath. "One is an absolute unbeliever; the other is such a thorough-going believer that he murders his friend to the tune of a prayer! Oh, prince, prince, that's too good for anything! You can't have invented it. It's the best thing I've heard!"

"Next morning I went out for a stroll through the town," continued the prince, so soon as Rogojin was a little quieter, though his laughter still burst out at intervals, "and soon observed a drunken-looking soldier staggering about the pavement. He came up to me and said, 'Buy my silver cross, sir! You shall have it for fourpence—it's real silver.' I looked, and there he held a cross, just taken off his own neck, evidently, a large tin one, made after the Byzantine pattern. I fished out fourpence, and put his cross on my own neck, and I could see by his face that he was as pleased as he could be at the thought that he had succeeded in cheating a foolish gentleman, and away he went to drink the value of his cross. At that time everything that I saw made a tremendous impression upon me. I had understood nothing about Russia before, and had only vague and fantastic memories of it. So I thought, 'I will wait awhile before I condemn this Judas. Only God knows what may be hidden in the hearts of drunkards.'

"Well, I went homewards, and near the hotel I came across a poor woman, carrying a child—a baby of some six weeks old. The mother was quite a girl herself. The baby was smiling up at her, for the first time in its life, just at that moment; and while I watched the woman she suddenly crossed herself, oh, so devoutly! 'What is it, my good woman?' I asked her. (I was never but asking questions then!) 'Exactly as is a mother's joy when her baby smiles for the first time into her eyes, so is God's joy when one of His children turns and prays to Him for the first time, with all his heart!' This is what that poor woman said to me, almost word for word; and such a deep, refined, truly religious thought it was—a thought in which the whole essence of Christianity was expressed in one flash—that is, the recognition of God as our Father, and of God's joy in men as His own children, which is the chief idea of Christ. She was a simple country-woman—a mother, it's true—and perhaps, who knows, she may have been the wife of the drunken soldier!

"Listen, Parfen; you put a question to me just now. This is my reply. The essence of religious feeling has nothing to do with reason, or atheism, or crime, or acts of any kind—it has nothing to do with these things—and never had. There is something besides all this, something which the arguments of the atheists can never touch. But the principal thing, and the conclusion of my argument, is that this is most clearly seen in the heart of a Russian. This is a conviction which I have gained while I have been in this Russia of ours. Yes, Parfen! there is work to be done; there is work to be done in this Russian world! Remember what talks we used to have in Moscow! And I never wished to come here at all; and I never thought to meet you like this, Parfen! Well, well—good-bye—good-bye! God be with you!"

He turned and went downstairs.

"Lef Nicolaievitch!" cried Parfen, before he had reached the next landing. "Have you got that cross you bought from the soldier with you?"

"Yes, I have," and the prince stopped again.

"Show it me, will you?"

A new fancy! The prince reflected, and then mounted the stairs once more. He pulled out the cross without taking it off his neck.

"Give it to me," said Parfen.

"Why? do you—"

The prince would rather have kept this particular cross.

"I'll wear it; and you shall have mine. I'll take it off at once."

"You wish to exchange crosses? Very well, Parfen, if that's the case, I'm glad enough—that makes us brothers, you know."

The prince took off his tin cross, Parfen his gold one, and the exchange was made.

Parfen was silent. With sad surprise the prince observed that the look of distrust, the bitter, ironical smile, had still not altogether left his newly-adopted brother's face. At moments, at all events, it showed itself but too plainly,

At last Rogojin took the prince's hand, and stood so for some moments, as though he could not make up his mind. Then he drew him along, murmuring almost inaudibly,

"Come!"

They stopped on the landing, and rang the bell at a door opposite to Parfen's own lodging.

An old woman opened to them and bowed low to Parfen, who asked her some questions hurriedly, but did not wait to hear her answer. He led the prince on through several dark, cold-looking rooms, spotlessly clean, with white covers over all the furniture.

Without the ceremony of knocking, Parfen entered a small apartment, furnished like a drawing-room, but with a polished mahogany partition dividing one half of it from what was probably a bedroom. In one corner of this room sat an old woman in an arm-chair, close to the stove. She did not look very old, and her face was a pleasant, round one; but she was white-haired and, as one could detect at the first glance, quite in her second childhood. She wore a black woollen dress, with a black handkerchief round her neck and shoulders, and a white cap with black ribbons. Her feet were raised on a footstool. Beside her sat another old woman, also dressed in mourning, and silently knitting a stocking; this was evidently a companion. They both looked as though they never broke the silence. The first old woman, so soon as she saw Rogojin and the prince, smiled and bowed courteously several times, in token of her gratification at their visit.

"Mother," said Rogojin, kissing her hand, "here is my great friend, Prince Muishkin; we have exchanged crosses; he was like a real brother to me at Moscow at one time, and did a great deal for me. Bless him, mother, as you would bless your own son. Wait a moment, let me arrange your hands for you."

But the old lady, before Parfen had time to touch her, raised her right hand, and, with three fingers held up, devoutly made the sign of the cross three times over the prince. She then nodded her head kindly at him once more.

"There, come along, Lef Nicolaievitch; that's all I brought you here for," said Rogojin.

When they reached the stairs again he added:

"She understood nothing of what I said to her, and did not know what I wanted her to do, and yet she blessed you; that shows she wished to do so herself. Well, goodbye; it's time you went, and I must go too."

He opened his own door.

"Well, let me at least embrace you and say goodbye, you strange fellow!" cried the prince, looking with gentle reproach at Rogojin, and advancing towards him. But the latter had hardly raised his arms when he dropped them again. He could not make up his mind to it; he turned away from the prince in order to avoid looking at him. He could not embrace him.

"Don't be afraid," he muttered, indistinctly, "though I have taken your cross, I shall not murder you for your watch." So saying, he laughed suddenly, and strangely. Then in a moment his face became transfigured; he grew deadly white, his lips trembled, his eyes burned like fire. He stretched out his arms and held the prince tightly to him, and said in a strangled voice:

"Well, take her! It's Fate! She's yours. I surrender her.... Remember Rogojin!" And pushing the prince from him, without looking back at him, he hurriedly entered his own flat, and banged the door.

CHAPTER V.

It was late now, nearly half-past two, and the prince did not find General Epanchin at home. He left a card, and determined to look up Colia, who had a room at a small hotel near. Colia was not in, but he was informed that he might be back shortly, and had left word that if he were not in by half-past three it was to be understood that he had gone to Pavlofsk to General Epanchin's, and would dine there. The prince decided to wait till half-past three, and ordered some dinner. At half-past three there was no sign of Colia. The prince waited until four o'clock, and then strolled off mechanically wherever his feet should carry him.

In early summer there are often magnificent days in St. Petersburg—bright, hot and still. This happened to be such a day.

For some time the prince wandered about without aim or object. He did not know the town well. He stopped to look about him on bridges, at street corners. He entered a confectioner's shop to rest, once. He was in a state of nervous excitement and perturbation; he noticed nothing and no one; and he felt a craving for solitude, to be alone with his thoughts and his emotions, and to give himself up to them passively. He loathed the idea of trying to answer the questions that would rise up in his heart and mind. "I am not to blame for all this," he thought to himself, half unconsciously.

Towards six o'clock he found himself at the station of the Tsarsko-Selski railway.

He was tired of solitude now; a new rush of feeling took hold of him, and a flood of light chased away the gloom, for a moment, from his soul. He took a ticket to Pavlofsk, and determined to get there as fast as he could, but something stopped him; a reality, and not a fantasy, as he was inclined to think it. He was about to take his place in a carriage, when he suddenly threw away his ticket and came out again, disturbed and thoughtful. A few moments later, in the street, he recalled something that had bothered him all the afternoon. He caught himself engaged in a strange occupation which he now recollected he had taken up at odd moments for the last few hours—it was looking about all around him for something, he did not know what. He had forgotten it for a while, half an hour or so, and now, suddenly, the uneasy search had recommenced.

But he had hardly become conscious of this curious phenomenon, when another recollection suddenly swam through his brain, interesting him for the moment, exceedingly. He remembered that the last time he had been engaged in looking around him for the unknown something, he was standing before a cutler's shop, in the window of which were exposed certain goods for sale. He was extremely anxious now to discover whether this shop and these goods really existed, or whether the whole thing had been a hallucination.

He felt in a very curious condition today, a condition similar to that which had preceded his fits in bygone years.

He remembered that at such times he had been particularly absentminded, and could not discriminate between objects and persons unless he concentrated special attention upon them.

He remembered seeing something in the window marked at sixty copecks. Therefore, if the shop existed and if this object were really in the window, it would prove that he had been able to concentrate his attention on this article at a moment when, as a general rule, his absence of mind would have been too great to admit of any such concentration; in fact, very shortly after he had left the railway station in such a state of agitation.

So he walked back looking about him for the shop, and his heart beat with intolerable impatience. Ah! here was the very shop, and there was the article marked "60 cop." Of course, it's sixty copecks, he thought, and certainly worth no more. This idea amused him and he laughed.

But it was a hysterical laugh; he was feeling terribly oppressed. He remembered clearly that just here, standing before this window, he had suddenly turned round, just as earlier in the day he had turned and found the dreadful eyes of Rogojin fixed upon him. Convinced, therefore, that in this respect at all events he had been under no delusion, he left the shop and went on.

This must be thought out; it was clear that there had been no hallucination at the station then, either; something had actually happened to him, on both occasions; there was no doubt of it. But again a loathing for all mental exertion overmastered him; he would not think it out now, he would put it off and think of something else. He remembered that during his epileptic fits, or rather immediately preceding them, he had always experienced a moment or two when his whole heart, and mind, and body seemed to wake up to vigour and light; when he became filled with joy and hope, and all his anxieties seemed to be swept away for ever; these moments were but presentiments, as it were, of the one final second (it was never more than a second) in which the fit came upon him. That second, of course, was inexpressible. When his attack was over, and the prince reflected on his symptoms, he used to say to himself: "These moments, short as they are, when I feel such extreme consciousness of myself, and consequently more of life than at other times, are due only to the disease—to the sudden rupture of normal conditions. Therefore they are not really a higher kind of life, but a lower." This reasoning, however, seemed to end in a paradox, and lead to the further consideration:—"What matter though it be only disease, an abnormal tension of the brain, if when I recall and analyze the moment, it seems to have been one of harmony and beauty in the highest degree—an instant of deepest sensation, overflowing with unbounded joy and rapture, ecstatic devotion, and completest life?" Vague though this sounds, it was perfectly comprehensible to Muishkin, though he knew that it was but a feeble expression of his sensations.

That there was, indeed, beauty and harmony in those abnormal moments, that they really contained the highest synthesis of life, he could not doubt, nor even admit the possibility of doubt. He felt that they were not analogous to the fantastic and unreal dreams due to intoxication by hashish, opium or wine. Of that he could judge, when the attack was over. These instants were characterized—to define it in a word—by an intense quickening of the sense of personality. Since, in the last conscious moment preceding the attack, he could say to himself, with full understanding of his words: "I would give my whole life for this one instant," then doubtless to him it really was worth a lifetime. For the rest, he thought the dialectical part of his argument of little worth; he saw only too clearly that the result of these ecstatic moments was stupefaction, mental darkness, idiocy. No argument was possible on that point. His conclusion, his estimate of the "moment," doubtless contained some error, yet the reality of the sensation troubled him. What's more unanswerable than a fact? And this fact had occurred. The prince had confessed unreservedly to himself that the feeling of intense beatitude in that crowded moment made the moment worth a lifetime. "I feel then," he said one day to Rogojin in Moscow, "I feel then as if I understood those amazing words—'There shall be no more time.'" And he added with a smile: "No doubt the epileptic Mahomet refers to that same moment when he says that he visited all the dwellings of Allah, in less time than was needed to empty his pitcher of water." Yes, he had often met Rogojin in Moscow, and many were the subjects they discussed. "He told me I had been a brother to him," thought the prince. "He said so today, for the first time."

He was sitting in the Summer Garden on a seat under a tree, and his mind dwelt on the matter. It was about seven o'clock, and the place was empty. The stifling atmosphere foretold a storm, and the prince felt a certain charm in the contemplative mood which possessed him. He found pleasure, too, in gazing at the exterior objects around him. All the time he was trying to forget some thing, to escape from some idea that haunted him; but melancholy thoughts came back, though he would so willingly have escaped from them. He remembered suddenly how he had been talking to the waiter, while he dined, about a recently committed murder which the whole town was discussing, and as he thought of it something strange came over him. He was seized all at once by a violent desire, almost a temptation, against which he strove in vain.

He jumped up and walked off as fast as he could towards the "Petersburg Side." [One of the quarters of St. Petersburg.] He had asked someone, a little while before, to show him which was the Petersburg Side, on the banks of the Neva. He had not gone there, however; and he knew very well that it was of no use to go now, for he would certainly not find Lebedeff's relation at home. He had the address, but she must certainly have gone to Pavlofsk, or Colia would have let him know. If he were to go now, it would merely be out of curiosity, but a sudden, new idea had come into his head.

However, it was something to move on and know where he was going. A minute later he was still moving on, but without knowing anything. He could no longer think out his new idea. He tried to take an interest in all he saw; in the sky, in the Neva. He spoke to some children he met.

He felt his epileptic condition becoming more and more developed. The evening was very close; thunder was heard some way off.

The prince was haunted all that day by the face of Lebedeff's nephew whom he had seen for the first time that morning, just as one is haunted at times by some persistent musical refrain. By a curious association of ideas, the young man always appeared as the murderer of whom Lebedeff had spoken when introducing him to Muishkin. Yes, he had read something about the murder, and that quite recently. Since he came to Russia, he had heard many stories of this kind, and was interested in them. His conversation with the waiter, an hour ago, chanced to be on the subject of this murder of the Zemarins, and the latter had agreed with him about it. He thought of the waiter again, and decided that he was no fool, but a steady, intelligent man: though, said he to himself, "God knows what he may really be; in a country with which one is unfamiliar it is difficult to understand the people one meets." He was beginning to have a passionate faith in the Russian soul, however, and what discoveries he had made in the last six months, what unexpected discoveries! But every soul is a mystery, and depths of mystery lie in the soul of a Russian. He had been intimate with Rogojin, for example, and a brotherly friendship had sprung up between them—yet did he really know him? What chaos and ugliness fills the world at times! What a self-satisfied rascal is that nephew of Lebedeff's! "But what am I thinking," continued the prince to himself. "Can he really have committed that crime? Did he kill those six persons? I seem to be confusing things... how strange it all is.... My head goes round... And Lebedeff's daughter—how sympathetic and charming her face was as she held the child in her arms! What an innocent look and child-like laugh she had! It is curious that I had forgotten her until now. I expect Lebedeff adores her—and I really believe, when I think of it, that as sure as two and two make four, he is fond of that nephew, too!"

Well, why should he judge them so hastily! Could he really say what they were, after one short visit? Even Lebedeff seemed an enigma today. Did he expect to find him so? He had never seen him like that before. Lebedeff and the Comtesse du Barry! Good Heavens! If Rogojin should really kill someone, it would not, at any rate, be such a senseless, chaotic affair. A knife made to a special pattern, and six people killed in a kind of delirium. But Rogojin also had a knife made to a special pattern. Can it be that Rogojin wishes to murder anyone? The prince began to tremble violently. "It is a crime on my part to imagine anything so base, with such cynical frankness." His face reddened with shame at the thought; and then there came across him as in a flash the memory of the incidents at the Pavlofsk station, and at the other station in the morning; and the question asked him by Rogojin about *the eyes* and Rogojin's cross, that he was even now wearing; and the benediction of Rogojin's mother; and his embrace on the darkened staircase—that last supreme renunciation—and now, to find himself full of this new "idea," staring into shop-windows, and looking round for things—how base he was!

Despair overmastered his soul; he would not go on, he would go back to his hotel; he even turned and went the other way; but a moment after he changed his mind again and went on in the old direction.

Why, here he was on the Petersburg Side already, quite close to the house! Where was his "idea"? He was marching along without it now. Yes, his malady was coming back, it was clear enough; all this gloom and heaviness, all these "ideas," were nothing more nor less than a fit coming on; perhaps he would have a fit this very day.

But just now all the gloom and darkness had fled, his heart felt full of joy and hope, there was no such thing as doubt. And yes, he hadn't seen her for so long; he really must see her. He wished he could meet Rogojin; he would take his hand, and they would go to her together. His heart was pure, he was no rival of Parfen's. Tomorrow, he would go and tell him that he had seen her. Why, he had only come for the sole purpose of seeing her, all the way from Moscow! Perhaps she might be here still, who knows? She might not have gone away to Pavlofsk yet.

Yes, all this must be put straight and above-board, there must be no more passionate renouncements, such as Rogojin's. It must all be clear as day. Cannot Rogojin's soul bear the light? He said he did not love her with sympathy and pity; true, he added that "your pity is greater than my love," but he was not quite fair on himself there. Kin! Rogojin reading a book—wasn't that sympathy beginning? Did it not show that he comprehended his relations with her? And his story of waiting day and night for her forgiveness? That didn't look quite like passion alone.

And as to her face, could it inspire nothing but passion? Could her face inspire passion at all now? Oh, it inspired suffering, grief, overwhelming grief of the soul! A poignant, agonizing memory swept over the prince's heart.

Yes, agonizing. He remembered how he had suffered that first day when he thought he observed in her the symptoms of madness. He had almost fallen into despair. How could he have lost his hold upon her when she ran away from him to Rogojin? He ought to have run after her himself, rather than wait for news as he had done. Can Rogojin have failed to observe, up to now, that she is mad? Rogojin attributes her strangeness to other causes, to passion! What insane jealousy! What was it he had hinted at in that suggestion of his? The prince suddenly blushed, and shuddered to his very heart.

But why recall all this? There was insanity on both sides. For him, the prince, to love this woman with passion, was unthinkable. It would be cruel and inhuman. Yes. Rogojin is not fair to himself; he has a large heart; he has aptitude for sympathy. When he learns the truth, and finds what a pitiable being is this injured, broken, half-insane creature, he will forgive her all the torment she has caused him. He will become her slave, her brother, her friend. Compassion will teach even Rogojin, it will show him how to reason. Compassion is the chief law of human existence. Oh, how guilty he felt towards Rogojin! And, for a few warm, hasty words spoken in Moscow, Parfen had called him "brother," while he—but no, this was delirium! It would all come right! That gloomy Parfen had implied that his faith was waning; he must suffer dreadfully. He said he liked to look at that picture; it was not that he liked it, but he felt the need of looking at it. Rogojin was not merely a passionate soul; he was a fighter. He was fighting for the restoration of his dying faith. He must have something to hold on to and believe, and someone to believe in. What a strange picture that of Holbein's is! Why, this is the street, and here's the house, No. 16.

The prince rang the bell, and asked for Nastasia Philipovna. The lady of the house came out, and stated that Nastasia had gone to stay with Daria Alexeyevna at Pavlofsk, and might be there some days.

Madame Filisoff was a little woman of forty, with a cunning face, and crafty, piercing eyes. When, with an air of mystery, she asked her visitor's name, he refused at first to answer, but in a moment he changed his mind, and left strict instructions that it should be given to Nastasia Philipovna. The urgency of his request seemed to impress Madame Filisoff, and she put on a knowing expression, as if to say, "You need not be afraid, I quite understand." The prince's name evidently was a great surprise to her. He stood and looked absently at her for a moment, then turned, and took the road back to his hotel. But he went away not as he came. A great change had suddenly come over him. He went blindly forward; his knees shook under him; he was tormented by "ideas"; his lips were blue, and trembled with a feeble, meaningless smile. His demon was upon him once more.

What had happened to him? Why was his brow clammy with drops of moisture, his knees shaking beneath him, and his soul oppressed with a cold gloom? Was it because he had just seen these dreadful eyes again? Why, he had left the Summer Garden on purpose to see them; that had been his "idea." He had wished to assure himself that he would see them once more at that house. Then why was he so overwhelmed now, having seen them as he expected? just as though he had not expected to see them! Yes, they were the very same eyes; and no doubt about it. The same that he had seen in the crowd that morning at the station, the same that he had surprised in Rogojin's rooms some hours later, when the latter had replied to his inquiry with a sneering laugh, "Well, whose eyes were they?" Then for the third time they had appeared just as he was getting into the train on his way to see Aglaya. He had had a strong impulse to rush up to Rogojin, and repeat his words of the morning "Whose eyes are they?" Instead he had fled from the station, and knew nothing more, until he found himself gazing into the window of a cutler's shop, and wondering if a knife with a staghorn handle would cost more than sixty copecks. And as the prince sat dreaming in the Summer Garden under a lime-tree, a wicked demon had come and whispered in his ear: "Rogojin has been spying upon you and watching you all the morning in a frenzy of desperation. When he finds you have not gone to Pavlofsk—a terrible discovery for him—he will surely go at once to that house in Petersburg Side, and watch for you there, although only this morning you gave your word of honour not to see *her*, and swore that you had not come to Petersburg for that purpose." And thereupon the prince had hastened off to that house, and what was there in the fact that he had met Rogojin there? He had only seen a wretched, suffering creature, whose state of mind was gloomy and miserable, but most comprehensible. In the morning Rogojin had seemed to be trying to keep out of the way; but at the station this afternoon he had stood out, he had concealed himself, indeed, less than the prince himself; at the house, now, he had stood fifty yards off on the other side of the road, with folded hands, watching, plainly in view and apparently desirous of being seen. He had stood there like an accuser, like a judge, not like a—a what?

And why had not the prince approached him and spoken to him, instead of turning away and pretending he had seen nothing, although their eyes met? (Yes, their eyes had met, and they had looked at each other.) Why, he had himself wished to take Rogojin by the hand and go in together, he had himself determined to go to him on the morrow and tell him that he had seen her, he had repudiated the demon as he walked to the house, and his heart had been full of joy.

Was there something in the whole aspect of the man, today, sufficient to justify the prince's terror, and the awful suspicions of his demon? Something seen, but indescribable, which filled him with dreadful presentiments? Yes, he was convinced of it—convinced of what? (Oh, how mean and hideous of him to feel this conviction, this presentiment! How he blamed himself for it!) "Speak if you dare, and tell me, what is the presentiment?" he repeated to himself, over and over again. "Put it into words, speak out clearly and distinctly. Oh, miserable coward that I am!" The prince flushed with shame for his own baseness. "How shall I ever look this man in the face again? My God, what a day! And what a nightmare, what a nightmare!"

There was a moment, during this long, wretched walk back from the Petersburg Side, when the prince felt an irresistible desire to go straight to Rogojin's, wait for him, embrace him with tears of shame and contrition, and tell him of his distrust, and finish with it—once for all.

But here he was back at his hotel.

How often during the day he had thought of this hotel with loathing—its corridor, its rooms, its stairs. How he had dreaded coming back to it, for some reason.

"What a regular old woman I am today," he had said to himself each time, with annoyance. "I believe in every foolish presentiment that comes into my head."

He stopped for a moment at the door; a great flush of shame came over him. "I am a coward, a wretched coward," he said, and moved forward again; but once more he paused.

Among all the incidents of the day, one recurred to his mind to the exclusion of the rest; although now that his self-control was regained, and he was no longer under the influence of a nightmare, he was able to think of it calmly. It concerned the knife on Rogojin's table. "Why should not Rogojin have as many knives on his table as he chooses?" thought the prince, wondering at his suspicions, as he had done when he found himself looking into the cutler's window. "What could it have to do with me?" he said to himself again, and stopped as if rooted to the ground by a kind of paralysis of limb such as attacks people under the stress of some humiliating recollection.

The doorway was dark and gloomy at any time; but just at this moment it was rendered doubly so by the fact that the thunder-storm had just broken, and the rain was coming down in torrents.

And in the semi-darkness the prince distinguished a man standing close to the stairs, apparently waiting.

There was nothing particularly significant in the fact that a man was standing back in the doorway, waiting to come out or go upstairs; but the prince felt an irresistible conviction that he knew this man, and that it was Rogojin. The man moved on up the stairs; a moment later the prince passed up them, too. His heart froze within him. "In a minute or two I shall know all," he thought.

The staircase led to the first and second corridors of the hotel, along which lay the guests' bedrooms. As is often the case in Petersburg houses, it was narrow and very dark, and turned around a massive stone column.

On the first landing, which was as small as the necessary turn of the stairs allowed, there was a niche in the column, about half a yard wide, and in this niche the prince felt convinced that a man stood concealed. He thought he could distinguish a figure standing there. He would pass by quickly and not look. He took a step forward, but could bear the uncertainty no longer and turned his head.

The eyes—the same two eyes—met his! The man concealed in the niche had also taken a step forward. For one second they stood face to face.

Suddenly the prince caught the man by the shoulder and twisted him round towards the light, so that he might see his face more clearly.

Rogojin's eyes flashed, and a smile of insanity distorted his countenance. His right hand was raised, and something glittered in it. The prince did not think of trying to stop it. All he could remember afterwards was that he seemed to have called out:

"Parfen! I won't believe it."

Next moment something appeared to burst open before him: a wonderful inner light illuminated his soul. This lasted perhaps half a second, yet he distinctly remembered hearing the beginning of the wail, the strange, dreadful wail, which burst from his lips of its own accord, and which no effort of will on his part could suppress.

Next moment he was absolutely unconscious; black darkness blotted out everything.

He had fallen in an epileptic fit.

As is well known, these fits occur instantaneously. The face, especially the eyes, become terribly disfigured, convulsions seize the limbs, a terrible cry breaks from the sufferer, a wail from which everything human seems to be blotted out, so that it is impossible to believe that the man who has just fallen is the same who emitted the dreadful cry. It seems more as though some other being, inside the stricken one, had cried. Many people have borne witness to this impression; and many cannot behold an epileptic fit without a feeling of mysterious terror and dread.

Such a feeling, we must suppose, overtook Rogojin at this moment, and saved the prince's life. Not knowing that it was a fit, and seeing his victim disappear head foremost into the darkness, hearing his head strike the stone steps below with a crash, Rogojin rushed downstairs, skirting the body, and flung himself headlong out of the hotel, like a raving madman.

The prince's body slipped convulsively down the steps till it rested at the bottom. Very soon, in five minutes or so, he was discovered, and a crowd collected around him.

A pool of blood on the steps near his head gave rise to grave fears. Was it a case of accident, or had there been a crime? It was, however, soon recognized as a case of epilepsy, and identification and proper measures for restoration followed one another, owing to a fortunate circumstance. Colia Ivolgin had come back to his hotel about seven o'clock, owing to a sudden impulse which made him refuse to dine at the Epanchins', and, finding a note from the prince awaiting him, had sped away to the latter's address. Arrived there, he ordered a cup of tea and sat sipping it in the coffee-room. While there he heard excited whispers of someone just found at the bottom of the stairs in a fit; upon which he had hurried to the spot, with a presentiment of evil, and at once recognized the prince.

The sufferer was immediately taken to his room, and though he partially regained consciousness, he lay long in a semi-dazed condition.

The doctor stated that there was no danger to be apprehended from the wound on the head, and as soon as the prince could understand what was going on around him, Colia hired a carriage and took him away to Lebedeff's. There he was received with much cordiality, and the departure to the country was hastened on his account. Three days later they were all at Pavlofsk.

CHAPTER VI.

Lebedeff's country-house was not large, but it was pretty and convenient, especially the part which was let to the prince.

A row of orange and lemon trees and jasmines, planted in green tubs, stood on the fairly wide terrace. According to Lebedeff, these trees gave the house a most delightful aspect. Some were there when he bought it, and he was so charmed with the effect that he promptly added to their number. When the tubs containing these plants arrived at the villa and were set in their places, Lebedeff kept running into the street to enjoy the view of the house, and every time he did so the rent to be demanded from the future tenant went up with a bound.

This country villa pleased the prince very much in his state of physical and mental exhaustion. On the day that they left for Pavlofsk, that is the day after his attack, he appeared almost well, though in reality he felt very far from it. The faces of those around him for the last three days had made a pleasant impression. He was pleased to see, not only Colia, who had become his inseparable companion, but Lebedeff himself and all the family, except the nephew, who had left the house. He was also glad to receive a visit from General Ivolgin, before leaving St. Petersburg.

It was getting late when the party arrived at Pavlofsk, but several people called to see the prince, and assembled in the verandah. Gania was the first to arrive. He had grown so pale and thin that the prince could hardly recognize him. Then came Varia and Ptitsin, who were rusticating in the neighbourhood. As to General Ivolgin, he scarcely budged from Lebedeff's house, and seemed to have moved to Pavlofsk with him. Lebedeff did his best to keep Ardalion Alexandrovitch by him, and to prevent him from invading the prince's quarters. He chatted with him confidentially, so that they might have been taken for old friends. During those three days the prince had noticed that they frequently held long conversations; he often heard their voices raised in argument on deep and learned subjects, which evidently pleased Lebedeff. He seemed as if he could not do without the general. But it was not only Ardalion Alexandrovitch whom Lebedeff kept out of the prince's way. Since they had come to the villa, he treated his own family the same. Upon the pretext that his tenant needed quiet, he kept him almost in isolation, and Muishkin protested in vain against this excess of zeal. Lebedeff stamped his feet at his daughters and drove them away if they attempted to join the prince on the terrace; not even Vera was excepted.

"They will lose all respect if they are allowed to be so free and easy; besides it is not proper for them," he declared at last, in answer to a direct question from the prince.

"Why on earth not?" asked the latter. "Really, you know, you are making yourself a nuisance, by keeping guard over me like this. I get bored all by myself; I have told you so over and over again, and you get on my nerves more than ever by waving your hands and creeping in and out in the mysterious way you do."

It was a fact that Lebedeff, though he was so anxious to keep everyone else from disturbing the patient, was continually in and out of the prince's room himself. He invariably began by opening the door a crack and peering in to see if the prince was there, or if he had escaped; then he would creep softly up to the arm-chair, sometimes making Muishkin jump by his sudden appearance. He always asked if the patient wanted anything, and when the latter replied that he only wanted to be left in peace, he would turn away obediently and make for the door on tip-toe, with deprecatory gestures to imply that he had only just looked in, that he would not speak a word, and would go away and not intrude again; which did not prevent him from reappearing in ten minutes or a quarter of an hour. Colia had free access to the prince, at which Lebedeff was quite disgusted and indignant. He would listen at the door for half an hour at a time while the two were talking. Colia found this out, and naturally told the prince of his discovery.

"Do you think yourself my master, that you try to keep me under lock and key like this?" said the prince to Lebedeff. "In the country, at least, I intend to be free, and you may make up your mind that I mean to see whom I like, and go where I please."

"Why, of course," replied the clerk, gesticulating with his hands.

The prince looked him sternly up and down.

"Well, Lukian Timofeyovitch, have you brought the little cupboard that you had at the head of your bed with you here?"

"No, I left it where it was."

"Impossible!"

"It cannot be moved; you would have to pull the wall down, it is so firmly fixed."

"Perhaps you have one like it here?"

"I have one that is even better, much better; that is really why I bought this house."

"Ah! What visitor did you turn away from my door, about an hour ago?"

"The-the general. I would not let him in; there is no need for him to visit you, prince... I have the deepest esteem for him, he is a—a great man. You don't believe it? Well, you will see, and yet, most excellent prince, you had much better not receive him."

"May I ask why? and also why you walk about on tiptoe and always seem as if you were going to whisper a secret in my ear whenever you come near me?"

"I am vile, vile; I know it!" cried Lebedeff, beating his breast with a contrite air. "But will not the general be too hospitable for you?"

"Too hospitable?"

"Yes. First, he proposes to come and live in my house. Well and good; but he sticks at nothing; he immediately makes himself one of the family. We have talked over our respective relations several times, and discovered that we are connected by marriage. It seems also that you are a sort of nephew on his mother's side; he was explaining it to me again only yesterday. If you are his nephew, it follows that I must also be a relation of yours, most excellent prince. Never mind about that, it is only a foible; but just now he assured me that all his life, from the day he was made an ensign to the 11th of last June, he has entertained at least two hundred guests at his table every day. Finally, he went so far as to say that they never rose from the table; they dined, supped, and had tea, for fifteen hours at a stretch. This went on for thirty years without a break; there was barely time to change the table-cloth; directly one person left, another took his place. On feast-days he entertained as many as three hundred guests, and they numbered seven hundred on the thousandth anniversary of the foundation of the Russian Empire. It amounts to a passion with him; it makes one uneasy to hear of it. It is terrible to have to entertain people who do things on such a scale. That is why I wonder whether such a man is not too hospitable for you and me."

"But you seem to be on the best of terms with him?"

"Quite fraternal—I look upon it as a joke. Let us be brothers-in-law, it is all the same to me,—rather an honour than not. But in spite of the two hundred guests and the thousandth anniversary of the Russian Empire, I can see that he is a very remarkable man. I am quite sincere. You said just now that I always looked as if I was going to tell you a secret; you are right. I have a secret to tell you: a certain person has just let me know that she is very anxious for a secret interview with you."

"Why should it be secret? Not at all; I will call on her myself tomorrow."

"No, oh no!" cried Lebedeff, waving his arms; "if she is afraid, it is not for the reason you think. By the way, do you know that the monster comes every day to inquire after your health?"

"You call him a monster so often that it makes me suspicious."

"You must have no suspicions, none whatever," said Lebedeff quickly. "I only want you to know that the person in question is not afraid of him, but of something quite, quite different."

"What on earth is she afraid of, then? Tell me plainly, without any more beating about the bush," said the prince, exasperated by the other's mysterious grimaces.

"Ah that is the secret," said Lebedeff, with a smile.

"Whose secret?"

"Yours. You forbade me yourself to mention it before you, most excellent prince," murmured Lebedeff. Then, satisfied that he had worked up Muishkin's curiosity to the highest pitch, he added abruptly: "She is afraid of Aglaya Ivanovna."

The prince frowned for a moment in silence, and then said suddenly:

"Really, Lebedeff, I must leave your house. Where are Gavrila Ardalionovitch and the Ptitsins? Are they here? Have you chased them away, too?"

"They are coming, they are coming; and the general as well. I will open all the doors; I will call all my daughters, all of them, this very minute," said Lebedeff in a low voice, thoroughly frightened, and waving his hands as he ran from door to door.

At that moment Colia appeared on the terrace; he announced that Lizabetha Prokofievna and her three daughters were close behind him.

Moved by this news, Lebedeff hurried up to the prince.

"Shall I call the Ptitsins, and Gavrila Ardalionovitch? Shall I let the general in?" he asked.

"Why not? Let in anyone who wants to see me. I assure you, Lebedeff, you have misunderstood my position from the very first; you have been wrong all along. I have not the slightest reason to hide myself from anyone," replied the prince gaily.

Seeing him laugh, Lebedeff thought fit to laugh also, and though much agitated his satisfaction was quite visible.

Colia was right; the Epanchin ladies were only a few steps behind him. As they approached the terrace other visitors appeared from Lebedeff's side of the house—the Ptitsins, Gania, and Ardalion Alexandrovitch.

The Epanchins had only just heard of the prince's illness and of his presence in Pavlofsk, from Colia; and up to this time had been in a state of considerable bewilderment about him. The general brought the prince's card down from town, and Mrs. Epanchin had felt convinced that he himself would follow his card at once; she was much excited.

In vain the girls assured her that a man who had not written for six months would not be in such a dreadful hurry, and that probably he had enough to do in town without needing to bustle down to Pavlofsk to see them. Their mother was quite angry at the very idea of such a thing, and announced her absolute conviction that he would turn up the next day at latest.

So next day the prince was expected all the morning, and at dinner, tea, and supper; and when he did not appear in the evening, Mrs. Epanchin quarrelled with everyone in the house, finding plenty of pretexts without so much as mentioning the prince's name.

On the third day there was no talk of him at all, until Aglaya remarked at dinner: "Mamma is cross because the prince hasn't turned up," to which the general replied that it was not his fault.

Mrs. Epanchin misunderstood the observation, and rising from her place she left the room in majestic wrath. In the evening, however, Colia came with the story of the prince's adventures, so far as he knew them. Mrs. Epanchin was triumphant; although Colia had to listen to a long lecture. "He idles about here the whole day long, one can't get rid of him; and then when he is wanted he does not come. He might have sent a line if he did not wish to inconvenience himself."

At the words "one can't get rid of him," Colia was very angry, and nearly flew into a rage; but he resolved to be quiet for the time and show his resentment later. If the words had been less offensive he might have forgiven them, so pleased was he to see Lizabetha Prokofievna worried and anxious about the prince's illness.

She would have insisted on sending to Petersburg at once, for a certain great medical celebrity; but her daughters dissuaded her, though they were not willing to stay behind when she at once prepared to go and visit the invalid. Aglaya, however, suggested that it was a little unceremonious to go *en masse* to see him.

"Very well then, stay at home," said Mrs. Epanchin, "and a good thing too, for Evgenie Pavlovitch is coming down and there will be no one at home to receive him."

Of course, after this, Aglaya went with the rest. In fact, she had never had the slightest intention of doing otherwise.

Prince S., who was in the house, was requested to escort the ladies. He had been much interested when he first heard of the prince from the Epanchins. It appeared that they had known one another before, and had spent some time together in a little provincial town three months ago. Prince S. had greatly taken to him, and was delighted with the opportunity of meeting him again.

The general had not come down from town as yet, nor had Evgenie Pavlovitch arrived.

It was not more than two or three hundred yards from the Epanchins' house to Lebedeff's. The first disagreeable impression experienced by Mrs. Epanchin was to find the prince surrounded by a whole assembly of other guests—not to mention the fact that some of those present were particularly detestable in her eyes. The next annoying circumstance was when an apparently strong and healthy young fellow, well dressed, and smiling, came forward to meet her on the terrace, instead of the half-dying unfortunate whom she had expected to see.

She was astonished and vexed, and her disappointment pleased Colia immensely. Of course he could have undeceived her before she started, but the mischievous boy had been careful not to do that, foreseeing the probably laughable disgust that she would experience when she found her dear friend, the prince, in good health. Colia was indelicate enough to voice the delight he felt at his success in managing to annoy Lizabetha Prokofievna, with whom, in spite of their really amicable relations, he was constantly sparring.

"Just wait a while, my boy!" said she; "don't be too certain of your triumph." And she sat down heavily, in the arm-chair pushed forward by the prince.

Lebedeff, Ptitsin, and General Ivolgin hastened to find chairs for the young ladies. Varia greeted them joyfully, and they exchanged confidences in ecstatic whispers.

"I must admit, prince, I was a little put out to see you up and about like this—I expected to find you in bed; but I give you my word, I was only annoyed for an instant, before I collected my thoughts properly. I am always wiser on second thoughts, and I dare say you are the same. I assure you I am as glad to see you well as though you were my own son,—yes, and more; and if you don't believe me the more shame to you, and it's not my fault. But that spiteful boy delights in playing all sorts of tricks. You are his patron, it seems. Well, I warn you that one fine morning I shall deprive myself of the pleasure of his further acquaintance."

"What have I done wrong now?" cried Colia. "What was the good of telling you that the prince was nearly well again? You would not have believed me; it was so much more interesting to picture him on his death-bed."

"How long do you remain here, prince?" asked Madame Epanchin.

"All the summer, and perhaps longer."

"You are alone, aren't you,—not married?"

"No, I'm not married!" replied the prince, smiling at the ingenuousness of this little feeler.

"Oh, you needn't laugh! These things do happen, you know! Now then—why didn't you come to us? We have a wing quite empty. But just as you like, of course. Do you lease it from *him?*—this fellow, I mean," she added, nodding towards Lebedeff. "And why does he always wriggle so?"

At that moment Vera, carrying the baby in her arms as usual, came out of the house, on to the terrace. Lebedeff kept fidgeting among the chairs, and did not seem to know what to do with himself, though he had no intention of going away. He no sooner caught sight of his daughter, than he rushed in her direction, waving his arms to keep her away; he even forgot himself so far as to stamp his foot.

"Is he mad?" asked Madame Epanchin suddenly.

"No, he..."

"Perhaps he is drunk? Your company is rather peculiar," she added, with a glance at the other guests....

"But what a pretty girl! Who is she?"

"That is Lebedeff's daughter—Vera Lukianovna."

"Indeed? She looks very sweet. I should like to make her acquaintance."

The words were hardly out of her mouth, when Lebedeff dragged Vera forward, in order to present her.

"Orphans, poor orphans!" he began in a pathetic voice.

"The child she carries is an orphan, too. She is Vera's sister, my daughter Luboff. The day this babe was born, six weeks ago, my wife died, by the will of God Almighty.... Yes... Vera takes her mother's place, though she is but her sister... nothing more... nothing more..."

"And you! You are nothing more than a fool, if you'll excuse me! Well! well! you know that yourself, I expect," said the lady indignantly.

Lebedeff bowed low. "It is the truth," he replied, with extreme respect.

"Oh, Mr. Lebedeff, I am told you lecture on the Apocalypse. Is it true?" asked Aglaya.

"Yes, that is so... for the last fifteen years."

"I have heard of you, and I think read of you in the newspapers."

"No, that was another commentator, whom the papers named. He is dead, however, and I have taken his place," said the other, much delighted.

"We are neighbours, so will you be so kind as to come over one day and explain the Apocalypse to me?" said Aglaya. "I do not understand it in the least."

"Allow me to warn you," interposed General Ivolgin, "that he is the greatest charlatan on earth." He had taken the chair next to the girl, and was impatient to begin talking. "No doubt there are pleasures and amusements peculiar to the country," he continued, "and to listen to a pretended student holding forth on the book of the Revelations may be as good as any other. It may even be original. But... you seem to be looking at me with some surprise—may I introduce myself—General Ivolgin—I carried you in my arms as a baby—"

"Delighted, I'm sure," said Aglaya; "I am acquainted with Varvara Ardalionovna and Nina Alexandrovna." She was trying hard to restrain herself from laughing.

Mrs. Epanchin flushed up; some accumulation of spleen in her suddenly needed an outlet. She could not bear this General Ivolgin whom she had once known, long ago—in society.

"You are deviating from the truth, sir, as usual!" she remarked, boiling over with indignation; "you never carried her in your life!"

"You have forgotten, mother," said Aglaya, suddenly. "He really did carry me about,—in Tver, you know. I was six years old, I remember. He made me a bow and arrow, and I shot a pigeon. Don't you remember shooting a pigeon, you and I, one day?"

"Yes, and he made me a cardboard helmet, and a little wooden sword—I remember!" said Adelaida.

"Yes, I remember too!" said Alexandra. "You quarrelled about the wounded pigeon, and Adelaida was put in the corner, and stood there with her helmet and sword and all."

The poor general had merely made the remark about having carried Aglaya in his arms because he always did so begin a conversation with young people. But it happened that this time he had really hit upon the truth, though he had himself entirely forgotten the fact. But when Adelaida and Aglaya recalled the episode of the pigeon, his mind became filled with memories, and it is impossible to describe how this poor old man, usually half drunk, was moved by the recollection.

"I remember—I remember it all!" he cried. "I was captain then. You were such a lovely little thing—Nina Alexandrovna!—Gania, listen! I was received then by General Epanchin."

"Yes, and look what you have come to now!" interrupted Mrs. Epanchin. "However, I see you have not quite drunk your better feelings away. But you've broken your wife's heart, sir—and instead of looking after your children, you have spent your time in public-houses and debtors' prisons! Go away, my friend, stand in some corner and weep, and bemoan your fallen dignity, and perhaps God will forgive you yet! Go, go! I'm serious! There's nothing so favourable for repentance as to think of the past with feelings of remorse!"

There was no need to repeat that she was serious. The general, like all drunkards, was extremely emotional and easily touched by recollections of his better days. He rose and walked quietly to the door, so meekly that Mrs. Epanchin was instantly sorry for him.

"Ardalion Alexandrovitch," she cried after him, "wait a moment, we are all sinners! When you feel that your conscience reproaches you a little less, come over to me and we'll have a talk about the past! I dare say I am fifty times more of a sinner than you are! And now go, go, good-bye, you had better not stay here!" she added, in alarm, as he turned as though to come back.

"Don't go after him just now, Colia, or he'll be vexed, and the benefit of this moment will be lost!" said the prince, as the boy was hurrying out of the room.

"Quite true! Much better to go in half an hour or so," said Mrs. Epanchin.

"That's what comes of telling the truth for once in one's life!" said Lebedeff. "It reduced him to tears."

"Come, come! the less *you* say about it the better—to judge from all I have heard about you!" replied Mrs. Epanchin.

The prince took the first opportunity of informing the Epanchin ladies that he had intended to pay them a visit that day, if they had not themselves come this afternoon, and Lizabetha Prokofievna replied that she hoped he would still do so.

By this time some of the visitors had disappeared.

Ptitsin had tactfully retreated to Lebedeff's wing; and Gania soon followed him.

The latter had behaved modestly, but with dignity, on this occasion of his first meeting with the Epanchins since the rupture. Twice Mrs. Epanchin had deliberately examined him from head to foot; but he had stood fire without flinching. He was certainly much changed, as anyone could see who had not met him for some time; and this fact seemed to afford Aglaya a good deal of satisfaction.

"That was Gavrila Ardalionovitch, who just went out, wasn't it?" she asked suddenly, interrupting somebody else's conversation to make the remark.

"Yes, it was," said the prince.

"I hardly knew him; he is much changed, and for the better!"

"I am very glad," said the prince.

"He has been very ill," added Varia.

"How has he changed for the better?" asked Mrs. Epanchin. "I don't see any change for the better! What's better in him? Where did you get *that* idea from? *what's* better?"

"There's nothing better than the 'poor knight'!" said Colia, who was standing near the last speaker's chair.

"I quite agree with you there!" said Prince S., laughing.

"So do I," said Adelaida, solemnly.

"*What* poor knight?" asked Mrs. Epanchin, looking round at the face of each of the speakers in turn. Seeing, however, that Aglaya was blushing, she added, angrily:

"What nonsense you are all talking! What do you mean by poor knight?"

"It's not the first time this urchin, your favourite, has shown his impudence by twisting other people's words," said Aglaya, haughtily.

Every time that Aglaya showed temper (and this was very often), there was so much childish pouting, such "school-girlishness," as it were, in her apparent wrath, that it was impossible to avoid smiling at her, to her own unutterable indignation. On these occasions she would say, "How can they, how *dare* they laugh at me?"

This time everyone laughed at her, her sisters, Prince S., Prince Muishkin (though he himself had flushed for some reason), and Colia. Aglaya was dreadfully indignant, and looked twice as pretty in her wrath.

"He's always twisting round what one says," she cried.

"I am only repeating your own exclamation!" said Colia. "A month ago you were turning over the pages of your Don Quixote, and suddenly called out 'there is nothing better than the poor knight.' I don't know whom you were referring to, of course, whether to Don Quixote, or Evgenie Pavlovitch, or someone else, but you certainly said these words, and afterwards there was a long conversation..."

"You are inclined to go a little too far, my good boy, with your guesses," said Mrs. Epanchin, with some show of annoyance.

"But it's not I alone," cried Colia. "They all talked about it, and they do still. Why, just now Prince S. and Adelaida Ivanovna declared that they upheld 'the poor knight'; so evidently there does exist a 'poor knight'; and if it were not for Adelaida Ivanovna, we should have known long ago who the 'poor knight' was."

"Why, how am I to blame?" asked Adelaida, smiling.

"You wouldn't draw his portrait for us, that's why you are to blame! Aglaya Ivanovna asked you to draw his portrait, and gave you the whole subject of the picture. She invented it herself; and you wouldn't."

"What was I to draw? According to the lines she quoted:

> *"'From his face he never lifted*
> *That eternal mask of steel.'"*

"What sort of a face was I to draw? I couldn't draw a mask."

"I don't know what you are driving at; what mask do you mean?" said Mrs. Epanchin, irritably. She began to see pretty clearly though what it meant, and whom they referred to by the generally accepted title of "poor knight." But what specially annoyed her was that the prince was looking so uncomfortable, and blushing like a ten-year-old child.

"Well, have you finished your silly joke?" she added, "and am I to be told what this 'poor knight' means, or is it a solemn secret which cannot be approached lightly?"

But they all laughed on.

"It's simply that there is a Russian poem," began Prince S., evidently anxious to change the conversation, "a strange thing, without beginning or end, and all about a 'poor knight.' A month or so ago, we were all talking and laughing, and looking up a subject for one of Adelaida's pictures—you know it is the principal business of this family to find subjects for Adelaida's pictures. Well, we happened upon this 'poor knight.' I don't remember who thought of it first—"

"Oh! Aglaya Ivanovna did," said Colia.

"Very likely—I don't recollect," continued Prince S.

"Some of us laughed at the subject; some liked it; but she declared that, in order to make a picture of the gentleman, she must first see his face. We then began to think over all our friends' faces to see if any of them would do, and none suited us, and so the matter stood; that's all. I don't know why Nicolai Ardalionovitch has brought up the joke now. What was appropriate and funny then, has quite lost all interest by this time."

"Probably there's some new silliness about it," said Mrs. Epanchin, sarcastically.

"There is no silliness about it at all—only the profoundest respect," said Aglaya, very seriously. She had quite recovered her temper; in fact, from certain signs, it was fair to conclude that she was delighted to see this joke going so far; and a careful observer might have remarked that her satisfaction dated from the moment when the fact of the prince's confusion became apparent to all.

"'Profoundest respect!' What nonsense! First, insane giggling, and then, all of a sudden, a display of 'profoundest respect.' Why respect? Tell me at once, why have you suddenly developed this 'profound respect,' eh?"

"Because," replied Aglaya gravely, "in the poem the knight is described as a man capable of living up to an ideal all his life. That sort of thing is not to be found every day among the men of our times. In the poem it is not stated exactly what the ideal was, but it was evidently some vision, some revelation of pure Beauty, and the knight wore round his neck, instead of a scarf, a rosary. A device—A. N. B.—the meaning of which is not explained, was inscribed on his shield—"

"No, A. N. D.," corrected Colia.

"I say A. N. B., and so it shall be!" cried Aglaya, irritably. "Anyway, the 'poor knight' did not care what his lady was, or what she did. He had chosen his ideal, and he was bound to serve her, and break lances for her, and acknowledge her as the ideal of pure Beauty, whatever she might say or do afterwards. If she had taken to stealing, he would have championed her just the same. I think the poet desired to embody in this one picture the whole spirit of medieval chivalry and the platonic love of a pure and high-souled knight. Of course it's all an ideal, and in the 'poor knight' that spirit reached the utmost limit of asceticism. He is a Don Quixote, only serious and not comical. I used not to understand him, and laughed at him, but now I love the 'poor knight,' and respect his actions."

So ended Aglaya; and, to look at her, it was difficult, indeed, to judge whether she was joking or in earnest.

"Pooh! he was a fool, and his actions were the actions of a fool," said Mrs. Epanchin; "and as for you, young woman, you ought to know better. At all events, you are not to talk like that again. What poem is it? Recite it! I want to hear this poem! I have hated poetry all my life. Prince, you must excuse this nonsense. We neither of us like this sort of thing! Be patient!"

They certainly were put out, both of them.

The prince tried to say something, but he was too confused, and could not get his words out. Aglaya, who had taken such liberties in her little speech, was the only person present, perhaps, who was not in the least embarrassed. She seemed, in fact, quite pleased.

She now rose solemnly from her seat, walked to the centre of the terrace, and stood in front of the prince's chair. All looked on with some surprise, and Prince S. and her sisters with feelings of decided alarm, to see what new frolic she was up to; it had gone quite far enough already, they thought. But Aglaya evidently thoroughly enjoyed the affectation and ceremony with which she was introducing her recitation of the poem.

Mrs. Epanchin was just wondering whether she would not forbid the performance after all, when, at the very moment that Aglaya commenced her declamation, two new guests, both talking loudly, entered from the street. The new arrivals were General Epanchin and a young man.

Their entrance caused some slight commotion.

CHAPTER VII.

The young fellow accompanying the general was about twenty-eight, tall, and well built, with a handsome and clever face, and bright black eyes, full of fun and intelligence.

Aglaya did not so much as glance at the new arrivals, but went on with her recitation, gazing at the prince the while in an affected manner, and at him alone. It was clear to him that she was doing all this with some special object.

But the new guests at least somewhat eased his strained and uncomfortable position. Seeing them approaching, he rose from his chair, and nodding amicably to the general, signed to him not to interrupt the recitation. He then got behind his chair, and stood there with his left hand resting on the back of it. Thanks to this change of position, he was able to listen to the ballad with far less embarrassment than before. Mrs. Epanchin had also twice motioned to the new arrivals to be quiet, and stay where they were.

The prince was much interested in the young man who had just entered. He easily concluded that this was Evgenie Pavlovitch Radomski, of whom he had already heard mention several times. He was puzzled, however, by the young man's plain clothes, for he had always heard of Evgenie Pavlovitch as a military man. An ironical smile played on Evgenie's lips all the while the recitation was proceeding, which showed that he, too, was probably in the secret of the 'poor knight' joke. But it had become quite a different matter with Aglaya. All the affectation of manner which she had displayed at the beginning disappeared as the ballad proceeded. She spoke the lines in so serious and exalted a manner, and with so much taste, that she even seemed to justify the exaggerated solemnity with which she had stepped forward. It was impossible to discern in her now anything but a deep feeling for the spirit of the poem which she had undertaken to interpret.

Her eyes were aglow with inspiration, and a slight tremor of rapture passed over her lovely features once or twice. She continued to recite:

> *"Once there came a vision glorious,*
> *Mystic, dreadful, wondrous fair;*
> *Burned itself into his spirit,*
> *And abode for ever there!*
>
> *"Never more—from that sweet moment—*
> *Gazéd he on womankind;*
> *He was dumb to love and wooing*
> *And to all their graces blind.*
>
> *"Full of love for that sweet vision,*
> *Brave and pure he took the field;*
> *With his blood he stained the letters*
> *N. P. B. upon his shield.*
>
> *"'Lumen caeli, sancta Rosa!'*
> *Shouting on the foe he fell,*
> *And like thunder rang his war-cry*
> *O'er the cowering infidel.*
>
> *"Then within his distant castle,*
> *Home returned, he dreamed his days—*
> *Silent, sad,—and when death took him*
> *He was mad, the legend says."*

When recalling all this afterwards the prince could not for the life of him understand how to reconcile the beautiful, sincere, pure nature of the girl with the irony of this jest. That it was a jest there was no doubt whatever; he knew that well enough, and had good reason, too, for his conviction; for during her recitation of the ballad Aglaya had deliberately changed the letters A. N. B. into N. P. B. He was quite sure she had not done this by accident, and that his ears had not deceived him. At all events her performance—which was a joke, of course, if rather a crude one,—was premeditated. They had evidently talked (and laughed) over the 'poor knight' for more than a month.

Yet Aglaya had brought out these letters N. P. B. not only without the slightest appearance of irony, or even any particular accentuation, but with so even and unbroken an appearance of seriousness that assuredly anyone might have supposed that these initials were the original ones written in the ballad. The thing made an uncomfortable impression upon the prince. Of course Mrs. Epanchin saw nothing either in the change of initials or in the insinuation embodied therein. General Epanchin only knew that there was a recitation of verses going on, and took no further interest in the matter. Of the rest of the audience, many had understood the allusion and wondered both at the daring of the lady and at the motive underlying it, but tried to show no sign of their feelings. But Evgenie Pavlovitch (as the prince was ready to wager) both comprehended and tried his best to show that he comprehended; his smile was too mocking to leave any doubt on that point.

"How beautiful that is!" cried Mrs. Epanchin, with sincere admiration. "Whose is it?"

"Pushkin's, mama, of course! Don't disgrace us all by showing your ignorance," said Adelaida.

"As soon as we reach home give it to me to read."

"I don't think we have a copy of Pushkin in the house."

"There are a couple of torn volumes somewhere; they have been lying about from time immemorial," added Alexandra.

"Send Feodor or Alexey up by the very first train to buy a copy, then.—Aglaya, come here—kiss me, dear, you recited beautifully! but," she added in a whisper, "if you were sincere I am sorry for you. If it was a joke, I do not approve of the feelings which prompted you to do it, and in any case you would have done far better not to recite it at all. Do you understand?—Now come along, young woman; we've sat here too long. I'll speak to you about this another time."

Meanwhile the prince took the opportunity of greeting General Epanchin, and the general introduced Evgenie Pavlovitch to him.

"I caught him up on the way to your house," explained the general. "He had heard that we were all here."

"Yes, and I heard that you were here, too," added Evgenie Pavlovitch; "and since I had long promised myself the pleasure of seeking not only your acquaintance but your friendship, I did not wish to waste time, but came straight on. I am sorry to hear that you are unwell."

"Oh, but I'm quite well now, thank you, and very glad to make your acquaintance. Prince S. has often spoken to me about you," said Muishkin, and for an instant the two men looked intently into one another's eyes.

The prince remarked that Evgenie Pavlovitch's plain clothes had evidently made a great impression upon the company present, so much so that all other interests seemed to be effaced before this surprising fact.

His change of dress was evidently a matter of some importance. Adelaida and Alexandra poured out a stream of questions; Prince S., a relative of the young man, appeared annoyed; and Ivan Fedorovitch quite excited. Aglaya alone was not interested. She merely looked closely at Evgenie for a minute, curious perhaps as to whether civil or military clothes became him best, then turned away and paid no more attention to him or his costume. Lizabetha Prokofievna asked no questions, but it was clear that she was uneasy, and the prince fancied that Evgenie was not in her good graces.

"He has astonished me," said Ivan Fedorovitch. "I nearly fell down with surprise. I could hardly believe my eyes when I met him in Petersburg just now. Why this haste? That's what I want to know. He has always said himself that there is no need to break windows."

Evgenie Pavlovitch remarked here that he had spoken of his intention of leaving the service long ago. He had, however, always made more or less of a joke about it, so no one had taken him seriously. For that matter he joked about everything, and his friends never knew what to believe, especially if he did not wish them to understand him.

"I have only retired for a time," said he, laughing. "For a few months; at most for a year."

"But there is no necessity for you to retire at all," complained the general, "as far as I know."

"I want to go and look after my country estates. You advised me to do that yourself," was the reply. "And then I wish to go abroad."

After a few more expostulations, the conversation drifted into other channels, but the prince, who had been an attentive listener, thought all this excitement about so small a matter very curious. "There must be more in it than appears," he said to himself.

"I see the 'poor knight' has come on the scene again," said Evgenie Pavlovitch, stepping to Aglaya's side.

To the amazement of the prince, who overheard the remark, Aglaya looked haughtily and inquiringly at the questioner, as though she would give him to know, once for all, that there could be no talk between them about the 'poor knight,' and that she did not understand his question.

"But not now! It is too late to send to town for a Pushkin now. It is much too late, I say!" Colia was exclaiming in a loud voice. "I have told you so at least a hundred times."

"Yes, it is really much too late to send to town now," said Evgenie Pavlovitch, who had escaped from Aglaya as rapidly as possible. "I am sure the shops are shut in Petersburg; it is past eight o'clock," he added, looking at his watch.

"We have done without him so far," interrupted Adelaida in her turn. "Surely we can wait until to-morrow."

"Besides," said Colia, "it is quite unusual, almost improper, for people in our position to take any interest in literature. Ask Evgenie Pavlovitch if I am not right. It is much more fashionable to drive a waggonette with red wheels."

"You got that from some magazine, Colia," remarked Adelaida.

"He gets most of his conversation in that way," laughed Evgenie Pavlovitch. "He borrows whole phrases from the reviews. I have long had the pleasure of knowing both Nicholai Ardalionovitch and his conversational methods, but this time he was not repeating something he had read; he was alluding, no doubt, to my yellow waggonette, which has, or had, red wheels. But I have exchanged it, so you are rather behind the times, Colia."

The prince had been listening attentively to Radomski's words, and thought his manner very pleasant. When Colia chaffed him about his waggonette he had replied with perfect equality and in a friendly fashion. This pleased Muishkin.

At this moment Vera came up to Lizabetha Prokofievna, carrying several large and beautifully bound books, apparently quite new.

"What is it?" demanded the lady.

"This is Pushkin," replied the girl. "Papa told me to offer it to you."

"What? Impossible!" exclaimed Mrs. Epanchin.

"Not as a present, not as a present! I should not have taken the liberty," said Lebedeff, appearing suddenly from behind his daughter. "It is our own Pushkin, our family copy, Annenkoff's edition; it could not be bought now. I beg to suggest, with great respect, that your excellency should buy it, and thus quench the noble literary thirst which is consuming you at this moment," he concluded grandiloquently.

"Oh! if you will sell it, very good—and thank you. You shall not be a loser! But for goodness' sake, don't twist about like that, sir! I have heard of you; they tell me you are a very learned person. We must have a talk one of these days. You will bring me the books yourself?"

"With the greatest respect... and... and veneration," replied Lebedeff, making extraordinary grimaces.

"Well, bring them, with or without respect, provided always you do not drop them on the way; but on the condition," went on the lady, looking full at him, "that you do not cross my threshold. I do not intend to receive you today. You may send your daughter Vera at once, if you like. I am much pleased with her."

"Why don't you tell him about them?" said Vera impatiently to her father. "They will come in, whether you announce them or not, and they are beginning to make a row. Lef Nicolaievitch,"— she addressed herself to the prince—"four men are here asking for you. They have waited some time, and are beginning to make a fuss, and papa will not bring them in."

"Who are these people?" said the prince.

"They say that they have come on business, and they are the kind of men, who, if you do not see them here, will follow you about the street. It would be better to receive them, and then you will get rid of them. Gavrila Ardalionovitch and Ptitsin are both there, trying to make them hear reason."

"Pavlicheff's son! It is not worth while!" cried Lebedeff. "There is no necessity to see them, and it would be most unpleasant for your excellency. They do not deserve..."

"What? Pavlicheff's son!" cried the prince, much perturbed. "I know... I know—but I entrusted this matter to Gavrila Ardalionovitch. He told me..."

At that moment Gania, accompanied by Ptitsin, came out to the terrace. From an adjoining room came a noise of angry voices, and General Ivolgin, in loud tones, seemed to be trying to shout them down. Colia rushed off at once to investigate the cause of the uproar.

"This is most interesting!" observed Evgenie Pavlovitch.

"I expect he knows all about it!" thought the prince.

"What, the son of Pavlicheff? And who may this son of Pavlicheff be?" asked General Epanchin with surprise; and looking curiously around him, he discovered that he alone had no clue to the mystery. Expectation and suspense were on every face, with the exception of that of the prince, who stood gravely wondering how an affair so entirely personal could have awakened such lively and widespread interest in so short a time.

Aglaya went up to him with a peculiarly serious look.

"It will be well," she said, "if you put an end to this affair yourself *at once*: but you must allow us to be your witnesses. They want to throw mud at you, prince, and you must be triumphantly vindicated. I give you joy beforehand!"

"And I also wish for justice to be done, once for all," cried Madame Epanchin, "about this impudent claim. Deal with them promptly, prince, and don't spare them! I am sick of hearing about the affair, and many a quarrel I have had in your cause. But I confess I am anxious to see what happens, so do make them come out here, and we will remain. You have heard people talking about it, no doubt?" she added, turning to Prince S.

"Of course," said he. "I have heard it spoken about at your house, and I am anxious to see these young men!"

"They are Nihilists, are they not?"

"No, they are not Nihilists," explained Lebedeff, who seemed much excited. "This is another lot—a special group. According to my nephew they are more advanced even than the Nihilists. You are quite wrong, excellency, if you think that your presence will intimidate them; nothing intimidates them. Educated men, learned men even, are to be found among Nihilists; these go further, in that they are men of action. The movement is, properly speaking, a derivative from Nihilism—though they are only known indirectly, and by hearsay, for they never advertise their doings in the papers. They go straight to the point. For them, it is not a question of showing that Pushkin is stupid, or that Russia must be torn in pieces. No; but if they have a great desire for anything, they believe they have a right to get it even at the cost of the lives, say, of eight persons. They are checked by no obstacles. In fact, prince, I should not advise you..."

But Muishkin had risen, and was on his way to open the door for his visitors.

"You are slandering them, Lebedeff," said he, smiling.

"You are always thinking about your nephew's conduct. Don't believe him, Lizabetha Prokofievna. I can assure you Gorsky and Daniloff are exceptions—and that these are only... mistaken. However, I do not care about receiving them here, in public. Excuse me, Lizabetha Prokofievna. They are coming, and you can see them, and then I will take them away. Please come in, gentlemen!"

Another thought tormented him: He wondered was this an arranged business—arranged to happen when he had guests in his house, and in anticipation of his humiliation rather than of his triumph? But he reproached himself bitterly for such a thought, and felt as if he should die of shame if it were discovered. When his new visitors appeared, he was quite ready to believe himself infinitely less to be respected than any of them.

Four persons entered, led by General Ivolgin, in a state of great excitement, and talking eloquently.

"He is for me, undoubtedly!" thought the prince, with a smile. Colia also had joined the party, and was talking with animation to Hippolyte, who listened with a jeering smile on his lips.

The prince begged the visitors to sit down. They were all so young that it made the proceedings seem even more extraordinary. Ivan Fedorovitch, who really understood nothing of what was going on, felt indignant at the sight of these youths, and would have interfered in some way had it not been for the extreme interest shown by his wife in the affair. He therefore remained, partly through curiosity, partly through good-nature, hoping that his presence might be of some use. But the bow with which General Ivolgin greeted him irritated him anew; he frowned, and decided to be absolutely silent.

As to the rest, one was a man of thirty, the retired officer, now a boxer, who had been with Rogojin, and in his happier days had given fifteen roubles at a time to beggars. Evidently he had joined the others as a comrade to give them moral, and if necessary material, support. The man who had been spoken of as "Pavlicheff's son," although he gave the name of Antip Burdovsky, was about twenty-two years of age, fair, thin and rather tall. He was remarkable for the poverty, not to say uncleanliness, of his personal appearance: the sleeves of his overcoat were greasy; his dirty waistcoat, buttoned up to his neck, showed not a trace of linen; a filthy black silk scarf, twisted till it resembled a cord, was round his neck, and his hands were unwashed. He looked round with an air of insolent effrontery. His face, covered with pimples, was neither thoughtful nor even contemptuous; it wore an expression of complacent satisfaction in demanding his rights and in being an aggrieved party. His voice trembled, and he spoke so fast, and with such stammerings, that he might have been taken for a foreigner, though the purest Russian blood ran in his veins. Lebedeff's nephew, whom the reader has seen already, accompanied him, and also the youth named Hippolyte Terentieff. The latter was only seventeen or eighteen. He had an intelligent face, though it was usually irritated and fretful in expression. His skeleton-like figure, his ghastly complexion, the brightness of his eyes, and the red spots of colour on his cheeks, betrayed the victim of consumption to the most casual glance. He coughed persistently, and panted for breath; it looked as though he had but a few weeks more to live. He was nearly dead with fatigue, and fell, rather than sat, into a chair. The rest bowed as they came in; and being more or less abashed, put on an air of extreme self-assurance. In short, their attitude was not that which one would have expected in men who professed to despise all trivialities, all foolish mundane conventions, and indeed everything, except their own personal interests.

"Antip Burdovsky," stuttered the son of Pavlicheff.

"Vladimir Doktorenko," said Lebedeff's nephew briskly, and with a certain pride, as if he boasted of his name.

"Keller," murmured the retired officer.

"Hippolyte Terentieff," cried the last-named, in a shrill voice.

They sat now in a row facing the prince, and frowned, and played with their caps. All appeared ready to speak, and yet all were silent; the defiant expression on their faces seemed to say, "No, sir, you don't take us in!" It could be felt that the first word spoken by anyone present would bring a torrent of speech from the whole deputation.

CHAPTER VIII.

"I *did* not expect you, gentlemen," began the prince. "I have been ill until to-day. A month ago," he continued, addressing himself to Antip Burdovsky, "I put your business into Gavrila Ardalionovitch Ivolgin's hands, as I told you then. I do not in the least object to having a personal interview... but you will agree with me that this is hardly the time... I propose that we go into another room, if you will not keep me long... As you see, I have friends here, and believe me..."

"Friends as many as you please, but allow me," interrupted the harsh voice of Lebedeff's nephew—"allow me to tell you that you might have treated us rather more politely, and not have kept us waiting at least two hours...

"No doubt... and I... is that acting like a prince? And you... you may be a general! But I... I am not your valet! And I... I..." stammered Antip Burdovsky.

He was extremely excited; his lips trembled, and the resentment of an embittered soul was in his voice. But he spoke so indistinctly that hardly a dozen words could be gathered.

"It was a princely action!" sneered Hippolyte.

"If anyone had treated me so," grumbled the boxer.

"I mean to say that if I had been in Burdovsky's place...I..."

"Gentlemen, I did not know you were there; I have only just been informed, I assure you," repeated Muishkin.

"We are not afraid of your friends, prince," remarked Lebedeff's nephew, "for we are within our rights."

The shrill tones of Hippolyte interrupted him. "What right have you... by what right do you demand us to submit this matter, about Burdovsky... to the judgment of your friends? We know only too well what the judgment of your friends will be!..."

This beginning gave promise of a stormy discussion. The prince was much discouraged, but at last he managed to make himself heard amid the vociferations of his excited visitors.

"If you," he said, addressing Burdovsky—"if you prefer not to speak here, I offer again to go into another room with you... and as to your waiting to see me, I repeat that I only this instant heard..."

"Well, you have no right, you have no right, no right at all!... Your friends indeed!"... gabbled Burdovsky, defiantly examining the faces round him, and becoming more and more excited. "You have no right!..." As he ended thus abruptly, he leant forward, staring at the prince with his short-sighted, bloodshot eyes. The latter was so astonished, that he did not reply, but looked steadily at him in return.

"Lef Nicolaievitch!" interposed Madame Epanchin, suddenly, "read this at once, this very moment! It is about this business."

She held out a weekly comic paper, pointing to an article on one of its pages. Just as the visitors were coming in, Lebedeff, wishing to ingratiate himself with the great lady, had pulled this paper from his pocket, and presented it to her, indicating a few columns marked in pencil. Lizabetha Prokofievna had had time to read some of it, and was greatly upset.

"Would it not be better to peruse it alone... later," asked the prince, nervously.

"No, no, read it—read it at once directly, and aloud, aloud!" cried she, calling Colia to her and giving him the journal.—"Read it aloud, so that everyone may hear it!"

An impetuous woman, Lizabetha Prokofievna sometimes weighed her anchors and put out to sea quite regardless of the possible storms she might encounter. Ivan Fedorovitch felt a sudden pang of alarm, but the others were merely curious, and somewhat surprised. Colia unfolded the paper, and began to read, in his clear, high-pitched voice, the following article:

"Proletarians and scions of nobility! An episode of the brigandage of today and every day! Progress! Reform! Justice!"

"Strange things are going on in our so-called Holy Russia in this age of reform and great enterprises; this age of patriotism in which hundreds of millions are yearly sent abroad; in which industry is encouraged, and the hands of Labour paralyzed, etc.; there is no end to this, gentlemen, so let us come to the point. A strange thing has happened to a scion of our defunct aristocracy. (De profundis!) The grandfathers of these scions ruined themselves at the gaming-tables; their fathers were forced to serve as officers or subalterns; some have died just as they were about to be tried for innocent thoughtlessness in the handling of public funds. Their children are sometimes congenital idiots, like the hero of our story; sometimes they are found in the dock at the Assizes, where they are generally acquitted by the jury for edifying motives; sometimes they distinguish themselves by one of those burning scandals that amaze the public and add another blot to the stained record of our age. Six months ago—that is, last winter—this particular scion returned to Russia, wearing gaiters like a foreigner, and shivering with cold in an old scantily-lined cloak. He had come from Switzerland, where he had just undergone a successful course of treatment for idiocy (sic!). Certainly Fortune favoured him, for, apart from the interesting malady of which he was cured in Switzerland (can there be a cure for idiocy?) his story proves the truth of the Russian proverb that 'happiness is the right of certain classes!' Judge for yourselves. Our subject was an infant in arms when he lost his father, an officer who died just as he was about to be court-martialled for gambling away the funds of his company, and perhaps also for flogging a subordinate to excess (remember the good old days, gentlemen). The orphan was brought up by the charity of a very rich Russian landowner. In the good old days, this man, whom we will call P——, owned four thousand souls as serfs (souls as serfs!—can you understand such an expression, gentlemen? I cannot; it must be looked up in a dictionary before one can understand it; these things of a bygone day are already unintelligible to us). He appears to have been one of those Russian parasites who lead an idle existence abroad, spending the summer at some spa, and the winter in Paris, to the greater profit of the organizers of public balls. It may safely be said that the manager of the Chateau des Fleurs (lucky man!) pocketed at least a third of the money paid by Russian peasants to their lords in the days of serfdom. However this may be, the gay P—— brought up the orphan like a prince, provided him with tutors and governesses (pretty, of course!) whom he chose himself in Paris. But the little aristocrat, the last of his noble race, was an idiot. The governesses, recruited at the Chateau des Fleurs, laboured in vain; at twenty years of age their pupil could not speak in any language, not even Russian. But ignorance of the latter was still excusable. At last P—— was seized with a strange notion; he imagined that in Switzerland they could change an idiot into a man of sense. After all, the idea was quite logical; a parasite and landowner naturally supposed that intelligence was a marketable commodity like everything else, and that in Switzerland especially it could be bought for money. The case was entrusted to a celebrated Swiss professor, and cost thousands of roubles; the treatment lasted five years. Needless to say, the idiot did not become intelligent, but it is alleged that he grew into something more or less resembling a man. At this stage P—— died suddenly, and, as usual, he had made no will and left his affairs in disorder. A crowd of eager claimants arose, who cared nothing about any last scion of a noble race undergoing treatment in Switzerland, at the expense of the deceased, as a congenital idiot. Idiot though he was, the noble scion tried to cheat his professor, and they say he succeeded in getting him to continue the treatment gratis for two years, by concealing the death of his benefactor. But the professor himself was a charlatan. Getting anxious at last when no money was forthcoming, and alarmed above all by his patient's appetite, he presented him with a pair of old gaiters and a shabby cloak and packed him off to Russia, third class. It would seem that Fortune had turned her back upon our hero. Not at all; Fortune, who lets whole populations die of hunger, showered all her gifts at once upon the little aristocrat, like Kryloff's Cloud which passes over an arid plain and empties itself into the sea. He had scarcely arrived in St. Petersburg, when a relation of his mother's (who was of bourgeois origin, of course), died at Moscow. He was a merchant, an Old Believer, and he had no children. He left a fortune of several millions in good current coin, and everything came to our noble scion, our gaitered baron, formerly treated for idiocy in a Swiss lunatic asylum. Instantly the scene changed, crowds of friends gathered round our baron, who meanwhile had lost his head over a celebrated demi-mondaine; he even discovered some relations; moreover a number of young girls of high birth burned to be united to him in lawful matrimony. Could anyone possibly imagine a better match?

Aristocrat, millionaire, and idiot, he has every advantage! One might hunt in vain for his equal, even with the lantern of Diogenes; his like is not to be had even by getting it made to order!"

"Oh, I don't know what this means" cried Ivan Fedorovitch, transported with indignation.

"Leave off, Colia," begged the prince. Exclamations arose on all sides.

"Let him go on reading at all costs!" ordered Lizabetha Prokofievna, evidently preserving her composure by a desperate effort. "Prince, if the reading is stopped, you and I will quarrel."

Colia had no choice but to obey. With crimson cheeks he read on unsteadily:

"But while our young millionaire dwelt as it were in the Empyrean, something new occurred. One fine morning a man called upon him, calm and severe of aspect, distinguished, but plainly dressed. Politely, but in dignified terms, as befitted his errand, he briefly explained the motive for his visit. He was a lawyer of enlightened views; his client was a young man who had consulted him in confidence. This young man was no other than the son of P——, though he bears another name. In his youth P——, the sensualist, had seduced a young girl, poor but respectable. She was a serf, but had received a European education. Finding that a child was expected, he hastened her marriage with a man of noble character who had loved her for a long time. He helped the young couple for a time, but he was soon obliged to give up, for the high-minded husband refused to accept anything from him. Soon the careless nobleman forgot all about his former mistress and the child she had borne him; then, as we know, he died intestate. P——'s son, born after his mother's marriage, found a true father in the generous man whose name he bore. But when he also died, the orphan was left to provide for himself, his mother now being an invalid who had lost the use of her limbs. Leaving her in a distant province, he came to the capital in search of pupils. By dint of daily toil he earned enough to enable him to follow the college courses, and at last to enter the university. But what can one earn by teaching the children of Russian merchants at ten copecks a lesson, especially with an invalid mother to keep? Even her death did not much diminish the hardships of the young man's struggle for existence. Now this is the question: how, in the name of justice, should our scion have argued the case? Our readers will think, no doubt, that he would say to himself: 'P—— showered benefits upon me all my life; he spent tens of thousands of roubles to educate me, to provide me with governesses, and to keep me under treatment in Switzerland. Now I am a millionaire, and P——'s son, a noble young man who is not responsible for the faults of his careless and forgetful father, is wearing himself out giving ill-paid lessons. According to justice, all that was done for me ought to have been done for him. The enormous sums spent upon me were not really mine; they came to me by an error of blind Fortune, when they ought to have gone to P——'s son. They should have gone to benefit him, not me, in whom P—— interested himself by a mere caprice, instead of doing his duty as a father. If I wished to behave nobly, justly, and with delicacy, I ought to bestow half my fortune upon the son of my benefactor; but as economy is my favourite virtue, and I know this is not a case in which the law can intervene, I will not give up half my millions. But it would be too openly vile, too flagrantly infamous, if I did not at least restore to P——'s son the tens of thousands of roubles spent in curing my idiocy. This is simply a case of conscience and of strict justice. Whatever would have become of me if P—— had not looked after my education, and had taken care of his own son instead of me?'

"No, gentlemen, our scions of the nobility do not reason thus. The lawyer, who had taken up the matter purely out of friendship to the young man, and almost against his will, invoked every consideration of justice, delicacy, honour, and even plain figures; in vain, the ex-patient of the Swiss lunatic asylum was inflexible. All this might pass, but the sequel is absolutely unpardonable, and not to be excused by any interesting malady. This millionaire, having but just discarded the old gaiters of his professor, could not even understand that the noble young man slaving away at his lessons was not asking for charitable help, but for his rightful due, though the debt was not a legal one; that, correctly speaking, he was not asking for anything, but it was merely his friends who had thought fit to bestir themselves on his behalf. With the cool insolence of a bloated capitalist, secure in his millions, he majestically drew a banknote for fifty roubles from his pocket-book and sent it to the noble young man as a humiliating piece of charity. You can hardly believe it, gentlemen! You are scandalized and disgusted; you cry out in indignation! But that is what he did! Needless to say, the money was returned, or rather flung back in his face. The case is not within the province of the law, it must be referred to the tribunal of public opinion; this is what we now do, guaranteeing the truth of all the details which we have related."

When Colia had finished reading, he handed the paper to the prince, and retired silently to a corner of the room, hiding his face in his hands. He was overcome by a feeling of inexpressible shame; his boyish sensitiveness was wounded beyond endurance. It seemed to him that something extraordinary, some sudden catastrophe had occurred, and that he was almost the cause of it, because he had read the article aloud.

Yet all the others were similarly affected. The girls were uncomfortable and ashamed. Lizabetha Prokofievna restrained her violent anger by a great effort; perhaps she bitterly regretted her interference in the matter; for the present she kept silence. The prince felt as very shy people often do in such a case; he was so ashamed of the conduct of other people, so humiliated for his guests, that he dared not look them in the face. Ptitsin, Varia, Gania, and Lebedeff himself, all looked rather confused. Stranger still, Hippolyte and the "son of Pavlicheff" also seemed slightly surprised, and Lebedeff's nephew was obviously far from pleased. The boxer alone was perfectly calm; he twisted his moustaches with affected dignity, and if his eyes were cast down it was certainly not in confusion, but rather in noble modesty, as if he did not wish to be insolent in his triumph. It was evident that he was delighted with the article.

"The devil knows what it means," growled Ivan Fedorovitch, under his breath; "it must have taken the united wits of fifty footmen to write it."

"May I ask your reason for such an insulting supposition, sir?" said Hippolyte, trembling with rage.

"You will admit yourself, general, that for an honourable man, if the author is an honourable man, that is an—an insult," growled the boxer suddenly, with convulsive jerkings of his shoulders.

"In the first place, it is not for you to address me as 'sir,' and, in the second place, I refuse to give you any explanation," said Ivan Fedorovitch vehemently; and he rose without another word, and went and stood on the first step of the flight that led from the verandah to the street, turning his back on the company. He was indignant with Lizabetha Prokofievna, who did not think of moving even now.

"Gentlemen, gentlemen, let me speak at last," cried the prince, anxious and agitated. "Please let us understand one another. I say nothing about the article, gentlemen, except that every word is false; I say this because you know it as well as I do. It is shameful. I should be surprised if any one of you could have written it."

"I did not know of its existence till this moment," declared Hippolyte. "I do not approve of it."

"I knew it had been written, but I would not have advised its publication," said Lebedeff's nephew, "because it is premature."

"I knew it, but I have a right. I... I..." stammered the "son of Pavlicheff."

"What! Did you write all that yourself? Is it possible?" asked the prince, regarding Burdovsky with curiosity.

"One might dispute your right to ask such questions," observed Lebedeff's nephew.

"I was only surprised that Mr. Burdovsky should have—however, this is what I have to say. Since you had already given the matter publicity, why did you object just now, when I began to speak of it to my friends?"

"At last!" murmured Lizabetha Prokofievna indignantly.

Lebedeff could restrain himself no longer; he made his way through the row of chairs.

"Prince," he cried, "you are forgetting that if you consented to receive and hear them, it was only because of your kind heart which has no equal, for they had not the least right to demand it, especially as you had placed the matter in the hands of Gavrila Ardalionovitch, which was also extremely kind of you. You are also forgetting, most excellent prince, that you are with friends, a select company; you cannot sacrifice them to these gentlemen, and it is only for you to have them turned out this instant. As the master of the house I shall have great pleasure ...."

"Quite right!" agreed General Ivolgin in a loud voice.

"That will do, Lebedeff, that will do—" began the prince, when an indignant outcry drowned his words.

"Excuse me, prince, excuse me, but now that will not do," shouted Lebedeff's nephew, his voice dominating all the others. "The matter must be clearly stated, for it is obviously not properly understood. They are calling in some legal chicanery, and upon that ground they are threatening to turn us out of the house! Really, prince, do you think we are such fools as not to be aware that this matter does not come within the law, and that legally we cannot claim a rouble from you? But we are also aware that if actual law is not on our side, human law is for us, natural law, the law of common-sense and conscience, which is no less binding upon every noble and honest man—that is, every man of sane judgment—because it is not to be found in miserable legal codes. If we come here without fear of being turned out (as was threatened just now) because of the imperative tone of our demand, and the unseemliness of such a visit at this late hour (though it was not late when we arrived, we were kept waiting in your anteroom), if, I say, we came in without fear, it is just because we expected to find you a man of sense; I mean, a man of honour and conscience. It is quite true that we did not present ourselves humbly, like your flatterers and parasites, but holding up our heads as befits independent men. We present no petition, but a proud and free demand (note it well, we do not beseech, we demand!). We ask you fairly and squarely in a dignified manner. Do you believe that in this affair of Burdovsky you have right on your side? Do you admit that Pavlicheff overwhelmed you with benefits, and perhaps saved your life? If you admit it (which we take for granted), do you intend, now that you are a millionaire, and do you not think it in conformity with justice, to indemnify Burdovsky? Yes or no? If it is yes, or, in other words, if you possess what you call honour and conscience, and we more justly call common-sense, then accede to our demand, and the matter is at an end. Give us satisfaction, without entreaties or thanks from us; do not expect thanks from us, for what you do will be done not for our sake, but for the sake of justice. If you refuse to satisfy us, that is, if your answer is no, we will go away at once, and there will be an end of the matter. But we will tell you to your face before the present company that you are a man of vulgar and undeveloped mind; we will openly deny you the right to speak in future of your honour and conscience, for you have not paid the fair price of such a right. I have no more to say—I have put the question before you. Now turn us out if you dare. You can do it; force is on your side. But remember that we do not beseech, we demand! We do not beseech, we demand!"

With these last excited words, Lebedeff's nephew was silent.

"We demand, we demand, we demand, we do not beseech," spluttered Burdovsky, red as a lobster.

The speech of Lebedeff's nephew caused a certain stir among the company; murmurs arose, though with the exception of Lebedeff, who was still very much excited, everyone was careful not to interfere in the matter. Strangely enough, Lebedeff, although on the prince's side, seemed quite proud of his nephew's eloquence. Gratified vanity was visible in the glances he cast upon the assembled company.

"In my opinion, Mr. Doktorenko," said the prince, in rather a low voice, "you are quite right in at least half of what you say. I would go further and say that you are altogether right, and that I quite agree with you, if there were not something lacking in your speech. I cannot undertake to say precisely what it is, but you have certainly omitted something, and you cannot be quite just while there is something lacking. But let us put that aside and return to the point. Tell me what induced you to publish this article. Every word of it is a calumny, and I think, gentlemen, that you have been guilty of a mean action."

"Allow me—"

"Sir—"

"What? What? What?" cried all the visitors at once, in violent agitation.

"As to the article," said Hippolyte in his croaking voice, "I have told you already that we none of us approve of it! There is the writer," he added, pointing to the boxer, who sat beside him. "I quite admit that he has written it in his old regimental manner, with an equal disregard for style and decency. I know he is a cross between a fool and an adventurer; I make no bones about telling him so to his face every day. But after all he is half justified; publicity is the lawful right of every man; consequently, Burdovsky is not excepted. Let him answer for his own blunders. As to the objection which I made just now in the name of all, to the presence of your friends, I think I ought to explain, gentlemen, that I only did so to assert our rights, though we really wished to have witnesses; we had

146

agreed unanimously upon the point before we came in. We do not care who your witnesses may be, or whether they are your friends or not. As they cannot fail to recognize Burdovsky's right (seeing that it is mathematically demonstrable), it is just as well that the witnesses should be your friends. The truth will only be more plainly evident."

"It is quite true; we had agreed upon that point," said Lebedeff's nephew, in confirmation.

"If that is the case, why did you begin by making such a fuss about it?" asked the astonished prince.

The boxer was dying to get in a few words; owing, no doubt, to the presence of the ladies, he was becoming quite jovial.

"As to the article, prince," he said, "I admit that I wrote it, in spite of the severe criticism of my poor friend, in whom I always overlook many things because of his unfortunate state of health. But I wrote and published it in the form of a letter, in the paper of a friend. I showed it to no one but Burdovsky, and I did not read it all through, even to him. He immediately gave me permission to publish it, but you will admit that I might have done so without his consent. Publicity is a noble, beneficent, and universal right. I hope, prince, that you are too progressive to deny this?"

"I deny nothing, but you must confess that your article—"

"Is a bit thick, you mean? Well, in a way that is in the public interest; you will admit that yourself, and after all one cannot overlook a blatant fact. So much the worse for the guilty parties, but the public welfare must come before everything. As to certain inaccuracies and figures of speech, so to speak, you will also admit that the motive, aim, and intention, are the chief thing. It is a question, above all, of making a wholesome example; the individual case can be examined afterwards; and as to the style—well, the thing was meant to be humorous, so to speak, and, after all, everybody writes like that; you must admit it yourself! Ha, ha!"

"But, gentlemen, I assure you that you are quite astray," exclaimed the prince. "You have published this article upon the supposition that I would never consent to satisfy Mr. Burdovsky. Acting on that conviction, you have tried to intimidate me by this publication and to be revenged for my supposed refusal. But what did you know of my intentions? It may be that I have resolved to satisfy Mr. Burdovsky's claim. I now declare openly, in the presence of these witnesses, that I will do so."

"The noble and intelligent word of an intelligent and most noble man, at last!" exclaimed the boxer.

"Good God!" exclaimed Lizabetha Prokofievna involuntarily.

"This is intolerable," growled the general.

"Allow me, gentlemen, allow me," urged the prince.

"I will explain matters to you. Five weeks ago I received a visit from Tchebaroff, your agent, Mr. Burdovsky. You have given a very flattering description of him in your article, Mr. Keller," he continued, turning to the boxer with a smile, "but he did not please me at all. I saw at once that Tchebaroff was the moving spirit in the matter, and, to speak frankly, I thought he might have induced you, Mr. Burdovsky, to make this claim, by taking advantage of your simplicity."

"You have no right.... I am not simple," stammered Burdovsky, much agitated.

"You have no sort of right to suppose such things," said Lebedeff's nephew in a tone of authority.

"It is most offensive!" shrieked Hippolyte; "it is an insulting suggestion, false, and most ill-timed."

"I beg your pardon, gentlemen; please excuse me," said the prince. "I thought absolute frankness on both sides would be best, but have it your own way. I told Tchebaroff that, as I was not in Petersburg, I would commission a friend to look into the matter without delay, and that I would let you know, Mr. Burdovsky. Gentlemen, I have no hesitation in telling you that it was the fact of Tchebaroff's intervention that made me suspect a fraud. Oh! do not take offence at my words, gentlemen, for Heaven's sake do not be so touchy!" cried the prince, seeing that Burdovsky was getting excited again, and that the rest were preparing to protest. "If I say I suspected a fraud, there is nothing personal in that. I had never seen any of you then; I did not even know your names; I only judged by Tchebaroff; I am speaking quite generally—if you only knew how I have been 'done' since I came into my fortune!"

"You are shockingly naive, prince," said Lebedeff's nephew in mocking tones.

"Besides, though you are a prince and a millionaire, and even though you may really be simple and good-hearted, you can hardly be outside the general law," Hippolyte declared loudly.

"Perhaps not; it is very possible," the prince agreed hastily, "though I do not know what general law you allude to. I will go on—only please do not take offence without good cause. I assure you I do not mean to offend you in the least. Really, it is impossible to speak three words sincerely without your flying into a rage! At first I was amazed when Tchebaroff told me that Pavlicheff had a son, and that he was in such a miserable position. Pavlicheff was my benefactor, and my father's friend. Oh, Mr. Keller, why does your article impute things to my father without the slightest foundation? He never squandered the funds of his company nor ill-treated his subordinates, I am absolutely certain of it; I cannot imagine how you could bring yourself to write such a calumny! But your assertions concerning Pavlicheff are absolutely intolerable! You do not scruple to make a libertine of that noble man; you call him a sensualist as coolly as if you were speaking the truth, and yet it would not be possible to find a chaster man. He was even a scholar of note, and in correspondence with several celebrated scientists, and spent large sums in the interests of science. As to his kind heart and his good actions, you were right indeed when you said that I was almost an idiot at that time, and could hardly understand anything—(I could speak and understand Russian, though),—but now I can appreciate what I remember—"

"Excuse me," interrupted Hippolyte, "is not this rather sentimental? You said you wished to come to the point; please remember that it is after nine o'clock."

"Very well, gentlemen—very well," replied the prince. "At first I received the news with mistrust, then I said to myself that I might be mistaken, and that Pavlicheff might possibly have had a son. But I was absolutely amazed at the readiness with which the son had revealed the secret of his birth at the expense of his mother's honour. For Tchebaroff had already menaced me with publicity in our interview...."

"What nonsense!" Lebedeff's nephew interrupted violently.

"You have no right—you have no right!" cried Burdovsky.

"The son is not responsible for the misdeeds of his father; and the mother is not to blame," added Hippolyte, with warmth.

"That seems to me all the more reason for sparing her," said the prince timidly.

"Prince, you are not only simple, but your simplicity is almost past the limit," said Lebedeff's nephew, with a sarcastic smile.

"But what right had you?" said Hippolyte in a very strange tone.

"None—none whatever," agreed the prince hastily. "I admit you are right there, but it was involuntary, and I immediately said to myself that my personal feelings had nothing to do with it,—that if I thought it right to satisfy the demands of Mr. Burdovsky, out of respect for the memory of Pavlicheff, I ought to do so in any case, whether I esteemed Mr. Burdovsky or not. I only mentioned this, gentlemen, because it seemed so unnatural to me for a son to betray his mother's secret in such a way. In short, that is what convinced me that Tchebaroff must be a rogue, and that he had induced Mr. Burdovsky to attempt this fraud."

"But this is intolerable!" cried the visitors, some of them starting to their feet.

"Gentlemen, I supposed from this that poor Mr. Burdovsky must be a simple-minded man, quite defenceless, and an easy tool in the hands of rogues. That is why I thought it my duty to try and help him as 'Pavlicheff's son'; in the first place by rescuing him from the influence of Tchebaroff, and secondly by making myself his friend. I have resolved to give him ten thousand roubles; that is about the sum which I calculate that Pavlicheff must have spent on me."

"What, only ten thousand!" cried Hippolyte.

"Well, prince, your arithmetic is not up to much, or else you are mighty clever at it, though you affect the air of a simpleton," said Lebedeff's nephew.

"I will not accept ten thousand roubles," said Burdovsky.

"Accept, Antip," whispered the boxer eagerly, leaning past the back of Hippolyte's chair to give his friend this piece of advice. "Take it for the present; we can see about more later on."

"Look here, Mr. Muishkin," shouted Hippolyte, "please understand that we are not fools, nor idiots, as your guests seem to imagine; these ladies who look upon us with such scorn, and especially this fine gentleman" (pointing to Evgenie Pavlovitch) "whom I have not the honour of knowing, though I think I have heard some talk about him—"

"Really, really, gentlemen," cried the prince in great agitation, "you are misunderstanding me again. In the first place, Mr. Keller, you have greatly overestimated my fortune in your article. I am far from being a millionaire. I have barely a tenth of what you suppose. Secondly, my treatment in Switzerland was very far from costing tens of thousands of roubles. Schneider received six hundred roubles a year, and he was only paid for the first three years. As to the pretty governesses whom Pavlicheff is supposed to have brought from Paris, they only exist in Mr. Keller's imagination; it is another calumny. According to my calculations, the sum spent on me was very considerably under ten thousand roubles, but I decided on that sum, and you must admit that in paying a debt I could not offer Mr. Burdovsky more, however kindly disposed I might be towards him; delicacy forbids it; I should seem to be offering him charity instead of rightful payment. I don't know how you cannot see that, gentlemen! Besides, I had no intention of leaving the matter there. I meant to intervene amicably later on and help to improve poor Mr. Burdovsky's position. It is clear that he has been deceived, or he would never have agreed to anything so vile as the scandalous revelations about his mother in Mr. Keller's article. But, gentlemen, why are you getting angry again? Are we never to come to an understanding? Well, the event has proved me right! I have just seen with my own eyes the proof that my conjecture was correct!" he added, with increasing eagerness.

He meant to calm his hearers, and did not perceive that his words had only increased their irritation.

"What do you mean? What are you convinced of?" they demanded angrily.

"In the first place, I have had the opportunity of getting a correct idea of Mr. Burdovsky. I see what he is for myself. He is an innocent man, deceived by everyone! A defenceless victim, who deserves indulgence! Secondly, Gavrila Ardalionovitch, in whose hands I had placed the matter, had his first interview with me barely an hour ago. I had not heard from him for some time, as I was away, and have been ill for three days since my return to St. Petersburg. He tells me that he has exposed the designs of Tchebaroff and has proof that justifies my opinion of him. I know, gentlemen, that many people think me an idiot. Counting upon my reputation as a man whose purse-strings are easily loosened, Tchebaroff thought it would be a simple matter to fleece me, especially by trading on my gratitude to Pavlicheff. But the main point is—listen, gentlemen, let me finish!—the main point is that Mr. Burdovsky is not Pavlicheff's son at all. Gavrila Ardalionovitch has just told me of his discovery, and assures me that he has positive proofs. Well, what do you think of that? It is scarcely credible, even after all the tricks that have been played upon me. Please note that we have positive proofs! I can hardly believe it myself, I assure you; I do not yet believe it; I am still doubtful, because Gavrila Ardalionovitch has not had time to go into details; but there can be no further doubt that Tchebaroff is a rogue! He has deceived poor Mr. Burdovsky, and all of you, gentlemen, who have come forward so nobly to support your friend—(he evidently needs support, I quite see that!). He has abused your credulity and involved you all in an attempted fraud, for when all is said and done this claim is nothing else!"

"What! a fraud? What, he is not Pavlicheff's son? Impossible!"

These exclamations but feebly expressed the profound bewilderment into which the prince's words had plunged Burdovsky's companions.

"Certainly it is a fraud! Since Mr. Burdovsky is not Pavlicheff's son, his claim is neither more nor less than attempted fraud (supposing, of course, that he had known the truth), but the fact is that he has been deceived. I insist on this point in order to justify him; I repeat that his simple-mindedness makes him worthy of pity, and that he cannot stand alone; otherwise he would have behaved like a scoundrel in this matter. But I feel certain that he does not understand it! I was just the same myself before I went to Switzerland; I stammered incoherently; one tries to express oneself and cannot. I understand that. I am all the better able to pity Mr. Burdovsky, because I know from experience what it is to be like that, and so I have a right to speak. Well, though there is no such person as

'Pavlicheff's son,' and it is all nothing but a humbug, yet I will keep to my decision, and I am prepared to give up ten thousand roubles in memory of Pavlicheff. Before Mr. Burdovsky made this claim, I proposed to found a school with this money, in memory of my benefactor, but I shall honour his memory quite as well by giving the ten thousand roubles to Mr. Burdovsky, because, though he was not Pavlicheff's son, he was treated almost as though he were. That is what gave a rogue the opportunity of deceiving him; he really did think himself Pavlicheff's son. Listen, gentlemen; this matter must be settled; keep calm; do not get angry; and sit down! Gavrila Ardalionovitch will explain everything to you at once, and I confess that I am very anxious to hear all the details myself. He says that he has even been to Pskoff to see your mother, Mr. Burdovsky; she is not dead, as the article which was just read to us makes out. Sit down, gentlemen, sit down!"

The prince sat down, and at length prevailed upon Burdovsky's company to do likewise. During the last ten or twenty minutes, exasperated by continual interruptions, he had raised his voice, and spoken with great vehemence. Now, no doubt, he bitterly regretted several words and expressions which had escaped him in his excitement. If he had not been driven beyond the limits of endurance, he would not have ventured to express certain conjectures so openly. He had no sooner sat down than his heart was torn by sharp remorse. Besides insulting Burdovsky with the supposition, made in the presence of witnesses, that he was suffering from the complaint for which he had himself been treated in Switzerland, he reproached himself with the grossest indelicacy in having offered him the ten thousand roubles before everyone. "I ought to have waited till to-morrow and offered him the money when we were alone," thought Muishkin. "Now it is too late, the mischief is done! Yes, I am an idiot, an absolute idiot!" he said to himself, overcome with shame and regret.

Till then Gavrila Ardalionovitch had sat apart in silence. When the prince called upon him, he came and stood by his side, and in a calm, clear voice began to render an account of the mission confided to him. All conversation ceased instantly. Everyone, especially the Burdovsky party, listened with the utmost curiosity.

CHAPTER IX.

"You will not deny, I am sure," said Gavrila Ardalionovitch, turning to Burdovsky, who sat looking at him with wide-open eyes, perplexed and astonished. "You will not deny, seriously, that you were born just two years after your mother's legal marriage to Mr. Burdovsky, your father. Nothing would be easier than to prove the date of your birth from well-known facts; we can only look on Mr. Keller's version as a work of imagination, and one, moreover, extremely offensive both to you and your mother. Of course he distorted the truth in order to strengthen your claim, and to serve your interests. Mr. Keller said that he previously consulted you about his article in the paper, but did not read it to you as a whole. Certainly he could not have read that passage..."

"As a matter of fact, I did not read it," interrupted the boxer, "but its contents had been given me on unimpeachable authority, and I..."

"Excuse me, Mr. Keller," interposed Gavrila Ardalionovitch. "Allow me to speak. I assure you your article shall be mentioned in its proper place, and you can then explain everything, but for the moment I would rather not anticipate. Quite accidentally, with the help of my sister, Varvara Ardalionovna Ptitsin, I obtained from one of her intimate friends, Madame Zoubkoff, a letter written to her twenty-five years ago, by Nicolai Andreevitch Pavlicheff, then abroad. After getting into communication with this lady, I went by her advice to Timofei Fedorovitch Viazovkin, a retired colonel, and one of Pavlicheff's oldest friends. He gave me two more letters written by the latter when he was still in foreign parts. These three documents, their dates, and the facts mentioned in them, prove in the most undeniable manner, that eighteen months before your birth, Nicolai Andreevitch went abroad, where he remained for three consecutive years. Your mother, as you are well aware, has never been out of Russia.... It is too late to read the letters now; I am content to state the fact. But if you desire it, come to me tomorrow morning, bring witnesses and writing experts with you, and I will prove the absolute truth of my story. From that moment the question will be decided."

These words caused a sensation among the listeners, and there was a general movement of relief. Burdovsky got up abruptly.

"If that is true," said he, "I have been deceived, grossly deceived, but not by Tchebaroff: and for a long time past, a long time. I do not wish for experts, not I, nor to go to see you. I believe you. I give it up.... But I refuse the ten thousand roubles. Good-bye."

"Wait five minutes more, Mr. Burdovsky," said Gavrila Ardalionovitch pleasantly. "I have more to say. Some rather curious and important facts have come to light, and it is absolutely necessary, in my opinion, that you should hear them. You will not regret, I fancy, to have the whole matter thoroughly cleared up."

Burdovsky silently resumed his seat, and bent his head as though in profound thought. His friend, Lebedeff's nephew, who had risen to accompany him, also sat down again. He seemed much disappointed, though as self-confident as ever. Hippolyte looked dejected and sulky, as well as surprised. He had just been attacked by a violent fit of coughing, so that his handkerchief was stained with blood. The boxer looked thoroughly frightened.

"Oh, Antip!" cried he in a miserable voice, "I did say to you the other day—the day before yesterday—that perhaps you were not really Pavlicheff's son!"

There were sounds of half-smothered laughter at this.

"Now, that is a valuable piece of information, Mr. Keller," replied Gania. "However that may be, I have private information which convinces me that Mr. Burdovsky, though doubtless aware of the date of his birth, knew nothing at all about Pavlicheff's sojourn abroad. Indeed, he passed the greater part of his life out of Russia, returning at intervals for short visits. The journey in question is in itself too unimportant for his friends to recollect it after more than twenty years; and of course Mr. Burdovsky could have known nothing about it, for he was not born. As the event has proved, it was not impossible to find evidence of his absence, though I must confess that chance has helped me in a quest which might very well have come to nothing. It was really almost impossible for

Burdovsky or Tchebaroff to discover these facts, even if it had entered their heads to try. Naturally they never dreamt..."

Here the voice of Hippolyte suddenly intervened.

"Allow me, Mr. Ivolgin," he said irritably. "What is the good of all this rigmarole? Pardon me. All is now clear, and we acknowledge the truth of your main point. Why go into these tedious details? You wish perhaps to boast of the cleverness of your investigation, to cry up your talents as detective? Or perhaps your intention is to excuse Burdovsky, by proving that he took up the matter in ignorance? Well, I consider that extremely impudent on your part! You ought to know that Burdovsky has no need of being excused or justified by you or anyone else! It is an insult! The affair is quite painful enough for him without that. Will nothing make you understand?"

"Enough! enough! Mr. Terentieff," interrupted Gania.

"Don't excite yourself; you seem very ill, and I am sorry for that. I am almost done, but there are a few facts to which I must briefly refer, as I am convinced that they ought to be clearly explained once for all...." A movement of impatience was noticed in his audience as he resumed: "I merely wish to state, for the information of all concerned, that the reason for Mr. Pavlicheff's interest in your mother, Mr. Burdovsky, was simply that she was the sister of a serf-girl with whom he was deeply in love in his youth, and whom most certainly he would have married but for her sudden death. I have proofs that this circumstance is almost, if not quite, forgotten. I may add that when your mother was about ten years old, Pavlicheff took her under his care, gave her a good education, and later, a considerable dowry. His relations were alarmed, and feared he might go so far as to marry her, but she gave her hand to a young land-surveyor named Burdovsky when she reached the age of twenty. I can even say definitely that it was a marriage of affection. After his wedding your father gave up his occupation as land-surveyor, and with his wife's dowry of fifteen thousand roubles went in for commercial speculations. As he had had no experience, he was cheated on all sides, and took to drink in order to forget his troubles. He shortened his life by his excesses, and eight years after his marriage he died. Your mother says herself that she was left in the direst poverty, and would have died of starvation had it not been for Pavlicheff, who generously allowed her a yearly pension of six hundred roubles. Many people recall his extreme fondness for you as a little boy. Your mother confirms this, and agrees with others in thinking that he loved you the more because you were a sickly child, stammering in your speech, and almost deformed—for it is known that all his life Nicolai Andreevitch had a partiality for unfortunates of every kind, especially children. In my opinion this is most important. I may add that I discovered yet another fact, the last on which I employed my detective powers. Seeing how fond Pavlicheff was of you,—it was thanks to him you went to school, and also had the advantage of special teachers—his relations and servants grew to believe that you were his son, and that your father had been betrayed by his wife. I may point out that this idea was only accredited generally during the last years of Pavlicheff's life, when his next-of-kin were trembling about the succession, when the earlier story was quite forgotten, and when all opportunity for discovering the truth had seemingly passed away. No doubt you, Mr. Burdovsky, heard this conjecture, and did not hesitate to accept it as true. I have had the honour of making your mother's acquaintance, and I find that she knows all about these reports. What she does not know is that you, her son, should have listened to them so complaisantly. I found your respected mother at Pskoff, ill and in deep poverty, as she has been ever since the death of your benefactor. She told me with tears of gratitude how you had supported her; she expects much of you, and believes fervently in your future success..."

"Oh, this is unbearable!" said Lebedeff's nephew impatiently. "What is the good of all this romancing?"

"It is revolting and unseemly!" cried Hippolyte, jumping up in a fury.

Burdovsky alone sat silent and motionless.

"What is the good of it?" repeated Gavrila Ardalionovitch, with pretended surprise. "Well, firstly, because now perhaps Mr. Burdovsky is quite convinced that Mr. Pavlicheff's love for him came simply from generosity of soul, and not from paternal duty. It was most necessary to impress this fact upon his mind, considering that he approved of the article written by Mr. Keller. I speak thus because I look on you, Mr. Burdovsky, as an honourable man. Secondly, it appears that there was no intention of cheating in this case, even on the part of Tchebaroff. I wish to say this quite plainly, because the prince hinted a while ago that I too thought it an attempt at robbery and extortion. On the contrary, everyone has been quite sincere in the matter, and although Tchebaroff may be somewhat of a rogue, in this business he has acted simply as any sharp lawyer would do under the circumstances. He looked at it as a case that might bring him in a lot of money, and he did not calculate badly; because on the one hand he speculated on the generosity of the prince, and his gratitude to the late Mr. Pavlicheff, and on the other to his chivalrous ideas as to the obligations of honour and conscience. As to Mr. Burdovsky, allowing for his principles, we may acknowledge that he engaged in the business with very little personal aim in view. At the instigation of Tchebaroff and his other friends, he decided to make the attempt in the service of truth, progress, and humanity. In short, the conclusion may be drawn that, in spite of all appearances, Mr. Burdovsky is a man of irreproachable character, and thus the prince can all the more readily offer him his friendship, and the assistance of which he spoke just now..."

"Hush! hush! Gavrila Ardalionovitch!" cried Muishkin in dismay, but it was too late.

"I said, and I have repeated it over and over again," shouted Burdovsky furiously, "that I did not want the money. I will not take it... why...I will not... I am going away!"

He was rushing hurriedly from the terrace, when Lebedeff's nephew seized his arms, and said something to him in a low voice. Burdovsky turned quickly, and drawing an addressed but unsealed envelope from his pocket, he threw it down on a little table beside the prince.

"There's the money!... How dare you?... The money!"

"Those are the two hundred and fifty roubles you dared to send him as a charity, by the hands of Tchebaroff," explained Doktorenko.

"The article in the newspaper put it at fifty!" cried Colia.

"I beg your pardon," said the prince, going up to Burdovsky. "I have done you a great wrong, but I did not send you that money as a charity, believe me. And now I am again to blame. I offended you just now." (The prince was much distressed; he seemed worn out with fatigue, and spoke almost incoherently.) "I spoke of swindling... but I did not apply that to you. I was deceived .... I said you were... afflicted... like me... But you are not like me... you give lessons... you support your mother. I said you had dishonoured your mother, but you love her. She says so herself... I did not know... Gavrila Ardalionovitch did not tell me that... Forgive me! I dared to offer you ten thousand roubles, but I was wrong. I ought to have done it differently, and now... there is no way of doing it, for you despise me..."

"I declare, this is a lunatic asylum!" cried Lizabetha Prokofievna.

"Of course it is a lunatic asylum!" repeated Aglaya sharply, but her words were overpowered by other voices. Everybody was talking loudly, making remarks and comments; some discussed the affair gravely, others laughed. Ivan Fedorovitch Epanchin was extremely indignant. He stood waiting for his wife with an air of offended dignity. Lebedeff's nephew took up the word again.

"Well, prince, to do you justice, you certainly know how to make the most of your—let us call it infirmity, for the sake of politeness; you have set about offering your money and friendship in such a way that no self-respecting man could possibly accept them. This is an excess of ingenuousness or of malice—you ought to know better than anyone which word best fits the case."

"Allow me, gentlemen," said Gavrila Ardalionovitch, who had just examined the contents of the envelope, "there are only a hundred roubles here, not two hundred and fifty. I point this out, prince, to prevent misunderstanding."

"Never mind, never mind," said the prince, signing to him to keep quiet.

"But we do mind," said Lebedeff's nephew vehemently. "Prince, your 'never mind' is an insult to us. We have nothing to hide; our actions can bear daylight. It is true that there are only a hundred roubles instead of two hundred and fifty, but it is all the same."

"Why, no, it is hardly the same," remarked Gavrila Ardalionovitch, with an air of ingenuous surprise.

"Don't interrupt, we are not such fools as you think, Mr. Lawyer," cried Lebedeff's nephew angrily. "Of course there is a difference between a hundred roubles and two hundred and fifty, but in this case the principle is the main point, and that a hundred and fifty roubles are missing is only a side issue. The point to be emphasized is that Burdovsky will not accept your highness's charity; he flings it back in your face, and it scarcely matters if there are a hundred roubles or two hundred and fifty. Burdovsky has refused ten thousand roubles; you heard him. He would not have returned even a hundred roubles if he was dishonest! The hundred and fifty roubles were paid to Tchebaroff for his travelling expenses. You may jeer at our stupidity and at our inexperience in business matters; you have done all you could already to make us look ridiculous; but do not dare to call us dishonest. The four of us will club together every day to repay the hundred and fifty roubles to the prince, if we have to pay it in instalments of a rouble at a time, but we will repay it, with interest. Burdovsky is poor, he has no millions. After his journey to see the prince Tchebaroff sent in his bill. We counted on winning... Who would not have done the same in such a case?"

"Who indeed?" exclaimed Prince S.

"I shall certainly go mad, if I stay here!" cried Lizabetha Prokofievna.

"It reminds me," said Evgenie Pavlovitch, laughing, "of the famous plea of a certain lawyer who lately defended a man for murdering six people in order to rob them. He excused his client on the score of poverty. 'It is quite natural,' he said in conclusion, 'considering the state of misery he was in, that he should have thought of murdering these six people; which of you, gentlemen, would not have done the same in his place?'"

"Enough," cried Lizabetha Prokofievna abruptly, trembling with anger, "we have had enough of this balderdash!"

In a state of terrible excitement she threw back her head, with flaming eyes, casting looks of contempt and defiance upon the whole company, in which she could no longer distinguish friend from foe. She had restrained herself so long that she felt forced to vent her rage on somebody. Those who knew Lizabetha Prokofievna saw at once how it was with her. "She flies into these rages sometimes," said Ivan Fedorovitch to Prince S. the next day, "but she is not often so violent as she was yesterday; it does not happen more than once in three years."

"Be quiet, Ivan Fedorovitch! Leave me alone!" cried Mrs. Epanchin. "Why do you offer me your arm now? You had not sense enough to take me away before. You are my husband, you are a father, it was your duty to drag me away by force, if in my folly I refused to obey you and go quietly. You might at least have thought of your daughters. We can find our way out now without your help. Here is shame enough for a year! Wait a moment 'till I thank the prince! Thank you, prince, for the entertainment you have given us! It was most amusing to hear these young men... It is vile, vile! A chaos, a scandal, worse than a nightmare! Is it possible that there can be many such people on earth? Be quiet, Aglaya! Be quiet, Alexandra! It is none of your business! Don't fuss round me like that, Evgenie Pavlovitch; you exasperate me! So, my dear," she cried, addressing the prince, "you go so far as to beg their pardon! He says, 'Forgive me for offering you a fortune.' And you, you mountebank, what are you laughing at?" she cried, turning suddenly on Lebedeff's nephew. "'We refuse ten thousand roubles; we do not beseech, we demand!' As if he did not know that this idiot will call on them tomorrow to renew his offers of money and friendship. You will, won't you? You will? Come, will you, or won't you?"

"I shall," said the prince, with gentle humility.

"You hear him! You count upon it, too," she continued, turning upon Doktorenko. "You are as sure of him now as if you had the money in your pocket. And there you are playing the swaggerer to throw dust in our eyes! No, my dear sir, you may take other people in! I can see through all your airs and graces, I see your game!"

"Lizabetha Prokofievna!" exclaimed the prince.

"Come, Lizabetha Prokofievna, it is quite time for us to be going, we will take the prince with us," said Prince S. with a smile, in the coolest possible way.

The girls stood apart, almost frightened; their father was positively horrified. Mrs. Epanchin's language astonished everybody. Some who stood a little way off smiled furtively, and talked in whispers. Lebedeff wore an expression of utmost ecstasy.

"Chaos and scandal are to be found everywhere, madame," remarked Doktorenko, who was considerably put out of countenance.

"Not like this! Nothing like the spectacle you have just given us, sir," answered Lizabetha Prokofievna, with a sort of hysterical rage. "Leave me alone, will you?" she cried violently to those around her, who were trying to keep her quiet. "No, Evgenie Pavlovitch, if, as you said yourself just now, a lawyer said in open court that he found it quite natural that a man should murder six people because he was in misery, the world must be coming to an end. I had not heard of it before. Now I understand everything. And this stutterer, won't he turn out a murderer?" she cried, pointing to Burdovsky, who was staring at her with stupefaction. "I bet he will! He will have none of your money, possibly, he will refuse it because his conscience will not allow him to accept it, but he will go murdering you by night and walking off with your cashbox, with a clear conscience! He does not call it a dishonest action but 'the impulse of a noble despair'; 'a negation'; or the devil knows what! Bah! everything is upside down, everyone walks head downwards. A young girl, brought up at home, suddenly jumps into a cab in the middle of the street, saying: 'Good-bye, mother, I married Karlitch, or Ivanitch, the other day!' And you think it quite right? You call such conduct estimable and natural? The 'woman question'? Look here," she continued, pointing to Colia, "the other day that whippersnapper told me that this was the whole meaning of the 'woman question.' But even supposing that your mother is a fool, you are none the less, bound to treat her with humanity. Why did you come here tonight so insolently? 'Give us our rights, but don't dare to speak in our presence. Show us every mark of deepest respect, while we treat you like the scum of the earth.' The miscreants have written a tissue of calumny in their article, and these are the men who seek for truth, and do battle for the right! 'We do not beseech, we demand, you will get no thanks from us, because you will be acting to satisfy your own conscience!' What morality! But, good heavens! if you declare that the prince's generosity will, excite no gratitude in you, he might answer that he is not, bound to be grateful to Pavlicheff, who also was only satisfying his own conscience. But you counted on the prince's, gratitude towards Pavlicheff; you never lent him any money; he owes you nothing; then what were you counting upon if not on his gratitude? And if you appeal to that sentiment in others, why should you expect to be exempted from it? They are mad! They say society is savage and inhuman because it despises a young girl who has been seduced. But if you call society inhuman you imply that the young girl is made to suffer by its censure. How then, can you hold her up to the scorn of society in the newspapers without realizing that you are making her suffering, still greater? Madmen! Vain fools! They don't believe in God, they don't believe in Christ! But you are so eaten up by pride and vanity, that you will end by devouring each other—that is my prophecy! Is not this absurd? Is it not monstrous chaos? And after all this, that shameless creature will go and beg their pardon! Are there many people like you? What are you smiling at? Because I am not ashamed to disgrace myself before you?—Yes, I am disgraced—it can't be helped now! But don't you jeer at me, you scum!" (this was aimed at Hippolyte). "He is almost at his last gasp, yet he corrupts others. You, have got hold of this lad—" (she pointed to Colia); "you, have turned his head, you have taught him to be an atheist, you don't believe in God, and you are not too old to be whipped, sir! A plague upon you! And so, Prince Lef Nicolaievitch, you will call on them tomorrow, will you?" she asked the prince breathlessly, for the second time.

"Yes."

"Then I will never speak to you again." She made a sudden movement to go, and then turned quickly back. "And you will call on that atheist?" she continued, pointing to Hippolyte. "How dare you grin at me like that?" she shouted furiously, rushing at the invalid, whose mocking smile drove her to distraction.

Exclamations arose on all sides.

"Lizabetha Prokofievna! Lizabetha Prokofievna! Lizabetha Prokofievna!"

"Mother, this is disgraceful!" cried Aglaya.

Mrs. Epanchin had approached Hippolyte and seized him firmly by the arm, while her eyes, blazing with fury, were fixed upon his face.

"Do not distress yourself, Aglaya Ivanovitch," he answered calmly; "your mother knows that one cannot strike a dying man. I am ready to explain why I was laughing. I shall be delighted if you will let me—"

A violent fit of coughing, which lasted a full minute, prevented him from finishing his sentence.

"He is dying, yet he will not stop holding forth!" cried Lizabetha Prokofievna. She loosed her hold on his arm, almost terrified, as she saw him wiping the blood from his lips. "Why do you talk? You ought to go home to bed."

"So I will," he whispered hoarsely. "As soon as I get home I will go to bed at once; and I know I shall be dead in a fortnight; Botkine told me so himself last week. That is why I should like to say a few farewell words, if you will let me."

"But you must be mad! It is ridiculous! You should take care of yourself; what is the use of holding a conversation now? Go home to bed, do!" cried Mrs. Epanchin in horror.

"When I do go to bed I shall never get up again," said Hippolyte, with a smile. "I meant to take to my bed yesterday and stay there till I died, but as my legs can still carry me, I put it off for two days, so as to come here with them to-day—but I am very tired."

"Oh, sit down, sit down, why are you standing?"

Lizabetha Prokofievna placed a chair for him with her own hands.

"Thank you," he said gently. "Sit opposite to me, and let us talk. We must have a talk now, Lizabetha Prokofievna; I am very anxious for it." He smiled at her once more. "Remember that today, for the last time, I am out in the air, and in the company of my fellow-men, and that in a fortnight I shall certainly be no longer in this world. So, in a way, this is my farewell to nature and to men. I am not very sentimental, but do you know, I am quite glad that all this has happened at Pavlofsk, where at least one can see a green tree."

"But why talk now?" replied Lizabetha Prokofievna, more and more alarmed; "You are quite feverish. Just now you would not stop shouting, and now you can hardly breathe. You are gasping."

"I shall have time to rest. Why will you not grant my last wish? Do you know, Lizabetha Prokofievna, that I have dreamed of meeting you for a long while? I had often heard of you from Colia; he is almost the only person who still comes to see me. You are an original and eccentric woman; I have seen that for myself—Do you know, I have even been rather fond of you?"

"Good heavens! And I very nearly struck him!"

"You were prevented by Aglaya Ivanovna. I think I am not mistaken? That is your daughter, Aglaya Ivanovna? She is so beautiful that I recognized her directly, although I had never seen her before. Let me, at least, look on beauty for the last time in my life," he said with a wry smile. "You are here with the prince, and your husband, and a large company. Why should you refuse to gratify my last wish?"

"Give me a chair!" cried Lizabetha Prokofievna, but she seized one for herself and sat down opposite to Hippolyte. "Colia, you must go home with him," she commanded, "and tomorrow I will come my self."

"Will you let me ask the prince for a cup of tea?... I am exhausted. Do you know what you might do, Lizabetha Prokofievna? I think you wanted to take the prince home with you for tea. Stay here, and let us spend the evening together. I am sure the prince will give us all some tea. Forgive me for being so free and easy—but I know you are kind, and the prince is kind, too. In fact, we are all good-natured people—it is really quite comical."

The prince bestirred himself to give orders. Lebedeff hurried out, followed by Vera.

"It is quite true," said Mrs. Epanchin decisively. "Talk, but not too loud, and don't excite yourself. You have made me sorry for you. Prince, you don't deserve that I should stay and have tea with you, yet I will, all the same, but I won't apologize. I apologize to nobody! Nobody! It is absurd! However, forgive me, prince, if I blew you up—that is, if you like, of course. But please don't let me keep anyone," she added suddenly to her husband and daughters, in a tone of resentment, as though they had grievously offended her. "I can come home alone quite well."

But they did not let her finish, and gathered round her eagerly. The prince immediately invited everyone to stay for tea, and apologized for not having thought of it before. The general murmured a few polite words, and asked Lizabetha Prokofievna if she did not feel cold on the terrace. He very nearly asked Hippolyte how long he had been at the University, but stopped himself in time. Evgenie Pavlovitch and Prince S. suddenly grew extremely gay and amiable. Adelaida and Alexandra had not recovered from their surprise, but it was now mingled with satisfaction; in short, everyone seemed very much relieved that Lizabetha Prokofievna had got over her paroxysm. Aglaya alone still frowned, and sat apart in silence. All the other guests stayed on as well; no one wanted to go, not even General Ivolgin, but Lebedeff said something to him in passing which did not seem to please him, for he immediately went and sulked in a corner. The prince took care to offer tea to Burdovsky and his friends as well as the rest. The invitation made them rather uncomfortable. They muttered that they would wait for Hippolyte, and went and sat by themselves in a distant corner of the verandah. Tea was served at once; Lebedeff had no doubt ordered it for himself and his family before the others arrived. It was striking eleven.

CHAPTER X.

After moistening his lips with the tea which Vera Lebedeff brought him, Hippolyte set the cup down on the table, and glanced round. He seemed confused and almost at a loss.

"Just look, Lizabetha Prokofievna," he began, with a kind of feverish haste; "these china cups are supposed to be extremely valuable. Lebedeff always keeps them locked up in his china-cupboard; they were part of his wife's dowry. Yet he has brought them out tonight—in your honour, of course! He is so pleased—" He was about to add something else, but could not find the words.

"There, he is feeling embarrassed; I expected as much," whispered Evgenie Pavlovitch suddenly in the prince's ear. "It is a bad sign; what do you think? Now, out of spite, he will come out with something so outrageous that even Lizabetha Prokofievna will not be able to stand it."

Muishkin looked at him inquiringly.

"You do not care if he does?" added Evgenie Pavlovitch. "Neither do I; in fact, I should be glad, merely as a proper punishment for our dear Lizabetha Prokofievna. I am very anxious that she should get it, without delay, and I shall stay till she does. You seem feverish."

"Never mind; by-and-by; yes, I am not feeling well," said the prince impatiently, hardly listening. He had just heard Hippolyte mention his own name.

"You don't believe it?" said the invalid, with a nervous laugh. "I don't wonder, but the prince will have no difficulty in believing it; he will not be at all surprised."

"Do you hear, prince—do you hear that?" said Lizabetha Prokofievna, turning towards him.

There was laughter in the group around her, and Lebedeff stood before her gesticulating wildly.

"He declares that your humbug of a landlord revised this gentleman's article—the article that was read aloud just now—in which you got such a charming dressing-down."

The prince regarded Lebedeff with astonishment.

"Why don't you say something?" cried Lizabetha Prokofievna, stamping her foot.

"Well," murmured the prince, with his eyes still fixed on Lebedeff, "I can see now that he did."

"Is it true?" she asked eagerly.

"Absolutely, your excellency," said Lebedeff, without the least hesitation.

Mrs. Epanchin almost sprang up in amazement at his answer, and at the assurance of his tone.

"He actually seems to boast of it!" she cried.

"I am base—base!" muttered Lebedeff, beating his breast, and hanging his head.

"What do I care if you are base or not? He thinks he has only to say, 'I am base,' and there is an end of it. As to you, prince, are you not ashamed?—I repeat, are you not ashamed, to mix with such riff-raff? I will never forgive you!"

"The prince will forgive me!" said Lebedeff with emotional conviction.

Keller suddenly left his seat, and approached Lizabetha Prokofievna.

"It was only out of generosity, madame," he said in a resonant voice, "and because I would not betray a friend in an awkward position, that I did not mention this revision before; though you heard him yourself threatening to kick us down the steps. To clear the matter up, I declare now that I did have recourse to his assistance, and that I paid him six roubles for it. But I did not ask him to correct my style; I simply went to him for information concerning the facts, of which I was ignorant to a great extent, and which he was competent to give. The story of the gaiters, the appetite in the Swiss professor's house, the substitution of fifty roubles for two hundred and fifty—all such details, in fact, were got from him. I paid him six roubles for them; but he did not correct the style."

"I must state that I only revised the first part of the article," interposed Lebedeff with feverish impatience, while laughter rose from all around him; "but we fell out in the middle over one idea, so I never corrected the second part. Therefore I cannot be held responsible for the numerous grammatical blunders in it."

"That is all he thinks of!" cried Lizabetha Prokofievna.

"May I ask when this article was revised?" said Evgenie Pavlovitch to Keller.

"Yesterday morning," he replied, "we had an interview which we all gave our word of honour to keep secret."

"The very time when he was cringing before you and making protestations of devotion! Oh, the mean wretches! I will have nothing to do with your Pushkin, and your daughter shall not set foot in my house!"

Lizabetha Prokofievna was about to rise, when she saw Hippolyte laughing, and turned upon him with irritation.

"Well, sir, I suppose you wanted to make me look ridiculous?"

"Heaven forbid!" he answered, with a forced smile. "But I am more than ever struck by your eccentricity, Lizabetha Prokofievna. I admit that I told you of Lebedeff's duplicity, on purpose. I knew the effect it would have on you,—on you alone, for the prince will forgive him. He has probably forgiven him already, and is racking his brains to find some excuse for him—is not that the truth, prince?"

He gasped as he spoke, and his strange agitation seemed to increase.

"Well?" said Mrs. Epanchin angrily, surprised at his tone; "well, what more?"

"I have heard many things of the kind about you...they delighted me... I have learned to hold you in the highest esteem," continued Hippolyte.

His words seemed tinged with a kind of sarcastic mockery, yet he was extremely agitated, casting suspicious glances around him, growing confused, and constantly losing the thread of his ideas. All this, together with his consumptive appearance, and the frenzied expression of his blazing eyes, naturally attracted the attention of everyone present.

"I might have been surprised (though I admit I know nothing of the world), not only that you should have stayed on just now in the company of such people as myself and my friends, who are not of your class, but that you should let these... young ladies listen to such a scandalous affair, though no doubt novel-reading has taught them all there is to know. I may be mistaken; I hardly know what I am saying; but surely no one but you would have stayed to please a whippersnapper (yes, a whippersnapper; I admit it) to spend the evening and take part in everything—only to be ashamed of it tomorrow. (I know I express myself badly.) I admire and appreciate it all extremely, though the expression on the face of his excellency, your husband, shows that he thinks it very improper. He-he!" He burst out laughing, and was seized with a fit of coughing which lasted for two minutes and prevented him from speaking.

"He has lost his breath now!" said Lizabetha Prokofievna coldly, looking at him with more curiosity than pity: "Come, my dear boy, that is quite enough—let us make an end of this."

Ivan Fedorovitch, now quite out of patience, interrupted suddenly. "Let me remark in my turn, sir," he said in tones of deep annoyance, "that my wife is here as the guest of Prince Lef Nicolaievitch, our friend and neighbour, and that in any case, young man, it is not for you to pass judgment on the conduct of Lizabetha Prokofievna, or to make remarks aloud in my presence concerning what feelings you think may be read in my face. Yes, my wife stayed here," continued the general, with increasing irritation, "more out of amazement than anything else. Everyone can understand that a collection of such strange young men would attract the attention of a person interested in contemporary life. I stayed myself, just as I sometimes stop to look on in the street when I see something that may be regarded as-as-as-"

"As a curiosity," suggested Evgenie Pavlovitch, seeing his excellency involved in a comparison which he could not complete.

"That is exactly the word I wanted," said the general with satisfaction—"a curiosity. However, the most astonishing and, if I may so express myself, the most painful, thing in this matter, is that you cannot even understand, young man, that Lizabetha Prokofievna, only stayed with you because you are ill,—if you really are dying—moved by the pity awakened by your plaintive appeal, and that her name, character, and social position place her above all risk of contamination. Lizabetha Prokofievna!" he continued, now crimson with rage, "if you are coming, we will say goodnight to the prince, and—"

"Thank you for the lesson, general," said Hippolyte, with unexpected gravity, regarding him thoughtfully.

"Two minutes more, if you please, dear Ivan Fedorovitch," said Lizabetha Prokofievna to her husband; "it seems to me that he is in a fever and delirious; you can see by his eyes what a state he is in; it is impossible to let him go back to Petersburg tonight. Can you put him up, Lef Nicolaievitch? I hope you are not bored, dear prince," she added suddenly to Prince S. "Alexandra, my dear, come here! Your hair is coming down."

She arranged her daughter's hair, which was not in the least disordered, and gave her a kiss. This was all that she had called her for.

"I thought you were capable of development," said Hippolyte, coming out of his fit of abstraction. "Yes, that is what I meant to say," he added, with the satisfaction of one who suddenly remembers something he had forgotten. "Here is Burdovsky, sincerely anxious to protect his mother; is not that so? And he himself is the cause of her disgrace. The prince is anxious to help Burdovsky and offers him friendship and a large sum of money, in the sincerity of his heart. And here they stand like two sworn enemies—ha, ha, ha! You all hate Burdovsky because his behaviour with regard to his mother is shocking and repugnant to you; do you not? Is not that true? Is it not true? You all have a passion for beauty and distinction in outward forms; that is all you care for, isn't it? I have suspected for a long time that you cared for nothing else! Well, let me tell you that perhaps there is not one of you who loved your mother as Burdovsky loved his. As to you, prince, I know that you have sent money secretly to Burdovsky's mother through Gania. Well, I bet now," he continued with an hysterical laugh, "that Burdovsky will accuse you of indelicacy, and reproach you with a want of respect for his mother! Yes, that is quite certain! Ha, ha, ha!"

He caught his breath, and began to cough once more.

"Come, that is enough! That is all now; you have no more to say? Now go to bed; you are burning with fever," said Lizabetha Prokofievna impatiently. Her anxious eyes had never left the invalid. "Good heavens, he is going to begin again!"

"You are laughing, I think? Why do you keep laughing at me?" said Hippolyte irritably to Evgenie Pavlovitch, who certainly was laughing.

"I only want to know, Mr. Hippolyte—excuse me, I forget your surname."

"Mr. Terentieff," said the prince.

"Oh yes, Mr. Terentieff. Thank you prince. I heard it just now, but had forgotten it. I want to know, Mr. Terentieff, if what I have heard about you is true. It seems you are convinced that if you could speak to the people from a window for a quarter of an hour, you could make them all adopt your views and follow you?"

"I may have said so," answered Hippolyte, as if trying to remember. "Yes, I certainly said so," he continued with sudden animation, fixing an unflinching glance on his questioner. "What of it?"

"Nothing. I was only seeking further information, to put the finishing touch."

Evgenie Pavlovitch was silent, but Hippolyte kept his eyes fixed upon him, waiting impatiently for more.

"Well, have you finished?" said Lizabetha Prokofievna to Evgenie. "Make haste, sir; it is time he went to bed. Have you more to say?" She was very angry.

"Yes, I have a little more," said Evgenie Pavlovitch, with a smile. "It seems to me that all you and your friends have said, Mr. Terentieff, and all you have just put forward with such undeniable talent, may be summed up in the triumph of right above all, independent of everything else, to the exclusion of everything else; perhaps even before having discovered what constitutes the right. I may be mistaken?"

"You are certainly mistaken; I do not even understand you. What else?"

Murmurs arose in the neighbourhood of Burdovsky and his companions; Lebedeff's nephew protested under his breath.

"I have nearly finished," replied Evgenie Pavlovitch.

"I will only remark that from these premises one could conclude that might is right—I mean the right of the clenched fist, and of personal inclination. Indeed, the world has often come to that conclusion. Prudhon upheld that might is right. In the American War some of the most advanced Liberals took sides with the planters on the score that the blacks were an inferior race to the whites, and that might was the right of the white race."

"Well?"

"You mean, no doubt, that you do not deny that might is right?"

"What then?"

"You are at least logical. I would only point out that from the right of might, to the right of tigers and crocodiles, or even Daniloff and Gorsky, is but a step."

"I know nothing about that; what else?"

Hippolyte was scarcely listening. He kept saying "well?" and "what else?" mechanically, without the least curiosity, and by mere force of habit.

"Why, nothing else; that is all."

"However, I bear you no grudge," said Hippolyte suddenly, and, hardly conscious of what he was doing, he held out his hand with a smile. The gesture took Evgenie Pavlovitch by surprise, but with the utmost gravity he touched the hand that was offered him in token of forgiveness.

"I can but thank you," he said, in a tone too respectful to be sincere, "for your kindness in letting me speak, for I have often noticed that our Liberals never allow other people to have an opinion of their own, and immediately answer their opponents with abuse, if they do not have recourse to arguments of a still more unpleasant nature."

"What you say is quite true," observed General Epanchin; then, clasping his hands behind his back, he returned to his place on the terrace steps, where he yawned with an air of boredom.

"Come, sir, that will do; you weary me," said Lizabetha Prokofievna suddenly to Evgenie Pavlovitch.

Hippolyte rose all at once, looking troubled and almost frightened.

"It is time for me to go," he said, glancing round in perplexity. "I have detained you... I wanted to tell you everything... I thought you all... for the last time... it was a whim..."

He evidently had sudden fits of returning animation, when he awoke from his semi-delirium; then, recovering full self-possession for a few moments, he would speak, in disconnected phrases which had perhaps haunted him for a long while on his bed of suffering, during weary, sleepless nights.

"Well, good-bye," he said abruptly. "You think it is easy for me to say good-bye to you? Ha, ha!"

Feeling that his question was somewhat gauche, he smiled angrily. Then as if vexed that he could not ever express what he really meant, he said irritably, in a loud voice:

"Excellency, I have the honour of inviting you to my funeral; that is, if you will deign to honour it with your presence. I invite you all, gentlemen, as well as the general."

He burst out laughing again, but it was the laughter of a madman. Lizabetha Prokofievna approached him anxiously and seized his arm. He stared at her for a moment, still laughing, but soon his face grew serious.

"Do you know that I came here to see those trees?" pointing to the trees in the park. "It is not ridiculous, is it? Say that it is not ridiculous!" he demanded urgently of Lizabetha Prokofievna. Then he seemed to be plunged in thought. A moment later he raised his head, and his eyes sought for someone. He was looking for Evgenie Pavlovitch, who was close by on his right as before, but he had forgotten this, and his eyes ranged over the assembled company. "Ah! you have not gone!" he said, when he caught sight of him at last. "You kept on laughing just now, because I thought of speaking to the people from the window for a quarter of an hour. But I am not eighteen, you know; lying on that bed, and looking out of that window, I have thought of all sorts of things for such a long time that... a dead man has no age, you know. I was saying that to myself only last week, when I was awake in the night. Do you know what you fear most? You fear our sincerity more than anything, although you despise us! The idea crossed my mind that night... You thought I was making fun of you just now, Lizabetha Prokofievna? No, the idea of mockery was far from me; I only meant to praise you. Colia told me the prince called you a child—very well—but let me see, I had something else to say..." He covered his face with his hands and tried to collect his thoughts.

"Ah, yes—you were going away just now, and I thought to myself: 'I shall never see these people again—never again! This is the last time I shall see the trees, too. I shall see nothing after this but the red brick wall of Meyer's house opposite my window. Tell them about it—try to tell them,' I thought. 'Here is a beautiful young girl—you are a dead man; make them understand that. Tell them that a dead man may say anything—and Mrs. Grundy will not be angry—ha-ha! You are not laughing?" He looked anxiously around. "But you know I get so many queer ideas, lying there in bed. I have grown convinced that nature is full of mockery—you called me an atheist just now, but you know this nature... why are you laughing again? You are very cruel!" he added suddenly, regarding them all with mournful reproach. "I have not corrupted Colia," he concluded in a different and very serious tone, as if remembering something again.

"Nobody here is laughing at you. Calm yourself," said Lizabetha Prokofievna, much moved. "You shall see a new doctor tomorrow; the other was mistaken; but sit down, do not stand like that! You are delirious—" Oh, what shall we do with him she cried in anguish, as she made him sit down again in the arm-chair.

A tear glistened on her cheek. At the sight of it Hippolyte seemed amazed. He lifted his hand timidly and, touched the tear with his finger, smiling like a child.

"I... you," he began joyfully. "You cannot tell how I... he always spoke so enthusiastically of you, Colia here; I liked his enthusiasm. I was not corrupting him! But I must leave him, too—I wanted to leave them all—there was not one of them—not one! I wanted to be a man of action—I had a right to be. Oh! what a lot of things I wanted! Now I want nothing; I renounce all my wants; I swore to myself that I would want nothing; let them seek the truth without me! Yes, nature is full of mockery! Why"—he continued with sudden warmth—"does she create the choicest beings only to mock at them? The only human being who is recognized as perfect, when nature showed him to mankind, was given the mission to say things which have caused the shedding of so much blood that it would have drowned mankind if it had all been shed at once! Oh! it is better for me to die! I should tell some dreadful lie too; nature would so contrive it! I have corrupted nobody. I wanted to live for the happiness of all men, to find and spread the truth. I used to look out of my window at the wall of Meyer's house, and say to myself that if I could speak for a quarter of an hour I would convince the whole world, and now for once in my life I have come into contact with... you—if not with the others! And what is the result? Nothing! The sole result is that you despise me! Therefore I must be a fool, I am useless, it is time I disappeared! And I shall leave not even a memory! Not a sound, not a trace, not a single deed! I have not spread a single truth!... Do not laugh at the fool! Forget him! Forget him forever! I beseech you, do not be so cruel as to remember! Do you know that if I were not consumptive, I would kill myself?"

Though he seemed to wish to say much more, he became silent. He fell back into his chair, and, covering his face with his hands, began to sob like a little child.

"Oh! what on earth are we to do with him?" cried Lizabetha Prokofievna. She hastened to him and pressed his head against her bosom, while he sobbed convulsively.

"Come, come, come! There, you must not cry, that will do. You are a good child! God will forgive you, because you knew no better. Come now, be a man! You know presently you will be ashamed."

Hippolyte raised his head with an effort, saying:

"I have little brothers and sisters, over there, poor avid innocent. She will corrupt them! You are a saint! You are a child yourself—save them! Snatch them from that... she is... it is shameful! Oh! help them! God will repay you a hundredfold. For the love of God, for the love of Christ!"

"Speak, Ivan Fedorovitch! What are we to do?" cried Lizabetha Prokofievna, irritably. "Please break your majestic silence! I tell you, if you cannot come to some decision, I will stay here all night myself. You have tyrannized over me enough, you autocrat!"

She spoke angrily, and in great excitement, and expected an immediate reply. But in such a case, no matter how many are present, all prefer to keep silence: no one will take the initiative, but all reserve their comments till afterwards. There were some present—Varvara Ardalionovna, for instance—who would have willingly sat there till morning without saying a word. Varvara had sat apart all the evening without opening her lips, but she listened to everything with the closest attention; perhaps she had her reasons for so doing.

"My dear," said the general, "it seems to me that a sick-nurse would be of more use here than an excitable person like you. Perhaps it would be as well to get some sober, reliable man for the night. In any case we must consult the prince, and leave the patient to rest at once. Tomorrow we can see what can be done for him."

"It is nearly midnight; we are going. Will he come with us, or is he to stay here?" Doktorenko asked crossly of the prince.

"You can stay with him if you like," said Muishkin.

"There is plenty of room here."

Suddenly, to the astonishment of all, Keller went quickly up to the general.

"Excellency," he said, impulsively, "if you want a reliable man for the night, I am ready to sacrifice myself for my friend—such a soul as he has! I have long thought him a great man, excellency! My article showed my lack of education, but when he criticizes he scatters pearls!"

Ivan Fedorovitch turned from the boxer with a gesture of despair.

"I shall be delighted if he will stay; it would certainly be difficult for him to get back to Petersburg," said the prince, in answer to the eager questions of Lizabetha Prokofievna.

"But you are half asleep, are you not? If you don't want him, I will take him back to my house! Why, good gracious! He can hardly stand up himself! What is it? Are you ill?"

Not finding the prince on his death-bed, Lizabetha Prokofievna had been misled by his appearance to think him much better than he was. But his recent illness, the painful memories attached to it, the fatigue of this evening, the incident with "Pavlicheff's son," and now this scene with Hippolyte, had all so worked on his oversensitive nature that he was now almost in a fever. Moreover, a new trouble, almost a fear, showed itself in his eyes; he watched Hippolyte anxiously as if expecting something further.

Suddenly Hippolyte arose. His face, shockingly pale, was that of a man overwhelmed with shame and despair. This was shown chiefly in the look of fear and hatred which he cast upon the assembled company, and in the wild smile upon his trembling lips. Then he cast down his eyes, and with the same smile, staggered towards Burdovsky and Doktorenko, who stood at the entrance to the verandah. He had decided to go with them.

"There! that is what I feared!" cried the prince. "It was inevitable!"

Hippolyte turned upon him, a prey to maniacal rage, which set all the muscles of his face quivering.

"Ah! that is what you feared! It was inevitable, you say! Well, let me tell you that if I hate anyone here—I hate you all," he cried, in a hoarse, strained voice—"but you, you, with your jesuitical soul, your soul of sickly sweetness, idiot, beneficent millionaire—I hate you worse than anything or anyone on earth! I saw through you and hated you long ago; from the day I first heard of you. I hated you with my whole heart. You have contrived all this! You have driven me into this state! You have made a dying man disgrace himself. You, you, you are the cause of my abject cowardice! I would kill you if I remained alive! I do not want your benefits; I will accept none from anyone; do you hear? Not from any one! I want nothing! I was delirious, do not dare to triumph! I curse every one of you, once for all!"

Breath failed him here, and he was obliged to stop.

"He is ashamed of his tears!" whispered Lebedeff to Lizabetha Prokofievna. "It was inevitable. Ah! what a wonderful man the prince is! He read his very soul."

But Mrs. Epanchin would not deign to look at Lebedeff. Drawn up haughtily, with her head held high, she gazed at the "riff-raff," with scornful curiosity. When Hippolyte had finished, Ivan Fedorovitch shrugged his shoulders, and his wife looked him angrily up and down, as if to demand the meaning of his movement. Then she turned to the prince.

"Thanks, prince, many thanks, eccentric friend of the family, for the pleasant evening you have provided for us. I am sure you are quite pleased that you have managed to mix us up with your extraordinary affairs. It is quite enough, dear family friend; thank you for giving us an opportunity of getting to know you so well."

She arranged her cloak with hands that trembled with anger as she waited for the "riff-raff" to go. The cab which Lebedeff's son had gone to fetch a quarter of an hour ago, by Doktorenko's order, arrived at that moment. The general thought fit to put in a word after his wife.

"Really, prince, I hardly expected after—after all our friendly intercourse—and you see, Lizabetha Prokofievna—"

"Papa, how can you?" cried Adelaida, walking quickly up to the prince and holding out her hand.

He smiled absently at her; then suddenly he felt a burning sensation in his ear as an angry voice whispered:

"If you do not turn those dreadful people out of the house this very instant, I shall hate you all my life—all my life!" It was Aglaya. She seemed almost in a frenzy, but she turned away before the prince could look at her. However, there was no one left to turn out of the house, for they had managed meanwhile to get Hippolyte into the cab, and it had driven off.

"Well, how much longer is this going to last, Ivan Fedorovitch? What do you think? Shall I soon be delivered from these odious youths?"

"My dear, I am quite ready; naturally... the prince."

Ivan Fedorovitch held out his hand to Muishkin, but ran after his wife, who was leaving with every sign of violent indignation, before he had time to shake it. Adelaida, her fiance, and Alexandra, said good-bye to their host with sincere friendliness. Evgenie Pavlovitch did the same, and he alone seemed in good spirits.

"What I expected has happened! But I am sorry, you poor fellow, that you should have had to suffer for it," he murmured, with a most charming smile.

Aglaya left without saying good-bye. But the evening was not to end without a last adventure. An unexpected meeting was yet in store for Lizabetha Prokofievna.

She had scarcely descended the terrace steps leading to the high road that skirts the park at Pavlofsk, when suddenly there dashed by a smart open carriage, drawn by a pair of beautiful white horses. Having passed some ten yards beyond the house, the carriage suddenly drew up, and one of the two ladies seated in it turned sharp round as though she had just caught sight of some acquaintance whom she particularly wished to see.

"Evgenie Pavlovitch! Is that you?" cried a clear, sweet voice, which caused the prince, and perhaps someone else, to tremble. "Well, I am glad I've found you at last! I've sent to town for you twice today myself! My messengers have been searching for you everywhere!"

Evgenie Pavlovitch stood on the steps like one struck by lightning. Mrs. Epanchin stood still too, but not with the petrified expression of Evgenie. She gazed haughtily at the audacious person who had addressed her companion, and then turned a look of astonishment upon Evgenie himself.

"There's news!" continued the clear voice. "You need not be anxious about Kupferof's IOU's— Rogojin has bought them up. I persuaded him to!—I dare say we shall settle Biscup too, so it's all right, you see! Au revoir, tomorrow! And don't worry!" The carriage moved on, and disappeared.

"The woman's mad!" cried Evgenie, at last, crimson with anger, and looking confusedly around. "I don't know what she's talking about! What IOU's? Who is she?" Mrs. Epanchin continued to watch his face for a couple of seconds; then she marched briskly and haughtily away towards her own house, the rest following her.

A minute afterwards, Evgenie Pavlovitch reappeared on the terrace, in great agitation.

"Prince," he said, "tell me the truth; do you know what all this means?"

"I know nothing whatever about it!" replied the latter, who was, himself, in a state of nervous excitement.

"No?"

"No!"

"Well, nor do I!" said Evgenie Pavlovitch, laughing suddenly. "I haven't the slightest knowledge of any such IOU's as she mentioned, I swear I haven't—What's the matter, are you fainting?"

"Oh, no—no—I'm all right, I assure you!"

CHAPTER XI.

The anger of the Epanchin family was unappeased for three days. As usual the prince reproached himself, and had expected punishment, but he was inwardly convinced that Lizabetha Prokofievna could not be seriously angry with him, and that she probably was more angry with herself. He was painfully surprised, therefore, when three days passed with no word from her. Other things also troubled and perplexed him, and one of these grew more important in his eyes as the days went by. He had begun to blame himself for two opposite tendencies—on the one hand to extreme, almost "senseless," confidence in his fellows, on the other to a "vile, gloomy suspiciousness."

By the end of the third day the incident of the eccentric lady and Evgenie Pavlovitch had attained enormous and mysterious proportions in his mind. He sorrowfully asked himself whether he had been the cause of this new "monstrosity," or was it... but he refrained from saying who else might be in fault. As for the letters N.P.B., he looked on that as a harmless joke, a mere childish piece of mischief—so childish that he felt it would be shameful, almost dishonourable, to attach any importance to it.

The day after these scandalous events, however, the prince had the honour of receiving a visit from Adelaida and her fiancé, Prince S. They came, ostensibly, to inquire after his health. They had wandered out for a walk, and called in "by accident," and talked for almost the whole of the time they were with him about a certain most lovely tree in the park, which Adelaida had set her heart upon for a picture. This, and a little amiable conversation on Prince S.'s part, occupied the time, and not a word was said about last evening's episodes. At length Adelaida burst out laughing, apologized, and explained that they had come incognito; from which, and from the circumstance that they said nothing about the prince's either walking back with them or coming to see them later on, the latter inferred that he was in Mrs. Epanchin's black books. Adelaida mentioned a watercolour that she would much like to show him, and explained that she would either send it by Colia, or bring it herself the next day—which to the prince seemed very suggestive.

At length, however, just as the visitors were on the point of departing, Prince S. seemed suddenly to recollect himself. "Oh yes, by-the-by," he said, "do you happen to know, my dear Lef Nicolaievitch, who that lady was who called out to Evgenie Pavlovitch last night, from the carriage?"

"It was Nastasia Philipovna," said the prince; "didn't you know that? I cannot tell you who her companion was."

"But what on earth did she mean? I assure you it is a real riddle to me—to me, and to others, too!" Prince S. seemed to be under the influence of sincere astonishment.

"She spoke of some bills of Evgenie Pavlovitch's," said the prince, simply, "which Rogojin had bought up from someone; and implied that Rogojin would not press him."

"Oh, I heard that much, my dear fellow! But the thing is so impossibly absurd! A man of property like Evgenie to give IOU's to a money-lender, and to be worried about them! It is ridiculous. Besides, he cannot possibly be on such intimate terms with Nastasia Philipovna as she gave us to understand; that's the principal part of the mystery! He has given me his word that he knows nothing whatever about the matter, and of course I believe him. Well, the question is, my dear prince, do you know anything about it? Has any sort of suspicion of the meaning of it come across you?"

"No, I know nothing whatever about it. I assure you I had nothing at all to do with it."

"Oh, prince, how strange you have become! I assure you, I hardly know you for your old self. How can you suppose that I ever suggested you could have had a finger in such a business? But you are not quite yourself today, I can see." He embraced the prince, and kissed him.

"What do you mean, though," asked Muishkin, "'by such a business'? I don't see any particular 'business' about it at all!"

"Oh, undoubtedly, this person wished somehow, and for some reason, to do Evgenie Pavlovitch a bad turn, by attributing to him—before witnesses—qualities which he neither has nor can have," replied Prince S. drily enough.

Muiskhin looked disturbed, but continued to gaze intently and questioningly into Prince S.'s face. The latter, however, remained silent.

"Then it was not simply a matter of bills?" Muishkin said at last, with some impatience. "It was not as she said?"

"But I ask you, my dear sir, how can there be anything in common between Evgenie Pavlovitch, and—her, and again Rogojin? I tell you he is a man of immense wealth—as I know for a fact; and he has further expectations from his uncle. Simply Nastasia Philipovna—"

Prince S. paused, as though unwilling to continue talking about Nastasia Philipovna.

"Then at all events he knows her!" remarked the prince, after a moment's silence.

"Oh, that may be. He may have known her some time ago—two or three years, at least. He used to know Totski. But it is impossible that there should be any intimacy between them. She has not even been in the place—many people don't even know that she has returned from Moscow! I have only observed her carriage about for the last three days or so."

"It's a lovely carriage," said Adelaida.

"Yes, it was a beautiful turn-out, certainly!"

The visitors left the house, however, on no less friendly terms than before. But the visit was of the greatest importance to the prince, from his own point of view. Admitting that he had his suspicions, from the moment of the occurrence of last night, perhaps even before, that Nastasia had some mysterious end in view, yet this visit confirmed his suspicions and justified his fears. It was all clear to him; Prince S. was wrong, perhaps, in his view of the matter, but he was somewhere near the truth, and was right in so far as that he understood there to be an intrigue of some sort going on. Perhaps Prince S. saw it all more clearly than he had allowed his hearers to understand. At all events, nothing could be plainer than that he and Adelaida had come for the express purpose of obtaining explanations, and that they suspected him of being concerned in the affair. And if all this were so, then *she* must have some terrible object in view! What was it? There was no stopping *her*, as Muishkin knew from experience, in the performance of anything she had set her mind on! "Oh, she is mad, mad!" thought the poor prince.

But there were many other puzzling occurrences that day, which required immediate explanation, and the prince felt very sad. A visit from Vera Lebedeff distracted him a little. She brought the infant Lubotchka with her as usual, and talked cheerfully for some time. Then came her younger sister, and later the brother, who attended a school close by. He informed Muishkin that his father had lately found a new interpretation of the star called "wormwood," which fell upon the water-springs, as described in the Apocalypse. He had decided that it meant the network of railroads spread over the face of Europe at the present time. The prince refused to believe that Lebedeff could have given such an interpretation, and they decided to ask him about it at the earliest opportunity. Vera related how Keller had taken up his abode with them on the previous evening. She thought he would remain for some time, as he was greatly pleased with the society of General Ivolgin and of the whole family. But he declared that he had only come to them in order to complete his education! The prince always enjoyed the company of Lebedeff's children, and today it was especially welcome, for Colia did not appear all day. Early that morning he had started for Petersburg. Lebedeff also was away on business. But Gavrila Ardalionovitch had promised to visit Muishkin, who eagerly awaited his coming.

About seven in the evening, soon after dinner, he arrived. At the first glance it struck the prince that he, at any rate, must know all the details of last night's affair. Indeed, it would have been impossible for him to remain in ignorance considering the intimate relationship between him, Varvara Ardalionovna, and Ptitsin. But although he and the prince were intimate, in a sense, and although the latter had placed the Burdovsky affair in his hands—and this was not the only mark of confidence he had received—it seemed curious how many matters there were that were tacitly avoided in their conversations. Muishkin thought that Gania at times appeared to desire more cordiality and frankness. It was apparent now, when he entered, that he was convinced that the moment for breaking the ice between them had come at last.

But all the same Gania was in haste, for his sister was waiting at Lebedeff's to consult him on an urgent matter of business. If he had anticipated impatient questions, or impulsive confidences, he was soon undeceived. The prince was thoughtful, reserved, even a little absent-minded, and asked none of the questions—one in particular—that Gania had expected. So he imitated the prince's demeanour, and talked fast and brilliantly upon all subjects but the one on which their thoughts were engaged. Among other things Gania told his host that Nastasia Philipovna had been only four days in Pavlofsk, and that everyone was talking about her already. She was staying with Daria Alexeyevna, in an ugly little house in Mattrossky Street, but drove about in the smartest carriage in the place. A crowd of followers had pursued her from the first, young and old. Some escorted her on horse-back when she took the air in her carriage.

She was as capricious as ever in the choice of her acquaintances, and admitted few into her narrow circle. Yet she already had a numerous following and many champions on whom she could depend in time of need. One gentleman on his holiday had broken off his engagement on her account, and an old general had quarrelled with his only son for the same reason.

She was accompanied sometimes in her carriage by a girl of sixteen, a distant relative of her hostess. This young lady sang very well; in fact, her music had given a kind of notoriety to their little house. Nastasia, however, was behaving with great discretion on the whole. She dressed quietly, though with such taste as to drive all the ladies in Pavlofsk mad with envy, of that, as well as of her beauty and her carriage and horses.

"As for yesterday's episode," continued Gania, "of course it was pre-arranged." Here he paused, as though expecting to be asked how he knew that. But the prince did not inquire. Concerning Evgenie Pavlovitch, Gania stated, without being asked, that he believed the former had not known Nastasia Philipovna in past years, but that he had probably been introduced to her by somebody in the park during these four days. As to the question of the IOU's she had spoken of, there might easily be something in that; for though Evgenie was undoubtedly a man of wealth, yet certain of his affairs were equally undoubtedly in disorder. Arrived at this interesting point, Gania suddenly broke off, and said no more about Nastasia's prank of the previous evening.

At last Varvara Ardalionovna came in search of her brother, and remained for a few minutes. Without Muishkin's asking her, she informed him that Evgenie Pavlovitch was spending the day in Petersburg, and perhaps would remain there over tomorrow; and that her husband had also gone to town, probably in connection with Evgenie Pavlovitch's affairs.

"Lizabetha Prokofievna is in a really fiendish temper today," she added, as she went out, "but the most curious thing is that Aglaya has quarrelled with her whole family; not only with her father and mother, but with her sisters also. It is not a good sign." She said all this quite casually, though it was extremely important in the eyes of the prince, and went off with her brother. Regarding the episode of "Pavlicheff's son," Gania had been absolutely silent, partly from a kind of false modesty, partly, perhaps, to "spare the prince's feelings." The latter, however, thanked him again for the trouble he had taken in the affair.

Muishkin was glad enough to be left alone. He went out of the garden, crossed the road, and entered the park. He wished to reflect, and to make up his mind as to a certain "step." This step was one of those things, however, which are not thought out, as a rule, but decided for or against hastily, and without much reflection. The fact is, he felt a longing to leave all this and go away—go anywhere, if only it were far enough, and at once, without bidding farewell to anyone. He felt a presentiment that if he remained but a few days more in this place, and among these people, he would be fixed there irrevocably and permanently. However, in a very few minutes he decided that to run away was impossible; that it would be cowardly; that great problems lay before him, and that he had no right to leave them unsolved, or at least to refuse to give all his energy and strength to the attempt to solve them. Having come to this determination, he turned and went home, his walk having lasted less than a quarter of an hour. At that moment he was thoroughly unhappy.

Lebedeff had not returned, so towards evening Keller managed to penetrate into the prince's apartments. He was not drunk, but in a confidential and talkative mood. He announced that he had come to tell the story of his life to Muishkin, and had only remained at Pavlofsk for that purpose. There was no means of turning him out; nothing short of an earthquake would have removed him.

In the manner of one with long hours before him, he began his history; but after a few incoherent words he jumped to the conclusion, which was that "having ceased to believe in God Almighty, he had lost every vestige of morality, and had gone so far as to commit a theft." "Could you imagine such a thing?" said he.

"Listen to me, Keller," returned the prince. "If I were in your place, I should not acknowledge that unless it were absolutely necessary for some reason. But perhaps you are making yourself out to be worse than you are, purposely?"

"I should tell it to no one but yourself, prince, and I only name it now as a help to my soul's evolution. When I die, that secret will die with me! But, excellency, if you knew, if you only had the least idea, how difficult it is to get money nowadays! Where to find it is the question. Ask for a loan, the answer is always the same: 'Give us gold, jewels, or diamonds, and it will be quite easy.' Exactly what one has not got! Can you picture that to yourself? I got angry at last, and said, 'I suppose you would accept emeralds?' 'Certainly, we accept emeralds with pleasure. Yes!' 'Well, that's all right,' said I. 'Go to the devil, you den of thieves!' And with that I seized my hat, and walked out."

"Had you any emeralds?" asked the prince.

"What? I have emeralds? Oh, prince! with what simplicity, with what almost pastoral simplicity, you look upon life!"

Could not something be made of this man under good influences? asked the prince of himself, for he began to feel a kind of pity for his visitor. He thought little of the value of his own personal influence, not from a sense of humility, but from his peculiar way of looking at things in general. Imperceptibly the conversation grew more animated and more interesting, so that neither of the two felt anxious to bring it to a close. Keller confessed, with apparent sincerity, to having been guilty of many acts of such a nature that it astonished the prince that he could mention them, even to him. At every fresh avowal he professed the deepest repentance, and described himself as being "bathed in tears"; but this did not prevent him from putting on a boastful air at times, and some of his stories were so absurdly comical that both he and the prince laughed like madmen.

"One point in your favour is that you seem to have a child-like mind, and extreme truthfulness," said the prince at last. "Do you know that that atones for much?"

"I am assuredly noble-minded, and chivalrous to a degree!" said Keller, much softened. "But, do you know, this nobility of mind exists in a dream, if one may put it so? It never appears in practice or deed. Now, why is that? I can never understand."

"Do not despair. I think we may say without fear of deceiving ourselves, that you have now given a fairly exact account of your life. I, at least, think it would be impossible to add much to what you have just told me."

"Impossible?" cried Keller, almost pityingly. "Oh prince, how little you really seem to understand human nature!"

"Is there really much more to be added?" asked the prince, with mild surprise. "Well, what is it you really want of me? Speak out; tell me why you came to make your confession to me?"

"What did I want? Well, to begin with, it is good to meet a man like you. It is a pleasure to talk over my faults with you. I know you for one of the best of men... and then... then..."

He hesitated, and appeared so much embarrassed that the prince helped him out.

"Then you wanted me to lend you money?"

The words were spoken in a grave tone, and even somewhat shyly.

Keller started, gave an astonished look at the speaker, and thumped the table with his fist.

"Well, prince, that's enough to knock me down! It astounds me! Here you are, as simple and innocent as a knight of the golden age, and yet... yet... you read a man's soul like a psychologist! Now, do explain it to me, prince, because I... I really do not understand!... Of course, my aim was to borrow money all along, and you... you asked the question as if there was nothing blameable in it—as if you thought it quite natural."

"Yes... from you it is quite natural."

"And you are not offended?"

"Why should I be offended?"

"Well, just listen, prince. I remained here last evening, partly because I have a great admiration for the French archbishop Bourdaloue. I enjoyed a discussion over him till three o'clock in the morning, with Lebedeff; and then... then—I swear by all I hold sacred that I am telling you the truth—then I wished to develop my soul in this frank and heartfelt confession to you. This was my thought as I was sobbing myself to sleep at dawn. Just as I was losing consciousness, tears in my soul, tears on my face (I remember how I lay there sobbing), an idea from hell struck me. 'Why not, after confessing, borrow money from him?' You see, this confession was a kind of masterstroke; I intended to use it as a means to your good grace and favour—and then—then I meant to walk off with a hundred and fifty roubles. Now, do you not call that base?"

"It is hardly an exact statement of the case," said the prince in reply. "You have confused your motives and ideas, as I need scarcely say too often happens to myself. I can assure you, Keller, I reproach myself bitterly for it sometimes. When you were talking just now I seemed to be listening to something about myself. At times I have imagined that all men were the same," he continued earnestly, for he appeared to be much interested in the conversation, "and that consoled me in a certain degree, for a *double* motive is a thing most difficult to fight against. I have tried, and I know. God knows whence they arise, these ideas that you speak of as base. I fear these double motives more than ever just now, but I am not your judge, and in my opinion it is going too far to give the name of baseness to it—what do you think? You were going to employ your tears as a ruse in order to borrow money, but you also say—in fact, you have sworn to the fact—that independently of this your confession was made with an honourable motive. As for the money, you want it for drink, do you not? After your confession, that is weakness, of course; but, after all, how can anyone give up a bad habit at a moment's notice? It is impossible. What can we do? It is best, I think, to leave the matter to your own conscience. How does it seem to you?" As he concluded the prince looked curiously at Keller; evidently this problem of double motives had often been considered by him before.

"Well, how anybody can call you an idiot after that, is more than I can understand!" cried the boxer.

The prince reddened slightly.

"Bourdaloue, the archbishop, would not have spared a man like me," Keller continued, "but you, you have judged me with humanity. To show how grateful I am, and as a punishment, I will not accept a hundred and fifty roubles. Give me twenty-five—that will be enough; it is all I really need, for a fortnight at least. I will not ask you for more for a fortnight. I should like to have given Agatha a present, but she does not really deserve it. Oh, my dear prince, God bless you!"

At this moment Lebedeff appeared, having just arrived from Petersburg. He frowned when he saw the twenty-five rouble note in Keller's hand, but the latter, having got the money, went away at once. Lebedeff began to abuse him.

"You are unjust; I found him sincerely repentant," observed the prince, after listening for a time.

"What is the good of repentance like that? It is the same exactly as mine yesterday, when I said, 'I am base, I am base,'—words, and nothing more!"

"Then they were only words on your part? I thought, on the contrary..."

"Well, I don't mind telling you the truth—you only! Because you see through a man somehow. Words and actions, truth and falsehood, are all jumbled up together in me, and yet I am perfectly sincere. I feel the deepest repentance, believe it or not, as you choose; but words and lies come out in the infernal craving to get the better of other people. It is always there—the notion of cheating people, and of using my repentant tears to my own advantage! I assure you this is the truth, prince! I would not tell any other man for the world! He would laugh and jeer at me—but you, you judge a man humanely."

"Why, Keller said the same thing to me nearly word for word a few minutes ago!" cried Muishkin. "And you both seem inclined to boast about it! You astonish me, but I think he is more sincere than you, for you make a regular trade of it. Oh, don't put on that pathetic expression, and don't put your hand on your heart! Have you anything to say to me? You have not come for nothing..."

Lebedeff grinned and wriggled.

"I have been waiting all day for you, because I want to ask you a question; and, for once in your life, please tell me the truth at once. Had you anything to do with that affair of the carriage yesterday?"

Lebedeff began to grin again, rubbed his hands, sneezed, but spoke not a word in reply.

"I see you had something to do with it."

"Indirectly, quite indirectly! I am speaking the truth—I am indeed! I merely told a certain person that I had people in my house, and that such and such personages might be found among them."

"I am aware that you sent your son to that house—he told me so himself just now, but what is this intrigue?" said the prince, impatiently.

"It is not my intrigue!" cried Lebedeff, waving his hand.

"It was engineered by other people, and is, properly speaking, rather a fantasy than an intrigue!"

"But what is it all about? Tell me, for Heaven's sake! Cannot you understand how nearly it touches me? Why are they blackening Evgenie Pavlovitch's reputation?"

Lebedeff grimaced and wriggled again.

"Prince!" said he. "Excellency! You won't let me tell you the whole truth; I have tried to explain; more than once I have begun, but you have not allowed me to go on..."

The prince gave no answer, and sat deep in thought. Evidently he was struggling to decide.

"Very well! Tell me the truth," he said, dejectedly.

"Aglaya Ivanovna..." began Lebedeff, promptly.

"Be silent! At once!" interrupted the prince, red with indignation, and perhaps with shame, too. "It is impossible and absurd! All that has been invented by you, or fools like you! Let me never hear you say a word again on that subject!"

Late in the evening Colia came in with a whole budget of Petersburg and Pavlofsk news. He did not dwell much on the Petersburg part of it, which consisted chiefly of intelligence about his friend Hippolyte, but passed quickly to the Pavlofsk tidings. He had gone straight to the Epanchins' from the station.

"There's the deuce and all going on there!" he said. "First of all about the row last night, and I think there must be something new as well, though I didn't like to ask. Not a word about *you*, prince, the whole time! The most interesting fact was that Aglaya had been quarrelling with her people about Gania. Colia did not know any details, except that it had been a terrible quarrel! Also Evgenie Pavlovitch had called, and met with an excellent reception all round. And another curious thing: Mrs. Epanchin was so angry that she called Varia to her—Varia was talking to the girls—and turned her out of the house 'once for all' she said. I heard it from Varia herself—Mrs. Epanchin was quite polite, but firm; and when Varia said good-bye to the girls, she told them nothing about it, and they didn't know they were saying goodbye for the last time. I'm sorry for Varia, and for Gania too; he isn't half a bad fellow, in spite of his faults, and I shall never forgive myself for not liking him before! I don't know whether I ought to continue to go to the Epanchins' now," concluded Colia—"I like to be quite independent of others, and of other people's quarrels if I can; but I must think over it."

"I don't think you need break your heart over Gania," said the prince; "for if what you say is true, he must be considered dangerous in the Epanchin household, and if so, certain hopes of his must have been encouraged."

"What? What hopes?" cried Colia; "you surely don't mean Aglaya?—oh, no!—"

"You're a dreadful sceptic, prince," he continued, after a moment's silence. "I have observed of late that you have grown sceptical about everything. You don't seem to believe in people as you did, and are always attributing motives and so on—am I using the word 'sceptic' in its proper sense?"

"I believe so; but I'm not sure."

"Well, I'll change it, right or wrong; I'll say that you are not sceptical, but *jealous*. There! you are deadly jealous of Gania, over a certain proud damsel! Come!" Colia jumped up, with these words, and burst out laughing. He laughed as he had perhaps never laughed before, and still more when he saw the prince flushing up to his temples. He was delighted that the prince should be jealous about Aglaya. However, he stopped immediately on seeing that the other was really hurt, and the conversation continued, very earnestly, for an hour or more.

Next day the prince had to go to town, on business. Returning in the afternoon, he happened upon General Epanchin at the station. The latter seized his hand, glancing around nervously, as if he were afraid of being caught in wrong-doing, and dragged him into a first-class compartment. He was burning to speak about something of importance.

"In the first place, my dear prince, don't be angry with me. I would have come to see you yesterday, but I didn't know how Lizabetha Prokofievna would take it. My dear fellow, my house is simply a hell just now, a sort of sphinx has taken up its abode there. We live in an atmosphere of riddles; I can't make head or tail of anything. As for you, I feel sure you are the least to blame of any of us, though you certainly have been the cause of a good deal of trouble. You see, it's all very pleasant to be a philanthropist; but it can be carried too far. Of course I admire kind-heartedness, and I esteem my wife, but—"

The general wandered on in this disconnected way for a long time; it was clear that he was much disturbed by some circumstance which he could make nothing of.

"It is plain to me, that *you* are not in it at all," he continued, at last, a little less vaguely, "but perhaps you had better not come to our house for a little while. I ask you in the friendliest manner, mind; just till the wind changes again. As for Evgenie Pavlovitch," he continued with some excitement, "the whole thing is a calumny, a dirty calumny. It is simply a plot, an intrigue, to upset our plans and to stir up a quarrel. You see, prince, I'll tell you privately, Evgenie and ourselves have not said a word yet, we have no formal understanding, we are in no way bound on either side, but the word may be said very soon, don't you see, *very* soon, and all this is most injurious, and is meant to be so. Why? I'm sure I can't tell you. She's an extraordinary woman, you see, an eccentric woman; I tell you I am so frightened of that woman that I can't sleep. What a carriage that was, and where did it come from, eh? I declare, I was base enough to suspect Evgenie at first; but it seems certain that that cannot be the case, and if so, why is she interfering here? That's the riddle, what does she want? Is it to keep Evgenie to herself? But, my dear fellow, I swear to you, I swear he doesn't even *know* her, and as for those bills, why, the whole thing is an invention! And the familiarity of the woman! It's quite clear we must treat the impudent creature's attempt with disdain, and redouble our courtesy towards Evgenie. I told my wife so.

"Now I'll tell you my secret conviction. I'm certain that she's doing this to revenge herself on me, on account of the past, though I assure you that all the time I was blameless. I blush at the very idea. And now she turns up again like this, when I thought she had finally disappeared! Where's Rogojin all this time? I thought she was Mrs. Rogojin, long ago."

The old man was in a state of great mental perturbation. The whole of the journey, which occupied nearly an hour, he continued in this strain, putting questions and answering them himself, shrugging his shoulders, pressing the prince's hand, and assuring the latter that, at all events, he had no suspicion whatever of *him*. This last assurance was satisfactory, at all events. The general finished by informing him that Evgenie's uncle was head of one of the civil service departments, and rich, very rich, and a gourmand. "And, well, Heaven preserve him, of course—but Evgenie gets his money, don't you see? But, for all this, I'm uncomfortable, I don't know why. There's something in the air, I feel there's something nasty in the air, like a bat, and I'm by no means comfortable."

And it was not until the third day that the formal reconciliation between the prince and the Epanchins took place, as said before.

CHAPTER XII.

It was seven in the evening, and the prince was just preparing to go out for a walk in the park, when suddenly Mrs. Epanchin appeared on the terrace.

"In the first place, don't dare to suppose," she began, "that I am going to apologize. Nonsense! You were entirely to blame."

The prince remained silent.

"Were you to blame, or not?"

"No, certainly not, no more than yourself, though at first I thought I was."

"Oh, very well, let's sit down, at all events, for I don't intend to stand up all day. And remember, if you say, one word about 'mischievous urchins,' I shall go away and break with you altogether. Now then, did you, or did you not, send a letter to Aglaya, a couple of months or so ago, about Easter-tide?"

"Yes!"

"What for? What was your object? Show me the letter." Mrs. Epanchin's eyes flashed; she was almost trembling with impatience.

"I have not got the letter," said the prince, timidly, extremely surprised at the turn the conversation had taken. "If anyone has it, if it still exists, Aglaya Ivanovna must have it."

"No finessing, please. What did you write about?"

"I am not finessing, and I am not in the least afraid of telling you; but I don't see the slightest reason why I should not have written."

"Be quiet, you can talk afterwards! What was the letter about? Why are you blushing?"

The prince was silent. At last he spoke.

"I don't understand your thoughts, Lizabetha Prokofievna; but I can see that the fact of my having written is for some reason repugnant to you. You must admit that I have a perfect right to refuse to answer your questions; but, in order to show you that I am neither ashamed of the letter, nor sorry that I wrote it, and that I am not in the least inclined to blush about it" (here the prince's blushes redoubled), "I will repeat the substance of my letter, for I think I know it almost by heart."

So saying, the prince repeated the letter almost word for word, as he had written it.

"My goodness, what utter twaddle, and what may all this nonsense have signified, pray? If it had any meaning at all!" said Mrs. Epanchin, cuttingly, after having listened with great attention.

"I really don't absolutely know myself; I know my feeling was very sincere. I had moments at that time full of life and hope."

"What sort of hope?"

"It is difficult to explain, but certainly not the hopes you have in your mind. Hopes—well, in a word, hopes for the future, and a feeling of joy that *there*, at all events, I was not entirely a stranger and a foreigner. I felt an ecstasy in being in my native land once more; and one sunny morning I took up a pen and wrote her that letter, but why to *her*, I don't quite know. Sometimes one longs to have a friend near, and I evidently felt the need of one then," added the prince, and paused.

"Are you in love with her?"

"N-no! I wrote to her as to a sister; I signed myself her brother."

"Oh yes, of course, on purpose! I quite understand."

"It is very painful to me to answer these questions, Lizabetha Prokofievna."

"I dare say it is; but that's no affair of mine. Now then, assure me truly as before Heaven, are you lying to me or not?"

"No, I am not lying."

"Are you telling the truth when you say you are not in love?"

"I believe it is the absolute truth."

"'I believe,' indeed! Did that mischievous urchin give it to her?"

"I asked Nicolai Ardalionovitch..."

"The urchin! the urchin!" interrupted Lizabetha Prokofievna in an angry voice. "I do not want to know if it were Nicolai Ardalionovitch! The urchin!"

"Nicolai Ardalionovitch..."

"The urchin, I tell you!"

"No, it was not the urchin: it was Nicolai Ardalionovitch," said the prince very firmly, but without raising his voice.

"Well, all right! All right, my dear! I shall put that down to your account."

She was silent a moment to get breath, and to recover her composure.

"Well!—and what's the meaning of the 'poor knight,' eh?"

"I don't know in the least; I wasn't present when the joke was made. It *is* a joke. I suppose, and that's all."

"Well, that's a comfort, at all events. You don't suppose she could take any interest in you, do you? Why, she called you an 'idiot' herself."

"I think you might have spared me that," murmured the prince reproachfully, almost in a whisper.

"Don't be angry; she is a wilful, mad, spoilt girl. If she likes a person she will pitch into him, and chaff him. I used to be just such another. But for all that you needn't flatter yourself, my boy; she is not for you. I don't believe it, and it is not to be. I tell you so at once, so that you may take proper precautions. Now, I want to hear you swear that you are not married to that woman?"

"Lizabetha Prokofievna, what are you thinking of?" cried the prince, almost leaping to his feet in amazement.

"Why? You very nearly were, anyhow."

"Yes—I nearly was," whispered the prince, hanging his head.

"Well then, have you come here for *her*? Are you in love with *her*? With *that* creature?"

"I did not come to marry at all," replied the prince.

"Is there anything you hold sacred?"

"There is."

"Then swear by it that you did not come here to marry *her!*"

"I'll swear it by whatever you please."

"I believe you. You may kiss me; I breathe freely at last. But you must know, my dear friend, Aglaya does not love you, and she shall never be your wife while I am out of my grave. So be warned in time. Do you hear me?"

"Yes, I hear."

The prince flushed up so much that he could not look her in the face.

"I have waited for you with the greatest impatience (not that you were worth it). Every night I have drenched my pillow with tears, not for you, my friend, not for you, don't flatter yourself! I have my own grief, always the same, always the same. But I'll tell you why I have been awaiting you so impatiently, because I believe that Providence itself sent you to be a friend and a brother to me. I haven't a friend in the world except Princess Bielokonski, and she is growing as stupid as a sheep from old age. Now then, tell me, yes or no? Do you know why she called out from her carriage the other night?"

"I give you my word of honour that I had nothing to do with the matter and know nothing about it."

"Very well, I believe you. I have my own ideas about it. Up to yesterday morning I thought it was really Evgenie Pavlovitch who was to blame; now I cannot help agreeing with the others. But why he was made such a fool of I cannot understand. However, he is not going to marry Aglaya, I can tell you that. He may be a very excellent fellow, but—so it shall be. I was not at all sure of accepting him before, but now I have quite made up my mind that I won't have him. 'Put me in my coffin first and then into my grave, and then you may marry my daughter to whomsoever you please,' so I said to the general this very morning. You see how I trust you, my boy."

"Yes, I see and understand."

Mrs. Epanchin gazed keenly into the prince's eyes. She was anxious to see what impression the news as to Evgenie Pavlovitch had made upon him.

"Do you know anything about Gavrila Ardalionovitch?" she asked at last.

"Oh yes, I know a good deal."

"Did you know he had communications with Aglaya?"

"No, I didn't," said the prince, trembling a little, and in great agitation. "You say Gavrila Ardalionovitch has private communications with Aglaya?—Impossible!"

"Only quite lately. His sister has been working like a rat to clear the way for him all the winter."

"I don't believe it!" said the prince abruptly, after a short pause. "Had it been so I should have known long ago."

"Oh, of course, yes; he would have come and wept out his secret on your bosom. Oh, you simpleton—you simpleton! Anyone can deceive you and take you in like a—like a,—aren't you ashamed to trust him? Can't you see that he humbugs you just as much as ever he pleases?"

"I know very well that he does deceive me occasionally, and he knows that I know it, but—" The prince did not finish his sentence.

"And that's why you trust him, eh? So I should have supposed. Good Lord, was there ever such a man as you? Tfu! and are you aware, sir, that this Gania, or his sister Varia, have brought her into correspondence with Nastasia Philipovna?"

"Brought whom?" cried Muishkin.

"Aglaya."

"I don't believe it! It's impossible! What object could they have?" He jumped up from his chair in his excitement.

"Nor do I believe it, in spite of the proofs. The girl is self-willed and fantastic, and insane! She's wicked, wicked! I'll repeat it for a thousand years that she's wicked; they *all* are, just now, all my daughters, even that 'wet hen' Alexandra. And yet I don't believe it. Because I don't choose to believe it, perhaps; but I don't. Why haven't you been?" she turned on the prince suddenly. "Why didn't you come near us all these three days, eh?"

The prince began to give his reasons, but she interrupted him again.

"Everybody takes you in and deceives you; you went to town yesterday. I dare swear you went down on your knees to that rogue, and begged him to accept your ten thousand roubles!"

"I never thought of doing any such thing. I have not seen him, and he is not a rogue, in my opinion. I have had a letter from him."

"Show it me!"

The prince took a paper from his pocket-book, and handed it to Lizabetha Prokofievna. It ran as follows:

"*Sir,*

"In the eyes of the world I am sure that I have no cause for pride or self-esteem. I am much too insignificant for that. But what may be so to other men's eyes is not so to yours. I am convinced that you are better than other people. Doktorenko disagrees with me, but I am content to differ from him on this point. I will never accept one single copeck from you, but you have helped my mother, and I am bound to be grateful to you for that, however weak it may seem. At any rate, I have changed my opinion about you, and I think right to inform you of the fact; but I also suppose that there can be no further intercourse between us.

"Antip Burdovsky.

"P.S.—The two hundred roubles I owe you shall certainly be repaid in time."

"How extremely stupid!" cried Mrs. Epanchin, giving back the letter abruptly. "It was not worth the trouble of reading. Why are you smiling?"

"Confess that you are pleased to have read it."

"What! Pleased with all that nonsense! Why, cannot you see that they are all infatuated with pride and vanity?"

"He has acknowledged himself to be in the wrong. Don't you see that the greater his vanity, the more difficult this admission must have been on his part? Oh, what a little child you are, Lizabetha Prokofievna!"

"Are you tempting me to box your ears for you, or what?"

"Not at all. I am only proving that you are glad about the letter. Why conceal your real feelings? You always like to do it."

"Never come near my house again!" cried Mrs. Epanchin, pale with rage. "Don't let me see as much as a *shadow* of you about the place! Do you hear?"

"Oh yes, and in three days you'll come and invite me yourself. Aren't you ashamed now? These are your best feelings; you are only tormenting yourself."

"I'll die before I invite you! I shall forget your very name! I've forgotten it already!"

She marched towards the door.

"But I'm forbidden your house as it is, without your added threats!" cried the prince after her.

"What? Who forbade you?"

She turned round so suddenly that one might have supposed a needle had been stuck into her.

The prince hesitated. He perceived that he had said too much now.

"*Who* forbade you?" cried Mrs. Epanchin once more.

"Aglaya Ivanovna told me—"

"When? Speak—quick!"

"She sent to say, yesterday morning, that I was never to dare to come near the house again."

Lizabetha Prokofievna stood like a stone.

"What did she send? Whom? Was it that boy? Was it a message?—quick!"

"I had a note," said the prince.

"Where is it? Give it here, at once."

The prince thought a moment. Then he pulled out of his waistcoat pocket an untidy slip of paper, on which was scrawled:

"*Prince Lef Nicolaievitch,*—If you think fit, after all that has passed, to honour our house with a visit, I can assure you you will not find me among the number of those who are in any way delighted to see you.

"Aglaya Epanchin."

Mrs. Epanchin reflected a moment. The next minute she flew at the prince, seized his hand, and dragged him after her to the door.

"Quick—come along!" she cried, breathless with agitation and impatience. "Come along with me this moment!"

"But you declared I wasn't—"

"Don't be a simpleton. You behave just as though you weren't a man at all. Come on! I shall see, now, with my own eyes. I shall see all."

"Well, let me get my hat, at least."

"Here's your miserable hat. He couldn't even choose a respectable shape for his hat! Come on! She did that because I took your part and said you ought to have come—little vixen!—else she would never have sent you that silly note. It's a most improper note, I call it; most improper for such an intelligent, well-brought-up girl to write. H'm! I dare say she was annoyed that you didn't come; but she ought to have known that one can't write like that to an idiot like you, for you'd be sure to take it literally." Mrs. Epanchin was dragging the prince along with her all the time, and never let go of his hand for an instant. "What are you listening for?" she added, seeing that she had committed herself a little. "She wants a clown like you—she hasn't seen one for some time—to play with. That's why she is anxious for you to come to the house. And right glad I am that she'll make a thorough good fool of you. You deserve it; and she can do it—oh! she can, indeed!—as well as most people."

PART III

Chapter I.

The Epanchin family, or at least the more serious members of it, were sometimes grieved because they seemed so unlike the rest of the world. They were not quite certain, but had at times a strong suspicion that things did not happen to them as they did to other people. Others led a quiet, uneventful life, while they were subject to continual upheavals. Others kept on the rails without difficulty; they ran off at the slightest obstacle. Other houses were governed by a timid routine; theirs was somehow different. Perhaps Lizabetha Prokofievna was alone in making these fretful observations; the girls, though not wanting in intelligence, were still young; the general was intelligent, too, but narrow, and in any difficulty he was content to say, "H'm!" and leave the matter to his wife. Consequently, on her fell the responsibility. It was not that they distinguished themselves as a family by any particular originality, or that their excursions off the track led to any breach of the proprieties. Oh no.

There was nothing premeditated, there was not even any conscious purpose in it all, and yet, in spite of everything, the family, although highly respected, was not quite what every highly respected family ought to be. For a long time now Lizabetha Prokofievna had had it in her mind that all the trouble was owing to her "unfortunate character," and this added to her distress. She blamed her own stupid unconventional "eccentricity." Always restless, always on the go, she constantly seemed to lose her way, and to get into trouble over the simplest and more ordinary affairs of life.

We said at the beginning of our story, that the Epanchins were liked and esteemed by their neighbours. In spite of his humble origin, Ivan Fedorovitch himself was received everywhere with respect. He deserved this, partly on account of his wealth and position, partly because, though limited, he was really a very good fellow. But a certain limitation of mind seems to be an indispensable asset, if not to all public personages, at least to all serious financiers. Added to this, his manner was modest and unassuming; he knew when to be silent, yet never allowed himself to be trampled upon. Also— and this was more important than all—he had the advantage of being under exalted patronage.

As to Lizabetha Prokofievna, she, as the reader knows, belonged to an aristocratic family. True, Russians think more of influential friends than of birth, but she had both. She was esteemed and even loved by people of consequence in society, whose example in receiving her was therefore followed by others. It seems hardly necessary to remark that her family worries and anxieties had little or no foundation, or that her imagination increased them to an absurd degree; but if you have a wart on your forehead or nose, you imagine that all the world is looking at it, and that people would make fun of you because of it, even if you had discovered America! Doubtless Lizabetha Prokofievna was considered "eccentric" in society, but she was none the less esteemed: the pity was that she was ceasing to believe in that esteem. When she thought of her daughters, she said to herself sorrowfully that she was a hindrance rather than a help to their future, that her character and temper were absurd, ridiculous, insupportable. Naturally, she put the blame on her surroundings, and from morning to night was quarrelling with her husband and children, whom she really loved to the point of self-sacrifice, even, one might say, of passion.

She was, above all distressed by the idea that her daughters might grow up "eccentric," like herself; she believed that no other society girls were like them. "They are growing into Nihilists!" she repeated over and over again. For years she had tormented herself with this idea, and with the question: "Why don't they get married?"

"It is to annoy their mother; that is their one aim in life; it can be nothing else. The fact is it is all of a piece with these modern ideas, that wretched woman's question! Six months ago Aglaya took a fancy to cut off her magnificent hair. Why, even I, when I was young, had nothing like it! The scissors were in her hand, and I had to go down on my knees and implore her... She did it, I know, from sheer mischief, to spite her mother, for she is a naughty, capricious girl, a real spoiled child spiteful and mischievous to a degree! And then Alexandra wanted to shave her head, not from caprice or mischief, but, like a little fool, simply because Aglaya persuaded her she would sleep better without her hair, and not suffer from headache! And how many suitors have they not had during the last five years! Excellent offers, too! What more do they want? Why don't they get married? For no other reason than to vex their mother—none—none!"

But Lizabetha Prokofievna felt somewhat consoled when she could say that one of her girls, Adelaida, was settled at last. "It will be one off our hands!" she declared aloud, though in private she expressed herself with greater tenderness. The engagement was both happy and suitable, and was therefore approved in society. Prince S. was a distinguished man, he had money, and his future wife was devoted to him; what more could be desired? Lizabetha Prokofievna had felt less anxious about this daughter, however, although she considered her artistic tastes suspicious. But to make up for them she was, as her mother expressed it, "merry," and had plenty of "common-sense." It was Aglaya's future which disturbed her most. With regard to her eldest daughter, Alexandra, the mother never quite knew whether there was cause for anxiety or not. Sometimes she felt as if there was nothing to be expected from her. She was twenty-five now, and must be fated to be an old maid, and "with such beauty, too!" The mother spent whole nights in weeping and lamenting, while all the time the cause of her grief slumbered peacefully. "What is the matter with her? Is she a Nihilist, or simply a fool?"

But Lizabetha Prokofievna knew perfectly well how unnecessary was the last question. She set a high value on Alexandra Ivanovna's judgment, and often consulted her in difficulties; but that she was a 'wet hen' she never for a moment doubted. "She is so calm; nothing rouses her—though wet hens are not always calm! Oh! I can't understand it!" Her eldest daughter inspired Lizabetha with a kind of puzzled compassion. She did not feel this in Aglaya's case, though the latter was her idol. It may be said that these outbursts and epithets, such as "wet hen" (in which the maternal solicitude usually showed itself), only made Alexandra laugh. Sometimes the most trivial thing annoyed Mrs. Epanchin, and drove her into a frenzy. For instance, Alexandra Ivanovna liked to sleep late, and was always dreaming, though her dreams had the peculiarity of being as innocent and naive as those of a child of seven; and the very innocence of her dreams annoyed her mother. Once she dreamt of nine hens, and this was the cause of quite a serious quarrel—no one knew why. Another time she had— it was most unusual—a dream with a spark of originality in it. She dreamt of a monk in a dark room, into which she was too frightened to go. Adelaida and Aglaya rushed off with shrieks of laughter to relate this to their mother, but she was quite angry, and said her daughters were all fools.

"H'm! she is as stupid as a fool! A veritable 'wet hen'! Nothing excites her; and yet she is not happy; some days it makes one miserable only to look at her! Why is she unhappy, I wonder?" At times Lizabetha Prokofievna put this question to her husband, and as usual she spoke in the threatening tone of one who demands an immediate answer. Ivan Fedorovitch would frown, shrug his shoulders, and at last give his opinion: "She needs a husband!"

"God forbid that he should share your ideas, Ivan Fedorovitch!" his wife flashed back. "Or that he should be as gross and churlish as you!"

The general promptly made his escape, and Lizabetha Prokofievna after a while grew calm again. That evening, of course, she would be unusually attentive, gentle, and respectful to her "gross and churlish" husband, her "dear, kind Ivan Fedorovitch," for she had never left off loving him. She was even still "in love" with him. He knew it well, and for his part held her in the greatest esteem.

But the mother's great and continual anxiety was Aglaya. "She is exactly like me—my image in everything," said Mrs. Epanchin to herself. "A tyrant! A real little demon! A Nihilist! Eccentric, senseless and mischievous! Good Lord, how unhappy she will be!"

But as we said before, the fact of Adelaida's approaching marriage was balm to the mother. For a whole month she forgot her fears and worries.

Adelaida's fate was settled; and with her name that of Aglaya's was linked, in society gossip. People whispered that Aglaya, too, was "as good as engaged;" and Aglaya always looked so sweet and behaved so well (during this period), that the mother's heart was full of joy. Of course, Evgenie Pavlovitch must be thoroughly studied first, before the final step should be taken; but, really, how lovely dear Aglaya had become—she actually grew more beautiful every day! And then—Yes, and then—this abominable prince showed his face again, and everything went topsy-turvy at once, and everyone seemed as mad as March hares.

What had really happened?

If it had been any other family than the Epanchins', nothing particular would have happened. But, thanks to Mrs. Epanchin's invariable fussiness and anxiety, there could not be the slightest hitch in the simplest matters of everyday life, but she immediately foresaw the most dreadful and alarming consequences, and suffered accordingly.

What then must have been her condition, when, among all the imaginary anxieties and calamities which so constantly beset her, she now saw looming ahead a serious cause for annoyance—something really likely to arouse doubts and suspicions!

"How dared they, how *dared* they write that hateful anonymous letter informing me that Aglaya is in communication with Nastasia Philipovna?" she thought, as she dragged the prince along towards her own house, and again when she sat him down at the round table where the family was already assembled. "How dared they so much as *think* of such a thing? I should *die* with shame if I thought there was a particle of truth in it, or if I were to show the letter to Aglaya herself! Who dares play these jokes upon *us*, the Epanchins? *Why* didn't we go to the Yelagin instead of coming down here? I *told* you we had better go to the Yelagin this summer, Ivan Fedorovitch. It's all your fault. I dare say it was that Varia who sent the letter. It's all Ivan Fedorovitch. *That* woman is doing it all for him, I know she is, to show she can make a fool of him now just as she did when he used to give her pearls.

"But after all is said, we are mixed up in it. Your daughters are mixed up in it, Ivan Fedorovitch; young ladies in society, young ladies at an age to be married; they were present, they heard everything there was to hear. They were mixed up with that other scene, too, with those dreadful youths. You must be pleased to remember they heard it all. I cannot forgive that wretched prince. I never shall forgive him! And why, if you please, has Aglaya had an attack of nerves for these last three days? Why has she all but quarrelled with her sisters, even with Alexandra—whom she respects so much that she always kisses her hands as though she were her mother? What are all these riddles of hers that we have to guess? What has Gavrila Ardalionovitch to do with it? Why did she take upon herself to champion him this morning, and burst into tears over it? Why is there an allusion to that cursed 'poor knight' in the anonymous letter? And why did I rush off to him just now like a lunatic, and drag him back here? I do believe I've gone mad at last. What on earth have I done now? To talk to a young man about my daughter's secrets—and secrets having to do with himself, too! Thank goodness, he's an idiot, and a friend of the house! Surely Aglaya hasn't fallen in love with such a gaby! What an idea! Pfu! we ought all to be put under glass cases—myself first of all—and be shown off as curiosities, at ten copecks a peep!"

"I shall never forgive you for all this, Ivan Fedorovitch—never! Look at her now. Why doesn't she make fun of him? She said she would, and she doesn't. Look there! She stares at him with all her eyes, and doesn't move; and yet she told him not to come. He looks pale enough; and that abominable chatterbox, Evgenie Pavlovitch, monopolizes the whole of the conversation. Nobody else can get a word in. I could soon find out all about everything if I could only change the subject."

The prince certainly was very pale. He sat at the table and seemed to be feeling, by turns, sensations of alarm and rapture.

Oh, how frightened he was of looking to one side—one particular corner—whence he knew very well that a pair of dark eyes were watching him intently, and how happy he was to think that he was once more among them, and occasionally hearing that well-known voice, although she had written and forbidden him to come again!

"What on earth will she say to me, I wonder?" he thought to himself.

He had not said a word yet; he sat silent and listened to Evgenie Pavlovitch's eloquence. The latter had never appeared so happy and excited as on this evening. The prince listened to him, but for a long time did not take in a word he said.

Excepting Ivan Fedorovitch, who had not as yet returned from town, the whole family was present. Prince S. was there; and they all intended to go out to hear the band very soon.

Colia arrived presently and joined the circle. "So he is received as usual, after all," thought the prince.

The Epanchins' country-house was a charming building, built after the model of a Swiss chalet, and covered with creepers. It was surrounded on all sides by a flower garden, and the family sat, as a rule, on the open verandah as at the prince's house.

The subject under discussion did not appear to be very popular with the assembly, and some would have been delighted to change it; but Evgenie would not stop holding forth, and the prince's arrival seemed to spur him on to still further oratorical efforts.

Lizabetha Prokofievna frowned, but had not as yet grasped the subject, which seemed to have arisen out of a heated argument. Aglaya sat apart, almost in the corner, listening in stubborn silence.

"Excuse me," continued Evgenie Pavlovitch hotly, "I don't say a word against liberalism. Liberalism is not a sin, it is a necessary part of a great whole, which whole would collapse and fall to pieces without it. Liberalism has just as much right to exist as has the most moral conservatism; but I am attacking *Russian* liberalism; and I attack it for the simple reason that a Russian liberal is not a Russian liberal, he is a non-Russian liberal. Show me a real Russian liberal, and I'll kiss him before you all, with pleasure."

"If he cared to kiss you, that is," said Alexandra, whose cheeks were red with irritation and excitement.

"Look at that, now," thought the mother to herself, "she does nothing but sleep and eat for a year at a time, and then suddenly flies out in the most incomprehensible way!"

The prince observed that Alexandra appeared to be angry with Evgenie, because he spoke on a serious subject in a frivolous manner, pretending to be in earnest, but with an under-current of irony.

"I was saying just now, before you came in, prince, that there has been nothing national up to now, about our liberalism, and nothing the liberals do, or have done, is in the least degree national. They are drawn from two classes only, the old landowning class, and clerical families—"

"How, nothing that they have done is Russian?" asked Prince S.

"It may be Russian, but it is not national. Our liberals are not Russian, nor are our conservatives, and you may be sure that the nation does not recognize anything that has been done by the landed gentry, or by the seminarists, or what is to be done either."

"Come, that's good! How can you maintain such a paradox? If you are serious, that is. I cannot allow such a statement about the landed proprietors to pass unchallenged. Why, you are a landed proprietor yourself!" cried Prince S. hotly.

"I suppose you'll say there is nothing national about our literature either?" said Alexandra.

"Well, I am not a great authority on literary questions, but I certainly do hold that Russian literature is not Russian, except perhaps Lomonosoff, Pouschkin and Gogol."

"In the first place, that is a considerable admission, and in the second place, one of the above was a peasant, and the other two were both landed proprietors!"

"Quite so, but don't be in such a hurry! For since it has been the part of these three men, and only these three, to say something absolutely their own, not borrowed, so by this very fact these three men become really national. If any Russian shall have done or said anything really and absolutely original, he is to be called national from that moment, though he may not be able to talk the Russian language; still he is a national Russian. I consider that an axiom. But we were not speaking of literature; we began by discussing the socialists. Very well then, I insist that there does not exist one single Russian socialist. There does not, and there has never existed such a one, because all socialists are derived from the two classes—the landed proprietors, and the seminarists. All our eminent socialists are merely old liberals of the class of landed proprietors, men who were liberals in the days of serfdom. Why do you laugh? Give me their books, give me their studies, their memoirs, and though I am not a literary critic, yet I will prove as clear as day that every chapter and every word of their writings has been the work of a former landed proprietor of the old school. You'll find that all their raptures, all their generous transports are proprietary, all their woes and their tears, proprietary; all proprietary or seminarist! You are laughing again, and you, prince, are smiling too. Don't you agree with me?"

It was true enough that everybody was laughing, the prince among them.

"I cannot tell you on the instant whether I agree with you or not," said the latter, suddenly stopping his laughter, and starting like a schoolboy caught at mischief. "But, I assure you, I am listening to you with extreme gratification."

So saying, he almost panted with agitation, and a cold sweat stood upon his forehead. These were his first words since he had entered the house; he tried to lift his eyes, and look around, but dared not; Evgenie Pavlovitch noticed his confusion, and smiled.

"I'll just tell you one fact, ladies and gentlemen," continued the latter, with apparent seriousness and even exaltation of manner, but with a suggestion of "chaff" behind every word, as though he were laughing in his sleeve at his own nonsense—"a fact, the discovery of which, I believe, I may claim to have made by myself alone. At all events, no other has ever said or written a word about it; and in this fact is expressed the whole essence of Russian liberalism of the sort which I am now considering.

"In the first place, what is liberalism, speaking generally, but an attack (whether mistaken or reasonable, is quite another question) upon the existing order of things? Is this so? Yes. Very well. Then my 'fact' consists in this, that *Russian* liberalism is not an attack upon the existing order of things, but an attack upon the very essence of things themselves—indeed, on the things themselves; not an attack on the Russian order of things, but on Russia itself. My Russian liberal goes so far as to reject Russia; that is, he hates and strikes his own mother. Every misfortune and mishap of the mother-country fills him with mirth, and even with ecstasy. He hates the national customs, Russian history, and everything. If he has a justification, it is that he does not know what he is doing, and believes that his hatred of Russia is the grandest and most profitable kind of liberalism. (You will often find a liberal who is applauded and esteemed by his fellows, but who is in reality the dreariest, blindest, dullest of conservatives, and is not aware of the fact.) This hatred for Russia has been mistaken by some of our 'Russian liberals' for sincere love of their country, and they boast that they see better than their neighbours what real love of one's country should consist in. But of late they have grown more candid and are ashamed of the expression 'love of country,' and have annihilated the very spirit of the words as something injurious and petty and undignified. This is the truth, and I hold by it; but at the same time it is a phenomenon which has not been repeated at any other time or place; and therefore, though I hold to it as a fact, yet I recognize that it is an accidental phenomenon, and may likely enough pass away. There can be no such thing anywhere else as a liberal who really hates his country; and how is this fact to be explained among *us?* By my original statement that a Russian liberal is *not* a *Russian* liberal—that's the only explanation that I can see."

"I take all that you have said as a joke," said Prince S. seriously.

"I have not seen all kinds of liberals, and cannot, therefore, set myself up as a judge," said Alexandra, "but I have heard all you have said with indignation. You have taken some accidental case and twisted it into a universal law, which is unjust."

"Accidental case!" said Evgenie Pavlovitch. "Do you consider it an accidental case, prince?"

"I must also admit," said the prince, "that I have not seen much, or been very far into the question; but I cannot help thinking that you are more or less right, and that Russian liberalism— that phase of it which you are considering, at least—really is sometimes inclined to hate Russia itself, and not only its existing order of things in general. Of course this is only *partially* the truth; you cannot lay down the law for all..."

The prince blushed and broke off, without finishing what he meant to say.

In spite of his shyness and agitation, he could not help being greatly interested in the conversation. A special characteristic of his was the naive candour with which he always listened to arguments which interested him, and with which he answered any questions put to him on the subject at issue. In the very expression of his face this naivete was unmistakably evident, this disbelief in the insincerity of others, and unsuspecting disregard of irony or humour in their words.

But though Evgenie Pavlovitch had put his questions to the prince with no other purpose but to enjoy the joke of his simple-minded seriousness, yet now, at his answer, he was surprised into some seriousness himself, and looked gravely at Muishkin as though he had not expected that sort of answer at all.

"Why, how strange!" he ejaculated. "You didn't answer me seriously, surely, did you?"

"Did not you ask me the question seriously" inquired the prince, in amazement.

Everybody laughed.

"Oh, trust *him* for that!" said Adelaida. "Evgenie Pavlovitch turns everything and everybody he can lay hold of to ridicule. You should hear the things he says sometimes, apparently in perfect seriousness."

"In my opinion the conversation has been a painful one throughout, and we ought never to have begun it," said Alexandra. "We were all going for a walk—"

"Come along then," said Evgenie; "it's a glorious evening. But, to prove that this time I was speaking absolutely seriously, and especially to prove this to the prince (for you, prince, have interested me exceedingly, and I swear to you that I am not quite such an ass as I like to appear sometimes, although I am rather an ass, I admit), and—well, ladies and gentlemen, will you allow me to put just one more question to the prince, out of pure curiosity? It shall be the last. This question came into my mind a couple of hours since (you see, prince, I do think seriously at times), and I made my own decision upon it; now I wish to hear what the prince will say to it."

"We have just used the expression 'accidental case.' This is a significant phrase; we often hear it. Well, not long since everyone was talking and reading about that terrible murder of six people on the part of a—young fellow, and of the extraordinary speech of the counsel for the defence, who observed that in the poverty-stricken condition of the criminal it must have come *naturally* into his head to kill these six people. I do not quote his words, but that is the sense of them, or something very like it. Now, in my opinion, the barrister who put forward this extraordinary plea was probably absolutely convinced that he was stating the most liberal, the most humane, the most enlightened view of the case that could possibly be brought forward in these days. Now, was this distortion, this capacity for a perverted way of viewing things, a special or accidental case, or is such a general rule?"

Everyone laughed at this.

"A special case—accidental, of course!" cried Alexandra and Adelaida.

"Let me remind you once more, Evgenie," said Prince S., "that your joke is getting a little threadbare."

"What do you think about it, prince?" asked Evgenie, taking no notice of the last remark, and observing Muishkin's serious eyes fixed upon his face. "What do you think—was it a special or a usual case—the rule, or an exception? I confess I put the question especially for you."

"No, I don't think it was a special case," said the prince, quietly, but firmly.

"My dear fellow!" cried Prince S., with some annoyance, "don't you see that he is chaffing you? He is simply laughing at you, and wants to make game of you."

"I thought Evgenie Pavlovitch was talking seriously," said the prince, blushing and dropping his eyes.

"My dear prince," continued Prince S. "remember what you and I were saying two or three months ago. We spoke of the fact that in our newly opened Law Courts one could already lay one's finger upon so many talented and remarkable young barristers. How pleased you were with the state of things as we found it, and how glad I was to observe your delight! We both said it was a matter to be proud of; but this clumsy defence that Evgenie mentions, this strange argument *can*, of course, only be an accidental case—one in a thousand!"

The prince reflected a little, but very soon he replied, with absolute conviction in his tone, though he still spoke somewhat shyly and timidly:

"I only wished to say that this 'distortion,' as Evgenie Pavlovitch expressed it, is met with very often, and is far more the general rule than the exception, unfortunately for Russia. So much so, that if this distortion were not the general rule, perhaps these dreadful crimes would be less frequent."

"Dreadful crimes? But I can assure you that crimes just as dreadful, and probably more horrible, have occurred before our times, and at all times, and not only here in Russia, but everywhere else as well. And in my opinion it is not at all likely that such murders will cease to occur for a very long time to come. The only difference is that in former times there was less publicity, while now everyone talks and writes freely about such things—which fact gives the impression that such crimes have only now sprung into existence. That is where your mistake lies—an extremely natural mistake, I assure you, my dear fellow!" said Prince S.

"I know that there were just as many, and just as terrible, crimes before our times. Not long since I visited a convict prison and made acquaintance with some of the criminals. There were some even more dreadful criminals than this one we have been speaking of—men who have murdered a dozen of their fellow-creatures, and feel no remorse whatever. But what I especially noticed was this, that the very most hopeless and remorseless murderer—however hardened a criminal he may be— still *knows that he is a criminal*; that is, he is conscious that he has acted wickedly, though he may feel no remorse whatever. And they were all like this. Those of whom Evgenie Pavlovitch has spoken, do not admit that they are criminals at all; they think they had a right to do what they did, and that they were even doing a good deed, perhaps. I consider there is the greatest difference between the two cases. And recollect—it was a *youth*, at the particular age which is most helplessly susceptible to the distortion of ideas!"

Prince S. was now no longer smiling; he gazed at the prince in bewilderment.

Alexandra, who had seemed to wish to put in her word when the prince began, now sat silent, as though some sudden thought had caused her to change her mind about speaking.

Evgenie Pavlovitch gazed at him in real surprise, and this time his expression of face had no mockery in it whatever.

"What are you looking so surprised about, my friend?" asked Mrs. Epanchin, suddenly. "Did you suppose he was stupider than yourself, and was incapable of forming his own opinions, or what?"

"No! Oh no! Not at all!" said Evgenie. "But—how is it, prince, that you—(excuse the question, will you?)—if you are capable of observing and seeing things as you evidently do, how is it that you saw nothing distorted or perverted in that claim upon your property, which you acknowledged a day or two since; and which was full of arguments founded upon the most distorted views of right and wrong?"

"I'll tell you what, my friend," cried Mrs. Epanchin, of a sudden, "here are we all sitting here and imagining we are very clever, and perhaps laughing at the prince, some of us, and meanwhile he has received a letter this very day in which that same claimant renounces his claim, and begs the prince's pardon. There! *we* don't often get that sort of letter; and yet we are not ashamed to walk with our noses in the air before him."

"And Hippolyte has come down here to stay," said Colia, suddenly.

"What! has he arrived?" said the prince, starting up.

"Yes, I brought him down from town just after you had left the house."

"There now! It's just like him," cried Lizabetha Prokofievna, boiling over once more, and entirely oblivious of the fact that she had just taken the prince's part. "I dare swear that you went up to town yesterday on purpose to get the little wretch to do you the great honour of coming to stay at your house. You did go up to town, you know you did—you said so yourself! Now then, did you, or did you not, go down on your knees and beg him to come, confess!"

"No, he didn't, for I saw it all myself," said Colia. "On the contrary, Hippolyte kissed his hand twice and thanked him; and all the prince said was that he thought Hippolyte might feel better here in the country!"

"Don't, Colia,—what is the use of saying all that?" cried the prince, rising and taking his hat.

"Where are you going to now?" cried Mrs. Epanchin.

"Never mind about him now, prince," said Colia. "He is all right and taking a nap after the journey. He is very happy to be here; but I think perhaps it would be better if you let him alone for today,—he is very sensitive now that he is so ill—and he might be embarrassed if you show him too much attention at first. He is decidedly better today, and says he has not felt so well for the last six months, and has coughed much less, too."

The prince observed that Aglaya came out of her corner and approached the table at this point.

He did not dare look at her, but he was conscious, to the very tips of his fingers, that she was gazing at him, perhaps angrily; and that she had probably flushed up with a look of fiery indignation in her black eyes.

"It seems to me, Mr. Colia, that you were very foolish to bring your young friend down—if he is the same consumptive boy who wept so profusely, and invited us all to his own funeral," remarked Evgenie Pavlovitch. "He talked so eloquently about the blank wall outside his bedroom window, that I'm sure he will never support life here without it."

"I think so too," said Mrs. Epanchin; "he will quarrel with you, and be off," and she drew her workbox towards her with an air of dignity, quite oblivious of the fact that the family was about to start for a walk in the park.

"Yes, I remember he boasted about the blank wall in an extraordinary way," continued Evgenie, "and I feel that without that blank wall he will never be able to die eloquently; and he does so long to die eloquently!"

"Oh, you must forgive him the blank wall," said the prince, quietly. "He has come down to see a few trees now, poor fellow."

"Oh, I forgive him with all my heart; you may tell him so if you like," laughed Evgenie.

"I don't think you should take it quite like that," said the prince, quietly, and without removing his eyes from the carpet. "I think it is more a case of his forgiving you."

"Forgiving me! why so? What have I done to need his forgiveness?"

"If you don't understand, then—but of course, you do understand. He wished—he wished to bless you all round and to have your blessing—before he died—that's all."

"My dear prince," began Prince S., hurriedly, exchanging glances with some of those present, "you will not easily find heaven on earth, and yet you seem to expect to. Heaven is a difficult thing to find anywhere, prince; far more difficult than appears to that good heart of yours. Better stop this conversation, or we shall all be growing quite disturbed in our minds, and—"

"Let's go and hear the band, then," said Lizabetha Prokofievna, angrily rising from her place.

The rest of the company followed her example.

CHAPTER II.

The prince suddenly approached Evgenie Pavlovitch.

"Evgenie Pavlovitch," he said, with strange excitement and seizing the latter's hand in his own, "be assured that I esteem you as a generous and honourable man, in spite of everything. Be assured of that."

Evgenie Pavlovitch fell back a step in astonishment. For one moment it was all he could do to restrain himself from bursting out laughing; but, looking closer, he observed that the prince did not seem to be quite himself; at all events, he was in a very curious state.

"I wouldn't mind betting, prince," he cried, "that you did not in the least mean to say that, and very likely you meant to address someone else altogether. What is it? Are you feeling unwell or anything?"

"Very likely, extremely likely, and you must be a very close observer to detect the fact that perhaps I did not intend to come up to *you* at all."

So saying he smiled strangely; but suddenly and excitedly he began again:

"Don't remind me of what I have done or said. Don't! I am very much ashamed of myself, I—"

"Why, what have you done? I don't understand you."

"I see you are ashamed of me, Evgenie Pavlovitch; you are blushing for me; that's a sign of a good heart. Don't be afraid; I shall go away directly."

"What's the matter with him? Do his fits begin like that?" said Lizabetha Prokofievna, in a high state of alarm, addressing Colia.

"No, no, Lizabetha Prokofievna, take no notice of me. I am not going to have a fit. I will go away directly; but I know I am afflicted. I was twenty-four years an invalid, you see—the first twenty-four years of my life—so take all I do and say as the sayings and actions of an invalid. I'm going away directly, I really am—don't be afraid. I am not blushing, for I don't think I need blush about it, need I? But I see that I am out of place in society—society is better without me. It's not vanity, I assure you. I have thought over it all these last three days, and I have made up my mind that I ought to unbosom myself candidly before you at the first opportunity. There are certain things, certain great ideas, which I must not so much as approach, as Prince S. has just reminded me, or I shall make you all laugh. I have no sense of proportion, I know; my words and gestures do not express my ideas—they are a humiliation and abasement of the ideas, and therefore, I have no right—and I am too sensitive. Still, I believe I am beloved in this household, and esteemed far more than I deserve. But I can't help knowing that after twenty-four years of illness there must be some trace left, so that it is impossible for people to refrain from laughing at me sometimes; don't you think so?"

He seemed to pause for a reply, for some verdict, as it were, and looked humbly around him.

All present stood rooted to the earth with amazement at this unexpected and apparently uncalled-for outbreak; but the poor prince's painful and rambling speech gave rise to a strange episode.

"Why do you say all this here?" cried Aglaya, suddenly. "Why do you talk like this to *them?*"

She appeared to be in the last stages of wrath and irritation; her eyes flashed. The prince stood dumbly and blindly before her, and suddenly grew pale.

"There is not one of them all who is worthy of these words of yours," continued Aglaya. "Not one of them is worth your little finger, not one of them has heart or head to compare with yours! You are more honest than all, and better, nobler, kinder, wiser than all. There are some here who are unworthy to bend and pick up the handkerchief you have just dropped. Why do you humiliate yourself like this, and place yourself lower than these people? Why do you debase yourself before them? Why have you no pride?"

"My God! Who would ever have believed this?" cried Mrs. Epanchin, wringing her hands.

"Hurrah for the 'poor knight'!" cried Colia.

"Be quiet! How dare they laugh at me in your house?" said Aglaya, turning sharply on her mother in that hysterical frame of mind that rides recklessly over every obstacle and plunges blindly through proprieties. "Why does everyone, everyone worry and torment me? Why have they all been bullying me these three days about you, prince? I will not marry you—never, and under no circumstances! Know that once and for all; as if anyone could marry an absurd creature like you! Just look in the glass and see what you look like, this very moment! Why, *why* do they torment me and say I am going to marry you? You must know it; you are in the plot with them!"

"No one ever tormented you on the subject," murmured Adelaida, aghast.

"No one ever thought of such a thing! There has never been a word said about it!" cried Alexandra.

"Who has been annoying her? Who has been tormenting the child? Who could have said such a thing to her? Is she raving?" cried Lizabetha Prokofievna, trembling with rage, to the company in general.

"Every one of them has been saying it—every one of them—all these three days! And I will never, never marry him!"

So saying, Aglaya burst into bitter tears, and, hiding her face in her handkerchief, sank back into a chair.

"But he has never even—"

"I have never asked you to marry me, Aglaya Ivanovna!" said the prince, of a sudden.

"*What?*" cried Mrs. Epanchin, raising her hands in horror. "*What's* that?"

She could not believe her ears.

"I meant to say—I only meant to say," said the prince, faltering, "I merely meant to explain to Aglaya Ivanovna—to have the honour to explain, as it were—that I had no intention—never had—to ask the honour of her hand. I assure you I am not guilty, Aglaya Ivanovna, I am not, indeed. I never did wish to—I never thought of it at all—and never shall—you'll see it yourself—you may be quite assured of it. Some wicked person has been maligning me to you; but it's all right. Don't worry about it."

So saying, the prince approached Aglaya.

She took the handkerchief from her face, glanced keenly at him, took in what he had said, and burst out laughing—such a merry, unrestrained laugh, so hearty and gay, that Adelaida could not contain herself. She, too, glanced at the prince's panic-stricken countenance, then rushed at her sister, threw her arms round her neck, and burst into as merry a fit of laughter as Aglaya's own. They laughed together like a couple of school-girls. Hearing and seeing this, the prince smiled happily, and in accents of relief and joy, he exclaimed "Well, thank God—thank God!"

Alexandra now joined in, and it looked as though the three sisters were going to laugh on for ever.

"They are insane," muttered Lizabetha Prokofievna. "Either they frighten one out of one's wits, or else—"

But Prince S. was laughing now, too, so was Evgenie Pavlovitch, so was Colia, and so was the prince himself, who caught the infection as he looked round radiantly upon the others.

"Come along, let's go out for a walk!" cried Adelaida. "We'll all go together, and the prince must absolutely go with us. You needn't go away, you dear good fellow! *Isn't* he a dear, Aglaya? Isn't he, mother? I must really give him a kiss for—for his explanation to Aglaya just now. Mother, dear, I may kiss him, mayn't I? Aglaya, may I kiss *your* prince?" cried the young rogue, and sure enough she skipped up to the prince and kissed his forehead.

He seized her hands, and pressed them so hard that Adelaida nearly cried out; he then gazed with delight into her eyes, and raising her right hand to his lips with enthusiasm, kissed it three times.

"Come along," said Aglaya. "Prince, you must walk with me. May he, mother? This young cavalier, who won't have me? You said you would *never* have me, didn't you, prince? No—no, not like that; *that's* not the way to give your arm to a lady yet?

There—so. Now, come along, you and I will lead the way. Would you like to lead the way with me alone, tête-à-tête?"

She went on talking and chatting without a pause, with occasional little bursts of laughter between.

"Thank God—thank God!" said Lizabetha Prokofievna to herself, without quite knowing why she felt so relieved.

"What extraordinary people they are!" thought Prince S., for perhaps the hundredth time since he had entered into intimate relations with the family; but—he liked these "extraordinary people," all the same. As for Prince Lef Nicolaievitch himself, Prince S. did not seem quite to like him, somehow. He was decidedly preoccupied and a little disturbed as they all started off.

Evgenie Pavlovitch seemed to be in a lively humour. He made Adelaida and Alexandra laugh all the way to the Vauxhall; but they both laughed so very readily and promptly that the worthy Evgenie began at last to suspect that they were not listening to him at all.

At this idea, he burst out laughing all at once, in quite unaffected mirth, and without giving any explanation.

The sisters, who also appeared to be in high spirits, never tired of glancing at Aglaya and the prince, who were walking in front. It was evident that their younger sister was a thorough puzzle to them both.

Prince S. tried hard to get up a conversation with Mrs. Epanchin upon outside subjects, probably with the good intention of distracting and amusing her; but he bored her dreadfully. She was absent-minded to a degree, and answered at cross purposes, and sometimes not at all.

But the puzzle and mystery of Aglaya was not yet over for the evening. The last exhibition fell to the lot of the prince alone. When they had proceeded some hundred paces or so from the house, Aglaya said to her obstinately silent cavalier in a quick half-whisper:

"Look to the right!"

The prince glanced in the direction indicated.

"Look closer. Do you see that bench, in the park there, just by those three big trees—that green bench?"

The prince replied that he saw it.

"Do you like the position of it? Sometimes of a morning early, at seven o'clock, when all the rest are still asleep, I come out and sit there alone."

The prince muttered that the spot was a lovely one.

"Now, go away, I don't wish to have your arm any longer; or perhaps, better, continue to give me your arm, and walk along beside me, but don't speak a word to me. I wish to think by myself."

The warning was certainly unnecessary; for the prince would not have said a word all the rest of the time whether forbidden to speak or not. His heart beat loud and painfully when Aglaya spoke of the bench; could she—but no! he banished the thought, after an instant's deliberation.

At Pavlofsk, on weekdays, the public is more select than it is on Sundays and Saturdays, when the townsfolk come down to walk about and enjoy the park.

The ladies dress elegantly, on these days, and it is the fashion to gather round the band, which is probably the best of our pleasure-garden bands, and plays the newest pieces. The behaviour of the public is most correct and proper, and there is an appearance of friendly intimacy among the usual frequenters. Many come for nothing but to look at their acquaintances, but there are others who come for the sake of the music. It is very seldom that anything happens to break the harmony of the proceedings, though, of course, accidents will happen everywhere.

On this particular evening the weather was lovely, and there were a large number of people present. All the places anywhere near the orchestra were occupied.

Our friends took chairs near the side exit. The crowd and the music cheered Mrs. Epanchin a little, and amused the girls; they bowed and shook hands with some of their friends and nodded at a distance to others; they examined the ladies' dresses, noticed comicalities and eccentricities among the people, and laughed and talked among themselves. Evgenie Pavlovitch, too, found plenty of friends to bow to. Several people noticed Aglaya and the prince, who were still together.

Before very long two or three young men had come up, and one or two remained to talk; all of these young men appeared to be on intimate terms with Evgenie Pavlovitch. Among them was a young officer, a remarkably handsome fellow—very good-natured and a great chatterbox. He tried to get up a conversation with Aglaya, and did his best to secure her attention. Aglaya behaved very graciously to him, and chatted and laughed merrily. Evgenie Pavlovitch begged the prince's leave to introduce their friend to him. The prince hardly realized what was wanted of him, but the introduction came off; the two men bowed and shook hands.

Evgenie Pavlovitch's friend asked the prince some question, but the latter did not reply, or if he did, he muttered something so strangely indistinct that there was nothing to be made of it. The officer stared intently at him, then glanced at Evgenie, divined why the latter had introduced him, and gave his undivided attention to Aglaya again. Only Evgenie Pavlovitch observed that Aglaya flushed up for a moment at this.

The prince did not notice that others were talking and making themselves agreeable to Aglaya; in fact, at moments, he almost forgot that he was sitting by her himself. At other moments he felt a longing to go away somewhere and be alone with his thoughts, and to feel that no one knew where he was.

Or if that were impossible he would like to be alone at home, on the terrace—without either Lebedeff or his children, or anyone else about him, and to lie there and think—a day and night and another day again! He thought of the mountains—and especially of a certain spot which he used to frequent, whence he would look down upon the distant valleys and fields, and see the waterfall, far off, like a little silver thread, and the old ruined castle in the distance. Oh! how he longed to be there now—alone with his thoughts—to think of one thing all his life—one thing! A thousand years would not be too much time! And let everyone here forget him—forget him utterly! How much better it would have been if they had never known him—if all this could but prove to be a dream. Perhaps it was a dream!

Now and then he looked at Aglaya for five minutes at a time, without taking his eyes off her face; but his expression was very strange; he would gaze at her as though she were an object a couple of miles distant, or as though he were looking at her portrait and not at herself at all.

"Why do you look at me like that, prince?" she asked suddenly, breaking off her merry conversation and laughter with those about her. "I'm afraid of you! You look as though you were just going to put out your hand and touch my face to see if it's real! Doesn't he, Evgenie Pavlovitch—doesn't he look like that?"

The prince seemed surprised that he should have been addressed at all; he reflected a moment, but did not seem to take in what had been said to him; at all events, he did not answer. But observing that she and the others had begun to laugh, he too opened his mouth and laughed with them.

The laughter became general, and the young officer, who seemed a particularly lively sort of person, simply shook with mirth.

Aglaya suddenly whispered angrily to herself the word—

"Idiot!"

"My goodness—surely she is not in love with such a—surely she isn't mad!" groaned Mrs. Epanchin, under her breath.

"It's all a joke, mamma; it's just a joke like the 'poor knight'—nothing more whatever, I assure you!" Alexandra whispered in her ear. "She is chaffing him—making a fool of him, after her own private fashion, that's all! But she carries it just a little too far—she is a regular little actress. How she frightened us just now—didn't she?—and all for a lark!"

"Well, it's lucky she has happened upon an idiot, then, that's all I can say!" whispered Lizabetha Prokofievna, who was somewhat comforted, however, by her daughter's remark.

The prince had heard himself referred to as "idiot," and had shuddered at the moment; but his shudder, it so happened, was not caused by the word applied to him. The fact was that in the crowd, not far from where he was sitting, a pale familiar face, with curly black hair, and a well-known smile

Sincerely,

Kelsey-Seybold Clinic

Kelsey-Seybold Clinic®
Changing the way health cares.™

Lisa Jenkins
5800 Jackson Rd
Montgomery TX 77316

Dear Lisa,

We would like to remind you of your appointment with Kimberly K Rosen, OD on 5/17/2022 at 10:40 am with the Optometry department at:

Cypress Clinic Clinic
13105 Wortham Center Dr
Houston TX, 77065-5611

and expression, had flashed across his vision for a moment, and disappeared again. Very likely he had imagined it! There only remained to him the impression of a strange smile, two eyes, and a bright green tie. Whether the man had disappeared among the crowd, or whether he had turned towards the Vauxhall, the prince could not say.

But a moment or two afterwards he began to glance keenly about him. That first vision might only too likely be the forerunner of a second; it was almost certain to be so. Surely he had not forgotten the possibility of such a meeting when he came to the Vauxhall? True enough, he had not remarked where he was coming to when he set out with Aglaya; he had not been in a condition to remark anything at all.

Had he been more careful to observe his companion, he would have seen that for the last quarter of an hour Aglaya had also been glancing around in apparent anxiety, as though she expected to see someone, or something particular, among the crowd of people. Now, at the moment when his own anxiety became so marked, her excitement also increased visibly, and when he looked about him, she did the same.

The reason for their anxiety soon became apparent. From that very side entrance to the Vauxhall, near which the prince and all the Epanchin party were seated, there suddenly appeared quite a large knot of persons, at least a dozen.

Heading this little band walked three ladies, two of whom were remarkably lovely; and there was nothing surprising in the fact that they should have had a large troop of admirers following in their wake.

But there was something in the appearance of both the ladies and their admirers which was peculiar, quite different for that of the rest of the public assembled around the orchestra.

Nearly everyone observed the little band advancing, and all pretended not to see or notice them, except a few young fellows who exchanged glances and smiled, saying something to one another in whispers.

It was impossible to avoid noticing them, however, in reality, for they made their presence only too conspicuous by laughing and talking loudly. It was to be supposed that some of them were more than half drunk, although they were well enough dressed, some even particularly well. There were one or two, however, who were very strange-looking creatures, with flushed faces and extraordinary clothes; some were military men; not all were quite young; one or two were middle-aged gentlemen of decidedly disagreeable appearance, men who are avoided in society like the plague, decked out in large gold studs and rings, and magnificently "got up," generally.

Among our suburban resorts there are some which enjoy a specially high reputation for respectability and fashion; but the most careful individual is not absolutely exempt from the danger of a tile falling suddenly upon his head from his neighbour's roof.

Such a tile was about to descend upon the elegant and decorous public now assembled to hear the music.

In order to pass from the Vauxhall to the band-stand, the visitor has to descend two or three steps. Just at these steps the group paused, as though it feared to proceed further; but very quickly one of the three ladies, who formed its apex, stepped forward into the charmed circle, followed by two members of her suite.

One of these was a middle-aged man of very respectable appearance, but with the stamp of parvenu upon him, a man whom nobody knew, and who evidently knew nobody. The other follower was younger and far less respectable-looking.

No one else followed the eccentric lady; but as she descended the steps she did not even look behind her, as though it were absolutely the same to her whether anyone were following or not. She laughed and talked loudly, however, just as before. She was dressed with great taste, but with rather more magnificence than was needed for the occasion, perhaps.

She walked past the orchestra, to where an open carriage was waiting, near the road.

The prince had not seen *her* for more than three months. All these days since his arrival from Petersburg he had intended to pay her a visit, but some mysterious presentiment had restrained him. He could not picture to himself what impression this meeting with her would make upon him, though he had often tried to imagine it, with fear and trembling. One fact was quite certain, and that was that the meeting would be painful.

Several times during the last six months he had recalled the effect which the first sight of this face had had upon him, when he only saw its portrait. He recollected well that even the portrait face had left but too painful an impression.

That month in the provinces, when he had seen this woman nearly every day, had affected him so deeply that he could not now look back upon it calmly. In the very look of this woman there was something which tortured him. In conversation with Rogojin he had attributed this sensation to pity—immeasurable pity, and this was the truth. The sight of the portrait face alone had filled his heart full of the agony of real sympathy; and this feeling of sympathy, nay, of actual *suffering*, for her, had never left his heart since that hour, and was still in full force. Oh yes, and more powerful than ever!

But the prince was not satisfied with what he had said to Rogojin. Only at this moment, when she suddenly made her appearance before him, did he realize to the full the exact emotion which she called up in him, and which he had not described correctly to Rogojin.

And, indeed, there were no words in which he could have expressed his horror, yes, *horror*, for he was now fully convinced from his own private knowledge of her, that the woman was mad.

If, loving a woman above everything in the world, or at least having a foretaste of the possibility of such love for her, one were suddenly to behold her on a chain, behind bars and under the lash of a keeper, one would feel something like what the poor prince now felt.

"What's the matter?" asked Aglaya, in a whisper, giving his sleeve a little tug.

He turned his head towards her and glanced at her black and (for some reason) flashing eyes, tried to smile, and then, apparently forgetting her in an instant, turned to the right once more, and continued to watch the startling apparition before him.

Nastasia Philipovna was at this moment passing the young ladies' chairs.

Evgenie Pavlovitch continued some apparently extremely funny and interesting anecdote to Alexandra, speaking quickly and with much animation. The prince remembered that at this moment Aglaya remarked in a half-whisper:

"*What a—*"

She did not finish her indefinite sentence; she restrained herself in a moment; but it was enough.

Nastasia Philipovna, who up to now had been walking along as though she had not noticed the Epanchin party, suddenly turned her head in their direction, as though she had just observed Evgenie Pavlovitch sitting there for the first time.

"Why, I declare, here he is!" she cried, stopping suddenly. "The man one can't find with all one's messengers sent about the place, sitting just under one's nose, exactly where one never thought of looking! I thought you were sure to be at your uncle's by this time."

Evgenie Pavlovitch flushed up and looked angrily at Nastasia Philipovna, then turned his back on her.

"What! don't you know about it yet? He doesn't know—imagine that! Why, he's shot himself. Your uncle shot himself this very morning. I was told at two this afternoon. Half the town must know it by now. They say there are three hundred and fifty thousand roubles, government money, missing; some say five hundred thousand. And I was under the impression that he would leave you a fortune! He's whistled it all away. A most depraved old gentleman, really! Well, ta, ta!—bonne chance! Surely you intend to be off there, don't you? Ha, ha! You've retired from the army in good time, I see! Plain clothes! Well done, sly rogue! Nonsense! I see—you knew it all before—I dare say you knew all about it yesterday-"

Although the impudence of this attack, this public proclamation of intimacy, as it were, was doubtless premeditated, and had its special object, yet Evgenie Pavlovitch at first seemed to intend to make no show of observing either his tormentor or her words. But Nastasia's communication struck him with the force of a thunderclap. On hearing of his uncle's death he suddenly grew as white as a sheet, and turned towards his informant.

At this moment, Lizabetha Prokofievna rose swiftly from her seat, beckoned her companions, and left the place almost at a run.

Only the prince stopped behind for a moment, as though in indecision; and Evgenie Pavlovitch lingered too, for he had not collected his scattered wits. But the Epanchins had not had time to get more than twenty paces away when a scandalous episode occurred. The young officer, Evgenie Pavlovitch's friend who had been conversing with Aglaya, said aloud in a great state of indignation:

"She ought to be whipped—that's the only way to deal with creatures like that—she ought to be whipped!"

This gentleman was a confidant of Evgenie's, and had doubtless heard of the carriage episode.

Nastasia turned to him. Her eyes flashed; she rushed up to a young man standing near, whom she did not know in the least, but who happened to have in his hand a thin cane. Seizing this from him, she brought it with all her force across the face of her insulter.

All this occurred, of course, in one instant of time.

The young officer, forgetting himself, sprang towards her. Nastasia's followers were not by her at the moment (the elderly gentleman having disappeared altogether, and the younger man simply standing aside and roaring with laughter).

In another moment, of course, the police would have been on the spot, and it would have gone hard with Nastasia Philipovna had not unexpected aid appeared.

Muishkin, who was but a couple of steps away, had time to spring forward and seize the officer's arms from behind.

The officer, tearing himself from the prince's grasp, pushed him so violently backwards that he staggered a few steps and then subsided into a chair.

But there were other defenders for Nastasia on the spot by this time. The gentleman known as the "boxer" now confronted the enraged officer.

"Keller is my name, sir; ex-lieutenant," he said, very loud. "If you will accept me as champion of the fair sex, I am at your disposal. English boxing has no secrets from me. I sympathize with you for the insult you have received, but I can't permit you to raise your hand against a woman in public. If you prefer to meet me—as would be more fitting to your rank—in some other manner, of course you understand me, captain."

But the young officer had recovered himself, and was no longer listening. At this moment Rogojin appeared, elbowing through the crowd; he took Nastasia's hand, drew it through his arm, and quickly led her away. He appeared to be terribly excited; he was trembling all over, and was as pale as a corpse. As he carried Nastasia off, he turned and grinned horribly in the officer's face, and with low malice observed:

"Tfu! look what the fellow got! Look at the blood on his cheek! Ha, ha!"

Recollecting himself, however, and seeing at a glance the sort of people he had to deal with, the officer turned his back on both his opponents, and courteously, but concealing his face with his handkerchief, approached the prince, who was now rising from the chair into which he had fallen.

"Prince Muishkin, I believe? The gentleman to whom I had the honour of being introduced?"

"She is mad, insane—I assure you, she is mad," replied the prince in trembling tones, holding out both his hands mechanically towards the officer.

"I cannot boast of any such knowledge, of course, but I wished to know your name."

He bowed and retired without waiting for an answer.

Five seconds after the disappearance of the last actor in this scene, the police arrived. The whole episode had not lasted more than a couple of minutes. Some of the spectators had risen from their places, and departed altogether; some merely exchanged their seats for others a little further off; some were delighted with the occurrence, and talked and laughed over it for a long time.

In a word, the incident closed as such incidents do, and the band began to play again. The prince walked away after the Epanchin party. Had he thought of looking round to the left after he had been pushed so unceremoniously into the chair, he would have observed Aglaya standing some twenty yards away. She had stayed to watch the scandalous scene in spite of her mother's and sisters' anxious cries to her to come away.

Prince S. ran up to her and persuaded her, at last, to come home with them.

Lizabetha Prokofievna saw that she returned in such a state of agitation that it was doubtful whether she had even heard their calls. But only a couple of minutes later, when they had reached the park, Aglaya suddenly remarked, in her usual calm, indifferent voice:

"I wanted to see how the farce would end."

CHAPTER III.

The occurrence at the Vauxhall had filled both mother and daughters with something like horror. In their excitement Lizabetha Prokofievna and the girls were nearly running all the way home.

In her opinion there was so much disclosed and laid bare by the episode, that, in spite of the chaotic condition of her mind, she was able to feel more or less decided on certain points which, up to now, had been in a cloudy condition.

However, one and all of the party realized that something important had happened, and that, perhaps fortunately enough, something which had hitherto been enveloped in the obscurity of guess-work had now begun to come forth a little from the mists. In spite of Prince S.'s assurances and explanations, Evgenie Pavlovitch's real character and position were at last coming to light. He was publicly convicted of intimacy with "that creature." So thought Lizabetha Prokofievna and her two elder daughters.

But the real upshot of the business was that the number of riddles to be solved was augmented. The two girls, though rather irritated at their mother's exaggerated alarm and haste to depart from the scene, had been unwilling to worry her at first with questions.

Besides, they could not help thinking that their sister Aglaya probably knew more about the whole matter than both they and their mother put together.

Prince S. looked as black as night, and was silent and moody. Mrs. Epanchin did not say a word to him all the way home, and he did not seem to observe the fact. Adelaida tried to pump him a little by asking, "who was the uncle they were talking about, and what was it that had happened in Petersburg?" But he had merely muttered something disconnected about "making inquiries," and that "of course it was all nonsense." "Oh, of course," replied Adelaida, and asked no more questions. Aglaya, too, was very quiet; and the only remark she made on the way home was that they were "walking much too fast to be pleasant."

Once she turned and observed the prince hurrying after them. Noticing his anxiety to catch them up, she smiled ironically, and then looked back no more. At length, just as they neared the house, General Epanchin came out and met them; he had only just arrived from town.

His first word was to inquire after Evgenie Pavlovitch. But Lizabetha stalked past him, and neither looked at him nor answered his question.

He immediately judged from the faces of his daughters and Prince S. that there was a thunderstorm brewing, and he himself already bore evidences of unusual perturbation of mind.

He immediately button-holed Prince S., and standing at the front door, engaged in a whispered conversation with him. By the troubled aspect of both of them, when they entered the house, and approached Mrs. Epanchin, it was evident that they had been discussing very disturbing news.

Little by little the family gathered together upstairs in Lizabetha Prokofievna's apartments, and Prince Muishkin found himself alone on the verandah when he arrived. He settled himself in a corner and sat waiting, though he knew not what he expected. It never struck him that he had better go away, with all this disturbance in the house. He seemed to have forgotten all the world, and to be ready to sit on where he was for years on end. From upstairs he caught sounds of excited conversation every now and then.

He could not say how long he sat there. It grew late and became quite dark.

Suddenly Aglaya entered the verandah. She seemed to be quite calm, though a little pale.

Observing the prince, whom she evidently did not expect to see there, alone in the corner, she smiled, and approached him:

"What are you doing there?" she asked.

The prince muttered something, blushed, and jumped up; but Aglaya immediately sat down beside him; so he reseated himself.

She looked suddenly, but attentively into his face, then at the window, as though thinking of something else, and then again at him.

"Perhaps she wants to laugh at me," thought the prince, "but no; for if she did she certainly would do so."

"Would you like some tea? I'll order some," she said, after a minute or two of silence.

"N-no thanks, I don't know—"

"Don't know! How can you not know? By-the-by, look here—if someone were to challenge you to a duel, what should you do? I wished to ask you this—some time ago—"

"Why? Nobody would ever challenge me to a duel!"

"But if they were to, would you be dreadfully frightened?"

"I dare say I should be—much alarmed!"

"Seriously? Then are you a coward?"

"N-no!—I don't think so. A coward is a man who is afraid and runs away; the man who is frightened but does not run away, is not quite a coward," said the prince with a smile, after a moment's thought.

"And you wouldn't run away?"

"No—I don't think I should run away," replied the prince, laughing outright at last at Aglaya's questions.

"Though I am a woman, I should certainly not run away for anything," said Aglaya, in a slightly pained voice. "However, I see you are laughing at me and twisting your face up as usual in order to make yourself look more interesting. Now tell me, they generally shoot at twenty paces, don't they? At ten, sometimes? I suppose if at ten they must be either wounded or killed, mustn't they?"

"I don't think they often kill each other at duels."

"They killed Pushkin that way."

"That may have been an accident."

"Not a bit of it; it was a duel to the death, and he was killed."

"The bullet struck so low down that probably his antagonist would never have aimed at that part of him—people never do; he would have aimed at his chest or head; so that probably the bullet hit him accidentally. I have been told this by competent authorities."

"Well, a soldier once told me that they were always ordered to aim at the middle of the body. So you see they don't aim at the chest or head; they aim lower on purpose. I asked some officer about this afterwards, and he said it was perfectly true."

"That is probably when they fire from a long distance."

"Can you shoot at all?"

"No, I have never shot in my life."

"Can't you even load a pistol?"

"No! That is, I understand how it's done, of course, but I have never done it."

"Then, you don't know how, for it is a matter that needs practice. Now listen and learn; in the first place buy good powder, not damp (they say it mustn't be at all damp, but very dry), some fine kind it is—you must ask for *pistol* powder, not the stuff they load cannons with. They say one makes the bullets oneself, somehow or other. Have you got a pistol?"

"No—and I don't want one," said the prince, laughing.

"Oh, what *nonsense!* You must buy one. French or English are the best, they say. Then take a little powder, about a thimbleful, or perhaps two, and pour it into the barrel. Better put plenty. Then push in a bit of felt (it *must* be felt, for some reason or other); you can easily get a bit off some old mattress, or off a door; it's used to keep the cold out. Well, when you have pushed the felt down, put the bullet in; do you hear now? The bullet last and the powder first, not the other way, or the pistol won't shoot. What are you laughing at? I wish you to buy a pistol and practise every day, and you must learn to hit a mark for *certain*; will you?"

The prince only laughed. Aglaya stamped her foot with annoyance.

Her serious air, however, during this conversation had surprised him considerably. He had a feeling that he ought to be asking her something, that there was something he wanted to find out far more important than how to load a pistol; but his thoughts had all scattered, and he was only aware that she was sitting by him, and talking to him, and that he was looking at her; as to what she happened to be saying to him, that did not matter in the least.

The general now appeared on the verandah, coming from upstairs. He was on his way out, with an expression of determination on his face, and of preoccupation and worry also.

"Ah! Lef Nicolaievitch, it's you, is it? Where are you off to now?" he asked, oblivious of the fact that the prince had not showed the least sign of moving. "Come along with me; I want to say a word or two to you."

"*Au revoir*, then!" said Aglaya, holding out her hand to the prince.

It was quite dark now, and Muishkin could not see her face clearly, but a minute or two later, when he and the general had left the villa, he suddenly flushed up, and squeezed his right hand tightly.

It appeared that he and the general were going in the same direction. In spite of the lateness of the hour, the general was hurrying away to talk to someone upon some important subject. Meanwhile he talked incessantly but disconnectedly to the prince, and continually brought in the name of Lizabetha Prokofievna.

If the prince had been in a condition to pay more attention to what the general was saying, he would have discovered that the latter was desirous of drawing some information out of him, or indeed of asking him some question outright; but that he could not make up his mind to come to the point.

Muishkin was so absent, that from the very first he could not attend to a word the other was saying; and when the general suddenly stopped before him with some excited question, he was obliged to confess, ignominiously, that he did not know in the least what he had been talking about.

The general shrugged his shoulders.

"How strange everyone, yourself included, has become of late," said he. "I was telling you that I cannot in the least understand Lizabetha Prokofievna's ideas and agitations. She is in hysterics up there, and moans and says that we have been 'shamed and disgraced.' How? Why? When? By whom? I confess that I am very much to blame myself; I do not conceal the fact; but the conduct, the outrageous behaviour of this woman, must really be kept within limits, by the police if necessary, and I am just on my way now to talk the question over and make some arrangements. It can all be managed quietly and gently, even kindly, and without the slightest fuss or scandal. I foresee that the future is pregnant with events, and that there is much that needs explanation. There is intrigue in the wind; but if on one side nothing is known, on the other side nothing will be explained. If I have heard nothing about it, nor have *you*, nor *he*, nor *she*—who *has* heard about it, I should like to know? How *can* all this be explained except by the fact that half of it is mirage or moonshine, or some hallucination of that sort?"

"*She* is insane," muttered the prince, suddenly recollecting all that had passed, with a spasm of pain at his heart.

"I too had that idea, and I slept in peace. But now I see that their opinion is more correct. I do not believe in the theory of madness! The woman has no common sense; but she is not only not insane, she is artful to a degree. Her outburst of this evening about Evgenie's uncle proves that conclusively. It was *villainous*, simply jesuitical, and it was all for some special purpose."

"What about Evgenie's uncle?"

"My goodness, Lef Nicolaievitch, why, you can't have heard a single word I said! Look at me, I'm still trembling all over with the dreadful shock! It is that that kept me in town so late. Evgenie Pavlovitch's uncle—"

"Well?" cried the prince.

"Shot himself this morning, at seven o'clock. A respected, eminent old man of seventy; and exactly point for point as she described it; a sum of money, a considerable sum of government money, missing!"

"Why, how could she—"

"What, know of it? Ha, ha, ha! Why, there was a whole crowd round her the moment she appeared on the scenes here. You know what sort of people surround her nowadays, and solicit the honour of her 'acquaintance.' Of course she might easily have heard the news from someone coming from town. All Petersburg, if not all Pavlofsk, knows it by now. Look at the slyness of her observation about Evgenie's uniform! I mean, her remark that he had retired just in time! There's a venomous hint for you, if you like! No, no! there's no insanity there! Of course I refuse to believe that Evgenie Pavlovitch could have known beforehand of the catastrophe; that is, that at such and such a day at seven o'clock, and all that; but he might well have had a presentiment of the truth. And I—all of us—Prince S. and everybody, believed that he was to inherit a large fortune from this uncle. It's dreadful, horrible! Mind, I don't suspect Evgenie of anything, be quite clear on that point; but the thing is a little suspicious, nevertheless. Prince S. can't get over it. Altogether it is a very extraordinary combination of circumstances."

"What suspicion attaches to Evgenie Pavlovitch?"

"Oh, none at all! He has behaved very well indeed. I didn't mean to drop any sort of hint. His own fortune is intact, I believe. Lizabetha Prokofievna, of course, refuses to listen to anything. That's the worst of it all, these family catastrophes or quarrels, or whatever you like to call them. You know, prince, you are a friend of the family, so I don't mind telling you; it now appears that Evgenie Pavlovitch proposed to Aglaya a month ago, and was refused."

"Impossible!" cried the prince.

"Why? Do you know anything about it? Look here," continued the general, more agitated than ever, and trembling with excitement, "maybe I have been letting the cat out of the bag too freely with you, if so, it is because you are—that sort of man, you know! Perhaps you have some special information?"

"I know nothing about Evgenie Pavlovitch!" said the prince.

"Nor do I! They always try to bury me underground when there's anything going on; they don't seem to reflect that it is unpleasant to a man to be treated so! I won't stand it! We have just had a terrible scene!—mind, I speak to you as I would to my own son! Aglaya laughs at her mother. Her sisters guessed about Evgenie having proposed and been rejected, and told Lizabetha.

"I tell you, my dear fellow, Aglaya is such an extraordinary, such a self-willed, fantastical little creature, you wouldn't believe it! Every high quality, every brilliant trait of heart and mind, are to be found in her, and, with it all, so much caprice and mockery, such wild fancies—indeed, a little devil! She has just been laughing at her mother to her very face, and at her sisters, and at Prince S., and everybody—and of course she always laughs at me! You know I love the child—I love her even when she laughs at me, and I believe the wild little creature has a special fondness for me for that very reason. She is fonder of me than any of the others. I dare swear she has had a good laugh at *you* before now! You were having a quiet talk just now, I observed, after all the thunder and lightning upstairs. She was sitting with you just as though there had been no row at all."

The prince blushed painfully in the darkness, and closed his right hand tightly, but he said nothing.

"My dear good Prince Lef Nicolaievitch," began the general again, suddenly, "both I and Lizabetha Prokofievna—(who has begun to respect you once more, and me through you, goodness knows why!)—we both love you very sincerely, and esteem you, in spite of any appearances to the contrary. But you'll admit what a riddle it must have been for us when that calm, cold, little spitfire, Aglaya—(for she stood up to her mother and answered her questions with inexpressible contempt, and mine still more so, because, like a fool, I thought it my duty to assert myself as head of the family)—when Aglaya stood up of a sudden and informed us that 'that madwoman' (strangely enough, she used exactly the same expression as you did) 'has taken it into her head to marry me to Prince Lef Nicolaievitch, and therefore is doing her best to choke Evgenie Pavlovitch off, and rid the house of him.' That's what she said. She would not give the slightest explanation; she burst out laughing, banged the door, and went away. We all stood there with our mouths open. Well, I was told afterwards of your little passage with Aglaya this afternoon, and—and—dear prince—you are a good, sensible fellow, don't be angry if I speak out—she is laughing at you, my boy! She is enjoying herself like a child, at your expense, and therefore, since she is a child, don't be angry with her, and don't think anything of it. I assure you, she is simply making a fool of you, just as she does with one and all of us out of pure lack of something better to do. Well—good-bye! You know our feelings, don't you—our sincere feelings for yourself? They are unalterable, you know, dear boy, under all circumstances, but—Well, here we part; I must go down to the right. Rarely have I sat so uncomfortably in my saddle, as they say, as I now sit. And people talk of the charms of a country holiday!"

Left to himself at the cross-roads, the prince glanced around him, quickly crossed the road towards the lighted window of a neighbouring house, and unfolded a tiny scrap of paper which he had held clasped in his right hand during the whole of his conversation with the general.

He read the note in the uncertain rays that fell from the window. It was as follows:

"Tomorrow morning, I shall be at the green bench in the park at seven, and shall wait there for you. I have made up my mind to speak to you about a most important matter which closely concerns yourself.

"P.S.—I trust that you will not show this note to anyone. Though I am ashamed of giving you such instructions, I feel that I must do so, considering what you are. I therefore write the words, and blush for your simple character.

"P.P.S.—It is the same green bench that I showed you before. There! aren't you ashamed of yourself? I felt that it was necessary to repeat even that information."

The note was written and folded anyhow, evidently in a great hurry, and probably just before Aglaya had come down to the verandah.

In inexpressible agitation, amounting almost to fear, the prince slipped quickly away from the window, away from the light, like a frightened thief, but as he did so he collided violently with some gentleman who seemed to spring from the earth at his feet.

"I was watching for you, prince," said the individual.

"Is that you, Keller?" said the prince, in surprise.

"Yes, I've been looking for you. I waited for you at the Epanchins' house, but of course I could not come in. I dogged you from behind as you walked along with the general. Well, prince, here is Keller, absolutely at your service—command him!—ready to sacrifice himself—even to die in case of need."

"But—why?"

"Oh, why?—Of course you'll be challenged! That was young Lieutenant Moloftsoff. I know him, or rather of him; he won't pass an insult. He will take no notice of Rogojin and myself, and, therefore, you are the only one left to account for. You'll have to pay the piper, prince. He has been asking about you, and undoubtedly his friend will call on you tomorrow—perhaps he is at your house already. If you would do me the honour to have me for a second, prince, I should be happy. That's why I have been looking for you now."

"Duel! You've come to talk about a duel, too!" The prince burst out laughing, to the great astonishment of Keller. He laughed unrestrainedly, and Keller, who had been on pins and needles, and in a fever of excitement to offer himself as "second," was very near being offended.

"You caught him by the arms, you know, prince. No man of proper pride can stand that sort of treatment in public."

"Yes, and he gave me a fearful dig in the chest," cried the prince, still laughing. "What are we to fight about? I shall beg his pardon, that's all. But if we must fight—we'll fight! Let him have a shot at me, by all means; I should rather like it. Ha, ha, ha! I know how to load a pistol now; do you know how to load a pistol, Keller? First, you have to buy the powder, you know; it mustn't be wet, and it mustn't be that coarse stuff that they load cannons with—it must be pistol powder. Then you pour the powder in, and get hold of a bit of felt from some door, and then shove the bullet in. But don't shove the bullet in before the powder, because the thing wouldn't go off—do you hear, Keller, the thing wouldn't go off! Ha, ha, ha! Isn't that a grand reason, Keller, my friend, eh? Do you know, my dear fellow, I really must kiss you, and embrace you, this very moment. Ha, ha! How was it you so suddenly popped up in front of me as you did? Come to my house as soon as you can, and we'll have some champagne. We'll all get drunk! Do you know I have a dozen of champagne in Lebedeff's cellar? Lebedeff sold them to me the day after I arrived. I took the lot. We'll invite everybody! Are you going to do any sleeping tonight?"

"As much as usual, prince—why?"

"Pleasant dreams then—ha, ha!"

The prince crossed the road, and disappeared into the park, leaving the astonished Keller in a state of ludicrous wonder. He had never before seen the prince in such a strange condition of mind, and could not have imagined the possibility of it.

"Fever, probably," he said to himself, "for the man is all nerves, and this business has been a little too much for him. He is not *afraid*, that's clear; that sort never funks! H'm! champagne! That was an interesting item of news, at all events!—Twelve bottles! Dear me, that's a very respectable little stock indeed! I bet anything Lebedeff lent somebody money on deposit of this dozen of champagne. Hum! he's a nice fellow, is this prince! I like this sort of man. Well, I needn't be wasting time here, and if it's a case of champagne, why—there's no time like the present!"

That the prince was almost in a fever was no more than the truth. He wandered about the park for a long while, and at last came to himself in a lonely avenue. He was vaguely conscious that he had already paced this particular walk—from that large, dark tree to the bench at the other end—about a hundred yards altogether—at least thirty times backwards and forwards.

As to recollecting what he had been thinking of all that time, he could not. He caught himself, however, indulging in one thought which made him roar with laughter, though there was nothing really to laugh at in it; but he felt that he must laugh, and go on laughing.

It struck him that the idea of the duel might not have occurred to Keller alone, but that his lesson in the art of pistol-loading might have been not altogether accidental! "Pooh! nonsense!" he said to himself, struck by another thought, of a sudden. "Why, she was immensely surprised to find me there on the verandah, and laughed and talked about *tea!* And yet she had this little note in her hand, therefore she must have known that I was sitting there. So why was she surprised? Ha, ha, ha!"

He pulled the note out and kissed it; then paused and reflected. "How strange it all is! how strange!" he muttered, melancholy enough now. In moments of great joy, he invariably felt a sensation of melancholy come over him—he could not tell why.

He looked intently around him, and wondered why he had come here; he was very tired, so he approached the bench and sat down on it. Around him was profound silence; the music in the Vauxhall was over. The park seemed quite empty, though it was not, in reality, later than half-past eleven. It was a quiet, warm, clear night—a real Petersburg night of early June; but in the dense avenue, where he was sitting, it was almost pitch dark.

If anyone had come up at this moment and told him that he was in love, passionately in love, he would have rejected the idea with astonishment, and, perhaps, with irritation. And if anyone had added that Aglaya's note was a love-letter, and that it contained an appointment to a lover's rendezvous, he would have blushed with shame for the speaker, and, probably, have challenged him to a duel.

All this would have been perfectly sincere on his part. He had never for a moment entertained the idea of the possibility of this girl loving him, or even of such a thing as himself falling in love with her. The possibility of being loved himself, "a man like me," as he put it, he ranked among ridiculous suppositions. It appeared to him that it was simply a joke on Aglaya's part, if there really were anything in it at all; but that seemed to him quite natural. His preoccupation was caused by something different.

As to the few words which the general had let slip about Aglaya laughing at everybody, and at himself most of all—he entirely believed them. He did not feel the slightest sensation of offence; on the contrary, he was quite certain that it was as it should be.

His whole thoughts were now as to next morning early; he would see her; he would sit by her on that little green bench, and listen to how pistols were loaded, and look at her. He wanted nothing more.

The question as to what she might have to say of special interest to himself occurred to him once or twice. He did not doubt, for a moment, that she really had some such subject of conversation in store, but so very little interested in the matter was he that it did not strike him to wonder what it could be. The crunch of gravel on the path suddenly caused him to raise his head.

A man, whose face it was difficult to see in the gloom, approached the bench, and sat down beside him. The prince peered into his face, and recognized the livid features of Rogojin.

"I knew you'd be wandering about somewhere here. I didn't have to look for you very long," muttered the latter between his teeth.

It was the first time they had met since the encounter on the staircase at the hotel.

Painfully surprised as he was at this sudden apparition of Rogojin, the prince, for some little while, was unable to collect his thoughts. Rogojin, evidently, saw and understood the impression he had made; and though he seemed more or less confused at first, yet he began talking with what looked like assumed ease and freedom. However, the prince soon changed his mind on this score, and thought that there was not only no affectation of indifference, but that Rogojin was not even particularly agitated. If there were a little apparent awkwardness, it was only in his words and gestures. The man could not change his heart.

"How did you—find me here?" asked the prince for the sake of saying something.

"Keller told me (I found him at your place) that you were in the park. 'Of course he is!' I thought."

"Why so?" asked the prince uneasily.

Rogojin smiled, but did not explain.

"I received your letter, Lef Nicolaievitch—what's the good of all that?—It's no use, you know. I've come to you from *her*,—she bade me tell you that she must see you, she has something to say to you. She told me to find you today."

"I'll come tomorrow. Now I'm going home—are you coming to my house?"

"Why should I? I've given you the message.—Goodbye!"

"Won't you come?" asked the prince in a gentle voice.

"What an extraordinary man you are! I wonder at you!" Rogojin laughed sarcastically.

"Why do you hate me so?" asked the prince, sadly. "You know yourself that all you suspected is quite unfounded. I felt you were still angry with me, though. Do you know why? Because you tried to kill me—that's why you can't shake off your wrath against me. I tell you that I only remember the Parfen Rogojin with whom I exchanged crosses, and vowed brotherhood. I wrote you this in yesterday's letter, in order that you might forget all that madness on your part, and that you might not feel called to talk about it when we met. Why do you avoid me? Why do you hold your hand back from me? I tell you again, I consider all that has passed a delirium, an insane dream. I can understand all you did, and all you felt that day, as if it were myself. What you were then imagining was not the case, and could never be the case. Why, then, should there be anger between us?"

"You don't know what anger is!" laughed Rogojin, in reply to the prince's heated words.

He had moved a pace or two away, and was hiding his hands behind him.

"No, it is impossible for me to come to your house again," he added slowly.

"Why? Do you hate me so much as all that?"

"I don't love you, Lef Nicolaievitch, and, therefore, what would be the use of my coming to see you? You are just like a child—you want a plaything, and it must be taken out and given you—and then you don't know how to work it. You are simply repeating all you said in your letter, and what's the use? Of course I believe every word you say, and I know perfectly well that you neither did or ever can deceive me in any way, and yet, I don't love you. You write that you've forgotten everything, and only remember your brother Parfen, with whom you exchanged crosses, and that you don't remember anything about the Rogojin who aimed a knife at your throat. What do you know about my feelings, eh?" (Rogojin laughed disagreeably.) "Here you are holding out your brotherly forgiveness to me for a thing that I have perhaps never repented of in the slightest degree. I did not think of it again all that evening; all my thoughts were centred on something else—"

"Not think of it again? Of course you didn't!" cried the prince. "And I dare swear that you came straight away down here to Pavlofsk to listen to the music and dog her about in the crowd, and stare at her, just as you did today. There's nothing surprising in that! If you hadn't been in that condition of mind that you could think of nothing but one subject, you would, probably, never have raised your knife against me. I had a presentiment of what you would do, that day, ever since I saw you first in the morning. Do you know yourself what you looked like? I knew you would try to murder me even at the very moment when we exchanged crosses. What did you take me to your mother for? Did you think to stay your hand by doing so? Perhaps you did not put your thoughts into words, but you and I were thinking the same thing, or feeling the same thing looming over us, at the same moment. What should you think of me now if you had not raised your knife to me— the knife which God averted from my throat? I would have been guilty of suspecting you all the same—and you would have intended the murder all the same; therefore we should have been mutually guilty in any case. Come, don't frown; you needn't laugh at me, either. You say you haven't 'repented.' Repented! You probably couldn't, if you were to try; you dislike me too much for that. Why, if I were an angel of light, and as innocent before you as a babe, you would still loathe me if you believed that *she* loved me, instead of loving yourself. That's jealousy—that is the real jealousy.

"But do you know what I have been thinking out during this last week, Parfen? I'll tell you. What if she loves you now better than anyone? And what if she torments you *because* she loves you, and in proportion to her love for you, so she torments you the more? She won't tell you this, of course; you must have eyes to see. Why do you suppose she consents to marry you? She must have a reason, and that reason she will tell you some day. Some women desire the kind of love you give her, and she is probably one of these. Your love and your wild nature impress her. Do you know that a woman is capable of driving a man crazy almost, with her cruelties and mockeries, and feels not one single pang of regret, because she looks at him and says to herself, 'There! I'll torment this man nearly into his grave, and then, oh! how I'll compensate him for it all with my love!'"

Rogojin listened to the end, and then burst out laughing:

"Why, prince, I declare you must have had a taste of this sort of thing yourself—haven't you? I have heard tell of something of the kind, you know; is it true?"

"What? What can you have heard?" said the prince, stammering.

Rogojin continued to laugh loudly. He had listened to the prince's speech with curiosity and some satisfaction. The speaker's impulsive warmth had surprised and even comforted him.

"Why, I've not only heard of it; I see it for myself," he said. "When have you ever spoken like that before? It wasn't like yourself, prince. Why, if I hadn't heard this report about you, I should never have come all this way into the park—at midnight, too!"

"I don't understand you in the least, Parfen."

"Oh, *she* told me all about it long ago, and tonight I saw for myself. I saw you at the music, you know, and whom you were sitting with. She swore to me yesterday, and again today, that you are madly in love with Aglaya Ivanovna. But that's all the same to me, prince, and it's not my affair at all; for if you have ceased to love *her*, *she* has not ceased to love *you*. You know, of course, that she wants to marry you to that girl? She's sworn to it! Ha, ha! She says to me, 'Until then I won't marry you. When they go to church, we'll go too—and not before.' What on earth does she mean by it? I don't know, and I never did. Either she loves you without limits or—yet, if she loves you, why does she wish to marry you to another girl? She says, 'I want to see him happy,' which is to say— she loves you."

"I wrote, and I say to you once more, that she is not in her right mind," said the prince, who had listened with anguish to what Rogojin said.

"Goodness knows—you may be wrong there! At all events, she named the day this evening, as we left the gardens. 'In three weeks,' says she, 'and perhaps sooner, we shall be married.' She swore to it, took off her cross and kissed it. So it all depends upon you now, prince, You see! Ha, ha!"

"That's all madness. What you say about me, Parfen, never can and never will be. Tomorrow, I shall come and see you—"

"How can she be mad," Rogojin interrupted, "when she is sane enough for other people and only mad for you? How can she write letters to *her*, if she's mad? If she were insane they would observe it in her letters."

"What letters?" said the prince, alarmed.

"She writes to *her*—and the girl reads the letters. Haven't you heard?—You are sure to hear; she's sure to show you the letters herself."

"I won't believe this!" cried the prince.

"Why, prince, you've only gone a few steps along this road, I perceive. You are evidently a mere beginner. Wait a bit! Before long, you'll have your own detectives, you'll watch day and night, and you'll know every little thing that goes on there—that is, if—"

"Drop that subject, Rogojin, and never mention it again. And listen: as I have sat here, and talked, and listened, it has suddenly struck me that tomorrow is my birthday. It must be about twelve o'clock, now; come home with me—do, and we'll see the day in! We'll have some wine, and you shall wish me—I don't know what—but you, especially you, must wish me a good wish, and I shall wish you full happiness in return. Otherwise, hand me my cross back again. You didn't return it to me next day. Haven't you got it on now?"

"Yes, I have," said Rogojin.

"Come along, then. I don't wish to meet my new year without you—my new life, I should say, for a new life is beginning for me. Did you know, Parfen, that a new life had begun for me?"

"I see for myself that it is so—and I shall tell *her*. But you are not quite yourself, Lef Nicolaievitch."

Chapter IV.

The prince observed with great surprise, as he approached his villa, accompanied by Rogojin, that a large number of people were assembled on his verandah, which was brilliantly lighted up. The company seemed merry and were noisily laughing and talking—even quarrelling, to judge from the sounds. At all events they were clearly enjoying themselves, and the prince observed further on closer investigation—that all had been drinking champagne. To judge from the lively condition of some of the party, it was to be supposed that a considerable quantity of champagne had been consumed already.

All the guests were known to the prince; but the curious part of the matter was that they had all arrived on the same evening, as though with one accord, although he had only himself recollected the fact that it was his birthday a few moments since.

"You must have told somebody you were going to trot out the champagne, and that's why they are all come!" muttered Rogojin, as the two entered the verandah. "We know all about that! You've only to whistle and they come up in shoals!" he continued, almost angrily. He was doubtless thinking of his own late experiences with his boon companions.

All surrounded the prince with exclamations of welcome, and, on hearing that it was his birthday, with cries of congratulation and delight; many of them were very noisy.

The presence of certain of those in the room surprised the prince vastly, but the guest whose advent filled him with the greatest wonder—almost amounting to alarm—was Evgenie Pavlovitch. The prince could not believe his eyes when he beheld the latter, and could not help thinking that something was wrong.

Lebedeff ran up promptly to explain the arrival of all these gentlemen. He was himself somewhat intoxicated, but the prince gathered from his long-winded periods that the party had assembled quite naturally, and accidentally.

First of all Hippolyte had arrived, early in the evening, and feeling decidedly better, had determined to await the prince on the verandah. There Lebedeff had joined him, and his household had followed—that is, his daughters and General Ivolgin. Burdovsky had brought Hippolyte, and stayed on with him. Gania and Ptitsin had dropped in accidentally later on; then came Keller, and he and Colia insisted on having champagne. Evgenie Pavlovitch had only dropped in half an hour or so ago. Lebedeff had served the champagne readily.

"My own though, prince, my own, mind," he said, "and there'll be some supper later on; my daughter is getting it ready now. Come and sit down, prince, we are all waiting for you, we want you with us. Fancy what we have been discussing! You know the question, 'to be or not to be,'—out of Hamlet! A contemporary theme! Quite up-to-date! Mr. Hippolyte has been eloquent to a degree. He won't go to bed, but he has only drunk a little champagne, and that can't do him any harm. Come along, prince, and settle the question. Everyone is waiting for you, sighing for the light of your luminous intelligence..."

The prince noticed the sweet, welcoming look on Vera Lebedeff's face, as she made her way towards him through the crowd. He held out his hand to her. She took it, blushing with delight, and wished him "a happy life from that day forward." Then she ran off to the kitchen, where her presence was necessary to help in the preparations for supper. Before the prince's arrival she had spent some time on the terrace, listening eagerly to the conversation, though the visitors, mostly under the influence of wine, were discussing abstract subjects far beyond her comprehension. In the next room her younger sister lay on a wooden chest, sound asleep, with her mouth wide open; but the boy, Lebedeff's son, had taken up his position close beside Colia and Hippolyte, his face lit up with interest in the conversation of his father and the rest, to which he would willingly have listened for ten hours at a stretch.

"I have waited for you on purpose, and am very glad to see you arrive so happy," said Hippolyte, when the prince came forward to press his hand, immediately after greeting Vera.

"And how do you know that I am 'so happy'?"

"I can see it by your face! Say 'how do you do' to the others, and come and sit down here, quick—I've been waiting for you!" he added, accentuating the fact that he had waited. On the prince's asking, "Will it not be injurious to you to sit out so late?" he replied that he could not believe that he had thought himself dying three days or so ago, for he never had felt better than this evening.

Burdovsky next jumped up and explained that he had come in by accident, having escorted Hippolyte from town. He murmured that he was glad he had "written nonsense" in his letter, and then pressed the prince's hand warmly and sat down again.

The prince approached Evgenie Pavlovitch last of all. The latter immediately took his arm.

"I have a couple of words to say to you," he began, "and those on a very important matter; let's go aside for a minute or two."

"Just a couple of words!" whispered another voice in the prince's other ear, and another hand took his other arm. Muishkin turned, and to his great surprise observed a red, flushed face and a droll-looking figure which he recognized at once as that of Ferdishenko. Goodness knows where he had turned up from!

"Do you remember Ferdishenko?" he asked.

"Where have you dropped from?" cried the prince.

"He is sorry for his sins now, prince," cried Keller. "He did not want to let you know he was here; he was hidden over there in the corner,—but he repents now, he feels his guilt."

"Why, what has he done?"

"I met him outside and brought him in—he's a gentleman who doesn't often allow his friends to see him, of late—but he's sorry now."

"Delighted, I'm sure!—I'll come back directly, gentlemen,—sit down there with the others, please,—excuse me one moment," said the host, getting away with difficulty in order to follow Evgenie.

"You are very gay here," began the latter, "and I have had quite a pleasant half-hour while I waited for you. Now then, my dear Lef Nicolaievitch, this is what's the matter. I've arranged it all with Moloftsoff, and have just come in to relieve your mind on that score. You need be under no apprehensions. He was very sensible, as he should be, of course, for I think he was entirely to blame himself."

"What Moloftsoff?"

"The young fellow whose arms you held, don't you know? He was so wild with you that he was going to send a friend to you tomorrow morning."

"What nonsense!"

"Of course it is nonsense, and in nonsense it would have ended, doubtless; but you know these fellows, they—"

"Excuse me, but I think you must have something else that you wished to speak about, Evgenie Pavlovitch?"

"Of course, I have!" said the other, laughing. "You see, my dear fellow, tomorrow, very early in the morning, I must be off to town about this unfortunate business (my uncle, you know!). Just imagine, my dear sir, it is all true—word for word—and, of course, everybody knew it excepting myself. All this has been such a blow to me that I have not managed to call in at the Epanchins'. Tomorrow I shall not see them either, because I shall be in town. I may not be here for three days or more; in a word, my affairs are a little out of gear. But though my town business is, of course, most pressing, still I determined not to go away until I had seen you, and had a clear understanding with you upon certain points; and that without loss of time. I will wait now, if you will allow me, until the company departs; I may just as well, for I have nowhere else to go to, and I shall certainly not do any sleeping tonight; I'm far too excited. And finally, I must confess that, though I know it is bad form to pursue a man in this way, I have come to beg your friendship, my dear prince. You are an unusual sort of a person; you don't lie at every step, as some men do; in fact, you don't lie at all, and there is a matter in which I need a true and sincere friend, for I really may claim to be among the number of bona fide unfortunates just now."

He laughed again.

"But the trouble is," said the prince, after a slight pause for reflection, "that goodness only knows when this party will break up. Hadn't we better stroll into the park? I'll excuse myself, there's no danger of their going away."

"No, no! I have my reasons for wishing them not to suspect us of being engaged in any specially important conversation. There are gentry present who are a little too much interested in us. You are not aware of that perhaps, prince? It will be a great deal better if they see that we are friendly just in an ordinary way. They'll all go in a couple of hours, and then I'll ask you to give me twenty minutes—half an hour at most."

"By all means! I assure you I am delighted—you need not have entered into all these explanations. As for your remarks about friendship with me—thanks, very much indeed. You must excuse my being a little absent this evening. Do you know, I cannot somehow be attentive to anything just now?"

"I see, I see," said Evgenie, smiling gently. His mirth seemed very near the surface this evening.

"What do you see?" said the prince, startled.

"I don't want you to suspect that I have simply come here to deceive you and pump information out of you!" said Evgenie, still smiling, and without making any direct reply to the question.

"Oh, but I haven't the slightest doubt that you did come to pump me," said the prince, laughing himself, at last; "and I dare say you are quite prepared to deceive me too, so far as that goes. But what of that? I'm not afraid of you; besides, you'll hardly believe it, I feel as though I really didn't care a scrap one way or the other, just now!—And—and—and as you are a capital fellow, I am convinced of that, I dare say we really shall end by being good friends. I like you very much Evgenie Pavlovitch; I consider you a very good fellow indeed."

"Well, in any case, you are a most delightful man to have to deal with, be the business what it may," concluded Evgenie. "Come along now, I'll drink a glass to your health. I'm charmed to have entered into alliance with you. By-the-by," he added suddenly, "has this young Hippolyte come down to stay with you?"

"Yes."

"He's not going to die at once, I should think, is he?"

"Why?"

"Oh, I don't know. I've been half an hour here with him, and he—"

Hippolyte had been waiting for the prince all this time, and had never ceased looking at him and Evgenie Pavlovitch as they conversed in the corner. He became much excited when they approached the table once more. He was disturbed in his mind, it seemed; perspiration stood in large drops on his forehead; in his gleaming eyes it was easy to read impatience and agitation; his gaze wandered from face to face of those present, and from object to object in the room, apparently without aim. He had taken a part, and an animated one, in the noisy conversation of the company; but his animation was clearly the outcome of fever. His talk was almost incoherent; he would break off in the middle of a sentence which he had begun with great interest, and forget what he had been saying. The prince discovered to his dismay that Hippolyte had been allowed to drink two large glasses of champagne; the one now standing by him being the third. All this he found out afterwards; at the moment he did not notice anything, very particularly.

"Do you know I am specially glad that today is your birthday!" cried Hippolyte.

"Why?"

"You'll soon see. D'you know I had a feeling that there would be a lot of people here tonight? It's not the first time that my presentiments have been fulfilled. I wish I had known it was your birthday, I'd have brought you a present—perhaps I have got a present for you! Who knows? Ha, ha! How long is it now before daylight?"

"Not a couple of hours," said Ptitsin, looking at his watch. "What's the good of daylight now? One can read all night in the open air without it," said someone.

"The good of it! Well, I want just to see a ray of the sun," said Hippolyte. "Can one drink to the sun's health, do you think, prince?"

"Oh, I dare say one can; but you had better be calm and lie down, Hippolyte—that's much more important."

"You are always preaching about resting; you are a regular nurse to me, prince. As soon as the sun begins to 'resound' in the sky—what poet said that? 'The sun resounded in the sky.' It is beautiful, though there's no sense in it!—then we will go to bed. Lebedeff, tell me, is the sun the source of life? What does the source, or 'spring,' of life really mean in the Apocalypse? You have heard of the 'Star that is called Wormwood,' prince?"

"I have heard that Lebedeff explains it as the railroads that cover Europe like a net."

Everybody laughed, and Lebedeff got up abruptly.

"No! Allow me, that is not what we are discussing!" he cried, waving his hand to impose silence. "Allow me! With these gentlemen... all these gentlemen," he added, suddenly addressing the prince, "on certain points... that is..." He thumped the table repeatedly, and the laughter increased. Lebedeff was in his usual evening condition, and had just ended a long and scientific argument, which had left him excited and irritable. On such occasions he was apt to evince a supreme contempt for his opponents.

"It is not right! Half an hour ago, prince, it was agreed among us that no one should interrupt, no one should laugh, that each person was to express his thoughts freely; and then at the end, when everyone had spoken, objections might be made, even by the atheists. We chose the general as president. Now without some such rule and order, anyone might be shouted down, even in the loftiest and most profound thought...."

"Go on! Go on! Nobody is going to interrupt you!" cried several voices.

"Speak, but keep to the point!"

"What is this 'star'?" asked another.

"I have no idea," replied General Ivolgin, who presided with much gravity.

"I love these arguments, prince," said Keller, also more than half intoxicated, moving restlessly in his chair. "Scientific and political." Then, turning suddenly towards Evgenie Pavlovitch, who was seated near him: "Do you know, I simply adore reading the accounts of the debates in the English parliament. Not that the discussions themselves interest me; I am not a politician, you know; but it delights me to see how they address each other 'the noble lord who agrees with me,' 'my honourable opponent who astonished Europe with his proposal,' 'the noble viscount sitting opposite'—all these expressions, all this parliamentarism of a free people, has an enormous attraction for me. It fascinates me, prince. I have always been an artist in the depths of my soul, I assure you, Evgenie Pavlovitch."

"Do you mean to say," cried Gania, from the other corner, "do you mean to say that railways are accursed inventions, that they are a source of ruin to humanity, a poison poured upon the earth to corrupt the springs of life?"

Gavrila Ardalionovitch was in high spirits that evening, and it seemed to the prince that his gaiety was mingled with triumph. Of course he was only joking with Lebedeff, meaning to egg him on, but he grew excited himself at the same time.

"Not the railways, oh dear, no!" replied Lebedeff, with a mixture of violent anger and extreme enjoyment. "Considered alone, the railways will not pollute the springs of life, but as a whole they are accursed. The whole tendency of our latest centuries, in its scientific and materialistic aspect, is most probably accursed."

"Is it certainly accursed?... or do you only mean it might be? That is an important point," said Evgenie Pavlovitch.

"It is accursed, certainly accursed!" replied the clerk, vehemently.

"Don't go so fast, Lebedeff; you are much milder in the morning," said Ptitsin, smiling.

"But, on the other hand, more frank in the evening! In the evening sincere and frank," repeated Lebedeff, earnestly. "More candid, more exact, more honest, more honourable, and... although I may show you my weak side, I challenge you all; you atheists, for instance! How are you going to save the world? How find a straight road of progress, you men of science, of industry, of cooperation, of trades unions, and all the rest? How are you going to save it, I say? By what? By credit? What is credit? To what will credit lead you?"

"You are too inquisitive," remarked Evgenie Pavlovitch.

"Well, anyone who does not interest himself in questions such as this is, in my opinion, a mere fashionable dummy."

"But it will lead at least to solidarity, and balance of interests," said Ptitsin.

"You will reach that with nothing to help you but credit? Without recourse to any moral principle, having for your foundation only individual selfishness, and the satisfaction of material desires? Universal peace, and the happiness of mankind as a whole, being the result! Is it really so that I may understand you, sir?"

"But the universal necessity of living, of drinking, of eating—in short, the whole scientific conviction that this necessity can only be satisfied by universal co-operation and the solidarity of interests—is, it seems to me, a strong enough idea to serve as a basis, so to speak, and a 'spring of life,' for humanity in future centuries," said Gavrila Ardalionovitch, now thoroughly roused.

"The necessity of eating and drinking, that is to say, solely the instinct of self-preservation..."

"Is not that enough? The instinct of self-preservation is the normal law of humanity..."

"Who told you that?" broke in Evgenie Pavlovitch.

"It is a law, doubtless, but a law neither more nor less normal than that of destruction, even self-destruction. Is it possible that the whole normal law of humanity is contained in this sentiment of self-preservation?"

"Ah!" cried Hippolyte, turning towards Evgenie Pavlovitch, and looking at him with a queer sort of curiosity.

Then seeing that Radomski was laughing, he began to laugh himself, nudged Colia, who was sitting beside him, with his elbow, and again asked what time it was. He even pulled Colia's silver watch out of his hand, and looked at it eagerly. Then, as if he had forgotten everything, he stretched himself out on the sofa, put his hands behind his head, and looked up at the sky. After a minute or two he got up and came back to the table to listen to Lebedeff's outpourings, as the latter passionately commentated on Evgenie Pavlovitch's paradox.

"That is an artful and traitorous idea. A smart notion," vociferated the clerk, "thrown out as an apple of discord. But it is just. You are a scoffer, a man of the world, a cavalry officer, and, though not without brains, you do not realize how profound is your thought, nor how true. Yes, the laws of self-preservation and of self-destruction are equally powerful in this world. The devil will hold his empire over humanity until a limit of time which is still unknown. You laugh? You do not believe in the devil? Scepticism as to the devil is a French idea, and it is also a frivolous idea. Do you know who the devil is? Do you know his name? Although you don't know his name you make a mockery of his form, following the example of Voltaire. You sneer at his hoofs, at his tail, at his horns—all of them the produce of your imagination! In reality the devil is a great and terrible spirit, with neither hoofs, nor tail, nor horns; it is you who have endowed him with these attributes! But... he is not the question just now!"

"How do you know he is not the question now?" cried Hippolyte, laughing hysterically.

"Another excellent idea, and worth considering!" replied Lebedeff. "But, again, that is not the question. The question at this moment is whether we have not weakened 'the springs of life' by the extension..."

"Of railways?" put in Colia eagerly.

"Not railways, properly speaking, presumptuous youth, but the general tendency of which railways may be considered as the outward expression and symbol. We hurry and push and hustle, for the good of humanity! 'The world is becoming too noisy, too commercial!' groans some solitary thinker. 'Undoubtedly it is, but the noise of waggons bearing bread to starving humanity is of more value than tranquillity of soul,' replies another triumphantly, and passes on with an air of pride. As for me, I don't believe in these waggons bringing bread to humanity. For, founded on no moral principle, these may well, even in the act of carrying bread to humanity, coldly exclude a considerable portion of humanity from enjoying it; that has been seen more than once."

"What, these waggons may coldly exclude?" repeated someone.

"That has been seen already," continued Lebedeff, not deigning to notice the interruption. "Malthus was a friend of humanity, but, with ill-founded moral principles, the friend of humanity is the devourer of humanity, without mentioning his pride; for, touch the vanity of one of these numberless philanthropists, and to avenge his self-esteem, he will be ready at once to set fire to the whole globe; and to tell the truth, we are all more or less like that. I, perhaps, might be the first to set a light to the fuel, and then run away. But, again, I must repeat, that is not the question."

"What is it then, for goodness' sake?"

"He is boring us!"

"The question is connected with the following anecdote of past times; for I am obliged to relate a story. In our times, and in our country, which I hope you love as much as I do, for as far as I am concerned, I am ready to shed the last drop of my blood..."

"Go on! Go on!"

"In our dear country, as indeed in the whole of Europe, a famine visits humanity about four times a century, as far as I can remember; once in every twenty-five years. I won't swear to this being the exact figure, but anyhow they have become comparatively rare."

"Comparatively to what?"

"To the twelfth century, and those immediately preceding and following it. We are told by historians that widespread famines occurred in those days every two or three years, and such was the condition of things that men actually had recourse to cannibalism, in secret, of course. One of these cannibals, who had reached a good age, declared of his own free will that during the course of his long and miserable life he had personally killed and eaten, in the most profound secrecy, sixty monks, not to mention several children; the number of the latter he thought was about six, an insignificant total when compared with the enormous mass of ecclesiastics consumed by him. As to adults, laymen that is to say, he had never touched them."

The president joined in the general outcry.

"That's impossible!" said he in an aggrieved tone. "I am often discussing subjects of this nature with him, gentlemen, but for the most part he talks nonsense enough to make one deaf: this story has no pretence of being true."

"General, remember the siege of Kars! And you, gentlemen, I assure you my anecdote is the naked truth. I may remark that reality, although it is governed by invariable law, has at times a resemblance to falsehood. In fact, the truer a thing is the less true it sounds."

"But could anyone possibly eat sixty monks?" objected the scoffing listeners.

"It is quite clear that he did not eat them all at once, but in a space of fifteen or twenty years: from that point of view the thing is comprehensible and natural..."

"Natural?"

"And natural," repeated Lebedeff with pedantic obstinacy. "Besides, a Catholic monk is by nature excessively curious; it would be quite easy therefore to entice him into a wood, or some secret place, on false pretences, and there to deal with him as said. But I do not dispute in the least that the number of persons consumed appears to denote a spice of greediness."

"It is perhaps true, gentlemen," said the prince, quietly. He had been listening in silence up to that moment without taking part in the conversation, but laughing heartily with the others from time to time. Evidently he was delighted to see that everybody was amused, that everybody was talking at once, and even that everybody was drinking. It seemed as if he were not intending to speak at all, when suddenly he intervened in such a serious voice that everyone looked at him with interest.

"It is true that there were frequent famines at that time, gentlemen. I have often heard of them, though I do not know much history. But it seems to me that it must have been so. When I was in Switzerland I used to look with astonishment at the many ruins of feudal castles perched on the top of steep and rocky heights, half a mile at least above sea-level, so that to reach them one had to climb many miles of stony tracks. A castle, as you know, is, a kind of mountain of stones—a dreadful, almost an impossible, labour! Doubtless the builders were all poor men, vassals, and had to pay heavy taxes, and to keep up the priesthood. How, then, could they provide for themselves, and when had they time to plough and sow their fields? The greater number must, literally, have died of starvation. I have sometimes asked myself how it was that these communities were not utterly swept off the face of the earth, and how they could possibly survive. Lebedeff is not mistaken, in my opinion, when he says that there were cannibals in those days, perhaps in considerable numbers; but I do not understand why he should have dragged in the monks, nor what he means by that."

"It is undoubtedly because, in the twelfth century, monks were the only people one could eat; they were the fat, among many lean," said Gavrila Ardalionovitch.

"A brilliant idea, and most true!" cried Lebedeff, "for he never even touched the laity. Sixty monks, and not a single layman! It is a terrible idea, but it is historic, it is statistic; it is indeed one of those facts which enables an intelligent historian to reconstruct the physiognomy of a special epoch, for it brings out this further point with mathematical accuracy, that the clergy were in those days sixty times richer and more flourishing than the rest of humanity and perhaps sixty times fatter also..."

"You are exaggerating, you are exaggerating, Lebedeff!" cried his hearers, amid laughter.

"I admit that it is an historic thought, but what is your conclusion?" asked the prince.

He spoke so seriously in addressing Lebedeff, that his tone contrasted quite comically with that of the others. They were very nearly laughing at him, too, but he did not notice it.

"Don't you see he is a lunatic, prince?" whispered Evgenie Pavlovitch in his ear. "Someone told me just now that he is a bit touched on the subject of lawyers, that he has a mania for making speeches and intends to pass the examinations. I am expecting a splendid burlesque now."

"My conclusion is vast," replied Lebedeff, in a voice like thunder. "Let us examine first the psychological and legal position of the criminal. We see that in spite of the difficulty of finding other food, the accused, or, as we may say, my client, has often during his peculiar life exhibited signs of repentance, and of wishing to give up this clerical diet. Incontrovertible facts prove this assertion. He has eaten five or six children, a relatively insignificant number, no doubt, but remarkable enough from another point of view. It is manifest that, pricked by remorse—for my client is religious, in his way, and has a conscience, as I shall prove later—and desiring to extenuate his sin as far as possible, he has tried six times at least to substitute lay nourishment for clerical. That this was merely an experiment we can hardly doubt: for if it had been only a question of gastronomic variety, six would have been too few; why only six? Why not thirty? But if we regard it as an experiment, inspired by the fear of committing new sacrilege, then this number six becomes intelligible. Six attempts to calm his remorse, and the pricking of his conscience, would amply suffice, for these attempts could scarcely have been happy ones. In my humble opinion, a child is too small; I should say, not sufficient; which would result in four or five times more lay children than monks being required in a given time. The sin, lessened on the one hand, would therefore be increased on the other, in quantity, not in quality. Please understand, gentlemen, that in reasoning thus, I am taking the point of view which might have been taken by a criminal of the middle ages. As for myself, a man of the late nineteenth century, I, of course, should reason differently; I say so plainly, and therefore you need not jeer at me nor mock me, gentlemen. As for you, general, it is still more unbecoming on your part. In the second place, and giving my own personal opinion, a child's flesh is not a satisfying diet; it is too insipid, too sweet; and the criminal, in making these experiments, could have satisfied neither his conscience nor his appetite. I am about to conclude, gentlemen; and my conclusion contains a reply to one of the most important questions of that day and of our own! This criminal ended at last by denouncing himself to the clergy, and giving himself up to justice. We cannot but ask, remembering the penal system of that day, and the tortures that awaited him—the wheel, the stake, the fire!—we cannot but ask, I repeat, what induced him to accuse himself of this crime? Why did he not simply stop short at the number sixty, and keep his secret until his last breath? Why could he not simply leave the monks alone, and go into the desert to repent? Or why not become a monk himself? That is where the puzzle comes in! There must have been something stronger than the stake or the fire, or even than the habits of twenty years! There must have been an idea more powerful than all the calamities and sorrows of this world, famine or torture, leprosy or plague—an idea which entered into the heart, directed and enlarged the springs of life, and made even that hell supportable to humanity! Show me a force, a power like that, in this our century of vices and railways! I might say, perhaps, in our century of steamboats and railways, but I repeat in our century of vices and railways, because I am drunk but truthful! Show me a single idea which unites men nowadays with half the strength that it had in those centuries, and dare to maintain that the 'springs of life' have not been polluted and weakened beneath this 'star,' beneath this network in which men are entangled! Don't talk to me about your prosperity, your riches, the rarity of famine, the rapidity of the means of transport! There is more of riches, but less of force. The idea uniting heart and soul to heart and soul exists no more. All is loose, soft, limp—we are all of us limp.... Enough, gentlemen! I have done. That is not the question. No, the question is now, excellency, I believe, to sit down to the banquet you are about to provide for us!"

Lebedeff had roused great indignation in some of his auditors (it should be remarked that the bottles were constantly uncorked during his speech); but this unexpected conclusion calmed even the most turbulent spirits. "That's how a clever barrister makes a good point!" said he, when speaking of his peroration later on. The visitors began to laugh and chatter once again; the committee left their seats, and stretched their legs on the terrace. Keller alone was still disgusted with Lebedeff and his speech; he turned from one to another, saying in a loud voice:

"He attacks education, he boasts of the fanaticism of the twelfth century, he makes absurd grimaces, and added to that he is by no means the innocent he makes himself out to be. How did he get the money to buy this house, allow me to ask?"

In another corner was the general, holding forth to a group of hearers, among them Ptitsin, whom he had buttonholed. "I have known," said he, "a real interpreter of the Apocalypse, the late Gregory Semeonovitch Burmistroff, and he—he pierced the heart like a fiery flash! He began by putting on his spectacles, then he opened a large black book; his white beard, and his two medals on his breast, recalling acts of charity, all added to his impressiveness. He began in a stern voice, and before him generals, hard men of the world, bowed down, and ladies fell to the ground fainting. But this one here—he ends by announcing a banquet! That is not the real thing!"

Ptitsin listened and smiled, then turned as if to get his hat; but if he had intended to leave, he changed his mind. Before the others had risen from the table, Gania had suddenly left off drinking, and pushed away his glass, a dark shadow seemed to come over his face. When they all rose, he went and sat down by Rogojin. It might have been believed that quite friendly relations existed between them. Rogojin, who had also seemed on the point of going away now sat motionless, his head bent, seeming to have forgotten his intention. He had drunk no wine, and appeared absorbed in reflection. From time to time he raised his eyes, and examined everyone present; one might have imagined that he was expecting something very important to himself, and that he had decided to wait for it. The prince had taken two or three glasses of champagne, and seemed cheerful. As he rose he noticed Evgenie Pavlovitch, and, remembering the appointment he had made with him, smiled pleasantly. Evgenie Pavlovitch made a sign with his head towards Hippolyte, whom he was attentively watching. The invalid was fast asleep, stretched out on the sofa.

"Tell me, prince, why on earth did this boy intrude himself upon you?" he asked, with such annoyance and irritation in his voice that the prince was quite surprised. "I wouldn't mind laying odds that he is up to some mischief."

"I have observed," said the prince, "that he seems to be an object of very singular interest to you, Evgenie Pavlovitch. Why is it?"

"You may add that I have surely enough to think of, on my own account, without him; and therefore it is all the more surprising that I cannot tear my eyes and thoughts away from his detestable physiognomy."

"Oh, come! He has a handsome face."

"Why, look at him—look at him now!"

The prince glanced again at Evgenie Pavlovitch with considerable surprise.

CHAPTER V.

Hippolyte, who had fallen asleep during Lebedeff's discourse, now suddenly woke up, just as though someone had jogged him in the side. He shuddered, raised himself on his arm, gazed around, and grew very pale. A look almost of terror crossed his face as he recollected.

"What! are they all off? Is it all over? Is the sun up?" He trembled, and caught at the prince's hand. "What time is it? Tell me, quick, for goodness' sake! How long have I slept?" he added, almost in despair, just as though he had overslept something upon which his whole fate depended.

"You have slept seven or perhaps eight minutes," said Evgenie Pavlovitch.

Hippolyte gazed eagerly at the latter, and mused for a few moments.

"Oh, is that all?" he said at last. "Then I—"

He drew a long, deep breath of relief, as it seemed. He realized that all was not over as yet, that the sun had not risen, and that the guests had merely gone to supper. He smiled, and two hectic spots appeared on his cheeks.

"So you counted the minutes while I slept, did you, Evgenie Pavlovitch?" he said, ironically. "You have not taken your eyes off me all the evening—I have noticed that much, you see! Ah, Rogojin! I've just been dreaming about him, prince," he added, frowning. "Yes, by the by," starting up, "where's the orator? Where's Lebedeff? Has he finished? What did he talk about? Is it true, prince, that you once declared that 'beauty would save the world'? Great Heaven! The prince says that beauty saves the world! And I declare that he only has such playful ideas because he's in love! Gentlemen, the prince is in love. I guessed it the moment he came in. Don't blush, prince; you make me sorry for you. What beauty saves the world? Colia told me that you are a zealous Christian; is it so? Colia says you call yourself a Christian."

The prince regarded him attentively, but said nothing.

"You don't answer me; perhaps you think I am very fond of you?" added Hippolyte, as though the words had been drawn from him.

"No, I don't think that. I know you don't love me."

"What, after yesterday? Wasn't I honest with you?"

"I knew yesterday that you didn't love me."

"Why so? why so? Because I envy you, eh? You always think that, I know. But do you know why I am saying all this? Look here! I must have some more champagne—pour me out some, Keller, will you?"

"No, you're not to drink any more, Hippolyte. I won't let you." The prince moved the glass away.

"Well perhaps you're right," said Hippolyte, musing. "They might say—yet, devil take them! what does it matter?—prince, what can it matter what people will say of us *then*, eh? I believe I'm half asleep. I've had such a dreadful dream—I've only just remembered it. Prince, I don't wish you such dreams as that, though sure enough, perhaps, I *don't* love you. Why wish a man evil, though you do not love him, eh? Give me your hand—let me press it sincerely. There—you've given me your hand—you must feel that I *do* press it sincerely, don't you? I don't think I shall drink any more. What time is it? Never mind, I know the time. The time has come, at all events. What! they are laying supper over there, are they? Then this table is free? Capital, gentlemen! I—hem! these gentlemen are not listening. Prince, I will just read over an article I have here. Supper is more interesting, of course, but—"

Here Hippolyte suddenly, and most unexpectedly, pulled out of his breast-pocket a large sealed paper. This imposing-looking document he placed upon the table before him.

The effect of this sudden action upon the company was instantaneous. Evgenie Pavlovitch almost bounded off his chair in excitement. Rogojin drew nearer to the table with a look on his face as if he knew what was coming. Gania came nearer too; so did Lebedeff and the others—the paper seemed to be an object of great interest to the company in general.

"What have you got there?" asked the prince, with some anxiety.

"At the first glimpse of the rising sun, prince, I will go to bed. I told you I would, word of honour! You shall see!" cried Hippolyte. "You think I'm not capable of opening this packet, do you?" He glared defiantly round at the audience in general.

The prince observed that he was trembling all over.

"None of us ever thought such a thing!" Muishkin replied for all. "Why should you suppose it of us? And what are you going to read, Hippolyte? What is it?"

"Yes, what is it?" asked others. The packet sealed with red wax seemed to attract everyone, as though it were a magnet.

"I wrote this yesterday, myself, just after I saw you, prince, and told you I would come down here. I wrote all day and all night, and finished it this morning early. Afterwards I had a dream."

"Hadn't we better hear it tomorrow?" asked the prince timidly.

"Tomorrow 'there will be no more time!'" laughed Hippolyte, hysterically. "You needn't be afraid; I shall get through the whole thing in forty minutes, at most an hour! Look how interested everybody is! Everybody has drawn near. Look! look at them all staring at my sealed packet! If I hadn't sealed it up it wouldn't have been half so effective! Ha, ha! that's mystery, that is! Now then, gentlemen, shall I break the seal or not? Say the word; it's a mystery, I tell you—a secret! Prince, you know who said there would be 'no more time'? It was the great and powerful angel in the Apocalypse."

"Better not read it now," said the prince, putting his hand on the packet.

"No, don't read it!" cried Evgenie suddenly. He appeared so strangely disturbed that many of those present could not help wondering.

"Reading? None of your reading now!" said somebody; "it's supper-time." "What sort of an article is it? For a paper? Probably it's very dull," said another. But the prince's timid gesture had impressed even Hippolyte.

"Then I'm not to read it?" he whispered, nervously. "Am I not to read it?" he repeated, gazing around at each face in turn. "What are you afraid of, prince?" he turned and asked the latter suddenly.

"What should I be afraid of?"

"Has anyone a coin about them? Give me a twenty-copeck piece, somebody!" And Hippolyte leapt from his chair.

"Here you are," said Lebedeff, handing him one; he thought the boy had gone mad.

"Vera Lukianovna," said Hippolyte, "toss it, will you? Heads, I read, tails, I don't."

Vera Lebedeff tossed the coin into the air and let it fall on the table.

It was "heads."

"Then I read it," said Hippolyte, in the tone of one bowing to the fiat of destiny. He could not have grown paler if a verdict of death had suddenly been presented to him.

"But after all, what is it? Is it possible that I should have just risked my fate by tossing up?" he went on, shuddering; and looked round him again. His eyes had a curious expression of sincerity. "That is an astonishing psychological fact," he cried, suddenly addressing the prince, in a tone of the most intense surprise. "It is... it is something quite inconceivable, prince," he repeated with growing animation, like a man regaining consciousness. "Take note of it, prince, remember it; you collect, I am told, facts concerning capital punishment... They told me so. Ha, ha! My God, how absurd!" He sat down on the sofa, put his elbows on the table, and laid his head on his hands. "It is shameful—though what does it matter to me if it is shameful?

"Gentlemen, gentlemen! I am about to break the seal," he continued, with determination. "I—I—of course I don't insist upon anyone listening if they do not wish to."

With trembling fingers he broke the seal and drew out several sheets of paper, smoothed them out before him, and began sorting them.

"What on earth does all this mean? What's he going to read?" muttered several voices. Others said nothing; but one and all sat down and watched with curiosity. They began to think something strange might really be about to happen. Vera stood and trembled behind her father's chair, almost in tears with fright; Colia was nearly as much alarmed as she was. Lebedeff jumped up and put a couple of candles nearer to Hippolyte, so that he might see better.

"Gentlemen, this—you'll soon see what this is," began Hippolyte, and suddenly commenced his reading.

"It's headed, 'A Necessary Explanation,' with the motto, '*Après moi le déluge!*' Oh, deuce take it all! Surely I can never have seriously written such a silly motto as that? Look here, gentlemen, I beg to give notice that all this is very likely terrible nonsense. It is only a few ideas of mine. If you think that there is anything mysterious coming—or in a word—"

"Better read on without any more beating about the bush," said Gania.

"Affectation!" remarked someone else.

"Too much talk," said Rogojin, breaking the silence for the first time.

Hippolyte glanced at him suddenly, and when their eyes met Rogojin showed his teeth in a disagreeable smile, and said the following strange words: "That's not the way to settle this business, my friend; that's not the way at all."

Of course nobody knew what Rogojin meant by this; but his words made a deep impression upon all. Everyone seemed to see in a flash the same idea.

As for Hippolyte, their effect upon him was astounding. He trembled so that the prince was obliged to support him, and would certainly have cried out, but that his voice seemed to have entirely left him for the moment. For a minute or two he could not speak at all, but panted and stared at Rogojin. At last he managed to ejaculate:

"Then it was *you* who came—*you—you?*"

"Came where? What do you mean?" asked Rogojin, amazed. But Hippolyte, panting and choking with excitement, interrupted him violently.

"*You* came to me last week, in the night, at two o'clock, the day I was with you in the morning! Confess it was you!"

"Last week? In the night? Have you gone cracked, my good friend?"

Hippolyte paused and considered a moment. Then a smile of cunning—almost triumph—crossed his lips.

"It was you," he murmured, almost in a whisper, but with absolute conviction. "Yes, it was you who came to my room and sat silently on a chair at my window for a whole hour—more! It was between one and two at night; you rose and went out at about three. It was you, you! Why you should have frightened me so, why you should have wished to torment me like that, I cannot tell—but you it was."

There was absolute hatred in his eyes as he said this, but his look of fear and his trembling had not left him.

"You shall hear all this directly, gentlemen. I—I—listen!"

He seized his paper in a desperate hurry; he fidgeted with it, and tried to sort it, but for a long while his trembling hands could not collect the sheets together. "He's either mad or delirious," murmured Rogojin. At last he began.

For the first five minutes the reader's voice continued to tremble, and he read disconnectedly and unevenly; but gradually his voice strengthened. Occasionally a violent fit of coughing stopped him, but his animation grew with the progress of the reading—as did also the disagreeable impression which it made upon his audience,—until it reached the highest pitch of excitement.

Here is the article.

MY NECESSARY EXPLANATION.

"Après moi le déluge.

"Yesterday morning the prince came to see me. Among other things he asked me to come down to his villa. I knew he would come and persuade me to this step, and that he would adduce the argument that it would be easier for me to die 'among people and green trees,'—as he expressed it. But today he did not say 'die,' he said 'live.' It is pretty much the same to me, in my position, which he says. When I asked him why he made such a point of his 'green trees,' he told me, to my astonishment, that he had heard that last time I was in Pavlofsk I had said that I had come 'to have a last look at the trees.'

"When I observed that it was all the same whether one died among trees or in front of a blank brick wall, as here, and that it was not worth making any fuss over a fortnight, he agreed at once. But he insisted that the good air at Pavlofsk and the greenness would certainly cause a physical change for the better, and that my excitement, and my *dreams*, would be perhaps relieved. I remarked to him, with a smile, that he spoke like a materialist, and he answered that he had always been one. As he never tells a lie, there must be something in his words. His smile is a pleasant one. I have had a good look at him. I don't know whether I like him or not; and I have no time to waste over the question. The hatred which I felt for him for five months has become considerably modified, I may say, during the last month. Who knows, perhaps I am going to Pavlofsk on purpose to see him! But why do I leave my chamber? Those who are sentenced to death should not leave their cells. If I had not formed a final resolve, but had decided to wait until the last minute, I should not leave my room, or accept his invitation to come and die at Pavlofsk. I must be quick and finish this explanation before tomorrow. I shall have no time to read it over and correct it, for I must read it tomorrow to the prince and two or three witnesses whom I shall probably find there.

"As it will be absolutely true, without a touch of falsehood, I am curious to see what impression it will make upon me myself at the moment when I read it out. This is my 'last and solemn'—but why need I call it that? There is no question about the truth of it, for it is not worthwhile lying for a fortnight; a fortnight of life is not itself worth having, which is a proof that I write nothing here but pure truth.

("N.B.—Let me remember to consider; am I mad at this moment, or not? or rather at these moments? I have been told that consumptives sometimes do go out of their minds for a while in the last stages of the malady. I can prove this tomorrow when I read it out, by the impression it makes upon the audience. I must settle this question once and for all, otherwise I can't go on with anything.)

"I believe I have just written dreadful nonsense; but there's no time for correcting, as I said before. Besides that, I have made myself a promise not to alter a single word of what I write in this paper, even though I find that I am contradicting myself every five lines. I wish to verify the working of the natural logic of my ideas tomorrow during the reading—whether I am capable of detecting logical errors, and whether all that I have meditated over during the last six months be true, or nothing but delirium.

"If two months since I had been called upon to leave my room and the view of Meyer's wall opposite, I verily believe I should have been sorry. But now I have no such feeling, and yet I am leaving this room and Meyer's brick wall *for ever*. So that my conclusion, that it is not worth while indulging in grief, or any other emotion, for a fortnight, has proved stronger than my very nature, and has taken over the direction of my feelings. But is it so? Is it the case that my nature is conquered entirely? If I were to be put on the rack now, I should certainly cry out. I should not say that it is not worth while to yell and feel pain because I have but a fortnight to live.

"But is it true that I have but a fortnight of life left to me? I know I told some of my friends that Doctor B. had informed me that this was the case; but I now confess that I lied; B. has not even seen me. However, a week ago, I called in a medical student, Kislorodoff, who is a Nationalist, an Atheist, and a Nihilist, by conviction, and that is why I had him. I needed a man who would tell me the bare truth without any humbug or ceremony—and so he did—indeed, almost with pleasure (which I thought was going a little too far).

"Well, he plumped out that I had about a month left me; it might be a little more, he said, under favourable circumstances, but it might also be considerably less. According to his opinion I might die quite suddenly—tomorrow, for instance—there had been such cases. Only a day or two since a young lady at Colomna who suffered from consumption, and was about on a par with myself in the march of the disease, was going out to market to buy provisions, when she suddenly felt faint, lay down on the sofa, gasped once, and died.

"Kislorodoff told me all this with a sort of exaggerated devil-may-care negligence, and as though he did me great honour by talking to me so, because it showed that he considered me the same sort of exalted Nihilistic being as himself, to whom death was a matter of no consequence whatever, either way.

"At all events, the fact remained—a month of life and no more! That he is right in his estimation I am absolutely persuaded.

"It puzzles me much to think how on earth the prince guessed yesterday that I have had bad dreams. He said to me, 'Your excitement and dreams will find relief at Pavlofsk.' Why did he say 'dreams'? Either he is a doctor, or else he is a man of exceptional intelligence and wonderful powers of observation. (But that he is an 'idiot,' at bottom there can be no doubt whatever.) It so happened that just before he arrived I had a delightful little dream; one of a kind that I have hundreds of just now. I had fallen asleep about an hour before he came in, and dreamed that I was in some room, not my own. It was a large room, well furnished, with a cupboard, chest of drawers, sofa, and my bed, a fine wide bed covered with a silken counterpane. But I observed in the room a dreadful-looking creature, a sort of monster. It was a little like a scorpion, but was not a scorpion, but far more horrible, and especially so, because there are no creatures anything like it in nature, and because it had appeared to me for a purpose, and bore some mysterious signification. I looked at the beast well; it was brown in colour and had a shell; it was a crawling kind of reptile, about eight inches long, and narrowed down from the head, which was about a couple of fingers in width, to the end of the tail, which came to a fine point. Out of its trunk, about a couple of inches below its head, came two legs at an angle of forty-five degrees, each about three inches long, so that the beast looked like a trident from above. It had eight hard needle-like whiskers coming out from different parts of its body; it went along like a snake, bending its body about in spite of the shell it wore, and its motion was very quick and very horrible to look at. I was dreadfully afraid it would sting me; somebody had told me, I thought, that it was venomous; but what tormented me most of all was the wondering and wondering as to who had sent it into my room, and what was the mystery which I felt it contained.

"It hid itself under the cupboard and under the chest of drawers, and crawled into the corners. I sat on a chair and kept my legs tucked under me. Then the beast crawled quietly across the room and disappeared somewhere near my chair. I looked about for it in terror, but I still hoped that as my feet were safely tucked away it would not be able to touch me.

"Suddenly I heard behind me, and about on a level with my head, a sort of rattling sound. I turned sharp round and saw that the brute had crawled up the wall as high as the level of my face, and that its horrible tail, which was moving incredibly fast from side to side, was actually touching my hair! I jumped up—and it disappeared. I did not dare lie down on my bed for fear it should creep under my pillow. My mother came into the room, and some friends of hers. They began to hunt for the reptile and were more composed than I was; they did not seem to be afraid of it. But they did not understand as I did.

"Suddenly the monster reappeared; it crawled slowly across the room and made for the door, as though with some fixed intention, and with a slow movement that was more horrible than ever.

"Then my mother opened the door and called my dog, Norma. Norma was a great Newfoundland, and died five years ago.

"She sprang forward and stood still in front of the reptile as if she had been turned to stone. The beast stopped too, but its tail and claws still moved about. I believe animals are incapable of feeling supernatural fright—if I have been rightly informed,—but at this moment there appeared to me to be something more than ordinary about Norma's terror, as though it must be supernatural; and as though she felt, just as I did myself, that this reptile was connected with some mysterious secret, some fatal omen.

"Norma backed slowly and carefully away from the brute, which followed her, creeping deliberately after her as though it intended to make a sudden dart and sting her.

"In spite of Norma's terror she looked furious, though she trembled in all her limbs. At length she slowly bared her terrible teeth, opened her great red jaws, hesitated—took courage, and seized the beast in her mouth. It seemed to try to dart out of her jaws twice, but Norma caught at it and half swallowed it as it was escaping. The shell cracked in her teeth; and the tail and legs stuck out of her mouth and shook about in a horrible manner. Suddenly Norma gave a piteous whine; the reptile had bitten her tongue. She opened her mouth wide with the pain, and I saw the beast lying across her tongue, and out of its body, which was almost bitten in two, came a hideous white-looking substance, oozing out into Norma's mouth; it was of the consistency of a crushed black-beetle. Just then I awoke and the prince entered the room."

"Gentlemen!" said Hippolyte, breaking off here, "I have not done yet, but it seems to me that I have written down a great deal here that is unnecessary,—this dream—"

"You have indeed!" said Gania.

"There is too much about myself, I know, but—" As Hippolyte said this his face wore a tired, pained look, and he wiped the sweat off his brow.

"Yes," said Lebedeff, "you certainly think a great deal too much about yourself."

"Well—gentlemen—I do not force anyone to listen! If any of you are unwilling to sit it out, please go away, by all means!"

"He turns people out of a house that isn't his own," muttered Rogojin.

"Suppose we all go away?" said Ferdishenko suddenly.

Hippolyte clutched his manuscript, and gazing at the last speaker with glittering eyes, said: "You don't like me at all!" A few laughed at this, but not all.

"Hippolyte," said the prince, "give me the papers, and go to bed like a sensible fellow. We'll have a good talk tomorrow, but you really mustn't go on with this reading; it is not good for you!"

"How can I? How can I?" cried Hippolyte, looking at him in amazement. "Gentlemen! I was a fool! I won't break off again. Listen, everyone who wants to!"

He gulped down some water out of a glass standing near, bent over the table, in order to hide his face from the audience, and recommenced.

"The idea that it is not worth while living for a few weeks took possession of me a month ago, when I was told that I had four weeks to live, but only partially so at that time. The idea quite overmastered me three days since, that evening at Pavlofsk. The first time that I felt really impressed with this thought was on the terrace at the prince's, at the very moment when I had taken it into my head to make a last trial of life. I wanted to see people and trees (I believe I said so myself), I got excited, I maintained Burdovsky's rights, 'my neighbour!'—I dreamt that one and all would open their arms, and embrace me, that there would be an indescribable exchange of forgiveness between us all! In a word, I behaved like a fool, and then, at that very same instant, I felt my 'last conviction.' I ask myself now how I could have waited six months for that conviction! I knew that I had a disease that spares no one, and I really had no illusions; but the more I realized my condition, the more I clung to life; I wanted to live at any price. I confess I might well have resented that blind, deaf fate, which, with no apparent reason, seemed to have decided to crush me like a fly; but why did I not stop at resentment? Why did I begin to live, knowing that it was not worthwhile to begin? Why did I attempt to do what I knew to be an impossibility? And yet I could not even read a book to the end; I had given up reading. What is the good of reading, what is the good of learning anything, for just six months? That thought has made me throw aside a book more than once.

"Yes, that wall of Meyer's could tell a tale if it liked. There was no spot on its dirty surface that I did not know by heart. Accursed wall! and yet it is dearer to me than all the Pavlofsk trees!—That is—it *would* be dearer if it were not all the same to me, now!

"I remember now with what hungry interest I began to watch the lives of other people—interest that I had never felt before! I used to wait for Colia's arrival impatiently, for I was so ill myself, then, that I could not leave the house. I so threw myself into every little detail of news, and took so much interest in every report and rumour, that I believe I became a regular gossip! I could not understand, among other things, how all these people—with so much life in and before them—do not become *rich*—and I don't understand it now. I remember being told of a poor wretch I once knew, who had died of hunger. I was almost beside myself with rage! I believe if I could have resuscitated him I would have done so for the sole purpose of murdering him!

"Occasionally I was so much better that I could go out; but the streets used to put me in such a rage that I would lock myself up for days rather than go out, even if I were well enough to do so! I could not bear to see all those preoccupied, anxious-looking creatures continuously surging along the streets past me! Why are they always anxious? What is the meaning of their eternal care and worry? It is their wickedness, their perpetual detestable malice—that's what it is—they are all full of malice, malice!

"Whose fault is it that they are all miserable, that they don't know how to live, though they have fifty or sixty years of life before them? Why did that fool allow himself to die of hunger with sixty years of unlived life before him?

"And everyone of them shows his rags, his toil-worn hands, and yells in his wrath: 'Here are we, working like cattle all our lives, and always as hungry as dogs, and there are others who do not work, and are fat and rich!' The eternal refrain! And side by side with them trots along some wretched fellow who has known better days, doing light porter's work from morn to night for a living, always blubbering and saying that 'his wife died because he had no money to buy medicine with,' and his children dying of cold and hunger, and his eldest daughter gone to the bad, and so on. Oh! I have no pity and no patience for these fools of people. Why can't they be Rothschilds? Whose fault is it that a man has not got millions of money like Rothschild? If he has life, all this must be in his power! Whose fault is it that he does not know how to live his life?

"Oh! it's all the same to me now—*now!* But at that time I would soak my pillow at night with tears of mortification, and tear at my blanket in my rage and fury. Oh, how I longed at that time to be turned out—*me*, eighteen years old, poor, half-clothed, turned out into the street, quite alone, without lodging, without work, without a crust of bread, without relations, without a single acquaintance, in some large town—hungry, beaten (if you like), but in good health—and *then* I would show them—

"What would I show them?

"Oh, don't think that I have no sense of my own humiliation! I have suffered already in reading so far. Which of you all does not think me a fool at this moment—a young fool who knows nothing of life—forgetting that to live as I have lived these last six months is to live longer than grey-haired old men. Well, let them laugh, and say it is all nonsense, if they please. They may say it is all fairy-tales, if they like; and I have spent whole nights telling myself fairy-tales. I remember them all. But how can I tell fairy-tales now? The time for them is over. They amused me when I found that there was not even time for me to learn the Greek grammar, as I wanted to do. 'I shall die before I get to the syntax,' I thought at the first page—and threw the book under the table. It is there still, for I forbade anyone to pick it up.

"If this 'Explanation' gets into anybody's hands, and they have patience to read it through, they may consider me a madman, or a schoolboy, or, more likely, a man condemned to die, who thought it only natural to conclude that all men, excepting himself, esteem life far too lightly, live it far too carelessly and lazily, and are, therefore, one and all, unworthy of it. Well, I affirm that my reader is wrong again, for my convictions have nothing to do with my sentence of death. Ask them, ask any one of them, or all of them, what they mean by happiness! Oh, you may be perfectly sure that if Columbus was happy, it was not after he had discovered America, but when he was discovering it! You may be quite sure that he reached the culminating point of his happiness three days before he saw the New World with his actual eyes, when his mutinous sailors wanted to tack about, and return to Europe! What did the New World matter after all? Columbus had hardly seen it when he died, and in reality he was entirely ignorant of what he had discovered. The important thing is life—life and nothing else! What is any 'discovery' whatever compared with the incessant, eternal discovery of life?

"But what is the use of talking? I'm afraid all this is so commonplace that my confession will be taken for a schoolboy exercise—the work of some ambitious lad writing in the hope of his work 'seeing the light'; or perhaps my readers will say that 'I had perhaps something to say, but did not know how to express it.'

"Let me add to this that in every idea emanating from genius, or even in every serious human idea—born in the human brain—there always remains something—some sediment—which cannot be expressed to others, though one wrote volumes and lectured upon it for five-and-thirty years. There is always a something, a remnant, which will never come out from your brain, but will remain there with you, and you alone, for ever and ever, and you will die, perhaps, without having imparted what may be the very essence of your idea to a single living soul.

"So that if I cannot now impart all that has tormented me for the last six months, at all events you will understand that, having reached my 'last convictions,' I must have paid a very dear price for them. That is what I wished, for reasons of my own, to make a point of in this my 'Explanation.'

"But let me resume."

CHAPTER VI.

"I will not deceive you. 'Reality' got me so entrapped in its meshes now and again during the past six months, that I forgot my 'sentence' (or perhaps I did not wish to think of it), and actually busied myself with affairs.

"A word as to my circumstances. When, eight months since, I became very ill, I threw up all my old connections and dropped all my old companions. As I was always a gloomy, morose sort of individual, my friends easily forgot me; of course, they would have forgotten me all the same, without that excuse. My position at home was solitary enough. Five months ago I separated myself entirely from the family, and no one dared enter my room except at stated times, to clean and tidy it, and so on, and to bring me my meals. My mother dared not disobey me; she kept the children quiet, for my sake, and beat them if they dared to make any noise and disturb me. I so often complained of them that I should think they must be very fond, indeed, of me by this time. I think I must have tormented 'my faithful Colia' (as I called him) a good deal too. He tormented me of late; I could see that he always bore my tempers as though he had determined to 'spare the poor invalid.' This annoyed me, naturally. He seemed to have taken it into his head to imitate the prince in Christian meekness! Surikoff, who lived above us, annoyed me, too. He was so miserably poor, and I used to prove to him that he had no one to blame but himself for his poverty. I used to be so angry that I think I frightened him eventually, for he stopped coming to see me. He was a most meek and humble fellow, was Surikoff. (N.B.—They say that meekness is a great power. I must ask the prince about this, for the expression is his.) But I remember one day in March, when I went up to his lodgings to see whether it was true that one of his children had been starved and frozen to death, I began to hold forth to him about his poverty being his own fault, and, in the course of my remarks, I accidentally smiled at the corpse of his child. Well, the poor wretch's lips began to tremble, and he caught me by the shoulder, and pushed me to the door. 'Go out,' he said, in a whisper. I went out, of course, and I declare I *liked* it. I liked it at the very moment when I was turned out. But his words filled me with a strange sort of feeling of disdainful pity for him whenever I thought of them—a feeling which I did not in the least desire to entertain. At the very moment of the insult (for I admit that I did insult him, though I did not mean to), this man could not lose his temper. His lips had trembled, but I swear it was not with rage. He had taken me by the arm, and said, 'Go out,' without the least anger. There was dignity, a great deal of dignity, about him, and it was so inconsistent with the look of him that, I assure you, it was quite comical. But there was no anger. Perhaps he merely began to despise me at that moment.

"Since that time he has always taken off his hat to me on the stairs, whenever I met him, which is a thing he never did before; but he always gets away from me as quickly as he can, as though he felt confused. If he did despise me, he despised me 'meekly,' after his own fashion.

"I dare say he only took his hat off out of fear, as it were, to the son of his creditor; for he always owed my mother money. I thought of having an explanation with him, but I knew that if I did, he would begin to apologize in a minute or two, so I decided to let him alone.

"Just about that time, that is, the middle of March, I suddenly felt very much better; this continued for a couple of weeks. I used to go out at dusk. I like the dusk, especially in March, when the night frost begins to harden the day's puddles, and the gas is burning.

"Well, one night in the Shestilavochnaya, a man passed me with a paper parcel under his arm. I did not take stock of him very carefully, but he seemed to be dressed in some shabby summer dust-coat, much too light for the season. When he was opposite the lamp-post, some ten yards away, I observed something fall out of his pocket. I hurried forward to pick it up, just in time, for an old wretch in a long kaftan rushed up too. He did not dispute the matter, but glanced at what was in my hand and disappeared.

"It was a large old-fashioned pocket-book, stuffed full; but I guessed, at a glance, that it had anything in the world inside it, except money.

"The owner was now some forty yards ahead of me, and was very soon lost in the crowd. I ran after him, and began calling out; but as I knew nothing to say excepting 'hey!' he did not turn round. Suddenly he turned into the gate of a house to the left; and when I darted in after him, the gateway was so dark that I could see nothing whatever. It was one of those large houses built in small tenements, of which there must have been at least a hundred.

"When I entered the yard I thought I saw a man going along on the far side of it; but it was so dark I could not make out his figure.

"I crossed to that corner and found a dirty dark staircase. I heard a man mounting up above me, some way higher than I was, and thinking I should catch him before his door would be opened to him, I rushed after him. I heard a door open and shut on the fifth storey, as I panted along; the stairs were narrow, and the steps innumerable, but at last I reached the door I thought the right one. Some moments passed before I found the bell and got it to ring.

"An old peasant woman opened the door; she was busy lighting the 'samovar' in a tiny kitchen. She listened silently to my questions, did not understand a word, of course, and opened another door leading into a little bit of a room, low and scarcely furnished at all, but with a large, wide bed in it, hung with curtains. On this bed lay one Terentich, as the woman called him, drunk, it appeared to me. On the table was an end of candle in an iron candlestick, and a half-bottle of vodka, nearly finished. Terentich muttered something to me, and signed towards the next room. The old woman had disappeared, so there was nothing for me to do but to open the door indicated. I did so, and entered the next room.

"This was still smaller than the other, so cramped that I could scarcely turn round; a narrow single bed at one side took up nearly all the room. Besides the bed there were only three common chairs, and a wretched old kitchen-table standing before a small sofa. One could hardly squeeze through between the table and the bed.

"On the table, as in the other room, burned a tallow candle-end in an iron candlestick; and on the bed there whined a baby of scarcely three weeks old. A pale-looking woman was dressing the child, probably the mother; she looked as though she had not as yet got over the trouble of childbirth, she seemed so weak and was so carelessly dressed. Another child, a little girl of about three years old, lay on the sofa, covered over with what looked like a man's old dress-coat.

"At the table stood a man in his shirt sleeves; he had thrown off his coat; it lay upon the bed; and he was unfolding a blue paper parcel in which were a couple of pounds of bread, and some little sausages.

"On the table along with these things were a few old bits of black bread, and some tea in a pot. From under the bed there protruded an open portmanteau full of bundles of rags. In a word, the confusion and untidiness of the room were indescribable.

"It appeared to me, at the first glance, that both the man and the woman were respectable people, but brought to that pitch of poverty where untidiness seems to get the better of every effort to cope with it, till at last they take a sort of bitter satisfaction in it. When I entered the room, the man, who had entered but a moment before me, and was still unpacking his parcels, was saying something to his wife in an excited manner. The news was apparently bad, as usual, for the woman began whimpering. The man's face seemed to me to be refined and even pleasant. He was dark-complexioned, and about twenty-eight years of age; he wore black whiskers, and his lip and chin were shaved. He looked morose, but with a sort of pride of expression. A curious scene followed.

"There are people who find satisfaction in their own touchy feelings, especially when they have just taken the deepest offence; at such moments they feel that they would rather be offended than not. These easily-ignited natures, if they are wise, are always full of remorse afterwards, when they reflect that they have been ten times as angry as they need have been.

"The gentleman before me gazed at me for some seconds in amazement, and his wife in terror; as though there was something alarmingly extraordinary in the fact that anyone could come to see them. But suddenly he fell upon me almost with fury; I had had no time to mutter more than a couple of words; but he had doubtless observed that I was decently dressed and, therefore, took deep offence because I had dared enter his den so unceremoniously, and spy out the squalor and untidiness of it.

"Of course he was delighted to get hold of someone upon whom to vent his rage against things in general.

"For a moment I thought he would assault me; he grew so pale that he looked like a woman about to have hysterics; his wife was dreadfully alarmed.

"'How dare you come in so? Be off!' he shouted, trembling all over with rage and scarcely able to articulate the words. Suddenly, however, he observed his pocketbook in my hand.

"'I think you dropped this,' I remarked, as quietly and drily as I could. (I thought it best to treat him so.) For some while he stood before me in downright terror, and seemed unable to understand. He then suddenly grabbed at his side-pocket, opened his mouth in alarm, and beat his forehead with his hand.

"'My God!' he cried, 'where did you find it? How?' I explained in as few words as I could, and as drily as possible, how I had seen it and picked it up; how I had run after him, and called out to him, and how I had followed him upstairs and groped my way to his door.

"'Gracious Heaven!' he cried, 'all our papers are in it! My dear sir, you little know what you have done for us. I should have been lost—lost!'

"I had taken hold of the door-handle meanwhile, intending to leave the room without reply; but I was panting with my run upstairs, and my exhaustion came to a climax in a violent fit of coughing, so bad that I could hardly stand.

"I saw how the man dashed about the room to find me an empty chair, how he kicked the rags off a chair which was covered up by them, brought it to me, and helped me to sit down; but my cough went on for another three minutes or so. When I came to myself he was sitting by me on another chair, which he had also cleared of the rubbish by throwing it all over the floor, and was watching me intently.

"'I'm afraid you are ill?' he remarked, in the tone which doctors use when they address a patient. 'I am myself a medical man' (he did not say 'doctor'), with which words he waved his hands towards the room and its contents as though in protest at his present condition. 'I see that you—'

"'I'm in consumption,' I said laconically, rising from my seat.

"He jumped up, too.

"'Perhaps you are exaggerating—if you were to take proper measures perhaps—'

"He was terribly confused and did not seem able to collect his scattered senses; the pocket-book was still in his left hand.

"'Oh, don't mind me,' I said. 'Dr. B—— saw me last week' (I lugged him in again), 'and my hash is quite settled; pardon me—' I took hold of the door-handle again. I was on the point of opening the door and leaving my grateful but confused medical friend to himself and his shame, when my damnable cough got hold of me again.

"My doctor insisted on my sitting down again to get my breath. He now said something to his wife who, without leaving her place, addressed a few words of gratitude and courtesy to me. She seemed very shy over it, and her sickly face flushed up with confusion. I remained, but with the air of a man who knows he is intruding and is anxious to get away. The doctor's remorse at last seemed to need a vent, I could see.

"'If I—' he began, breaking off abruptly every other moment, and starting another sentence. 'I—I am so very grateful to you, and I am so much to blame in your eyes, I feel sure, I—you see—' (he pointed to the room again) 'at this moment I am in such a position—'

"'Oh!' I said, 'there's nothing to see; it's quite a clear case—you've lost your post and have come up to make explanations and get another, if you can!'

"'How do you know that?' he asked in amazement.

"'Oh, it was evident at the first glance,' I said ironically, but not intentionally so. 'There are lots of people who come up from the provinces full of hope, and run about town, and have to live as best they can.'

"He began to talk at once excitedly and with trembling lips; he began complaining and telling me his story. He interested me, I confess; I sat there nearly an hour. His story was a very ordinary one. He had been a provincial doctor; he had a civil appointment, and had no sooner taken it up than intrigues began. Even his wife was dragged into these. He was proud, and flew into a passion; there was a change of local government which acted in favour of his opponents; his position was undermined, complaints were made against him; he lost his post and came up to Petersburg with his last remaining money, in order to appeal to higher authorities. Of course nobody would listen to him for a long time; he would come and tell his story one day and be refused promptly; another day he would be fed on false promises; again he would be treated harshly; then he would be told to sign some documents; then he would sign the paper and hand it in, and they would refuse to receive it, and tell him to file a formal petition. In a word he had been driven about from office to office for five months and had spent every farthing he had; his wife's last rags had just been pawned; and meanwhile a child had been born to them and—and today I have a final refusal to my petition, and I have hardly a crumb of bread left—I have nothing left; my wife has had a baby lately—and I—I—'

"He sprang up from his chair and turned away. His wife was crying in the corner; the child had begun to moan again. I pulled out my note-book and began writing in it. When I had finished and rose from my chair he was standing before me with an expression of alarmed curiosity.

"'I have jotted down your name,' I told him, 'and all the rest of it—the place you served at, the district, the date, and all. I have a friend, Bachmatoff, whose uncle is a councillor of state and has to do with these matters, one Peter Matveyevitch Bachmatoff.'

"'Peter Matveyevitch Bachmatoff!' he cried, trembling all over with excitement. 'Why, nearly everything depends on that very man!'

"It is very curious, this story of the medical man, and my visit, and the happy termination to which I contributed by accident! Everything fitted in, as in a novel. I told the poor people not to put much hope in me, because I was but a poor schoolboy myself—(I am not really, but I humiliated myself as much as possible in order to make them less hopeful)—but that I would go at once to the Vassili Ostroff and see my friend; and that as I knew for certain that his uncle adored him, and was absolutely devoted to him as the last hope and branch of the family, perhaps the old man might do something to oblige his nephew.

"'If only they would allow me to explain all to his excellency! If I could but be permitted to tell my tale to him!' he cried, trembling with feverish agitation, and his eyes flashing with excitement. I repeated once more that I could not hold out much hope—that it would probably end in smoke, and if I did not turn up next morning they must make up their minds that there was no more to be done in the matter.

"They showed me out with bows and every kind of respect; they seemed quite beside themselves. I shall never forget the expression of their faces!

"I took a droshky and drove over to the Vassili Ostroff at once. For some years I had been at enmity with this young Bachmatoff, at school. We considered him an aristocrat; at all events I called him one. He used to dress smartly, and always drove to school in a private trap. He was a good companion, and was always merry and jolly, sometimes even witty, though he was not very intellectual, in spite of the fact that he was always top of the class; I myself was never top in anything! All his companions were very fond of him, excepting myself. He had several times during those years come up to me and tried to make friends; but I had always turned sulkily away and refused to have anything to do with him. I had not seen him for a whole year now; he was at the university. When, at nine o'clock, or so, this evening, I arrived and was shown up to him with great ceremony, he first received me with astonishment, and not too affably, but he soon cheered up, and suddenly gazed intently at me and burst out laughing.

"'Why, what on earth can have possessed you to come and see *me*, Terentieff?' he cried, with his usual pleasant, sometimes audacious, but never offensive familiarity, which I liked in reality, but for which I also detested him. 'Why what's the matter?' he cried in alarm. 'Are you ill?'

"That confounded cough of mine had come on again; I fell into a chair, and with difficulty recovered my breath. 'It's all right, it's only consumption' I said. 'I have come to you with a petition!'

"He sat down in amazement, and I lost no time in telling him the medical man's history; and explained that he, with the influence which he possessed over his uncle, might do some good to the poor fellow.

"'I'll do it—I'll do it, of course!' he said. 'I shall attack my uncle about it tomorrow morning, and I'm very glad you told me the story. But how was it that you thought of coming to me about it, Terentieff?'

"'So much depends upon your uncle,' I said. 'And besides we have always been enemies, Bachmatoff; and as you are a generous sort of fellow, I thought you would not refuse my request because I was your enemy!' I added with irony.

"'Like Napoleon going to England, eh?' cried he, laughing. 'I'll do it though—of course, and at once, if I can!' he added, seeing that I rose seriously from my chair at this point.

"And sure enough the matter ended as satisfactorily as possible. A month or so later my medical friend was appointed to another post. He got his travelling expenses paid, and something to help him to start life with once more. I think Bachmatoff must have persuaded the doctor to accept a loan from himself. I saw Bachmatoff two or three times, about this period, the third time being when he gave a farewell dinner to the doctor and his wife before their departure, a champagne dinner.

"Bachmatoff saw me home after the dinner and we crossed the Nicolai bridge. We were both a little drunk. He told me of his joy, the joyful feeling of having done a good action; he said that it was all thanks to myself that he could feel this satisfaction; and held forth about the foolishness of the theory that individual charity is useless.

"I, too, was burning to have my say!

"'In Moscow,' I said, 'there was an old state counsellor, a civil general, who, all his life, had been in the habit of visiting the prisons and speaking to criminals. Every party of convicts on its way to Siberia knew beforehand that on the Vorobeef Hills the "old general" would pay them a visit. He did all he undertook seriously and devotedly. He would walk down the rows of the unfortunate prisoners, stop before each individual and ask after his needs—he never sermonized them; he spoke kindly to them—he gave them money; he brought them all sorts of necessaries for the journey, and gave them devotional books, choosing those who could read, under the firm conviction that they would read to those who could not, as they went along.

"'He scarcely ever talked about the particular crimes of any of them, but listened if any volunteered information on that point. All the convicts were equal for him, and he made no distinction. He spoke to all as to brothers, and every one of them looked upon him as a father. When he observed among the exiles some poor woman with a child, he would always come forward and fondle the little one, and make it laugh. He continued these acts of mercy up to his very death; and by that time all the criminals, all over Russia and Siberia, knew him!

"'A man I knew who had been to Siberia and returned, told me that he himself had been a witness of how the very most hardened criminals remembered the old general, though, in point of fact, he could never, of course, have distributed more than a few pence to each member of a party. Their recollection of him was not sentimental or particularly devoted. Some wretch, for instance, who had been a murderer—cutting the throat of a dozen fellow-creatures, for instance; or stabbing six little children for his own amusement (there have been such men!)—would perhaps, without rhyme or reason, suddenly give a sigh and say, "I wonder whether that old general is alive still!" Although perhaps he had not thought of mentioning him for a dozen years before! How can one say what seed of good may have been dropped into his soul, never to die?'

"I continued in that strain for a long while, pointing out to Bachmatoff how impossible it is to follow up the effects of any isolated good deed one may do, in all its influences and subtle workings upon the heart and after-actions of others.

"'And to think that you are to be cut off from life!' remarked Bachmatoff, in a tone of reproach, as though he would like to find someone to pitch into on my account.

"We were leaning over the balustrade of the bridge, looking into the Neva at this moment.

"'Do you know what has suddenly come into my head?' said I, suddenly—leaning further and further over the rail.

"'Surely not to throw yourself into the river?' cried Bachmatoff in alarm. Perhaps he read my thought in my face.

"'No, not yet. At present nothing but the following consideration. You see I have some two or three months left me to live—perhaps four; well, supposing that when I have but a month or two more, I take a fancy for some "good deed" that needs both trouble and time, like this business of our doctor friend, for instance: why, I shall have to give up the idea of it and take to something else—some *little* good deed, *more within my means*, eh? Isn't that an amusing idea!'

"Poor Bachmatoff was much impressed—painfully so. He took me all the way home; not attempting to console me, but behaving with the greatest delicacy. On taking leave he pressed my hand warmly and asked permission to come and see me. I replied that if he came to me as a 'comforter,' so to speak (for he would be in that capacity whether he spoke to me in a soothing manner or only kept silence, as I pointed out to him), he would but remind me each time of my approaching death! He shrugged his shoulders, but quite agreed with me; and we parted better friends than I had expected.

"But that evening and that night were sown the first seeds of my 'last conviction.' I seized greedily on my new idea; I thirstily drank in all its different aspects (I did not sleep a wink that night!), and the deeper I went into it the more my being seemed to merge itself in it, and the more alarmed I became. A dreadful terror came over me at last, and did not leave me all next day.

"Sometimes, thinking over this, I became quite numb with the terror of it; and I might well have deduced from this fact, that my 'last conviction' was eating into my being too fast and too seriously, and would undoubtedly come to its climax before long. And for the climax I needed greater determination than I yet possessed.

"However, within three weeks my determination was taken, owing to a very strange circumstance.

"Here on my paper, I make a note of all the figures and dates that come into my explanation. Of course, it is all the same to me, but just now—and perhaps only at this moment—I desire that all those who are to judge of my action should see clearly out of how logical a sequence of deductions has at length proceeded my 'last conviction.'

"I have said above that the determination needed by me for the accomplishment of my final resolve, came to hand not through any sequence of causes, but thanks to a certain strange circumstance which had perhaps no connection whatever with the matter at issue. Ten days ago Rogojin called upon me about certain business of his own with which I have nothing to do at present. I had never seen Rogojin before, but had often heard about him.

"I gave him all the information he needed, and he very soon took his departure; so that, since he only came for the purpose of gaining the information, the matter might have been expected to end there.

"But he interested me too much, and all that day I was under the influence of strange thoughts connected with him, and I determined to return his visit the next day.

"Rogojin was evidently by no means pleased to see me, and hinted, delicately, that he saw no reason why our acquaintance should continue. For all that, however, I spent a very interesting hour, and so, I dare say, did he. There was so great a contrast between us that I am sure we must both have felt it; anyhow, I felt it acutely. Here was I, with my days numbered, and he, a man in the full vigour of life, living in the present, without the slightest thought for 'final convictions,' or numbers, or days, or, in fact, for anything but that which-which—well, which he was mad about, if he will excuse me the expression—as a feeble author who cannot express his ideas properly.

"In spite of his lack of amiability, I could not help seeing, in Rogojin a man of intellect and sense; and although, perhaps, there was little in the outside world which was of interest to him, still he was clearly a man with eyes to see.

"I hinted nothing to him about my 'final conviction,' but it appeared to me that he had guessed it from my words. He remained silent—he is a terribly silent man. I remarked to him, as I rose to depart, that, in spite of the contrast and the wide differences between us two, les extremites se touchent ('extremes meet,' as I explained to him in Russian); so that maybe he was not so far from my final conviction as appeared.

"His only reply to this was a sour grimace. He rose and looked for my cap, and placed it in my hand, and led me out of the house—that dreadful gloomy house of his—to all appearances, of course, as though I were leaving of my own accord, and he were simply seeing me to the door out of politeness. His house impressed me much; it is like a burial-ground, he seems to like it, which is, however, quite natural. Such a full life as he leads is so overflowing with absorbing interests that he has little need of assistance from his surroundings.

"The visit to Rogojin exhausted me terribly. Besides, I had felt ill since the morning; and by evening I was so weak that I took to my bed, and was in high fever at intervals, and even delirious. Colia sat with me until eleven o'clock.

"Yet I remember all he talked about, and every word we said, though whenever my eyes closed for a moment I could picture nothing but the image of Surikoff just in the act of finding a million roubles. He could not make up his mind what to do with the money, and tore his hair over it. He trembled with fear that somebody would rob him, and at last he decided to bury it in the ground. I persuaded him that, instead of putting it all away uselessly underground, he had better melt it down and make a golden coffin out of it for his starved child, and then dig up the little one and put her into the golden coffin. Surikoff accepted this suggestion, I thought, with tears of gratitude, and immediately commenced to carry out my design.

"I thought I spat on the ground and left him in disgust. Colia told me, when I quite recovered my senses, that I had not been asleep for a moment, but that I had spoken to him about Surikoff the whole while.

"At moments I was in a state of dreadful weakness and misery, so that Colia was greatly disturbed when he left me.

"When I arose to lock the door after him, I suddenly called to mind a picture I had noticed at Rogojin's in one of his gloomiest rooms, over the door. He had pointed it out to me himself as we walked past it, and I believe I must have stood a good five minutes in front of it. There was nothing artistic about it, but the picture made me feel strangely uncomfortable. It represented Christ just taken down from the cross. It seems to me that painters as a rule represent the Saviour, both on the cross and taken down from it, with great beauty still upon His face. This marvellous beauty they strive to preserve even in His moments of deepest agony and passion. But there was no such beauty in Rogojin's picture. This was the presentment of a poor mangled body which had evidently suffered unbearable anguish even before its crucifixion, full of wounds and bruises, marks of the violence of soldiers and people, and of the bitterness of the moment when He had fallen with the cross—all this combined with the anguish of the actual crucifixion.

"The face was depicted as though still suffering; as though the body, only just dead, was still almost quivering with agony. The picture was one of pure nature, for the face was not beautified by the artist, but was left as it would naturally be, whosoever the sufferer, after such anguish.

"I know that the earliest Christian faith taught that the Saviour suffered actually and not figuratively, and that nature was allowed her own way even while His body was on the cross.

"It is strange to look on this dreadful picture of the mangled corpse of the Saviour, and to put this question to oneself: 'Supposing that the disciples, the future apostles, the women who had followed Him and stood by the cross, all of whom believed in and worshipped Him—supposing that they saw this tortured body, this face so mangled and bleeding and bruised (and they *must* have so seen it)—how could they have gazed upon the dreadful sight and yet have believed that He would rise again?'

"The thought steps in, whether one likes it or no, that death is so terrible and so powerful, that even He who conquered it in His miracles during life was unable to triumph over it at the last. He who called to Lazarus, 'Lazarus, come forth!' and the dead man lived—He was now Himself a prey to nature and death. Nature appears to one, looking at this picture, as some huge, implacable, dumb monster; or still better—a stranger simile—some enormous mechanical engine of modern days which has seized and crushed and swallowed up a great and invaluable Being, a Being worth nature and all her laws, worth the whole earth, which was perhaps created merely for the sake of the advent of that Being.

"This blind, dumb, implacable, eternal, unreasoning force is well shown in the picture, and the absolute subordination of all men and things to it is so well expressed that the idea unconsciously arises in the mind of anyone who looks at it. All those faithful people who were gazing at the cross and its mutilated occupant must have suffered agony of mind that evening; for they must have felt that all their hopes and almost all their faith had been shattered at a blow. They must have separated in terror and dread that night, though each perhaps carried away with him one great thought which was never eradicated from his mind for ever afterwards. If this great Teacher of theirs could have seen Himself after the Crucifixion, how could He have consented to mount the Cross and to die as He did? This thought also comes into the mind of the man who gazes at this picture. I thought of all this by snatches probably between my attacks of delirium—for an hour and a half or so before Colia's departure.

"Can there be an appearance of that which has no form? And yet it seemed to me, at certain moments, that I beheld in some strange and impossible form, that dark, dumb, irresistibly powerful, eternal force.

"I thought someone led me by the hand and showed me, by the light of a candle, a huge, loathsome insect, which he assured me was that very force, that very almighty, dumb, irresistible Power, and laughed at the indignation with which I received this information. In my room they always light the little lamp before my icon for the night; it gives a feeble flicker of light, but it is strong enough to see by dimly, and if you sit just under it you can even read by it. I think it was about twelve or a little past that night. I had not slept a wink, and was lying with my eyes wide open, when suddenly the door opened, and in came Rogojin.

"He entered, and shut the door behind him. Then he silently gazed at me and went quickly to the corner of the room where the lamp was burning and sat down underneath it.

"I was much surprised, and looked at him expectantly.

"Rogojin only leaned his elbow on the table and silently stared at me. So passed two or three minutes, and I recollect that his silence hurt and offended me very much. Why did he not speak?

"That his arrival at this time of night struck me as more or less strange may possibly be the case; but I remember I was by no means amazed at it. On the contrary, though I had not actually told him my thought in the morning, yet I know he understood it; and this thought was of such a character that it would not be anything very remarkable, if one were to come for further talk about it at any hour of night, however late.

"I thought he must have come for this purpose.

"In the morning we had parted not the best of friends; I remember he looked at me with disagreeable sarcasm once or twice; and this same look I observed in his eyes now—which was the cause of the annoyance I felt.

"I did not for a moment suspect that I was delirious and that this Rogojin was but the result of fever and excitement. I had not the slightest idea of such a theory at first.

"Meanwhile he continued to sit and stare jeeringly at me.

"I angrily turned round in bed and made up my mind that I would not say a word unless he did; so I rested silently on my pillow determined to remain dumb, if it were to last till morning. I felt resolved that he should speak first. Probably twenty minutes or so passed in this way. Suddenly the idea struck me—what if this is an apparition and not Rogojin himself?

"Neither during my illness nor at any previous time had I ever seen an apparition;—but I had always thought, both when I was a little boy, and even now, that if I were to see one I should die on the spot—though I don't believe in ghosts. And yet *now*, when the idea struck me that this was a ghost and not Rogojin at all, I was not in the least alarmed. Nay—the thought actually irritated me. Strangely enough, the decision of the question as to whether this were a ghost or Rogojin did not, for some reason or other, interest me nearly so much as it ought to have done;—I think I began to muse about something altogether different. For instance, I began to wonder why Rogojin, who had been in dressing-gown and slippers when I saw him at home, had now put on a dress-coat and white waistcoat and tie? I also thought to myself, I remember—'if this is a ghost, and I am not afraid of it, why don't I approach it and verify my suspicions? Perhaps I am afraid—' And no sooner did this last idea enter my head than an icy blast blew over me; I felt a chill down my backbone and my knees shook.

"At this very moment, as though divining my thoughts, Rogojin raised his head from his arm and began to part his lips as though he were going to laugh—but he continued to stare at me as persistently as before.

"I felt so furious with him at this moment that I longed to rush at him; but as I had sworn that he should speak first, I continued to lie still—and the more willingly, as I was still by no means satisfied as to whether it really was Rogojin or not.

"I cannot remember how long this lasted; I cannot recollect, either, whether consciousness forsook me at intervals, or not. But at last Rogojin rose, staring at me as intently as ever, but not smiling any longer,—and walking very softly, almost on tip-toes, to the door, he opened it, went out, and shut it behind him.

"I did not rise from my bed, and I don't know how long I lay with my eyes open, thinking. I don't know what I thought about, nor how I fell asleep or became insensible; but I awoke next morning after nine o'clock when they knocked at my door. My general orders are that if I don't open the door and call, by nine o'clock, Matreona is to come and bring my tea. When I now opened the door to her, the thought suddenly struck me—how could he have come in, since the door was locked? I made inquiries and found that Rogojin himself could not possibly have come in, because all our doors were locked for the night.

"Well, this strange circumstance—which I have described with so much detail—was the ultimate cause which led me to taking my final determination. So that no logic, or logical deductions, had anything to do with my resolve;—it was simply a matter of disgust.

"It was impossible for me to go on living when life was full of such detestable, strange, tormenting forms. This ghost had humiliated me;—nor could I bear to be subordinate to that dark, horrible force which was embodied in the form of the loathsome insect. It was only towards evening, when I had quite made up my mind on this point, that I began to feel easier."

CHAPTER VII.

"I had a small pocket pistol. I had procured it while still a boy, at that droll age when the stories of duels and highwaymen begin to delight one, and when one imagines oneself nobly standing fire at some future day, in a duel.

"There were a couple of old bullets in the bag which contained the pistol, and powder enough in an old flask for two or three charges.

"The pistol was a wretched thing, very crooked and wouldn't carry farther than fifteen paces at the most. However, it would send your skull flying well enough if you pressed the muzzle of it against your temple.

"I determined to die at Pavlofsk at sunrise, in the park—so as to make no commotion in the house.

"This 'explanation' will make the matter clear enough to the police. Students of psychology, and anyone else who likes, may make what they please of it. I should not like this paper, however, to be made public. I request the prince to keep a copy himself, and to give a copy to Aglaya Ivanovna Epanchin. This is my last will and testament. As for my skeleton, I bequeath it to the Medical Academy for the benefit of science.

"I recognize no jurisdiction over myself, and I know that I am now beyond the power of laws and judges.

"A little while ago a very amusing idea struck me. What if I were now to commit some terrible crime—murder ten fellow-creatures, for instance, or anything else that is thought most shocking and dreadful in this world—what a dilemma my judges would be in, with a criminal who only has a fortnight to live in any case, now that the rack and other forms of torture are abolished! Why, I should die comfortably in their own hospital—in a warm, clean room, with an attentive doctor—probably much more comfortably than I should at home.

"I don't understand why people in my position do not oftener indulge in such ideas—if only for a joke! Perhaps they do! Who knows! There are plenty of merry souls among us!

"But though I do not recognize any jurisdiction over myself, still I know that I shall be judged, when I am nothing but a voiceless lump of clay; therefore I do not wish to go before I have left a word of reply—the reply of a free man—not one forced to justify himself—oh no! I have no need to ask forgiveness of anyone. I wish to say a word merely because I happen to desire it of my own free will.

"Here, in the first place, comes a strange thought!

"Who, in the name of what Law, would think of disputing my full personal right over the fortnight of life left to me? What jurisdiction can be brought to bear upon the case? Who would wish me, not only to be sentenced, but to endure the sentence to the end? Surely there exists no man who would wish such a thing—why should anyone desire it? For the sake of morality? Well, I can understand that if I were to make an attempt upon my own life while in the enjoyment of full health and vigour—my life which might have been 'useful,' etc., etc.—morality might reproach me, according to the old routine, for disposing of my life without permission—or whatever its tenet may be. But now, *now*, when my sentence is out and my days numbered! How can morality have need of my last breaths, and why should I die listening to the consolations offered by the prince, who, without doubt, would not omit to demonstrate that death is actually a benefactor to me? (Christians like him always end up with that—it is their pet theory.) And what do they want with their ridiculous 'Pavlofsk trees'? To sweeten my last hours? Cannot they understand that the more I forget myself, the more I let myself become attached to these last illusions of life and love, by means of which they try to hide from me Meyer's wall, and all that is so plainly written on it—the more unhappy they make me? What is the use of all your nature to me—all your parks and trees, your sunsets and sunrises, your blue skies and your self-satisfied faces—when all this wealth of beauty and happiness begins with the fact that it accounts me—only me—one too many! What is the good of all this beauty and glory to me, when every second, every moment, I cannot but be aware that this little fly which buzzes around my head in the sun's rays—even this little fly is a sharer and participator in all the glory of the universe, and knows its place and is happy in it;—while I—only I, am an outcast, and have been blind to the fact hitherto, thanks to my simplicity! Oh! I know well how the prince and others would like me, instead of indulging in all these wicked words of my own, to sing, to the glory and triumph of morality, that well-known verse of Gilbert's:

"'O, puissent voir longtemps votre beauté sacrée
Tant d'amis, sourds à mes adieux!
Qu'ils meurent pleins de jours, que leur mort soit pleurée,
Qu'un ami leur ferme les yeux!'

"But believe me, believe me, my simple-hearted friends, that in this highly moral verse, in this academical blessing to the world in general in the French language, is hidden the intensest gall and bitterness; but so well concealed is the venom, that I dare say the poet actually persuaded himself that his words were full of the tears of pardon and peace, instead of the bitterness of disappointment and malice, and so died in the delusion.

"Do you know there is a limit of ignominy, beyond which man's consciousness of shame cannot go, and after which begins satisfaction in shame? Well, of course humility is a great force in that sense, I admit that—though not in the sense in which religion accounts humility to be strength!

"Religion!—I admit eternal life—and perhaps I always did admit it.

"Admitted that consciousness is called into existence by the will of a Higher Power; admitted that this consciousness looks out upon the world and says 'I am;' and admitted that the Higher Power wills that the consciousness so called into existence, be suddenly extinguished (for so—for some unexplained reason—it is and must be)—still there comes the eternal question—why must I be humble through all this? Is it not enough that I am devoured, without my being expected to bless the power that devours me? Surely—surely I need not suppose that Somebody—there—will be offended because I do not wish to live out the fortnight allowed me? I don't believe it.

"It is much simpler, and far more likely, to believe that my death is needed—the death of an insignificant atom—in order to fulfil the general harmony of the universe—in order to make even some plus or minus in the sum of existence. Just as every day the death of numbers of beings is necessary because without their annihilation the rest cannot live on—(although we must admit that the idea is not a particularly grand one in itself!)

"However—admit the fact! Admit that without such perpetual devouring of one another the world cannot continue to exist, or could never have been organized—I am ever ready to confess that I cannot understand why this is so—but I'll tell you what I *do* know, for certain. If I have once been given to understand and realize that I *am*—what does it matter to me that the world is organized on a system full of errors and that otherwise it cannot be organized at all? Who will or can judge me after this? Say what you like—the thing is impossible and unjust!

"And meanwhile I have never been able, in spite of my great desire to do so, to persuade myself that there is no future existence, and no Providence.

"The fact of the matter is that all this *does* exist, but that we know absolutely nothing about the future life and its laws!

"But it is so difficult, and even impossible to understand, that surely I am not to be blamed because I could not fathom the incomprehensible?

"Of course I know they say that one must be obedient, and of course, too, the prince is one of those who say so: that one must be obedient without questions, out of pure goodness of heart, and that for my worthy conduct in this matter I shall meet with reward in another world. We degrade God when we attribute our own ideas to Him, out of annoyance that we cannot fathom His ways.

"Again, I repeat, I cannot be blamed because I am unable to understand that which it is not given to mankind to fathom. Why am I to be judged because I could not comprehend the Will and Laws of Providence? No, we had better drop religion.

"And enough of this. By the time I have got so far in the reading of my document the sun will be up and the huge force of his rays will be acting upon the living world. So be it. I shall die gazing straight at the great Fountain of life and power; I do not want this life!

"If I had had the power to prevent my own birth I should certainly never have consented to accept existence under such ridiculous conditions. However, I have the power to end my existence, although I do but give back days that are already numbered. It is an insignificant gift, and my revolt is equally insignificant.

"Final explanation: I die, not in the least because I am unable to support these next three weeks. Oh no, I should find strength enough, and if I wished it I could obtain consolation from the thought of the injury that is done me. But I am not a French poet, and I do not desire such consolation. And finally, nature has so limited my capacity for work or activity of any kind, in allotting me but three weeks of time, that suicide is about the only thing left that I can begin and end in the time of my own free will.

"Perhaps then I am anxious to take advantage of my last chance of doing something for myself. A protest is sometimes no small thing."

The explanation was finished; Hippolyte paused at last.

There is, in extreme cases, a final stage of cynical candour when a nervous man, excited, and beside himself with emotion, will be afraid of nothing and ready for any sort of scandal, nay, glad of it. The extraordinary, almost unnatural, tension of the nerves which upheld Hippolyte up to this point, had now arrived at this final stage. This poor feeble boy of eighteen—exhausted by disease—looked for all the world as weak and frail as a leaflet torn from its parent tree and trembling in the breeze; but no sooner had his eye swept over his audience, for the first time during the whole of the last hour, than the most contemptuous, the most haughty expression of repugnance lighted up his face. He defied them all, as it were. But his hearers were indignant, too; they rose to their feet with annoyance. Fatigue, the wine consumed, the strain of listening so long, all added to the disagreeable impression which the reading had made upon them.

Suddenly Hippolyte jumped up as though he had been shot.

"The sun is rising," he cried, seeing the gilded tops of the trees, and pointing to them as to a miracle. "See, it is rising now!"

"Well, what then? Did you suppose it wasn't going to rise?" asked Ferdishenko.

"It's going to be atrociously hot again all day," said Gania, with an air of annoyance, taking his hat. "A month of this... Are you coming home, Ptitsin?" Hippolyte listened to this in amazement, almost amounting to stupefaction. Suddenly he became deadly pale and shuddered.

"You manage your composure too awkwardly. I see you wish to insult me," he cried to Gania. "You—you are a cur!" He looked at Gania with an expression of malice.

"What on earth is the matter with the boy? What phenomenal feeble-mindedness!" exclaimed Ferdishenko.

"Oh, he's simply a fool," said Gania.

Hippolyte braced himself up a little.

"I understand, gentlemen," he began, trembling as before, and stumbling over every word, "that I have deserved your resentment, and—and am sorry that I should have troubled you with this raving nonsense" (pointing to his article), "or rather, I am sorry that I have not troubled you enough." He smiled feebly. "Have I troubled you, Evgenie Pavlovitch?" He suddenly turned on Evgenie with this question. "Tell me now, have I troubled you or not?"

"Well, it was a little drawn out, perhaps; but—"

"Come, speak out! Don't lie, for once in your life—speak out!" continued Hippolyte, quivering with agitation.

"Oh, my good sir, I assure you it's entirely the same to me. Please leave me in peace," said Evgenie, angrily, turning his back on him.

"Good-night, prince," said Ptitsin, approaching his host.

"What are you thinking of? Don't go, he'll blow his brains out in a minute!" cried Vera Lebedeff, rushing up to Hippolyte and catching hold of his hands in a torment of alarm. "What are you thinking of? He said he would blow his brains out at sunrise."

"Oh, he won't shoot himself!" cried several voices, sarcastically.

"Gentlemen, you'd better look out," cried Colia, also seizing Hippolyte by the hand. "Just look at him! Prince, what are you thinking of?" Vera and Colia, and Keller, and Burdovsky were all crowding round Hippolyte now and holding him down.

"He has the right—the right—" murmured Burdovsky. "Excuse me, prince, but what are your arrangements?" asked Lebedeff, tipsy and exasperated, going up to Muishkin.

"What do you mean by 'arrangements'?"

"No, no, excuse me! I'm master of this house, though I do not wish to lack respect towards you. You are master of the house too, in a way; but I can't allow this sort of thing—"

"He won't shoot himself; the boy is only playing the fool," said General Ivolgin, suddenly and unexpectedly, with indignation.

"I know he won't, I know he won't, general; but I—I'm master here!"

"Listen, Mr. Terentieff," said Ptitsin, who had bidden the prince good-night, and was now holding out his hand to Hippolyte; "I think you remark in that manuscript of yours, that you bequeath your skeleton to the Academy. Are you referring to your own skeleton—I mean, your very bones?"

"Yes, my bones, I—"

"Quite so, I see; because, you know, little mistakes have occurred now and then. There was a case—"

"Why do you tease him?" cried the prince, suddenly.

"You've moved him to tears," added Ferdishenko. But Hippolyte was by no means weeping. He was about to move from his place, when his four guards rushed at him and seized him once more. There was a laugh at this.

"He led up to this on purpose. He took the trouble of writing all that so that people should come and grab him by the arm," observed Rogojin. "Good-night, prince. What a time we've sat here, my very bones ache!"

"If you really intended to shoot yourself, Terentieff," said Evgenie Pavlovitch, laughing, "if I were you, after all these compliments, I should just not shoot myself in order to vex them all."

"They are very anxious to see me blow my brains out," said Hippolyte, bitterly.

"Yes, they'll be awfully annoyed if they don't see it."

"Then you think they won't see it?"

"I am not trying to egg you on. On the contrary, I think it very likely that you may shoot yourself; but the principal thing is to keep cool," said Evgenie with a drawl, and with great condescension.

"I only now perceive what a terrible mistake I made in reading this article to them," said Hippolyte, suddenly, addressing Evgenie, and looking at him with an expression of trust and confidence, as though he were applying to a friend for counsel.

"Yes, it's a droll situation; I really don't know what advice to give you," replied Evgenie, laughing. Hippolyte gazed steadfastly at him, but said nothing. To look at him one might have supposed that he was unconscious at intervals.

"Excuse me," said Lebedeff, "but did you observe the young gentleman's style? 'I'll go and blow my brains out in the park,' says he, 'so as not to disturb anyone.' He thinks he won't disturb anybody if he goes three yards away, into the park, and blows his brains out there."

"Gentlemen—" began the prince.

"No, no, excuse me, most revered prince," Lebedeff interrupted, excitedly. "Since you must have observed yourself that this is no joke, and since at least half your guests must also have concluded that after all that has been said this youth *must* blow his brains out for honour's sake—I—as master of this house, and before these witnesses, now call upon you to take steps."

"Yes, but what am I to do, Lebedeff? What steps am I to take? I am ready."

"I'll tell you. In the first place he must immediately deliver up the pistol which he boasted of, with all its appurtenances. If he does this I shall consent to his being allowed to spend the night in this house—considering his feeble state of health, and of course conditionally upon his being under proper supervision. But tomorrow he must go elsewhere. Excuse me, prince! Should he refuse to deliver up his weapon, then I shall instantly seize one of his arms and General Ivolgin the other, and we shall hold him until the police arrive and take the matter into their own hands. Mr. Ferdishenko will kindly fetch them."

At this there was a dreadful noise; Lebedeff danced about in his excitement; Ferdishenko prepared to go for the police; Gania frantically insisted that it was all nonsense, "for nobody was going to shoot themselves." Evgenie Pavlovitch said nothing.

"Prince," whispered Hippolyte, suddenly, his eyes all ablaze, "you don't suppose that I did not foresee all this hatred?" He looked at the prince as though he expected him to reply, for a moment. "Enough!" he added at length, and addressing the whole company, he cried: "It's all my fault, gentlemen! Lebedeff, here's the key," (he took out a small bunch of keys); "this one, the last but one—Colia will show you—Colia, where's Colia?" he cried, looking straight at Colia and not seeing him. "Yes, he'll show you; he packed the bag with me this morning. Take him up, Colia; my bag is upstairs in the prince's study, under the table. Here's the key, and in the little case you'll find my pistol and the powder, and all. Colia packed it himself, Mr. Lebedeff; he'll show you; but it's on condition that tomorrow morning, when I leave for Petersburg, you will give me back my pistol, do you hear? I do this for the prince's sake, not yours."

"Capital, that's much better!" cried Lebedeff, and seizing the key he made off in haste.

Colia stopped a moment as though he wished to say something; but Lebedeff dragged him away.

Hippolyte looked around at the laughing guests. The prince observed that his teeth were chattering as though in a violent attack of ague.

"What brutes they all are!" he whispered to the prince. Whenever he addressed him he lowered his voice.

"Let them alone, you're too weak now—"

"Yes, directly; I'll go away directly. I'll—"

Suddenly he embraced Muishkin.

"Perhaps you think I am mad, eh?" he asked him, laughing very strangely.

"No, but you—"

"Directly, directly! Stand still a moment, I wish to look in your eyes; don't speak—stand so— let me look at you! I am bidding farewell to mankind."

He stood so for ten seconds, gazing at the prince, motionless, deadly pale, his temples wet with perspiration; he held the prince's hand in a strange grip, as though afraid to let him go.

"Hippolyte, Hippolyte, what is the matter with you?" cried Muishkin.

"Directly! There, that's enough. I'll lie down directly. I must drink to the sun's health. I wish to—I insist upon it! Let go!"

He seized a glass from the table, broke away from the prince, and in a moment had reached the terrace steps.

The prince made after him, but it so happened that at this moment Evgenie Pavlovitch stretched out his hand to say good-night. The next instant there was a general outcry, and then followed a few moments of indescribable excitement.

Reaching the steps, Hippolyte had paused, holding the glass in his left hand while he put his right hand into his coat pocket.

Keller insisted afterwards that he had held his right hand in his pocket all the while, when he was speaking to the prince, and that he had held the latter's shoulder with his left hand only. This circumstance, Keller affirmed, had led him to feel some suspicion from the first. However this may be, Keller ran after Hippolyte, but he was too late.

He caught sight of something flashing in Hippolyte's right hand, and saw that it was a pistol. He rushed at him, but at that very instant Hippolyte raised the pistol to his temple and pulled the trigger. There followed a sharp metallic click, but no report.

When Keller seized the would-be suicide, the latter fell forward into his arms, probably actually believing that he was shot. Keller had hold of the pistol now. Hippolyte was immediately placed in a chair, while the whole company thronged around excitedly, talking and asking each other questions. Every one of them had heard the snap of the trigger, and yet they saw a live and apparently unharmed man before them.

Hippolyte himself sat quite unconscious of what was going on, and gazed around with a senseless expression.

Lebedeff and Colia came rushing up at this moment.

"What is it?" someone asked, breathlessly—"A misfire?"

"Perhaps it wasn't loaded," said several voices.

"It's loaded all right," said Keller, examining the pistol, "but—"

"What! did it miss fire?"

"There was no cap in it," Keller announced.

It would be difficult to describe the pitiable scene that now followed. The first sensation of alarm soon gave place to amusement; some burst out laughing loud and heartily, and seemed to find a malicious satisfaction in the joke. Poor Hippolyte sobbed hysterically; he wrung his hands; he approached everyone in turn—even Ferdishenko—and took them by both hands, and swore solemnly that he had forgotten—absolutely forgotten—"accidentally, and not on purpose,"—to put a cap in—that he "had ten of them, at least, in his pocket." He pulled them out and showed them to everyone; he protested that he had not liked to put one in beforehand for fear of an accidental explosion in his pocket. That he had thought he would have lots of time to put it in afterwards—when required—and, that, in the heat of the moment, he had forgotten all about it. He threw himself upon the prince, then on Evgenie Pavlovitch. He entreated Keller to give him back the pistol, and he'd soon show them all that "his honour—his honour,"—but he was "dishonoured, now, for ever!"

He fell senseless at last—and was carried into the prince's study.

Lebedeff, now quite sobered down, sent for a doctor; and he and his daughter, with Burdovsky and General Ivolgin, remained by the sick man's couch.

When he was carried away unconscious, Keller stood in the middle of the room, and made the following declaration to the company in general, in a loud tone of voice, with emphasis upon each word.

"Gentlemen, if any one of you casts any doubt again, before me, upon Hippolyte's good faith, or hints that the cap was forgotten intentionally, or suggests that this unhappy boy was acting a part before us, I beg to announce that the person so speaking shall account to me for his words."

No one replied.

The company departed very quickly, in a mass. Ptitsin, Gania, and Rogojin went away together.

The prince was much astonished that Evgenie Pavlovitch changed his mind, and took his departure without the conversation he had requested.

"Why, you wished to have a talk with me when the others left?" he said.

"Quite so," said Evgenie, sitting down suddenly beside him, "but I have changed my mind for the time being. I confess, I am too disturbed, and so, I think, are you; and the matter as to which I wished to consult you is too serious to tackle with one's mind even a little disturbed; too serious both for myself and for you. You see, prince, for once in my life I wish to perform an absolutely honest action, that is, an action with no ulterior motive; and I think I am hardly in a condition to talk of it just at this moment, and—and—well, we'll discuss it another time. Perhaps the matter may gain in clearness if we wait for two or three days—just the two or three days which I must spend in Petersburg."

Here he rose again from his chair, so that it seemed strange that he should have thought it worth while to sit down at all.

The prince thought, too, that he looked vexed and annoyed, and not nearly so friendly towards himself as he had been earlier in the night.

"I suppose you will go to the sufferer's bedside now?" he added.

"Yes, I am afraid..." began the prince.

"Oh, you needn't fear! He'll live another six weeks all right. Very likely he will recover altogether; but I strongly advise you to pack him off tomorrow."

"I think I may have offended him by saying nothing just now. I am afraid he may suspect that I doubted his good faith,—about shooting himself, you know. What do you think, Evgenie Pavlovitch?"

"Not a bit of it! You are much too good to him; you shouldn't care a hang about what he thinks. I have heard of such things before, but never came across, till tonight, a man who would actually shoot himself in order to gain a vulgar notoriety, or blow out his brains for spite, if he finds that people don't care to pat him on the back for his sanguinary intentions. But what astonishes me more than anything is the fellow's candid confession of weakness. You'd better get rid of him tomorrow, in any case."

"Do you think he will make another attempt?"

"Oh no, not he, not now! But you have to be very careful with this sort of gentleman. Crime is too often the last resource of these petty nonentities. This young fellow is quite capable of cutting the throats of ten people, simply for a lark, as he told us in his 'explanation.' I assure you those confounded words of his will not let me sleep."

"I think you disturb yourself too much."

"What an extraordinary person you are, prince! Do you mean to say that you doubt the fact that he is capable of murdering ten men?"

"I daren't say, one way or the other; all this is very strange—but—"

"Well, as you like, just as you like," said Evgenie Pavlovitch, irritably. "Only you are such a plucky fellow, take care you don't get included among the ten victims!"

"Oh, he is much more likely not to kill anyone at all," said the prince, gazing thoughtfully at Evgenie. The latter laughed disagreeably.

"Well, *au revoir!* Did you observe that he 'willed' a copy of his confession to Aglaya Ivanovna?"

"Yes, I did; I am thinking of it."

"In connection with 'the ten,' eh?" laughed Evgenie, as he left the room.

An hour later, towards four o'clock, the prince went into the park. He had endeavoured to fall asleep, but could not, owing to the painful beating of his heart.

He had left things quiet and peaceful; the invalid was fast asleep, and the doctor, who had been called in, had stated that there was no special danger. Lebedeff, Colia, and Burdovsky were lying down in the sick-room, ready to take it in turns to watch. There was nothing to fear, therefore, at home.

But the prince's mental perturbation increased every moment. He wandered about the park, looking absently around him, and paused in astonishment when he suddenly found himself in the empty space with the rows of chairs round it, near the Vauxhall. The look of the place struck him as dreadful now: so he turned round and went by the path which he had followed with the Epanchins on the way to the band, until he reached the green bench which Aglaya had pointed out for their rendezvous. He sat down on it and suddenly burst into a loud fit of laughter, immediately followed by a feeling of irritation. His disturbance of mind continued; he felt that he must go away somewhere, anywhere.

Above his head some little bird sang out, of a sudden; he began to peer about for it among the leaves. Suddenly the bird darted out of the tree and away, and instantly he thought of the "fly buzzing about in the sun's rays" that Hippolyte had talked of; how that it knew its place and was a participator in the universal life, while he alone was an "outcast." This picture had impressed him at the time,

235

and he meditated upon it now. An old, forgotten memory awoke in his brain, and suddenly burst into clearness and light. It was a recollection of Switzerland, during the first year of his cure, the very first months. At that time he had been pretty nearly an idiot still; he could not speak properly, and had difficulty in understanding when others spoke to him. He climbed the mountain-side, one sunny morning, and wandered long and aimlessly with a certain thought in his brain, which would not become clear. Above him was the blazing sky, below, the lake; all around was the horizon, clear and infinite. He looked out upon this, long and anxiously. He remembered how he had stretched out his arms towards the beautiful, boundless blue of the horizon, and wept, and wept. What had so tormented him was the idea that he was a stranger to all this, that he was outside this glorious festival.

What was this universe? What was this grand, eternal pageant to which he had yearned from his childhood up, and in which he could never take part? Every morning the same magnificent sun; every morning the same rainbow in the waterfall; every evening the same glow on the snow-mountains.

Every little fly that buzzed in the sun's rays was a singer in the universal chorus, "knew its place, and was happy in it." Every blade of grass grew and was happy. Everything knew its path and loved it, went forth with a song and returned with a song; only he knew nothing, understood nothing, neither men nor words, nor any of nature's voices; he was a stranger and an outcast.

Oh, he could not then speak these words, or express all he felt! He had been tormented dumbly; but now it appeared to him that he must have said these very words—even then—and that Hippolyte must have taken his picture of the little fly from his tears and words of that time.

He was sure of it, and his heart beat excitedly at the thought, he knew not why.

He fell asleep on the bench; but his mental disquiet continued through his slumbers.

Just before he dozed off, the idea of Hippolyte murdering ten men flitted through his brain, and he smiled at the absurdity of such a thought.

Around him all was quiet; only the flutter and whisper of the leaves broke the silence, but broke it only to cause it to appear yet more deep and still.

He dreamed many dreams as he sat there, and all were full of disquiet, so that he shuddered every moment.

At length a woman seemed to approach him. He knew her, oh! he knew her only too well. He could always name her and recognize her anywhere; but, strange, she seemed to have quite a different face from hers, as he had known it, and he felt a tormenting desire to be able to say she was not the same woman. In the face before him there was such dreadful remorse and horror that he thought she must be a criminal, that she must have just committed some awful crime.

Tears were trembling on her white cheek. She beckoned him, but placed her finger on her lip as though to warn him that he must follow her very quietly. His heart froze within him. He wouldn't, he *couldn't* confess her to be a criminal, and yet he felt that something dreadful would happen the next moment, something which would blast his whole life.

She seemed to wish to show him something, not far off, in the park.

He rose from his seat in order to follow her, when a bright, clear peal of laughter rang out by his side. He felt somebody's hand suddenly in his own, seized it, pressed it hard, and awoke. Before him stood Aglaya, laughing aloud.

CHAPTER VIII.

She laughed, but she was rather angry too.

"He's asleep! You were asleep," she said, with contemptuous surprise.

"Is it really you?" muttered the prince, not quite himself as yet, and recognizing her with a start of amazement. "Oh yes, of course," he added, "this is our rendezvous. I fell asleep here."

"So I saw."

"Did no one awake me besides yourself? Was there no one else here? I thought there was another woman."

"There was another woman here?"

At last he was wide awake.

"It was a dream, of course," he said, musingly. "Strange that I should have a dream like that at such a moment. Sit down—"

He took her hand and seated her on the bench; then sat down beside her and reflected.

Aglaya did not begin the conversation, but contented herself with watching her companion intently.

He looked back at her, but at times it was clear that he did not see her and was not thinking of her.

Aglaya began to flush up.

"Oh yes!" cried the prince, starting. "Hippolyte's suicide—"

"What? At your house?" she asked, but without much surprise. "He was alive yesterday evening, wasn't he? How could you sleep here after that?" she cried, growing suddenly animated.

"Oh, but he didn't kill himself; the pistol didn't go off." Aglaya insisted on hearing the whole story. She hurried the prince along, but interrupted him with all sorts of questions, nearly all of which were irrelevant. Among other things, she seemed greatly interested in every word that Evgenie Pavlovitch had said, and made the prince repeat that part of the story over and over again.

"Well, that'll do; we must be quick," she concluded, after hearing all. "We have only an hour here, till eight; I must be home by then without fail, so that they may not find out that I came and sat here with you; but I've come on business. I have a great deal to say to you. But you have bowled me over considerably with your news. As to Hippolyte, I think his pistol was bound not to go off; it was more consistent with the whole affair. Are you sure he really wished to blow his brains out, and that there was no humbug about the matter?"

"No humbug at all."

"Very likely. So he wrote that you were to bring me a copy of his confession, did he? Why didn't you bring it?"

"Why, he didn't die! I'll ask him for it, if you like."

"Bring it by all means; you needn't ask him. He will be delighted, you may be sure; for, in all probability, he shot at himself simply in order that I might read his confession. Don't laugh at what I say, please, Lef Nicolaievitch, because it may very well be the case."

"I'm not laughing. I am convinced, myself, that that may have been partly the reason."

"You are convinced? You don't really mean to say you think that honestly?" asked Aglaya, extremely surprised.

She put her questions very quickly and talked fast, every now and then forgetting what she had begun to say, and not finishing her sentence. She seemed to be impatient to warn the prince about something or other. She was in a state of unusual excitement, and though she put on a brave and even defiant air, she seemed to be rather alarmed. She was dressed very simply, but this suited her well. She continually trembled and blushed, and she sat on the very edge of the seat.

The fact that the prince confirmed her idea, about Hippolyte shooting himself that she might read his confession, surprised her greatly.

"Of course," added the prince, "he wished us all to applaud his conduct—besides yourself."

"How do you mean—applaud?"

"Well—how am I to explain? He was very anxious that we should all come around him, and say we were so sorry for him, and that we loved him very much, and all that; and that we hoped he wouldn't kill himself, but remain alive. Very likely he thought more of you than the rest of us, because he mentioned you at such a moment, though perhaps he did not know himself that he had you in his mind's eye."

"I don't understand you. How could he have me in view, and not be aware of it himself? And yet, I don't know—perhaps I do. Do you know I have intended to poison myself at least thirty times—ever since I was thirteen or so—and to write to my parents before I did it? I used to think how nice it would be to lie in my coffin, and have them all weeping over me and saying it was all their fault for being so cruel, and all that—what are you smiling at?" she added, knitting her brow. "What do *you* think of when you go mooning about alone? I suppose you imagine yourself a field-marshal, and think you have conquered Napoleon?"

"Well, I really have thought something of the sort now and then, especially when just dozing off," laughed the prince. "Only it is the Austrians whom I conquer—not Napoleon."

"I don't wish to joke with you, Lef Nicolaievitch. I shall see Hippolyte myself. Tell him so. As for you, I think you are behaving very badly, because it is not right to judge a man's soul as you are judging Hippolyte's. You have no gentleness, but only justice—so you are unjust."

The prince reflected.

"I think you are unfair towards me," he said. "There is nothing wrong in the thoughts I ascribe to Hippolyte; they are only natural. But of course I don't know for certain what he thought. Perhaps he thought nothing, but simply longed to see human faces once more, and to hear human praise and feel human affection. Who knows? Only it all came out wrong, somehow. Some people have luck, and everything comes out right with them; others have none, and never a thing turns out fortunately."

"I suppose you have felt that in your own case," said Aglaya.

"Yes, I have," replied the prince, quite unsuspicious of any irony in the remark.

"H'm—well, at all events, I shouldn't have fallen asleep here, in your place. It wasn't nice of you, that. I suppose you fall asleep wherever you sit down?"

"But I didn't sleep a wink all night. I walked and walked about, and went to where the music was—"

"What music?"

"Where they played last night. Then I found this bench and sat down, and thought and thought—and at last I fell fast asleep."

"Oh, is that it? That makes a difference, perhaps. What did you go to the bandstand for?"

"I don't know; I—"

"Very well—afterwards. You are always interrupting me. What woman was it you were dreaming about?"

"It was—about—you saw her—"

"Quite so; I understand. I understand quite well. You are very—Well, how did she appear to you? What did she look like? No, I don't want to know anything about her," said Aglaya, angrily; "don't interrupt me—"

She paused a moment as though getting breath, or trying to master her feeling of annoyance.

"Look here; this is what I called you here for. I wish to make you a—to ask you to be my friend. What do you stare at me like that for?" she added, almost angrily.

The prince certainly had darted a rather piercing look at her, and now observed that she had begun to blush violently. At such moments, the more Aglaya blushed, the angrier she grew with herself; and this was clearly expressed in her eyes, which flashed like fire. As a rule, she vented her wrath on her unfortunate companion, be it who it might. She was very conscious of her own shyness, and was not nearly so talkative as her sisters for this reason—in fact, at times she was much too quiet. When, therefore, she was bound to talk, especially at such delicate moments as this, she invariably did so with an air of haughty defiance. She always knew beforehand when she was going to blush, long before the blush came.

"Perhaps you do not wish to accept my proposition?" she asked, gazing haughtily at the prince.

"Oh yes, I do; but it is so unnecessary. I mean, I did not think you need make such a proposition," said the prince, looking confused.

"What did you suppose, then? Why did you think I invited you out here? I suppose you think me a 'little fool,' as they all call me at home?"

"I didn't know they called you a fool. I certainly don't think you one."

"You don't think me one! Oh, dear me!—that's very clever of you; you put it so neatly, too."

"In my opinion, you are far from a fool sometimes—in fact, you are very intelligent. You said a very clever thing just now about my being unjust because I had *only* justice. I shall remember that, and think about it."

Aglaya blushed with pleasure. All these changes in her expression came about so naturally and so rapidly—they delighted the prince; he watched her, and laughed.

"Listen," she began again; "I have long waited to tell you all this, ever since the time when you sent me that letter—even before that. Half of what I have to say you heard yesterday. I consider you the most honest and upright of men—more honest and upright than any other man; and if anybody says that your mind is—is sometimes affected, you know—it is unfair. I always say so and uphold it, because even if your surface mind be a little affected (of course you will not feel angry with me for talking so—I am speaking from a higher point of view) yet your real mind is far better than all theirs put together. Such a mind as they have never even *dreamed* of; because really, there are *two* minds—the kind that matters, and the kind that doesn't matter. Isn't it so?"

"May be! may be so!" said the prince, faintly; his heart was beating painfully.

"I knew you would not misunderstand me," she said, triumphantly. "Prince S. and Evgenie Pavlovitch and Alexandra don't understand anything about these two kinds of mind, but, just fancy, mamma does!"

"You are very like Lizabetha Prokofievna."

"What! surely not?" said Aglaya.

"Yes, you are, indeed."

"Thank you; I am glad to be like mamma," she said, thoughtfully. "You respect her very much, don't you?" she added, quite unconscious of the naiveness of the question.

"*Very* much; and I am so glad that you have realized the fact."

"I am very glad, too, because she is often laughed at by people. But listen to the chief point. I have long thought over the matter, and at last I have chosen you. I don't wish people to laugh at me; I don't wish people to think me a 'little fool.' I don't want to be chaffed. I felt all this of a sudden, and I refused Evgenie Pavlovitch flatly, because I am not going to be forever thrown at people's heads to be married. I want—I want—well, I'll tell you, I wish to run away from home, and I have chosen you to help me."

"Run away from home?" cried the prince.

"Yes—yes—yes! Run away from home!" she repeated, in a transport of rage. "I won't, I won't be made to blush every minute by them all! I don't want to blush before Prince S. or Evgenie Pavlovitch, or anyone, and therefore I have chosen you. I shall tell you everything, *everything*, even the most important things of all, whenever I like, and you are to hide nothing from me on your side. I want to speak to at least one person, as I would to myself. They have suddenly begun to say that I am waiting for you, and in love with you. They began this before you arrived here, and so I didn't show them the letter, and now they all say it, every one of them. I want to be brave, and be afraid of nobody. I don't want to go to their balls and things—I want to do good. I have long desired to run away, for I have been kept shut up for twenty years, and they are always trying to marry me off.

I wanted to run away when I was fourteen years old—I was a little fool then, I know—but now I have worked it all out, and I have waited for you to tell me about foreign countries. I have never seen a single Gothic cathedral. I must go to Rome; I must see all the museums; I must study in Paris. All this last year I have been preparing and reading forbidden books. Alexandra and Adelaida are allowed to read anything they like, but I mayn't. I don't want to quarrel with my sisters, but I told my parents long ago that I wish to change my social position. I have decided to take up teaching, and I count on you because you said you loved children. Can we go in for education together—if not at once, then afterwards? We could do good together. I won't be a general's daughter any more! Tell me, are you a very learned man?"

"Oh no; not at all."

"Oh-h-h! I'm sorry for that. I thought you were. I wonder why I always thought so—but at all events you'll help me, won't you? Because I've chosen you, you know."

"Aglaya Ivanovna, it's absurd."

"But I will, I *will* run away!" she cried—and her eyes flashed again with anger—"and if you don't agree I shall go and marry Gavrila Ardalionovitch! I won't be considered a horrible girl, and accused of goodness knows what."

"Are you out of your mind?" cried the prince, almost starting from his seat. "What do they accuse you of? Who accuses you?"

"At home, everybody, mother, my sisters, Prince S., even that detestable Colia! If they don't say it, they think it. I told them all so to their faces. I told mother and father and everybody. Mamma was ill all the day after it, and next day father and Alexandra told me that I didn't understand what nonsense I was talking. I informed them that they little knew me—I was not a small child—I understood every word in the language—that I had read a couple of Paul de Kok's novels two years since on purpose, so as to know all about everything. No sooner did mamma hear me say this than she nearly fainted!"

A strange thought passed through the prince's brain; he gazed intently at Aglaya and smiled.

He could not believe that this was the same haughty young girl who had once so proudly shown him Gania's letter. He could not understand how that proud and austere beauty could show herself to be such an utter child—a child who probably did not even now understand some words.

"Have you always lived at home, Aglaya Ivanovna?" he asked. "I mean, have you never been to school, or college, or anything?"

"No—never—nowhere! I've been at home all my life, corked up in a bottle; and they expect me to be married straight out of it. What are you laughing at again? I observe that you, too, have taken to laughing at me, and range yourself on their side against me," she added, frowning angrily. "Don't irritate me—I'm bad enough without that—I don't know what I am doing sometimes. I am persuaded that you came here today in the full belief that I am in love with you, and that I arranged this meeting because of that," she cried, with annoyance.

"I admit I was afraid that that was the case, yesterday," blundered the prince (he was rather confused), "but today I am quite convinced that—"

"How?" cried Aglaya—and her lower lip trembled violently. "You were *afraid* that I—you dared to think that I—good gracious! you suspected, perhaps, that I sent for you to come here in order to catch you in a trap, so that they should find us here together, and make you marry me—"

"Aglaya Ivanovna, aren't you ashamed of saying such a thing? How could such a horrible idea enter your sweet, innocent heart? I am certain you don't believe a word of what you say, and probably you don't even know what you are talking about."

Aglaya sat with her eyes on the ground; she seemed to have alarmed even herself by what she had said.

"No, I'm not; I'm not a bit ashamed!" she murmured. "And how do you know my heart is innocent? And how dared you send me a love-letter that time?"

"*Love-letter?* My letter a love-letter? That letter was the most respectful of letters; it went straight from my heart, at what was perhaps the most painful moment of my life! I thought of you at the time as a kind of light. I—"

"Well, very well, very well!" she said, but quite in a different tone. She was remorseful now, and bent forward to touch his shoulder, though still trying not to look him in the face, as if the more persuasively to beg him not to be angry with her. "Very well," she continued, looking thoroughly ashamed of herself, "I feel that I said a very foolish thing. I only did it just to try you. Take it as unsaid, and if I offended you, forgive me. Don't look straight at me like that, please; turn your head away. You called it a 'horrible idea'; I only said it to shock you. Very often I am myself afraid of saying what I intend to say, and out it comes all the same. You have just told me that you wrote that letter at the most painful moment of your life. I know what moment that was!" she added softly, looking at the ground again.

"Oh, if you could know all!"

"I *do* know all!" she cried, with another burst of indignation. "You were living in the same house as that horrible woman with whom you ran away." She did not blush as she said this; on the contrary, she grew pale, and started from her seat, apparently oblivious of what she did, and immediately sat down again. Her lip continued to tremble for a long time.

There was silence for a moment. The prince was taken aback by the suddenness of this last reply, and did not know to what he should attribute it.

"I don't love you a bit!" she said suddenly, just as though the words had exploded from her mouth.

The prince did not answer, and there was silence again. "I love Gavrila Ardalionovitch," she said, quickly; but hardly audibly, and with her head bent lower than ever.

"That is *not* true," said the prince, in an equally low voice.

"What! I tell stories, do I? It is true! I gave him my promise a couple of days ago on this very seat."

The prince was startled, and reflected for a moment.

"It is not true," he repeated, decidedly; "you have just invented it!"

"You are wonderfully polite. You know he is greatly improved. He loves me better than his life. He let his hand burn before my very eyes in order to prove to me that he loved me better than his life!"

"He burned his hand!"

"Yes, believe it or not! It's all the same to me!"

The prince sat silent once more. Aglaya did not seem to be joking; she was too angry for that.

"What! he brought a candle with him to this place? That is, if the episode happened here; otherwise I can't."

"Yes, a candle! What's there improbable about that?"

"A whole one, and in a candlestick?"

"Yes—no—half a candle—an end, you know—no, it was a whole candle; it's all the same. Be quiet, can't you! He brought a box of matches too, if you like, and then lighted the candle and held his finger in it for half an hour and more!—There! Can't that be?"

"I saw him yesterday, and his fingers were all right!"

Aglaya suddenly burst out laughing, as simply as a child.

"Do you know why I have just told you these lies?" She appealed to the prince, of a sudden, with the most childlike candour, and with the laugh still trembling on her lips. "Because when one tells a lie, if one insists on something unusual and eccentric—something too 'out of the way' for anything, you know—the more impossible the thing is, the more plausible does the lie sound. I've noticed this. But I managed it badly; I didn't know how to work it." She suddenly frowned again at this point as though at some sudden unpleasant recollection.

"If"—she began, looking seriously and even sadly at him—"if when I read you all that about the 'poor knight,' I wished to-to praise you for one thing—I also wished to show you that I knew all—and did not approve of your conduct."

"You are very unfair to me, and to that unfortunate woman of whom you spoke just now in such dreadful terms, Aglaya."

"Because I know all, all—and that is why I speak so. I know very well how you—half a year since—offered her your hand before everybody. Don't interrupt me. You see, I am merely stating facts without any comment upon them. After that she ran away with Rogojin. Then you lived with her at some village or town, and she ran away from you." (Aglaya blushed dreadfully.) "Then she returned to Rogojin again, who loves her like a madman. Then you—like a wise man as you are—came back here after her as soon as ever you heard that she had returned to Petersburg. Yesterday evening you sprang forward to protect her, and just now you dreamed about her. You see, I know all. You did come back here for her, for her—now didn't you?"

"Yes—for her!" said the prince softly and sadly, and bending his head down, quite unconscious of the fact that Aglaya was gazing at him with eyes which burned like live coals. "I came to find out something—I don't believe in her future happiness as Rogojin's wife, although—in a word, I did not know how to help her or what to do for her—but I came, on the chance."

He glanced at Aglaya, who was listening with a look of hatred on her face.

"If you came without knowing why, I suppose you love her very much indeed!" she said at last.

"No," said the prince, "no, I do not love her. Oh! if you only knew with what horror I recall the time I spent with her!"

A shudder seemed to sweep over his whole body at the recollection.

"Tell me about it," said Aglaya.

"There is nothing which you might not hear. Why I should wish to tell you, and only you, this experience of mine, I really cannot say; perhaps it really is because I love you very much. This unhappy woman is persuaded that she is the most hopeless, fallen creature in the world. Oh, do not condemn her! Do not cast stones at her! She has suffered too much already in the consciousness of her own undeserved shame.

"And she is not guilty—oh God!—Every moment she bemoans and bewails herself, and cries out that she does not admit any guilt, that she is the victim of circumstances—the victim of a wicked libertine.

"But whatever she may say, remember that she does not believe it herself,—remember that she will believe nothing but that she is a guilty creature.

"When I tried to rid her soul of this gloomy fallacy, she suffered so terribly that my heart will never be quite at peace so long as I can remember that dreadful time!—Do you know why she left me? Simply to prove to me what is not true—that she is base. But the worst of it is, she did not realize herself that that was all she wanted to prove by her departure! She went away in response to some inner prompting to do something disgraceful, in order that she might say to herself—'There—you've done a new act of shame—you degraded creature!'

"Oh, Aglaya—perhaps you cannot understand all this. Try to realize that in the perpetual admission of guilt she probably finds some dreadful unnatural satisfaction—as though she were revenging herself upon someone.

"Now and then I was able to persuade her almost to see light around her again; but she would soon fall, once more, into her old tormenting delusions, and would go so far as to reproach me for placing myself on a pedestal above her (I never had an idea of such a thing!), and informed me, in reply to my proposal of marriage, that she 'did not want condescending sympathy or help from anybody.' You saw her last night. You don't suppose she can be happy among such people as those—you cannot suppose that such society is fit for her? You have no idea how well-educated she is, and what an intellect she has! She astonished me sometimes."

"And you preached her sermons there, did you?"

"Oh no," continued the prince thoughtfully, not noticing Aglaya's mocking tone, "I was almost always silent there. I often wished to speak, but I really did not know what to say. In some cases it is best to say nothing, I think. I loved her, yes, I loved her very much indeed; but afterwards—afterwards she guessed all."

"What did she guess?"

"That I only *pitied* her—and—and loved her no longer!"

"How do you know that? How do you know that she is not really in love with that—that rich cad—the man she eloped with?"

"Oh no! I know she only laughs at him; she has made a fool of him all along."

"Has she never laughed at you?"

"No—in anger, perhaps. Oh yes! she reproached me dreadfully in anger; and suffered herself, too! But afterwards—oh! don't remind me—don't remind me of that!"

He hid his face in his hands.

"Are you aware that she writes to me almost every day?"

"So that is true, is it?" cried the prince, greatly agitated. "I had heard a report of it, but would not believe it."

"Whom did you hear it from?" asked Aglaya, alarmed. "Rogojin said something about it yesterday, but nothing definite."

"Yesterday! Morning or evening? Before the music or after?"

"After—it was about twelve o'clock."

"Ah! Well, if it was Rogojin—but do you know what she writes to me about?"

"I should not be surprised by anything. She is mad!"

"There are the letters." (Aglaya took three letters out of her pocket and threw them down before the prince.) "For a whole week she has been entreating and worrying and persuading me to marry you. She—well, she is clever, though she may be mad—much cleverer than I am, as you say. Well, she writes that she is in love with me herself, and tries to see me every day, if only from a distance. She writes that you love me, and that she has long known it and seen it, and that you and she talked about me—there. She wishes to see you happy, and she says that she is certain only I can ensure you the happiness you deserve. She writes such strange, wild letters—I haven't shown them to anyone. Now, do you know what all this means? Can you guess anything?"

"It is madness—it is merely another proof of her insanity!" said the prince, and his lips trembled.

"You are crying, aren't you?"

"No, Aglaya. No, I'm not crying." The prince looked at her.

"Well, what am I to do? What do you advise me? I cannot go on receiving these letters, you know."

"Oh, let her alone, I entreat you!" cried the prince. "What can you do in this dark, gloomy mystery? Let her alone, and I'll use all my power to prevent her writing you any more letters."

"If so, you are a heartless man!" cried Aglaya. "As if you can't see that it is not myself she loves, but you, you, and only you! Surely you have not remarked everything else in her, and only not *this*? Do you know what these letters mean? They mean jealousy, sir—nothing but pure jealousy! She—do you think she will ever really marry this Rogojin, as she says here she will? She would take her own life the day after you and I were married."

The prince shuddered; his heart seemed to freeze within him. He gazed at Aglaya in wonderment; it was difficult for him to realize that this child was also a woman.

"God knows, Aglaya, that to restore her peace of mind and make her happy I would willingly give up my life. But I cannot love her, and she knows that."

"Oh, make a sacrifice of yourself! That sort of thing becomes you well, you know. Why not do it? And don't call me 'Aglaya'; you have done it several times lately. You are bound, it is your *duty* to 'raise' her; you must go off somewhere again to soothe and pacify her. Why, you love her, you know!"

"I cannot sacrifice myself so, though I admit I did wish to do so once. Who knows, perhaps I still wish to! But I know for *certain*, that if she married me it would be her ruin; I know this and therefore I leave her alone. I ought to go to see her today; now I shall probably not go. She is proud, she would never forgive me the nature of the love I bear her, and we should both be ruined. This may be unnatural, I don't know; but everything seems unnatural. You say she loves me, as if this were *love!* As if she could love *me*, after what I have been through! No, no, it is not love."

"How pale you have grown!" cried Aglaya in alarm.

"Oh, it's nothing. I haven't slept, that's all, and I'm rather tired. I—we certainly did talk about you, Aglaya."

"Oh, indeed, it is true then! *You could actually talk about me with her,* and—and how could you have been fond of me when you had only seen me once?"

"I don't know. Perhaps it was that I seemed to come upon light in the midst of my gloom. I told you the truth when I said I did not know why I thought of you before all others. Of course it was all a sort of dream, a dream amidst the horrors of reality. Afterwards I began to work. I did not intend to come back here for two or three years—"

"Then you came for her sake?" Aglaya's voice trembled.

"Yes, I came for her sake."

There was a moment or two of gloomy silence. Aglaya rose from her seat.

"If you say," she began in shaky tones, "if you say that this woman of yours is mad—at all events I have nothing to do with her insane fancies. Kindly take these three letters, Lef Nicolaievitch, and throw them back to her, from me. And if she dares," cried Aglaya suddenly, much louder than before, "if she dares so much as write me one word again, tell her I shall tell my father, and that she shall be taken to a lunatic asylum."

The prince jumped up in alarm at Aglaya's sudden wrath, and a mist seemed to come before his eyes.

"You cannot really feel like that! You don't mean what you say. It is not true," he murmured.

"It *is* true, it *is* true," cried Aglaya, almost beside herself with rage.

"What's true? What's all this? What's true?" said an alarmed voice just beside them.

Before them stood Lizabetha Prokofievna.

"Why, it's true that I am going to marry Gavrila Ardalionovitch, that I love him and intend to elope with him tomorrow," cried Aglaya, turning upon her mother. "Do you hear? Is your curiosity satisfied? Are you pleased with what you have heard?"

Aglaya rushed away homewards with these words.

"H'm! well, *you* are not going away just yet, my friend, at all events," said Lizabetha, stopping the prince. "Kindly step home with me, and let me have a little explanation of the mystery. Nice goings on, these! I haven't slept a wink all night as it is."

The prince followed her.

CHAPTER IX.

Arrived at her house, Lizabetha Prokofievna paused in the first room. She could go no farther, and subsided on to a couch quite exhausted; too feeble to remember so much as to ask the prince to take a seat. This was a large reception-room, full of flowers, and with a glass door leading into the garden.

Alexandra and Adelaida came in almost immediately, and looked inquiringly at the prince and their mother.

The girls generally rose at about nine in the morning in the country; Aglaya, of late, had been in the habit of getting up rather earlier and having a walk in the garden, but not at seven o'clock; about eight or a little later was her usual time.

Lizabetha Prokofievna, who really had not slept all night, rose at about eight on purpose to meet Aglaya in the garden and walk with her; but she could not find her either in the garden or in her own room.

This agitated the old lady considerably; and she awoke her other daughters. Next, she learned from the maid that Aglaya had gone into the park before seven o'clock. The sisters made a joke of Aglaya's last freak, and told their mother that if she went into the park to look for her, Aglaya would probably be very angry with her, and that she was pretty sure to be sitting reading on the green bench that she had talked of two or three days since, and about which she had nearly quarrelled with Prince S., who did not see anything particularly lovely in it.

Arrived at the rendezvous of the prince and her daughter, and hearing the strange words of the latter, Lizabetha Prokofievna had been dreadfully alarmed, for many reasons. However, now that she had dragged the prince home with her, she began to feel a little frightened at what she had undertaken. Why should not Aglaya meet the prince in the park and have a talk with him, even if such a meeting should be by appointment?

"Don't suppose, prince," she began, bracing herself up for the effort, "don't suppose that I have brought you here to ask questions. After last night, I assure you, I am not so exceedingly anxious to see you at all; I could have postponed the pleasure for a long while." She paused.

"But at the same time you would be very glad to know how I happened to meet Aglaya Ivanovna this morning?" The prince finished her speech for her with the utmost composure.

"Well, what then? Supposing I should like to know?" cried Lizabetha Prokofievna, blushing. "I'm sure I am not afraid of plain speaking. I'm not offending anyone, and I never wish to, and—"

"Pardon me, it is no offence to wish to know this; you are her mother. We met at the green bench this morning, punctually at seven o'clock,—according to an agreement made by Aglaya Ivanovna with myself yesterday. She said that she wished to see me and speak to me about something important. We met and conversed for an hour about matters concerning Aglaya Ivanovna herself, and that's all."

"Of course it is all, my friend. I don't doubt you for a moment," said Lizabetha Prokofievna with dignity.

"Well done, prince, capital!" cried Aglaya, who entered the room at this moment. "Thank you for assuming that I would not demean myself with lies. Come, is that enough, mamma, or do you intend to put any more questions?"

"You know I have never needed to blush before you, up to this day, though perhaps you would have been glad enough to make me," said Lizabetha Prokofievna,—with majesty. "Good-bye, prince; forgive me for bothering you. I trust you will rest assured of my unalterable esteem for you."

The prince made his bows and retired at once. Alexandra and Adelaida smiled and whispered to each other, while Lizabetha Prokofievna glared severely at them. "We are only laughing at the prince's beautiful bows, mamma," said Adelaida. "Sometimes he bows just like a meal-sack, but to-day he was like—like Evgenie Pavlovitch!"

"It is the *heart* which is the best teacher of refinement and dignity, not the dancing-master," said her mother, sententiously, and departed upstairs to her own room, not so much as glancing at Aglaya.

When the prince reached home, about nine o'clock, he found Vera Lebedeff and the maid on the verandah. They were both busy trying to tidy up the place after last night's disorderly party.

"Thank goodness, we've just managed to finish it before you came in!" said Vera, joyfully.

"Good-morning! My head whirls so; I didn't sleep all night. I should like to have a nap now."

"Here, on the verandah? Very well, I'll tell them all not to come and wake you. Papa has gone out somewhere."

The servant left the room. Vera was about to follow her, but returned and approached the prince with a preoccupied air.

"Prince!" she said, "have pity on that poor boy; don't turn him out today."

"Not for the world; he shall do just as he likes."

"He won't do any harm now; and—and don't be too severe with him."

"Oh dear no! Why—"

"And—and you won't *laugh* at him? That's the chief thing."

"Oh no! Never."

"How foolish I am to speak of such things to a man like you," said Vera, blushing. "Though you *do* look tired," she added, half turning away, "your eyes are so splendid at this moment—so full of happiness."

"Really?" asked the prince, gleefully, and he laughed in delight.

But Vera, simple-minded little girl that she was (just like a boy, in fact), here became dreadfully confused, of a sudden, and ran hastily out of the room, laughing and blushing.

"What a dear little thing she is," thought the prince, and immediately forgot all about her.

He walked to the far end of the verandah, where the sofa stood, with a table in front of it. Here he sat down and covered his face with his hands, and so remained for ten minutes. Suddenly he put his hand in his coat-pocket and hurriedly produced three letters.

But the door opened again, and out came Colia.

The prince actually felt glad that he had been interrupted,—and might return the letters to his pocket. He was glad of the respite.

"Well," said Colia, plunging *in medias res*, as he always did, "here's a go! What do you think of Hippolyte now? Don't respect him any longer, eh?"

"Why not? But look here, Colia, I'm tired; besides, the subject is too melancholy to begin upon again. How is he, though?"

"Asleep—he'll sleep for a couple of hours yet. I quite understand—you haven't slept—you walked about the park, I know. Agitation—excitement—all that sort of thing—quite natural, too!"

"How do you know I walked in the park and didn't sleep at home?"

"Vera just told me. She tried to persuade me not to come, but I couldn't help myself, just for one minute. I have been having my turn at the bedside for the last two hours; Kostia Lebedeff is there now. Burdovsky has gone. Now, lie down, prince, make yourself comfortable, and sleep well! I'm awfully impressed, you know."

"Naturally, all this—"

"No, no, I mean with the 'explanation,' especially that part of it where he talks about Providence and a future life. There is a gigantic thought there."

The prince gazed affectionately at Colia, who, of course, had come in solely for the purpose of talking about this "gigantic thought."

"But it is not any one particular thought, only; it is the general circumstances of the case. If Voltaire had written this now, or Rousseau, I should have just read it and thought it remarkable, but should not have been so *impressed* by it. But a man who knows for certain that he has but ten minutes to live and can talk like that—why—it's—it's *pride*, that is! It is really a most extraordinary, exalted assertion of personal dignity, it's—it's *defiant!* What a *gigantic* strength of will, eh? And to accuse a fellow like that of not putting in the cap on purpose; it's base and mean! You know he deceived us last night, the cunning rascal. I never packed his bag for him, and I never saw his pistol. He packed it himself. But he put me off my guard like that, you see. Vera says you are going to let him stay on; I swear there's no danger, especially as we are always with him."

"Who was by him at night?"

"I, and Burdovsky, and Kostia Lebedeff. Keller stayed a little while, and then went over to Lebedeff's to sleep. Ferdishenko slept at Lebedeff's, too; but he went away at seven o'clock. My father is always at Lebedeff's; but he has gone out just now. I dare say Lebedeff will be coming in here directly; he has been looking for you; I don't know what he wants. Shall we let him in or not, if you are asleep? I'm going to have a nap, too. By-the-by, such a curious thing happened. Burdovsky woke me at seven, and I met my father just outside the room, so drunk, he didn't even know me. He stood before me like a log, and when he recovered himself, asked hurriedly how Hippolyte was. 'Yes,' he said, when I told him, 'that's all very well, but I *really* came to warn you that you must be very careful what you say before Ferdishenko.' Do you follow me, prince?"

"Yes. Is it really so? However, it's all the same to us, of course."

"Of course it is; we are not a secret society; and that being the case, it is all the more curious that the general should have been on his way to wake me up in order to tell me this."

"Ferdishenko has gone, you say?"

"Yes, he went at seven o'clock. He came into the room on his way out; I was watching just then. He said he was going to spend 'the rest of the night' at Wilkin's; there's a tipsy fellow, a friend of his, of that name. Well, I'm off. Oh, here's Lebedeff himself! The prince wants to go to sleep, Lukian Timofeyovitch, so you may just go away again."

"One moment, my dear prince, just one. I must absolutely speak to you about something which is most grave," said Lebedeff, mysteriously and solemnly, entering the room with a bow and looking extremely important. He had but just returned, and carried his hat in his hand. He looked preoccupied and most unusually dignified.

The prince begged him to take a chair.

"I hear you have called twice; I suppose you are still worried about yesterday's affair."

"What, about that boy, you mean? Oh dear no, yesterday my ideas were a little—well—mixed. Today, I assure you, I shall not oppose in the slightest degree any suggestions it may please you to make."

"What's up with you this morning, Lebedeff? You look so important and dignified, and you choose your words so carefully," said the prince, smiling.

"Nicolai Ardalionovitch!" said Lebedeff, in a most amiable tone of voice, addressing the boy. "As I have a communication to make to the prince which concerns only myself—"

"Of course, of course, not my affair. All right," said Colia, and away he went.

"I love that boy for his perception," said Lebedeff, looking after him. "My dear prince," he continued, "I have had a terrible misfortune, either last night or early this morning. I cannot tell the exact time."

"What is it?"

"I have lost four hundred roubles out of my side pocket! They're gone!" said Lebedeff, with a sour smile.

"You've lost four hundred roubles? Oh! I'm sorry for that."

"Yes, it is serious for a poor man who lives by his toil."

"Of course, of course! How was it?"

"Oh, the wine is to blame, of course. I confess to you, prince, as I would to Providence itself. Yesterday I received four hundred roubles from a debtor at about five in the afternoon, and came down here by train. I had my purse in my pocket. When I changed, I put the money into the pocket of my plain clothes, intending to keep it by me, as I expected to have an applicant for it in the evening."

"It's true then, Lebedeff, that you advertise to lend money on gold or silver articles?"

"Yes, through an agent. My own name doesn't appear. I have a large family, you see, and at a small percentage—"

"Quite so, quite so. I only asked for information—excuse the question. Go on."

"Well, meanwhile that sick boy was brought here, and those guests came in, and we had tea, and—well, we made merry—to my ruin! Hearing of your birthday afterwards, and excited with the circumstances of the evening, I ran upstairs and changed my plain clothes once more for my uniform [Civil Service clerks in Russia wear uniform.]—you must have noticed I had my uniform on all the evening? Well, I forgot the money in the pocket of my old coat—you know when God will ruin a man he first of all bereaves him of his senses—and it was only this morning at half-past seven that I woke up and grabbed at my coat pocket, first thing. The pocket was empty—the purse gone, and not a trace to be found!"

"Dear me! This is very unpleasant!"

"Unpleasant! Indeed it is. You have found a very appropriate expression," said Lebedeff, politely, but with sarcasm.

"But what's to be done? It's a serious matter," said the prince, thoughtfully. "Don't you think you may have dropped it out of your pocket whilst intoxicated?"

"Certainly. Anything is possible when one is intoxicated, as you neatly express it, prince. But consider—if I, intoxicated or not, dropped an object out of my pocket on to the ground, that object ought to remain on the ground. Where is the object, then?"

"Didn't you put it away in some drawer, perhaps?"

"I've looked everywhere, and turned out everything."

"I confess this disturbs me a good deal. Someone must have picked it up, then."

"Or taken it out of my pocket—two alternatives."

"It is very distressing, because *who*—? That's the question!"

"Most undoubtedly, excellent prince, you have hit it—that is the very question. How wonderfully you express the exact situation in a few words!"

"Come, come, Lebedeff, no sarcasm! It's a serious—"

"Sarcasm!" cried Lebedeff, wringing his hands. "All right, all right, I'm not angry. I'm only put out about this. Whom do you suspect?"

"That is a very difficult and complicated question. I cannot suspect the servant, for she was in the kitchen the whole evening, nor do I suspect any of my children."

"I should think not. Go on."

"Then it must be one of the guests."

"Is such a thing possible?"

"Absolutely and utterly impossible—and yet, so it must be. But one thing I am sure of, if it be a theft, it was committed, not in the evening when we were all together, but either at night or early in the morning; therefore, by one of those who slept here. Burdovsky and Colia I except, of course. They did not even come into my room."

"Yes, or even if they had! But who did sleep with you?"

"Four of us, including myself, in two rooms. The general, myself, Keller, and Ferdishenko. One of us four it must have been. I don't suspect myself, though such cases have been known."

"Oh! *do* go on, Lebedeff! Don't drag it out so."

"Well, there are three left, then—Keller firstly. He is a drunkard to begin with, and a liberal (in the sense of other people's pockets), otherwise with more of the ancient knight about him than of the modern liberal. He was with the sick man at first, but came over afterwards because there was no place to lie down in the room and the floor was so hard."

"You suspect him?"

"I *did* suspect him. When I woke up at half-past seven and tore my hair in despair for my loss and carelessness, I awoke the general, who was sleeping the sleep of innocence near me. Taking into consideration the sudden disappearance of Ferdishenko, which was suspicious in itself, we decided to search Keller, who was lying there sleeping like a top. Well, we searched his clothes thoroughly, and not a farthing did we find; in fact, his pockets all had holes in them. We found a dirty handkerchief, and a love-letter from some scullery-maid. The general decided that he was innocent. We awoke him for further inquiries, and had the greatest difficulty in making him understand what was up. He opened his mouth and stared—he looked so stupid and so absurdly innocent. It wasn't Keller."

"Oh, I'm so glad!" said the prince, joyfully. "I was so afraid."

"Afraid! Then you had some grounds for supposing he might be the culprit?" said Lebedeff, frowning.

"Oh no—not a bit! It was foolish of me to say I was afraid! Don't repeat it please, Lebedeff, don't tell anyone I said that!"

"My dear prince! your words lie in the lowest depth of my heart—it is their tomb!" said Lebedeff, solemnly, pressing his hat to the region of his heart.

"Thanks; very well. Then I suppose it's Ferdishenko; that is, I mean, you suspect Ferdishenko?"

"Whom else?" said Lebedeff, softly, gazing intently into the prince s face.

"Of course—quite so, whom else? But what are the proofs?"

"We have evidence. In the first place, his mysterious disappearance at seven o'clock, or even earlier."

"I know, Colia told me that he had said he was off to—I forget the name, some friend of his, to finish the night."

"H'm! then Colia has spoken to you already?"

"Not about the theft."

"He does not know of it; I have kept it a secret. Very well, Ferdishenko went off to Wilkin's. That is not so curious in itself, but here the evidence opens out further. He left his address, you see, when he went. Now prince, consider, why did he leave his address? Why do you suppose he went out of his way to tell Colia that he had gone to Wilkin's? Who cared to know that he was going to Wilkin's? No, no! prince, this is finesse, thieves' finesse! This is as good as saying, 'There, how can I be a thief when I leave my address? I'm not concealing my movements as a thief would.' Do you understand, prince?"

"Oh yes, but that is not enough."

"Second proof. The scent turns out to be false, and the address given is a sham. An hour after—that is at about eight, I went to Wilkin's myself, and there was no trace of Ferdishenko. The maid did tell me, certainly, that an hour or so since someone had been hammering at the door, and had smashed the bell; she said she would not open the door because she didn't want to wake her master; probably she was too lazy to get up herself. Such phenomena are met with occasionally!"

"But is that all your evidence? It is not enough!"

"Well, prince, whom are we to suspect, then? Consider!" said Lebedeff with almost servile amiability, smiling at the prince. There was a look of cunning in his eyes, however.

"You should search your room and all the cupboards again," said the prince, after a moment or two of silent reflection.

"But I have done so, my dear prince!" said Lebedeff, more sweetly than ever.

"H'm! why must you needs go up and change your coat like that?" asked the prince, banging the table with his fist, in annoyance.

"Oh, don't be so worried on my account, prince! I assure you I am not worth it! At least, not I alone. But I see you are suffering on behalf of the criminal too, for wretched Ferdishenko, in fact!"

"Of course you have given me a disagreeable enough thing to think about," said the prince, irritably, "but what are you going to do, since you are so sure it was Ferdishenko?"

"But who else *could* it be, my very dear prince?" repeated Lebedeff, as sweet as sugar again. "If you don't wish me to suspect Mr. Burdovsky?"

"Of course not."

"Nor the general? Ha, ha, ha!"

"Nonsense!" said the prince, angrily, turning round upon him.

"Quite so, nonsense! Ha, ha, ha! dear me! He did amuse me, did the general! We went off on the hot scent to Wilkin's together, you know; but I must first observe that the general was even more thunderstruck than I myself this morning, when I awoke him after discovering the theft; so much so that his very face changed—he grew red and then pale, and at length flew into a paroxysm of such noble wrath that I assure you I was quite surprised! He is a most generous-hearted man! He tells lies by the thousands, I know, but it is merely a weakness; he is a man of the highest feelings; a simple-minded man too, and a man who carries the conviction of innocence in his very appearance. I love that man, sir; I may have told you so before; it is a weakness of mine. Well—he suddenly stopped in the middle of the road, opened out his coat and bared his breast. 'Search me,' he says, 'you searched Keller; why don't you search me too? It is only fair!' says he. And all the while his legs and hands were trembling with anger, and he as white as a sheet all over! So I said to him, 'Nonsense, general; if anybody but yourself had said that to me, I'd have taken my head, my own head, and put it on a large dish and carried it round to anyone who suspected you; and I should have said: "There, you see that head? It's my head, and I'll go bail with that head for him! Yes, and walk through the fire for him, too." There,' says I, 'that's how I'd answer for you, general!' Then he embraced me, in the middle of the street, and hugged me so tight (crying over me all the while) that I coughed fit to choke! 'You are the one friend left to me amid all my misfortunes,' says he. Oh, he's a man of sentiment, that! He went on to tell me a story of how he had been accused, or suspected, of stealing five hundred thousand roubles once, as a young man; and how, the very next day, he had rushed into a burning, blazing house and saved the very count who suspected him, and Nina Alexandrovna (who was then a young girl), from a fiery death. The count embraced him, and that was how he came to marry Nina Alexandrovna, he said. As for the money, it was found among the ruins next day in an English iron box with a secret lock; it had got under the floor somehow, and if it had not been for the fire it would never have been found! The whole thing is, of course, an absolute fabrication, though when he spoke of Nina Alexandrovna he wept! She's a grand woman, is Nina Alexandrovna, though she is very angry with me!"

"Are you acquainted with her?"

"Well, hardly at all. I wish I were, if only for the sake of justifying myself in her eyes. Nina Alexandrovna has a grudge against me for, as she thinks, encouraging her husband in drinking; whereas in reality I not only do not encourage him, but I actually keep him out of harm's way, and out of bad company. Besides, he's my friend, prince, so that I shall not lose sight of him, again. Where he goes, I go. He's quite given up visiting the captain's widow, though sometimes he thinks sadly of her, especially in the morning, when he's putting on his boots. I don't know why it's at that time. But he has no money, and it's no use his going to see her without. Has he borrowed any money from you, prince?"

"No, he has not."

"Ah, he's ashamed to! He *meant* to ask you, I know, for he said so. I suppose he thinks that as you gave him some once (you remember), you would probably refuse if he asked you again."

"Do you ever give him money?"

"Prince! Money! Why I would give that man not only my money, but my very life, if he wanted it. Well, perhaps that's exaggeration; not life, we'll say, but some illness, a boil or a bad cough, or anything of that sort, I would stand with pleasure, for his sake; for I consider him a great man fallen—money, indeed!"

"H'm, then you *do* give him money?"

"N-no, I have never given him money, and he knows well that I will never give him any; because I am anxious to keep him out of intemperate ways. He is going to town with me now; for you must know I am off to Petersburg after Ferdishenko, while the scent is hot; I'm certain he is there. I shall let the general go one way, while I go the other; we have so arranged matters in order to pop out upon Ferdishenko, you see, from different sides. But I am going to follow that naughty old general and catch him, I know where, at a certain widow's house; for I think it will be a good lesson, to put him to shame by catching him with the widow."

"Oh, Lebedeff, don't, don't make any scandal about it!" said the prince, much agitated, and speaking in a low voice.

"Not for the world, not for the world! I merely wish to make him ashamed of himself. Oh, prince, great though this misfortune be to myself, I cannot help thinking of his morals! I have a great favour to ask of you, esteemed prince; I confess that it is the chief object of my visit. You know the Ivolgins, you have even lived in their house; so if you would lend me your help, honoured prince, in the general's own interest and for his good."

Lebedeff clasped his hands in supplication.

"What help do you want from me? You may be certain that I am most anxious to understand you, Lebedeff."

"I felt sure of that, or I should not have come to you. We might manage it with the help of Nina Alexandrovna, so that he might be closely watched in his own house. Unfortunately I am not on terms... otherwise... but Nicolai Ardalionovitch, who adores you with all his youthful soul, might help, too."

"No, no! Heaven forbid that we should bring Nina Alexandrovna into this business! Or Colia, either. But perhaps I have not yet quite understood you, Lebedeff?"

Lebedeff made an impatient movement.

"But there is nothing to understand! Sympathy and tenderness, that is all—that is all our poor invalid requires! You will permit me to consider him an invalid?"

"Yes, it shows delicacy and intelligence on your part."

"I will explain my idea by a practical example, to make it clearer. You know the sort of man he is. At present his only failing is that he is crazy about that captain's widow, and he cannot go to her without money, and I mean to catch him at her house today—for his own good; but supposing it was not only the widow, but that he had committed a real crime, or at least some very dishonourable action (of which he is, of course, incapable), I repeat that even in that case, if he were treated with what I may call generous tenderness, one could get at the whole truth, for he is very soft-hearted! Believe me, he would betray himself before five days were out; he would burst into tears, and make a clean breast of the matter; especially if managed with tact, and if you and his family watched his every step, so to speak. Oh, my dear prince," Lebedeff added most emphatically, "I do not positively assert that he has... I am ready, as the saying is, to shed my last drop of blood for him this instant; but you will admit that debauchery, drunkenness, and the captain's widow, all these together may lead him very far."

"I am, of course, quite ready to add my efforts to yours in such a case," said the prince, rising; "but I confess, Lebedeff, that I am terribly perplexed. Tell me, do you still think... plainly, you say yourself that you suspect Mr. Ferdishenko?"

Lebedeff clasped his hands once more.

"Why, who else could I possibly suspect? Who else, most outspoken prince?" he replied, with an unctuous smile.

Muishkin frowned, and rose from his seat.

"You see, Lebedeff, a mistake here would be a dreadful thing. This Ferdishenko, I would not say a word against him, of course; but, who knows? Perhaps it really was he? I mean he really does seem to be a more likely man than... than any other."

Lebedeff strained his eyes and ears to take in what the prince was saying. The latter was frowning more and more, and walking excitedly up and down, trying not to look at Lebedeff.

"You see," he said, "I was given to understand that Ferdishenko was that sort of man,—that one can't say everything before him. One has to take care not to say too much, you understand? I say this to prove that he really is, so to speak, more likely to have done this than anyone else, eh? You understand? The important thing is, not to make a mistake."

"And who told you this about Ferdishenko?"

"Oh, I was told. Of course I don't altogether believe it. I am very sorry that I should have had to say this, because I assure you I don't believe it myself; it is all nonsense, of course. It was stupid of me to say anything about it."

"You see, it is very important, it is most important to know where you got this report from," said Lebedeff, excitedly. He had risen from his seat, and was trying to keep step with the prince, running after him, up and down. "Because look here, prince, I don't mind telling you now that as we were going along to Wilkin's this morning, after telling me what you know about the fire, and saving the count and all that, the general was pleased to drop certain hints to the same effect about Ferdishenko, but so vaguely and clumsily that I thought better to put a few questions to him on the matter, with the result that I found the whole thing was an invention of his excellency's own mind. Of course, he only lies with the best intentions; still, he lies. But, such being the case, where could you have heard the same report? It was the inspiration of the moment with him, you understand, so who could have told *you*? It is an important question, you see!"

"It was Colia told me, and his father told *him* at about six this morning. They met at the threshold, when Colia was leaving the room for something or other." The prince told Lebedeff all that Colia had made known to himself, in detail.

"There now, that's what we may call *scent!*" said Lebedeff, rubbing his hands and laughing silently. "I thought it must be so, you see. The general interrupted his innocent slumbers, at six o'clock, in order to go and wake his beloved son, and warn him of the dreadful danger of companionship with Ferdishenko. Dear me! what a dreadfully dangerous man Ferdishenko must be, and what touching paternal solicitude, on the part of his excellency, ha! ha! ha!"

"Listen, Lebedeff," began the prince, quite overwhelmed; "*do* act quietly—don't make a scandal, Lebedeff, I ask you—I entreat you! No one must know—*no one*, mind! In that case only, I will help you."

"Be assured, most honourable, most worthy of princes—be assured that the whole matter shall be buried within my heart!" cried Lebedeff, in a paroxysm of exaltation. "I'd give every drop of my blood... Illustrious prince, I am a poor wretch in soul and spirit, but ask the veriest scoundrel whether he would prefer to deal with one like himself, or with a noble-hearted man like you, and there is no doubt as to his choice! He'll answer that he prefers the noble-hearted man—and there you have the triumph of virtue! *Au revoir*, honoured prince! You and I together—softly! softly!"

CHAPTER X.

The prince understood at last why he shivered with dread every time he thought of the three letters in his pocket, and why he had put off reading them until the evening.

When he fell into a heavy sleep on the sofa on the verandah, without having had the courage to open a single one of the three envelopes, he again dreamed a painful dream, and once more that poor, "sinful" woman appeared to him. Again she gazed at him with tears sparkling on her long lashes, and beckoned him after her; and again he awoke, as before, with the picture of her face haunting him.

He longed to get up and go to her at once—but he *could not*. At length, almost in despair, he unfolded the letters, and began to read them.

These letters, too, were like a dream. We sometimes have strange, impossible dreams, contrary to all the laws of nature. When we awake we remember them and wonder at their strangeness. You remember, perhaps, that you were in full possession of your reason during this succession of fantastic images; even that you acted with extraordinary logic and cunning while surrounded by murderers who hid their intentions and made great demonstrations of friendship, while waiting for an opportunity to cut your throat. You remember how you escaped them by some ingenious stratagem; then you doubted if they were really deceived, or whether they were only pretending not to know your hiding-place; then you thought of another plan and hoodwinked them once again. You remember all this quite clearly, but how is it that your reason calmly accepted all the manifest absurdities and impossibilities that crowded into your dream? One of the murderers suddenly changed into a woman before your very eyes; then the woman was transformed into a hideous, cunning little dwarf; and you believed it, and accepted it all almost as a matter of course—while at the same time your intelligence seemed unusually keen, and accomplished miracles of cunning, sagacity, and logic! Why is it that when you awake to the world of realities you nearly always feel, sometimes very vividly, that the vanished dream has carried with it some enigma which you have failed to solve? You smile at the extravagance of your dream, and yet you feel that this tissue of absurdity contained some real idea, something that belongs to your true life,—something that exists, and has always existed, in your heart. You search your dream for some prophecy that you were expecting. It has left a deep impression upon you, joyful or cruel, but what it means, or what has been predicted to you in it, you can neither understand nor remember.

The reading of these letters produced some such effect upon the prince. He felt, before he even opened the envelopes, that the very fact of their existence was like a nightmare. How could she ever have made up her mind to write to her? he asked himself. How could she write about that at all? And how could such a wild idea have entered her head? And yet, the strangest part of the matter was, that while he read the letters, he himself almost believed in the possibility, and even in the justification, of the idea he had thought so wild. Of course it was a mad dream, a nightmare, and yet there was something cruelly real about it. For hours he was haunted by what he had read. Several passages returned again and again to his mind, and as he brooded over them, he felt inclined to say to himself that he had foreseen and known all that was written here; it even seemed to him that he had read the whole of this some time or other, long, long ago; and all that had tormented and grieved him up to now was to be found in these old, long since read, letters.

"When you open this letter" (so the first began), "look first at the signature. The signature will tell you all, so that I need explain nothing, nor attempt to justify myself. Were I in any way on a footing with you, you might be offended at my audacity; but who am I, and who are you? We are at such extremes, and I am so far removed from you, that I could not offend you if I wished to do so."

Farther on, in another place, she wrote: "Do not consider my words as the sickly ecstasies of a diseased mind, but you are, in my opinion—perfection! I have seen you—I see you every day. I do not judge you; I have not weighed you in the scales of Reason and found you Perfection—it is simply an article of faith. But I must confess one sin against you—I love you. One should not love perfection. One should only look on it as perfection—yet I am in love with you. Though love equalizes, do not fear. I have not lowered you to my level, even in my most secret thoughts. I have written 'Do not fear,' as if you could fear. I would kiss your footprints if I could; but, oh! I am not putting myself on a level with you!—Look at the signature—quick, look at the signature!"

"However, observe" (she wrote in another of the letters), "that although I couple you with him, yet I have not once asked you whether you love him. He fell in love with you, though he saw you but once. He spoke of you as of 'the light.' These are his own words—I heard him use them. But I understood without his saying it that you were all that light is to him. I lived near him for a whole month, and I understood then that you, too, must love him. I think of you and him as one."

"What was the matter yesterday?" (she wrote on another sheet). "I passed by you, and you seemed to me to *blush*. Perhaps it was only my fancy. If I were to bring you to the most loathsome den, and show you the revelation of undisguised vice—you should not blush. You can never feel the sense of personal affront. You may hate all who are mean, or base, or unworthy—but not for yourself—only for those whom they wrong. No one can wrong *you*. Do you know, I think you ought to love me—for you are the same in my eyes as in his—you are as light. An angel cannot hate, perhaps cannot love, either. I often ask myself—is it possible to love everybody? Indeed it is not; it is not in nature. Abstract love of humanity is nearly always love of self. But you are different. You cannot help loving all, since you can compare with none, and are above all personal offence or anger. Oh! how bitter it would be to me to know that you felt anger or shame on my account, for that would be your fall—you would become comparable at once with such as me.

"Yesterday, after seeing you, I went home and thought out a picture.

"Artists always draw the Saviour as an actor in one of the Gospel stories. I should do differently. I should represent Christ alone—the disciples did leave Him alone occasionally. I should paint one little child left with Him. This child has been playing about near Him, and had probably just been telling the Saviour something in its pretty baby prattle. Christ had listened to it, but was now musing—one hand reposing on the child's bright head. His eyes have a far-away expression. Thought, great as the Universe, is in them—His face is sad. The little one leans its elbow upon Christ's knee, and with its cheek resting on its hand, gazes up at Him, pondering as children sometimes do ponder. The sun is setting. There you have my picture.

"You are innocent—and in your innocence lies all your perfection—oh, remember that! What is my passion to you?—you are mine now; I shall be near you all my life—I shall not live long!"

At length, in the last letter of all, he found:

"For Heaven's sake, don't misunderstand me! Do not think that I humiliate myself by writing thus to you, or that I belong to that class of people who take a satisfaction in humiliating themselves—from pride. I have my consolation, though it would be difficult to explain it—but I do not humiliate myself.

"Why do I wish to unite you two? For your sakes or my own? For my own sake, naturally. All the problems of my life would thus be solved; I have thought so for a long time. I know that once when your sister Adelaida saw my portrait she said that such beauty could overthrow the world. But I have renounced the world. You think it strange that I should say so, for you saw me decked with lace and diamonds, in the company of drunkards and wastrels. Take no notice of that; I know that I have almost ceased to exist. God knows what it is dwelling within me now—it is not myself. I can see it every day in two dreadful eyes which are always looking at me, even when not present. These eyes are silent now, they say nothing; but I know their secret. His house is gloomy, and there is a secret in it. I am convinced that in some box he has a razor hidden, tied round with silk, just like the one that Moscow murderer had. This man also lived with his mother, and had a razor hidden away, tied round with white silk, and with this razor he intended to cut a throat.

"All the while I was in their house I felt sure that somewhere beneath the floor there was hidden away some dreadful corpse, wrapped in oil-cloth, perhaps buried there by his father, who knows? Just as in the Moscow case. I could have shown you the very spot!

"He is always silent, but I know well that he loves me so much that he must hate me. My wedding and yours are to be on the same day; so I have arranged with him. I have no secrets from him. I would kill him from very fright, but he will kill me first. He has just burst out laughing, and says that I am raving. He knows I am writing to you."

There was much more of this delirious wandering in the letters—one of them was very long.

At last the prince came out of the dark, gloomy park, in which he had wandered about for hours just as yesterday. The bright night seemed to him to be lighter than ever. "It must be quite early," he thought. (He had forgotten his watch.) There was a sound of distant music somewhere. "Ah," he thought, "the Vauxhall! They won't be there today, of course!" At this moment he noticed that he was close to their house; he had felt that he must gravitate to this spot eventually, and, with a beating heart, he mounted the verandah steps.

No one met him; the verandah was empty, and nearly pitch dark. He opened the door into the room, but it, too, was dark and empty. He stood in the middle of the room in perplexity. Suddenly the door opened, and in came Alexandra, candle in hand. Seeing the prince she stopped before him in surprise, looking at him questioningly.

It was clear that she had been merely passing through the room from door to door, and had not had the remotest notion that she would meet anyone.

"How did you come here?" she asked, at last.

"I—I—came in—"

"Mamma is not very well, nor is Aglaya. Adelaida has gone to bed, and I am just going. We were alone the whole evening. Father and Prince S. have gone to town."

"I have come to you—now—to—"

"Do you know what time it is?"

"N—no!"

"Half-past twelve. We are always in bed by one."

"I—I thought it was half-past nine!"

"Never mind!" she laughed, "but why didn't you come earlier? Perhaps you were expected!"

"I thought" he stammered, making for the door.

"*Au revoir!* I shall amuse them all with this story tomorrow!"

He walked along the road towards his own house. His heart was beating, his thoughts were confused, everything around seemed to be part of a dream.

And suddenly, just as twice already he had awaked from sleep with the same vision, that very apparition now seemed to rise up before him. The woman appeared to step out from the park, and stand in the path in front of him, as though she had been waiting for him there.

He shuddered and stopped; she seized his hand and pressed it frenziedly.

No, this was no apparition!

There she stood at last, face to face with him, for the first time since their parting.

She said something, but he looked silently back at her. His heart ached with anguish. Oh! never would he banish the recollection of this meeting with her, and he never remembered it but with the same pain and agony of mind.

She went on her knees before him—there in the open road—like a madwoman. He retreated a step, but she caught his hand and kissed it, and, just as in his dream, the tears were sparkling on her long, beautiful lashes.

"Get up!" he said, in a frightened whisper, raising her. "Get up at once!"

"Are you happy—are you happy?" she asked. "Say this one word. Are you happy now? Today, this moment? Have you just been with her? What did she say?"

She did not rise from her knees; she would not listen to him; she put her questions hurriedly, as though she were pursued.

"I am going away tomorrow, as you bade me—I won't write—so that this is the last time I shall see you, the last time! This is really the *last time!*"

"Oh, be calm—be calm! Get up!" he entreated, in despair.

She gazed thirstily at him and clutched his hands.

"Good-bye!" she said at last, and rose and left him, very quickly.

The prince noticed that Rogojin had suddenly appeared at her side, and had taken her arm and was leading her away.

"Wait a minute, prince," shouted the latter, as he went. "I shall be back in five minutes."

He reappeared in five minutes as he had said. The prince was waiting for him.

"I've put her in the carriage," he said; "it has been waiting round the corner there since ten o'clock. She expected that you would be with *them* all the evening. I told her exactly what you wrote me. She won't write to the girl any more, she promises; and tomorrow she will be off, as you wish. She desired to see you for the last time, although you refused, so we've been sitting and waiting on that bench till you should pass on your way home."

"Did she bring you with her of her own accord?"

"Of course she did!" said Rogojin, showing his teeth; "and I saw for myself what I knew before. You've read her letters, I suppose?"

"Did you read them?" asked the prince, struck by the thought.

"Of course—she showed them to me herself. You are thinking of the razor, eh? Ha, ha, ha!"

"Oh, she is mad!" cried the prince, wringing his hands.

"Who knows? Perhaps she is not so mad after all," said Rogojin, softly, as though thinking aloud.

The prince made no reply.

"Well, good-bye," said Rogojin. "I'm off tomorrow too, you know. Remember me kindly! By-the-by," he added, turning round sharply again, "did you answer her question just now? Are you happy, or not?"

"No, no, no!" cried the prince, with unspeakable sadness.

"Ha, ha! I never supposed you would say 'yes,'" cried Rogojin, laughing sardonically.

And he disappeared, without looking round again.

PART IV

Chapter I.

A week had elapsed since the rendezvous of our two friends on the green bench in the park, when, one fine morning at about half-past ten o'clock, Varvara Ardalionovna, otherwise Mrs. Ptitsin, who had been out to visit a friend, returned home in a state of considerable mental depression.

There are certain people of whom it is difficult to say anything which will at once throw them into relief—in other words, describe them graphically in their typical characteristics. These are they who are generally known as "commonplace people," and this class comprises, of course, the immense majority of mankind. Authors, as a rule, attempt to select and portray types rarely met with in their entirety, but these types are nevertheless more real than real life itself.

"Podkoleosin" [A character in Gogol's comedy, The Wedding.] was perhaps an exaggeration, but he was by no means a non-existent character; on the contrary, how many intelligent people, after hearing of this Podkoleosin from Gogol, immediately began to find that scores of their friends were exactly like him! They knew, perhaps, before Gogol told them, that their friends were like Podkoleosin, but they did not know what name to give them. In real life, young fellows seldom jump out of the window just before their weddings, because such a feat, not to speak of its other aspects, must be a decidedly unpleasant mode of escape; and yet there are plenty of bridegrooms, intelligent fellows too, who would be ready to confess themselves Podkoleosins in the depths of their consciousness, just before marriage. Nor does every husband feel bound to repeat at every step, "*Tu l'as voulu, Georges Dandin!*" like another typical personage; and yet how many millions and billions of Georges Dandins there are in real life who feel inclined to utter this soul-drawn cry after their honeymoon, if not the day after the wedding! Therefore, without entering into any more serious examination of the question, I will content myself with remarking that in real life typical characters are "watered down," so to speak; and all these Dandins and Podkoleosins actually exist among us every day, but in a diluted form. I will just add, however, that Georges Dandin might have existed exactly as Molière presented him, and probably does exist now and then, though rarely; and so I will end this scientific examination, which is beginning to look like a newspaper criticism. But for all this, the question remains,—what are the novelists to do with commonplace people, and how are they to be presented to the reader in such a form as to be in the least degree interesting? They cannot be left out altogether, for commonplace people meet one at every turn of life, and to leave them out would be to destroy the whole reality and probability of the story. To fill a novel with typical characters only, or with merely strange and uncommon people, would render the book unreal and improbable, and would very likely destroy the interest. In my opinion, the duty of the novelist is to seek out points of interest and instruction even in the characters of commonplace people.

For instance, when the whole essence of an ordinary person's nature lies in his perpetual and unchangeable commonplaceness; and when in spite of all his endeavours to do something out of the common, this person ends, eventually, by remaining in his unbroken line of routine—. I think such an individual really does become a type of his own—a type of commonplaceness which will not for the world, if it can help it, be contented, but strains and yearns to be something original and independent, without the slightest possibility of being so. To this class of commonplace people belong several characters in this novel;—characters which—I admit—I have not drawn very vividly up to now for my reader's benefit.

Such were, for instance, Varvara Ardalionovna Ptitsin, her husband, and her brother, Gania.

There is nothing so annoying as to be fairly rich, of a fairly good family, pleasing presence, average education, to be "not stupid," kind-hearted, and yet to have no talent at all, no originality, not a single idea of one's own—to be, in fact, "just like everyone else."

Of such people there are countless numbers in this world—far more even than appear. They can be divided into two classes as all men can—that is, those of limited intellect, and those who are much cleverer. The former of these classes is the happier.

To a commonplace man of limited intellect, for instance, nothing is simpler than to imagine himself an original character, and to revel in that belief without the slightest misgiving.

Many of our young women have thought fit to cut their hair short, put on blue spectacles, and call themselves Nihilists. By doing this they have been able to persuade themselves, without further trouble, that they have acquired new convictions of their own. Some men have but felt some little qualm of kindness towards their fellow-men, and the fact has been quite enough to persuade them that they stand alone in the van of enlightenment and that no one has such humanitarian feelings as they. Others have but to read an idea of somebody else's, and they can immediately assimilate it and believe that it was a child of their own brain. The "impudence of ignorance," if I may use the expression, is developed to a wonderful extent in such cases;—unlikely as it appears, it is met with at every turn.

This confidence of a stupid man in his own talents has been wonderfully depicted by Gogol in the amazing character of Pirogoff. Pirogoff has not the slightest doubt of his own genius,—nay, of his *superiority* of genius,—so certain is he of it that he never questions it. How many Pirogoffs have there not been among our writers—scholars, propagandists? I say "have been," but indeed there are plenty of them at this very day.

Our friend, Gania, belonged to the other class—to the "much cleverer" persons, though he was from head to foot permeated and saturated with the longing to be original. This class, as I have said above, is far less happy. For the "clever commonplace" person, though he may possibly imagine himself a man of genius and originality, none the less has within his heart the deathless worm of suspicion and doubt; and this doubt sometimes brings a clever man to despair. (As a rule, however, nothing tragic happens;—his liver becomes a little damaged in the course of time, nothing more serious. Such men do not give up their aspirations after originality without a severe struggle,—and there have been men who, though good fellows in themselves, and even benefactors to humanity, have sunk to the level of base criminals for the sake of originality).

Gania was a beginner, as it were, upon this road. A deep and unchangeable consciousness of his own lack of talent, combined with a vast longing to be able to persuade himself that he was original, had rankled in his heart, even from childhood.

He seemed to have been born with overwrought nerves, and in his passionate desire to excel, he was often led to the brink of some rash step; and yet, having resolved upon such a step, when the moment arrived, he invariably proved too sensible to take it. He was ready, in the same way, to do a base action in order to obtain his wished-for object; and yet, when the moment came to do it, he found that he was too honest for any great baseness. (Not that he objected to acts of petty meanness—he was always ready for *them*.) He looked with hate and loathing on the poverty and downfall of his family, and treated his mother with haughty contempt, although he knew that his whole future depended on her character and reputation.

Aglaya had simply frightened him; yet he did not give up all thoughts of her—though he never seriously hoped that she would condescend to him. At the time of his "adventure" with Nastasia Philipovna he had come to the conclusion that money was his only hope—money should do all for him.

At the moment when he lost Aglaya, and after the scene with Nastasia, he had felt so low in his own eyes that he actually brought the money back to the prince. Of this returning of the money given to him by a madwoman who had received it from a madman, he had often repented since—though he never ceased to be proud of his action. During the short time that Muishkin remained in Petersburg Gania had had time to come to hate him for his sympathy, though the prince told him that it was "not everyone who would have acted so nobly" as to return the money. He had long pondered, too, over his relations with Aglaya, and had persuaded himself that with such a strange, childish, innocent character as hers, things might have ended very differently. Remorse then seized him; he threw up his post, and buried himself in self-torment and reproach.

He lived at Ptitsin's, and openly showed contempt for the latter, though he always listened to his advice, and was sensible enough to ask for it when he wanted it. Gavrila Ardalionovitch was angry with Ptitsin because the latter did not care to become a Rothschild. "If you are to be a Jew," he said, "do it properly—squeeze people right and left, show some character; be the King of the Jews while you are about it."

Ptitsin was quiet and not easily offended—he only laughed. But on one occasion he explained seriously to Gania that he was no Jew, that he did nothing dishonest, that he could not help the market price of money, that, thanks to his accurate habits, he had already a good footing and was respected, and that his business was flourishing.

"I shan't ever be a Rothschild, and there is no reason why I should," he added, smiling; "but I shall have a house in the Liteynaya, perhaps two, and that will be enough for me." "Who knows but what I may have three!" he concluded to himself; but this dream, cherished inwardly, he never confided to a soul.

Nature loves and favours such people. Ptitsin will certainly have his reward, not three houses, but four, precisely because from childhood up he had realized that he would never be a Rothschild. That will be the limit of Ptitsin's fortune, and, come what may, he will never have more than four houses.

Varvara Ardalionovna was not like her brother. She too, had passionate desires, but they were persistent rather than impetuous. Her plans were as wise as her methods of carrying them out. No doubt she also belonged to the category of ordinary people who dream of being original, but she soon discovered that she had not a grain of true originality, and she did not let it trouble her too much. Perhaps a certain kind of pride came to her help. She made her first concession to the demands of practical life with great resolution when she consented to marry Ptitsin. However, when she married she did not say to herself, "Never mind a mean action if it leads to the end in view," as her brother would certainly have said in such a case; it is quite probable that he may have said it when he expressed his elder-brotherly satisfaction at her decision. Far from this; Varvara Ardalionovna did not marry until she felt convinced that her future husband was unassuming, agreeable, almost cultured, and that nothing on earth would tempt him to a really dishonourable deed. As to small meannesses, such trifles did not trouble her. Indeed, who is free from them? It is absurd to expect the ideal! Besides, she knew that her marriage would provide a refuge for all her family. Seeing Gania unhappy, she was anxious to help him, in spite of their former disputes and misunderstandings. Ptitsin, in a friendly way, would press his brother-in-law to enter the army. "You know," he said sometimes, jokingly, "you despise generals and generaldom, but you will see that 'they' will all end by being generals in their turn. You will see it if you live long enough!"

"But why should they suppose that I despise generals?" Gania thought sarcastically to himself.

To serve her brother's interests, Varvara Ardalionovna was constantly at the Epanchins' house, helped by the fact that in childhood she and Gania had played with General Ivan Fedorovitch's daughters. It would have been inconsistent with her character if in these visits she had been pursuing a chimera; her project was not chimerical at all; she was building on a firm basis—on her knowledge of the character of the Epanchin family, especially Aglaya, whom she studied closely. All Varvara's efforts were directed towards bringing Aglaya and Gania together. Perhaps she achieved some result; perhaps, also, she made the mistake of depending too much upon her brother, and expecting more from him than he would ever be capable of giving. However this may be, her manoeuvres were skilful enough. For weeks at a time she would never mention Gania. Her attitude was modest but dignified, and she was always extremely truthful and sincere. Examining the depths of her conscience, she found nothing to reproach herself with, and this still further strengthened her in her designs. But Varvara Ardalionovna sometimes remarked that she felt spiteful; that there was a good deal of vanity in her, perhaps even of wounded vanity. She noticed this at certain times more than at others, and especially after her visits to the Epanchins.

Today, as I have said, she returned from their house with a heavy feeling of dejection. There was a sensation of bitterness, a sort of mocking contempt, mingled with it.

Arrived at her own house, Varia heard a considerable commotion going on in the upper storey, and distinguished the voices of her father and brother. On entering the salon she found Gania pacing up and down at frantic speed, pale with rage and almost tearing his hair. She frowned, and subsided on to the sofa with a tired air, and without taking the trouble to remove her hat. She very well knew that if she kept quiet and asked her brother nothing about his reason for tearing up and down the room, his wrath would fall upon her head. So she hastened to put the question:

"The old story, eh?"

"Old story? No! Heaven knows what's up now—I don't! Father has simply gone mad; mother's in floods of tears. Upon my word, Varia, I must kick him out of the house; or else go myself," he added, probably remembering that he could not well turn people out of a house which was not his own.

"You must make allowances," murmured Varia.

"Make allowances? For whom? Him—the old blackguard? No, no, Varia—that won't do! It won't do, I tell you! And look at the swagger of the man! He's all to blame himself, and yet he puts on so much 'side' that you'd think—my word!—'It's too much trouble to go through the gate, you must break the fence for me!' That's the sort of air he puts on; but what's the matter with you, Varia? What a curious expression you have!"

"I'm all right," said Varia, in a tone that sounded as though she were all wrong.

Gania looked more intently at her.

"You've been *there?*" he asked, suddenly.

"Yes."

"Did you find out anything?"

"Nothing unexpected. I discovered that it's all true. My husband was wiser than either of us. Just as he suspected from the beginning, so it has fallen out. Where is he?"

"Out. Well—what has happened?—go on."

"The prince is formally engaged to her—that's settled. The elder sisters told me about it. Aglaya has agreed. They don't attempt to conceal it any longer; you know how mysterious and secret they have all been up to now. Adelaida's wedding is put off again, so that both can be married on one day. Isn't that delightfully romantic? Somebody ought to write a poem on it. Sit down and write an ode instead of tearing up and down like that. This evening Princess Bielokonski is to arrive; she comes just in time—they have a party tonight. He is to be presented to old Bielokonski, though I believe he knows her already; probably the engagement will be openly announced. They are only afraid that he may knock something down, or trip over something when he comes into the room. It would be just like him."

Gania listened attentively, but to his sister's astonishment he was by no means so impressed by this news (which should, she thought, have been so important to him) as she had expected.

"Well, it was clear enough all along," he said, after a moment's reflection. "So that's the end," he added, with a disagreeable smile, continuing to walk up and down the room, but much slower than before, and glancing slyly into his sister's face.

"It's a good thing that you take it philosophically, at all events," said Varia. "I'm really very glad of it."

"Yes, it's off our hands—off *yours*, I should say."

"I think I have served you faithfully. I never even asked you what happiness you expected to find with Aglaya."

"Did I ever expect to find happiness with Aglaya?"

"Come, come, don't overdo your philosophy. Of course you did. Now it's all over, and a good thing, too; pair of fools that we have been! I confess I have never been able to look at it seriously. I busied myself in it for your sake, thinking that there was no knowing what might happen with a funny girl like that to deal with. There were ninety to one chances against it. To this moment I can't make out why you wished for it."

"H'm! now, I suppose, you and your husband will never weary of egging me on to work again. You'll begin your lectures about perseverance and strength of will, and all that. I know it all by heart," said Gania, laughing.

"He's got some new idea in his head," thought Varia. "Are they pleased over there—the parents?" asked Gania, suddenly.

"N-no, I don't think they are. You can judge for yourself. I think the general is pleased enough; her mother is a little uneasy. She always loathed the idea of the prince as a *husband*; everybody knows that."

"Of course, naturally. The bridegroom is an impossible and ridiculous one. I mean, has *she* given her formal consent?"

"She has not said 'no,' up to now, and that's all. It was sure to be so with her. You know what she is like. You know how absurdly shy she is. You remember how she used to hide in a cupboard as a child, so as to avoid seeing visitors, for hours at a time. She is just the same now; but, do you know, I think there is something serious in the matter, even from her side; I feel it, somehow. She laughs at the prince, they say, from morn to night in order to hide her real feelings; but you may be sure she finds occasion to say something or other to him on the sly, for he himself is in a state of radiant happiness. He walks in the clouds; they say he is extremely funny just now; I heard it from themselves. They seemed to be laughing at me in their sleeves—those elder girls—I don't know why."

Gania had begun to frown, and probably Varia added this last sentence in order to probe his thought. However, at this moment, the noise began again upstairs.

"I'll turn him out!" shouted Gania, glad of the opportunity of venting his vexation. "I shall just turn him out—we can't have this."

"Yes, and then he'll go about the place and disgrace us as he did yesterday."

"How 'as he did yesterday'? What do you mean? What did he do yesterday?" asked Gania, in alarm.

"Why, goodness me, don't you know?" Varia stopped short.

"What? You don't mean to say that he went there yesterday!" cried Gania, flushing red with shame and anger. "Good heavens, Varia! Speak! You have just been there. *Was* he there or not, *quick*?" And Gania rushed for the door. Varia followed and caught him by both hands.

"What are you doing? Where are you going to? You can't let him go now; if you do he'll go and do something worse."

"What did he do there? What did he say?"

"They couldn't tell me themselves; they couldn't make head or tail of it; but he frightened them all. He came to see the general, who was not at home; so he asked for Lizabetha Prokofievna. First of all, he begged her for some place, or situation, for work of some kind, and then he began to complain about *us*, about me and my husband, and you, especially *you*; he said a lot of things."

"Oh! couldn't you find out?" muttered Gania, trembling hysterically.

"No—nothing more than that. Why, they couldn't understand him themselves; and very likely didn't tell me all."

Gania seized his head with both hands and tottered to the window; Varia sat down at the other window.

"Funny girl, Aglaya," she observed, after a pause. "When she left me she said, 'Give my special and personal respects to your parents; I shall certainly find an opportunity to see your father one day,' and so serious over it. She's a strange creature."

"Wasn't she joking? She was speaking sarcastically!"

"Not a bit of it; that's just the strange part of it."

"Does she know about father, do you think—or not?"

"That they do *not* know about it in the house is quite certain, the rest of them, I mean; but you have given me an idea. Aglaya perhaps knows. She alone, though, if anyone; for the sisters were as astonished as I was to hear her speak so seriously. If she knows, the prince must have told her."

"Oh! it's not a great matter to guess who told her. A thief! A thief in our family, and the head of the family, too!"

"Oh! nonsense!" cried Varia, angrily. "That was nothing but a drunkard's tale. Nonsense! Why, who invented the whole thing—Lebedeff and the prince—a pretty pair! Both were probably drunk."

"Father is a drunkard and a thief; I am a beggar, and the husband of my sister is a usurer," continued Gania, bitterly. "There was a pretty list of advantages with which to enchant the heart of Aglaya."

"That same husband of your sister, the usurer—"

"Feeds me? Go on. Don't stand on ceremony, pray."

"Don't lose your temper. You are just like a schoolboy. You think that all this sort of thing would harm you in Aglaya's eyes, do you? You little know her character. She is capable of refusing the most brilliant party, and running away and starving in a garret with some wretched student; that's the sort of girl she is. You never could or did understand how interesting you would have seen in her eyes if you had come firmly and proudly through our misfortunes. The prince has simply caught her with hook and line; firstly, because he never thought of fishing for her, and secondly, because he is an idiot in the eyes of most people. It's quite enough for her that by accepting him she puts her family out and annoys them all round—that's what she likes. You don't understand these things."

"We shall see whether I understand or no!" said Gania, enigmatically. "But I shouldn't like her to know all about father, all the same. I thought the prince would manage to hold his tongue about this, at least. He prevented Lebedeff spreading the news—he wouldn't even tell me all when I asked him—"

"Then you must see that he is not responsible. What does it matter to you now, in any case? What are you hoping for still? If you *have* a hope left, it is that your suffering air may soften her heart towards you."

"Oh, she would funk a scandal like anyone else. You are all tarred with one brush!"

"What! *Aglaya* would have funked? You are a chicken-hearted fellow, Gania!" said Varia, looking at her brother with contempt. "Not one of us is worth much. Aglaya may be a wild sort of a girl, but she is far nobler than any of us, a thousand times nobler!"

"Well—come! there's nothing to get cross about," said Gania.

"All I'm afraid of is—mother. I'm afraid this scandal about father may come to her ears; perhaps it has already. I am dreadfully afraid."

"It undoubtedly has already!" observed Gania.

Varia had risen from her place and had started to go upstairs to her mother; but at this observation of Gania's she turned and gazed at him attentively.

"Who could have told her?"

"Hippolyte, probably. He would think it the most delightful amusement in the world to tell her of it the instant he moved over here; I haven't a doubt of it."

"But how could he know anything of it? Tell me that. Lebedeff and the prince determined to tell no one—even Colia knows nothing."

"What, Hippolyte? He found it out himself, of course. Why, you have no idea what a cunning little animal he is; dirty little gossip! He has the most extraordinary nose for smelling out other people's secrets, or anything approaching to scandal. Believe it or not, but I'm pretty sure he has got round Aglaya. If he hasn't, he soon will. Rogojin is intimate with him, too. How the prince doesn't notice it, I can't understand. The little wretch considers me his enemy now and does his best to catch me tripping. What on earth does it matter to him, when he's dying? However, you'll see; I shall catch *him* tripping yet, and not he me."

"Why did you get him over here, if you hate him so? And is it really worth your while to try to score off him?"

"Why, it was yourself who advised me to bring him over!"

"I thought he might be useful. You know he is in love with Aglaya himself, now, and has written to her; he has even written to Lizabetha Prokofievna!"

"Oh! he's not dangerous there!" cried Gania, laughing angrily. "However, I believe there is something of that sort in the air; he is very likely to be in love, for he is a mere boy. But he won't write anonymous letters to the old lady; that would be too audacious a thing for him to attempt; but I dare swear the very first thing he did was to show me up to Aglaya as a base deceiver and intriguer. I confess I was fool enough to attempt something through him at first. I thought he would throw himself into my service out of revengeful feelings towards the prince, the sly little beast! But I know him better now. As for the theft, he may have heard of it from the widow in Petersburg, for if the old man committed himself to such an act, he can have done it for no other object but to give the money to her. Hippolyte said to me, without any prelude, that the general had promised the widow four hundred roubles. Of course I understood, and the little wretch looked at me with a nasty sort of satisfaction. I know him; you may depend upon it he went and told mother too, for the pleasure of wounding her. And why doesn't he die, I should like to know? He undertook to die within three weeks, and here he is getting fatter. His cough is better, too. It was only yesterday that he said that was the second day he hadn't coughed blood."

"Well, turn him out!"

"I don't *hate*, I despise him," said Gania, grandly. "Well, I do hate him, if you like!" he added, with a sudden access of rage, "and I'll tell him so to his face, even when he's dying! If you had but read his confession—good Lord! what refinement of impudence! Oh, but I'd have liked to whip him then and there, like a schoolboy, just to see how surprised he would have been! Now he hates everybody because he—Oh, I say, what on earth are they doing there! Listen to that noise! I really can't stand this any longer. Ptitsin!" he cried, as the latter entered the room, "what in the name of goodness are we coming to? Listen to that—"

But the noise came rapidly nearer, the door burst open, and old General Ivolgin, raging, furious, purple-faced, and trembling with anger, rushed in. He was followed by Nina Alexandrovna, Colia, and behind the rest, Hippolyte.

Chapter II.

Hippolyte had now been five days at the Ptitsins'. His flitting from the prince's to these new quarters had been brought about quite naturally and without many words. He did not quarrel with the prince—in fact, they seemed to part as friends. Gania, who had been hostile enough on that eventful evening, had himself come to see him a couple of days later, probably in obedience to some sudden impulse. For some reason or other, Rogojin too had begun to visit the sick boy. The prince thought it might be better for him to move away from his (the prince's) house. Hippolyte informed him, as he took his leave, that Ptitsin "had been kind enough to offer him a corner," and did not say a word about Gania, though Gania had procured his invitation, and himself came to fetch him away. Gania noticed this at the time, and put it to Hippolyte's debit on account.

Gania was right when he told his sister that Hippolyte was getting better; that he was better was clear at the first glance. He entered the room now last of all, deliberately, and with a disagreeable smile on his lips.

Nina Alexandrovna came in, looking frightened. She had changed much since we last saw her, half a year ago, and had grown thin and pale. Colia looked worried and perplexed. He could not understand the vagaries of the general, and knew nothing of the last achievement of that worthy, which had caused so much commotion in the house. But he could see that his father had of late changed very much, and that he had begun to behave in so extraordinary a fashion both at home and abroad that he was not like the same man. What perplexed and disturbed him as much as anything was that his father had entirely given up drinking during the last few days. Colia knew that he had quarrelled with both Lebedeff and the prince, and had just bought a small bottle of vodka and brought it home for his father.

"Really, mother," he had assured Nina Alexandrovna upstairs, "really you had better let him drink. He has not had a drop for three days; he must be suffering agonies—" The general now entered the room, threw the door wide open, and stood on the threshold trembling with indignation.

"Look here, my dear sir," he began, addressing Ptitsin in a very loud tone of voice; "if you have really made up your mind to sacrifice an old man—your father too or at all events father of your wife—an old man who has served his emperor—to a wretched little atheist like this, all I can say is, sir, my foot shall cease to tread your floors. Make your choice, sir; make your choice quickly, if you please! Me or this—screw! Yes, screw, sir; I said it accidentally, but let the word stand—this screw, for he screws and drills himself into my soul—"

"Hadn't you better say corkscrew?" said Hippolyte.

"No, sir, *not* corkscrew. I am a general, not a bottle, sir. Make your choice, sir—me or him."

Here Colia handed him a chair, and he subsided into it, breathless with rage.

"Hadn't you better—better—take a nap?" murmured the stupefied Ptitsin.

"A nap?" shrieked the general. "I am not drunk, sir; you insult me! I see," he continued, rising, "I see that all are against me here. Enough—I go; but know, sirs—know that—"

He was not allowed to finish his sentence. Somebody pushed him back into his chair, and begged him to be calm. Nina Alexandrovna trembled, and cried quietly. Gania retired to the window in disgust.

"But what have I done? What is his grievance?" asked Hippolyte, grinning.

"What have you done, indeed?" put in Nina Alexandrovna. "You ought to be ashamed of yourself, teasing an old man like that—and in your position, too."

"And pray what *is* my position, madame? I have the greatest respect for you, personally; but—"

"He's a little screw," cried the general; "he drills holes in my heart and soul. He wishes me to be a pervert to atheism. Know, you young greenhorn, that I was covered with honours before ever you were born; and you are nothing better than a wretched little worm, torn in two with coughing, and dying slowly of your own malice and unbelief. What did Gavrila bring you over here for? They're all against me, even to my own son—all against me."

"Oh, come—nonsense!" cried Gania; "if you did not go shaming us all over the town, things might be better for all parties."

"What—shame you? I?—what do you mean, you young calf? I shame you? I can only do you honour, sir; I cannot shame you."

He jumped up from his chair in a fit of uncontrollable rage. Gania was very angry too.

"Honour, indeed!" said the latter, with contempt.

"What do you say, sir?" growled the general, taking a step towards him.

"I say that I have but to open my mouth, and you—"

Gania began, but did not finish. The two—father and son—stood before one another, both unspeakably agitated, especially Gania.

"Gania, Gania, reflect!" cried his mother, hurriedly.

"It's all nonsense on both sides," snapped out Varia. "Let them alone, mother."

"It's only for mother's sake that I spare him," said Gania, tragically.

"Speak!" said the general, beside himself with rage and excitement; "speak—under the penalty of a father's curse!"

"Oh, father's curse be hanged—you don't frighten me that way!" said Gania. "Whose fault is it that you have been as mad as a March hare all this week? It is just a week—you see, I count the days. Take care now; don't provoke me too much, or I'll tell all. Why did you go to the Epanchins' yesterday—tell me that? And you call yourself an old man, too, with grey hair, and father of a family! H'm—nice sort of a father."

"Be quiet, Gania," cried Colia. "Shut up, you fool!"

"Yes, but how have I offended him?" repeated Hippolyte, still in the same jeering voice. "Why does he call me a screw? You all heard it. He came to me himself and began telling me about some Captain Eropegoff. I don't wish for your company, general. I always avoided you—you know that. What have I to do with Captain Eropegoff? All I did was to express my opinion that probably Captain Eropegoff never existed at all!"

"Of course he never existed!" Gania interrupted.

But the general only stood stupefied and gazed around in a dazed way. Gania's speech had impressed him, with its terrible candour. For the first moment or two he could find no words to answer him, and it was only when Hippolyte burst out laughing, and said:

"There, you see! Even your own son supports my statement that there never was such a person as Captain Eropegoff!" that the old fellow muttered confusedly:

"Kapiton Eropegoff—not Captain Eropegoff!—Kapiton—major retired—Eropegoff—Kapiton."

"Kapiton didn't exist either!" persisted Gania, maliciously.

"What? Didn't exist?" cried the poor general, and a deep blush suffused his face.

"That'll do, Gania!" cried Varia and Ptitsin.

"Shut up, Gania!" said Colia.

But this intercession seemed to rekindle the general.

"What did you mean, sir, that he didn't exist? Explain yourself," he repeated, angrily.

"Because he *didn't* exist—never could and never did—there! You'd better drop the subject, I warn you!"

"And this is my son—my own son—whom I—oh, gracious Heaven! Eropegoff—Eroshka Eropegoff didn't exist!"

"Ha, ha! it's Eroshka now," laughed Hippolyte.

"No, sir, Kapitoshka—not Eroshka. I mean, Kapiton Alexeyevitch—retired major—married Maria Petrovna Lu—Lu—he was my friend and companion—Lutugoff—from our earliest beginnings. I closed his eyes for him—he was killed. Kapiton Eropegoff never existed! tfu!"

The general shouted in his fury; but it was to be concluded that his wrath was not kindled by the expressed doubt as to Kapiton's existence. This was his scapegoat; but his excitement was caused by something quite different. As a rule he would have merely shouted down the doubt as to Kapiton, told a long yarn about his friend, and eventually retired upstairs to his room. But today, in the strange uncertainty of human nature, it seemed to require but so small an offence as this to make his cup to overflow. The old man grew purple in the face, he raised his hands. "Enough of this!" he yelled. "My curse—away, out of the house I go! Colia, bring my bag away!" He left the room hastily and in a paroxysm of rage.

His wife, Colia, and Ptitsin ran out after him.

"What have you done now?" said Varia to Gania. "He'll probably be making off *there* again! What a disgrace it all is!"

"Well, he shouldn't steal," cried Gania, panting with fury. And just at this moment his eye met Hippolyte's.

"As for you, sir," he cried, "you should at least remember that you are in a strange house and—receiving hospitality; you should not take the opportunity of tormenting an old man, sir, who is too evidently out of his mind."

Hippolyte looked furious, but he restrained himself.

"I don't quite agree with you that your father is out of his mind," he observed, quietly. "On the contrary, I cannot help thinking he has been less demented of late. Don't you think so? He has grown so cunning and careful, and weighs his words so deliberately; he spoke to me about that Kapiton fellow with an object, you know! Just fancy—he wanted me to—"

"Oh, devil take what he wanted you to do! Don't try to be too cunning with me, young man!" shouted Gania. "If you are aware of the real reason for my father's present condition (and you have kept such an excellent spying watch during these last few days that you are sure to be aware of it)—you had no right whatever to torment the—unfortunate man, and to worry my mother by your exaggerations of the affair; because the whole business is nonsense—simply a drunken freak, and nothing more, quite unproved by any evidence, and I don't believe that much of it!" (he snapped his fingers). "But you must needs spy and watch over us all, because you are a—a—"

"Screw!" laughed Hippolyte.

"Because you are a humbug, sir; and thought fit to worry people for half an hour, and tried to frighten them into believing that you would shoot yourself with your little empty pistol, pirouetting about and playing at suicide! I gave you hospitality, you have fattened on it, your cough has left you, and you repay all this—"

"Excuse me—two words! I am Varvara Ardalionovna's guest, not yours; *you* have extended no hospitality to me. On the contrary, if I am not mistaken, I believe you are yourself indebted to Mr. Ptitsin's hospitality. Four days ago I begged my mother to come down here and find lodgings, because I certainly do feel better here, though I am not fat, nor have I ceased to cough. I am today informed that my room is ready for me; therefore, having thanked your sister and mother for their kindness to me, I intend to leave the house this evening. I beg your pardon—I interrupted you—I think you were about to add something?"

"Oh—if that is the state of affairs—" began Gania.

"Excuse me—I will take a seat," interrupted Hippolyte once more, sitting down deliberately; "for I am not strong yet. Now then, I am ready to hear you. Especially as this is the last chance we shall have of a talk, and very likely the last meeting we shall ever have at all."

Gania felt a little guilty.

"I assure you I did not mean to reckon up debits and credits," he began, "and if you—"

"I don't understand your condescension," said Hippolyte. "As for me, I promised myself, on the first day of my arrival in this house, that I would have the satisfaction of settling accounts with you in a very thorough manner before I said good-bye to you. I intend to perform this operation now, if you like; after you, though, of course."

"May I ask you to be so good as to leave this room?"

"You'd better speak out. You'll be sorry afterwards if you don't."

"Hippolyte, stop, please! It's so dreadfully undignified," said Varia.

"Well, only for the sake of a lady," said Hippolyte, laughing. "I am ready to put off the reckoning, but only put it off, Varvara Ardalionovna, because an explanation between your brother and myself has become an absolute necessity, and I could not think of leaving the house without clearing up all misunderstandings first."

"In a word, you are a wretched little scandal-monger," cried Gania, "and you cannot go away without a scandal!"

"You see," said Hippolyte, coolly, "you can't restrain yourself. You'll be dreadfully sorry afterwards if you don't speak out now. Come, you shall have the first say. I'll wait."

Gania was silent and merely looked contemptuously at him.

"You won't? Very well. I shall be as short as possible, for my part. Two or three times to-day I have had the word 'hospitality' pushed down my throat; this is not fair. In inviting me here you yourself entrapped me for your own use; you thought I wished to revenge myself upon the prince. You heard that Aglaya Ivanovna had been kind to me and read my confession. Making sure that I should give myself up to your interests, you hoped that you might get some assistance out of me. I will not go into details. I don't ask either admission or confirmation of this from yourself; I am quite content to leave you to your conscience, and to feel that we understand one another capitally."

"What a history you are weaving out of the most ordinary circumstances!" cried Varia.

"I told you the fellow was nothing but a scandal-monger," said Gania.

"Excuse me, Varia Ardalionovna, I will proceed. I can, of course, neither love nor respect the prince, though he is a good-hearted fellow, if a little queer. But there is no need whatever for me to hate him. I quite understood your brother when he first offered me aid against the prince, though I did not show it; I knew well that your brother was making a ridiculous mistake in me. I am ready to spare him, however, even now; but solely out of respect for yourself, Varvara Ardalionovna.

"Having now shown you that I am not quite such a fool as I look, and that I have to be fished for with a rod and line for a good long while before I am caught, I will proceed to explain why I specially wished to make your brother look a fool. That my motive power is hate, I do not attempt to conceal. I have felt that before dying (and I am dying, however much fatter I may appear to you), I must absolutely make a fool of, at least, one of that class of men which has dogged me all my life, which I hate so cordially, and which is so prominently represented by your much esteemed brother. I should not enjoy paradise nearly so much without having done this first. I hate you, Gavrila Ardalionovitch, solely (this may seem curious to you, but I repeat)—solely because you are the type, and incarnation, and head, and crown of the most impudent, the most self-satisfied, the most vulgar and detestable form of commonplaceness. You are ordinary of the ordinary; you have no chance of ever fathering the pettiest idea of your own. And yet you are as jealous and conceited as you can possibly be; you consider yourself a great genius; of this you are persuaded, although there are dark moments of doubt and rage, when even this fact seems uncertain. There are spots of darkness on your horizon, though they will disappear when you become completely stupid. But a long and chequered path lies before you, and of this I am glad. In the first place you will never gain a certain person."

"Come, come! This is intolerable! You had better stop, you little mischief-making wretch!" cried Varia. Gania had grown very pale; he trembled, but said nothing.

Hippolyte paused, and looked at him intently and with great gratification. He then turned his gaze upon Varia, bowed, and went out, without adding another word.

Gania might justly complain of the hardness with which fate treated him. Varia dared not speak to him for a long while, as he strode past her, backwards and forwards. At last he went and stood at the window, looking out, with his back turned towards her. There was a fearful row going on upstairs again.

"Are you off?" said Gania, suddenly, remarking that she had risen and was about to leave the room. "Wait a moment—look at this."

He approached the table and laid a small sheet of paper before her. It looked like a little note.

"Good heavens!" cried Varia, raising her hands.

This was the note:

"*Gavrila Ardolionovitch*,—persuaded of your kindness of heart, I have determined to ask your advice on a matter of great importance to myself. I should like to meet you tomorrow morning at seven o'clock by the green bench in the park. It is not far from our house. Varvara Ardalionovna, who must accompany you, knows the place well.

"*A. E.*"

"What on earth is one to make of a girl like that?" said Varia.

Gania, little as he felt inclined for swagger at this moment, could not avoid showing his triumph, especially just after such humiliating remarks as those of Hippolyte. A smile of self-satisfaction beamed on his face, and Varia too was brimming over with delight.

"And this is the very day that they were to announce the engagement! What will she do next?"

"What do you suppose she wants to talk about tomorrow?" asked Gania.

"Oh, *that's* all the same! The chief thing is that she wants to see you after six months' absence. Look here, Gania, this is a *serious* business. Don't swagger again and lose the game—play carefully, but don't funk, do you understand? As if she could possibly avoid seeing what I have been working for all this last six months! And just imagine, I was there this morning and not a word of this! I was there, you know, on the sly. The old lady did not know, or she would have kicked me out. I ran some risk for you, you see. I did so want to find out, at all hazards."

Here there was a frantic noise upstairs once more; several people seemed to be rushing downstairs at once.

"Now, Gania," cried Varia, frightened, "we can't let him go out! We can't afford to have a breath of scandal about the town at this moment. Run after him and beg his pardon—quick."

But the father of the family was out in the road already. Colia was carrying his bag for him; Nina Alexandrovna stood and cried on the doorstep; she wanted to run after the general, but Ptitsin kept her back.

"You will only excite him more," he said. "He has nowhere else to go to—he'll be back here in half an hour. I've talked it all over with Colia; let him play the fool a bit, it will do him good."

"What are you up to? Where are you off to? You've nowhere to go to, you know," cried Gania, out of the window.

"Come back, father; the neighbours will hear!" cried Varia.

The general stopped, turned round, raised his hands and remarked: "My curse be upon this house!"

"Which observation should always be made in as theatrical a tone as possible," muttered Gania, shutting the window with a bang.

The neighbours undoubtedly did hear. Varia rushed out of the room.

No sooner had his sister left him alone, than Gania took the note out of his pocket, kissed it, and pirouetted around.

CHAPTER III.

As a general rule, old General Ivolgin's paroxysms ended in smoke. He had before this experienced fits of sudden fury, but not very often, because he was really a man of peaceful and kindly disposition. He had tried hundreds of times to overcome the dissolute habits which he had contracted of late years. He would suddenly remember that he was "a father," would be reconciled with his wife, and shed genuine tears. His feeling for Nina Alexandrovna amounted almost to adoration; she had pardoned so much in silence, and loved him still in spite of the state of degradation into which he had fallen. But the general's struggles with his own weakness never lasted very long. He was, in his way, an impetuous man, and a quiet life of repentance in the bosom of his family soon became insupportable to him. In the end he rebelled, and flew into rages which he regretted, perhaps, even as he gave way to them, but which were beyond his control. He picked quarrels with everyone, began to hold forth eloquently, exacted unlimited respect, and at last disappeared from the house, and sometimes did not return for a long time. He had given up interfering in the affairs of his family for two years now, and knew nothing about them but what he gathered from hearsay.

But on this occasion there was something more serious than usual. Everyone seemed to know something, but to be afraid to talk about it.

The general had turned up in the bosom of his family two or three days before, but not, as usual, with the olive branch of peace in his hand, not in the garb of penitence—in which he was usually clad on such occasions—but, on the contrary, in an uncommonly bad temper. He had arrived in a quarrelsome mood, pitching into everyone he came across, and talking about all sorts and kinds of subjects in the most unexpected manner, so that it was impossible to discover what it was that was really putting him out. At moments he would be apparently quite bright and happy; but as a rule he would sit moody and thoughtful. He would abruptly commence to hold forth about the Epanchins, about Lebedeff, or the prince, and equally abruptly would stop short and refuse to speak another word, answering all further questions with a stupid smile, unconscious that he was smiling, or that he had been asked a question. The whole of the previous night he had spent tossing about and groaning, and poor Nina Alexandrovna had been busy making cold compresses and warm fomentations and so on, without being very clear how to apply them. He had fallen asleep after a while, but not for long, and had awaked in a state of violent hypochondria which had ended in his quarrel with Hippolyte, and the solemn cursing of Ptitsin's establishment generally. It was also observed during those two or three days that he was in a state of morbid self-esteem, and was specially touchy on all points of honour. Colia insisted, in discussing the matter with his mother, that all this was but the outcome of abstinence from drink, or perhaps of pining after Lebedeff, with whom up to this time the general had been upon terms of the greatest friendship; but with whom, for some reason or other, he had quarrelled a few days since, parting from him in great wrath. There had also been a scene with the prince. Colia had asked an explanation of the latter, but had been forced to conclude that he was not told the whole truth.

If Hippolyte and Nina Alexandrovna had, as Gania suspected, had some special conversation about the general's actions, it was strange that the malicious youth, whom Gania had called a scandal-monger to his face, had not allowed himself a similar satisfaction with Colia.

The fact is that probably Hippolyte was not quite so black as Gania painted him; and it was hardly likely that he had informed Nina Alexandrovna of certain events, of which we know, for the mere pleasure of giving her pain. We must never forget that human motives are generally far more complicated than we are apt to suppose, and that we can very rarely accurately describe the motives of another. It is much better for the writer, as a rule, to content himself with the bare statement of events; and we shall take this line with regard to the catastrophe recorded above, and shall state the remaining events connected with the general's trouble shortly, because we feel that we have already given to this secondary character in our story more attention than we originally intended.

The course of events had marched in the following order. When Lebedeff returned, in company with the general, after their expedition to town a few days since, for the purpose of investigation, he brought the prince no information whatever. If the latter had not himself been occupied with other thoughts and impressions at the time, he must have observed that Lebedeff not only was very uncommunicative, but even appeared anxious to avoid him.

When the prince did give the matter a little attention, he recalled the fact that during these days he had always found Lebedeff to be in radiantly good spirits, when they happened to meet; and further, that the general and Lebedeff were always together. The two friends did not seem ever to be parted for a moment.

Occasionally the prince heard loud talking and laughing upstairs, and once he detected the sound of a jolly soldier's song going on above, and recognized the unmistakable bass of the general's voice. But the sudden outbreak of song did not last; and for an hour afterwards the animated sound of apparently drunken conversation continued to be heard from above. At length there was the clearest evidence of a grand mutual embracing, and someone burst into tears. Shortly after this, however, there was a violent but short-lived quarrel, with loud talking on both sides.

All these days Colia had been in a state of great mental preoccupation. Muishkin was usually out all day, and only came home late at night. On his return he was invariably informed that Colia had been looking for him. However, when they did meet, Colia never had anything particular to tell him, excepting that he was highly dissatisfied with the general and his present condition of mind and behaviour.

"They drag each other about the place," he said, "and get drunk together at the pub close by here, and quarrel in the street on the way home, and embrace one another after it, and don't seem to part for a moment."

When the prince pointed out that there was nothing new about that, for that they had always behaved in this manner together, Colia did not know what to say; in fact he could not explain what it was that specially worried him, just now, about his father.

On the morning following the bacchanalian songs and quarrels recorded above, as the prince stepped out of the house at about eleven o'clock, the general suddenly appeared before him, much agitated.

"I have long sought the honour and opportunity of meeting you—much-esteemed Lef Nicolaievitch," he murmured, pressing the prince's hand very hard, almost painfully so; "long—very long."

The prince begged him to step in and sit down.

"No—I will not sit down,—I am keeping you, I see,—another time!—I think I may be permitted to congratulate you upon the realization of your heart's best wishes, is it not so?"

"What best wishes?"

The prince blushed. He thought, as so many in his position do, that nobody had seen, heard, noticed, or understood anything.

"Oh—be easy, sir, be easy! I shall not wound your tenderest feelings. I've been through it all myself, and I know well how unpleasant it is when an outsider sticks his nose in where he is not wanted. I experience this every morning. I came to speak to you about another matter, though, an important matter. A very important matter, prince."

The latter requested him to take a seat once more, and sat down himself.

"Well—just for one second, then. The fact is, I came for advice. Of course I live now without any very practical objects in life; but, being full of self-respect, in which quality the ordinary Russian is so deficient as a rule, and of activity, I am desirous, in a word, prince, of placing myself and my wife and children in a position of—in fact, I want advice."

The prince commended his aspirations with warmth.

"Quite so—quite so! But this is all mere nonsense. I came here to speak of something quite different, something very important, prince. And I have determined to come to you as to a man in whose sincerity and nobility of feeling I can trust like—like—are you surprised at my words, prince?"

The prince was watching his guest, if not with much surprise, at all events with great attention and curiosity.

The old man was very pale; every now and then his lips trembled, and his hands seemed unable to rest quietly, but continually moved from place to place. He had twice already jumped up from his chair and sat down again without being in the least aware of it. He would take up a book from the table and open it—talking all the while,—look at the heading of a chapter, shut it and put it back again, seizing another immediately, but holding it unopened in his hand, and waving it in the air as he spoke.

"But enough!" he cried, suddenly. "I see I have been boring you with my—"

"Not in the least—not in the least, I assure you. On the contrary, I am listening most attentively, and am anxious to guess—"

"Prince, I wish to place myself in a respectable position—I wish to esteem myself—and to—"

"My dear sir, a man of such noble aspirations is worthy of all esteem by virtue of those aspirations alone."

The prince brought out his "copy-book sentence" in the firm belief that it would produce a good effect. He felt instinctively that some such well-sounding humbug, brought out at the proper moment, would soothe the old man's feelings, and would be specially acceptable to such a man in such a position. At all hazards, his guest must be despatched with heart relieved and spirit comforted; that was the problem before the prince at this moment.

The phrase flattered the general, touched him, and pleased him mightily. He immediately changed his tone, and started off on a long and solemn explanation. But listen as he would, the prince could make neither head nor tail of it.

The general spoke hotly and quickly for ten minutes; he spoke as though his words could not keep pace with his crowding thoughts. Tears stood in his eyes, and yet his speech was nothing but a collection of disconnected sentences, without beginning and without end—a string of unexpected words and unexpected sentiments—colliding with one another, and jumping over one another, as they burst from his lips.

"Enough!" he concluded at last, "you understand me, and that is the great thing. A heart like yours cannot help understanding the sufferings of another. Prince, you are the ideal of generosity; what are other men beside yourself? But you are young—accept my blessing! My principal object is to beg you to fix an hour for a most important conversation—that is my great hope, prince. My heart needs but a little friendship and sympathy, and yet I cannot always find means to satisfy it."

"But why not now? I am ready to listen, and—"

"No, no—prince, not now! Now is a dream! And it is too, too important! It is to be the hour of Fate to me—*my own* hour. Our interview is not to be broken in upon by every chance comer, every impertinent guest—and there are plenty of such stupid, impertinent fellows"—(he bent over and whispered mysteriously, with a funny, frightened look on his face)—"who are unworthy to tie your shoe, prince. I don't say *mine*, mind—you will understand me, prince. Only *you* understand me, prince—no one else. *He* doesn't understand me, he is absolutely—*absolutely* unable to sympathize. The first qualification for understanding another is Heart."

The prince was rather alarmed at all this, and was obliged to end by appointing the same hour of the following day for the interview desired. The general left him much comforted and far less agitated than when he had arrived.

At seven in the evening, the prince sent to request Lebedeff to pay him a visit. Lebedeff came at once, and "esteemed it an honour," as he observed, the instant he entered the room. He acted as though there had never been the slightest suspicion of the fact that he had systematically avoided the prince for the last three days.

He sat down on the edge of his chair, smiling and making faces, and rubbing his hands, and looking as though he were in delighted expectation of hearing some important communication, which had been long guessed by all.

The prince was instantly covered with confusion; for it appeared to be plain that everyone expected something of him—that everyone looked at him as though anxious to congratulate him, and greeted him with hints, and smiles, and knowing looks.

Keller, for instance, had run into the house three times of late, "just for a moment," and each time with the air of desiring to offer his congratulations. Colia, too, in spite of his melancholy, had once or twice begun sentences in much the same strain of suggestion or insinuation.

The prince, however, immediately began, with some show of annoyance, to question Lebedeff categorically, as to the general's present condition, and his opinion thereon. He described the morning's interview in a few words.

"Everyone has his worries, prince, especially in these strange and troublous times of ours," Lebedeff replied, drily, and with the air of a man disappointed of his reasonable expectations.

"Dear me, what a philosopher you are!" laughed the prince.

"Philosophy is necessary, sir—very necessary—in our day. It is too much neglected. As for me, much esteemed prince, I am sensible of having experienced the honour of your confidence in a certain matter up to a certain point, but never beyond that point. I do not for a moment complain—"

"Lebedeff, you seem to be angry for some reason!" said the prince.

"Not the least bit in the world, esteemed and revered prince! Not the least bit in the world!" cried Lebedeff, solemnly, with his hand upon his heart. "On the contrary, I am too painfully aware that neither by my position in the world, nor by my gifts of intellect and heart, nor by my riches, nor by any former conduct of mine, have I in any way deserved your confidence, which is far above my highest aspirations and hopes. Oh no, prince; I may serve you, but only as your humble slave! I am not angry, oh no! Not angry; pained perhaps, but nothing more.

"My dear Lebedeff, I—"

"Oh, nothing more, nothing more! I was saying to myself but now... 'I am quite unworthy of friendly relations with him,' say I; 'but perhaps as landlord of this house I may, at some future date, in his good time, receive information as to certain imminent and much to be desired changes—'"

So saying Lebedeff fixed the prince with his sharp little eyes, still in hope that he would get his curiosity satisfied.

The prince looked back at him in amazement.

"I don't understand what you are driving at!" he cried, almost angrily, "and, and—what an intriguer you are, Lebedeff!" he added, bursting into a fit of genuine laughter.

Lebedeff followed suit at once, and it was clear from his radiant face that he considered his prospects of satisfaction immensely improved.

"And do you know," the prince continued, "I am amazed at your naive ways, Lebedeff! Don't be angry with me—not only yours, everybody else's also! You are waiting to hear something from me at this very moment with such simplicity that I declare I feel quite ashamed of myself for having nothing whatever to tell you. I swear to you solemnly, that there is nothing to tell. There! Can you take that in?" The prince laughed again.

Lebedeff assumed an air of dignity. It was true enough that he was sometimes naive to a degree in his curiosity; but he was also an excessively cunning gentleman, and the prince was almost converting him into an enemy by his repeated rebuffs. The prince did not snub Lebedeff's curiosity, however, because he felt any contempt for him; but simply because the subject was too delicate to talk about. Only a few days before he had looked upon his own dreams almost as crimes. But Lebedeff considered the refusal as caused by personal dislike to himself, and was hurt accordingly. Indeed, there was at this moment a piece of news, most interesting to the prince, which Lebedeff knew and even had wished to tell him, but which he now kept obstinately to himself.

"And what can I do for you, esteemed prince? Since I am told you sent for me just now," he said, after a few moments' silence.

"Oh, it was about the general," began the prince, waking abruptly from the fit of musing which he too had indulged in "and—and about the theft you told me of."

"That is—er—about—what theft?"

"Oh come! just as if you didn't understand, Lukian Timofeyovitch! What are you up to? I can't make you out! The money, the money, sir! The four hundred roubles that you lost that day. You came and told me about it one morning, and then went off to Petersburg. There, *now* do you understand?"

"Oh—h—h! You mean the four hundred roubles!" said Lebedeff, dragging the words out, just as though it had only just dawned upon him what the prince was talking about. "Thanks very much, prince, for your kind interest—you do me too much honour. I found the money, long ago!"

"You found it? Thank God for that!"

"Your exclamation proves the generous sympathy of your nature, prince; for four hundred roubles—to a struggling family man like myself—is no small matter!"

"I didn't mean that; at least, of course, I'm glad for your sake, too," added the prince, correcting himself, "but—how did you find it?"

"Very simply indeed! I found it under the chair upon which my coat had hung; so that it is clear the purse simply fell out of the pocket and on to the floor!"

"Under the chair? Impossible! Why, you told me yourself that you had searched every corner of the room? How could you not have looked in the most likely place of all?"

"Of course I looked there,—of course I did! Very much so! I looked and scrambled about, and felt for it, and wouldn't believe it was not there, and looked again and again. It is always so in such cases. One longs and expects to find a lost article; one sees it is not there, and the place is as bare as one's palm; and yet one returns and looks again and again, fifteen or twenty times, likely enough!"

"Oh, quite so, of course. But how was it in your case?—I don't quite understand," said the bewildered prince. "You say it wasn't there at first, and that you searched the place thoroughly, and yet it turned up on that very spot!"

"Yes, sir—on that very spot." The prince gazed strangely at Lebedeff. "And the general?" he asked, abruptly.

"The—the general? How do you mean, the general?" said Lebedeff, dubiously, as though he had not taken in the drift of the prince's remark.

"Oh, good heavens! I mean, what did the general say when the purse turned up under the chair? You and he had searched for it together there, hadn't you?"

"Quite so—together! But the second time I thought better to say nothing about finding it. I found it alone."

"But—why in the world—and the money? Was it all there?"

"I opened the purse and counted it myself; right to a single rouble."

"I think you might have come and told me," said the prince, thoughtfully.

"Oh—I didn't like to disturb you, prince, in the midst of your private and doubtless most interesting personal reflections. Besides, I wanted to appear, myself, to have found nothing. I took the purse, and opened it, and counted the money, and shut it and put it down again under the chair."

"What in the world for?"

"Oh, just out of curiosity," said Lebedeff, rubbing his hands and sniggering.

"What, it's still there then, is it? Ever since the day before yesterday?"

"Oh no! You see, I was half in hopes the general might find it. Because if I found it, why should not he too observe an object lying before his very eyes? I moved the chair several times so as to expose the purse to view, but the general never saw it. He is very absent just now, evidently. He talks and laughs and tells stories, and suddenly flies into a rage with me, goodness knows why."

"Well, but—have you taken the purse away now?"

"No, it disappeared from under the chair in the night."

"Where is it now, then?"

"Here," laughed Lebedeff, at last, rising to his full height and looking pleasantly at the prince, "here, in the lining of my coat. Look, you can feel it for yourself, if you like!"

Sure enough there was something sticking out of the front of the coat—something large. It certainly felt as though it might well be the purse fallen through a hole in the pocket into the lining.

"I took it out and had a look at it; it's all right. I've let it slip back into the lining now, as you see, and so I have been walking about ever since yesterday morning; it knocks against my legs when I walk along."

"H'm! and you take no notice of it?"

"Quite so, I take no notice of it. Ha, ha! and think of this, prince, my pockets are always strong and whole, and yet, here in one night, is a huge hole. I know the phenomenon is unworthy of your notice; but such is the case. I examined the hole, and I declare it actually looks as though it had been made with a pen-knife, a most improbable contingency."

"And—and—the general?"

"Ah, very angry all day, sir; all yesterday and all today. He shows decided bacchanalian predilections at one time, and at another is tearful and sensitive, but at any moment he is liable to paroxysms of such rage that I assure you, prince, I am quite alarmed. I am not a military man, you know. Yesterday we were sitting together in the tavern, and the lining of my coat was—quite accidentally, of course—sticking out right in front. The general squinted at it, and flew into a rage. He never looks me quite in the face now, unless he is very drunk or maudlin; but yesterday he looked at me in such a way that a shiver went all down my back. I intend to find the purse tomorrow; but till then I am going to have another night of it with him."

"What's the good of tormenting him like this?" cried the prince.

"I don't torment him, prince, I don't indeed!" cried Lebedeff, hotly. "I love him, my dear sir, I esteem him; and believe it or not, I love him all the better for this business, yes—and value him more."

Lebedeff said this so seriously that the prince quite lost his temper with him.

"Nonsense! love him and torment him so! Why, by the very fact that he put the purse prominently before you, first under the chair and then in your lining, he shows that he does not wish to deceive you, but is anxious to beg your forgiveness in this artless way. Do you hear? He is asking your pardon. He confides in the delicacy of your feelings, and in your friendship for him. And you can allow yourself to humiliate so thoroughly honest a man!"

"Thoroughly honest, quite so, prince, thoroughly honest!" said Lebedeff, with flashing eyes. "And only you, prince, could have found so very appropriate an expression. I honour you for it, prince. Very well, that's settled; I shall find the purse now and not tomorrow. Here, I find it and take it out before your eyes! And the money is all right. Take it, prince, and keep it till tomorrow, will you? Tomorrow or next day I'll take it back again. I think, prince, that the night after its disappearance it was buried under a bush in the garden. So I believe—what do you think of that?"

"Well, take care you don't tell him to his face that you have found the purse. Simply let him see that it is no longer in the lining of your coat, and form his own conclusions."

"Do you think so? Had I not just better tell him I have found it, and pretend I never guessed where it was?"

"No, I don't think so," said the prince, thoughtfully; "it's too late for that—that would be dangerous now. No, no! Better say nothing about it. Be nice with him, you know, but don't show him—oh, *you* know well enough—"

"I know, prince, of course I know, but I'm afraid I shall not carry it out; for to do so one needs a heart like your own. He is so very irritable just now, and so proud. At one moment he will embrace me, and the next he flies out at me and sneers at me, and then I stick the lining forward on purpose. Well, *au revoir*, prince, I see I am keeping you, and boring you, too, interfering with your most interesting private reflections."

"Now, do be careful! Secrecy, as before!"

"Oh, silence isn't the word! Softly, softly!"

But in spite of this conclusion to the episode, the prince remained as puzzled as ever, if not more so. He awaited next morning's interview with the general most impatiently.

CHAPTER IV.

The time appointed was twelve o'clock, and the prince, returning home unexpectedly late, found the general waiting for him. At the first glance, he saw that the latter was displeased, perhaps because he had been kept waiting. The prince apologized, and quickly took a seat. He seemed strangely timid before the general this morning, for some reason, and felt as though his visitor were some piece of china which he was afraid of breaking.

On scrutinizing him, the prince soon saw that the general was quite a different man from what he had been the day before; he looked like one who had come to some momentous resolve. His calmness, however, was more apparent than real. He was courteous, but there was a suggestion of injured innocence in his manner.

"I've brought your book back," he began, indicating a book lying on the table. "Much obliged to you for lending it to me."

"Ah, yes. Well, did you read it, general? It's curious, isn't it?" said the prince, delighted to be able to open up conversation upon an outside subject.

"Curious enough, yes, but crude, and of course dreadful nonsense; probably the man lies in every other sentence."

The general spoke with considerable confidence, and dragged his words out with a conceited drawl.

"Oh, but it's only the simple tale of an old soldier who saw the French enter Moscow. Some of his remarks were wonderfully interesting. Remarks of an eye-witness are always valuable, whoever he be, don't you think so?"

"Had I been the publisher I should not have printed it. As to the evidence of eye-witnesses, in these days people prefer impudent lies to the stories of men of worth and long service. I know of some notes of the year 1812, which—I have determined, prince, to leave this house, Mr. Lebedeff's house."

The general looked significantly at his host.

"Of course you have your own lodging at Pavlofsk at—at your daughter's house," began the prince, quite at a loss what to say. He suddenly recollected that the general had come for advice on a most important matter, affecting his destiny.

"At my wife's; in other words, at my own place, my daughter's house."

"I beg your pardon, I—"

"I leave Lebedeff's house, my dear prince, because I have quarrelled with this person. I broke with him last night, and am very sorry that I did not do so before. I expect respect, prince, even from those to whom I give my heart, so to speak. Prince, I have often given away my heart, and am nearly always deceived. This person was quite unworthy of the gift."

"There is much that might be improved in him," said the prince, moderately, "but he has some qualities which—though amid them one cannot but discern a cunning nature—reveal what is often a diverting intellect."

The prince's tone was so natural and respectful that the general could not possibly suspect him of any insincerity.

"Oh, that he possesses good traits, I was the first to show, when I very nearly made him a present of my friendship. I am not dependent upon his hospitality, and upon his house; I have my own family. I do not attempt to justify my own weakness. I have drunk with this man, and perhaps I deplore the fact now, but I did not take him up for the sake of drink alone (excuse the crudeness of the expression, prince); I did not make friends with him for that alone. I was attracted by his good qualities; but when the fellow declares that he was a child in 1812, and had his left leg cut off, and buried in the Vagarkoff cemetery, in Moscow, such a cock-and-bull story amounts to disrespect, my dear sir, to—to impudent exaggeration."

"Oh, he was very likely joking; he said it for fun."

"I quite understand you. You mean that an innocent lie for the sake of a good joke is harmless, and does not offend the human heart. Some people lie, if you like to put it so, out of pure friendship, in order to amuse their fellows; but when a man makes use of extravagance in order to show his disrespect and to make clear how the intimacy bores him, it is time for a man of honour to break off the said intimacy, and to teach the offender his place."

The general flushed with indignation as he spoke.

"Oh, but Lebedeff cannot have been in Moscow in 1812. He is much too young; it is all nonsense."

"Very well, but even if we admit that he *was* alive in 1812, can one believe that a French chasseur pointed a cannon at him for a lark, and shot his left leg off? He says he picked his own leg up and took it away and buried it in the cemetery. He swore he had a stone put up over it with the inscription: 'Here lies the leg of Collegiate Secretary Lebedeff,' and on the other side, 'Rest, beloved ashes, till the morn of joy,' and that he has a service read over it every year (which is simply sacrilege), and goes to Moscow once a year on purpose. He invites me to Moscow in order to prove his assertion, and show me his leg's tomb, and the very cannon that shot him; he says it's the eleventh from the gate of the Kremlin, an old-fashioned falconet taken from the French afterwards."

"And, meanwhile both his legs are still on his body," said the prince, laughing. "I assure you, it is only an innocent joke, and you need not be angry about it."

"Excuse me—wait a minute—he says that the leg we see is a wooden one, made by Tchernosvitoff."

"They do say one can dance with those!"

"Quite so, quite so; and he swears that his wife never found out that one of his legs was wooden all the while they were married. When I showed him the ridiculousness of all this, he said, 'Well, if you were one of Napoleon's pages in 1812, you might let me bury my leg in the Moscow cemetery.'"

"Why, did you say—" began the prince, and paused in confusion.

The general gazed at his host disdainfully.

"Oh, go on," he said, "finish your sentence, by all means. Say how odd it appears to you that a man fallen to such a depth of humiliation as I, can ever have been the actual eye-witness of great events. Go on, *I* don't mind! Has *he* found time to tell you scandal about me?"

"No, I've heard nothing of this from Lebedeff, if you mean Lebedeff."

"H'm; I thought differently. You see, we were talking over this period of history. I was criticizing a current report of something which then happened, and having been myself an eye-witness of the occurrence—you are smiling, prince—you are looking at my face as if—"

"Oh no! not at all—I—"

"I am rather young-looking, I know; but I am actually older than I appear to be. I was ten or eleven in the year 1812. I don't know my age exactly, but it has always been a weakness of mine to make it out less than it really is."

"I assure you, general, I do not in the least doubt your statement. One of our living autobiographers states that when he was a small baby in Moscow in 1812 the French soldiers fed him with bread."

"Well, there you see!" said the general, condescendingly. "There is nothing whatever unusual about my tale. Truth very often appears to be impossible. I was a page—it sounds strange, I dare say. Had I been fifteen years old I should probably have been terribly frightened when the French arrived, as my mother was (who had been too slow about clearing out of Moscow); but as I was only just ten I was not in the least alarmed, and rushed through the crowd to the very door of the palace when Napoleon alighted from his horse."

"Undoubtedly, at ten years old you would not have felt the sense of fear, as you say," blurted out the prince, horribly uncomfortable in the sensation that he was just about to blush.

"Of course; and it all happened so easily and naturally. And yet, were a novelist to describe the episode, he would put in all kinds of impossible and incredible details."

"Oh," cried the prince, "I have often thought that! Why, I know of a murder, for the sake of a watch. It's in all the papers now. But if some writer had invented it, all the critics would have jumped down his throat and said the thing was too improbable for anything. And yet you read it in the paper, and you can't help thinking that out of these strange disclosures is to be gained the full knowledge of Russian life and character. You said that well, general; it is so true," concluded the prince, warmly, delighted to have found a refuge from the fiery blushes which had covered his face.

"Yes, it's quite true, isn't it?" cried the general, his eyes sparkling with gratification. "A small boy, a child, would naturally realize no danger; he would shove his way through the crowds to see the shine and glitter of the uniforms, and especially the great man of whom everyone was speaking, for at that time all the world had been talking of no one but this man for some years past. The world was full of his name; I—so to speak—drew it in with my mother's milk. Napoleon, passing a couple of paces from me, caught sight of me accidentally. I was very well dressed, and being all alone, in that crowd, as you will easily imagine..."

"Oh, of course! Naturally the sight impressed him, and proved to him that not *all* the aristocracy had left Moscow; that at least some nobles and their children had remained behind."

"Just so! just so! He wanted to win over the aristocracy! When his eagle eye fell on me, mine probably flashed back in response. '*Voilà un garçon bien éveillé! Qui est ton père?*' I immediately replied, almost panting with excitement, 'A general, who died on the battle-fields of his country!' '*Le fils d'un boyard et d'un brave, pardessus le marché. J'aime les boyards. M'aimes-tu, petit?*'

"To this keen question I replied as keenly, 'The Russian heart can recognize a great man even in the bitter enemy of his country.' At least, I don't remember the exact words, you know, but the idea was as I say. Napoleon was struck; he thought a minute and then said to his suite: 'I like that boy's pride; if all Russians think like this child, then—' he didn't finish, but went on and entered the palace. I instantly mixed with his suite, and followed him. I was already in high favour. I remember when he came into the first hall, the emperor stopped before a portrait of the Empress Katherine, and after a thoughtful glance remarked, 'That was a great woman,' and passed on.

"Well, in a couple of days I was known all over the palace and the Kremlin as 'le petit boyard.' I only went home to sleep. They were nearly out of their minds about me at home. A couple of days after this, Napoleon's page, De Bazancour, died; he had not been able to stand the trials of the campaign. Napoleon remembered me; I was taken away without explanation; the dead page's uniform was tried on me, and when I was taken before the emperor, dressed in it, he nodded his head to me, and I was told that I was appointed to the vacant post of page.

"Well, I was glad enough, for I had long felt the greatest sympathy for this man; and then the pretty uniform and all that—only a child, you know—and so on. It was a dark green dress coat with gold buttons—red facings, white trousers, and a white silk waistcoat—silk stockings, shoes with buckles, and top-boots if I were riding out with his majesty or with the suite.

"Though the position of all of us at that time was not particularly brilliant, and the poverty was dreadful all round, yet the etiquette at court was strictly preserved, and the more strictly in proportion to the growth of the forebodings of disaster."

"Quite so, quite so, of course!" murmured the poor prince, who didn't know where to look. "Your memoirs would be most interesting."

The general was, of course, repeating what he had told Lebedeff the night before, and thus brought it out glibly enough, but here he looked suspiciously at the prince out of the corners of his eyes.

"My memoirs!" he began, with redoubled pride and dignity. "Write my memoirs? The idea has not tempted me. And yet, if you please, my memoirs have long been written, but they shall not see the light until dust returns to dust. Then, I doubt not, they will be translated into all languages, not of course on account of their actual literary merit, but because of the great events of which I was the actual witness, though but a child at the time. As a child, I was able to penetrate into the secrecy of the great man's private room. At nights I have heard the groans and wailings of this 'giant in distress.' He could feel no shame in weeping before such a mere child as I was, though I understood even then that the reason for his suffering was the silence of the Emperor Alexander."

"Yes, of course; he had written letters to the latter with proposals of peace, had he not?" put in the prince.

"We did not know the details of his proposals, but he wrote letter after letter, all day and every day. He was dreadfully agitated. Sometimes at night I would throw myself upon his breast with tears (Oh, how I loved that man!). 'Ask forgiveness, Oh, ask forgiveness of the Emperor Alexander!' I would cry. I should have said, of course, 'Make peace with Alexander,' but as a child I expressed my idea in the naive way recorded. 'Oh, my child,' he would say (he loved to talk to me and seemed to forget my tender years), 'Oh, my child, I am ready to kiss Alexander's feet, but I hate and abominate the King of Prussia and the Austrian Emperor, and—and—but you know nothing of politics, my child.' He would pull up, remembering whom he was speaking to, but his eyes would sparkle for a long while after this. Well now, if I were to describe all this, and I have seen greater events than these, all these critical gentlemen of the press and political parties—Oh, no thanks! I'm their very humble servant, but no thanks!"

"Quite so—parties—you are very right," said the prince. "I was reading a book about Napoleon and the Waterloo campaign only the other day, by Charasse, in which the author does not attempt to conceal his joy at Napoleon's discomfiture at every page. Well now, I don't like that; it smells of 'party,' you know. You are quite right. And were you much occupied with your service under Napoleon?"

The general was in ecstasies, for the prince's remarks, made, as they evidently were, in all seriousness and simplicity, quite dissipated the last relics of his suspicion.

"I know Charasse's book! Oh! I was so angry with his work! I wrote to him and said—I forget what, at this moment. You ask whether I was very busy under the Emperor? Oh no! I was called 'page,' but hardly took my duty seriously. Besides, Napoleon very soon lost hope of conciliating the Russians, and he would have forgotten all about me had he not loved me—for personal reasons—I don't mind saying so now. My heart was greatly drawn to him, too. My duties were light. I merely had to be at the palace occasionally to escort the Emperor out riding, and that was about all. I rode very fairly well. He used to have a ride before dinner, and his suite on those occasions were generally Davoust, myself, and Roustan."

"Constant?" said the prince, suddenly, and quite involuntarily.

"No; Constant was away then, taking a letter to the Empress Josephine. Instead of him there were always a couple of orderlies—and that was all, excepting, of course, the generals and marshals whom Napoleon always took with him for the inspection of various localities, and for the sake of consultation generally. I remember there was one—Davoust—nearly always with him—a big man with spectacles. They used to argue and quarrel sometimes. Once they were in the Emperor's study together—just those two and myself—I was unobserved—and they argued, and the Emperor seemed to be agreeing to something under protest. Suddenly his eye fell on me and an idea seemed to flash across him.

"'Child,' he said, abruptly. 'If I were to recognize the Russian orthodox religion and emancipate the serfs, do you think Russia would come over to me?'"

"'Never!' I cried, indignantly."

"The Emperor was much struck."

"'In the flashing eyes of this patriotic child I read and accept the fiat of the Russian people. Enough, Davoust, it is mere phantasy on our part. Come, let's hear your other project.'"

"Yes, but that was a great idea," said the prince, clearly interested. "You ascribe it to Davoust, do you?"

"Well, at all events, they were consulting together at the time. Of course it was the idea of an eagle, and must have originated with Napoleon; but the other project was good too—it was the 'Conseil du lion!' as Napoleon called it. This project consisted in a proposal to occupy the Kremlin with the whole army; to arm and fortify it scientifically, to kill as many horses as could be got, and salt their flesh, and spend the winter there; and in spring to fight their way out. Napoleon liked the idea—it attracted him. We rode round the Kremlin walls every day, and Napoleon used to give orders where they were to be patched, where built up, where pulled down and so on. All was decided at last. They were alone together—those two and myself.

"Napoleon was walking up and down with folded arms. I could not take my eyes off his face—my heart beat loudly and painfully.

"'I'm off,' said Davoust. 'Where to?' asked Napoleon.

"'To salt horse-flesh,' said Davoust. Napoleon shuddered—his fate was being decided.

"'Child,' he addressed me suddenly, 'what do you think of our plan?' Of course he only applied to me as a sort of toss-up, you know. I turned to Davoust and addressed my reply to him. I said, as though inspired:

"'Escape, general! Go home!—'

"The project was abandoned; Davoust shrugged his shoulders and went out, whispering to himself—'Bah, il devient superstitieux!' Next morning the order to retreat was given."

"All this is most interesting," said the prince, very softly, "if it really was so—that is, I mean—" he hastened to correct himself.

"Oh, my dear prince," cried the general, who was now so intoxicated with his own narrative that he probably could not have pulled up at the most patent indiscretion. "You say, 'if it really was so!' There was more—much more, I assure you! These are merely a few little political acts. I tell you I was the eye-witness of the nightly sorrow and groanings of the great man, and of that no one can speak but myself. Towards the end he wept no more, though he continued to emit an occasional groan; but his face grew more overcast day by day, as though Eternity were wrapping its gloomy mantle about him. Occasionally we passed whole hours of silence together at night, Roustan snoring in the next room—that fellow slept like a pig. 'But he's loyal to me and my dynasty,' said Napoleon of him.

"Sometimes it was very painful to me, and once he caught me with tears in my eyes. He looked at me kindly. 'You are sorry for me,' he said, 'you, my child, and perhaps one other child—my son, the King of Rome—may grieve for me. All the rest hate me; and my brothers are the first to betray me in misfortune.' I sobbed and threw myself into his arms. He could not resist me—he burst into tears, and our tears mingled as we folded each other in a close embrace.

"'Write, oh, write a letter to the Empress Josephine!' I cried, sobbing. Napoleon started, reflected, and said, 'You remind me of a third heart which loves me. Thank you, my friend;' and then and there he sat down and wrote that letter to Josephine, with which Constant was sent off next day."

"You did a good action," said the prince, "for in the midst of his angry feelings you insinuated a kind thought into his heart."

"Just so, prince, just so. How well you bring out that fact! Because your own heart is good!" cried the ecstatic old gentleman, and, strangely enough, real tears glistened in his eyes. "Yes, prince, it was a wonderful spectacle. And, do you know, I all but went off to Paris, and should assuredly have shared his solitary exile with him; but, alas, our destinies were otherwise ordered! We parted, he to his island, where I am sure he thought of the weeping child who had embraced him so affectionately at parting in Moscow; and I was sent off to the cadet corps, where I found nothing but roughness and harsh discipline. Alas, my happy days were done!"

"'I do not wish to deprive your mother of you, and, therefore, I will not ask you to go with me,' he said, the morning of his departure, 'but I should like to do something for you.' He was mounting his horse as he spoke. 'Write something in my sister's album for me,' I said rather timidly, for he was in a state of great dejection at the moment. He turned, called for a pen, took the album. 'How old is your sister?' he asked, holding the pen in his hand. 'Three years old,' I said. 'Ah, petite fille alors!' and he wrote in the album:

"'Ne mentez jamais! Napoléon (votre ami sincère).'

"Such advice, and at such a moment, you must allow, prince, was—"

"Yes, quite so; very remarkable."

"This page of the album, framed in gold, hung on the wall of my sister's drawing-room all her life, in the most conspicuous place, till the day of her death; where it is now, I really don't know. Heavens! it's two o'clock! How I have kept you, prince! It is really most unpardonable of me."

The general rose.

"Oh, not in the least," said the prince. "On the contrary, I have been so much interested, I'm really very much obliged to you."

"Prince," said the general, pressing his hand, and looking at him with flashing eyes, and an expression as though he were under the influence of a sudden thought which had come upon him with stunning force. "Prince, you are so kind, so simple-minded, that sometimes I really feel sorry for you! I gaze at you with a feeling of real affection. Oh, Heaven bless you! May your life blossom and fructify in love. Mine is over. Forgive me, forgive me!"

He left the room quickly, covering his face with his hands.

The prince could not doubt the sincerity of his agitation. He understood, too, that the old man had left the room intoxicated with his own success. The general belonged to that class of liars, who, in spite of their transports of lying, invariably suspect that they are not believed. On this occasion, when he recovered from his exaltation, he would probably suspect Muishkin of pitying him, and feel insulted.

"Have I been acting rightly in allowing him to develop such vast resources of imagination?" the prince asked himself. But his answer was a fit of violent laughter which lasted ten whole minutes. He tried to reproach himself for the laughing fit, but eventually concluded that he needn't do so, since in spite of it he was truly sorry for the old man. The same evening he received a strange letter, short but decided. The general informed him that they must part for ever; that he was grateful, but that even from him he could not accept "signs of sympathy which were humiliating to the dignity of a man already miserable enough."

When the prince heard that the old man had gone to Nina Alexandrovna, though, he felt almost easy on his account.

We have seen, however, that the general paid a visit to Lizabetha Prokofievna and caused trouble there, the final upshot being that he frightened Mrs. Epanchin, and angered her by bitter hints as to his son Gania.

He had been turned out in disgrace, eventually, and this was the cause of his bad night and quarrelsome day, which ended in his sudden departure into the street in a condition approaching insanity, as recorded before.

Colia did not understand the position. He tried severity with his father, as they stood in the street after the latter had cursed the household, hoping to bring him round that way.

"Well, where are we to go to now, father?" he asked. "You don't want to go to the prince's; you have quarrelled with Lebedeff; you have no money; I never have any; and here we are in the middle of the road, in a nice sort of mess."

"Better to be of a mess than in a mess! I remember making a joke something like that at the mess in eighteen hundred and forty—forty—I forget. 'Where is my youth, where is my golden youth?' Who was it said that, Colia?"

"It was Gogol, in Dead Souls, father," cried Colia, glancing at him in some alarm.

"'Dead Souls,' yes, of course, dead. When I die, Colia, you must engrave on my tomb:

> "*Here lies a Dead Soul,*
> *Shame pursues me.*'

"Who said that, Colia?"

"I don't know, father."

"There was no Eropegoff? Eroshka Eropegoff?" he cried, suddenly, stopping in the road in a frenzy. "No Eropegoff! And my own son to say it! Eropegoff was in the place of a brother to me for eleven months. I fought a duel for him. He was married afterwards, and then killed on the field of battle. The bullet struck the cross on my breast and glanced off straight into his temple. 'I'll never forget you,' he cried, and expired. I served my country well and honestly, Colia, but shame, shame has pursued me! You and Nina will come to my grave, Colia; poor Nina, I always used to call her Nina in the old days, and how she loved.... Nina, Nina, oh, Nina. What have I ever done to deserve your forgiveness and long-suffering? Oh, Colia, your mother has an angelic spirit, an angelic spirit, Colia!"

"I know that, father. Look here, dear old father, come back home! Let's go back to mother. Look, she ran after us when we came out. What have you stopped her for, just as though you didn't take in what I said? Why are you crying, father?"

Poor Colia cried himself, and kissed the old man's hands

"You kiss my hands, *mine?*"

"Yes, yes, yours, yours! What is there to surprise anyone in that? Come, come, you mustn't go on like this, crying in the middle of the road; and you a general too, a military man! Come, let's go back."

"God bless you, dear boy, for being respectful to a disgraced man. Yes, to a poor disgraced old fellow, your father. You shall have such a son yourself; le roi de Rome. Oh, curses on this house!"

"Come, come, what does all this mean?" cried Colia beside himself at last. "What is it? What has happened to you? Why don't you wish to come back home? Why have you gone out of your mind, like this?"

"I'll explain it, I'll explain all to you. Don't shout! You shall hear. Le roi de Rome. Oh, I am sad, I am melancholy!

"'Nurse, where is your tomb?'"

"Who said that, Colia?"

"I don't know, I don't know who said it. Come home at once; come on! I'll punch Gania's head myself, if you like—only come. Oh, where *are* you off to again?" The general was dragging him away towards the door of a house nearby. He sat down on the step, still holding Colia by the hand.

"Bend down—bend down your ear. I'll tell you all—disgrace—bend down, I'll tell you in your ear."

"What are you dreaming of?" said poor, frightened Colia, stooping down towards the old man, all the same.

"Le roi de Rome," whispered the general, trembling all over.

"What? What *do* you mean? What roi de Rome?"

"I—I," the general continued to whisper, clinging more and more tightly to the boy's shoulder. "I—wish—to tell you—all—Maria—Maria Petrovna—Su—Su—Su......."

Colia broke loose, seized his father by the shoulders, and stared into his eyes with frenzied gaze. The old man had grown livid—his lips were shaking, convulsions were passing over his features. Suddenly he leant over and began to sink slowly into Colia's arms.

"He's got a stroke!" cried Colia, loudly, realizing what was the matter at last.

CHAPTER V.

In point of fact, Varia had rather exaggerated the certainty of her news as to the prince's betrothal to Aglaya. Very likely, with the perspicacity of her sex, she gave out as an accomplished fact what she felt was pretty sure to become a fact in a few days. Perhaps she could not resist the satisfaction of pouring one last drop of bitterness into her brother Gania's cup, in spite of her love for him. At all events, she had been unable to obtain any definite news from the Epanchin girls—the most she could get out of them being hints and surmises, and so on. Perhaps Aglaya's sisters had merely been pumping Varia for news while pretending to impart information; or perhaps, again, they had been unable to resist the feminine gratification of teasing a friend—for, after all this time, they could scarcely have helped divining the aim of her frequent visits.

On the other hand, the prince, although he had told Lebedeff,—as we know, that nothing had happened, and that he had nothing to impart,—the prince may have been in error. Something strange seemed to have happened, without anything definite having actually happened. Varia had guessed that with her true feminine instinct.

How or why it came about that everyone at the Epanchins' became imbued with one conviction—that something very important had happened to Aglaya, and that her fate was in process of settlement—it would be very difficult to explain. But no sooner had this idea taken root, than all at once declared that they had seen and observed it long ago; that they had remarked it at the time of the "poor knight" joke, and even before, though they had been unwilling to believe in such nonsense.

So said the sisters. Of course, Lizabetha Prokofievna had foreseen it long before the rest; her "heart had been sore" for a long while, she declared, and it was now so sore that she appeared to be quite overwhelmed, and the very thought of the prince became distasteful to her.

There was a question to be decided—most important, but most difficult; so much so, that Mrs. Epanchin did not even see how to put it into words. Would the prince do or not? Was all this good or bad? If good (which might be the case, of course), *why* good? If bad (which was hardly doubtful), *wherein*, especially, bad? Even the general, the paterfamilias, though astonished at first, suddenly declared that, "upon his honour, he really believed he had fancied something of the kind, after all. At first, it seemed a new idea, and then, somehow, it looked as familiar as possible." His wife frowned him down there. This was in the morning; but in the evening, alone with his wife, he had given tongue again.

"Well, really, you know"—(silence)—"of course, you know all this is very strange, if true, which I cannot deny; but"—(silence).—"But, on the other hand, if one looks things in the face, you know—upon my honour, the prince is a rare good fellow—and—and—and—well, his name, you know—your family name—all this looks well, and perpetuates the name and title and all that—which at this moment is not standing so high as it might—from one point of view—don't you know? The world, the world is the world, of course—and people will talk—and—and—the prince has property, you know—if it is not very large—and then he—he—" (Continued silence, and collapse of the general.)

Hearing these words from her husband, Lizabetha Prokofievna was driven beside herself.

According to her opinion, the whole thing had been one huge, fantastical, absurd, unpardonable mistake. "First of all, this prince is an idiot, and, secondly, he is a fool—knows nothing of the world, and has no place in it. Whom can he be shown to? Where can you take him to? What will old Bielokonski say? We never thought of such a husband as *that* for our Aglaya!"

Of course, the last argument was the chief one. The maternal heart trembled with indignation to think of such an absurdity, although in that heart there rose another voice, which said: "And *why* is not the prince such a husband as you would have desired for Aglaya?" It was this voice which annoyed Lizabetha Prokofievna more than anything else.

For some reason or other, the sisters liked the idea of the prince. They did not even consider it very strange; in a word, they might be expected at any moment to range themselves strongly on his side. But both of them decided to say nothing either way. It had always been noticed in the family that the stronger Mrs. Epanchin's opposition was to any project, the nearer she was, in reality, to giving in.

Alexandra, however, found it difficult to keep absolute silence on the subject. Long since holding, as she did, the post of "confidential adviser to mamma," she was now perpetually called in council, and asked her opinion, and especially her assistance, in order to recollect "how on earth all this happened?" Why did no one see it? Why did no one say anything about it? What did all that wretched "poor knight" joke mean? Why was she, Lizabetha Prokofievna, driven to think, and foresee, and worry for everybody, while they all sucked their thumbs, and counted the crows in the garden, and did nothing? At first, Alexandra had been very careful, and had merely replied that perhaps her father's remark was not so far out: that, in the eyes of the world, probably the choice of the prince as a husband for one of the Epanchin girls would be considered a very wise one. Warming up, however, she added that the prince was by no means a fool, and never had been; and that as to "place in the world," no one knew what the position of a respectable person in Russia would imply in a few years—whether it would depend on successes in the government service, on the old system, or what.

To all this her mother replied that Alexandra was a freethinker, and that all this was due to that "cursed woman's rights question."

Half an hour after this conversation, she went off to town, and thence to the Kammenny Ostrof, ["Stone Island," a suburb and park of St. Petersburg] to see Princess Bielokonski, who had just arrived from Moscow on a short visit. The princess was Aglaya's godmother.

"Old Bielokonski" listened to all the fevered and despairing lamentations of Lizabetha Prokofievna without the least emotion; the tears of this sorrowful mother did not evoke answering sighs—in fact, she laughed at her. She was a dreadful old despot, this princess; she could not allow equality in anything, not even in friendship of the oldest standing, and she insisted on treating Mrs. Epanchin as her *protégée*, as she had been thirty-five years ago. She could never put up with the independence and energy of Lizabetha's character. She observed that, as usual, the whole family had gone much too far ahead, and had converted a fly into an elephant; that, so far as she had heard their story, she was persuaded that nothing of any seriousness had occurred; that it would surely be better to wait until something *did* happen; that the prince, in her opinion, was a very decent young fellow, though perhaps a little eccentric, through illness, and not quite as weighty in the world as one could wish. The worst feature was, she said, Nastasia Philipovna.

Lizabetha Prokofievna well understood that the old lady was angry at the failure of Evgenie Pavlovitch—her own recommendation. She returned home to Pavlofsk in a worse humour than when she left, and of course everybody in the house suffered. She pitched into everyone, because, she declared, they had 'gone mad.' Why were things always mismanaged in her house? Why had everybody been in such a frantic hurry in this matter? So far as she could see, nothing whatever had happened. Surely they had better wait and see what was to happen, instead of making mountains out of molehills.

And so the conclusion of the matter was that it would be far better to take it quietly, and wait coolly to see what would turn up. But, alas! peace did not reign for more than ten minutes. The first blow dealt to its power was in certain news communicated to Lizabetha Prokofievna as to events which had happened during her trip to see the princess. (This trip had taken place the day after that on which the prince had turned up at the Epanchins at nearly one o'clock at night, thinking it was nine.)

The sisters replied candidly and fully enough to their mother's impatient questions on her return. They said, in the first place, that nothing particular had happened since her departure; that the prince had been, and that Aglaya had kept him waiting a long while before she appeared—half an hour, at least; that she had then come in, and immediately asked the prince to have a game of chess; that the prince did not know the game, and Aglaya had beaten him easily; that she had been in a wonderfully merry mood, and had laughed at the prince, and chaffed him so unmercifully that one was quite sorry to see his wretched expression.

She had then asked him to play cards—the game called "little fools." At this game the tables were turned completely, for the prince had shown himself a master at it. Aglaya had cheated and changed cards, and stolen others, in the most bare-faced way, but, in spite of everything the prince had beaten her hopelessly five times running, and she had been left "little fool" each time.

Aglaya then lost her temper, and began to say such awful things to the prince that he laughed no more, but grew dreadfully pale, especially when she said that she should not remain in the house with him, and that he ought to be ashamed of coming to their house at all, especially at night, "*after all that had happened.*"

So saying, she had left the room, banging the door after her, and the prince went off, looking as though he were on his way to a funeral, in spite of all their attempts at consolation.

Suddenly, a quarter of an hour after the prince's departure, Aglaya had rushed out of her room in such a hurry that she had not even wiped her eyes, which were full of tears. She came back because Colia had brought a hedgehog. Everybody came in to see the hedgehog. In answer to their questions Colia explained that the hedgehog was not his, and that he had left another boy, Kostia Lebedeff, waiting for him outside. Kostia was too shy to come in, because he was carrying a hatchet; they had bought the hedgehog and the hatchet from a peasant whom they had met on the road. He had offered to sell them the hedgehog, and they had paid fifty copecks for it; and the hatchet had so taken their fancy that they had made up their minds to buy it of their own accord. On hearing this, Aglaya urged Colia to sell her the hedgehog; she even called him "dear Colia," in trying to coax him. He refused for a long time, but at last he could hold out no more, and went to fetch Kostia Lebedeff. The latter appeared, carrying his hatchet, and covered with confusion. Then it came out that the hedgehog was not theirs, but the property of a schoolmate, one Petroff, who had given them some money to buy Schlosser's History for him, from another schoolfellow who at that moment was driven to raising money by the sale of his books. Colia and Kostia were about to make this purchase for their friend when chance brought the hedgehog to their notice, and they had succumbed to the temptation of buying it. They were now taking Petroff the hedgehog and hatchet which they had bought with his money, instead of Schlosser's History. But Aglaya so entreated them that at last they consented to sell her the hedgehog. As soon as she had got possession of it, she put it in a wicker basket with Colia's help, and covered it with a napkin. Then she said to Colia: "Go and take this hedgehog to the prince from me, and ask him to accept it as a token of my profound respect." Colia joyfully promised to do the errand, but he demanded explanations. "What does the hedgehog mean? What is the meaning of such a present?" Aglaya replied that it was none of his business. "I am sure that there is some allegory about it," Colia persisted. Aglaya grew angry, and called him "a silly boy." "If I did not respect all women in your person," replied Colia, "and if my own principles would permit it, I would soon prove to you, that I know how to answer such an insult!" But, in the end, Colia went off with the hedgehog in great delight, followed by Kostia Lebedeff. Aglaya's annoyance was soon over, and seeing that Colia was swinging the hedgehog's basket violently to and fro, she called out to him from the verandah, as if they had never quarrelled: "Colia, dear, please take care not to drop him!" Colia appeared to have no grudge against her, either, for he stopped, and answered most cordially: "No, I will not drop him! Don't be afraid, Aglaya Ivanovna!" After which he went on his way. Aglaya burst out laughing and ran up to her room, highly delighted. Her good spirits lasted the whole day.

All this filled poor Lizabetha's mind with chaotic confusion. What on earth did it all mean? The most disturbing feature was the hedgehog. What was the symbolic signification of a hedgehog? What did they understand by it? What underlay it? Was it a cryptic message?

Poor General Epanchin "put his foot in it" by answering the above questions in his own way. He said there was no cryptic message at all. As for the hedgehog, it was just a hedgehog, which meant nothing—unless, indeed, it was a pledge of friendship,—the sign of forgetting of offences and so on. At all events, it was a joke, and, of course, a most pardonable and innocent one.

We may as well remark that the general had guessed perfectly accurately.

The prince, returning home from the interview with Aglaya, had sat gloomy and depressed for half an hour. He was almost in despair when Colia arrived with the hedgehog.

Then the sky cleared in a moment. The prince seemed to arise from the dead; he asked Colia all about it, made him repeat the story over and over again, and laughed and shook hands with the boys in his delight.

It seemed clear to the prince that Aglaya forgave him, and that he might go there again this very evening; and in his eyes that was not only the main thing, but everything in the world.

"What children we are still, Colia!" he cried at last, enthusiastically,—"and how delightful it is that we can be children still!"

"Simply—my dear prince,—simply she is in love with you,—that's the whole of the secret!" replied Colia, with authority.

The prince blushed, but this time he said nothing. Colia burst out laughing and clapped his hands. A minute later the prince laughed too, and from this moment until the evening he looked at his watch every other minute to see how much time he had to wait before evening came.

But the situation was becoming rapidly critical.

Mrs. Epanchin could bear her suspense no longer, and in spite of the opposition of husband and daughters, she sent for Aglaya, determined to get a straightforward answer out of her, once for all.

"Otherwise," she observed hysterically, "I shall die before evening."

It was only now that everyone realized to what a ridiculous dead-lock the whole matter had been brought. Excepting feigned surprise, indignation, laughter, and jeering—both at the prince and at everyone who asked her questions,—nothing could be got out of Aglaya.

Lizabetha Prokofievna went to bed and only rose again in time for tea, when the prince might be expected.

She awaited him in trembling agitation; and when he at last arrived she nearly went off into hysterics.

Muishkin himself came in very timidly. He seemed to feel his way, and looked in each person's eyes in a questioning way,—for Aglaya was absent, which fact alarmed him at once.

This evening there were no strangers present—no one but the immediate members of the family. Prince S. was still in town, occupied with the affairs of Evgenie Pavlovitch's uncle.

"I wish at least *he* would come and say something!" complained poor Lizabetha Prokofievna.

The general sat still with a most preoccupied air. The sisters were looking very serious and did not speak a word, and Lizabetha Prokofievna did not know how to commence the conversation.

At length she plunged into an energetic and hostile criticism of railways, and glared at the prince defiantly.

Alas Aglaya still did not come—and the prince was quite lost. He had the greatest difficulty in expressing his opinion that railways were most useful institutions,—and in the middle of his speech Adelaida laughed, which threw him into a still worse state of confusion.

At this moment in marched Aglaya, as calm and collected as could be. She gave the prince a ceremonious bow and solemnly took up a prominent position near the big round table. She looked at the prince questioningly.

All present realized that the moment for the settlement of perplexities had arrived.

"Did you get my hedgehog?" she inquired, firmly and almost angrily.

"Yes, I got it," said the prince, blushing.

"Tell us now, at once, what you made of the present? I must have you answer this question for mother's sake; she needs pacifying, and so do all the rest of the family!"

"Look here, Aglaya—" began the general.

"This—this is going beyond all limits!" said Lizabetha Prokofievna, suddenly alarmed.

"It is not in the least beyond all limits, mamma!" said her daughter, firmly. "I sent the prince a hedgehog this morning, and I wish to hear his opinion of it. Go on, prince."

"What—what sort of opinion, Aglaya Ivanovna?"

"About the hedgehog."

"That is—I suppose you wish to know how I received the hedgehog, Aglaya Ivanovna,—or, I should say, how I regarded your sending him to me? In that case, I may tell you—in a word—that I—in fact—"

He paused, breathless.

"Come—you haven't told us much!" said Aglaya, after waiting some five seconds. "Very well, I am ready to drop the hedgehog, if you like; but I am anxious to be able to clear up this accumulation of misunderstandings. Allow me to ask you, prince,—I wish to hear from you, personally—are you making me an offer, or not?"

"Gracious heavens!" exclaimed Lizabetha Prokofievna. The prince started. The general stiffened in his chair; the sisters frowned.

"Don't deceive me now, prince—tell the truth. All these people persecute me with astounding questions—about you. Is there any ground for all these questions, or not? Come!"

"I have not asked you to marry me yet, Aglaya Ivanovna," said the prince, becoming suddenly animated; "but you know yourself how much I love you and trust you."

"No—I asked you this—answer this! Do you intend to ask for my hand, or not?"

"Yes—I do ask for it!" said the prince, more dead than alive now.

There was a general stir in the room.

"No—no—my dear girl," began the general. "You cannot proceed like this, Aglaya, if that's how the matter stands. It's impossible. Prince, forgive it, my dear fellow, but—Lizabetha Prokofievna!"—he appealed to his spouse for help—"you must really—"

"Not I—not I! I retire from all responsibility," said Lizabetha Prokofievna, with a wave of the hand.

"Allow me to speak, please, mamma," said Aglaya. "I think I ought to have something to say in the matter. An important moment of my destiny is about to be decided"—(this is how Aglaya expressed herself)—"and I wish to find out how the matter stands, for my own sake, though I am glad you are all here. Allow me to ask you, prince, since you cherish those intentions, how you consider that you will provide for my happiness?"

"I—I don't quite know how to answer your question, Aglaya Ivanovna. What is there to say to such a question? And—and must I answer?"

"I think you are rather overwhelmed and out of breath. Have a little rest, and try to recover yourself. Take a glass of water, or—but they'll give you some tea directly."

"I love you, Aglaya Ivanovna,—I love you very much. I love only you—and—please don't jest about it, for I do love you very much."

"Well, this matter is important. We are not children—we must look into it thoroughly. Now then, kindly tell me—what does your fortune consist of?"

"No—Aglaya—come, enough of this, you mustn't behave like this," said her father, in dismay.

"It's disgraceful," said Lizabetha Prokofievna in a loud whisper.

"She's mad—quite!" said Alexandra.

"Fortune—money—do you mean?" asked the prince in some surprise.

"Just so."

"I have now—let's see—I have a hundred and thirty-five thousand roubles," said the prince, blushing violently.

"Is that all, really?" said Aglaya, candidly, without the slightest show of confusion. "However, it's not so bad, especially if managed with economy. Do you intend to serve?"

"I—I intended to try for a certificate as private tutor."

"Very good. That would increase our income nicely. Have you any intention of being a Kammer-junker?"

"A Kammer-junker? I had not thought of it, but—"

But here the two sisters could restrain themselves no longer, and both of them burst into irrepressible laughter.

Adelaida had long since detected in Aglaya's features the gathering signs of an approaching storm of laughter, which she restrained with amazing self-control.

Aglaya looked menacingly at her laughing sisters, but could not contain herself any longer, and the next minute she too had burst into an irrepressible, and almost hysterical, fit of mirth. At length she jumped up, and ran out of the room.

"I knew it was all a joke!" cried Adelaida. "I felt it ever since—since the hedgehog."

"No, no! I cannot allow this,—this is a little too much," cried Lizabetha Prokofievna, exploding with rage, and she rose from her seat and followed Aglaya out of the room as quickly as she could.

The two sisters hurriedly went after her.

The prince and the general were the only two persons left in the room.

"It's—it's really—now could you have imagined anything like it, Lef Nicolaievitch?" cried the general. He was evidently so much agitated that he hardly knew what he wished to say. "Seriously now, seriously I mean—"

"I only see that Aglaya Ivanovna is laughing at me," said the poor prince, sadly.

"Wait a bit, my boy, I'll just go—you stay here, you know. But do just explain, if you can, Lef Nicolaievitch, how in the world has all this come about? And what does it all mean? You must understand, my dear fellow; I am a father, you see, and I ought to be allowed to understand the matter—do explain, I beg you!"

"I love Aglaya Ivanovna—she knows it,—and I think she must have long known it."

The general shrugged his shoulders.

"Strange—it's strange," he said, "and you love her very much?"

"Yes, very much."

"Well—it's all most strange to me. That is—my dear fellow, it is such a surprise—such a blow—that... You see, it is not your financial position (though I should not object if you were a bit richer)— I am thinking of my daughter's happiness, of course, and the thing is—are you able to give her the happiness she deserves? And then—is all this a joke on her part, or is she in earnest? I don't mean on your side, but on hers."

At this moment Alexandra's voice was heard outside the door, calling out "Papa!"

"Wait for me here, my boy—will you? Just wait and think it all over, and I'll come back directly," he said hurriedly, and made off with what looked like the rapidity of alarm in response to Alexandra's call.

He found the mother and daughter locked in one another's arms, mingling their tears.

These were the tears of joy and peace and reconciliation. Aglaya was kissing her mother's lips and cheeks and hands; they were hugging each other in the most ardent way.

"There, look at her now—Ivan Fedorovitch! Here she is—all of her! This is our *real* Aglaya at last!" said Lizabetha Prokofievna.

Aglaya raised her happy, tearful face from her mother's breast, glanced at her father, and burst out laughing. She sprang at him and hugged him too, and kissed him over and over again. She then rushed back to her mother and hid her face in the maternal bosom, and there indulged in more tears. Her mother covered her with a corner of her shawl.

"Oh, you cruel little girl! How will you treat us all next, I wonder?" she said, but she spoke with a ring of joy in her voice, and as though she breathed at last without the oppression which she had felt so long.

"Cruel?" sobbed Aglaya. "Yes, I *am* cruel, and worthless, and spoiled—tell father so,—oh, here he is—I forgot Father, listen!" She laughed through her tears.

"My darling, my little idol," cried the general, kissing and fondling her hands (Aglaya did not draw them away); "so you love this young man, do you?"

"No, no, no, can't *bear* him, I can't *bear* your young man!" cried Aglaya, raising her head. "And if you dare say that *once* more, papa—I'm serious, you know, I'm,—do you hear me—I'm serious!"

She certainly did seem to be serious enough. She had flushed up all over and her eyes were blazing.

The general felt troubled and remained silent, while Lizabetha Prokofievna telegraphed to him from behind Aglaya to ask no questions.

"If that's the case, darling—then, of course, you shall do exactly as you like. He is waiting alone downstairs. Hadn't I better hint to him gently that he can go?" The general telegraphed to Lizabetha Prokofievna in his turn.

"No, no, you needn't do anything of the sort; you mustn't hint gently at all. I'll go down myself directly. I wish to apologize to this young man, because I hurt his feelings."

"Yes, *seriously*," said the general, gravely.

"Well, you'd better stay here, all of you, for a little, and I'll go down to him alone to begin with. I'll just go in and then you can follow me almost at once. That's the best way."

She had almost reached the door when she turned round again.

"I shall laugh—I know I shall; I shall die of laughing," she said, lugubriously.

However, she turned and ran down to the prince as fast as her feet could carry her.

"Well, what does it all mean? What do you make of it?" asked the general of his spouse, hurriedly.

"I hardly dare say," said Lizabetha, as hurriedly, "but I think it's as plain as anything can be."

"I think so too, as clear as day; she loves him."

"Loves him? She is head over ears in love, that's what she is," put in Alexandra.

"Well, God bless her, God bless her, if such is her destiny," said Lizabetha, crossing herself devoutly.

"H'm destiny it is," said the general, "and there's no getting out of destiny."

With these words they all moved off towards the drawing-room, where another surprise awaited them. Aglaya had not only not laughed, as she had feared, but had gone to the prince rather timidly, and said to him:

"Forgive a silly, horrid, spoilt girl"—(she took his hand here)—"and be quite assured that we all of us esteem you beyond all words. And if I dared to turn your beautiful, admirable simplicity to ridicule, forgive me as you would a little child its mischief. Forgive me all my absurdity of just now, which, of course, meant nothing, and could not have the slightest consequence." She spoke these words with great emphasis.

Her father, mother, and sisters came into the room and were much struck with the last words, which they just caught as they entered—"absurdity which of course meant nothing"—and still more so with the emphasis with which Aglaya had spoken.

They exchanged glances questioningly, but the prince did not seem to have understood the meaning of Aglaya's words; he was in the highest heaven of delight.

"Why do you speak so?" he murmured. "Why do you ask my forgiveness?"

He wished to add that he was unworthy of being asked for forgiveness by her, but paused. Perhaps he did understand Aglaya's sentence about "absurdity which meant nothing," and like the strange fellow that he was, rejoiced in the words.

Undoubtedly the fact that he might now come and see Aglaya as much as he pleased again was quite enough to make him perfectly happy; that he might come and speak to her, and see her, and sit by her, and walk with her—who knows, but that all this was quite enough to satisfy him for the whole of his life, and that he would desire no more to the end of time?

(Lizabetha Prokofievna felt that this might be the case, and she didn't like it; though very probably she could not have put the idea into words.)

It would be difficult to describe the animation and high spirits which distinguished the prince for the rest of the evening.

He was so happy that "it made one feel happy to look at him," as Aglaya's sisters expressed it afterwards. He talked, and told stories just as he had done once before, and never since, namely on the very first morning of his acquaintance with the Epanchins, six months ago. Since his return to Petersburg from Moscow, he had been remarkably silent, and had told Prince S. on one occasion, before everyone, that he did not think himself justified in degrading any thought by his unworthy words.

But this evening he did nearly all the talking himself, and told stories by the dozen, while he answered all questions put to him clearly, gladly, and with any amount of detail.

There was nothing, however, of love-making in his talk. His ideas were all of the most serious kind; some were even mystical and profound.

He aired his own views on various matters, some of his most private opinions and observations, many of which would have seemed rather funny, so his hearers agreed afterwards, had they not been so well expressed.

The general liked serious subjects of conversation; but both he and Lizabetha Prokofievna felt that they were having a little too much of a good thing tonight, and as the evening advanced, they both grew more or less melancholy; but towards night, the prince fell to telling funny stories, and was always the first to burst out laughing himself, which he invariably did so joyously and simply that the rest laughed just as much at him as at his stories.

As for Aglaya, she hardly said a word all the evening; but she listened with all her ears to Lef Nicolaievitch's talk, and scarcely took her eyes off him.

"She looked at him, and stared and stared, and hung on every word he said," said Lizabetha afterwards, to her husband, "and yet, tell her that she loves him, and she is furious!"

"What's to be done? It's fate," said the general, shrugging his shoulders, and, for a long while after, he continued to repeat: "It's fate, it's fate!"

We may add that to a business man like General Epanchin the present position of affairs was most unsatisfactory. He hated the uncertainty in which they had been, perforce, left. However, he decided to say no more about it, and merely to look on, and take his time and tune from Lizabetha Prokofievna.

The happy state in which the family had spent the evening, as just recorded, was not of very long duration. Next day Aglaya quarrelled with the prince again, and so she continued to behave for the next few days. For whole hours at a time she ridiculed and chaffed the wretched man, and made him almost a laughing-stock.

It is true that they used to sit in the little summer-house together for an hour or two at a time, very often, but it was observed that on these occasions the prince would read the paper, or some book, aloud to Aglaya.

"Do you know," Aglaya said to him once, interrupting the reading, "I've remarked that you are dreadfully badly educated. You never know anything thoroughly, if one asks you; neither anyone's name, nor dates, nor about treaties and so on. It's a great pity, you know!"

"I told you I had not had much of an education," replied the prince.

"How am I to respect you, if that's the case? Read on now. No—don't! Stop reading!"

And once more, that same evening, Aglaya mystified them all. Prince S. had returned, and Aglaya was particularly amiable to him, and asked a great deal after Evgenie Pavlovitch. (Muishkin had not come in as yet.)

Suddenly Prince S. hinted something about "a new and approaching change in the family." He was led to this remark by a communication inadvertently made to him by Lizabetha Prokofievna, that Adelaida's marriage must be postponed a little longer, in order that the two weddings might come off together.

It is impossible to describe Aglaya's irritation. She flared up, and said some indignant words about "all these silly insinuations." She added that "she had no intentions as yet of replacing anybody's mistress."

These words painfully impressed the whole party; but especially her parents. Lizabetha Prokofievna summoned a secret council of two, and insisted upon the general's demanding from the prince a full explanation of his relations with Nastasia Philipovna. The general argued that it was only a whim of Aglaya's; and that, had not Prince S. unfortunately made that remark, which had confused the child and made her blush, she never would have said what she did; and that he was sure Aglaya knew well that anything she might have heard of the prince and Nastasia Philipovna was merely the fabrication of malicious tongues, and that the woman was going to marry Rogojin. He insisted that the prince had nothing whatever to do with Nastasia Philipovna, so far as any liaison was concerned; and, if the truth were to be told about it, he added, never had had.

Meanwhile nothing put the prince out, and he continued to be in the seventh heaven of bliss. Of course he could not fail to observe some impatience and ill-temper in Aglaya now and then; but he believed in something else, and nothing could now shake his conviction. Besides, Aglaya's frowns never lasted long; they disappeared of themselves.

Perhaps he was too easy in his mind. So thought Hippolyte, at all events, who met him in the park one day.

"Didn't I tell you the truth now, when I said you were in love?" he said, coming up to Muishkin of his own accord, and stopping him.

The prince gave him his hand and congratulated him upon "looking so well."

Hippolyte himself seemed to be hopeful about his state of health, as is often the case with consumptives.

He had approached the prince with the intention of talking sarcastically about his happy expression of face, but very soon forgot his intention and began to talk about himself. He began complaining about everything, disconnectedly and endlessly, as was his wont.

"You wouldn't believe," he concluded, "how irritating they all are there. They are such wretchedly small, vain, egotistical, *commonplace* people! Would you believe it, they invited me there under the express condition that I should die quickly, and they are all as wild as possible with me for not having died yet, and for being, on the contrary, a good deal better! Isn't it a comedy? I don't mind betting that you don't believe me!"

The prince said nothing.

"I sometimes think of coming over to you again," said Hippolyte, carelessly. "So you *don't* think them capable of inviting a man on the condition that he is to look sharp and die?"

"I certainly thought they invited you with quite other views."

"Ho, ho! you are not nearly so simple as they try to make you out! This is not the time for it, or I would tell you a thing or two about that beauty, Gania, and his hopes. You are being undermined, pitilessly undermined, and—and it is really melancholy to see you so calm about it. But alas! it's your nature—you can't help it!"

"My word! what a thing to be melancholy about! Why, do you think I should be any happier if I were to feel disturbed about the excavations you tell me of?"

"It is better to be unhappy and know the worst, than to be happy in a fool's paradise! I suppose you don't believe that you have a rival in that quarter?"

"Your insinuations as to rivalry are rather cynical, Hippolyte. I'm sorry to say I have no right to answer you! As for Gania, I put it to you, *can* any man have a happy mind after passing through what he has had to suffer? I think that is the best way to look at it. He will change yet, he has lots of time before him, and life is rich; besides—besides..." the prince hesitated. "As to being undermined, I don't know what in the world you are driving at, Hippolyte. I think we had better drop the subject!"

"Very well, we'll drop it for a while. You can't look at anything but in your exalted, generous way. You must put out your finger and touch a thing before you'll believe it, eh? Ha! ha! ha! I suppose you despise me dreadfully, prince, eh? What do you think?"

"Why? Because you have suffered more than we have?"

"No; because I am unworthy of my sufferings, if you like!"

"Whoever *can* suffer is worthy to suffer, I should think. Aglaya Ivanovna wished to see you, after she had read your confession, but—"

"She postponed the pleasure—I see—I quite understand!" said Hippolyte, hurriedly, as though he wished to banish the subject. "I hear—they tell me—that you read her all that nonsense aloud? Stupid bosh it was—written in delirium. And I can't understand how anyone can be so—I won't say *cruel*, because the word would be humiliating to myself, but we'll say childishly vain and revengeful, as to *reproach* me with this confession, and use it as a weapon against me. Don't be afraid, I'm not referring to yourself."

"Oh, but I'm sorry you repudiate the confession, Hippolyte—it is sincere; and, do you know, even the absurd parts of it—and these are many" (here Hippolyte frowned savagely) "are, as it were, redeemed by suffering—for it must have cost you something to admit what you there say—great torture, perhaps, for all I know. Your motive must have been a very noble one all through. Whatever may have appeared to the contrary, I give you my word, I see this more plainly every day. I do not judge you; I merely say this to have it off my mind, and I am only sorry that I did not say it all *then*—"

Hippolyte flushed hotly. He had thought at first that the prince was "humbugging" him; but on looking at his face he saw that he was absolutely serious, and had no thought of any deception. Hippolyte beamed with gratification.

"And yet I must die," he said, and almost added: "a man like me!"

"And imagine how that Gania annoys me! He has developed the idea—or pretends to believe—that in all probability three or four others who heard my confession will die before I do. There's an idea for you—and all this by way of *consoling* me! Ha! ha! ha! In the first place they haven't died yet; and in the second, if they *did* die—all of them—what would be the satisfaction to me in that? He judges me by himself. But he goes further, he actually pitches into me because, as he declares, 'any decent fellow' would die quietly, and that 'all this' is mere egotism on my part. He doesn't see what refinement of egotism it is on his own part—and at the same time, what ox-like coarseness! Have you ever read of the death of one Stepan Gleboff, in the eighteenth century? I read of it yesterday by chance."

"Who was he?"

"He was impaled on a stake in the time of Peter."

"I know, I know! He lay there fifteen hours in the hard frost, and died with the most extraordinary fortitude—I know—what of him?"

"Only that God gives that sort of dying to some, and not to others. Perhaps you think, though, that I could not die like Gleboff?"

"Not at all!" said the prince, blushing. "I was only going to say that you—not that you could not be like Gleboff—but that you would have been more like—"

"I guess what you mean—I should be an Osterman, not a Gleboff—eh? Is that what you meant?"

"What Osterman?" asked the prince in some surprise.

"Why, Osterman—the diplomatist. Peter's Osterman," muttered Hippolyte, confused. There was a moment's pause of mutual confusion.

"Oh, no, no!" said the prince at last, "that was not what I was going to say—oh no! I don't think you would ever have been like Osterman."

Hippolyte frowned gloomily.

"I'll tell you why I draw the conclusion," explained the prince, evidently desirous of clearing up the matter a little. "Because, though I often think over the men of those times, I cannot for the life of me imagine them to be like ourselves. It really appears to me that they were of another race altogether than ourselves of today. At that time people seemed to stick so to one idea; now, they are more nervous, more sensitive, more enlightened—people of two or three ideas at once—as it were. The man of today is a broader man, so to speak—and I declare I believe that is what prevents him from being so self-contained and independent a being as his brother of those earlier days. Of course my remark was only made under this impression, and not in the least—"

"I quite understand. You are trying to comfort me for the naiveness with which you disagreed with me—eh? Ha! ha! ha! You are a regular child, prince! However, I cannot help seeing that you always treat me like—like a fragile china cup. Never mind, never mind, I'm not a bit angry! At all events we have had a very funny talk. Do you know, all things considered, I should like to be something better than Osterman! I wouldn't take the trouble to rise from the dead to be an Osterman. However, I see I must make arrangements to die soon, or I myself—. Well—leave me now! *Au revoir*. Look here—before you go, just give me your opinion: how do you think I ought to die, now? I mean—the best, the most virtuous way? Tell me!"

"You should pass us by and forgive us our happiness," said the prince in a low voice.

"Ha! ha! ha! I thought so. I thought I should hear something like that. Well, you are—you really are—oh dear me! Eloquence, eloquence! Good-bye!"

Chapter VI.

As to the evening party at the Epanchins' at which Princess Bielokonski was to be present, Varia had reported with accuracy; though she had perhaps expressed herself too strongly.

The thing was decided in a hurry and with a certain amount of quite unnecessary excitement, doubtless because "nothing could be done in this house like anywhere else."

The impatience of Lizabetha Prokofievna "to get things settled" explained a good deal, as well as the anxiety of both parents for the happiness of their beloved daughter. Besides, Princess Bielokonski was going away soon, and they hoped that she would take an interest in the prince. They were anxious that he should enter society under the auspices of this lady, whose patronage was the best of recommendations for any young man.

Even if there seems something strange about the match, the general and his wife said to each other, the "world" will accept Aglaya's fiance without any question if he is under the patronage of the princess. In any case, the prince would have to be "shown" sooner or later; that is, introduced into society, of which he had, so far, not the least idea. Moreover, it was only a question of a small gathering of a few intimate friends. Besides Princess Bielokonski, only one other lady was expected, the wife of a high dignitary. Evgenie Pavlovitch, who was to escort the princess, was the only young man.

Muishkin was told of the princess's visit three days beforehand, but nothing was said to him about the party until the night before it was to take place.

He could not help observing the excited and agitated condition of all members of the family, and from certain hints dropped in conversation he gathered that they were all anxious as to the impression he should make upon the princess. But the Epanchins, one and all, believed that Muishkin, in his simplicity of mind, was quite incapable of realizing that they could be feeling any anxiety on his account, and for this reason they all looked at him with dread and uneasiness.

In point of fact, he did attach marvellously little importance to the approaching event. He was occupied with altogether different thoughts. Aglaya was growing hourly more capricious and gloomy, and this distressed him. When they told him that Evgenie Pavlovitch was expected, he evinced great delight, and said that he had long wished to see him—and somehow these words did not please anyone.

Aglaya left the room in a fit of irritation, and it was not until late in the evening, past eleven, when the prince was taking his departure, that she said a word or two to him, privately, as she accompanied him as far as the front door.

"I should like you," she said, "not to come here tomorrow until evening, when the guests are all assembled. You know there are to be guests, don't you?"

She spoke impatiently and with severity; this was the first allusion she had made to the party of tomorrow.

She hated the idea of it, everyone saw that; and she would probably have liked to quarrel about it with her parents, but pride and modesty prevented her from broaching the subject.

The prince jumped to the conclusion that Aglaya, too, was nervous about him, and the impression he would make, and that she did not like to admit her anxiety; and this thought alarmed him.

"Yes, I am invited," he replied.

She was evidently in difficulties as to how best to go on. "May I speak of something serious to you, for once in my life?" she asked, angrily. She was irritated at she knew not what, and could not restrain her wrath.

"Of course you may; I am very glad to listen," replied Muishkin.

Aglaya was silent a moment and then began again with evident dislike of her subject:

"I do not wish to quarrel with them about this; in some things they won't be reasonable. I always did feel a loathing for the laws which seem to guide mamma's conduct at times. I don't speak of father, for he cannot be expected to be anything but what he is. Mother is a noble-minded woman, I know; you try to suggest anything mean to her, and you'll see! But she is such a slave to these miserable creatures! I don't mean old Bielokonski alone. She is a contemptible old thing, but she is able to twist people round her little finger, and I admire that in her, at all events! How mean it all is, and how foolish! We were always middle-class, thoroughly middle-class, people. Why should we attempt to climb into the giddy heights of the fashionable world? My sisters are all for it. It's Prince S. they have to thank for poisoning their minds. Why are you so glad that Evgenie Pavlovitch is coming?"

"Listen to me, Aglaya," said the prince, "I do believe you are nervous lest I shall make a fool of myself tomorrow at your party?"

"Nervous about you?" Aglaya blushed. "Why should I be nervous about you? What would it matter to me if you were to make ever such a fool of yourself? How can you say such a thing? What do you mean by 'making a fool of yourself'? What a vulgar expression! I suppose you intend to talk in that sort of way tomorrow evening? Look up a few more such expressions in your dictionary; do, you'll make a grand effect! I'm sorry that you seem to be able to come into a room as gracefully as you do; where did you learn the art? Do you think you can drink a cup of tea decently, when you know everybody is looking at you, on purpose to see how you do it?"

"Yes, I think I can."

"Can you? I'm sorry for it then, for I should have had a good laugh at you otherwise. Do break *something* at least, in the drawing-room! Upset the Chinese vase, won't you? It's a valuable one; *do* break it. Mamma values it, and she'll go out of her mind—it was a present. She'll cry before everyone, you'll see! Wave your hand about, you know, as you always do, and just smash it. Sit down near it on purpose."

"On the contrary, I shall sit as far from it as I can. Thanks for the hint."

"Ha, ha! Then you are afraid you *will* wave your arms about! I wouldn't mind betting that you'll talk about some lofty subject, something serious and learned. How delightful, how tactful that will be!"

"I should think it would be very foolish indeed, unless it happened to come in appropriately."

"Look here, once for all," cried Aglaya, boiling over, "if I hear you talking about capital punishment, or the economical condition of Russia, or about Beauty redeeming the world, or anything of that sort, I'll—well, of course I shall laugh and seem very pleased, but I warn you beforehand, don't look me in the face again! I'm serious now, mind, this time I *am really* serious." She certainly did say this very seriously, so much so, that she looked quite different from what she usually was, and the prince could not help noticing the fact. She did not seem to be joking in the slightest degree.

"Well, you've put me into such a fright that I shall certainly make a fool of myself, and very likely break something too. I wasn't a bit alarmed before, but now I'm as nervous as can be."

"Then don't speak at all. Sit still and don't talk."

"Oh, I can't do that, you know! I shall say something foolish out of pure 'funk,' and break something for the same excellent reason; I know I shall. Perhaps I shall slip and fall on the slippery floor; I've done that before now, you know. I shall dream of it all night now. Why did you say anything about it?"

Aglaya looked blackly at him.

"Do you know what, I had better not come at all tomorrow! I'll plead sick-list and stay away," said the prince, with decision.

Aglaya stamped her foot, and grew quite pale with anger.

"Oh, my goodness! Just listen to that! 'Better not come,' when the party is on purpose for him! Good Lord! What a delightful thing it is to have to do with such a—such a stupid as you are!"

"Well, I'll come, I'll come," interrupted the prince, hastily, "and I'll give you my word of honour that I will sit the whole evening and not say a word."

"I believe that's the best thing you can do. You said you'd 'plead sick-list' just now; where in the world do you get hold of such expressions? Why do you talk to me like this? Are you trying to irritate me, or what?"

"Forgive me, it's a schoolboy expression. I won't do it again. I know quite well, I see it, that you are anxious on my account (now, don't be angry), and it makes me very happy to see it. You wouldn't believe how frightened I am of misbehaving somehow, and how glad I am of your instructions. But all this panic is simply nonsense, you know, Aglaya! I give you my word it is; I am so pleased that you are such a child, such a dear good child. How *charming* you can be if you like, Aglaya."

Aglaya wanted to be angry, of course, but suddenly some quite unexpected feeling seized upon her heart, all in a moment.

"And you won't reproach me for all these rude words of mine—some day—afterwards?" she asked, of a sudden.

"What an idea! Of course not. And what are you blushing for again? And there comes that frown once more! You've taken to looking too gloomy sometimes, Aglaya, much more than you used to. I know why it is."

"Be quiet, do be quiet!"

"No, no, I had much better speak out. I have long wished to say it, and *have* said it, but that's not enough, for you didn't believe me. Between us two there stands a being who—"

"Be quiet, be quiet, be quiet, be quiet!" Aglaya struck in, suddenly, seizing his hand in hers, and gazing at him almost in terror.

At this moment she was called by someone. She broke loose from him with an air of relief and ran away.

The prince was in a fever all night. It was strange, but he had suffered from fever for several nights in succession. On this particular night, while in semi-delirium, he had an idea: what if on the morrow he were to have a fit before everybody? The thought seemed to freeze his blood within him. All night he fancied himself in some extraordinary society of strange persons. The worst of it was that he was talking nonsense; he knew that he ought not to speak at all, and yet he talked the whole time; he seemed to be trying to persuade them all to something. Evgenie and Hippolyte were among the guests, and appeared to be great friends.

He awoke towards nine o'clock with a headache, full of confused ideas and strange impressions. For some reason or other he felt most anxious to see Rogojin, to see and talk to him, but what he wished to say he could not tell. Next, he determined to go and see Hippolyte. His mind was in a confused state, so much so that the incidents of the morning seemed to be imperfectly realized, though acutely felt.

One of these incidents was a visit from Lebedeff. Lebedeff came rather early—before ten—but he was tipsy already. Though the prince was not in an observant condition, yet he could not avoid seeing that for at least three days—ever since General Ivolgin had left the house Lebedeff had been behaving very badly. He looked untidy and dirty at all times of the day, and it was said that he had begun to rage about in his own house, and that his temper was very bad. As soon as he arrived this morning, he began to hold forth, beating his breast and apparently blaming himself for something.

"I've—I've had a reward for my meanness—I've had a slap in the face," he concluded, tragically.

"A slap in the face? From whom? And so early in the morning?"

"Early?" said Lebedeff, sarcastically. "Time counts for nothing, even in physical chastisement; but my slap in the face was not physical, it was moral."

He suddenly took a seat, very unceremoniously, and began his story. It was very disconnected; the prince frowned, and wished he could get away; but suddenly a few words struck him. He sat stiff with wonder—Lebedeff said some extraordinary things.

In the first place he began about some letter; the name of Aglaya Ivanovna came in. Then suddenly he broke off and began to accuse the prince of something; he was apparently offended with him. At first he declared that the prince had trusted him with his confidences as to "a certain person" (Nastasia Philipovna), but that of late his friendship had been thrust back into his bosom, and his innocent question as to "approaching family changes" had been curtly put aside, which Lebedeff declared, with tipsy tears, he could not bear; especially as he knew so much already both from Rogojin and Nastasia Philipovna and her friend, and from Varvara Ardalionovna, and even from Aglaya Ivanovna, through his daughter Vera. "And who told Lizabetha Prokofievna something in secret, by letter? Who told her all about the movements of a certain person called Nastasia Philipovna? Who was the anonymous person, eh? Tell me!"

"Surely not you?" cried the prince.

"Just so," said Lebedeff, with dignity; "and only this very morning I have sent up a letter to the noble lady, stating that I have a matter of great importance to communicate. She received the letter; I know she got it; and she received *me*, too."

"Have you just seen Lizabetha Prokofievna?" asked the prince, scarcely believing his ears.

"Yes, I saw her, and got the said slap in the face as mentioned. She chucked the letter back to me unopened, and kicked me out of the house, morally, not physically, although not far off it."

"What letter do you mean she returned unopened?"

"What! didn't I tell you? Ha, ha, ha! I thought I had. Why, I received a letter, you know, to be handed over—"

"From whom? To whom?"

But it was difficult, if not impossible, to extract anything from Lebedeff. All the prince could gather was, that the letter had been received very early, and had a request written on the outside that it might be sent on to the address given.

"Just as before, sir, just as before! To a certain person, and from a certain hand. The individual's name who wrote the letter is to be represented by the letter A.—"

"What? Impossible! To Nastasia Philipovna? Nonsense!" cried the prince.

"It was, I assure you, and if not to her then to Rogojin, which is the same thing. Mr. Hippolyte has had letters, too, and all from the individual whose name begins with an A.," smirked Lebedeff, with a hideous grin.

As he kept jumping from subject to subject, and forgetting what he had begun to talk about, the prince said nothing, but waited, to give him time.

It was all very vague. Who had taken the letters, if letters there were? Probably Vera—and how could Lebedeff have got them? In all probability, he had managed to steal the present letter from Vera, and had himself gone over to Lizabetha Prokofievna with some idea in his head. So the prince concluded at last.

"You are mad!" he cried, indignantly.

"Not quite, esteemed prince," replied Lebedeff, with some acerbity. "I confess I thought of doing you the service of handing the letter over to yourself, but I decided that it would pay me better to deliver it up to the noble lady aforesaid, as I had informed her of everything hitherto by anonymous letters; so when I sent her up a note from myself, with the letter, you know, in order to fix a meeting for eight o'clock this morning, I signed it 'your secret correspondent.' They let me in at once—very quickly—by the back door, and the noble lady received me."

"Well? Go on."

"Oh, well, when I saw her she almost punched my head, as I say; in fact so nearly that one might almost say she did punch my head. She threw the letter in my face; she seemed to reflect first, as if she would have liked to keep it, but thought better of it and threw it in my face instead. 'If anybody can have been such a fool as to trust a man like you to deliver the letter,' says she, 'take it and deliver it!' Hey! she was grandly indignant. A fierce, fiery lady that, sir!"

"Where's the letter now?"

"Oh, I've still got it, here!"

And he handed the prince the very letter from Aglaya to Gania, which the latter showed with so much triumph to his sister at a later hour.

"This letter cannot be allowed to remain in your hands."

"It's for you—for you! I've brought it you on purpose!" cried Lebedeff, excitedly. "Why, I'm yours again now, heart and hand, your slave; there was but a momentary pause in the flow of my love and esteem for you. Mea culpa, mea culpa! as the Pope of Rome says."

"This letter should be sent on at once," said the prince, disturbed. "I'll hand it over myself."

"Wouldn't it be better, esteemed prince, wouldn't it be better—to—don't you know—"

Lebedeff made a strange and very expressive grimace; he twisted about in his chair, and did something, apparently symbolical, with his hands.

"What do you mean?" said the prince.

"Why, open it, for the time being, don't you know?" he said, most confidentially and mysteriously.

The prince jumped up so furiously that Lebedeff ran towards the door; having gained which strategic position, however, he stopped and looked back to see if he might hope for pardon.

"Oh, Lebedeff, Lebedeff! Can a man really sink to such depths of meanness?" said the prince, sadly.

Lebedeff's face brightened.

"Oh, I'm a mean wretch—a mean wretch!" he said, approaching the prince once more, and beating his breast, with tears in his eyes.

"It's abominable dishonesty, you know!"

"Dishonesty—it is, it is! That's the very word!"

"What in the world induces you to act so? You are nothing but a spy. Why did you write anonymously to worry so noble and generous a lady? Why should not Aglaya Ivanovna write a note to whomever she pleases? What did you mean to complain of today? What did you expect to get by it? What made you go at all?"

"Pure amiable curiosity,—I assure you—desire to do a service. That's all. Now I'm entirely yours again, your slave; hang me if you like!"

"Did you go before Lizabetha Prokofievna in your present condition?" inquired the prince.

"No—oh no, fresher—more the correct card. I only became this like after the humiliation I suffered there."

"Well—that'll do; now leave me."

This injunction had to be repeated several times before the man could be persuaded to move. Even then he turned back at the door, came as far as the middle of the room, and there went through his mysterious motions designed to convey the suggestion that the prince should open the letter. He did not dare put his suggestion into words again.

After this performance, he smiled sweetly and left the room on tiptoe.

All this had been very painful to listen to. One fact stood out certain and clear, and that was that poor Aglaya must be in a state of great distress and indecision and mental torment ("from jealousy," the prince whispered to himself). Undoubtedly in this inexperienced, but hot and proud little head, there were all sorts of plans forming, wild and impossible plans, maybe; and the idea of this so frightened the prince that he could not make up his mind what to do. Something must be done, that was clear.

He looked at the address on the letter once more. Oh, he was not in the least degree alarmed about Aglaya writing such a letter; he could trust her. What he did not like about it was that he could not trust Gania.

However, he made up his mind that he would himself take the note and deliver it. Indeed, he went so far as to leave the house and walk up the road, but changed his mind when he had nearly reached Ptitsin's door. However, he there luckily met Colia, and commissioned him to deliver the letter to his brother as if direct from Aglaya. Colia asked no questions but simply delivered it, and Gania consequently had no suspicion that it had passed through so many hands.

Arrived home again, the prince sent for Vera Lebedeff and told her as much as was necessary, in order to relieve her mind, for she had been in a dreadful state of anxiety since she had missed the letter. She heard with horror that her father had taken it. Muishkin learned from her that she had on several occasions performed secret missions both for Aglaya and for Rogojin, without, however, having had the slightest idea that in so doing she might injure the prince in any way.

The latter, with one thing and another, was now so disturbed and confused, that when, a couple of hours or so later, a message came from Colia that the general was ill, he could hardly take the news in.

However, when he did master the fact, it acted upon him as a tonic by completely distracting his attention. He went at once to Nina Alexandrovna's, whither the general had been carried, and stayed there until the evening. He could do no good, but there are people whom to have near one is a blessing at such times. Colia was in an almost hysterical state; he cried continuously, but was running about all day, all the same; fetching doctors, of whom he collected three; going to the chemist's, and so on.

The general was brought round to some extent, but the doctors declared that he could not be said to be out of danger. Varia and Nina Alexandrovna never left the sick man's bedside; Gania was excited and distressed, but would not go upstairs, and seemed afraid to look at the patient. He wrung his hands when the prince spoke to him, and said that "such a misfortune at such a moment" was terrible.

The prince thought he knew what Gania meant by "such a moment."

Hippolyte was not in the house. Lebedeff turned up late in the afternoon; he had been asleep ever since his interview with the prince in the morning. He was quite sober now, and cried with real sincerity over the sick general—mourning for him as though he were his own brother. He blamed himself aloud, but did not explain why. He repeated over and over again to Nina Alexandrovna that he alone was to blame—no one else—but that he had acted out of "pure amiable curiosity," and that "the deceased," as he insisted upon calling the still living general, had been the greatest of geniuses.

He laid much stress on the genius of the sufferer, as if this idea must be one of immense solace in the present crisis.

Nina Alexandrovna—seeing his sincerity of feeling—said at last, and without the faintest suspicion of reproach in her voice: "Come, come—don't cry! God will forgive you!"

Lebedeff was so impressed by these words, and the tone in which they were spoken, that he could not leave Nina Alexandrovna all the evening—in fact, for several days. Till the general's death, indeed, he spent almost all his time at his side.

Twice during the day a messenger came to Nina Alexandrovna from the Epanchins to inquire after the invalid.

When—late in the evening—the prince made his appearance in Lizabetha Prokofievna's drawing-room, he found it full of guests. Mrs. Epanchin questioned him very fully about the general as soon as he appeared; and when old Princess Bielokonski wished to know "who this general was, and who was Nina Alexandrovna," she proceeded to explain in a manner which pleased the prince very much.

He himself, when relating the circumstances of the general's illness to Lizabetha Prokofievna, "spoke beautifully," as Aglaya's sisters declared afterwards—"modestly, quietly, without gestures or too many words, and with great dignity." He had entered the room with propriety and grace, and he was perfectly dressed; he not only did not "fall down on the slippery floor," as he had expressed it, but evidently made a very favourable impression upon the assembled guests.

As for his own impression on entering the room and taking his seat, he instantly remarked that the company was not in the least such as Aglaya's words had led him to fear, and as he had dreamed of—in nightmare form—all night.

This was the first time in his life that he had seen a little corner of what was generally known by the terrible name of "society." He had long thirsted, for reasons of his own, to penetrate the mysteries of the magic circle, and, therefore, this assemblage was of the greatest possible interest to him.

His first impression was one of fascination. Somehow or other he felt that all these people must have been born on purpose to be together! It seemed to him that the Epanchins were not having a party at all; that these people must have been here always, and that he himself was one of them—returned among them after a long absence, but one of them, naturally and indisputably.

It never struck him that all this refined simplicity and nobility and wit and personal dignity might possibly be no more than an exquisite artistic polish. The majority of the guests—who were somewhat empty-headed, after all, in spite of their aristocratic bearing—never guessed, in their self-satisfied composure, that much of their superiority was mere veneer, which indeed they had adopted unconsciously and by inheritance.

The prince would never so much as suspect such a thing in the delight of his first impression.

He saw, for instance, that one important dignitary, old enough to be his grandfather, broke off his own conversation in order to listen to *him*—a young and inexperienced man; and not only listened, but seemed to attach value to his opinion, and was kind and amiable, and yet they were strangers and had never seen each other before. Perhaps what most appealed to the prince's impressionability was the refinement of the old man's courtesy towards him. Perhaps the soil of his susceptible nature was really predisposed to receive a pleasant impression.

Meanwhile all these people—though friends of the family and of each other to a certain extent—were very far from being such intimate friends of the family and of each other as the prince concluded. There were some present who never would think of considering the Epanchins their equals. There were even some who hated one another cordially. For instance, old Princess Bielokonski had all her life despised the wife of the "dignitary," while the latter was very far from loving Lizabetha Prokofievna. The dignitary himself had been General Epanchin's protector from his youth up; and the general considered him so majestic a personage that he would have felt a hearty contempt for himself if he had even for one moment allowed himself to pose as the great man's equal, or to think of him—in his fear and reverence—as anything less than an Olympic God! There were others present who had not met for years, and who had no feeling whatever for each other, unless it were dislike; and yet they met tonight as though they had seen each other but yesterday in some friendly and intimate assembly of kindred spirits.

It was not a large party, however. Besides Princess Bielokonski and the old dignitary (who was really a great man) and his wife, there was an old military general—a count or baron with a German name, a man reputed to possess great knowledge and administrative ability. He was one of those Olympian administrators who know everything except Russia, pronounce a word of extraordinary wisdom, admired by all, about once in five years, and, after being an eternity in the service, generally die full of honour and riches, though they have never done anything great, and have even been hostile to all greatness. This general was Ivan Fedorovitch's immediate superior in the service; and it pleased the latter to look upon him also as a patron. On the other hand, the great man did not at all consider himself Epanchin's patron. He was always very cool to him, while taking advantage of his ready services, and would instantly have put another in his place if there had been the slightest reason for the change.

Another guest was an elderly, important-looking gentleman, a distant relative of Lizabetha Prokofievna's. This gentleman was rich, held a good position, was a great talker, and had the reputation of being "one of the dissatisfied," though not belonging to the dangerous sections of that class. He had the manners, to some extent, of the English aristocracy, and some of their tastes (especially in the matter of under-done roast beef, harness, men-servants, etc.). He was a great friend of the dignitary's, and Lizabetha Prokofievna, for some reason or other, had got hold of the idea that this worthy intended at no distant date to offer the advantages of his hand and heart to Alexandra.

Besides the elevated and more solid individuals enumerated, there were present a few younger though not less elegant guests. Besides Prince S. and Evgenie Pavlovitch, we must name the eminent and fascinating Prince N.—once the vanquisher of female hearts all over Europe. This gentleman was no longer in the first bloom of youth—he was forty-five, but still very handsome. He was well off, and lived, as a rule, abroad, and was noted as a good teller of stories. Then came a few guests belonging to a lower stratum of society—people who, like the Epanchins themselves, moved only occasionally in this exalted sphere. The Epanchins liked to draft among their more elevated guests a few picked representatives of this lower stratum, and Lizabetha Prokofievna received much praise for this practice, which proved, her friends said, that she was a woman of tact. The Epanchins prided themselves upon the good opinion people held of them.

One of the representatives of the middle-class present today was a colonel of engineers, a very serious man and a great friend of Prince S., who had introduced him to the Epanchins. He was extremely silent in society, and displayed on the forefinger of his right hand a large ring, probably bestowed upon him for services of some sort. There was also a poet, German by name, but a Russian poet; very presentable, and even handsome—the sort of man one could bring into society with impunity. This gentleman belonged to a German family of decidedly bourgeois origin, but he had a knack of acquiring the patronage of "big-wigs," and of retaining their favour. He had translated some great German poem into Russian verse, and claimed to have been a friend of a famous Russian poet, since dead. (It is strange how great a multitude of literary people there are who have had the advantages of friendship with some great man of their own profession who is, unfortunately, dead.) The dignitary's wife had introduced this worthy to the Epanchins. This lady posed as the patroness of literary people, and she certainly had succeeded in obtaining pensions for a few of them, thanks to her influence with those in authority on such matters. She was a lady of weight in her own way. Her age was about forty-five, so that she was a very young wife for such an elderly husband as the dignitary. She had been a beauty in her day and still loved, as many ladies of forty-five do love, to dress a little too smartly. Her intellect was nothing to boast of, and her literary knowledge very doubtful. Literary patronage was, however, with her as much a mania as was the love of gorgeous clothes. Many books and translations were dedicated to her by her proteges, and a few of these talented individuals had published some of their own letters to her, upon very weighty subjects.

This, then, was the society that the prince accepted at once as true coin, as pure gold without alloy.

It so happened, however, that on this particular evening all these good people were in excellent humour and highly pleased with themselves. Every one of them felt that they were doing the Epanchins the greatest possible honour by their presence. But alas! the prince never suspected any such subtleties! For instance, he had no suspicion of the fact that the Epanchins, having in their mind so important a step as the marriage of their daughter, would never think of presuming to take it without having previously "shown off" the proposed husband to the dignitary—the recognized patron of the family. The latter, too, though he would probably have received news of a great disaster to the Epanchin family with perfect composure, would nevertheless have considered it a personal offence if they had dared to marry their daughter without his advice, or we might almost say, his leave.

The amiable and undoubtedly witty Prince N. could not but feel that he was as a sun, risen for one night only to shine upon the Epanchin drawing-room. He accounted them immeasurably his inferiors, and it was this feeling which caused his special amiability and delightful ease and grace towards them. He knew very well that he must tell some story this evening for the edification of the company, and led up to it with the inspiration of anticipatory triumph.

The prince, when he heard the story afterwards, felt that he had never yet come across so wonderful a humorist, or such remarkable brilliancy as was shown by this man; and yet if he had only known it, this story was the oldest, stalest, and most worn-out yarn, and every drawing-room in town was sick to death of it. It was only in the innocent Epanchin household that it passed for a new and brilliant tale—as a sudden and striking reminiscence of a splendid and talented man.

Even the German poet, though as amiable as possible, felt that he was doing the house the greatest of honours by his presence in it.

But the prince only looked at the bright side; he did not turn the coat and see the shabby lining.

Aglaya had not foreseen that particular calamity. She herself looked wonderfully beautiful this evening. All three sisters were dressed very tastefully, and their hair was done with special care.

Aglaya sat next to Evgenie Pavlovitch, and laughed and talked to him with an unusual display of friendliness. Evgenie himself behaved rather more sedately than usual, probably out of respect to the dignitary. Evgenie had been known in society for a long while. He had appeared at the Epanchins' today with crape on his hat, and Princess Bielokonski had commended this action on his part. Not every society man would have worn crape for "such an uncle." Lizabetha Prokofievna had liked it also, but was too preoccupied to take much notice. The prince remarked that Aglaya looked attentively at him two or three times, and seemed to be satisfied with his behaviour.

Little by little he became very happy indeed. All his late anxieties and apprehensions (after his conversation with Lebedeff) now appeared like so many bad dreams—impossible, and even laughable.

He did not speak much, only answering such questions as were put to him, and gradually settled down into unbroken silence, listening to what went on, and steeped in perfect satisfaction and contentment.

Little by little a sort of inspiration, however, began to stir within him, ready to spring into life at the right moment. When he did begin to speak, it was accidentally, in response to a question, and apparently without any special object.

CHAPTER VII.

While he feasted his eyes upon Aglaya, as she talked merrily with Evgenie and Prince N., suddenly the old anglomaniac, who was talking to the dignitary in another corner of the room, apparently telling him a story about something or other—suddenly this gentleman pronounced the name of "Nicolai Andreevitch Pavlicheff" aloud. The prince quickly turned towards him, and listened.

The conversation had been on the subject of land, and the present disorders, and there must have been something amusing said, for the old man had begun to laugh at his companion's heated expressions.

The latter was describing in eloquent words how, in consequence of recent legislation, he was obliged to sell a beautiful estate in the N. province, not because he wanted ready money—in fact, he was obliged to sell it at half its value. "To avoid another lawsuit about the Pavlicheff estate, I ran away," he said. "With a few more inheritances of that kind I should soon be ruined!"

At this point General Epanchin, noticing how interested Muishkin had become in the conversation, said to him, in a low tone:

"That gentleman—Ivan Petrovitch—is a relation of your late friend, Mr. Pavlicheff. You wanted to find some of his relations, did you not?"

The general, who had been talking to his chief up to this moment, had observed the prince's solitude and silence, and was anxious to draw him into the conversation, and so introduce him again to the notice of some of the important personages.

"Lef Nicolaievitch was a ward of Nicolai Andreevitch Pavlicheff, after the death of his own parents," he remarked, meeting Ivan Petrovitch's eye.

"Very happy to meet him, I'm sure," remarked the latter. "I remember Lef Nicolaievitch well. When General Epanchin introduced us just now, I recognized you at once, prince. You are very little changed, though I saw you last as a child of some ten or eleven years old. There was something in your features, I suppose, that—"

"You saw me as a child!" exclaimed the prince, with surprise.

"Oh! yes, long ago," continued Ivan Petrovitch, "while you were living with my cousin at Zlatoverhoff. You don't remember me? No, I dare say you don't; you had some malady at the time, I remember. It was so serious that I was surprised—"

"No; I remember nothing!" said the prince. A few more words of explanation followed, words which were spoken without the smallest excitement by his companion, but which evoked the greatest agitation in the prince; and it was discovered that two old ladies to whose care the prince had been left by Pavlicheff, and who lived at Zlatoverhoff, were also relations of Ivan Petrovitch.

The latter had no idea and could give no information as to why Pavlicheff had taken so great an interest in the little prince, his ward.

"In point of fact I don't think I thought much about it," said the old fellow. He seemed to have a wonderfully good memory, however, for he told the prince all about the two old ladies, Pavlicheff's cousins, who had taken care of him, and whom, he declared, he had taken to task for being too severe with the prince as a small sickly boy—the elder sister, at least; the younger had been kind, he recollected. They both now lived in another province, on a small estate left to them by Pavlicheff. The prince listened to all this with eyes sparkling with emotion and delight.

He declared with unusual warmth that he would never forgive himself for having travelled about in the central provinces during these last six months without having hunted up his two old friends.

He declared, further, that he had intended to go every day, but had always been prevented by circumstances; but that now he would promise himself the pleasure—however far it was, he would find them out. And so Ivan Petrovitch *really* knew Natalia Nikitishna!—what a saintly nature was hers!—and Martha Nikitishna! Ivan Petrovitch must excuse him, but really he was not quite fair on dear old Martha. She was severe, perhaps; but then what else could she be with such a little idiot as he was then? (Ha, ha.) He really was an idiot then, Ivan Petrovitch must know, though he might not believe it. (Ha, ha.) So he had really seen him there! Good heavens! And was he really and truly and actually a cousin of Pavlicheff's?

"I assure you of it," laughed Ivan Petrovitch, gazing amusedly at the prince.

"Oh! I didn't say it because I *doubt* the fact, you know. (Ha, ha.) How could I doubt such a thing? (Ha, ha, ha.) I made the remark because—because Nicolai Andreevitch Pavlicheff was such a splendid man, don't you see! Such a high-souled man, he really was, I assure you."

The prince did not exactly pant for breath, but he "seemed almost to *choke* out of pure simplicity and goodness of heart," as Adelaida expressed it, on talking the party over with her fiance, the Prince S., next morning.

"But, my goodness me," laughed Ivan Petrovitch, "why can't I be cousin to even a splendid man?"

"Oh, dear!" cried the prince, confused, trying to hurry his words out, and growing more and more eager every moment: "I've gone and said another stupid thing. I don't know what to say. I—I didn't mean that, you know—I—I—he really was such a splendid man, wasn't he?"

The prince trembled all over. Why was he so agitated? Why had he flown into such transports of delight without any apparent reason? He had far outshot the measure of joy and emotion consistent with the occasion. Why this was it would be difficult to say.

He seemed to feel warmly and deeply grateful to someone for something or other—perhaps to Ivan Petrovitch; but likely enough to all the guests, individually, and collectively. He was much too happy.

Ivan Petrovitch began to stare at him with some surprise; the dignitary, too, looked at him with considerable attention; Princess Bielokonski glared at him angrily, and compressed her lips. Prince N., Evgenie, Prince S., and the girls, all broke off their own conversations and listened. Aglaya seemed a little startled; as for Lizabetha Prokofievna, her heart sank within her.

This was odd of Lizabetha Prokofievna and her daughters. They had themselves decided that it would be better if the prince did not talk all the evening. Yet seeing him sitting silent and alone, but perfectly happy, they had been on the point of exerting themselves to draw him into one of the groups of talkers around the room. Now that he was in the midst of a talk they became more than ever anxious and perturbed.

"That he was a splendid man is perfectly true; you are quite right," repeated Ivan Petrovitch, but seriously this time. "He was a fine and a worthy fellow—worthy, one may say, of the highest respect," he added, more and more seriously at each pause; "and it is agreeable to see, on your part, such—"

"Wasn't it this same Pavlicheff about whom there was a strange story in connection with some abbot? I don't remember who the abbot was, but I remember at one time everybody was talking about it," remarked the old dignitary.

"Yes—Abbot Gurot, a Jesuit," said Ivan Petrovitch. "Yes, that's the sort of thing our best men are apt to do. A man of rank, too, and rich—a man who, if he had continued to serve, might have done anything; and then to throw up the service and everything else in order to go over to Roman Catholicism and turn Jesuit—openly, too—almost triumphantly. By Jove! it was positively a mercy that he died when he did—it was indeed—everyone said so at the time."

The prince was beside himself.

"Pavlicheff?—Pavlicheff turned Roman Catholic? Impossible!" he cried, in horror.

"H'm! impossible is rather a strong word," said Ivan Petrovitch. "You must allow, my dear prince... However, of course you value the memory of the deceased so very highly; and he certainly was the kindest of men; to which fact, by the way, I ascribe, more than to anything else, the success of the abbot in influencing his religious convictions. But you may ask me, if you please, how much trouble and worry I, personally, had over that business, and especially with this same Gurot! Would you believe it," he continued, addressing the dignitary, "they actually tried to put in a claim under the deceased's will, and I had to resort to the very strongest measures in order to bring them to their senses? I assure you they knew their cue, did these gentlemen—wonderful! Thank goodness all this was in Moscow, and I got the Court, you know, to help me, and we soon brought them to their senses."

"You wouldn't believe how you have pained and astonished me," cried the prince.

"Very sorry; but in point of fact, you know, it was all nonsense and would have ended in smoke, as usual—I'm sure of that. Last year,"—he turned to the old man again,—"Countess K. joined some Roman Convent abroad. Our people never seem to be able to offer any resistance so soon as they get into the hands of these—intriguers—especially abroad."

"That is all thanks to our lassitude, I think," replied the old man, with authority. "And then their way of preaching; they have a skilful manner of doing it! And they know how to startle one, too. I got quite a fright myself in '32, in Vienna, I assure you; but I didn't cave in to them, I ran away instead, ha, ha!"

"Come, come, I've always heard that you ran away with the beautiful Countess Levitsky that time—throwing up everything in order to do it—and not from the Jesuits at all," said Princess Bielokonski, suddenly.

"Well, yes—but we call it from the Jesuits, you know; it comes to the same thing," laughed the old fellow, delighted with the pleasant recollection.

"You seem to be very religious," he continued, kindly, addressing the prince, "which is a thing one meets so seldom nowadays among young people."

The prince was listening open-mouthed, and still in a condition of excited agitation. The old man was evidently interested in him, and anxious to study him more closely.

"Pavlicheff was a man of bright intellect and a good Christian, a sincere Christian," said the prince, suddenly. "How could he possibly embrace a faith which is unchristian? Roman Catholicism is, so to speak, simply the same thing as unchristianity," he added with flashing eyes, which seemed to take in everybody in the room.

"Come, that's a little *too* strong, isn't it?" murmured the old man, glancing at General Epanchin in surprise.

"How do you make out that the Roman Catholic religion is *unchristian?* What is it, then?" asked Ivan Petrovitch, turning to the prince.

"It is not a Christian religion, in the first place," said the latter, in extreme agitation, quite out of proportion to the necessity of the moment. "And in the second place, Roman Catholicism is, in my opinion, worse than Atheism itself. Yes—that is my opinion. Atheism only preaches a negation, but Romanism goes further; it preaches a disfigured, distorted Christ—it preaches Anti-Christ—I assure you, I swear it! This is my own personal conviction, and it has long distressed me. The Roman Catholic believes that the Church on earth cannot stand without universal temporal Power. He cries 'non possumus!' In my opinion the Roman Catholic religion is not a faith at all, but simply a continuation of the Roman Empire, and everything is subordinated to this idea—beginning with faith. The Pope has seized territories and an earthly throne, and has held them with the sword. And so the thing has gone on, only that to the sword they have added lying, intrigue, deceit, fanaticism, superstition, swindling;—they have played fast and loose with the most sacred and sincere feelings of men;—they have exchanged everything—everything for money, for base earthly *power!* And is this not the teaching of Anti-Christ? How could the upshot of all this be other than Atheism? Atheism is the child of Roman Catholicism—it proceeded from these Romans themselves, though perhaps they would not believe it. It grew and fattened on hatred of its parents; it is the progeny of their lies and spiritual feebleness. Atheism! In our country it is only among the upper classes that you find unbelievers; men who have lost the root or spirit of their faith; but abroad whole masses of the people are beginning to profess unbelief—at first because of the darkness and lies by which they were surrounded; but now out of fanaticism, out of loathing for the Church and Christianity!"

The prince paused to get breath. He had spoken with extraordinary rapidity, and was very pale.

All present interchanged glances, but at last the old dignitary burst out laughing frankly. Prince N. took out his eye-glass to have a good look at the speaker. The German poet came out of his corner and crept nearer to the table, with a spiteful smile.

"You exaggerate the matter very much," said Ivan Petrovitch, with rather a bored air. "There are, in the foreign Churches, many representatives of their faith who are worthy of respect and esteem."

"Oh, but I did not speak of individual representatives. I was merely talking about Roman Catholicism, and its essence—of Rome itself. A Church can never entirely disappear; I never hinted at that!"

"Agreed that all this may be true; but we need not discuss a subject which belongs to the domain of theology."

"Oh, no; oh, no! Not to theology alone, I assure you! Why, Socialism is the progeny of Romanism and of the Romanistic spirit. It and its brother Atheism proceed from Despair in opposition to Catholicism. It seeks to replace in itself the moral power of religion, in order to appease the spiritual thirst of parched humanity and save it; not by Christ, but by force. 'Don't dare to believe in God, don't dare to possess any individuality, any property! *Fraternité ou la Mort*; two million heads. 'By their works ye shall know them'—we are told. And we must not suppose that all this is harmless and without danger to ourselves. Oh, no; we must resist, and quickly, quickly! We must let our Christ shine forth upon the Western nations, our Christ whom we have preserved intact, and whom they have never known. Not as slaves, allowing ourselves to be caught by the hooks of the Jesuits, but carrying our Russian civilization to *them*, we must stand before them, not letting it be said among us that their preaching is 'skilful,' as someone expressed it just now."

"But excuse me, excuse me;" cried Ivan Petrovitch considerably disturbed, and looking around uneasily. "Your ideas are, of course, most praiseworthy, and in the highest degree patriotic; but you exaggerate the matter terribly. It would be better if we dropped the subject."

"No, sir, I do not exaggerate, I understate the matter, if anything, undoubtedly understate it; simply because I cannot express myself as I should like, but—"

"Allow me!"

The prince was silent. He sat straight up in his chair and gazed fervently at Ivan Petrovitch.

"It seems to me that you have been too painfully impressed by the news of what happened to your good benefactor," said the old dignitary, kindly, and with the utmost calmness of demeanour. "You are excitable, perhaps as the result of your solitary life. If you would make up your mind to live more among your fellows in society, I trust, I am sure, that the world would be glad to welcome you, as a remarkable young man; and you would soon find yourself able to look at things more calmly. You would see that all these things are much simpler than you think; and, besides, these rare cases come about, in my opinion, from ennui and from satiety."

"Exactly, exactly! That is a true thought!" cried the prince. "From ennui, from our ennui but not from satiety! Oh, no, you are wrong there! Say from *thirst* if you like; the thirst of fever! And please do not suppose that this is so small a matter that we may have a laugh at it and dismiss it; we must be able to foresee our disasters and arm against them. We Russians no sooner arrive at the brink of the water, and realize that we are really at the brink, than we are so delighted with the outlook that in we plunge and swim to the farthest point we can see. Why is this? You say you are surprised at Pavlicheff's action; you ascribe it to madness, to kindness of heart, and what not, but it is not so.

"Our Russian intensity not only astonishes ourselves; all Europe wonders at our conduct in such cases! For, if one of us goes over to Roman Catholicism, he is sure to become a Jesuit at once, and a rabid one into the bargain. If one of us becomes an Atheist, he must needs begin to insist on the prohibition of faith in God by force, that is, by the sword. Why is this? Why does he then exceed all bounds at once? Because he has found land at last, the fatherland that he sought in vain before; and, because his soul is rejoiced to find it, he throws himself upon it and kisses it! Oh, it is not from vanity alone, it is not from feelings of vanity that Russians become Atheists and Jesuits! But from spiritual thirst, from anguish of longing for higher things, for dry firm land, for foothold on a fatherland which they never believed in because they never knew it. It is easier for a Russian to become an Atheist, than for any other nationality in the world. And not only does a Russian 'become an Atheist,' but he actually *believes in* Atheism, just as though he had found a new faith, not perceiving that he has pinned his faith to a negation. Such is our anguish of thirst! 'Whoso has no country has no God.' That is not my own expression; it is the expression of a merchant, one of the Old Believers, whom I once met while travelling. He did not say exactly these words. I think his expression was:

"'Whoso forsakes his country forsakes his God.'

"But let these thirsty Russian souls find, like Columbus' discoverers, a new world; let them find the Russian world, let them search and discover all the gold and treasure that lies hid in the bosom of their own land! Show them the restitution of lost humanity, in the future, by Russian thought alone, and by means of the God and of the Christ of our Russian faith, and you will see how mighty and just and wise and good a giant will rise up before the eyes of the astonished and frightened world; astonished because they expect nothing but the sword from us, because they think they will get nothing out of us but barbarism. This has been the case up to now, and the longer matters go on as they are now proceeding, the more clear will be the truth of what I say; and I—"

But at this moment something happened which put a most unexpected end to the orator's speech. All this heated tirade, this outflow of passionate words and ecstatic ideas which seemed to hustle and tumble over each other as they fell from his lips, bore evidence of some unusually disturbed mental condition in the young fellow who had "boiled over" in such a remarkable manner, without any apparent reason.

Of those who were present, such as knew the prince listened to his outburst in a state of alarm, some with a feeling of mortification. It was so unlike his usual timid self-constraint; so inconsistent with his usual taste and tact, and with his instinctive feeling for the higher proprieties. They could not understand the origin of the outburst; it could not be simply the news of Pavlicheff's perversion. By the ladies the prince was regarded as little better than a lunatic, and Princess Bielokonski admitted afterwards that "in another minute she would have bolted."

The two old gentlemen looked quite alarmed. The old general (Epanchin's chief) sat and glared at the prince in severe displeasure. The colonel sat immovable. Even the German poet grew a little pale, though he wore his usual artificial smile as he looked around to see what the others would do.

In point of fact it is quite possible that the matter would have ended in a very commonplace and natural way in a few minutes. The undoubtedly astonished, but now more collected, General Epanchin had several times endeavoured to interrupt the prince, and not having succeeded he was now preparing to take firmer and more vigorous measures to attain his end. In another minute or two he would probably have made up his mind to lead the prince quietly out of the room, on the plea of his being ill (and it was more than likely that the general was right in his belief that the prince *was* actually ill), but it so happened that destiny had something different in store.

At the beginning of the evening, when the prince first came into the room, he had sat down as far as possible from the Chinese vase which Aglaya had spoken of the day before.

Will it be believed that, after Aglaya's alarming words, an ineradicable conviction had taken possession of his mind that, however he might try to avoid this vase next day, he must certainly break it? But so it was.

During the evening other impressions began to awaken in his mind, as we have seen, and he forgot his presentiment. But when Pavlicheff was mentioned and the general introduced him to Ivan Petrovitch, he had changed his place, and went over nearer to the table; when, it so happened, he took the chair nearest to the beautiful vase, which stood on a pedestal behind him, just about on a level with his elbow.

As he spoke his last words he had risen suddenly from his seat with a wave of his arm, and there was a general cry of horror.

The huge vase swayed backwards and forwards; it seemed to be uncertain whether or no to topple over on to the head of one of the old men, but eventually determined to go the other way, and came crashing over towards the German poet, who darted out of the way in terror.

The crash, the cry, the sight of the fragments of valuable china covering the carpet, the alarm of the company—what all this meant to the poor prince it would be difficult to convey to the mind of the reader, or for him to imagine.

But one very curious fact was that all the shame and vexation and mortification which he felt over the accident were less powerful than the deep impression of the almost supernatural truth of his premonition. He stood still in alarm—in almost superstitious alarm, for a moment; then all mists seemed to clear away from his eyes; he was conscious of nothing but light and joy and ecstasy; his breath came and went; but the moment passed. Thank God it was not that! He drew a long breath and looked around.

For some minutes he did not seem to comprehend the excitement around him; that is, he comprehended it and saw everything, but he stood aside, as it were, like someone invisible in a fairy tale, as though he had nothing to do with what was going on, though it pleased him to take an interest in it.

He saw them gather up the broken bits of china; he heard the loud talking of the guests and observed how pale Aglaya looked, and how very strangely she was gazing at him. There was no hatred in her expression, and no anger whatever. It was full of alarm for him, and sympathy and affection, while she looked around at the others with flashing, angry eyes. His heart filled with a sweet pain as he gazed at her.

At length he observed, to his amazement, that all had taken their seats again, and were laughing and talking as though nothing had happened. Another minute and the laughter grew louder—they were laughing at him, at his dumb stupor—laughing kindly and merrily. Several of them spoke to him, and spoke so kindly and cordially, especially Lizabetha Prokofievna—she was saying the kindest possible things to him.

Suddenly he became aware that General Epanchin was tapping him on the shoulder; Ivan Petrovitch was laughing too, but still more kind and sympathizing was the old dignitary. He took the prince by the hand and pressed it warmly; then he patted it, and quietly urged him to recollect himself—speaking to him exactly as he would have spoken to a little frightened child, which pleased the prince wonderfully; and next seated him beside himself.

The prince gazed into his face with pleasure, but still seemed to have no power to speak. His breath failed him. The old man's face pleased him greatly.

"Do you really forgive me?" he said at last. "And—and Lizabetha Prokofievna too?" The laugh increased, tears came into the prince's eyes, he could not believe in all this kindness—he was enchanted.

"The vase certainly was a very beautiful one. I remember it here for fifteen years—yes, quite that!" remarked Ivan Petrovitch.

"Oh, what a dreadful calamity! A wretched vase smashed, and a man half dead with remorse about it," said Lizabetha Prokofievna, loudly. "What made you so dreadfully startled, Lef Nicolaievitch?" she added, a little timidly. "Come, my dear boy! cheer up. You really alarm me, taking the accident so to heart."

"Do you forgive me all—*all*, besides the vase, I mean?" said the prince, rising from his seat once more, but the old gentleman caught his hand and drew him down again—he seemed unwilling to let him go.

"*C'est très-curieux et c'est très-sérieux*," he whispered across the table to Ivan Petrovitch, rather loudly. Probably the prince heard him.

"So that I have not offended any of you? You will not believe how happy I am to be able to think so. It is as it should be. As if I *could* offend anyone here! I should offend you again by even suggesting such a thing."

"Calm yourself, my dear fellow. You are exaggerating again; you really have no occasion to be so grateful to us. It is a feeling which does you great credit, but an exaggeration, for all that."

"I am not exactly thanking you, I am only feeling a growing admiration for you—it makes me happy to look at you. I dare say I am speaking very foolishly, but I must speak—I must explain, if it be out of nothing better than self-respect."

All he said and did was abrupt, confused, feverish—very likely the words he spoke, as often as not, were not those he wished to say. He seemed to inquire whether he *might* speak. His eyes lighted on Princess Bielokonski.

"All right, my friend, talk away, talk away!" she remarked. "Only don't lose your breath; you were in such a hurry when you began, and look what you've come to now! Don't be afraid of speaking—all these ladies and gentlemen have seen far stranger people than yourself; you don't astonish *them*. You are nothing out-of-the-way remarkable, you know. You've done nothing but break a vase, and give us all a fright."

The prince listened, smiling.

"Wasn't it you," he said, suddenly turning to the old gentleman, "who saved the student Porkunoff and a clerk called Shoabrin from being sent to Siberia, two or three months since?"

The old dignitary blushed a little, and murmured that the prince had better not excite himself further.

"And I have heard of *you*," continued the prince, addressing Ivan Petrovitch, "that when some of your villagers were burned out you gave them wood to build up their houses again, though they were no longer your serfs and had behaved badly towards you."

"Oh, come, come! You are exaggerating," said Ivan Petrovitch, beaming with satisfaction, all the same. He was right, however, in this instance, for the report had reached the prince's ears in an incorrect form.

"And you, princess," he went on, addressing Princess Bielokonski, "was it not you who received me in Moscow, six months since, as kindly as though I had been your own son, in response to a letter from Lizabetha Prokofievna; and gave me one piece of advice, again as to your own son, which I shall never forget? Do you remember?"

"What are you making such a fuss about?" said the old lady, with annoyance. "You are a good fellow, but very silly. One gives you a halfpenny, and you are as grateful as though one had saved your life. You think this is praiseworthy on your part, but it is not—it is not, indeed."

She seemed to be very angry, but suddenly burst out laughing, quite good-humouredly.

Lizabetha Prokofievna's face brightened up, too; so did that of General Epanchin.

"I told you Lef Nicolaievitch was a man—a man—if only he would not be in such a hurry, as the princess remarked," said the latter, with delight.

Aglaya alone seemed sad and depressed; her face was flushed, perhaps with indignation.

"He really is very charming," whispered the old dignitary to Ivan Petrovitch.

"I came into this room with anguish in my heart," continued the prince, with ever-growing agitation, speaking quicker and quicker, and with increasing strangeness. "I—I was afraid of you all, and afraid of myself. I was most afraid of myself. When I returned to Petersburg, I promised myself to make a point of seeing our greatest men, and members of our oldest families—the old families like my own. I am now among princes like myself, am I not? I wished to know you, and it was necessary, very, very necessary. I had always heard so much that was evil said of you all—more evil than good; as to how small and petty were your interests, how absurd your habits, how shallow your education, and so on. There is so much written and said about you! I came here today with anxious curiosity; I wished to see for myself and form my own convictions as to whether it were true that the whole of this upper stratum of Russian society is *worthless*, has outlived its time, has existed too long, and is only fit to die—and yet is dying with petty, spiteful warring against that which is destined to supersede it and take its place—hindering the Coming Men, and knowing not that itself is in a dying condition. I did not fully believe in this view even before, for there never was such a class among us—excepting perhaps at court, by accident—or by uniform; but now there is not even that, is there? It has vanished, has it not?"

"No, not a bit of it," said Ivan Petrovitch, with a sarcastic laugh.

"Good Lord, he's off again!" said Princess Bielokonski, impatiently.

"Laissez-le dire! He is trembling all over," said the old man, in a warning whisper.

The prince certainly was beside himself.

"Well? What have I seen?" he continued. "I have seen men of graceful simplicity of intellect; I have seen an old man who is not above speaking kindly and even *listening* to a boy like myself; I see before me persons who can understand, who can forgive—kind, good Russian hearts—hearts almost as kind and cordial as I met abroad. Imagine how delighted I must have been, and how surprised! Oh, let me express this feeling! I have so often heard, and I have even believed, that in society there was nothing but empty forms, and that reality had vanished; but I now see for myself that this can never be the case *here*, among us—it may be the order elsewhere, but not in Russia. Surely you are not all Jesuits and deceivers! I heard Prince N.'s story just now. Was it not simple-minded, spontaneous humour? Could such words come from the lips of a man who is dead?—a man whose heart and talents are dried up? Could dead men and women have treated me so kindly as you have all been treating me to-day? Is there not material for the future in all this—for hope? Can such people fail to *understand*? Can such men fall away from reality?"

"Once more let us beg you to be calm, my dear boy. We'll talk of all this another time—I shall do so with the greatest pleasure, for one," said the old dignitary, with a smile.

Ivan Petrovitch grunted and twisted round in his chair. General Epanchin moved nervously. The latter's chief had started a conversation with the wife of the dignitary, and took no notice whatever of the prince, but the old lady very often glanced at him, and listened to what he was saying.

"No, I had better speak," continued the prince, with a new outburst of feverish emotion, and turning towards the old man with an air of confidential trustfulness. "Yesterday, Aglaya Ivanovna forbade me to talk, and even specified the particular subjects I must not touch upon—she knows well enough that I am odd when I get upon these matters. I am nearly twenty-seven years old, and yet I know I am little better than a child. I have no right to express my ideas, and said so long ago. Only in Moscow, with Rogojin, did I ever speak absolutely freely! He and I read Pushkin together—all his works. Rogojin knew nothing of Pushkin, had not even heard his name. I am always afraid of spoiling a great Thought or Idea by my absurd manner. I have no eloquence, I know. I always make the wrong gestures—inappropriate gestures—and therefore I degrade the Thought, and raise a laugh instead of doing my subject justice. I have no sense of proportion either, and that is the chief thing. I know it would be much better if I were always to sit still and say nothing. When I do so, I appear to be quite a sensible sort of a person, and what's more, I think about things. But now I must speak; it is better that I should. I began to speak because you looked so kindly at me; you have such a beautiful face. I promised Aglaya Ivanovna yesterday that I would not speak all the evening."

"Really?" said the old man, smiling.

"But, at times, I can't help thinking that I am wrong in feeling so about it, you know. Sincerity is more important than elocution, isn't it?"

"Sometimes."

"I want to explain all to you—everything—everything! I know you think me Utopian, don't you—an idealist? Oh, no! I'm not, indeed—my ideas are all so simple. You don't believe me? You are smiling. Do you know, I am sometimes very wicked—for I lose my faith? This evening as I came here, I thought to myself, 'What shall I talk about? How am I to begin, so that they may be able to understand partially, at all events?' How afraid I was—dreadfully afraid! And yet, how *could* I be afraid—was it not shameful of me? Was I afraid of finding a bottomless abyss of empty selfishness? Ah! that's why I am so happy at this moment, because I find there is no bottomless abyss at all—but good, healthy material, full of life.

"It is not such a very dreadful circumstance that we are odd people, is it? For we really are odd, you know—careless, reckless, easily wearied of anything. We don't look thoroughly into matters—don't care to understand things. We are all like this—you and I, and all of them! Why, here are you, now—you are not a bit angry with me for calling you 'odd,' are you? And, if so, surely there is good material in you? Do you know, I sometimes think it is a good thing to be odd. We can forgive one another more easily, and be more humble. No one can begin by being perfect—there is much one cannot understand in life at first. In order to attain to perfection, one must begin by failing to understand much. And if we take in knowledge too quickly, we very likely are not taking it in at all. I say all this to you—you who by this time understand so much—and doubtless have failed to understand so much, also. I am not afraid of you any longer. You are not angry that a mere boy should say such words to you, are you? Of course not! You know how to forget and to forgive. You are laughing, Ivan Petrovitch? You think I am a champion of other classes of people—that I am *their* advocate, a democrat, and an orator of Equality?" The prince laughed hysterically; he had several times burst into these little, short nervous laughs. "Oh, no—it is for you, for myself, and for all of us together, that I am alarmed. I am a prince of an old family myself, and I am sitting among my peers; and I am talking like this in the hope of saving us all; in the hope that our class will not

310

disappear altogether—into the darkness—unguessing its danger—blaming everything around it, and losing ground every day. Why should we disappear and give place to others, when we may still, if we choose, remain in the front rank and lead the battle? Let us be servants, that we may become lords in due season!"

He tried to get upon his feet again, but the old man still restrained him, gazing at him with increasing perturbation as he went on.

"Listen—I know it is best not to speak! It is best simply to give a good example—simply to begin the work. I have done this—I have begun, and—and—oh! *can* anyone be unhappy, really? Oh! what does grief matter—what does misfortune matter, if one knows how to be happy? Do you know, I cannot understand how anyone can pass by a green tree, and not feel happy only to look at it! How anyone can talk to a man and not feel happy in loving him! Oh, it is my own fault that I cannot express myself well enough! But there are lovely things at every step I take—things which even the most miserable man must recognize as beautiful. Look at a little child—look at God's day dawn—look at the grass growing—look at the eyes that love you, as they gaze back into your eyes!"

He had risen, and was speaking standing up. The old gentleman was looking at him now in unconcealed alarm. Lizabetha Prokofievna wrung her hands. "Oh, my God!" she cried. She had guessed the state of the case before anyone else.

Aglaya rushed quickly up to him, and was just in time to receive him in her arms, and to hear with dread and horror that awful, wild cry as he fell writhing to the ground.

There he lay on the carpet, and someone quickly placed a cushion under his head.

No one had expected this.

In a quarter of an hour or so Prince N. and Evgenie Pavlovitch and the old dignitary were hard at work endeavouring to restore the harmony of the evening, but it was of no avail, and very soon after the guests separated and went their ways.

A great deal of sympathy was expressed; a considerable amount of advice was volunteered; Ivan Petrovitch expressed his opinion that the young man was "a Slavophile, or something of that sort"; but that it was not a dangerous development. The old dignitary said nothing.

True enough, most of the guests, next day and the day after, were not in very good humour. Ivan Petrovitch was a little offended, but not seriously so. General Epanchin's chief was rather cool towards him for some while after the occurrence. The old dignitary, as patron of the family, took the opportunity of murmuring some kind of admonition to the general, and added, in flattering terms, that he was most interested in Aglaya's future. He was a man who really did possess a kind heart, although his interest in the prince, in the earlier part of the evening, was due, among other reasons, to the latter's connection with Nastasia Philipovna, according to popular report. He had heard a good deal of this story here and there, and was greatly interested in it, so much so that he longed to ask further questions about it.

Princess Bielokonski, as she drove away on this eventful evening, took occasion to say to Lizabetha Prokofievna:

"Well—he's a good match—and a bad one; and if you want my opinion, more bad than good. You can see for yourself the man is an invalid."

Lizabetha therefore decided that the prince was impossible as a husband for Aglaya; and during the ensuing night she made a vow that never while she lived should he marry Aglaya. With this resolve firmly impressed upon her mind, she awoke next day; but during the morning, after her early lunch, she fell into a condition of remarkable inconsistency.

In reply to a very guarded question of her sisters', Aglaya had answered coldly, but exceedingly haughtily:

"I have never given him my word at all, nor have I ever counted him as my future husband—never in my life. He is just as little to me as all the rest."

Lizabetha Prokofievna suddenly flared up.

"I did not expect that of you, Aglaya," she said. "He is an impossible husband for you,—I know it; and thank God that we agree upon that point; but I did not expect to hear such words from you.

I thought I should hear a very different tone from you. I would have turned out everyone who was in the room last night and kept him,—that's the sort of man he is, in my opinion!"

Here she suddenly paused, afraid of what she had just said. But she little knew how unfair she was to her daughter at that moment. It was all settled in Aglaya's mind. She was only waiting for the hour that would bring the matter to a final climax; and every hint, every careless probing of her wound, did but further lacerate her heart.

CHAPTER VIII.

This same morning dawned for the prince pregnant with no less painful presentiments,—which fact his physical state was, of course, quite enough to account for; but he was so indefinably melancholy,—his sadness could not attach itself to anything in particular, and this tormented him more than anything else. Of course certain facts stood before him, clear and painful, but his sadness went beyond all that he could remember or imagine; he realized that he was powerless to console himself unaided. Little by little he began to develop the expectation that this day something important, something decisive, was to happen to him.

His attack of yesterday had been a slight one. Excepting some little heaviness in the head and pain in the limbs, he did not feel any particular effects. His brain worked all right, though his soul was heavy within him.

He rose late, and immediately upon waking remembered all about the previous evening; he also remembered, though not quite so clearly, how, half an hour after his fit, he had been carried home.

He soon heard that a messenger from the Epanchins' had already been to inquire after him. At half-past eleven another arrived; and this pleased him.

Vera Lebedeff was one of the first to come to see him and offer her services. No sooner did she catch sight of him than she burst into tears; but when he tried to soothe her she began to laugh. He was quite struck by the girl's deep sympathy for him; he seized her hand and kissed it. Vera flushed crimson.

"Oh, don't, don't!" she exclaimed in alarm, snatching her hand away. She went hastily out of the room in a state of strange confusion.

Lebedeff also came to see the prince, in a great hurry to get away to the "deceased," as he called General Ivolgin, who was alive still, but very ill. Colia also turned up, and begged the prince for pity's sake to tell him all he knew about his father which had been concealed from him till now. He said he had found out nearly everything since yesterday; the poor boy was in a state of deep affliction. With all the sympathy which he could bring into play, the prince told Colia the whole story without reserve, detailing the facts as clearly as he could. The tale struck Colia like a thunderbolt. He could not speak. He listened silently, and cried softly to himself the while. The prince perceived that this was an impression which would last for the whole of the boy's life. He made haste to explain his view of the matter, and pointed out that the old man's approaching death was probably brought on by horror at the thought of his action; and that it was not everyone who was capable of such a feeling.

Colia's eyes flashed as he listened.

"Gania and Varia and Ptitsin are a worthless lot! I shall not quarrel with them; but from this moment our feet shall not travel the same road. Oh, prince, I have felt much that is quite new to me since yesterday! It is a lesson for me. I shall now consider my mother as entirely my responsibility; though she may be safe enough with Varia. Still, meat and drink is not everything."

He jumped up and hurried off, remembering suddenly that he was wanted at his father's bedside; but before he went out of the room he inquired hastily after the prince's health, and receiving the latter's reply, added:

"Isn't there something else, prince? I heard yesterday, but I have no right to talk about this... If you ever want a true friend and servant—neither you nor I are so very happy, are we?—come to me. I won't ask you questions, though."

He ran off and left the prince more dejected than ever.

Everyone seemed to be speaking prophetically, hinting at some misfortune or sorrow to come; they had all looked at him as though they knew something which he did not know. Lebedeff had asked questions, Colia had hinted, and Vera had shed tears. What was it?

At last, with a sigh of annoyance, he said to himself that it was nothing but his own cursed sickly suspicion. His face lighted up with joy when, at about two o'clock, he espied the Epanchins coming along to pay him a short visit, "just for a minute." They really had only come for a minute.

Lizabetha Prokofievna had announced, directly after lunch, that they would all take a walk together. The information was given in the form of a command, without explanation, drily and abruptly. All had issued forth in obedience to the mandate; that is, the girls, mamma, and Prince S. Lizabetha Prokofievna went off in a direction exactly contrary to the usual one, and all understood very well what she was driving at, but held their peace, fearing to irritate the good lady. She, as though anxious to avoid any conversation, walked ahead, silent and alone. At last Adelaida remarked that it was no use racing along at such a pace, and that she could not keep up with her mother.

"Look here," said Lizabetha Prokofievna, turning round suddenly; "we are passing his house. Whatever Aglaya may think, and in spite of anything that may happen, he is not a stranger to us; besides which, he is ill and in misfortune. I, for one, shall call in and see him. Let anyone follow me who cares to."

Of course every one of them followed her.

The prince hastened to apologize, very properly, for yesterday's mishap with the vase, and for the scene generally.

"Oh, that's nothing," replied Lizabetha; "I'm not sorry for the vase, I'm sorry for you. H'm! so you can see that there was a 'scene,' can you? Well, it doesn't matter much, for everyone must realize now that it is impossible to be hard on you. Well, *au revoir*. I advise you to have a walk, and then go to sleep again if you can. Come in as usual, if you feel inclined; and be assured, once for all, whatever happens, and whatever may have happened, you shall always remain the friend of the family—mine, at all events. I can answer for myself."

In response to this challenge all the others chimed in and re-echoed mamma's sentiments.

And so they took their departure; but in this hasty and kindly designed visit there was hidden a fund of cruelty which Lizabetha Prokofievna never dreamed of. In the words "as usual," and again in her added, "mine, at all events," there seemed an ominous knell of some evil to come.

The prince began to think of Aglaya. She had certainly given him a wonderful smile, both at coming and again at leave-taking, but had not said a word, not even when the others all professed their friendship for him. She had looked very intently at him, but that was all. Her face had been paler than usual; she looked as though she had slept badly.

The prince made up his mind that he would make a point of going there "as usual," tonight, and looked feverishly at his watch.

Vera came in three minutes after the Epanchins had left. "Lef Nicolaievitch," she said, "Aglaya Ivanovna has just given me a message for you."

The prince trembled.

"Is it a note?"

"No, a verbal message; she had hardly time even for that. She begs you earnestly not to go out of the house for a single moment all to-day, until seven o'clock in the evening. It may have been nine; I didn't quite hear."

"But—but, why is this? What does it mean?"

"I don't know at all; but she said I was to tell you particularly."

"Did she say that?"

"Not those very words. She only just had time to whisper as she went by; but by the way she looked at me I knew it was important. She looked at me in a way that made my heart stop beating."

The prince asked a few more questions, and though he learned nothing else, he became more and more agitated.

Left alone, he lay down on the sofa, and began to think.

"Perhaps," he thought, "someone is to be with them until nine tonight and she is afraid that I may come and make a fool of myself again, in public." So he spent his time longing for the evening and looking at his watch. But the clearing-up of the mystery came long before the evening, and came in the form of a new and agonizing riddle.

Half an hour after the Epanchins had gone, Hippolyte arrived, so tired that, almost unconscious, he sank into a chair, and broke into such a fit of coughing that he could not stop. He coughed till the blood came. His eyes glittered, and two red spots on his cheeks grew brighter and brighter. The prince murmured something to him, but Hippolyte only signed that he must be left alone for a while, and sat silent. At last he came to himself.

"I am off," he said, hoarsely, and with difficulty.

"Shall I see you home?" asked the prince, rising from his seat, but suddenly stopping short as he remembered Aglaya's prohibition against leaving the house. Hippolyte laughed.

"I don't mean that I am going to leave your house," he continued, still gasping and coughing. "On the contrary, I thought it absolutely necessary to come and see you; otherwise I should not have troubled you. I am off there, you know, and this time I believe, seriously, that I am off! It's all over. I did not come here for sympathy, believe me. I lay down this morning at ten o'clock with the intention of not rising again before that time; but I thought it over and rose just once more in order to come here; from which you may deduce that I had some reason for wishing to come."

"It grieves me to see you so, Hippolyte. Why didn't you send me a message? I would have come up and saved you this trouble."

"Well, well! Enough! You've pitied me, and that's all that good manners exact. I forgot, how are you?"

"I'm all right; yesterday I was a little—"

"I know, I heard; the china vase caught it! I'm sorry I wasn't there. I've come about something important. In the first place I had, the pleasure of seeing Gavrila Ardalionovitch and Aglaya Ivanovna enjoying a rendezvous on the green bench in the park. I was astonished to see what a fool a man can look. I remarked upon the fact to Aglaya Ivanovna when he had gone. I don't think anything ever surprises you, prince!" added Hippolyte, gazing incredulously at the prince's calm demeanour. "To be astonished by nothing is a sign, they say, of a great intellect. In my opinion it would serve equally well as a sign of great foolishness. I am not hinting about you; pardon me! I am very unfortunate today in my expressions."

"I knew yesterday that Gavrila Ardalionovitch—" began the prince, and paused in evident confusion, though Hippolyte had shown annoyance at his betraying no surprise.

"You knew it? Come, that's news! But no—perhaps better not tell me. And were you a witness of the meeting?"

"If you were there yourself you must have known that I was *not* there!"

"Oh! but you may have been sitting behind the bushes somewhere. However, I am very glad, on your account, of course. I was beginning to be afraid that Mr. Gania—might have the preference!"

"May I ask you, Hippolyte, not to talk of this subject? And not to use such expressions?"

"Especially as you know all, eh?"

"You are wrong. I know scarcely anything, and Aglaya Ivanovna is aware that I know nothing. I knew nothing whatever about this meeting. You say there was a meeting. Very well; let's leave it so—"

"Why, what do you mean? You said you knew, and now suddenly you know nothing! You say 'very well; let's leave it so.' But I say, don't be so confiding, especially as you know nothing. You are confiding simply *because* you know nothing. But do you know what these good people have in their minds' eye—Gania and his sister? Perhaps you are suspicious? Well, well, I'll drop the subject!" he added, hastily, observing the prince's impatient gesture. "But I've come to you on my own business; I wish to make you a clear explanation. What a nuisance it is that one cannot die without explanations! I have made such a quantity of them already. Do you wish to hear what I have to say?"

"Speak away, I am listening."

"Very well, but I'll change my mind, and begin about Gania. Just fancy to begin with, if you can, that I, too, was given an appointment at the green bench today! However, I won't deceive you; I asked for the appointment. I said I had a secret to disclose. I don't know whether I came there too early, I think I must have; but scarcely had I sat down beside Aglaya Ivanovna than I saw Gavrila Ardalionovitch and his sister Varia coming along, arm in arm, just as though they were enjoying a morning walk together. Both of them seemed very much astonished, not to say disturbed, at seeing me; they evidently had not expected the pleasure. Aglaya Ivanovna blushed up, and was actually a little confused. I don't know whether it was merely because I was there, or whether Gania's beauty was too much for her! But anyway, she turned crimson, and then finished up the business in a very funny manner. She jumped up from her seat, bowed back to Gania, smiled to Varia, and suddenly observed: 'I only came here to express my gratitude for all your kind wishes on my behalf, and to say that if I find I need your services, believe me—' Here she bowed them away, as it were, and they both marched off again, looking very foolish. Gania evidently could not make head nor tail of the matter, and turned as red as a lobster; but Varia understood at once that they must get away as quickly as they could, so she dragged Gania away; she is a great deal cleverer than he is. As for myself, I went there to arrange a meeting to be held between Aglaya Ivanovna and Nastasia Philipovna."

"Nastasia Philipovna!" cried the prince.

"Aha! I think you are growing less cool, my friend, and are beginning to be a trifle surprised, aren't you? I'm glad that you are not above ordinary human feelings, for once. I'll console you a little now, after your consternation. See what I get for serving a young and high-souled maiden! This morning I received a slap in the face from the lady!"

"A—a moral one?" asked the prince, involuntarily.

"Yes—not a physical one! I don't suppose anyone—even a woman—would raise a hand against me now. Even Gania would hesitate! I did think at one time yesterday, that he would fly at me, though. I bet anything that I know what you are thinking of now! You are thinking: 'Of course one can't strike the little wretch, but one could suffocate him with a pillow, or a wet towel, when he is asleep! One *ought* to get rid of him somehow.' I can see in your face that you are thinking that at this very second."

"I never thought of such a thing for a moment," said the prince, with disgust.

"I don't know—I dreamed last night that I was being suffocated with a wet cloth by—somebody. I'll tell you who it was—Rogojin! What do you think, can a man be suffocated with a wet cloth?"

"I don't know."

"I've heard so. Well, we'll leave that question just now. Why am I a scandal-monger? Why did she call me a scandal-monger? And mind, *after* she had heard every word I had to tell her, and had asked all sorts of questions besides—but such is the way of women. For *her* sake I entered into relations with Rogojin—an interesting man! At *her* request I arranged a personal interview between herself and Nastasia Philipovna. Could she have been angry because I hinted that she was enjoying Nastasia Philipovna's 'leavings'? Why, I have been impressing it upon her all this while for her own good. Two letters have I written her in that strain, and I began straight off today about its being humiliating for her. Besides, the word 'leavings' is not my invention. At all events, they all used it at Gania's, and she used it herself. So why am I a scandal-monger? I see—I see you are tremendously amused, at this moment! Probably you are laughing at me and fitting those silly lines to my case—

"'Maybe sad Love upon his setting smiles, And with vain hopes his farewell hour beguiles.'

"Ha, ha, ha!"

Hippolyte suddenly burst into a fit of hysterical laughter, which turned into a choking cough.

"Observe," he gasped, through his coughing, "what a fellow Gania is! He talks about Nastasia's 'leavings,' but what does he want to take himself?"

The prince sat silent for a long while. His mind was filled with dread and horror.

"You spoke of a meeting with Nastasia Philipovna," he said at last, in a low voice.

"Oh—come! Surely you must know that there is to be a meeting today between Nastasia and Aglaya Ivanovna, and that Nastasia has been sent for on purpose, through Rogojin, from St. Petersburg? It has been brought about by invitation of Aglaya Ivanovna and my own efforts, and Nastasia is at this moment with Rogojin, not far from here—at Dana Alexeyevna's—that curious friend of hers; and to this questionable house Aglaya Ivanovna is to proceed for a friendly chat with Nastasia Philipovna, and for the settlement of several problems. They are going to play at arithmetic—didn't you know about it? Word of honour?"

"It's a most improbable story."

"Oh, very well! if it's improbable—it is—that's all! And yet—where should you have heard it? Though I must say, if a fly crosses the room it's known all over the place here. However, I've warned you, and you may be grateful to me. Well—*au revoir*—probably in the next world! One more thing—don't think that I am telling you all this for your sake. Oh, dear, no! Do you know that I dedicated my confession to Aglaya Ivanovna? I did though, and how she took it, ha, ha! Oh, no! I am not acting from any high, exalted motives. But though I may have behaved like a cad to you, I have not done *her* any harm. I don't apologize for my words about 'leavings' and all that. I am atoning for that, you see, by telling you the place and time of the meeting. Goodbye! You had better take your measures, if you are worthy the name of a man! The meeting is fixed for this evening—that's certain."

Hippolyte walked towards the door, but the prince called him back and he stopped.

"Then you think Aglaya Ivanovna herself intends to go to Nastasia Philipovna's tonight?" he asked, and bright hectic spots came out on his cheeks and forehead.

"I don't know absolutely for certain; but in all probability it is so," replied Hippolyte, looking round. "Nastasia would hardly go to her; and they can't meet at Gania's, with a man nearly dead in the house."

"It's impossible, for that very reason," said the prince. "How would she get out if she wished to? You don't know the habits of that house—she *could* not get away alone to Nastasia Philipovna's! It's all nonsense!"

"Look here, my dear prince, no one jumps out of the window if they can help it; but when there's a fire, the dandiest gentleman or the finest lady in the world will skip out! When the moment comes, and there's nothing else to be done—our young lady will go to Nastasia Philipovna's! Don't they let the young ladies out of the house alone, then?"

"I didn't mean that exactly."

"If you didn't mean that, then she has only to go down the steps and walk off, and she need never come back unless she chooses: Ships are burned behind one sometimes, and one doesn't care to return whence one came. Life need not consist only of lunches, and dinners, and Prince S's. It strikes me you take Aglaya Ivanovna for some conventional boarding-school girl. I said so to her, and she quite agreed with me. Wait till seven or eight o'clock. In your place I would send someone there to keep watch, so as to seize the exact moment when she steps out of the house. Send Colia. He'll play the spy with pleasure—for you at least. Ha, ha, ha!"

Hippolyte went out.

There was no reason for the prince to set anyone to watch, even if he had been capable of such a thing. Aglaya's command that he should stay at home all day seemed almost explained now. Perhaps she meant to call for him, herself, or it might be, of course, that she was anxious to make sure of his not coming there, and therefore bade him remain at home. His head whirled; the whole room seemed to be turning round. He lay down on the sofa, and closed his eyes.

One way or the other the question was to be decided at last—finally.

Oh, no, he did not think of Aglaya as a boarding-school miss, or a young lady of the conventional type! He had long since feared that she might take some such step as this. But why did she wish to see Nastasia?

He shivered all over as he lay; he was in high fever again.

No! he did not account her a child. Certain of her looks, certain of her words, of late, had filled him with apprehension. At times it had struck him that she was putting too great a restraint upon herself, and he remembered that he had been alarmed to observe this. He had tried, all these days, to drive away the heavy thoughts that oppressed him; but what was the hidden mystery of that soul? The question had long tormented him, although he implicitly trusted that soul. And now it was all to be cleared up. It was a dreadful thought. And "that woman" again! Why did he always feel as though "that woman" were fated to appear at each critical moment of his life, and tear the thread of his destiny like a bit of rotten string? That he always *had* felt this he was ready to swear, although he was half delirious at the moment. If he had tried to forget her, all this time, it was simply because he was afraid of her. Did he love the woman or hate her? This question he did not once ask himself today; his heart was quite pure. He knew whom he loved. He was not so much afraid of this meeting, nor of its strangeness, nor of any reasons there might be for it, unknown to himself; he was afraid of the woman herself, Nastasia Philipovna. He remembered, some days afterwards, how during all those fevered hours he had seen but *her* eyes, *her* look, had heard *her* voice, strange words of hers; he remembered that this was so, although he could not recollect the details of his thoughts.

He could remember that Vera brought him some dinner, and that he took it; but whether he slept after dinner, or no, he could not recollect.

He only knew that he began to distinguish things clearly from the moment when Aglaya suddenly appeared, and he jumped up from the sofa and went to meet her. It was just a quarter past seven then.

Aglaya was quite alone, and dressed, apparently hastily, in a light mantle. Her face was pale, as it had been in the morning, and her eyes were ablaze with bright but subdued fire. He had never seen that expression in her eyes before.

She gazed attentively at him.

"You are quite ready, I observe," she said, with absolute composure, "dressed, and your hat in your hand. I see somebody has thought fit to warn you, and I know who. Hippolyte?"

"Yes, he told me," said the prince, feeling only half alive.

"Come then. You know, I suppose, that you must escort me there? You are well enough to go out, aren't you?"

"I am well enough; but is it really possible?—"

He broke off abruptly, and could not add another word. This was his one attempt to stop the mad child, and, after he had made it, he followed her as though he had no will of his own. Confused as his thoughts were, he was, nevertheless, capable of realizing the fact that if he did not go with her, she would go alone, and so he must go with her at all hazards. He guessed the strength of her determination; it was beyond him to check it.

They walked silently, and said scarcely a word all the way. He only noticed that she seemed to know the road very well; and once, when he thought it better to go by a certain lane, and remarked to her that it would be quieter and less public, she only said, "it's all the same," and went on.

When they were almost arrived at Daria Alexeyevna's house (it was a large wooden structure of ancient date), a gorgeously-dressed lady and a young girl came out of it. Both these ladies took their seats in a carriage, which was waiting at the door, talking and laughing loudly the while, and drove away without appearing to notice the approaching couple.

No sooner had the carriage driven off than the door opened once more; and Rogojin, who had apparently been awaiting them, let them in and closed it after them.

"There is not another soul in the house now excepting our four selves," he said aloud, looking at the prince in a strange way.

Nastasia Philipovna was waiting for them in the first room they went into. She was dressed very simply, in black.

She rose at their entrance, but did not smile or give her hand, even to the prince. Her anxious eyes were fixed upon Aglaya. Both sat down, at a little distance from one another—Aglaya on the sofa, in the corner of the room, Nastasia by the window. The prince and Rogojin remained standing, and were not invited to sit.

Muishkin glanced at Rogojin in perplexity, but the latter only smiled disagreeably, and said nothing. The silence continued for some few moments.

An ominous expression passed over Nastasia Philipovna's face, of a sudden. It became obstinate-looking, hard, and full of hatred; but she did not take her eyes off her visitors for a moment.

Aglaya was clearly confused, but not frightened. On entering she had merely glanced momentarily at her rival, and then had sat still, with her eyes on the ground, apparently in thought. Once or twice she glanced casually round the room. A shade of disgust was visible in her expression; she looked as though she were afraid of contamination in this place.

She mechanically arranged her dress, and fidgeted uncomfortably, eventually changing her seat to the other end of the sofa. Probably she was unconscious of her own movements; but this very unconsciousness added to the offensiveness of their suggested meaning.

At length she looked straight into Nastasia's eyes, and instantly read all there was to read in her rival's expression. Woman understood woman! Aglaya shuddered.

"You know of course why I requested this meeting?" she said at last, quietly, and pausing twice in the delivery of this very short sentence.

"No—I know nothing about it," said Nastasia, drily and abruptly.

Aglaya blushed. Perhaps it struck her as very strange and impossible that she should really be sitting here and waiting for "that woman's" reply to her question.

At the first sound of Nastasia's voice a shudder ran through her frame. Of course "that woman" observed and took in all this.

"You know quite well, but you are pretending to be ignorant," said Aglaya, very low, with her eyes on the ground.

"Why should I?" asked Nastasia Philipovna, smiling slightly.

"You want to take advantage of my position, now that I am in your house," continued Aglaya, awkwardly.

"For that position *you* are to blame and not I," said Nastasia, flaring up suddenly. "*I* did not invite *you*, but you me; and to this moment I am quite ignorant as to why I am thus honoured."

Aglaya raised her head haughtily.

"Restrain your tongue!" she said. "I did not come here to fight you with your own weapons."

"Oh! then you did come 'to fight,' I may conclude? Dear me!—and I thought you were cleverer—"

They looked at one another with undisguised malice. One of these women had written to the other, so lately, such letters as we have seen; and it all was dispersed at their first meeting. Yet it appeared that not one of the four persons in the room considered this in any degree strange.

The prince who, up to yesterday, would not have believed that he could even dream of such an impossible scene as this, stood and listened and looked on, and felt as though he had long foreseen it all. The most fantastic dream seemed suddenly to have been metamorphosed into the most vivid reality.

One of these women so despised the other, and so longed to express her contempt for her (perhaps she had only come for that very purpose, as Rogojin said next day), that howsoever fantastical was the other woman, howsoever afflicted her spirit and disturbed her understanding, no preconceived idea of hers could possibly stand up against that deadly feminine contempt of her rival. The prince felt sure that Nastasia would say nothing about the letters herself; but he could judge by her flashing eyes and the expression of her face what the thought of those letters must be costing her at this moment. He would have given half his life to prevent Aglaya from speaking of them. But Aglaya suddenly braced herself up, and seemed to master herself fully, all in an instant.

"You have not quite understood," she said. "I did not come to quarrel with you, though I do not like you. I came to speak to you as... as one human being to another. I came with my mind made up as to what I had to say to you, and I shall not change my intention, although you may misunderstand me. So much the worse for you, not for myself! I wished to reply to all you have written to me and to reply personally, because I think that is the more convenient way. Listen to my reply to all your letters. I began to be sorry for Prince Lef Nicolaievitch on the very day I made his acquaintance, and when I heard—afterwards—of all that took place at your house in the evening, I was sorry for him because he was such a simple-minded man, and because he, in the simplicity of his soul, believed that he could be happy with a woman of your character. What I feared actually took place; you could not love him, you tortured him, and threw him over. You could not love him because you are too proud—no, not proud, that is an error; because you are too vain—no, not quite that either; too self-loving; you are self-loving to madness. Your letters to me are a proof of it. You could not love so simple a soul as his, and perhaps in your heart you despised him and laughed at him. All you could love was your shame and the perpetual thought that you were disgraced and insulted. If you were less shameful, or had no cause at all for shame, you would be still more unhappy than you are now."

Aglaya brought out these thronging words with great satisfaction. They came from her lips hurriedly and impetuously, and had been prepared and thought out long ago, even before she had ever dreamed of the present meeting. She watched with eagerness the effect of her speech as shown in Nastasia's face, which was distorted with agitation.

"You remember," she continued, "he wrote me a letter at that time; he says you know all about that letter and that you even read it. I understand all by means of this letter, and understand it correctly. He has since confirmed it all to me—what I now say to you, word for word. After receiving his letter I waited; I guessed that you would soon come back here, because you could never do without Petersburg; you are still too young and lovely for the provinces. However, this is not my own idea," she added, blushing dreadfully; and from this moment the colour never left her cheeks to the end of her speech. "When I next saw the prince I began to feel terribly pained and hurt on his account. Do not laugh; if you laugh you are unworthy of understanding what I say."

"Surely you see that I am not laughing," said Nastasia, sadly and sternly.

"However, it's all the same to me; laugh or not, just as you please. When I asked him about you, he told me that he had long since ceased to love you, that the very recollection of you was a torture to him, but that he was sorry for you; and that when he thought of you his heart was pierced. I ought to tell you that I never in my life met a man anything like him for noble simplicity of mind and for boundless trustfulness. I guessed that anyone who liked could deceive him, and that he would immediately forgive anyone who did deceive him; and it was for this that I grew to love him—"

Aglaya paused for a moment, as though suddenly brought up in astonishment that she could have said these words, but at the same time a great pride shone in her eyes, like a defiant assertion that it would not matter to her if "this woman" laughed in her face for the admission just made.

"I have told you all now, and of course you understand what I wish of you."

"Perhaps I do; but tell me yourself," said Nastasia Philipovna, quietly.

Aglaya flushed up angrily.

"I wished to find out from you," she said, firmly, "by what right you dare to meddle with his feelings for me? By what right you dared send me those letters? By what right do you continually remind both me and him that you love him, after you yourself threw him over and ran away from him in so insulting and shameful a way?"

"I never told either him or you that I loved him!" replied Nastasia Philipovna, with an effort. "And—and I did run away from him—you are right there," she added, scarcely audibly.

"Never told either him or me?" cried Aglaya. "How about your letters? Who asked you to try to persuade me to marry him? Was not that a declaration from you? Why do you force yourself upon us in this way? I confess I thought at first that you were anxious to arouse an aversion for him in my heart by your meddling, in order that I might give him up; and it was only afterwards that I guessed the truth. You imagined that you were doing an heroic action! How could you spare any love for him, when you love your own vanity to such an extent? Why could you not simply go away from here, instead of writing me those absurd letters? Why do you not *now* marry that generous man who loves you, and has done you the honour of offering you his hand? It is plain enough why; if you marry Rogojin you lose your grievance; you will have nothing more to complain of. You will be receiving too much honour. Evgenie Pavlovitch was saying the other day that you had read too many poems and are too well educated for—your position; and that you live in idleness. Add to this your vanity, and, there you have reason enough—"

"And do you not live in idleness?"

Things had come to this unexpected point too quickly. Unexpected because Nastasia Philipovna, on her way to Pavlofsk, had thought and considered a good deal, and had expected something different, though perhaps not altogether good, from this interview; but Aglaya had been carried away by her own outburst, just as a rolling stone gathers impetus as it careers downhill, and could not restrain herself in the satisfaction of revenge.

It was strange, Nastasia Philipovna felt, to see Aglaya like this. She gazed at her, and could hardly believe her eyes and ears for a moment or two.

Whether she were a woman who had read too many poems, as Evgenie Pavlovitch supposed, or whether she were mad, as the prince had assured Aglaya, at all events, this was a woman who, in spite of her occasionally cynical and audacious manner, was far more refined and trustful and sensitive than appeared. There was a certain amount of romantic dreaminess and caprice in her, but with the fantastic was mingled much that was strong and deep.

The prince realized this, and great suffering expressed itself in his face.

Aglaya observed it, and trembled with anger.

"How dare you speak so to me?" she said, with a haughtiness which was quite indescribable, replying to Nastasia's last remark.

"You must have misunderstood what I said," said Nastasia, in some surprise.

"If you wished to preserve your good name, why did you not give up your—your 'guardian,' Totski, without all that theatrical posturing?" said Aglaya, suddenly a propos of nothing.

"What do you know of my position, that you dare to judge me?" cried Nastasia, quivering with rage, and growing terribly white.

"I know this much, that you did not go out to honest work, but went away with a rich man, Rogojin, in order to pose as a fallen angel. I don't wonder that Totski was nearly driven to suicide by such a fallen angel."

"Silence!" cried Nastasia Philipovna. "You are about as fit to understand me as the housemaid here, who bore witness against her lover in court the other day. She would understand me better than you do."

"Probably an honest girl living by her own toil. Why do you speak of a housemaid so contemptuously?"

"I do not despise toil; I despise you when you speak of toil."

"If you had cared to be an honest woman, you would have gone out as a laundress."

Both had risen, and were gazing at one another with pallid faces.

"Aglaya, don't! This is unfair," cried the prince, deeply distressed.

Rogojin was not smiling now; he sat and listened with folded arms, and lips tight compressed.

"There, look at her," cried Nastasia, trembling with passion. "Look at this young lady! And I imagined her an angel! Did you come to me without your governess, Aglaya Ivanovna? Oh, fie, now shall I just tell you why you came here today? Shall I tell you without any embellishments? You came because you were afraid of me!"

"Afraid of *you*?" asked Aglaya, beside herself with naive amazement that the other should dare talk to her like this.

"Yes, me, of course! Of course you were afraid of me, or you would not have decided to come. You cannot despise one you fear. And to think that I have actually esteemed you up to this very moment! Do you know why you are afraid of me, and what is your object now? You wished to satisfy yourself with your own eyes as to which he loves best, myself or you, because you are fearfully jealous."

"He has told me already that he hates you," murmured Aglaya, scarcely audibly.

"Perhaps, perhaps! I am not worthy of him, I know. But I think you are lying, all the same. He cannot hate me, and he cannot have said so. I am ready to forgive you, in consideration of your position; but I confess I thought better of you. I thought you were wiser, and more beautiful, too; I did, indeed! Well, take your treasure! See, he is gazing at you, he can't recollect himself. Take him, but on one condition; go away at once, this instant!"

She fell back into a chair, and burst into tears. But suddenly some new expression blazed in her eyes. She stared fixedly at Aglaya, and rose from her seat.

"Or would you like me to bid him, *bid him*, do you hear, *command him*, now, at once, to throw you up, and remain mine for ever? Shall I? He will stay, and he will marry me too, and you shall trot home all alone. Shall I?—shall I say the word?" she screamed like a madwoman, scarcely believing herself that she could really pronounce such wild words.

Aglaya had made for the door in terror, but she stopped at the threshold, and listened. "Shall I turn Rogojin off? Ha! ha! you thought I would marry him for your benefit, did you? Why, I'll call out *now*, if you like, in your presence, 'Rogojin, get out!' and say to the prince, 'Do you remember what you promised me?' Heavens! what a fool I have been to humiliate myself before them! Why, prince, you yourself gave me your word that you would marry me whatever happened, and would never abandon me. You said you loved me and would forgive me all, and—and resp—yes, you even said that! I only ran away from you in order to set you free, and now I don't care to let you go again. Why does she treat me so—so shamefully? I am not a loose woman—ask Rogojin there! He'll tell you. Will you go again now that she has insulted me, before your eyes, too; turn away from me and lead her away, arm-in-arm? May you be accursed too, for you were the only one I trusted among them all! Go away, Rogojin, I don't want you," she continued, blind with fury, and forcing the words out with dry lips and distorted features, evidently not believing a single word of her own tirade, but, at the same time, doing her utmost to prolong the moment of self-deception.

The outburst was so terribly violent that the prince thought it would have killed her.

"There he is!" she shrieked again, pointing to the prince and addressing Aglaya. "There he is! and if he does not approach me at once and take *me* and throw you over, then have him for your own—I give him up to you! I don't want him!"

Both she and Aglaya stood and waited as though in expectation, and both looked at the prince like madwomen.

But he, perhaps, did not understand the full force of this challenge; in fact, it is certain he did not. All he could see was the poor despairing face which, as he had said to Aglaya, "had pierced his heart for ever."

He could bear it no longer, and with a look of entreaty, mingled with reproach, he addressed Aglaya, pointing to Nastasia the while:

"How can you?" he murmured; "she is so unhappy."

But he had no time to say another word before Aglaya's terrible look bereft him of speech. In that look was embodied so dreadful a suffering and so deadly a hatred, that he gave a cry and flew to her; but it was too late.

She could not hold out long enough even to witness his movement in her direction. She had hidden her face in her hands, cried once "Oh, my God!" and rushed out of the room. Rogojin followed her to undo the bolts of the door and let her out into the street.

The prince made a rush after her, but he was caught and held back. The distorted, livid face of Nastasia gazed at him reproachfully, and her blue lips whispered:

"What? Would you go to her—to her?"

She fell senseless into his arms.

He raised her, carried her into the room, placed her in an arm-chair, and stood over her, stupefied. On the table stood a tumbler of water. Rogojin, who now returned, took this and sprinkled a little in her face. She opened her eyes, but for a moment she understood nothing.

Suddenly she looked around, shuddered, gave a loud cry, and threw herself in the prince's arms.

"Mine, mine!" she cried. "Has the proud young lady gone? Ha, ha, ha!" she laughed hysterically. "And I had given him up to her! Why—why did I? Mad—mad! Get away, Rogojin! Ha, ha, ha!"

Rogojin stared intently at them; then he took his hat, and without a word, left the room.

A few moments later, the prince was seated by Nastasia on the sofa, gazing into her eyes and stroking her face and hair, as he would a little child's. He laughed when she laughed, and was ready to cry when she cried. He did not speak, but listened to her excited, disconnected chatter, hardly understanding a word of it the while. No sooner did he detect the slightest appearance of complaining, or weeping, or reproaching, than he would smile at her kindly, and begin stroking her hair and her cheeks, soothing and consoling her once more, as if she were a child.

CHAPTER IX.

A fortnight had passed since the events recorded in the last chapter, and the position of the actors in our story had become so changed that it is almost impossible for us to continue the tale without some few explanations. Yet we feel that we ought to limit ourselves to the simple record of facts, without much attempt at explanation, for a very patent reason: because we ourselves have the greatest possible difficulty in accounting for the facts to be recorded. Such a statement on our part may appear strange to the reader. How is anyone to tell a story which he cannot understand himself? In order to keep clear of a false position, we had perhaps better give an example of what we mean; and probably the intelligent reader will soon understand the difficulty. More especially are we inclined to take this course since the example will constitute a distinct march forward of our story, and will not hinder the progress of the events remaining to be recorded.

During the next fortnight—that is, through the early part of July—the history of our hero was circulated in the form of strange, diverting, most unlikely-sounding stories, which passed from mouth to mouth, through the streets and villas adjoining those inhabited by Lebedeff, Ptitsin, Nastasia Philipovna and the Epanchins; in fact, pretty well through the whole town and its environs. All society—both the inhabitants of the place and those who came down of an evening for the music—had got hold of one and the same story, in a thousand varieties of detail—as to how a certain young prince had raised a terrible scandal in a most respectable household, had thrown over a daughter of the family, to whom he was engaged, and had been captured by a woman of shady reputation whom he was determined to marry at once—breaking off all old ties for the satisfaction of his insane idea; and, in spite of the public indignation roused by his action, the marriage was to take place in Pavlofsk openly and publicly, and the prince had announced his intention of going through with it with head erect and looking the whole world in the face. The story was so artfully adorned with scandalous details, and persons of so great eminence and importance were apparently mixed up in it, while, at the same time, the evidence was so circumstantial, that it was no wonder the matter gave food for plenty of curiosity and gossip.

According to the reports of the most talented gossip-mongers—those who, in every class of society, are always in haste to explain every event to their neighbours—the young gentleman concerned was of good family—a prince—fairly rich—weak of intellect, but a democrat and a dabbler in the Nihilism of the period, as exposed by Mr. Turgenieff. He could hardly talk Russian, but had fallen in love with one of the Miss Epanchins, and his suit met with so much encouragement that he had been received in the house as the recognized bridegroom-to-be of the young lady. But like the Frenchman of whom the story is told that he studied for holy orders, took all the oaths, was ordained priest, and next morning wrote to his bishop informing him that, as he did not believe in God and considered it wrong to deceive the people and live upon their pockets, he begged to surrender the orders conferred upon him the day before, and to inform his lordship that he was sending this letter to the public press,—like this Frenchman, the prince played a false game. It was rumoured that he had purposely waited for the solemn occasion of a large evening party at the house of his future bride, at which he was introduced to several eminent persons, in order publicly to make known his ideas and opinions, and thereby insult the "big-wigs," and to throw over his bride as offensively as possible; and that, resisting the servants who were told off to turn him out of the house, he had seized and thrown down a magnificent china vase. As a characteristic addition to the above, it was currently reported that the young prince really loved the lady to whom he was engaged, and had thrown her over out of purely Nihilistic motives, with the intention of giving himself the satisfaction of marrying a fallen woman in the face of all the world, thereby publishing his opinion that there is no distinction between virtuous and disreputable women, but that all women are alike, free; and a "fallen" woman, indeed, somewhat superior to a virtuous one.

It was declared that he believed in no classes or anything else, excepting "the woman question."

All this looked likely enough, and was accepted as fact by most of the inhabitants of the place, especially as it was borne out, more or less, by daily occurrences.

Of course much was said that could not be determined absolutely. For instance, it was reported that the poor girl had so loved her future husband that she had followed him to the house of the other woman, the day after she had been thrown over; others said that he had insisted on her coming, himself, in order to shame and insult her by his taunts and Nihilistic confessions when she reached the house. However all these things might be, the public interest in the matter grew daily, especially as it became clear that the scandalous wedding was undoubtedly to take place.

So that if our readers were to ask an explanation, not of the wild reports about the prince's Nihilistic opinions, but simply as to how such a marriage could possibly satisfy his real aspirations, or as to the spiritual condition of our hero at this time, we confess that we should have great difficulty in giving the required information.

All we know is, that the marriage really was arranged, and that the prince had commissioned Lebedeff and Keller to look after all the necessary business connected with it; that he had requested them to spare no expense; that Nastasia herself was hurrying on the wedding; that Keller was to be the prince's best man, at his own earnest request; and that Burdovsky was to give Nastasia away, to his great delight. The wedding was to take place before the middle of July.

But, besides the above, we are cognizant of certain other undoubted facts, which puzzle us a good deal because they seem flatly to contradict the foregoing.

We suspect, for instance, that having commissioned Lebedeff and the others, as above, the prince immediately forgot all about masters of ceremonies and even the ceremony itself; and we feel quite certain that in making these arrangements he did so in order that he might absolutely escape all thought of the wedding, and even forget its approach if he could, by detailing all business concerning it to others.

What did he think of all this time, then? What did he wish for? There is no doubt that he was a perfectly free agent all through, and that as far as Nastasia was concerned, there was no force of any kind brought to bear on him. Nastasia wished for a speedy marriage, true!—but the prince agreed at once to her proposals; he agreed, in fact, so casually that anyone might suppose he was but acceding to the most simple and ordinary suggestion.

There are many strange circumstances such as this before us; but in our opinion they do but deepen the mystery, and do not in the smallest degree help us to understand the case.

However, let us take one more example. Thus, we know for a fact that during the whole of this fortnight the prince spent all his days and evenings with Nastasia; he walked with her, drove with her; he began to be restless whenever he passed an hour without seeing her—in fact, to all appearances, he sincerely loved her. He would listen to her for hours at a time with a quiet smile on his face, scarcely saying a word himself. And yet we know, equally certainly, that during this period he several times set off, suddenly, to the Epanchins', not concealing the fact from Nastasia Philipovna, and driving the latter to absolute despair. We know also that he was not received at the Epanchins' so long as they remained at Pavlofsk, and that he was not allowed an interview with Aglaya;—but next day he would set off once more on the same errand, apparently quite oblivious of the fact of yesterday's visit having been a failure,—and, of course, meeting with another refusal. We know, too, that exactly an hour after Aglaya had fled from Nastasia Philipovna's house on that fateful evening, the prince was at the Epanchins',—and that his appearance there had been the cause of the greatest consternation and dismay; for Aglaya had not been home, and the family only discovered then, for the first time, that the two of them had been to Nastasia's house together.

It was said that Elizabetha Prokofievna and her daughters had there and then denounced the prince in the strongest terms, and had refused any further acquaintance and friendship with him; their rage and denunciations being redoubled when Varia Ardalionovna suddenly arrived and stated that Aglaya had been at her house in a terrible state of mind for the last hour, and that she refused to come home.

This last item of news, which disturbed Lizabetha Prokofievna more than anything else, was perfectly true. On leaving Nastasia's, Aglaya had felt that she would rather die than face her people, and had therefore gone straight to Nina Alexandrovna's. On receiving the news, Lizabetha and her daughters and the general all rushed off to Aglaya, followed by Prince Lef Nicolaievitch—undeterred by his recent dismissal; but through Varia he was refused a sight of Aglaya here also. The end of the episode was that when Aglaya saw her mother and sisters crying over her and not uttering a word of reproach, she had flung herself into their arms and gone straight home with them.

It was said that Gania managed to make a fool of himself even on this occasion; for, finding himself alone with Aglaya for a minute or two when Varia had gone to the Epanchins', he had thought it a fitting opportunity to make a declaration of his love, and on hearing this Aglaya, in spite of her state of mind at the time, had suddenly burst out laughing, and had put a strange question to him. She asked him whether he would consent to hold his finger to a lighted candle in proof of his devotion! Gania—it was said—looked so comically bewildered that Aglaya had almost laughed herself into hysterics, and had rushed out of the room and upstairs,—where her parents had found her.

Hippolyte told the prince this last story, sending for him on purpose. When Muishkin heard about the candle and Gania's finger he had laughed so that he had quite astonished Hippolyte,—and then shuddered and burst into tears. The prince's condition during those days was strange and perturbed. Hippolyte plainly declared that he thought he was out of his mind;—this, however, was hardly to be relied upon.

Offering all these facts to our readers and refusing to explain them, we do not for a moment desire to justify our hero's conduct. On the contrary, we are quite prepared to feel our share of the indignation which his behaviour aroused in the hearts of his friends. Even Vera Lebedeff was angry with him for a while; so was Colia; so was Keller, until he was selected for best man; so was Lebedeff himself,—who began to intrigue against him out of pure irritation;—but of this anon. In fact we are in full accord with certain forcible words spoken to the prince by Evgenie Pavlovitch, quite unceremoniously, during the course of a friendly conversation, six or seven days after the events at Nastasia Philipovna's house.

We may remark here that not only the Epanchins themselves, but all who had anything to do with them, thought it right to break with the prince in consequence of his conduct. Prince S. even went so far as to turn away and cut him dead in the street. But Evgenie Pavlovitch was not afraid to compromise himself by paying the prince a visit, and did so, in spite of the fact that he had recommenced to visit at the Epanchins', where he was received with redoubled hospitality and kindness after the temporary estrangement.

Evgenie called upon the prince the day after that on which the Epanchins left Pavlofsk. He knew of all the current rumours,—in fact, he had probably contributed to them himself. The prince was delighted to see him, and immediately began to speak of the Epanchins;—which simple and straightforward opening quite took Evgenie's fancy, so that he melted at once, and plunged *in medias res* without ceremony.

The prince did not know, up to this, that the Epanchins had left the place. He grew very pale on hearing the news; but a moment later he nodded his head, and said thoughtfully:

"I knew it was bound to be so." Then he added quickly:

"Where have they gone to?"

Evgenie meanwhile observed him attentively, and the rapidity of the questions, their simplicity, the prince's candour, and at the same time, his evident perplexity and mental agitation, surprised him considerably. However, he told Muishkin all he could, kindly and in detail. The prince hardly knew anything, for this was the first informant from the household whom he had met since the estrangement.

Evgenie reported that Aglaya had been really ill, and that for two nights she had not slept at all, owing to high fever; that now she was better and out of serious danger, but still in a nervous, hysterical state.

"It's a good thing that there is peace in the house, at all events," he continued. "They never utter a hint about the past, not only in Aglaya's presence, but even among themselves. The old people are talking of a trip abroad in the autumn, immediately after Adelaida's wedding; Aglaya received the news in silence."

Evgenie himself was very likely going abroad also; so were Prince S. and his wife, if affairs allowed of it; the general was to stay at home. They were all at their estate of Colmina now, about twenty miles or so from St. Petersburg. Princess Bielokonski had not returned to Moscow yet, and was apparently staying on for reasons of her own. Lizabetha Prokofievna had insisted that it was quite impossible to remain in Pavlofsk after what had happened. Evgenie had told her of all the rumours current in town about the affair; so that there could be no talk of their going to their house on the Yelagin as yet.

"And in point of fact, prince," added Evgenie Pavlovitch, "you must allow that they could hardly have stayed here, considering that they knew of all that went on at your place, and in the face of your daily visits to their house, visits which you insisted upon making in spite of their refusal to see you."

"Yes—yes, quite so; you are quite right. I wished to see Aglaya Ivanovna, you know!" said the prince, nodding his head.

"Oh, my dear fellow," cried Evgenie, warmly, with real sorrow in his voice, "how could you permit all that to come about as it has? Of course, of course, I know it was all so unexpected. I admit that you, only naturally, lost your head, and—and could not stop the foolish girl; that was not in your power. I quite see so much; but you really should have understood how seriously she cared for you. She could not bear to share you with another; and you could bring yourself to throw away and shatter such a treasure! Oh, prince, prince!"

"Yes, yes, you are quite right again," said the poor prince, in anguish of mind. "I was wrong, I know. But it was only Aglaya who looked on Nastasia Philipovna so; no one else did, you know."

"But that's just the worst of it all, don't you see, that there was absolutely nothing serious about the matter in reality!" cried Evgenie, beside himself. "Excuse me, prince, but I have thought over all this; I have thought a great deal over it; I know all that had happened before; I know all that took place six months since; and I know there was *nothing* serious about the matter, it was but fancy, smoke, fantasy, distorted by agitation, and only the alarmed jealousy of an absolutely inexperienced girl could possibly have mistaken it for serious reality."

Here Evgenie Pavlovitch quite let himself go, and gave the reins to his indignation.

Clearly and reasonably, and with great psychological insight, he drew a picture of the prince's past relations with Nastasia Philipovna. Evgenie Pavlovitch always had a ready tongue, but on this occasion his eloquence, surprised himself. "From the very beginning," he said, "you began with a lie; what began with a lie was bound to end with a lie; such is the law of nature. I do not agree, in fact I am angry, when I hear you called an idiot; you are far too intelligent to deserve such an epithet; but you are so far *strange* as to be unlike others; that you must allow, yourself. Now, I have come to the conclusion that the basis of all that has happened, has been first of all your innate inexperience (remark the expression 'innate,' prince). Then follows your unheard-of simplicity of heart; then comes your absolute want of sense of proportion (to this want you have several times confessed); and lastly, a mass, an accumulation, of intellectual convictions which you, in your unexampled honesty of soul, accept unquestionably as also innate and natural and true. Admit, prince, that in your relations with Nastasia Philipovna there has existed, from the very first, something democratic, and the fascination, so to speak, of the 'woman question'? I know all about that scandalous scene at Nastasia Philipovna's house when Rogojin brought the money, six months ago. I'll show you yourself as in a looking-glass, if you like. I know exactly all that went on, in every detail, and why things have turned out as they have. You thirsted, while in Switzerland, for your home-country, for Russia; you read, doubtless, many books about Russia, excellent books, I dare say, but hurtful to *you*; and you arrived here; as it were, on fire with the longing to be of service. Then, on the very day of your arrival, they tell you a sad story of an ill-used woman; they tell *you*, a knight, pure and without reproach, this tale of a poor woman! The same day you actually *see* her; you are attracted by her beauty, her fantastic, almost demoniacal, beauty—(I admit her beauty, of course).

"Add to all this your nervous nature, your epilepsy, and your sudden arrival in a strange town—the day of meetings and of exciting scenes, the day of unexpected acquaintanceships, the day of sudden actions, the day of meeting with the three lovely Epanchin girls, and among them Aglaya—add your fatigue, your excitement; add Nastasia' s evening party, and the tone of that party, and—what were you to expect of yourself at such a moment as that?"

"Yes, yes, yes!" said the prince, once more, nodding his head, and blushing slightly. "Yes, it was so, or nearly so—I know it. And besides, you see, I had not slept the night before, in the train, or the night before that, either, and I was very tired."

"Of course, of course, quite so; that's what I am driving at!" continued Evgenie, excitedly. "It is as clear as possible, and most comprehensible, that you, in your enthusiasm, should plunge headlong into the first chance that came of publicly airing your great idea that you, a prince, and a pure-living man, did not consider a woman disgraced if the sin were not her own, but that of a disgusting social libertine! Oh, heavens! it's comprehensible enough, my dear prince, but that is not the question, unfortunately! The question is, was there any reality and truth in your feelings? Was it nature, or nothing but intellectual enthusiasm? What do you think yourself? We are told, of course, that a far worse woman was *forgiven*, but we don't find that she was told that she had done well, or that she was worthy of honour and respect! Did not your common-sense show you what was the real state of the case, a few months later? The question is now, not whether she is an innocent woman (I do not insist one way or the other—I do not wish to); but can her whole career justify such intolerable pride, such insolent, rapacious egotism as she has shown? Forgive me, I am too violent, perhaps, but—"

"Yes—I dare say it is all as you say; I dare say you are quite right," muttered the prince once more. "She is very sensitive and easily put out, of course; but still, she..."

"She is worthy of sympathy? Is that what you wished to say, my good fellow? But then, for the mere sake of vindicating her worthiness of sympathy, you should not have insulted and offended a noble and generous girl in her presence! This is a terrible exaggeration of sympathy! How can you love a girl, and yet so humiliate her as to throw her over for the sake of another woman, before the very eyes of that other woman, when you have already made her a formal proposal of marriage? And you *did* propose to her, you know; you did so before her parents and sisters. Can you be an honest man, prince, if you act so? I ask you! And did you not deceive that beautiful girl when you assured her of your love?"

"Yes, you are quite right. Oh! I feel that I am very guilty!" said Muishkin, in deepest distress.

"But as if that is enough!" cried Evgenie, indignantly. "As if it is enough simply to say: 'I know I am very guilty!' You are to blame, and yet you persevere in evil-doing. Where was your heart, I should like to know, your *christian heart*, all that time? Did she look as though she were suffering less, at that moment? You saw her face—was she suffering less than the other woman? How could you see her suffering and allow it to continue? How could you?"

"But I did not allow it," murmured the wretched prince.

"How—what do you mean you didn't allow?"

"Upon my word, I didn't! To this moment I don't know how it all happened. I—I ran after Aglaya Ivanovna, but Nastasia Philipovna fell down in a faint; and since that day they won't let me see Aglaya—that's all I know."

"It's all the same; you ought to have run after Aglaya though the other was fainting."

"Yes, yes, I ought—but I couldn't! She would have died—she would have killed herself. You don't know her; and I should have told Aglaya everything afterwards—but I see, Evgenie Pavlovitch, you don't know all. Tell me now, why am I not allowed to see Aglaya? I should have cleared it all up, you know. Neither of them kept to the real point, you see. I could never explain what I mean to you, but I think I could to Aglaya. Oh! my God, my God! You spoke just now of Aglaya's face at the moment when she ran away. Oh, my God! I remember it! Come along, come along—quick!" He pulled at Evgenie's coat-sleeve nervously and excitedly, and rose from his chair.

"Where to?"

"Come to Aglaya—quick, quick!"

"But I told you she is not at Pavlofsk. And what would be the use if she were?"

"Oh, she'll understand, she'll understand!" cried the prince, clasping his hands. "She would understand that all this is not the point—not a bit the real point—it is quite foreign to the real question."

"How can it be foreign? You *are* going to be married, are you not? Very well, then you are persisting in your course. *Are* you going to marry her or not?"

"Yes, I shall marry her—yes."

"Then why is it 'not the point'?"

"Oh, no, it is not the point, not a bit. It makes no difference, my marrying her—it means nothing."

"How 'means nothing'? You are talking nonsense, my friend. You are marrying the woman you love in order to secure her happiness, and Aglaya sees and knows it. How can you say that it's 'not the point'?"

"Her happiness? Oh, no! I am only marrying her—well, because she wished it. It means nothing—it's all the same. She would certainly have died. I see now that that marriage with Rogojin was an insane idea. I understand all now that I did not understand before; and, do you know, when those two stood opposite to one another, I could not bear Nastasia Philipovna's face! You must know, Evgenie Pavlovitch, I have never told anyone before—not even Aglaya—that I cannot bear Nastasia Philipovna's face." (He lowered his voice mysteriously as he said this.) "You described that evening at Nastasia Philipovna's (six months since) very accurately just now; but there is one thing which you did not mention, and of which you took no account, because you do not know. I mean her *face*—I looked at her face, you see. Even in the morning when I saw her portrait, I felt that I could not *bear* to look at it. Now, there's Vera Lebedeff, for instance, her eyes are quite different, you know. I'm *afraid* of her face!" he added, with real alarm.

"You are *afraid* of it?"

"Yes—she's mad!" he whispered, growing pale.

"Do you know this for certain?" asked Evgenie, with the greatest curiosity.

"Yes, for certain—quite for certain, now! I have discovered it *absolutely* for certain, these last few days."

"What are you doing, then?" cried Evgenie, in horror. "You must be marrying her solely out of *fear*, then! I can't make head or tail of it, prince. Perhaps you don't even love her?"

"Oh, no; I love her with all my soul. Why, she is a child! She's a child now—a real child. Oh! you know nothing about it at all, I see."

"And are you assured, at the same time, that you love Aglaya too?"

"Yes—yes—oh; yes!"

"How so? Do you want to make out that you love them *both?*"

"Yes—yes—both! I do!"

"Excuse me, prince, but think what you are saying! Recollect yourself!"

"Without Aglaya—I—I *must* see Aglaya!—I shall die in my sleep very soon—I thought I was dying in my sleep last night. Oh! if Aglaya only knew all—I mean really, *really* all! Because she must know *all*—that's the first condition towards understanding. Why cannot we ever know all about another, especially when that other has been guilty? But I don't know what I'm talking about—I'm so confused. You pained me so dreadfully. Surely—surely Aglaya has not the same expression now as she had at the moment when she ran away? Oh, yes! I am guilty and I know it—I know it! Probably I am in fault all round—I don't quite know how—but I am in fault, no doubt. There is something else, but I cannot explain it to you, Evgenie Pavlovitch. I have no words; but Aglaya will understand. I have always believed Aglaya will understand—I am assured she will."

"No, prince, she will not. Aglaya loved like a woman, like a human being, not like an abstract spirit. Do you know what, my poor prince? The most probable explanation of the matter is that you never loved either the one or the other in reality."

"I don't know—perhaps you are right in much that you have said, Evgenie Pavlovitch. You are very wise, Evgenie Pavlovitch—oh! how my head is beginning to ache again! Come to her, quick—for God's sake, come!"

"But I tell you she is not in Pavlofsk! She's in Colmina."

"Oh, come to Colmina, then! Come—let us go at once!"

"No—no, impossible!" said Evgenie, rising.

"Look here—I'll write a letter—take a letter for me!"

"No—no, prince; you must forgive me, but I can't undertake any such commissions! I really can't."

And so they parted.

Evgenie Pavlovitch left the house with strange convictions. He, too, felt that the prince must be out of his mind.

"And what did he mean by that *face*—a face which he so fears, and yet so loves? And meanwhile he really may die, as he says, without seeing Aglaya, and she will never know how devotedly he loves her! Ha, ha, ha! How does the fellow manage to love two of them? Two different kinds of love, I suppose! This is very interesting—poor idiot! What on earth will become of him now?"

Chapter X.

The prince did not die before his wedding—either by day or night, as he had foretold that he might. Very probably he passed disturbed nights, and was afflicted with bad dreams; but, during the daytime, among his fellow-men, he seemed as kind as ever, and even contented; only a little thoughtful when alone.

The wedding was hurried on. The day was fixed for exactly a week after Evgenie's visit to the prince. In the face of such haste as this, even the prince's best friends (if he had had any) would have felt the hopelessness of any attempt to save "the poor madman." Rumour said that in the visit of Evgenie Pavlovitch was to be discerned the influence of Lizabetha Prokofievna and her husband... But if those good souls, in the boundless kindness of their hearts, were desirous of saving the eccentric young fellow from ruin, they were unable to take any stronger measures to attain that end. Neither their position, nor their private inclination, perhaps (and only naturally), would allow them to use any more pronounced means.

We have observed before that even some of the prince's nearest neighbours had begun to oppose him. Vera Lebedeff's passive disagreement was limited to the shedding of a few solitary tears; to more frequent sitting alone at home, and to a diminished frequency in her visits to the prince's apartments.

Colia was occupied with his father at this time. The old man died during a second stroke, which took place just eight days after the first. The prince showed great sympathy in the grief of the family, and during the first days of their mourning he was at the house a great deal with Nina Alexandrovna. He went to the funeral, and it was observable that the public assembled in church greeted his arrival and departure with whisperings, and watched him closely.

The same thing happened in the park and in the street, wherever he went. He was pointed out when he drove by, and he often overheard the name of Nastasia Philipovna coupled with his own as he passed. People looked out for her at the funeral, too, but she was not there; and another conspicuous absentee was the captain's widow, whom Lebedeff had prevented from coming.

The funeral service produced a great effect on the prince. He whispered to Lebedeff that this was the first time he had ever heard a Russian funeral service since he was a little boy. Observing that he was looking about him uneasily, Lebedeff asked him whom he was seeking.

"Nothing. I only thought I—"

"Is it Rogojin?"

"Why—is he here?"

"Yes, he's in church."

"I thought I caught sight of his eyes!" muttered the prince, in confusion. "But what of it!—Why is he here? Was he asked?"

"Oh, dear, no! Why, they don't even know him! Anyone can come in, you know. Why do you look so amazed? I often meet him; I've seen him at least four times, here at Pavlofsk, within the last week."

"I haven't seen him once—since that day!" the prince murmured.

As Nastasia Philipovna had not said a word about having met Rogojin since "that day," the prince concluded that the latter had his own reasons for wishing to keep out of sight. All the day of the funeral our hero was in a deeply thoughtful state, while Nastasia Philipovna was particularly merry, both in the daytime and in the evening.

Colia had made it up with the prince before his father's death, and it was he who urged him to make use of Keller and Burdovsky, promising to answer himself for the former's behaviour. Nina Alexandrovna and Lebedeff tried to persuade him to have the wedding in St. Petersburg, instead of in the public fashion contemplated, down here at Pavlofsk in the height of the season. But the prince only said that Nastasia Philipovna desired to have it so, though he saw well enough what prompted their arguments.

The next day Keller came to visit the prince. He was in a high state of delight with the post of honour assigned to him at the wedding.

Before entering he stopped on the threshold, raised his hand as if making a solemn vow, and cried:

"I won't drink!"

Then he went up to the prince, seized both his hands, shook them warmly, and declared that he had at first felt hostile towards the project of this marriage, and had openly said so in the billiard-rooms, but that the reason simply was that, with the impatience of a friend, he had hoped to see the prince marry at least a Princess de Rohan or de Chabot; but that now he saw that the prince's way of thinking was ten times more noble than that of "all the rest put together." For he desired neither pomp nor wealth nor honour, but only the truth! The sympathies of exalted personages were well known, and the prince was too highly placed by his education, and so on, not to be in some sense an exalted personage!

"But all the common herd judge differently; in the town, at the meetings, in the villas, at the band, in the inns and the billiard-rooms, the coming event has only to be mentioned and there are shouts and cries from everybody. I have even heard talk of getting up a 'charivari' under the windows on the wedding-night. So if 'you have need of the pistol' of an honest man, prince, I am ready to fire half a dozen shots even before you rise from your nuptial couch!"

Keller also advised, in anticipation of the crowd making a rush after the ceremony, that a fire-hose should be placed at the entrance to the house; but Lebedeff was opposed to this measure, which he said might result in the place being pulled down.

"I assure you, prince, that Lebedeff is intriguing against you. He wants to put you under control. Imagine that! To take 'from you the use of your free-will and your money'—that is to say, the two things that distinguish us from the animals! I have heard it said positively. It is the sober truth."

The prince recollected that somebody had told him something of the kind before, and he had, of course, scoffed at it. He only laughed now, and forgot the hint at once.

Lebedeff really had been busy for some little while; but, as usual, his plans had become too complex to succeed, through sheer excess of ardour. When he came to the prince—the very day before the wedding—to confess (for he always confessed to the persons against whom he intrigued, especially when the plan failed), he informed our hero that he himself was a born Talleyrand, but for some unknown reason had become simple Lebedeff. He then proceeded to explain his whole game to the prince, interesting the latter exceedingly.

According to Lebedeff's account, he had first tried what he could do with General Epanchin. The latter informed him that he wished well to the unfortunate young man, and would gladly do what he could to "save him," but that he did not think it would be seemly for him to interfere in this matter. Lizabetha Prokofievna would neither hear nor see him. Prince S. and Evgenie Pavlovitch only shrugged their shoulders, and implied that it was no business of theirs. However, Lebedeff had not lost heart, and went off to a clever lawyer,—a worthy and respectable man, whom he knew well. This old gentleman informed him that the thing was perfectly feasible if he could get hold of competent witnesses as to Muishkin's mental incapacity. Then, with the assistance of a few influential persons, he would soon see the matter arranged.

Lebedeff immediately procured the services of an old doctor, and carried the latter away to Pavlofsk to see the prince, by way of viewing the ground, as it were, and to give him (Lebedeff) counsel as to whether the thing was to be done or not. The visit was not to be official, but merely friendly.

Muishkin remembered the doctor's visit quite well. He remembered that Lebedeff had said that he looked ill, and had better see a doctor; and although the prince scouted the idea, Lebedeff had turned up almost immediately with his old friend, explaining that they had just met at the bedside of Hippolyte, who was very ill, and that the doctor had something to tell the prince about the sick man.

The prince had, of course, at once received him, and had plunged into a conversation about Hippolyte. He had given the doctor an account of Hippolyte's attempted suicide; and had proceeded thereafter to talk of his own malady,—of Switzerland, of Schneider, and so on; and so deeply was the old man interested by the prince's conversation and his description of Schneider's system, that he sat on for two hours.

Muishkin gave him excellent cigars to smoke, and Lebedeff, for his part, regaled him with liqueurs, brought in by Vera, to whom the doctor—a married man and the father of a family—addressed such compliments that she was filled with indignation. They parted friends, and, after leaving the prince, the doctor said to Lebedeff: "If all such people were put under restraint, there would be no one left for keepers." Lebedeff then, in tragic tones, told of the approaching marriage, whereupon the other nodded his head and replied that, after all, marriages like that were not so rare; that he had heard that the lady was very fascinating and of extraordinary beauty, which was enough to explain the infatuation of a wealthy man; that, further, thanks to the liberality of Totski and of Rogojin, she possessed—so he had heard—not only money, but pearls, diamonds, shawls, and furniture, and consequently she could not be considered a bad match. In brief, it seemed to the doctor that the prince's choice, far from being a sign of foolishness, denoted, on the contrary, a shrewd, calculating, and practical mind. Lebedeff had been much struck by this point of view, and he terminated his confession by assuring the prince that he was ready, if need be, to shed his very life's blood for him.

Hippolyte, too, was a source of some distraction to the prince at this time; he would send for him at any and every hour of the day. They lived,—Hippolyte and his mother and the children,—in a small house not far off, and the little ones were happy, if only because they were able to escape from the invalid into the garden. The prince had enough to do in keeping the peace between the irritable Hippolyte and his mother, and eventually the former became so malicious and sarcastic on the subject of the approaching wedding, that Muishkin took offence at last, and refused to continue his visits.

A couple of days later, however, Hippolyte's mother came with tears in her eyes, and begged the prince to come back, "or *he* would eat her up bodily." She added that Hippolyte had a great secret to disclose. Of course the prince went. There was no secret, however, unless we reckon certain pantings and agitated glances around (probably all put on) as the invalid begged his visitor to "beware of Rogojin."

"He is the sort of man," he continued, "who won't give up his object, you know; he is not like you and me, prince—he belongs to quite a different order of beings. If he sets his heart on a thing he won't be afraid of anything—" and so on.

Hippolyte was very ill, and looked as though he could not long survive. He was tearful at first, but grew more and more sarcastic and malicious as the interview proceeded.

The prince questioned him in detail as to his hints about Rogojin. He was anxious to seize upon some facts which might confirm Hippolyte's vague warnings; but there were none; only Hippolyte's own private impressions and feelings.

However, the invalid—to his immense satisfaction—ended by seriously alarming the prince.

At first Muishkin had not cared to make any reply to his sundry questions, and only smiled in response to Hippolyte's advice to "run for his life—abroad, if necessary. There are Russian priests everywhere, and one can get married all over the world."

But it was Hippolyte's last idea which upset him.

"What I am really alarmed about, though," he said, "is Aglaya Ivanovna. Rogojin knows how you love her. Love for love. You took Nastasia Philipovna from him. He will murder Aglaya Ivanovna; for though she is not yours, of course, now, still such an act would pain you,—wouldn't it?"

He had attained his end. The prince left the house beside himself with terror.

These warnings about Rogojin were expressed on the day before the wedding. That evening the prince saw Nastasia Philipovna for the last time before they were to meet at the altar; but Nastasia was not in a position to give him any comfort or consolation. On the contrary, she only added to his mental perturbation as the evening went on. Up to this time she had invariably done her best to cheer him—she was afraid of his looking melancholy; she would try singing to him, and telling him every sort of funny story or reminiscence that she could recall. The prince nearly always pretended to be amused, whether he were so actually or no; but often enough he laughed sincerely, delighted by the brilliancy of her wit when she was carried away by her narrative, as she very often was. Nastasia would be wild with joy to see the impression she had made, and to hear his laugh of real amusement; and she would remain the whole evening in a state of pride and happiness. But this evening her melancholy and thoughtfulness grew with every hour.

The prince had told Evgenie Pavlovitch with perfect sincerity that he loved Nastasia Philipovna with all his soul. In his love for her there was the sort of tenderness one feels for a sick, unhappy child which cannot be left alone. He never spoke of his feelings for Nastasia to anyone, not even to herself. When they were together they never discussed their "feelings," and there was nothing in their cheerful, animated conversation which an outsider could not have heard. Daria Alexeyevna, with whom Nastasia was staying, told afterwards how she had been filled with joy and delight only to look at them, all this time.

Thanks to the manner in which he regarded Nastasia's mental and moral condition, the prince was to some extent freed from other perplexities. She was now quite different from the woman he had known three months before. He was not astonished, for instance, to see her now so impatient to marry him—she who formerly had wept with rage and hurled curses and reproaches at him if he mentioned marriage! "It shows that she no longer fears, as she did then, that she would make me unhappy by marrying me," he thought. And he felt sure that so sudden a change could not be a natural one. This rapid growth of self-confidence could not be due only to her hatred for Aglaya. To suppose that would be to suspect the depth of her feelings. Nor could it arise from dread of the fate that awaited her if she married Rogojin. These causes, indeed, as well as others, might have played a part in it, but the true reason, Muishkin decided, was the one he had long suspected—that the poor sick soul had come to the end of its forces. Yet this was an explanation that did not procure him any peace of mind. At times he seemed to be making violent efforts to think of nothing, and one would have said that he looked on his marriage as an unimportant formality, and on his future happiness as a thing not worth considering. As to conversations such as the one held with Evgenie Pavlovitch, he avoided them as far as possible, feeling that there were certain objections to which he could make no answer.

The prince had observed that Nastasia knew well enough what Aglaya was to him. He never spoke of it, but he had seen her face when she had caught him starting off for the Epanchins' house on several occasions. When the Epanchins left Pavlofsk, she had beamed with radiance and happiness. Unsuspicious and unobservant as he was, he had feared at that time that Nastasia might have some scheme in her mind for a scene or scandal which would drive Aglaya out of Pavlofsk. She had encouraged the rumours and excitement among the inhabitants of the place as to her marriage with the prince, in order to annoy her rival; and, finding it difficult to meet the Epanchins anywhere, she had, on one occasion, taken him for a drive past their house. He did not observe what was happening until they were almost passing the windows, when it was too late to do anything. He said nothing, but for two days afterwards he was ill.

Nastasia did not try that particular experiment again. A few days before that fixed for the wedding, she grew grave and thoughtful. She always ended by getting the better of her melancholy, and becoming merry and cheerful again, but not quite so unaffectedly happy as she had been some days earlier.

The prince redoubled his attentive study of her symptoms. It was a most curious circumstance, in his opinion, that she never spoke of Rogojin. But once, about five days before the wedding, when the prince was at home, a messenger arrived begging him to come at once, as Nastasia Philipovna was very ill.

He had found her in a condition approaching to absolute madness. She screamed, and trembled, and cried out that Rogojin was hiding out there in the garden—that she had seen him herself—and that he would murder her in the night—that he would cut her throat. She was terribly agitated all day. But it so happened that the prince called at Hippolyte's house later on, and heard from his mother that she had been in town all day, and had there received a visit from Rogojin, who had made inquiries about Pavlofsk. On inquiry, it turned out that Rogojin visited the old lady in town at almost the same moment when Nastasia declared that she had seen him in the garden; so that the whole thing turned out to be an illusion on her part. Nastasia immediately went across to Hippolyte's to inquire more accurately, and returned immensely relieved and comforted.

On the day before the wedding, the prince left Nastasia in a state of great animation. Her wedding-dress and all sorts of finery had just arrived from town. Muishkin had not imagined that she would be so excited over it, but he praised everything, and his praise rendered her doubly happy.

But Nastasia could not hide the cause of her intense interest in her wedding splendour. She had heard of the indignation in the town, and knew that some of the populace was getting up a sort of charivari with music, that verses had been composed for the occasion, and that the rest of Pavlofsk society more or less encouraged these preparations. So, since attempts were being made to humiliate her, she wanted to hold her head even higher than usual, and to overwhelm them all with the beauty and taste of her toilette. "Let them shout and whistle, if they dare!" Her eyes flashed at the thought. But, underneath this, she had another motive, of which she did not speak. She thought that possibly Aglaya, or at any rate someone sent by her, would be present incognito at the ceremony, or in the crowd, and she wished to be prepared for this eventuality.

The prince left her at eleven, full of these thoughts, and went home. But it was not twelve o'clock when a messenger came to say that Nastasia was very bad, and he must come at once.

On hurrying back he found his bride locked up in her own room and could hear her hysterical cries and sobs. It was some time before she could be made to hear that the prince had come, and then she opened the door only just sufficiently to let him in, and immediately locked it behind him. She then fell on her knees at his feet. (So at least Dana Alexeyevna reported.)

"What am I doing? What am I doing to you?" she sobbed convulsively, embracing his knees.

The prince was a whole hour soothing and comforting her, and left her, at length, pacified and composed. He sent another messenger during the night to inquire after her, and two more next morning. The last brought back a message that Nastasia was surrounded by a whole army of dressmakers and maids, and was as happy and as busy as such a beauty should be on her wedding morning, and that there was not a vestige of yesterday's agitation remaining. The message concluded with the news that at the moment of the bearer's departure there was a great confabulation in progress as to which diamonds were to be worn, and how.

This message entirely calmed the prince's mind.

The following report of the proceedings on the wedding day may be depended upon, as coming from eye-witnesses.

The wedding was fixed for eight o'clock in the evening. Nastasia Philipovna was ready at seven. From six o'clock groups of people began to gather at Nastasia's house, at the prince's, and at the church door, but more especially at the former place. The church began to fill at seven.

Colia and Vera Lebedeff were very anxious on the prince's account, but they were so busy over the arrangements for receiving the guests after the wedding, that they had not much time for the indulgence of personal feelings.

There were to be very few guests besides the best men and so on; only Dana Alexeyevna, the Ptitsins, Gania, and the doctor. When the prince asked Lebedeff why he had invited the doctor, who was almost a stranger, Lebedeff replied:

"Why, he wears an 'order,' and it looks so well!"

This idea amused the prince.

Keller and Burdovsky looked wonderfully correct in their dress-coats and white kid gloves, although Keller caused the bridegroom some alarm by his undisguisedly hostile glances at the gathering crowd of sight-seers outside.

At about half-past seven the prince started for the church in his carriage.

We may remark here that he seemed anxious not to omit a single one of the recognized customs and traditions observed at weddings. He wished all to be done as openly as possible, and "in due order."

Arrived at the church, Muishkin, under Keller's guidance, passed through the crowd of spectators, amid continuous whispering and excited exclamations. The prince stayed near the altar, while Keller made off once more to fetch the bride.

On reaching the gate of Daria Alexeyevna's house, Keller found a far denser crowd than he had encountered at the prince's. The remarks and exclamations of the spectators here were of so irritating a nature that Keller was very near making them a speech on the impropriety of their conduct, but was luckily caught by Burdovsky, in the act of turning to address them, and hurried indoors.

Nastasia Philipovna was ready. She rose from her seat, looked into the glass and remarked, as Keller told the tale afterwards, that she was "as pale as a corpse." She then bent her head reverently, before the ikon in the corner, and left the room.

A torrent of voices greeted her appearance at the front door. The crowd whistled, clapped its hands, and laughed and shouted; but in a moment or two isolated voices were distinguishable.

"What a beauty!" cried one.

"Well, she isn't the first in the world, nor the last," said another.

"Marriage covers everything," observed a third.

"I defy you to find another beauty like that," said a fourth.

"She's a real princess! I'd sell my soul for such a princess as that!"

Nastasia came out of the house looking as white as any handkerchief; but her large dark eyes shone upon the vulgar crowd like blazing coals. The spectators' cries were redoubled, and became more exultant and triumphant every moment. The door of the carriage was open, and Keller had given his hand to the bride to help her in, when suddenly with a loud cry she rushed from him, straight into the surging crowd. Her friends about her were stupefied with amazement; the crowd parted as she rushed through it, and suddenly, at a distance of five or six yards from the carriage, appeared Rogojin. It was his look that had caught her eyes.

Nastasia rushed to him like a madwoman, and seized both his hands.

"Save me!" she cried. "Take me away, anywhere you like, quick!"

Rogojin seized her in his arms and almost carried her to the carriage. Then, in a flash, he tore a hundred-rouble note out of his pocket and held it to the coachman.

"To the station, quick! If you catch the train you shall have another. Quick!"

He leaped into the carriage after Nastasia and banged the door. The coachman did not hesitate a moment; he whipped up the horses, and they were off.

"One more second and I should have stopped him," said Keller, afterwards. In fact, he and Burdovsky jumped into another carriage and set off in pursuit; but it struck them as they drove along that it was not much use trying to bring Nastasia back by force.

"Besides," said Burdovsky, "the prince would not like it, would he?" So they gave up the pursuit.

Rogojin and Nastasia Philipovna reached the station just in time for the train. As he jumped out of the carriage and was almost on the point of entering the train, Rogojin accosted a young girl standing on the platform and wearing an old-fashioned, but respectable-looking, black cloak and a silk handkerchief over her head.

"Take fifty roubles for your cloak?" he shouted, holding the money out to the girl. Before the astonished young woman could collect her scattered senses, he pushed the money into her hand, seized the mantle, and threw it and the handkerchief over Nastasia's head and shoulders. The latter's wedding-array would have attracted too much attention, and it was not until some time later that the girl understood why her old cloak and kerchief had been bought at such a price.

The news of what had happened reached the church with extraordinary rapidity. When Keller arrived, a host of people whom he did not know thronged around to ask him questions. There was much excited talking, and shaking of heads, even some laughter; but no one left the church, all being anxious to observe how the now celebrated bridegroom would take the news. He grew very pale upon hearing it, but took it quite quietly.

"I was afraid," he muttered, scarcely audibly, "but I hardly thought it would come to this." Then after a short silence, he added: "However, in her state, it is quite consistent with the natural order of things."

Even Keller admitted afterwards that this was "extraordinarily philosophical" on the prince's part. He left the church quite calm, to all appearances, as many witnesses were found to declare afterwards. He seemed anxious to reach home and be left alone as quickly as possible; but this was not to be. He was accompanied by nearly all the invited guests, and besides this, the house was almost besieged by excited bands of people, who insisted upon being allowed to enter the verandah. The prince heard Keller and Lebedeff remonstrating and quarrelling with these unknown individuals, and soon went out himself. He approached the disturbers of his peace, requested courteously to be told what was desired; then politely putting Lebedeff and Keller aside, he addressed an old gentleman who was standing on the verandah steps at the head of the band of would-be guests, and courteously requested him to honour him with a visit. The old fellow was quite taken aback by this, but entered, followed by a few more, who tried to appear at their ease. The rest remained outside, and presently the whole crowd was censuring those who had accepted the invitation. The prince offered seats to his strange visitors, tea was served, and a general conversation sprang up. Everything was done most decorously, to the considerable surprise of the intruders. A few tentative attempts were made to turn the conversation to the events of the day, and a few indiscreet questions were asked; but Muishkin replied to everybody with such simplicity and good-humour, and at the same time with so much dignity, and showed such confidence in the good breeding of his guests, that the indiscreet talkers were quickly silenced. By degrees the conversation became almost serious. One gentleman suddenly exclaimed, with great vehemence: "Whatever happens, I shall not sell my property; I shall wait. Enterprise is better than money, and there, sir, you have my whole system of economy, if you wish!" He addressed the prince, who warmly commended his sentiments, though Lebedeff whispered in his ear that this gentleman, who talked so much of his "property," had never had either house or home.

Nearly an hour passed thus, and when tea was over the visitors seemed to think that it was time to go. As they went out, the doctor and the old gentleman bade Muishkin a warm farewell, and all the rest took their leave with hearty protestations of good-will, dropping remarks to the effect that "it was no use worrying," and that "perhaps all would turn out for the best," and so on. Some of the younger intruders would have asked for champagne, but they were checked by the older ones. When all had departed, Keller leaned over to Lebedeff, and said:

"With you and me there would have been a scene. We should have shouted and fought, and called in the police. But he has simply made some new friends—and such friends, too! I know them!"

Lebedeff, who was slightly intoxicated, answered with a sigh:

"Things are hidden from the wise and prudent, and revealed unto babes. I have applied those words to him before, but now I add that God has preserved the babe himself from the abyss, He and all His saints."

At last, about half-past ten, the prince was left alone. His head ached. Colia was the last to go, after having helped him to change his wedding clothes. They parted on affectionate terms, and, without speaking of what had happened, Colia promised to come very early the next day. He said later that the prince had given no hint of his intentions when they said good-bye, but had hidden them even from him. Soon there was hardly anyone left in the house. Burdovsky had gone to see Hippolyte; Keller and Lebedeff had wandered off together somewhere.

Only Vera Lebedeff remained hurriedly rearranging the furniture in the rooms. As she left the verandah, she glanced at the prince. He was seated at the table, with both elbows upon it, and his head resting on his hands. She approached him, and touched his shoulder gently. The prince started and looked at her in perplexity; he seemed to be collecting his senses for a minute or so, before he could remember where he was. As recollection dawned upon him, he became violently agitated. All he did, however, was to ask Vera very earnestly to knock at his door and awake him in time for the first train to Petersburg next morning. Vera promised, and the prince entreated her not to tell anyone of his intention. She promised this, too; and at last, when she had half-closed the door, he called her back a third time, took her hands in his, kissed them, then kissed her forehead, and in a rather peculiar manner said to her, "Until tomorrow!"

Such was Vera's story afterwards.

She went away in great anxiety about him, but when she saw him in the morning, he seemed to be quite himself again, greeted her with a smile, and told her that he would very likely be back by the evening. It appears that he did not consider it necessary to inform anyone excepting Vera of his departure for town.

CHAPTER XI.

An hour later he was in St. Petersburg, and by ten o'clock he had rung the bell at Rogojin's.

He had gone to the front door, and was kept waiting a long while before anyone came. At last the door of old Mrs. Rogojin's flat was opened, and an aged servant appeared.

"Parfen Semionovitch is not at home," she announced from the doorway. "Whom do you want?"

"Parfen Semionovitch."

"He is not in."

The old woman examined the prince from head to foot with great curiosity.

"At all events tell me whether he slept at home last night, and whether he came alone?"

The old woman continued to stare at him, but said nothing.

"Was not Nastasia Philipovna here with him, yesterday evening?"

"And, pray, who are you yourself?"

"Prince Lef Nicolaievitch Muishkin; he knows me well."

"He is not at home."

The woman lowered her eyes.

"And Nastasia Philipovna?"

"I know nothing about it."

"Stop a minute! When will he come back?"

"I don't know that either."

The door was shut with these words, and the old woman disappeared. The prince decided to come back within an hour. Passing out of the house, he met the porter.

"Is Parfen Semionovitch at home?" he asked.

"Yes."

"Why did they tell me he was not at home, then?"

"Where did they tell you so,—at his door?"

"No, at his mother's flat; I rang at Parfen Semionovitch's door and nobody came."

"Well, he may have gone out. I can't tell. Sometimes he takes the keys with him, and leaves the rooms empty for two or three days."

"Do you know for certain that he was at home last night?"

"Yes, he was."

"Was Nastasia Philipovna with him?"

"I don't know; she doesn't come often. I think I should have known if she had come."

The prince went out deep in thought, and walked up and down the pavement for some time. The windows of all the rooms occupied by Rogojin were closed, those of his mother's apartments were open. It was a hot, bright day. The prince crossed the road in order to have a good look at the windows again; not only were Rogojin's closed, but the white blinds were all down as well.

He stood there for a minute and then, suddenly and strangely enough, it seemed to him that a little corner of one of the blinds was lifted, and Rogojin's face appeared for an instant and then vanished. He waited another minute, and decided to go and ring the bell once more; however, he thought better of it again and put it off for an hour.

The chief object in his mind at this moment was to get as quickly as he could to Nastasia Philipovna's lodging. He remembered that, not long since, when she had left Pavlofsk at his request, he had begged her to put up in town at the house of a respectable widow, who had well-furnished rooms to let, near the Ismailofsky barracks. Probably Nastasia had kept the rooms when she came down to Pavlofsk this last time; and most likely she would have spent the night in them, Rogojin having taken her straight there from the station.

The prince took a droshky. It struck him as he drove on that he ought to have begun by coming here, since it was most improbable that Rogojin should have taken Nastasia to his own house last night. He remembered that the porter said she very rarely came at all, so that it was still less likely that she would have gone there so late at night.

Vainly trying to comfort himself with these reflections, the prince reached the Ismailofsky barracks more dead than alive.

To his consternation the good people at the lodgings had not only heard nothing of Nastasia, but all came out to look at him as if he were a marvel of some sort. The whole family, of all ages, surrounded him, and he was begged to enter. He guessed at once that they knew perfectly well who he was, and that yesterday ought to have been his wedding-day; and further that they were dying to ask about the wedding, and especially about why he should be here now, inquiring for the woman who in all reasonable human probability might have been expected to be with him in Pavlofsk.

He satisfied their curiosity, in as few words as possible, with regard to the wedding, but their exclamations and sighs were so numerous and sincere that he was obliged to tell the whole story— in a short form, of course. The advice of all these agitated ladies was that the prince should go at once and knock at Rogojin's until he was let in: and when let in insist upon a substantial explanation of everything. If Rogojin was really not at home, the prince was advised to go to a certain house, the address of which was given, where lived a German lady, a friend of Nastasia Philipovna's. It was possible that she might have spent the night there in her anxiety to conceal herself.

The prince rose from his seat in a condition of mental collapse. The good ladies reported afterwards that "his pallor was terrible to see, and his legs seemed to give way underneath him." With difficulty he was made to understand that his new friends would be glad of his address, in order to act with him if possible. After a moment's thought he gave the address of the small hotel, on the stairs of which he had had a fit some five weeks since. He then set off once more for Rogojin's.

This time they neither opened the door at Rogojin's flat nor at the one opposite. The prince found the porter with difficulty, but when found, the man would hardly look at him or answer his questions, pretending to be busy. Eventually, however, he was persuaded to reply so far as to state that Rogojin had left the house early in the morning and gone to Pavlofsk, and that he would not return today at all.

"I shall wait; he may come back this evening."

"He may not be home for a week."

"Then, at all events, he *did* sleep here, did he?"

"Well—he did sleep here, yes."

All this was suspicious and unsatisfactory. Very likely the porter had received new instructions during the interval of the prince's absence; his manner was so different now. He had been obliging— now he was as obstinate and silent as a mule. However, the prince decided to call again in a couple of hours, and after that to watch the house, in case of need. His hope was that he might yet find Nastasia at the address which he had just received. To that address he now set off at full speed.

But alas! at the German lady's house they did not even appear to understand what he wanted. After a while, by means of certain hints, he was able to gather that Nastasia must have had a quarrel with her friend two or three weeks ago, since which date the latter had neither heard nor seen anything of her. He was given to understand that the subject of Nastasia's present whereabouts was not of the slightest interest to her; and that Nastasia might marry all the princes in the world for all she cared! So Muishkin took his leave hurriedly. It struck him now that she might have gone away to Moscow just as she had done the last time, and that Rogojin had perhaps gone after her, or even *with* her. If only he could find some trace!

However, he must take his room at the hotel; and he started off in that direction. Having engaged his room, he was asked by the waiter whether he would take dinner; replying mechanically in the affirmative, he sat down and waited; but it was not long before it struck him that dining would delay him. Enraged at this idea, he started up, crossed the dark passage (which filled him with horrible impressions and gloomy forebodings), and set out once more for Rogojin's. Rogojin had not returned, and no one came to the door. He rang at the old lady's door opposite, and was informed that Parfen Semionovitch would not return for three days. The curiosity with which the old servant stared at him again impressed the prince disagreeably. He could not find the porter this time at all.

As before, he crossed the street and watched the windows from the other side, walking up and down in anguish of soul for half an hour or so in the stifling heat. Nothing stirred; the blinds were motionless; indeed, the prince began to think that the apparition of Rogojin's face could have been nothing but fancy. Soothed by this thought, he drove off once more to his friends at the Ismailofsky barracks. He was expected there. The mother had already been to three or four places to look for Nastasia, but had not found a trace of any kind.

The prince said nothing, but entered the room, sat down silently, and stared at them, one after the other, with the air of a man who cannot understand what is being said to him. It was strange— one moment he seemed to be so observant, the next so absent; his behaviour struck all the family as most remarkable. At length he rose from his seat, and begged to be shown Nastasia's rooms. The ladies reported afterwards how he had examined everything in the apartments. He observed an open book on the table, Madam Bovary, and requested the leave of the lady of the house to take it with him. He had turned down the leaf at the open page, and pocketed it before they could explain that it was a library book. He had then seated himself by the open window, and seeing a card-table, he asked who played cards.

He was informed that Nastasia used to play with Rogojin every evening, either at "preference" or "little fool," or "whist"; that this had been their practice since her last return from Pavlofsk; that she had taken to this amusement because she did not like to see Rogojin sitting silent and dull for whole evenings at a time; that the day after Nastasia had made a remark to this effect, Rogojin had whipped a pack of cards out of his pocket. Nastasia had laughed, but soon they began playing. The prince asked where were the cards, but was told that Rogojin used to bring a new pack every day, and always carried it away in his pocket.

The good ladies recommended the prince to try knocking at Rogojin's once more—not at once, but in the evening. Meanwhile, the mother would go to Pavlofsk to inquire at Dana Alexeyevna's whether anything had been heard of Nastasia there. The prince was to come back at ten o'clock and meet her, to hear her news and arrange plans for the morrow.

In spite of the kindly-meant consolations of his new friends, the prince walked to his hotel in inexpressible anguish of spirit, through the hot, dusty streets, aimlessly staring at the faces of those who passed him. Arrived at his destination, he determined to rest awhile in his room before he started for Rogojin's once more. He sat down, rested his elbows on the table and his head on his hands, and fell to thinking.

Heaven knows how long and upon what subjects he thought. He thought of many things—of Vera Lebedeff, and of her father; of Hippolyte; of Rogojin himself, first at the funeral, then as he had met him in the park, then, suddenly, as they had met in this very passage, outside, when Rogojin had watched in the darkness and awaited him with uplifted knife. The prince remembered his enemy's eyes as they had glared at him in the darkness. He shuddered, as a sudden idea struck him.

This idea was, that if Rogojin were in Petersburg, though he might hide for a time, yet he was quite sure to come to him—the prince—before long, with either good or evil intentions, but probably with the same intention as on that other occasion. At all events, if Rogojin were to come at all he would be sure to seek the prince here—he had no other town address—perhaps in this same corridor; he might well seek him here if he needed him. And perhaps he did need him. This idea seemed quite natural to the prince, though he could not have explained why he should so suddenly have become necessary to Rogojin. Rogojin would not come if all were well with him, that was part of the thought; he would come if all were not well; and certainly, undoubtedly, all would not be well with him. The prince could not bear this new idea; he took his hat and rushed out towards the street. It was almost dark in the passage.

"What if he were to come out of that corner as I go by and—and stop me?" thought the prince, as he approached the familiar spot. But no one came out.

He passed under the gateway and into the street. The crowds of people walking about—as is always the case at sunset in Petersburg, during the summer—surprised him, but he walked on in the direction of Rogojin's house.

About fifty yards from the hotel, at the first cross-road, as he passed through the crowd of foot-passengers sauntering along, someone touched his shoulder, and said in a whisper into his ear:

"Lef Nicolaievitch, my friend, come along with me." It was Rogojin.

The prince immediately began to tell him, eagerly and joyfully, how he had but the moment before expected to see him in the dark passage of the hotel.

"I was there," said Rogojin, unexpectedly. "Come along." The prince was surprised at this answer; but his astonishment increased a couple of minutes afterwards, when he began to consider it. Having thought it over, he glanced at Rogojin in alarm. The latter was striding along a yard or so ahead, looking straight in front of him, and mechanically making way for anyone he met.

"Why did you not ask for me at my room if you were in the hotel?" asked the prince, suddenly.

Rogojin stopped and looked at him; then reflected, and replied as though he had not heard the question:

"Look here, Lef Nicolaievitch, you go straight on to the house; I shall walk on the other side. See that we keep together."

So saying, Rogojin crossed the road.

Arrived on the opposite pavement, he looked back to see whether the prince were moving, waved his hand in the direction of the Gorohovaya, and strode on, looking across every moment to see whether Muishkin understood his instructions. The prince supposed that Rogojin desired to look out for someone whom he was afraid to miss; but if so, why had he not told *him* whom to look out for? So the two proceeded for half a mile or so. Suddenly the prince began to tremble from some unknown cause. He could not bear it, and signalled to Rogojin across the road.

The latter came at once.

"Is Nastasia Philipovna at your house?"

"Yes."

"And was it you looked out of the window under the blind this morning?"

"Yes."

"Then why did—"

But the prince could not finish his question; he did not know what to say. Besides this, his heart was beating so that he found it difficult to speak at all. Rogojin was silent also and looked at him as before, with an expression of deep thoughtfulness.

"Well, I'm going," he said, at last, preparing to recross the road. "You go along here as before; we will keep to different sides of the road; it's better so, you'll see."

When they reached the Gorohovaya, and came near the house, the prince's legs were trembling so that he could hardly walk. It was about ten o'clock. The old lady's windows were open, as before; Rogojin's were all shut, and in the darkness the white blinds showed whiter than ever. Rogojin and the prince each approached the house on his respective side of the road; Rogojin, who was on the near side, beckoned the prince across. He went over to the doorway.

"Even the porter does not know that I have come home now. I told him, and told them at my mother's too, that I was off to Pavlofsk," said Rogojin, with a cunning and almost satisfied smile. "We'll go in quietly and nobody will hear us."

He had the key in his hand. Mounting the staircase he turned and signalled to the prince to go more softly; he opened the door very quietly, let the prince in, followed him, locked the door behind him, and put the key in his pocket.

"Come along," he whispered.

He had spoken in a whisper all the way. In spite of his apparent outward composure, he was evidently in a state of great mental agitation. Arrived in a large salon, next to the study, he went to the window and cautiously beckoned the prince up to him.

"When you rang the bell this morning I thought it must be you. I went to the door on tip-toe and heard you talking to the servant opposite. I had told her before that if anyone came and rang—especially you, and I gave her your name—she was not to tell about me. Then I thought, what if he goes and stands opposite and looks up, or waits about to watch the house? So I came to this very window, looked out, and there you were staring straight at me. That's how it came about."

"Where is Nastasia Philipovna?" asked the prince, breathlessly.

"She's here," replied Rogojin, slowly, after a slight pause.

"Where?"

Rogojin raised his eyes and gazed intently at the prince.

"Come," he said.

He continued to speak in a whisper, very deliberately as before, and looked strangely thoughtful and dreamy. Even while he told the story of how he had peeped through the blind, he gave the impression of wishing to say something else. They entered the study. In this room some changes had taken place since the prince last saw it. It was now divided into two equal parts by a heavy green silk curtain stretched across it, separating the alcove beyond, where stood Rogojin's bed, from the rest of the room.

The heavy curtain was drawn now, and it was very dark. The bright Petersburg summer nights were already beginning to close in, and but for the full moon, it would have been difficult to distinguish anything in Rogojin's dismal room, with the drawn blinds. They could just see one anothers faces, however, though not in detail. Rogojin's face was white, as usual. His glittering eyes watched the prince with an intent stare.

"Had you not better light a candle?" said Muishkin.

"No, I needn't," replied Rogojin, and taking the other by the hand he drew him down to a chair. He himself took a chair opposite and drew it up so close that he almost pressed against the prince's knees. At their side was a little round table.

"Sit down," said Rogojin; "let's rest a bit." There was silence for a moment.

"I knew you would be at that hotel," he continued, just as men sometimes commence a serious conversation by discussing any outside subject before leading up to the main point. "As I entered the passage it struck me that perhaps you were sitting and waiting for me, just as I was waiting for you. Have you been to the old lady at Ismailofsky barracks?"

"Yes," said the prince, squeezing the word out with difficulty owing to the dreadful beating of his heart.

"I thought you would. 'They'll talk about it,' I thought; so I determined to go and fetch you to spend the night here—'We will be together,' I thought, 'for this one night—'"

"Rogojin, *where* is Nastasia Philipovna?" said the prince, suddenly rising from his seat. He was quaking in all his limbs, and his words came in a scarcely audible whisper. Rogojin rose also.

"There," he whispered, nodding his head towards the curtain.

"Asleep?" whispered the prince.

Rogojin looked intently at him again, as before.

"Let's go in—but you mustn't—well—let's go in."

He lifted the curtain, paused—and turned to the prince. "Go in," he said, motioning him to pass behind the curtain. Muishkin went in.

"It's so dark," he said.

"You can see quite enough," muttered Rogojin.

"I can just see there's a bed—"

"Go nearer," suggested Rogojin, softly.

The prince took a step forward—then another—and paused. He stood and stared for a minute or two.

Neither of the men spoke a word while at the bedside. The prince's heart beat so loud that its knocking seemed to be distinctly audible in the deathly silence.

But now his eyes had become so far accustomed to the darkness that he could distinguish the whole of the bed. Someone was asleep upon it—in an absolutely motionless sleep. Not the slightest movement was perceptible, not the faintest breathing could be heard. The sleeper was covered with a white sheet; the outline of the limbs was hardly distinguishable. He could only just make out that a human being lay outstretched there.

All around, on the bed, on a chair beside it, on the floor, were scattered the different portions of a magnificent white silk dress, bits of lace, ribbons and flowers. On a small table at the bedside glittered a mass of diamonds, torn off and thrown down anyhow. From under a heap of lace at the end of the bed peeped a small white foot, which looked as though it had been chiselled out of marble; it was terribly still.

The prince gazed and gazed, and felt that the more he gazed the more death-like became the silence. Suddenly a fly awoke somewhere, buzzed across the room, and settled on the pillow. The prince shuddered.

"Let's go," said Rogojin, touching his shoulder. They left the alcove and sat down in the two chairs they had occupied before, opposite to one another. The prince trembled more and more violently, and never took his questioning eyes off Rogojin's face.

"I see you are shuddering, Lef Nicolaievitch," said the latter, at length, "almost as you did once in Moscow, before your fit; don't you remember? I don't know what I shall do with you—"

The prince bent forward to listen, putting all the strain he could muster upon his understanding in order to take in what Rogojin said, and continuing to gaze at the latter's face.

"Was it you?" he muttered, at last, motioning with his head towards the curtain.

"Yes, it was I," whispered Rogojin, looking down.

Neither spoke for five minutes.

"Because, you know," Rogojin recommenced, as though continuing a former sentence, "if you were ill now, or had a fit, or screamed, or anything, they might hear it in the yard, or even in the street, and guess that someone was passing the night in the house. They would all come and knock and want to come in, because they know I am not at home. I didn't light a candle for the same reason. When I am not here—for two or three days at a time, now and then—no one comes in to tidy the house or anything; those are my orders. So that I want them to not know we are spending the night here—"

"Wait," interrupted the prince. "I asked both the porter and the woman whether Nastasia Philipovna had spent last night in the house; so they knew—"

"I know you asked. I told them that she had called in for ten minutes, and then gone straight back to Pavlofsk. No one knows she slept here. Last night we came in just as carefully as you and I did today. I thought as I came along with her that she would not like to creep in so secretly, but I was quite wrong. She whispered, and walked on tip-toe; she carried her skirt over her arm, so that it shouldn't rustle, and she held up her finger at me on the stairs, so that I shouldn't make a noise—it was you she was afraid of. She was mad with terror in the train, and she begged me to bring her to this house. I thought of taking her to her rooms at the Ismailofsky barracks first; but she wouldn't hear of it. She said, 'No—not there; he'll find me out at once there. Take me to your own house, where you can hide me, and tomorrow we'll set off for Moscow.' Thence she would go to Orel, she said. When she went to bed, she was still talking about going to Orel."

"Wait! What do you intend to do now, Parfen?"

"Well, I'm afraid of you. You shudder and tremble so. We'll pass the night here together. There are no other beds besides that one; but I've thought how we'll manage. I'll take the cushions off all the sofas, and lay them down on the floor, up against the curtain here—for you and me—so that we shall be together. For if they come in and look about now, you know, they'll find her, and carry her away, and they'll be asking me questions, and I shall say I did it, and then they'll take me away, too, don't you see? So let her lie close to us—close to you and me."

"Yes, yes," agreed the prince, warmly.

"So we will not say anything about it, or let them take her away?"

"Not for anything!" cried the other; "no, no, no!"

"So I had decided, my friend; not to give her up to anyone," continued Rogojin. "We'll be very quiet. I have only been out of the house one hour all day, all the rest of the time I have been with her. I dare say the air is very bad here. It is so hot. Do you find it bad?"

"I don't know—perhaps—by morning it will be."

"I've covered her with oilcloth—best American oilcloth, and put the sheet over that, and four jars of disinfectant, on account of the smell—as they did at Moscow—you remember? And she's lying so still; you shall see, in the morning, when it's light. What! can't you get up?" asked Rogojin, seeing the other was trembling so that he could not rise from his seat.

"My legs won't move," said the prince; "it's fear, I know. When my fear is over, I'll get up—"

"Wait a bit—I'll make the bed, and you can lie down. I'll lie down, too, and we'll listen and watch, for I don't know yet what I shall do... I tell you beforehand, so that you may be ready in case I—"

Muttering these disconnected words, Rogojin began to make up the beds. It was clear that he had devised these beds long before; last night he slept on the sofa. But there was no room for two on the sofa, and he seemed anxious that he and the prince should be close to one another; therefore, he now dragged cushions of all sizes and shapes from the sofas, and made a sort of bed of them close by the curtain. He then approached the prince, and gently helped him to rise, and led him towards the bed. But the prince could now walk by himself, so that his fear must have passed; for all that, however, he continued to shudder.

"It's hot weather, you see," continued Rogojin, as he lay down on the cushions beside Muishkin, "and, naturally, there will be a smell. I daren't open the window. My mother has some beautiful flowers in pots; they have a delicious scent; I thought of fetching them in, but that old servant will find out, she's very inquisitive."

"Yes, she is inquisitive," assented the prince.

"I thought of buying flowers, and putting them all round her; but I was afraid it would make us sad to see her with flowers round her."

"Look here," said the prince; he was bewildered, and his brain wandered. He seemed to be continually groping for the questions he wished to ask, and then losing them. "Listen—tell me—how did you—with a knife?—That same one?"

"Yes, that same one."

"Wait a minute, I want to ask you something else, Parfen; all sorts of things; but tell me first, did you intend to kill her before my wedding, at the church door, with your knife?"

"I don't know whether I did or not," said Rogojin, drily, seeming to be a little astonished at the question, and not quite taking it in.

"Did you never take your knife to Pavlofsk with you?"

"No. As to the knife," he added, "this is all I can tell you about it." He was silent for a moment, and then said, "I took it out of the locked drawer this morning about three, for it was in the early morning all this—happened. It has been inside the book ever since—and—and—this is what is such a marvel to me, the knife only went in a couple of inches at most, just under her left breast, and there wasn't more than half a tablespoonful of blood altogether, not more."

"Yes—yes—yes—" The prince jumped up in extraordinary agitation. "I know, I know, I've read of that sort of thing—it's internal haemorrhage, you know. Sometimes there isn't a drop—if the blow goes straight to the heart—"

"Wait—listen!" cried Rogojin, suddenly, starting up. "Somebody's walking about, do you hear? In the hall." Both sat up to listen.

"I hear," said the prince in a whisper, his eyes fixed on Rogojin.

"Footsteps?"

"Yes."

"Shall we shut the door, and lock it, or not?"

"Yes, lock it."

They locked the door, and both lay down again. There was a long silence.

"Yes, by-the-by," whispered the prince, hurriedly and excitedly as before, as though he had just seized hold of an idea and was afraid of losing it again. "I—I wanted those cards! They say you played cards with her?"

"Yes, I played with her," said Rogojin, after a short silence.

"Where are the cards?"

"Here they are," said Rogojin, after a still longer pause.

He pulled out a pack of cards, wrapped in a bit of paper, from his pocket, and handed them to the prince. The latter took them, with a sort of perplexity. A new, sad, helpless feeling weighed on his heart; he had suddenly realized that not only at this moment, but for a long while, he had not been saying what he wanted to say, had not been acting as he wanted to act; and that these cards which he held in his hand, and which he had been so delighted to have at first, were now of no use—no use... He rose, and wrung his hands. Rogojin lay motionless, and seemed neither to hear nor see his movements; but his eyes blazed in the darkness, and were fixed in a wild stare.

The prince sat down on a chair, and watched him in alarm. Half an hour went by.

Suddenly Rogojin burst into a loud abrupt laugh, as though he had quite forgotten that they must speak in whispers.

"That officer, eh!—that young officer—don't you remember that fellow at the band? Eh? Ha, ha, ha! Didn't she whip him smartly, eh?"

The prince jumped up from his seat in renewed terror. When Rogojin quieted down (which he did at once) the prince bent over him, sat down beside him, and with painfully beating heart and still more painful breath, watched his face intently. Rogojin never turned his head, and seemed to have forgotten all about him. The prince watched and waited. Time went on—it began to grow light.

Rogojin began to wander—muttering disconnectedly; then he took to shouting and laughing. The prince stretched out a trembling hand and gently stroked his hair and his cheeks—he could do nothing more. His legs trembled again and he seemed to have lost the use of them. A new sensation came over him, filling his heart and soul with infinite anguish.

Meanwhile the daylight grew full and strong; and at last the prince lay down, as though overcome by despair, and laid his face against the white, motionless face of Rogojin. His tears flowed on to Rogojin's cheek, though he was perhaps not aware of them himself.

At all events when, after many hours, the door was opened and people thronged in, they found the murderer unconscious and in a raging fever. The prince was sitting by him, motionless, and each time that the sick man gave a laugh, or a shout, he hastened to pass his own trembling hand over his companion's hair and cheeks, as though trying to soothe and quiet him. But alas! he understood nothing of what was said to him, and recognized none of those who surrounded him.

If Schneider himself had arrived then and seen his former pupil and patient, remembering the prince's condition during the first year in Switzerland, he would have flung up his hands, despairingly, and cried, as he did then:

"An idiot!"

CHAPTER XII.

When the widow hurried away to Pavlofsk, she went straight to Daria Alexeyevna's house, and telling all she knew, threw her into a state of great alarm. Both ladies decided to communicate at once with Lebedeff, who, as the friend and landlord of the prince, was also much agitated. Vera Lebedeff told all she knew, and by Lebedeff's advice it was decided that all three should go to Petersburg as quickly as possible, in order to avert "what might so easily happen."

This is how it came about that at eleven o'clock next morning Rogojin's flat was opened by the police in the presence of Lebedeff, the two ladies, and Rogojin's own brother, who lived in the wing.

The evidence of the porter went further than anything else towards the success of Lebedeff in gaining the assistance of the police. He declared that he had seen Rogojin return to the house last night, accompanied by a friend, and that both had gone upstairs very secretly and cautiously. After this there was no hesitation about breaking open the door, since it could not be got open in any other way.

Rogojin suffered from brain fever for two months. When he recovered from the attack he was at once brought up on trial for murder.

He gave full, satisfactory, and direct evidence on every point; and the prince's name was, thanks to this, not brought into the proceedings. Rogojin was very quiet during the progress of the trial. He did not contradict his clever and eloquent counsel, who argued that the brain fever, or inflammation of the brain, was the cause of the crime; clearly proving that this malady had existed long before the murder was perpetrated, and had been brought on by the sufferings of the accused.

But Rogojin added no words of his own in confirmation of this view, and as before, he recounted with marvellous exactness the details of his crime. He was convicted, but with extenuating circumstances, and condemned to hard labour in Siberia for fifteen years. He heard his sentence grimly, silently, and thoughtfully. His colossal fortune, with the exception of the comparatively small portion wasted in the first wanton period of his inheritance, went to his brother, to the great satisfaction of the latter.

The old lady, Rogojin's mother, is still alive, and remembers her favourite son Parfen sometimes, but not clearly. God spared her the knowledge of this dreadful calamity which had overtaken her house.

Lebedeff, Keller, Gania, Ptitsin, and many other friends of ours continue to live as before. There is scarcely any change in them, so that there is no need to tell of their subsequent doings.

Hippolyte died in great agitation, and rather sooner than he expected, about a fortnight after Nastasia Philipovna's death. Colia was much affected by these events, and drew nearer to his mother in heart and sympathy. Nina Alexandrovna is anxious, because he is "thoughtful beyond his years," but he will, we think, make a useful and active man.

The prince's further fate was more or less decided by Colia, who selected, out of all the persons he had met during the last six or seven months, Evgenie Pavlovitch, as friend and confidant. To him he made over all that he knew as to the events above recorded, and as to the present condition of the prince. He was not far wrong in his choice. Evgenie Pavlovitch took the deepest interest in the fate of the unfortunate "idiot," and, thanks to his influence, the prince found himself once more with Dr. Schneider, in Switzerland.

Evgenie Pavlovitch, who went abroad at this time, intending to live a long while on the continent, being, as he often said, quite superfluous in Russia, visits his sick friend at Schneider's every few months.

But Dr. Schneider frowns ever more and more and shakes his head; he hints that the brain is fatally injured; he does not as yet declare that his patient is incurable, but he allows himself to express the gravest fears.

Evgenie takes this much to heart, and he has a heart, as is proved by the fact that he receives and even answers letters from Colia. But besides this, another trait in his character has become apparent, and as it is a good trait we will make haste to reveal it. After each visit to Schneider's establishment, Evgenie Pavlovitch writes another letter, besides that to Colia, giving the most minute particulars concerning the invalid's condition. In these letters is to be detected, and in each one more than the last, a growing feeling of friendship and sympathy.

The individual who corresponds thus with Evgenie Pavlovitch, and who engages so much of his attention and respect, is Vera Lebedeff. We have never been able to discover clearly how such relations sprang up. Of course the root of them was in the events which we have already recorded, and which so filled Vera with grief on the prince's account that she fell seriously ill. But exactly how the acquaintance and friendship came about, we cannot say.

We have spoken of these letters chiefly because in them is often to be found some news of the Epanchin family, and of Aglaya in particular. Evgenie Pavlovitch wrote of her from Paris, that after a short and sudden attachment to a certain Polish count, an exile, she had suddenly married him, quite against the wishes of her parents, though they had eventually given their consent through fear of a terrible scandal. Then, after a six months' silence, Evgenie Pavlovitch informed his correspondent, in a long letter, full of detail, that while paying his last visit to Dr. Schneider's establishment, he had there come across the whole Epanchin family (excepting the general, who had remained in St. Petersburg) and Prince S. The meeting was a strange one. They all received Evgenie Pavlovitch with effusive delight; Adelaida and Alexandra were deeply grateful to him for his "angelic kindness to the unhappy prince."

Lizabetha Prokofievna, when she saw poor Muishkin, in his enfeebled and humiliated condition, had wept bitterly. Apparently all was forgiven him.

Prince S. had made a few just and sensible remarks. It seemed to Evgenie Pavlovitch that there was not yet perfect harmony between Adelaida and her fiance, but he thought that in time the impulsive young girl would let herself be guided by his reason and experience. Besides, the recent events that had befallen her family had given Adelaida much to think about, especially the sad experiences of her younger sister. Within six months, everything that the family had dreaded from the marriage with the Polish count had come to pass. He turned out to be neither count nor exile— at least, in the political sense of the word—but had had to leave his native land owing to some rather dubious affair of the past. It was his noble patriotism, of which he made a great display, that had rendered him so interesting in Aglaya's eyes. She was so fascinated that, even before marrying him, she joined a committee that had been organized abroad to work for the restoration of Poland; and further, she visited the confessional of a celebrated Jesuit priest, who made an absolute fanatic of her. The supposed fortune of the count had dwindled to a mere nothing, although he had given almost irrefutable evidence of its existence to Lizabetha Prokofievna and Prince S.

Besides this, before they had been married half a year, the count and his friend the priest managed to bring about a quarrel between Aglaya and her family, so that it was now several months since they had seen her. In a word, there was a great deal to say; but Mrs. Epanchin, and her daughters, and even Prince S., were still so much distressed by Aglaya's latest infatuations and adventures, that they did not care to talk of them, though they must have known that Evgenie knew much of the story already.

Poor Lizabetha Prokofievna was most anxious to get home, and, according to Evgenie's account, she criticized everything foreign with much hostility.

"They can't bake bread anywhere, decently; and they all freeze in their houses, during winter, like a lot of mice in a cellar. At all events, I've had a good Russian cry over this poor fellow," she added, pointing to the prince, who had not recognized her in the slightest degree. "So enough of this nonsense; it's time we faced the truth. All this continental life, all this Europe of yours, and all the trash about 'going abroad' is simply foolery, and it is mere foolery on our part to come. Remember what I say, my friend; you'll live to agree with me yourself."

So spoke the good lady, almost angrily, as she took leave of Evgenie Pavlovitch.

Made in the USA
Monee, IL
27 December 2021

87193293R00206